16 June 2007

For Jayne: A fellow RN! It was great to meet you; I hope you enjoy —

When Europa Rode the Bull

All the best,

Barbara Bérot

a novel
by
Barbara Bérot

This book is a work of fiction. Names, characters, busi-nesses, organizations, places, events, and incidents are either the product of the author's imagination or are used fictitiously. Any similarity to living persons or actual events is coincidental and not intended by the author.

cover design by Renee Leister
cover photo of St. Andrews Cathedral by Barbara Bérot
photo of Ms. Bérot by Patricia Gershanick, C.P.P.

Published by Streetcar Books
Mechanicsville, Pennsylvania 18943

www.BarbaraBerot.com

ISBN 0-9748899-0-3

LCCN 2003195003

Second Edition

Printed by BookMasters, Inc.,
in the United States of America

The Myth

Zeus's voracious sexual appetite was matched only by his wife's appetite for revenge, which she frequently wielded on his lovers. But his passion for the mortal Europa would not be denied, and he would find a way to shield her from Hera's wrath.

The beautiful daughter of the King of Sidon, Europa awoke early one morning from a disturbing dream; two continents, each in the shape of a woman, were trying to possess her. Rather than return to sleep, Europa roused her friends, all fair maidens of noble birth, and together they walked to the sea. Zeus watched admiringly from his vantage point at Olympus, while the girls gathered the fragrant flowers that carpeted the spring meadow. But it was Europa who most profoundly captured his attention, for although the others were lovely, she was as Aphrodite to the sister Graces. And while he reveled in the joy of beholding her, the mischievous Eros sent an arrow straight for his heart.

So that Hera would not know of his desire, Zeus disguised himself as a bull—a chestnut bull with horns like crescent moons, whose scent was sweeter than the hyacinth that bloomed in the meadow. Europa was enchanted by his comeliness and gentle nature and as she approached him, he bowed low before her. She fashioned a garland from her flowers and laid it upon him, then climbed onto his back. To the astonishment of her friends, the magnificent creature leaped into the air and over the sea, as though he was possessed of wings. Europa cried out in terror but he gently reassured her, confessing that he was the mighty Zeus and everything he did was for love of her. He carried her to the island of Crete where he ravished her and gave her his three sons to carry.

Europa later married Asterius, the king of Crete, who cherished her and adopted her sons. But Zeus loved her always, and throughout her life she remained a favorite of the father of gods and men.

* * *

Self is the only prison that can ever bind the soul;
Love is the only angel who can bid the gates unroll;
And when he comes to call thee, arise and follow fast;
His way may lie through darkness,
but it leads to light at last.

Henry Van Dyke, *The Prison and the Angel*

Acknowledgments

Writing is such a lonely and frustrating occupation. Many days the task seemed so mammoth, I might have chucked my computer in the pond. But angels of inspiration were hovering about me, guiding and buoying me, lifting me through to the end. To these special people, I will always be grateful. And while it is impossible to acknowledge everyone who helped me, I will make special mention of the more involved.

Early on there was Maryann Bérot, to whom I sent each chapter as it was completed. Her urgent messages of, "When are you sending the next one, you're not going to make me wait, are you?" infused me with confidence.

And there was the sound advice of James Rahn, who also provided entrée to Sheila Dolan. Despite seeing my manuscript at its raw and rambling worst, she did not flinch, but rather approached it with skill and patience. But for her critical guidance, I might still be in search of a story.

Then came Sarah Farnsworth, whose intelligent editorial assistance was just what my characters needed, and Helene Mathern, whose friendship and enthusiasm for the novel nurtured me through the painful editing process. The team at BookMasters was exceptionally helpful. I thank Anne Clarke for her fine copyediting and Kristen Butler for her skillful management of the overall project.

My family and friends were an ongoing source of encouragement, and there were generous strangers along the way, such as the Montfords and Innes' in St. Andrews, Betty in Oxford, and Malcolm in Kilmartin.

Were it not for the courage of Marilyn Paige at Barnes & Noble and the boundless energy and persistence of Deborah Ruriani from Smith Publicity, this novel might have languished; I'm eternally grateful to them and the many Community Relations Managers at B&N who have supported me. I'm also most thankful for the creative talent of Renee Leister, who came into my life just in time to redesign the cover.

My son Alexis was there throughout, prodding me with "When are you going to finish that book?" His loving and forgiving nature has been a mother's blessing, and his insightful humor has helped me to laugh my way through the bleakest, most discouraging days.

My husband and ardent supporter, the steadfast Robbie, never failed me; his unconditional love has given me license to be myself and chase my dreams.

But perhaps most important of all was my stepfather, a founding member and vice president of the hay-chewers club. His belief in me was a gift, one that allowed me to see myself as unique and capable, even lovable. He was my archangel, the man who delivered us all from the bonds of mediocrity; without him, I shudder to think.

This is for you, Pop. I miss you.

* * *

For Frederick James Digby
(1919–1993)

Part I

Chapter 1

When Annie d'Inard looked back upon that day, she realized that she had been delivered an omen.

It was going to be another one of those meetings, with a smug client encouraged into obnoxiousness by her ass-kissing colleagues. They had asked for her, they had sought her creative talent for their ad campaign, but that wouldn't stop them.

She knew how the meeting would go. They would sit relatively quietly as she delivered her presentation, twirling Montblanc pens, adjusting a French cuff here or there, crossing and uncrossing legs. When she concluded, one of them—probably the one with the slicked-back coiffure—would clear his throat and close the folder. Then, in a voice as greased-up as his hair and with a smile so patronizing she'd want to puke, he would pound her ideas to the ground. When he'd knocked her around enough to get his rocks off, he'd propose his own ingenious concept and ask Annie what she thought of it. Instead of telling slick-head to go fuck himself, she'd be obliged to respond that she would give it due consideration.

She so dreaded the upcoming hour that she contemplated pleading illness, though she knew that would merely postpone the inevitable. Craving a distraction, she picked up a newspaper someone had left on the conference table. Fastest-growing segment of the HIV-infected population, she read—heterosexual women. She felt an overwhelming nausea for a few seconds. Then she put the article down, preferring to think about the meeting.

At the end of the day, when Annie drove to meet her lover, that sick feeling returned. It wasn't unusual for her to feel that way; their encounters never left her with any sense of satisfaction. She would often wonder after she left, why she had gone there, and ask herself what she had gotten from it. She'd sometimes drive aimlessly for hours afterward, her mind turned off, her body feeling heavy, burdened. Now and again she'd even resolve to stop seeing him. But inevitably, and usually in the lonely night as she waited for her perennially late husband to return home, the need would resurface. It would drive her to pick up the telephone and make that call, the one in which she asked timidly, "When can I see you?" Before long she would find herself with him again, like an animal that cannot stop itself from biting at a wound, though it merely overlays one pain with another.

The carefully placed photos of Glenn Winters's wife and children greeted her, grinned at her, as she entered his office. He was on the telephone and raised a single finger to indicate that he'd be a minute. She lifted a corner of her mouth in an almost-smile, then went to the bar to pour a drink. By the time he concluded his conversation, she had guzzled the Jack Daniels and was stretched across the leather couch. He grinned seductively as he approached her, leaving his tie, shirt, and slacks strewn behind him.

They had to hurry on this Friday evening, because Annie was to meet her husband at a reception for one of his law partners. The lovers wasted no time in putting their naked bodies together and little on foreplay. It was that moment of penetration that she longed for anyway, the instant of connection, when something deep inside turned on and obliterated everything else. It was then that she felt the hope—however fleeting—the hope that it could happen again, that she might know the depths of a man and the rapturous embrace of kindred souls.

But everything stopped the day the letter came.

It was after midnight when Annie and her husband headed home from Philadelphia. A powdery snow had begun to fall, and the wind organized it into pinwheels that spun furiously in their headlights before being scattered asunder by the speeding Mercedes. Mike seemed deep in thought and kept his eyes fixed on the road as he drove. Annie leaned her head back and closed her eyes from time to time.

When they walked into the kitchen of their old farm-house, the floorboards creaked beneath their feet. The aromas of wood smoke and the day's cooking lingered; Marc's overburdened backpack and an open schoolbook lay on the table where he'd left them. Lucy, their house-keeper, had placed the mail on the pine sideboard, and Mike went to it first thing. On the top of the pile was a postal notice of attempted delivery; as he shuffled through the envelopes, it got moved to the bottom.

Annie went to her son's room before turning in. His face, so sweet in repose, drew her to kiss it softly. Still asleep, he brushed at the spot, then turned away from her. His dog, an obese beagle named Buddy, lay curled on the covers. He lifted his head and enthusiastically wagged his tail in anticipation of his own kiss. She delivered one to his head, whispering, "You're such a spoiled baby," then scratched under his chin. His tail continued to beat against the mattress as he watched her close the door.

Eager for the warmth of their bed, she wasted no time in donning her nightgown and taking refuge under the piles of covers. Mike, however, removed his clothing methodically in what seemed to be slow motion. She watched as he gradually revealed his body in the dim light, his back taut and strong, his legs all muscle.

He'd barely spoken to her since leaving the reception, so when he asked, "How was your day?" it seemed forced and unnatural.

She watched him smooth the creases of his trousers, then carefully clamp them in the suit hanger. "A pain in my ass," she answered, "that's how it was."

He had gone into the bathroom and called back to her now, "You seem to have a lot of those lately."

She sighed in exasperation and waited for him to return. "You know, it was the most fateful day of my career, the day that *Ad Week* decided to spotlight my work. Now every asshole-run corporation out there wants me do their campaign, and it's goddamn painful dealing with them, because Rich just doesn't get it. Just because a client has an ad budget large enough to end starvation in the third world, that doesn't mean we should do whatever asinine thing they ask—we need to maintain some standards."

He pulled his jogging clothes from the dresser and laid them on an upholstered bench—as was his habit—so he could slip into them in the morning without awakening her. "Why don't you leave then, strike out on your own?" he proposed. "Then you could do things your way."

"Are you kidding me?" she frowned. "You know how I am; I'd alienate more clients than I'd win. The good thing about Rich—there's nobody better at sucking up. He wrote the book."

Knowing Rich as he did, Mike might have chuckled at her comment, but his mind was too burdened for laughter.

Her tone softened. "Besides," she continued, "I don't want to work that hard. There are other things I'd like to do with my life, like spend time with my husband."

When he turned to face her, he smiled vacantly. Annie pushed the covers aside with a warm, inviting smile. He dropped his eyes to the floor and climbed in beside her, settling on his back, his arms folded behind his head.

She propped herself on an elbow and rubbed his chest with one hand. "Too tired?" she questioned softly.

"Too distracted," he answered.

"Want to talk about it?"

He shook his head no.

She rolled to her back, and they both lay staring at the ceiling. The wind whistled through the frail windows, and the radiators clicked softly. Every so often, a slight gust actually blew through the room.

"This is the only time of year I ever think about moving to a new, insulated house," he told her.

"We could get new windows," she responded, "if we had the heart to do that to the place." As ineffectual as they were, they were mostly the original leaded glass of the two hundred-year-old structure. "Shall I get up and light the fire?"

"Don't bother." He turned and pulled her close. "We'll be warm in a few minutes."

She kissed his forehead. "That was a nice party the firm gave Rod, but I can't see him retired. He's as much a workaholic as you are."

"He's not exactly retiring," he explained. "He'll be of consul and probably at the firm as much as ever, at least in the beginning."

"Then why bother?"

"It gives him more freedom. He can travel with Val and be gone for weeks if he's a mind to."

She stroked her husband's graying hair. "Would you consider doing that? Would you retire early?"

He exhaled in a short burst and appeared to be contemplating the idea.

Seeing that, her face lit and the green in her eyes seemed to deepen. "Think about the things we could do! I saw an ad the other day for a villa in the Tuscan hills, complete with staff. We could rent it for the summer— God, wouldn't that be wonderful? You and me and Marc, we could even take Lucy if she'd go! Think of how marvelous it would be to wake up every morning with nothing to do except whatever brought us pleasure."

He cut her off. "I'm not ready for that. Besides, it would be professional suicide," he answered. "I'm forty-five years old, Annie. I'm at the peak of my career."

She leaned over him and looked into his eyes, eyes that were speckled and softly colored, like a fawn. "You work too hard, sweetheart. We hardly see each other anymore."

Mike looked away. It was always difficult to withstand the intensity of her gaze. "It's the only way I can keep up. You know what my caseload is like. The conference table in my office is stacked two feet high with depositions."

"But you can change that if you want to," she persisted. "It's not like we need the money."

"It's not the money."

Her voice became softer. "Then what is it, honey? Life is too short. The way we're going about it, I worry that one of these days we're going to wake up and realize we're out of time."

Rather abruptly, he turned his back on his wife.

Annie felt that all-too-familiar sensation shoot through her now, like something cold tearing into her chest. "Please, Mike," she pleaded.

His voice was slightly strained. "Why do you always do that? Why do you push and push, trying to get me to talk about things you know I don't want to discuss?"

"I'm sorry," she said, as she kissed the back of his neck. "Please don't be mad. We need to talk. As time goes by it seems we do that less and less."

"I'm not mad, I just don't want to talk," he insisted. "It's late and I'm very tired."

"It's more than that, I can feel it." The stinging emptiness in her chest grew as her husband pulled away and locked himself up. But a sudden realization about the time of year and the memories it evoked for Mike broke through her distress. She whispered to him now, "I'm sorry, I forgot."

"I haven't," he murmured.

She reached her arms around him, but he remained stiff and unyielding.

Toward dawn, Mike awakened. He lay on his back, looking around the room, listening as the wind rippled the tin roof over their heads. He listened also to the sound of his wife's breathing. Her breaths came slowly, deeply, and in them he heard the venting of the anguish he'd caused her. He understood that pain. He hated that he always seemed to bring it to her, but he could never help himself. Cautiously, he reached to stroke her dark hair, then he brought his face close to take in the scent of it. He heard her moan slightly and he waited, knowing that she was awakening.

She turned to him and opened her eyes. "Having trouble sleeping, honey?" she asked in a husky, nighttime voice.

"The wind woke me." He went back to stroking her hair.

"I love that sound," she responded. "I always have. Wind like that reminds me of Scotland."

He smiled slightly. "It's a wonder you've never gone back after all these years."

"It's a damn shame, that's what it is. But before I met you, I didn't have the time or the money, and since we've been married, well, I haven't wanted to go without you."

He reached for one of her hands. "You could take Marc. I know he'd love to see the places he's always heard his mother speak of."

"It'd be better with all of us. That's the way I'd like to go back." She smiled so sweetly it drew him to kiss her lips. "That was nice," she said, as he took his mouth away.

"I'm sorry about earlier," he sighed. "It's just so damned hard. Sometimes the memories are so fresh, it seems like yesterday."

"It's all right, sweetheart, I understand," she answered, just as she always did, trying to make it easier for him.

He took her in an embrace and pressed his erection between her legs.

He passed into sleep as he held her in his arms, but Annie's heart and conscience kept her eyes from closing. Her soul was scorched by the agonizing realization that only hours earlier she had betrayed her husband once again and allowed another man entrance to that private part of herself. But even as she experienced that gnawing, burning pain, her flesh grew colder, until she felt as frigid and unprotected as one of the bare trees outside their window that quietly endured this winter night. For their coming together had happened as it always did—as she was beginning to believe it always would—with his heart locked safely away from hers and hers left untouched, futilely beating on its own.

When her husband turned away and onto his stomach, falling deeper into his slumber, the action reminded her of something from her past. As she finally began to sleep, that memory ignited a dream. It was one she'd had on and off throughout the years, and she always awakened from it feeling anxious and disturbed—sick inside.

She was standing outside the enormous iron gates of a cemetery, watching a white-haired man as he tended to the graves, each of which were carefully planted like tiny, perfect gardens. From time to time he looked up and smiled at her. She clung to the gates with clenched fists and pleaded with him to open them, to allow her entrance to that special, beautiful place, but he would not.

Then she was in the gloom of a dark woods, outstretched upon leaves, juices trickling from her vagina. She wanted to sit up, but when she tried to move her hands seemed shackled to the ground, her body encumbered by an enormous weight. Something cold grasped her leg and drew it away from the other, separating her tender labia. She felt the cold creep up one thigh, wrapping itself around and around like a snake, until it reached the moisture it sought and slid into it, wriggling its large, hooded head against her insides—before it finally halted and slithered out.

* * *

Before anyone else was up, Mike ate a toasted bagel, washing it down with a glass of grapefruit juice, then plunged into the cold darkness to begin his run. The snowfall had ended and the plow had already cleared the narrow country road, so it was easy going. He spied a herd of deer making a feast of the rhododendron that lined his neighbor's drive, their graceful forms visible in the growing, pearl light. They paused long enough to look up and follow his movements as he jogged past, and he slowed so that he might enjoy the moment with them. As long as he had lived in this countryside near the Delaware River, and it was more than nine years now, he never ceased to be taken with scenes like these. Although moving here meant a long, often difficult commute from his office, he had never regretted it. It was the kind of home Annie had always dreamed of having, and in his love for her and her son, he had adopted it as his dream, too. He picked up speed after he passed the deer to tackle the hill that came before the river.

Annie sat at the table with her thirteen-year-old son while Lucy prepared his breakfast. She had lit a fire in the walk-in fireplace that was the focal point of the kitchen, and it roared and crackled, brightening the large room.

"Did you remember I have basketball practice this morning, Mom?"

"I did. How's it going? Don't you have a big game this Friday?"

"Yup. Are you and Mike coming?"

"Lucy and I are planning on it, but we'll have to wait and see about Mike."

Lucy placed his plate of scrambled eggs and toast in front of Marc, and he looked at his watch. "Never mind that," she grumbled, "you've got time to eat. You can't play on an empty stomach."

"Coach makes you run laps if you're late," he complained before diving into his food.

"Take your time," his mother told him. "I'll get your jacket and warm up the car."

"Annie, wait," Lucy called to her. She went to the sideboard and shuffled through the prior day's mail, looking for the yellow slip of paper. "When I went for the mail yesterday Joyce gave me this. She wouldn't let me sign for it. She said you had to."

Annie took it from her and tucked it into her pocket.

"Morning, Joyce," Annie greeted the postmistress.

"Mornin'. How's everything?" Knowing what Annie had stopped in for, Joyce had already turned to one of the sorting tables. She passed it over the counter with their other mail and a simple, "Here you go."

Annie stared at the envelope, and her heart immediately picked up speed. Joyce held out a pen and Annie took it with a trembling hand. The signature she left was illegible, and she forgot to say good-bye.

As she read the words, the air in her lungs was suddenly, forcefully expelled, as though she'd been punched. When her hands began to shake, she laid the letter on the passenger seat, then sat a moment grasping the steering wheel, trying to steady herself enough to drive. It was less than ten minutes before she was home, but the drive seemed interminable.

Mike had returned from his run and was drinking coffee by the kitchen fire while the dog slept near the hearth. He sat in one of the wing back chairs with his feet propped on a small stool, his thoughts drifting while he gazed into the flames.

Not unexpectedly, Michele came first to mind. He remembered the candlelit dinner she had prepared for him on the day she learned that she was pregnant. It had been a true expression of love, preparing his favorite foods when she'd been so nauseated and tired. Still, she had wanted to make the day as special as she could, one that he would always recall—the day he learned that he would become a father. She had accomplished that, undoubtedly, though she had never intended the remembrance to be so bittersweet, so persistently painful. He forced the recollection away, and in its place came the memory of last evening.

When Annie walked into the lobby of the Four Seasons to meet him, she had turned heads, as usual, with her strikingly pretty face and tall, shapely form. In the minute that she watched her cross the room and come to him—her dark hair prismatic in the lights, her hazel eyes lit with green—he felt it all: the pride, the love, the intense physical attraction, the joy of simply being near her. But by the time she reached him those feelings were overshadowed by his creeping guilt, his constant and unpredictable companion. It all too frequently ambushed him in moments like this, insisting that it was wrong for him to be this happy, telling him he had no right.

He looked up when Annie came into the kitchen and immediately discerned something in her face. "What's the matter? Marc's all right, isn't he?" he questioned.

She halted near the table, then stood rigidly a few feet in front of him, afraid to take another step. "He's fine," she barely got out, "I dropped him off at basketball practice."

He was uncomforted by her words and rose from his chair to search her terror-struck eyes. "What's wrong? Something's wrong."

She handed over the letter from the Red Cross. "This came for me." As his eyes scanned the document, she watched the color drain from his face.

He had to read it twice, because it didn't sink in the first time. "My God," he finally uttered, "my God." His eyes remained fixed on the piece of paper in his hands. "It says you've tested positive in their screening for HIV, and that you should see a doctor immediately." He lifted his eyes to hers now. "How can this be?" he asked, though the possibilities were already whirling through his head.

She took the letter from him, then sank into a chair. The glimmer of hope that she had grasped onto—the possibility that she had misinterpreted what she read—vanished, and she was suddenly dizzy and disoriented.

Mike had remained standing, seemingly unable to move. "It must be a mistake," he forced himself to say, but it sounded more like a question.

In the last ten minutes her world had begun collapsing in on itself, at first in small, barely noticeable pieces, but now in larger and larger chunks, one after the other, with the thundering momentum of a rock slide. She glanced over the paper again, then read the words aloud to make certain she understood them. "The last two times you donated blood, you tested positive in our screening for HIV antibodies. But both times you were negative in the test for the virus itself. I don't understand this. I don't understand what this means." Her heart was galloping, her breaths becoming increasingly shallow.

"Let me see it again." Mike held his hand out and Annie gladly gave the thing over. He had to clear his throat first.

"The wording—it's a warning. It sounds as though they think you're in the early stages of the disease."

The gray spots in her vision told her that she wasn't getting enough oxygen. She looked around for her handbag and her husband understood. He quickly located her inhaler and watched as she used it, then waited a few moments while she tried to slow her breathing down.

He pulled a chair next to her, then sat and rested a hand on her thigh. "Better now?"

She nodded slightly.

He read the letter yet again. "But this can't be," he said, lifting his eyes to hers. "You'd have to have had a blood transfusion or—" As the next few words formed in his mind, he looked away and shook his head to dispel them. "We've been married nine and a half years." His voice trailed off, but he focused on his wife again.

She met his eyes for a second, then she covered her face with her hands.

That action spoke volumes to him. But still he insisted, "Annie—Annie look at me—we've been married for more than nine years."

She kept her face hidden.

"Either this is some God-awful mistake, or—" He couldn't bring himself to accuse her, so he said, "I know I've been faithful."

The palms of her hands were wet with tears and perspiration, and when she spoke into them, her voice was muffled and barely coherent. "I'm so sorry—so very, very sorry. I don't know how to tell you."

In anticipation of the blow to come, he stiffened and demanded, "Tell me what?"

She took several deep breaths before uncovering her face. "I haven't been."

"Haven't been what?"

"Faithful."

"Annie."

"Please forgive me."

Mike stood and let the letter fall to her lap, then took a few backward steps away from his wife, closing his eyes tightly. After a long, painful moment, he looked at her again. "Who? Who is it?"

"Glenn Winters," she whispered.

The reality of a name, someone he knew existed but had never met, was like a fist in the gut, and it was in that second that he lost hope. "You told me you were just friends."

"We were."

"Do you sleep with all your friends?" he retorted.

It was hard enough to think, let alone explain something she didn't understand herself. "I didn't mean for it to happen. I only went to him to talk. I needed someone to talk to."

"I suppose talking to your husband was out of the question," he lashed back, with so much bitterness it curled his lip. He waited for her to respond. When she said nothing, he demanded to know, "And who else? Has there been anyone else?"

The mascara was washing down her cheeks, giving her a pathetic, crazed look. "No one else, just Glenn," she managed to answer.

"How long?"

"Two years—no three, maybe three."

He nodded as though he understood something, then closed his eyes as the pain overwhelmed him. They heard a noise behind them and were both startled to see Lucy descending the stairs that led from her apartment. When she was near the couple, she halted and stared gap-mouthed, like someone who had come upon an accident. "Has something happened to Marc?" she asked anxiously.

The shame she felt made Annie hide her face again.

"No," Mike told her. "Marc's fine." Then he asked, "Were you going to your son's this weekend?"

Although baffled as to why he would ask such a question, she nodded at him, for it was her custom to stay with her son and his family on her day off.

He put superhuman effort into restraining his anger. "I wonder, do you think you could stick around? I'd like you to pick up Marc and be here with him over the next few days. Do you think you could do that?"

Lucy spoke in an uncharacteristically quiet voice. "Sure," she said. "Is there anything else I can do?"

"I've got to go away for a few days," Mike answered. "Something unexpected has come up and I need to leave."

Annie looked up now, her tear-streaked face wild with fear. "You're leaving? You're going?"

He couldn't bring himself to respond to her. "I'll call you with a number, Lucy, where I can be reached." He stumbled into a chair as he made his way out of the kitchen and away from his faithless wife.

Annie's stunned eyes followed her husband until he was gone from the room. Then she turned to Lucy, the woman who had cared for her family these nine years like it was her own.

"Oh Lucy, oh God, what have I done?" she asked, and began to sob.

Lucy moved closer to Annie and patted her head. "Listen to me, you don't have time for that. Whatever's happened, you can't let him leave like this. Go after him, make him stay so you can talk this out. Get up," she pulled on one of Annie's arms. "Go on, get after him." Annie didn't move, so she plucked the letter from her lap. "Is it in here? Is what he's mad about in here?"

"It's the end result of what I've done, it's the hell I've brought on us both," she cried out.

"Whatever it is, it can't be the end of the world. Go after him and try to fix it. Go on." She yanked at Annie's arm again. "Hurry up now, before he leaves!"

Annie suppressed her sobs as she recovered the letter from Lucy and returned it to its envelope. Then she went to the sink and splashed icy water on her face before following her husband upstairs.

The bedroom was empty, so she went to his study and knocked softly.

He cried out, "Have the decency to leave me alone, will you?"

She opened the door anyway and found him sitting behind his desk, his face ravaged by tears. "Please, please let me talk to you," she pleaded. "You don't have to say anything, but I need to tell you why I did it."

"And that's something I don't need to hear," he railed at her. "I can figure that out for myself, thank you."

She took a few tentative steps closer to her husband. "I never stopped loving you, Mike. I never stopped."

"Spare me," he scoffed, "spare me the meaningless sentiment. Your actions have spoken loudly and clearly, and I don't need to hear another fucking thing from you."

She swallowed her pride and her desire to crawl away and die. "Please don't leave me, Mike. I'm so scared. I'm frightened for you as well as for myself. If I'm infected, oh God, dear God! Please, at least stay long enough to go to the doctor with me. We'll call Matt Bennett, we'll go see him. We need to make certain you're all right."

He'd been looking out the window while she spoke, but he jerked his head around to glare at her. "Why in God's name didn't you use protection? Why in God's name didn't you have the sense to do that?"

Though she was putting everything she had into holding them back, a few more tears escaped, running straight down her cheeks and dropping onto her bosom. "I didn't think it was necessary. I trusted him, Mike. We've been friends for so long. I thought I could trust him." A mixed expression of hurt and shame overcame her, and it evoked pangs of sympathy in her husband.

He didn't want her to do that to him, so he tried to dismiss her. "Fine," he blurted out, "I'll stay until you get medical help. Now will you go and leave me in peace?"

Annie sniveled and reached for a tissue from the box on his desk. "I've no right to ask you for anything, but I need you Mike. I need you more than I ever have—and if I'm sick, God—Marc! Please stay for Marc, he loves you so much. It'll devastate him if you leave. If anyone should leave, it should be me; I'm the one who did this, I'm the one who caused all of this."

He was trying to fight it, but simple compassion was quelling his anger. Besides, she was right in what she'd said about her son. He had to do what he could for Marc, protect him as much as possible. If his mother had contracted a fatal disease—God—he couldn't even imagine how he'd handle that. "All right, let's table the talk of leaving for now. The priority is the medical part of this. We need to get you to a doctor and get more information before we make decisions."

She broke in, "And you, you need to be tested."

"Fine." He took a few deep breaths before asking, "And what about him? What are you going to do about him?" He couldn't bring himself to say the man's name.

"I don't know. I can't think of that right now."

During the course of their conversation Annie's face had assumed a growing pallor. Mike frowned at her, wondering, "Have you eaten anything at all this morning?"

She shook her head slightly.

"Go lie down. I'll ask Lucy to bring you something."

"I'm not hungry," she murmured. Her hands trembled as she reached to discard the used tissue.

No, he reprimanded himself, don't let her do that to you. He stood, and in a commanding voice insisted, "Go and lie down, Annie. You've had a hell of a shock and you don't look well."

Slowly, she turned away. In her heart, she longed for him to follow, to reach a supportive arm around her waist and see her safely to bed. In her mind, she understood that he would stay where he was, standing securely behind his desk, his expression guarded, his eyes impregnable. She felt those eyes upon her as she left the study, felt them burn into her flesh. Her breathing became labored again, and by the time she reached their bedroom, it was all she could do to open the bathroom cabinet that held her inhaler and tranquilizers.

The doors between them had been left open so Mike could hear his wife struggling for air. He forced himself into his chair and grabbed hold of the desk's edge as a flood of emotion rushed over him, trying to sweep him away.

As the medication took hold, Annie fell back on their bed. She reached for the pillow that had only this morning cradled her husband's head, and pulled it to her chest, wishing that it was his body covering hers in an embrace, shielding her from the ravages of her pain. But the futility of her wish pierced her through, and she brought the pillow to her face to smother her cries with his scent.

With her breathing settling down, Mike was able to loosen his hold on the desk. The tide had passed and he had escaped this time, but he wondered about the next time, about the heartache and misery yet to come. He felt sick at the thought, and questioned his ability to handle it. To answer himself, he opened the small drawer that held his treasured photographs of Michele. With one look, the sobs were upon him, and he moved quickly to close his office door lest his grief be discovered.

Along the hallway that separated them, the chimes of the tall clock sounded, announcing the hour. When it concluded, husband and wife were stilled in their private anguish and blankly staring, both of them pondering the unknown future, that had embarked today from the irrecoverable past.

Chapter 2

Mike composed himself enough to greet his stepson after basketball practice. He knew that seeing his mother in her present state would not be wise, so he told Marc that Annie had come down with the flu, and advised him not to go in to see her lest he catch it. With the upcoming important game, Marc didn't want to be ill, so he sent her get-well wishes via Mike and kept his distance.

Mike kept his distance, too. He canceled the plans they had for the evening, then left for the gym, staying until it closed. Afterward he drove the dark, country roads for hours, until hunger and fatigue compelled him to return to the home he now felt brutally exiled from.

Only Buddy and Lucy visited Annie during that day, the latter bringing her food, the former eating most of it. Lucy offered her ear but Annie declined, explaining that the extremely personal nature of what had happened made it impossible to share with anyone. Inside the four walls of her bedroom, she paced and rocked like a prisoner, then stared out the windows into the gray, foreboding sky. Mike didn't come to see her when he returned, and he stayed in the guest room Saturday night. But late Sunday morning, with his thoughts somewhat collected, he decided it was time to talk.

Natural sleep was impossible, so Annie had taken another of the tranquilizers that were prescribed for her bouts of anxiety. It afforded her no more than three hours of rest, however, and left her eyes unfocused and puffy. When her husband walked into their bedroom, she was perched in the window seat and covered with a quilt, a box of tissues in her lap. Buddy lay on the floor near her and upon seeing Mike, he exerted himself in a burst of tail action.

He didn't greet her; he merely sat in the overstuffed chair. "Lucy says you've eaten next to nothing."

"I'm not hungry," she answered, sounding hoarse and defeated.

"Marc slept at a friend's house last night," he informed her.

"I know."

He looked around the room, then let his eyes rest on the dog. "Does he need to go out?"

"Lucy let him out this morning."

The room filled with oppressive silence, then Mike sighed. "You can't stay locked up here forever."

"I know you can't stand the sight of me," she said. "I didn't want to force myself on you."

Shaking his head, he responded, "You'll have to tell Marc something."

"I know, but not now. The last thing I'm up to is seeing him. He'll know something's terribly wrong the minute he sees me. I won't be able to fool him, no matter what I try."

"No, you won't. He's much too perceptive." He shifted his position and crossed his legs. "I've been trying to get a handle on this," he said, his tone deliberately cool and professional.

"Me, too," she answered meekly.

"I decided to call Matt Bennett at home. He'll have his scheduling secretary phone tomorrow with a time for you."

She gasped slightly.

"Do you have a problem with that?"

"No, it's just the idea of facing up to it so quickly." She pursed her lips as she exhaled. "What did he say?"

"He says it's a standard letter."

Her heart began to pound as she asked, "What does it mean? Does it mean I have it?"

"He said that there's a chance you don't," he answered, "but there are things that need to be done to rule it out.

For one, you should be retested immediately. And he said I need to be tested, but you already knew that."

"Did you tell him? Did you mention Glenn?" she asked. She was concerned about that because the two men knew each other—Glenn, in effect, was Matt's boss.

"No," he glared at her. "I'll leave that up to you. I've had all the humiliation I can take, thank you."

"I'm sorry," she whispered.

"Aren't we all?" he quipped. He let his eyes close in a long blink before informing her, "He asked me if I donated blood and when I said I did, he was relieved. He said the fact that I haven't also been contacted makes it unlikely that I have a problem."

She lowered her head and murmured, "Thank you, God."

Mike watched her for a moment, then questioned, "Have you decided what you're going to do about him?" Mike would not say Glenn's name.

She looked out the window again. "I'll go and see him in a day or two. I'll make certain he gets tested."

Yes, I'm sure you will—he thought, and his anger welled up at the idea of her seeing him. He struggled to regain his composure. "Matt said that even if you are negative in the definitive test, the Western blot, they recommend a follow-up in six months to be certain."

That was worrisome, and it renewed her fear. "Why? Why six months?"

"Because they don't know enough about this disease," he explained. "He says it can hide in tissue, like lymph glands, and be undetectable for a time. That's why the Red Cross worries when they see positive results in the screening. It's a red flag."

She was obviously confused but she said nothing.

He struggled to maintain detachment. "In the meantime, for everyone's safety, you need to proceed as though you do have it and take precautions with your blood, like if you cut yourself or when you have your period, and during sex, of course."

Annie almost smiled, as she thought of how unnecessary that warning was. Having sex with Glenn was the last thing she wanted, and she was certain that her husband would never want to make love with her again. The couple locked eyes for a few seconds, then Mike turned his away.

A long, painful minute passed between them. Then, in a voice disturbing for its tremulous quality, he asked her, "Was it all a lie, Annie? Was our marriage nothing but a lie?"

The medication she took had lingering effects. Her defenses had been lowered by it, and she found herself answering her husband bluntly, without the usual censoring she employed to protect his feelings. "Not for me. I've told you lies and I've kept the truth from you, but all the while I've loved you. As hard as it is for you to believe, love has always been behind my actions."

He leaned back in his chair and glared at the ceiling. The tension in his jaw made his speech even more terse. "Do you take me for a complete idiot? Do you realize how absurd a concept that is? Everything about you, about us, is a falsehood. It's fiction, and bad fiction at that!"

No matter what would become of them in the weeks and months ahead, she would not let him denigrate the love that had bound her so deeply to him. Pushing the comforter away, she stood on unsteady legs to face him. "There's no sense in holding anything back now, is there?"

When he answered, it was with increasing rancor. "No. I'd say now's the time for complete honesty, if you know what that is—if that word has any meaning for you."

Wincing, she closed her eyes. "I deserve that," she whispered, then looked at her husband again. "But I do know the truth, my truth anyway."

"Then by all means, let's hear your version," he sneered.

She fortified herself with a deep breath. "You gave me everything, Mike, in the beginning. You opened your heart to me and my son and you loved and protected us. You gave us the most secure and happy days we'd ever known. Without you, I don't know what would have happened to us; I don't know where we'd be today." Reflecting on that time, she paused briefly. "And that wasn't all you did for me. You encouraged me to take risks and make something of myself that I couldn't have been without your support." She struggled with the tears that were forming in her throat. "But something happened to you, to us, years ago, and I look back now and see that it was just about the time my career took off. I can't really explain it, but once you'd gotten us on our feet, you backed away. You distanced yourself from me—and even from Marc—though not to the same degree. I tried to understand, I made excuses for you, but it continued. And I got lonelier and lonelier, until I couldn't stand it anymore, until I had to do something about it."

"So you did what every woman in love with her husband does, right? You went out and had an affair."

"I went to Glenn as a friend," she said. "We sat together and we talked, about you much of the time, about how much I loved you and how concerned I was about you."

"Spare me," he scoffed.

"Let me finish, Mike. Give me that now, please!"

"Go ahead, what difference does it make anyway?"

"I didn't go there for sex, but the sex happened," she found the courage to say. "It happened because we talked intimately, because we shared things with one another. It didn't make me feel very good, but it gave me something I needed. That's why I went back, that's why I kept it up." She could feel the impact her words were having on him, so it was with a bowed head that she added, "There was something I needed that I wasn't getting here, with you."

"And he fulfilled you," he said bitterly. "How nice for you—how nice for you both!"

She responded with sober certainty, "No, he didn't. But his wanting to be with me, it made me feel less alone."

Mike grasped the arms of the chair. "So you're blaming me, are you? You're making me responsible for what you've done?"

She was suddenly overcome with exhaustion and slumped back upon the window seat. "I blame no one but myself. But if you don't understand anything else, please know that I didn't just say to hell with you and our marriage, then deliberately set out to betray you."

"I got that, thank you," he spat at her. "I've got the picture." His heartache was deepening, growing more deadly. It was pushing upward into his throat, making it difficult for him to breathe, let alone swallow.

When she saw what was in his face, she pleaded, "God forgive me for the pain I've brought you, but I was trying to save what we had. I was trying to find a way we could stay together without sacrificing—" she hesitated. "It sounds so intolerably selfish now to say it."

"Your needs? Is that what you want to say?"

"It sounds like a bad word, doesn't it?" she realized. "Why does it have to seem like that? Why is it that trying to satisfy them seems so wrong, so evil?"

The response came swiftly, like a powerful and unanticipated blow to her face. "It's because of the reckless way you went about it—the underhanded, dangerous way you went about it. Those needs may have brought you to the brink of disaster, and they've most certainly brought our marriage there." The anger suddenly, inexplicably fled his face and voice, leaving the heartache on its own, and making it much more evident.

Her tears came in torrents. "Please, Mike," she begged, "please forgive me."

In that moment, with all her heart and soul, she wanted to reach out and embrace her husband and to be embraced by him. She wanted to comfort him, to say that it would be all right, and to hear him say those words to her. She loathed herself for bringing him this anguish; in the years they'd been married, she'd done her best not to bring him any more. It was the reason she'd kept her own feelings hidden from him, why she'd gone to Glenn for the venting of them. But loving her husband in that way, hiding herself from him while seeking to protect him, only added to her suffering, and in recent years her feelings for him had come to afflict her, like the incessant aching of a wound that had never been allowed to properly heal.

Mixing in with her thoughts was concern about what was going on inside Mike. She'd have done anything to help him now, given anything to hear him open his heart and tell her how he felt, even if hearing it tore her apart. But he was so good at camouflaging his feelings, so practiced and skilled at their concealment. The only thing she could be certain about at this moment was that it wasn't love for her that he was feeling.

Slowly, Mike rose from his seat. He kept his eyes trained downward out of fear that she might see what he fought so valiantly to shroud, and made his way to the door. With the sound of the latch closing between them, both their hearts slowed and nearly stopped.

When she was able to move again, when the numbness his leaving had brought on subsided, Annie went to her desk and switched on the lamp. Tucked away in one of the drawers was a leather-bound journal that Mike had given her years ago, and in which she had never written. The burning need to express her emotions drove her to seek it out, and as she opened it to the first blank page, she felt those emotions fester and swell, like the abscessed mass they'd become.

27 February, 1994

I have not believed in a beneficent, almighty God since I was a child. I envision instead the petulant, vengeful gods of the ancient Greeks, who amuse their immortal selves by toying with us, giving and taking as they will to provide themselves with sport. They delight in the turns of fate they deal us, laying bets on our survival and endurance, using our insignificant little lives for momentary distractions from their endlessness.

Chapter 3

The wind started up again at dusk. The temperature fell rather drastically in the bedroom, and Annie decided to lay a fire. Once it began to blaze, she sat cross-legged in front of it, cloaking her back with the comforter. She had taken another tranquilizer and boosted its effects with a large glass of Armagnac hoping to free her mind of the trap it had been caught in these twenty-four hours. After a few minutes, she fell back on some pillows and closed her eyes as her muscles began to relax and her thoughts started to drift.

They went first to her brother Timmy, a place they'd been wanting to visit but had been forcibly kept from. It was impossible not to think of him now, so she gave in and released the tears that always accompanied the memories. But that wasn't what she needed or wanted, so she sat up and took several more sips of her drink. The fire captured her attention as it hissed and popped, sending fine sparks shooting through the screen. It was followed by the distinctive sound of wind rolling over the tin roof. As the objects in the room became hazy, Annie began to feel lighter, and when the next gust bowed the trees and rattled the shutters, she let her mind go with it.

The wind carried her to the cliffs of St. Andrews, just beyond the cathedral gate.

It was winter when she arrived. The days were filled with fleeting, gray passages, clouds in perpetual flux, flashes of brilliant blue sky. The wind was ever present.

Her hair was straight and long and when she was out-doors, it was never quiet. She was forever moving stray bits from her face, wisps catching in her mouth as she spoke to greet friends and passersby.

Time had no meaning or authority then; days were scored by the rising and falling of the sun, the race of clouds across the sea. Meaning was found in the company of friends and the sharing of hearts, the warmth of a smile that welcomed one in. And there was no place more wel-coming than that little cottage, with its musty aromas, its worn furnishings, its glowing hearth, so often lit for her. There was nothing more meaningful or important to that young Annie than the face that came alive whenever it saw hers, and no sound more dear than the ring of his voice, the Scottish accent dancing softly in and out of his words, like the ebb and flow of a gentle tide.

A smile came to her lips as she lay next to the burn-ing wood, lost in her memories. She imagined herself as she was then, twenty years old, standing tall and straight, a face as fresh as the salt air, eyes as fine as a spring morning. She tried to conjure up his face. There had never been a photograph so the memory surfaced slowly, less vividly, more like an impressionistic rendering than a rec-ollection. With the wash of twenty-two years, the visage had faded, the distinct lines of it now all tenderness and acceptance, kindness and admiration, with a smile that brightened the day, no matter how rainy, and eyes that stole the blue from the heavens. Simply imagining it brought her solace, and she did her best to hold it in her mind. But it was not long before the images began to diminish and float away, leaving her once again in the grips of cruel reality. How ever did I lose that young woman, she wondered, as the memory faded. And him, whatever became of Andrew?

She looked into the empty snifter, then reached for the bottle beside her. They belong to the past, she answered her-self, and I'm left with the mess I've made of tomorrow. And tomorrow will come, no matter what. It will come like a toll taker, a tax collector, a sheriff with a warrant, and there will be no dispensations. The Armagnac glowed amber and clung to the sides of the glass as she swirled it. The question of what she would do with the days ahead plagued her as much as the irrepressible thought she harbored—that time was running out.

As Annie lay alone, Mike paced the floor of the guest room. His thoughts, too, were focused on tomorrow. He would rise at five as usual, run for a half hour, then be on his way by six. At seven-thirty, he would meet with his team and prepare for court. He would spend hours in the courtroom, hours in meetings, hours on the telephone. Everything would be so damned urgent, everyone wanting a piece of him. And then he would return home sometime around ten, exhausted and hungry, and ensconce himself in his favorite chair. His stepson would be happy to see him, and Marc would amuse him with a story about something that had happened at school. Lucy would have kept his dinner warm. And Annie, his beautiful Annie, she'd throw her arms around him, give him a hug that said welcome home. No, what was he thinking? It wasn't going to happen that way tomorrow. It wasn't going to happen that way ever again. He halted his pacing and sat on the edge of the bed, then buried his face in his hands.

* * *

In the morning, Annie waited until her son left for school to come downstairs. With Lucy off to the grocery store, she sat alone at the kitchen table, distractedly sipping coffee before remembering to phone her secretary.

"Morning, Jack."

"Morning, Annie. What's up?"

"I'm not coming in today."

"Not feeling well?"

"No, I'm not, and I won't be in for the next couple of days, either."

"Touch of the flu or something?"

"Something like that."

"Well, you take care. Oh, want your messages?"

"Not really, but give them to me anyway."

"Slick-head himself called, left a voice mail on Sunday of all days."

She was instantly irritated. "What the hell did he want?"

"It was rather nasty, actually. He said he had the feeling from the meeting on Friday that you weren't too keen on his idea, and he wants it understood that this is the direction they want you to take, and you're not to waste their time on Thursday with anything else."

"Christ."

"And Rich wanted to meet with you this morning, but I'll handle that."

"Tell him I've got laryngitis or something to keep him from calling me."

He laughed.

"Anything else?" Annie asked.

"Nothing that can't wait. Do you want me to come out and help you at home so you'll be ready when you return?"

"You're a dear to offer, but I'll be fine."

"If you change your mind, just give me a ring. Hope you feel better."

Feeling the need for some fresh air, she bundled up and walked in the direction of the ice-covered pond. Buddy refused to follow her, his earlier outing having left him licking his paws to thaw them, so he backed away from the door clearly saying, "No way."

The air stung as it entered her lungs, making her cough at first, but she quickly adapted to it. The crystallized snow crunched with her footfalls, and the morning light made it glisten. She walked directly to the bench that overlooked the water and cleared a place to sit. The trees that flanked her were silver skeletons, frozen in the barren landscape, and they clattered whenever the wind brushed against them.

In the days when her anxiety had been at its worst, she had learned to change the focus of her thoughts using a kind of self-hypnosis. She practiced it now, taking deep, frosty breaths with closed eyelids. It wasn't long before she felt her mind slip out of the stranglehold of tension.

Free to go where it pleased, it returned to the place it had gone last night. It took her back to Scotland, to the bench at the high point of the cliffs.

It had been her favorite spot to sit, a place where she often met him. It was a mystical location, with an unparalleled view of the North Sea and the towering cathedral ruins behind them. They would hold hands and look out over the water, while the enchantment of the place induced them to speak their hearts, to share their innermost thoughts as they had never before. And there had been that night, with the town all tucked in bed, that they had been visited by the gods. They had opened their souls to one another and were bestowed with the magic of love, the blessing of forgiveness. The sky had glittered and crackled and danced in celebration.

Annie remained on the bench for the better part of an hour. Her nose was bright red, her hands and feet so frigid she could barely move them. A flock of chattering crows flew overhead, then staked out the branches of a nearby sycamore. They called to one another in their hoarse, cranky tones, and hopped nervously from limb to limb. The slamming sound of the back door sent them off again, in a flurry of ebony wings.

Lucy came to find her, muttering and cursing as she traversed the icy lawn. "Damn, it's cold!" She clutched at her jacket collar with thickly gloved hands. "Your doctor's office just phoned. They said they can fit you in at three." She waited for a response. "Are you sick, Annie? I know you told Marc you were, but I thought that was to avoid him.

She turned her face away. "I can't talk about it, Lucy."

Lucy patted her head. "Come on inside and let me fix you something hot to eat."

"No thanks."

The older woman's hands went to her hips. "Now you stop that. You've been moping around all weekend, and enough is enough. You need to eat, and I'm not taking no for an answer. You get yourself inside this minute."

"All right. Jesus! Anything to shut you up!"

* * *

Dr. Bennett began by reading the letter, then confirming what Mike had already conveyed to Annie. He kept his face and voice expressionless as he doled out the facts.

"I want you to relax, because it's basically good news. In the last two screenings of the blood you donated, they found that you had antibodies to the HIV virus. But when they went to the next step, they found nothing."

"I'm confused about the two different tests."

"They don't do the second test, the Western blot, on all the blood, because it's time-consuming and costly, so they use an easier, less expensive method, an enzyme immunoassay. It's not foolproof, but if you have the virus, you'll show positive results there, so it's a reliable screen. When that test is positive, they move on to the second test, which looks for specific protein components of the HIV virus. You were reactive both times in the screening and negative both times in the other."

"I'm still confused," she admitted.

"Roughly two percent of all reactive screening tests are false positives; that is, the patient never turns up with the disease. But here's the problem—the HIV virus is a very clever entity. It seems to deliberately hide in lymph glands soon after it's been introduced, which can make it undetectable for a time. While it's hiding, it's multiplying and subversively destroying the patient's immune system. When it comes out again, the damage has been done."

Annie shivered. "God, it's diabolical."

"That's why the Red Cross has told you that you can't donate blood any longer. The fear is that you may be in the hiding stage, if you will, and that in time, you'll turn up positive."

In the pit of her stomach, she felt the impact of his words. "But you said it was basically good news."

"You're not in one of the high-risk groups," he explained. "You're not an IV drug abuser, gay male or hemophiliac, or someone who's had a blood transfusion in the last ten years. How often do you donate blood?"

"At least twice a year, it depends."

"How long have you been doing that?"

"Since I started working here—about twelve years." Annie had been an associate director of public relations for the hospital; she was working there when she met Mike, and it was how she knew Matt Bennett personally.

For the first time, he smiled. "Well, that's good to know. They've been testing the blood supply for many years now, and if you haven't shown up positive before, that's good. And you've been in a stable relationship. You and Mike have been married for how long?"

The lid of her right eye began to twitch. "There's something I need to tell you." She shifted her position on the chair, then grabbed at the upholstered arms. "Since we've been married, Mike's been faithful but I haven't."

One brow lifted as he responded, "I see." It relaxed when he said, "That changes the picture, then. Does Mike know?"

"I told him."

When he exhaled, it made a slight whistling sound. "Must have been pretty tough," he offered.

"It was horrendous." She reached to rub at the twitch.

He picked up a pen and began scribbling with it. "Are we talking more than one contact, Annie?"

"No. It's been the same man, someone I've known for a long time, since before Mike and I married."

"I see," he repeated.

"And he's married, too."

He sighed quietly. "You know, of course, that every person you've had contact with increases your chances of contracting the disease exponentially."

She closed her eyes as she answered, "I know, and it has occurred to me that I'm not the only one he's had on the side."

Matt shook his head slightly. "All of you should be tested, you know. Your contact and his wife, as well as Mike."

Her eyes opened widely now. "Are you worried about Mike?"

"He said he gives blood regularly, too."

"That's right."

"No, I'm not concerned about him. If he were infected, the Red Cross would have picked up on that. Testing him is just a precaution and a way of ruling out who the carrier is."

When he said the word *carrier*, it rang ominously. "Do you think I have it? Tell me the truth, Matt."

He cleared his throat. "Given what you've just told me, I'd say it's possible that you've become infected. But let's not jump to any conclusions. Let's proceed carefully, get your blood drawn, and I'll do an examination to look for any signs of the disease. The blood donations were three months apart, and the first positive screen was in late October. When would you have donated before that?"

She searched her mind. "The spring, I think, or early summer. I can't remember exactly."

"OK, so we go back to March. Have you had any viral-type illness since then, any flulike symptoms with a fever, swollen glands? I ask because it often initially presents in that fashion."

She kept her head down, shaking it as she answered. "I get the flu shot every year. I started doing that when I worked here, too."

He made a notation on her chart. "I'll call the nurse and we can get started with the exam, all right?"

Annie nodded. "Matt, if the man I've been with is positive, what happens then? Is it a given that I've contracted it, too?"

"No, it's not a given, but if your contact has the virus, the CDC recommends six months to a year of negative tests before you can safely say that you haven't been infected."

"Jesus, that's a long wait." She rubbed at her throbbing forehead. "And if he's negative, then what? Do I still have to worry?"

"Not as much, though they still recommend a retest at six months. And in the meantime, you should take precautions— you know, refrain from or have only well-protected sex. The reason for that is pretty simple: Your contact could be negative now, then turn up positive at a later testing."

"Six months to a year," she sighed. "In terms of the rest of your life it seems so little, but waiting to know if you have a rest of your life, it's forever."

Keeping his focus on her chart, he answered, "Yes, I imagine so." He felt foolish after he said that, but anything he said to patients in this circumstance always sounded trite and inadequate. "How's the anxiety? Any episodes lately?"

"I had trouble breathing on Saturday."

"How bad was it? Did you need to medicate?"

"I used the inhaler and took a few pills."

He looked her directly in the eyes. "I've no need to tell you to be careful with those pills, to use them only in extreme circumstances."

She frowned as she answered, "I consider these circumstances extreme."

He acknowledged that with a slight nod. "How many do you have left? Shall I write you a new prescription?"

"Please," she answered. "God knows I'm likely to need them in the weeks ahead."

She didn't have to go far when she was finished in Dr. Bennett's office. She had merely to traverse a long corridor, round a few corners, then take the executive elevator to the top floor suite of offices that housed the hospital's CEO. Annie was relieved to discover that Glenn's guard-dog secretary was gone for the day. With his office door slightly ajar, she could hear that he was in and talking on the telephone, telling his wife that he'd be home in an hour. She waited for him to hang up, then she pushed the door open.

He was startled when he saw her. "This is a surprise—why didn't you call first?"

She didn't answer as she turned and shut the door. She remained with her back to him as she tried to compose herself.

"What is it? Is something wrong?" he asked.

When she faced him, her complexion was flushed. "I've known you for fifteen years," she began, "and I've counted you as one of my best friends. You hired me here and gave me my start—after my divorce—when everything seemed so bleak. It was you I went to when I got into so much trouble those years ago. You helped me find my way out of it."

Worry evidenced itself on his face. "Sit down, will you, and tell me what's wrong."

She remained on her feet, her coat draped over one arm. "And it was you, again, that I went to when things in my marriage weren't going right, when my husband started to pull away from me and I felt so lost. You were the only one I even thought of talking to about it, because I knew you cared about me, and I knew you'd help me find a way."

He softened his voice. "What is it? What's happened?"

"I trusted you."

"I know that. I trust you, too, and I count you as one of my closest friends."

"You betrayed that trust."

He scrunched his face. "How?"

It was instinct, not reason, that told her what to say. "I'm not the only one, am I? I thought I was something special to you, but I was deluded, wasn't I?"

The cryptic way in which she spoke was beginning to annoy him. "Of course you're special. I love you, you know that! What the hell is the problem?"

"You see other women, don't you Glenn?"

The color fled his face as he began searching his memory, trying to discover how it was she found out.

There was no denying her outrage. "I know you fuck other women."

It took courage to meet her eyes. "I had a brief thing, very brief, and it's over. It was someone I met at a meeting. We spent a couple of nights together, and that was it."

Her next breath was a gasp. "You didn't use protection, did you? You screwed some woman you'd never met before and you didn't use protection."

The furrows in his forehead deepened.

Closing her eyes, Annie expelled the air from her lungs and realized her worst fear. "Jesus Christ," she hissed, "you didn't."

"It was just a passing attraction. There was nothing to it. I told you it's over," he continued to protest.

Her voice cracked as she screamed, "Nothing to it? It's over? It's not over! It's far from over! That little attraction may have infected us with HIV!"

As she told him, Annie's tremulous voice sounded more and more distant to Glenn, as though they were standing at opposite ends of a tunnel.

The muscles that held Glenn Winters upright were the first to be affected, then it was his heart, which felt as though it had been cut loose from its attachments and thrown down a crevasse. The office began to spin, and he slumped into his chair. He swallowed hard as he listened, putting his elbows on the desk, then letting his forehead come to rest in his palms.

"God in heaven, what have I done," he murmured. It sounded like a prayer.

"You've fucked us all, that's what you've done—Mike, your wife, me—you've fucked us all!" Anger was choking her, and she needed to get out of there and away from it. She pulled on her coat with such vehemence that she ripped through the sleeve lining. Then she moved toward the door, but turned back to him before she reached it. "Was it worth it, Glenn? Was it worth sticking your dick in some good-looking woman because she smiled at you and gave you a hard-on?"

"I'm such an ass," he whispered.

"Why couldn't you have used your brains and put on a rubber? Were you so hot and bothered that you couldn't stop for three goddamn minutes in the gift shop?"

"Annie, please."

"Was it worth it? Was it the greatest fuck of your life? Because for what it may have cost you, cost us all, I sure as hell hope it was!"

She waited for him to respond, but he wouldn't.

"Didn't you even once think about the rest of us? We're one big, happy family you know—your wife, my husband, you and me—we fuck each other and then we go home and fuck them." The raw anger was depleting Annie's energy. She had to let it go, let it pass, or it would take her sanity with it. "You should have thought about the rest of us. You owed us that. I trusted you. I never asked you to use a rubber because I trusted you. Now I've risked my husband's life, my own life, because I trusted you to be responsible."

A fire of shame and regret burned through his gut, and every movement he made, every thought he had, made it burn brighter. "There's nothing I can say. I'm an asshole, a fucking asshole."

"If you think I'm going to disagree with you—" Her insides simmered with the desire to lash out and hurt him, but she managed to maintain some control. "Listen to me. You've got to get tested, and you need to tell your wife, because she should be tested too. I've already told my husband."

His eyes widened with disbelief. "God, you told him?"

"Of course, I told him! This affects him as much as it does me! God in heaven, the morning I got the letter we made love. We made love only hours after you and I were together!"

"Oh God, did you tell him that, too?"

She looked, and felt, utterly disgusted. "Christ, no! I spared him that detail. I'd already ripped his heart out, I wasn't going to tear his guts out, too!"

"What did he say?" he asked, though he feared the answer.

"What did he say? What the hell do you think? I've not only betrayed him and abused his trust in the worst possible way, I might have passed a fatal disease on to him! What the hell do you think he said: It's all right, honey?"

"Dear God." The word *fatal* resonated in his head.

The private line rang and he ignored it, but listening to it quieted them for a few moments. The muted sounds of traffic and car horns coming through the thick glass added an air of unreality to everything. It made them feel isolated from the world—held down in deep water.

Annie's voice pierced the quiet. "I've destroyed my marriage. It's over. Mike can't stand the sight of me, and

I don't blame him for one damn minute, because I can't either. I can't even look in a goddamn mirror."

Glenn's focus drifted off as the fear of death settled in, displacing all of his other concerns. His mind's eye began running scenes from the future. "My God, what if I'm sick. How am I going to tell Sandi? She'll never forgive me, and my children, my God, my family will be torn apart!" He was trying hard, but he could not stop the tears. "How could this happen? I never meant to hurt anyone. I kept it in its place," he explained to no one but himself.

Annie exhaled loudly as self-loathing and disgust welled up within her. "We're both such stupid, selfish idiots—both of us thinking that it was OK, that we had a right to do what we did!" She spat her words. "And Christ, the arrogance of it all, thinking we weren't hurting anybody."

Glenn was sobbing openly now, and the lonesome sound of it made Annie hungry for air. She started for the door again, but something made her turn around to look one more time upon the man who had been her lover. She saw him slumped in his chair, seeming so frightened, so regretful, so alone—entangled in the same web of bitter emotion that she had become trapped in. As irate as she was, compassion got the better of her. How could she not offer him something, if only a modicum of comfort? She remembered too well what it felt like—needing Mike more than she ever had, desperately wanting his reassurance, then watching him walk away. She went back to where Glenn sat and wrapped her arms around him, then pulled him to her. Their embrace was tentative, wary.

"We're such pathetic, weak creatures," she finally said.

"I'm sorry," he whispered to her. "I'm so very sorry for this."

"I know."

"Sandi will leave me."

"If that's the worst thing that happens, you'll be lucky."

The thought of losing his wife made him tremble, and he looked to Annie for solace. "At least we have each other to get through this."

She pushed away from him. The idea of continuing any sort of relationship, even if it were just two suffering human beings comforting one another, repulsed her. "No, we don't."

He stared at her in puzzlement. "Why?"

"Because I can't do this anymore."

"But we need each other."

"I need something, Glenn, but it's not this." Looking away from him, Annie focused on the couch where they had so often lain. It now seemed like a crime scene, a place that should be cordoned off with yellow tape while photographers exploded flashbulbs and police collected evidence. "You sleeping with someone else, this whole horrible nightmare that's come crashing down on us, it's made everything too clear. What we've done, it's been nothing but betrayal, pure and simple. I deluded myself into thinking that it was meaningful, that it gave me something, served some absurd purpose."

He looked into her eyes; determination had clouded them, and he knew Annie well enough to understand that there was no going past that. Besides, he had never begged a woman for anything, and he was not going to start now. He felt a sudden, powerful urge for a drink. He walked to the bar and poured a large Scotch, keeping his back to Annie. She moved away from his desk and back to the center of the room. Still with her coat on, she slipped her hands into the pockets and stood by expectantly. Glenn said nothing while he was at the bar, but his mind was working at light speed.

Sandi, his wife of twenty-six years, she could be sick, too. No, he wasn't going to think that way. Annie said they didn't find the virus in her blood, so maybe this is all some dreadful mistake, a false positive bad dream. First things first, he told himself. I'll get tested tomorrow, no, what am I thinking? I can't do that, not here, not even in this city. It'd be too easy for someone to find out, too juicy a tidbit for some disgruntled lab technician. Guess who's getting himself tested for HIV? Jesus, what grist for the hospital rumor mill. I'll have to go away and do it discreetly, he thought, someplace where I'm not known. I could go to Hopkins and ask my internist cousin to check me out and run the tests. That's what I'll do—take a few days and go to Baltimore. I'll tell Sandi I've got a meeting. It'll mean a wait. I can't up and go right away or it won't look legit. In the meantime, I won't tell Sandi. There's no sense in upsetting her yet. If I'm negative, she'll never have to know, and the nightmare will be over.

When he finished his drink, he returned to his desk chair, then clasped his hands together, bringing the tips of his index fingers to his lips. The photograph of Sandi captured his attention and put her foremost in his thoughts again. *If I am sick, I'll have to find a way to tell her so that she'll forgive me—find a way to explain it without destroying everything. I can't lose her. She's the one I'll need; she's the one who'll be there for me, who'll take care of me. If for no other reason, she'll do it for the sake of the children, because that's the kind of woman she is.*

"You're right, of course," he finally said to Annie. "I need to put all my efforts into my marriage and do whatever I can to save it." *Even if it means lying,* he completed in his head, *even if it means more deception.*

Annie nodded slightly and only partially heard him. She was thinking back to what she'd said about betrayal, realizing that the person she'd most grievously forsaken was herself.

He looked up to where she stood, straight and stiff in her winter coat. "Are you certain yours is over?"

She nodded again.

"What will you do? How will you manage alone?"

That question had crept up on her Saturday afternoon when Mike had gone away and she had retreated to her room. She had refused to hear it out then, refused to allow it to take hold of her consciousness. But Glenn asking it now gave it new strength, and the thought gained a foothold. It whirled around in her mind until it anchored on a response, an idea, and that idea set something else in motion.

"I may go away for a while, out of the country."

Her answer surprised him. "Out of the country? Why?"

"Since this happened, my thoughts," she paused and took a long breath, "they keep going back to a time when I was different. It's made me question everything about myself, made me wonder how I got like this, how I got to be the kind of woman who cheats on the husband she loves."

"I don't understand. What's that got to do with going out of the country?"

"Never mind," she answered, and it was something of a put-down. "Whatever I do with the days ahead, it has to be real. I've no time or patience left for anything that isn't."

The evening rush hour was coming to an end. The sounds of traffic and movement diminished substantially, and the building, the world, seemed suddenly deeply quiet. Annie turned her gaze to the large window behind Glenn's desk; it revealed nothing of the outside, only the blackness of the winter night. But the light from a single lamp allowed for the reflection of a shadowy inside, the interior space of an elite, protected world. At the center of that image a curious, singular figure stood apart and unmoving. She stared into the reflection, and wondered who that woman was.

When they parted, Annie walked very slowly to her car, then drove the streets of Center City for a time. She went past her husband's well-lit law offices, then to the places she and Mike had lived when they first met. It was almost her son's bedtime when she pulled into the drive of their home, but her husband, as usual, had not yet returned.

Chapter 4

On Tuesday afternoon, Annie baked her son's favorite cookies in time for his return from school. The aroma filled the house, and the warmth of the kitchen fire was particularly welcome on what proved to be the coldest day of the year. To give mother and son time alone, Lucy had gone to her apartment to watch Oprah. As Marc ate, Buddy wagged and waited alongside his chair, hoping for a wayward crumb. Her son seemed unusually excited about something, and when Annie questioned him, he blushed.

"Is it a girl?" his mother asked.

He blushed again and gulped half a glass of milk.

"What's her name?"

"Jen."

"Is she cute?"

He grinned from ear to ear. "She's going to the dance with me on Saturday."

"Smart girl," his mother offered.

"Why do you say that?" he asked after he inhaled another cookie.

"Because you're the sweetest, most intelligent, most handsome boy in the school, that's why."

"Geez, give me a break, will you?"

They laughed together.

"Everything else going OK?"

"Yup, everything's great. Why do you ask?" He lifted an eyebrow and looked a little skeptical, a gesture that he had learned from his father. "You seem like you've got something on your mind."

Hesitating now, she considered her response. "I do, actually. I need to ask you how you'd feel about something, about my going away for a little while."

"How long?"

"At least a month, maybe more, but that would depend on you."

"On me, how?"

"Well, I thought I'd plan on a month at first, then if I wanted to stay longer and you didn't miss me too much, I might do that. But if you wanted me home, I'd come back sooner." She'd been watching his face carefully. "How do you feel about that?"

"Where would you go?"

"Scotland."

"St. Andrews?"

"Exactly."

He held onto his milk glass and looked into it. "Can I ask you something?"

"Sure."

"Are you and Mike breaking up?"

Annie reached for the hand that held the glass, and he gave it to her. "We're going through something right now, and we need time apart. I'm thinking that it makes more sense for me to leave than him. I'm not happy with my job, anyway, and he can't leave his."

He looked very thoughtful. "You weren't sick this weekend, were you?"

Talking with her son now, Annie realized that she owed him the truth, at least as much of it as he could handle. "No, not physically, anyway. But I was and still am very sick at heart."

He digested what she said, then asked, "What'd Mike do?"

"Actually, it wasn't something Mike did. It's more a matter of us drifting apart for some time now, and both of us realizing that we need to do something about it." She had taken the truth as far as she could.

It didn't make sense to him. "So you think that separating is the way to fix it?"

"Sometimes that's all it takes, sweetheart, for people to appreciate what they take for granted on a day-to-day basis." If only it were that simple, she thought. I'd give anything to have it be that simple.

Marc took his hand away and traced a finger along the rim of the cookie plate.

His mother allowed him time to think before offering, "I won't go if you don't want me to. It seems like this is too upsetting for you."

He looked up at her. "It's not your leaving, I'm OK with that, really. It's not like we haven't gotten used to being away from each other for months at a time." He was referring to the fact that he spent summers with his father and had once stayed with him for six months. "It's Mike, Mom. I love him, and I don't want to lose him." There was a decided lump in his throat when he swallowed again.

"Oh, honey," Annie's throat also tightened. "I know that, and I want you to know that I love him, too. That hasn't changed. But what I'm doing, I'm not giving up and walking away, I'm going away to try to get my bearings. But I intend to do everything I can to keep us together, to keep us a family. I give you my word on that. I want you to feel secure in that."

Buddy put his front paws on Marc's lap and begged for the crumbs. "So if you leave, it'll be me and Mike and Lucy here?"

"And Bud. Don't forget Buddy," she gently teased. Upon hearing his name, he went to Annie, and she gave him a whole cookie.

"Geez, Mom, don't do that! He's fat enough as it is."

"I know, but I can't help it. Food is what he lives for. That's basically all his life's about, right? How can I deny him the one passion of his life?"

"You're such a pushover."

The day had been coming to an end as they talked, and now the last rays of sunlight angled through the windows, casting long shadows from everything they touched. The house was still but for the occasional crack from the fire and the muted sound of Lucy's television.

"Any more thoughts on what we've talked about?" Annie asked softly.

"Scotland, huh? I think I know why you're going there." He looked a little smug in his ensuing grin.

"Oh, yeah?"

"Yup. All my life I've heard about what a neat place it is and how happy you were when you were there. I think you're going back to remember what that felt like or something."

Annie smiled the first real smile she'd known in quite some time. "You're something else, you know that? You never cease to amaze me, and I don't think there's a prouder mother on the face of this earth. And man, but that Jen's a lucky girl."

The blush that comment brought on was as bright as the embers that glowed in the hearth.

* * *

Though he'd slept at home on Monday night, Annie hadn't seen Mike that day. Nor had she seen him on Tuesday, because he'd eaten at the office and arrived home after everyone had turned in. On Wednesday she set her alarm for five to make certain she'd catch him, and she did, just as he was going out for his run.

He glared at her without greeting.

"I've missed you," she said.

"Have you?" he quipped.

"You know I have. How much longer are we to go on like this?" she asked.

"I've no answer for that." He knew he sounded petulant, even childish, but it was what he needed to do to keep his distance.

She made an attempt at softening the atmosphere. "I saw Matt on Monday."

"I know, he told me. I was an hour behind you."

That surprised her. "I wish I'd known, I'd have waited for you."

"Oh? Where would you have waited? In Glenn's office?"

For an instant, she felt like opening the kitchen door and walking barefooted into the snow—it would have been warmer there. "I went to see him. There was no point in waiting. I had to know if he'd been with anyone else."

"And had he?" he fired back, his heart suddenly racing in anticipation.

"Yes," she answered and bowed her head.

The underhanded bastard—goddamn him, goddamn him to hell. He had to keep himself steady; it wouldn't do to have her see how that news had upset him. He moved toward the refrigerator and poured another glass of juice. "And how'd it go between you?" he flippantly inquired. "You two console each other as usual?"

She cringed. "There is no consolation in this."

"No?"

"I said good-bye to him, Mike. The only thing left between us is communication about his tests. He needs to let me know the results when he gets them. That's all that's left."

"Pity, one would have thought that this whole thing might make you closer."

"It's done anything but."

"And why's that? Feel betrayed, do you?"

His remarks were caustic. They were eating through her like acid. "Please, can we stop this? Can't we talk civilly, without the daggers?"

He drank more juice and kept his eyes on her.

"What did Matt say to you?" she asked.

"He said I shouldn't lose any sleep worrying about my health."

Annie closed her eyes. "I thank God for that."

"Apparently it's much harder for a man to contract it from a woman than the other way around." His tone was a little less abrasive. "And you?"

For an instant, she felt a glimmer of hope, thinking that the same would apply to Glenn. But the hopeful feeling passed when she recalled all the other things Dr. Bennett had said. "He confirmed what he'd already told you."

Mike looked at the floor, then his watch. "I need to get going."

"Please, can you come home at a decent hour tonight so we can talk?"

He pulled on his sweatshirt and gloves before responding. "Fine," he said, just before he went out.

Annie worked all that day on the presentation she was to give on Thursday. It was not an easy task, trying to keep focused on something that seemed so trivial, so insignificant, when her life was in total disarray and so many critical decisions needed to be made. But she struggled through it and managed to put something together by supper time.

She helped Marc with his math homework, then waited alone in the living room. When she heard the sound of her husband's car, it was after ten. She didn't go to the door to greet him. She stayed where she was, curled up on the sofa with a glass of wine. After about ten minutes in the kitchen, he entered the room.

"Hi," she said, softly.

He exhaled loudly.

"Tough day?"

"No tougher than usual." That was an outright lie. Since Saturday morning, everything, even the most routine of tasks, had become inordinately difficult.

"Have you eaten? Lucy's kept something warm for you."

"I grabbed a sandwich."

"Want a drink or something? Glass of wine, maybe? I just opened a bottle."

"No thanks. You wanted to talk," he said, taking a seat across from her. "Let's get it over with so I can get to bed."

He had intended that to hurt, and it did. She lowered her head. "We can't go on like this."

"You're the one who wanted me to stay."

"I know. That's what I want to talk about."

Thinking he understood, he rose abruptly. "Fine. I'll pack and be gone on the weekend."

"No, please, I wasn't going to ask you to leave. What I was going to say—I need your help with something, though I know I've no right to ask you for anything."

Her words were met with obvious skepticism, and he folded his arms and glared.

"Please sit down. Let's not make this harder than it has to be."

Reluctantly, he sat again, but he would not look at her now.

She began boldly. "You've been considerate enough to not mention divorce, but I know you must be thinking about it; it's what I deserve, after all." She waited for a response, and when none came she continued. "The next few months aren't going to be easy for me, waiting to hear if I'm sick or not. I doubt I'll handle it well. I don't want my son to watch me go through that. I remember too well what it was like for him before."

Mike understood the reference. His thoughts were drawn to the time when he and Annie first met and the difficulties she was fighting her way through then.

She set her glass on the end table and pulled her knees in, then wrapped her arms around them. "There are two parts to this. The first is a request that you hold off on any divorce actions for now, while I wait this thing out. The added strain of that, I don't think I could manage." She kept her eyes trained on him. "Do you think you could do that for me?"

His arms stayed folded as he answered curtly, "I don't see why not."

"Thank you." Annie waited to see if he would add anything. "The second part of my request is a little tougher. With the way you feel about me, it's very clear that you and I can't go on living in the same house."

He wasted no time in answering, "I agree."

His words stung, and she reeled from them. "When this first happened, you wanted to leave, and I begged you not to. I said I should be the one to go." She tried to catch his eyes, but he would not allow it. "I've decided to do that."

He looked at her, searching her face to see if this was some kind of ploy, some attempt at manipulating him. He scanned the lines of it, then zeroed in on her eyes in the way he would a client or witness to discern whether or not he was being lied to. "What are you up to?" he asked.

That question hurt most of all. "Nothing, Mike. I'm not trying to pull anything, if that's what you're worried about." She blinked away the burning in her eyes.

"Then what is it?"

"Marc loves you," she sighed, "sometimes I think more than his own father. He looks up to you; he needs you. Your relationship is crucial to him at this stage of his life. You're his role model and so much more than that."

His expression softened somewhat. "I love that boy. I always have," he declared, then added, "and whatever becomes of us, that isn't going to change."

Hearing him say that drew powerful emotions. To distract herself from them, she reached again for her wine. "What I'm going to ask you is—when I leave, would you consider staying here, with him, so that his life won't be disrupted? I ask because he adores you, Mike, and I believe he'll be much better off over the next few months in his home with you and Lucy taking care of him than being around his wreck of a mother."

Like the lawyer he was, he considered his response carefully before answering. "I'm not asking you to leave this house. You can stay here with Marc and Lucy."

She smiled, albeit briefly. "I know that, and I thank you for it, but that's not the issue. The issue is me—Marc being around me."

Unfolding his arms, he brought a hand to his forehead to rub it while he contemplated her request. He saw the wisdom in what she was proposing, but he was uncertain as to the overall plan. "He's going to miss his mother, and he's not going to understand."

"We've already discussed it. We talked about it yesterday, actually. He knows something bad is happening between us, and I told him that I would be going away to get my bearings with the hope that you and I can find a way to solve our problems. He's OK with my leaving. What upset him was the thought of losing you."

He looked concerned. "What else did you tell him?"

"Nothing else. Nothing about my health or what I did."

"Good, because he doesn't need to be worried about you," he replied with audible relief.

"No, he doesn't, and that's the main reason I want to be away from him."

Mike rose from his seat and walked to the bar in the keeping room. He poured a glass of the wine Annie had opened and then returned with the bottle. She watched his face as he refilled her glass.

He remained on his feet, looking down at her. "Where will you go?"

She wiped at her cheeks, at the few tears that had rolled there when he was out of the room. "I'm thinking of Scotland."

That came as something of a shock. "Scotland?"

"Since everything happened, my thoughts keep going back there. I keep remembering, reliving things. I know this sounds strange, but it feels as though I'm being pulled there."

"It's not so strange," he responded. "It was a very significant place and time for you."

She bit her lower lip and nodded. "It's where I found myself once before." Her focus drifted off momentarily. "I got on the phone today and spoke with a real estate agent in St. Andrews to ask about renting a cottage or apartment. He said he has several places to show me."

Abruptly, Mike turned his face away. "Sounds as though you've decided."

"But not without your consent. This all hinges on your willingness to stay with Marc."

He would never say it, but he felt as though he'd been granted a reprieve, now that he knew he would not have to tear himself away from everyone that he loved. "I've no problem with that."

With the utterance of those words, Annie sighed and rested her head on the sofa back. She closed her eyes and breathed in and out slowly as the reality of separation began to take hold. It was happening now. Things were being set in motion that would take her away from her son, remove her from her home, and put even more distance between herself and her husband. The sensation of it was almost more than she could endure, and she reached for the wine to flush it out.

"What about your job? How are you going to handle that?" Mike wanted to know.

"I'm going to ask Rich for a leave of absence, starting immediately, tomorrow. If he says no, I'll resign."

Tomorrow—Mike heard that word very distinctly. He had remained standing during this last part of their conversation, but when his knees weakened, he knew he should leave before she noticed anything. "You'll be needing money to live on. I'll help you with your expenses," he said.

She shook her head. "I can't take your money."

"Don't be silly."

"Mike," a sad, brief, almost-smile came upon her, "thank you for the offer. It's very generous and I do appreciate it, but I need to stand on my own. I've got a fair amount set aside, so I'll manage." At his insistence, she had saved almost everything she'd made in the last six years. "Besides, I'm leaving my son in your hands. Your looking after him is all the help I need."

He feared revealing himself if he stood there and argued with her, so he responded tersely, "All right, have it your way, but don't be pigheaded about it. If you change your mind, you only have to ask." He set the glass down and made his way to the stairs, then mounted them quickly. When he reached the top the tears began, and he barely made it to the guest room in time to conceal them.

In her mind, Annie followed his footsteps as he left her. She saw him going past Marc's bedroom, past theirs, then beyond the study. He rounded the corner and took the two steps down to the wing that housed the extra bedrooms. She waited until she heard the distant click of the door latch. Then she listened, hoping to hear something else, though she didn't know what.

But for the ticking of the eighteenth-century tall case clock, a hush fell over the house. She looked now to its painted dial, and recalled the day she and Mike bought it; they had seen it in an antique store and were instantly taken with its whimsical sun-face. It was a few weeks before their wedding and their first purchase as a couple, something special for their new life together. Until today, it had been a happy reminder, a discreet presence whose entrancing chimes were always welcomed. But now, on the night it had been decided that she would separate from her husband, it became melancholy company. As Annie sat alone in the large room, it insinuated itself in the stillness like a living thing, a judgmental witness to the past nine years, cruelly reminding her of the time that had gone by and all the precious opportunities that had been laid to waste.

Unable to fall asleep, she once again pulled the journal from her desk.

2 March, 1994

Time is more powerful than any god. It rules everything, it spares nothing. It is not mindful of joy or peace or pain, or anything we might wish more or less of. It is ruthless, it is a tyrant, it is inexorable.

It mocks our mortality. It deceives us when we are young into thinking it moves slowly and believing that there are endless stores of it to waste. And then, when we have squandered much of it, it imperceptibly begins to run with us, laughing, plunging ahead on its one-way journey, ever faster.

Time's one concession is memory, but it is a treacherous gift. Memories have their own power, as they direct and distort the present, and keep us bound to what cannot be undone. I am compelled by memories to return, to sit on the bench at the high point of the cliffs, and wander into that place again, into that battle-worn and scarred corner of myself, where last I saw him.

Chapter 5

Thursday morning pretended to be ordinary. Annie had breakfast with her son, then dropped him off at school on her way to work. When she arrived at the Princeton office of Haymaker Agency, her secretary greeted her with his usual cordiality.

Jack followed Annie into her office and closed the door behind them. "You have several important messages."

"They'll have to wait."

"One is from your doctor's office. They have lab results for you."

That got her attention. "Did they give them to you?"

"No."

She breathed a little easier.

"And the client meeting has been moved up to ten."

She looked at her watch. It was already half past nine. "Christ."

"Rich wants to meet with you first."

"I figured." She was seated at her desk, staring at the piles of paper that had accumulated there during the three days she was out. "Oh, Jack—"

He was leaving her office, but he turned back, letting his hips follow his body in the way that only gay men can. "Yes?" His smile brought her a little warmth.

She could tell him. He'd understand if anyone would; he had friends with the disease. No, she couldn't tell him. She couldn't tell a soul. "I just wanted to say—I think you're the hardest working, most honest person in this company and I don't know if I've said it enough, but I appreciate everything you've done for me."

"That's very nice of you, and you've said it often, but I still thank you." He lingered a moment in her doorway. "Is everything all right?"

She looked at her desk again. "No, it's not. But it's nothing for you to worry about."

Rich didn't take the time to greet her, but that wasn't unusual. Things had grown increasingly tense between the two in recent months as they found themselves arguing more and more over creative issues. He was the president of a small, up-and-coming ad agency, whose main talent was a headstrong, independent woman, and he quite simply resented that.

"Let's see what you've got," was the first thing he said to her.

Annie laid a copy of her presentation on his desk. "And good morning to you, too," she responded.

He opened the folder. "Slides?"

"None."

He looked up. "What do you mean, none?"

"I mean I have no slides."

"You have to have slides," he insisted.

"Not necessary," she glibly answered. "I want them to use their imaginations."

As he read through the summary, his complexion turned pink. Slamming the folder shut, he glanced at his Rolex, then glared at Annie. "Get to your office right now and get busy. I'll stall them as long as I can while you do something else up." His tone and facial expression reminded her of a school principal disciplining an errant student.

She had been standing in front of him, and she nonchalantly took a seat. "I'm not going to do that," she said in a softened voice. "You've been strong-arming me into too many compromises lately, and it's no good. I don't want to do that anymore."

He gritted his teeth. "This is not your decision to make."

"I beg to differ. Whatever I create has to be mine by its very nature."

"You're pushing me, Annie. Dammit, but I should never have let you at this on your own!"

"You had no choice. They came here because of me. They didn't come for Carter or Helene or Chuck. They wanted my work, and that's what I'm obliged to give them. That's why I can't compromise. Don't you get that?"

"You're a member of a team, my team," he reminded her. "You seem to forget that all too often."

She closed her eyes in a sustained blink. "They can walk out of here into any agency they choose and get the kind of garbage they talked about the other day. Why hell, why bother doing that? They can have their own PR department spit that crap out, so why do you think they came looking for me?"

"Get over yourself, will you? Jesus! Your fifteen minutes has turned you into the worst kind of prima donna."

That remark astonished her. "If that fame has changed anybody, it's you! You used to give me full rein, then stand behind whatever I came up with. Now that we're getting the monster accounts, you're breathing down my neck and dictating to me, forcing me to do things that insult my intelligence and defame the agency. That's why we're butting heads all the time."

"We're butting heads because you refuse to look at the big picture. Those accounts put us in a whole new ball game."

She exhaled frustration. "And that, my dear Rich, is precisely what you're not hearing me say. I don't want to be in that game! As for the prima donna comment, I've always been that way about my work, and you know it. I'd be the same goddamn way whatever I did! If I made shoes, they wouldn't be flashy, pointy-toed numbers that fell apart after a couple of wearings. They'd be the classic, custom-made kind, durable and useful, and I'd be as stubborn about making them that way as I am about this!"

He had cooled somewhat. "That doesn't change the fact that we're going to lose them if you continue on in this vein."

She was growing tired of this argument, so she made a decision to end it. "Listen Rich, I've made up my mind about something, and we might as well discuss it here and now."

"We've got twenty goddamn minutes before we meet," he said with impatience.

Undaunted, she continued, "I'd like to take an extended leave of absence, starting today. If you can't grant me that, I intend to resign."

His jaw dropped. "Have you lost your mind?"

"Maybe," she answered in a subdued, thoughtful voice.

He had reached his breaking point. "I'm not going to tolerate this. I'm not going to be bullied by you!"

"I'm not bullying you. I'm trying to maintain my creative integrity, and if you can't tell the difference between the two things, then you've got a problem."

"You listen to me." It was a down and dirty tone that he used. "You go to your office this minute and put your mind to giving them what they want. I'm going to stall them, tell them how sick you've been, set them up to come back next week. This is only the largest, most important account the agency has ever seen, and we're not going to lose it because of your willfulness and obstinacy!"

Annie shook her head, then turned and left the room.

She took a file box from the closet in her office and began to fill it with her personal things. At ten o'clock, she walked into the conference room where a caterer had set out a California-style brunch. The client representatives were helping themselves to fresh fruit and breakfast burritos, being careful not to spill anything on their Armani suits. The aromas of breakfast and corporate arrogance were strong.

Saccharine smiles greeted her, and for a moment she felt as though she would vomit. But she took her place quietly, forgoing the usual platitudes. Rich shot her a disapproving glance before beginning his ingratiating speech. Annie was not listening, and he had to ask her twice to begin her presentation. She stood mechanically and passed folders around the table.

"Good morning. Thank you for coming. I'll begin by saying that there will be no slide show today, no fantasy audio-video presentation. My approach to what you've brought us will be simple and straightforward."

Rich cleared his throat and shifted nervously in his seat. In his mind, he was rehearsing the spin he would put on everything if she went her own way.

"You came to us because you're being vilified in the press. In our meeting last week, you rejected my preliminary ideas in favor of your own. You want us to launch a campaign that makes no mention of the incident and portrays you as environmentally friendly." She frowned sarcastically. "Let's get real, shall we? I don't think there's a person sitting at this table who doesn't see that for what it is—total bullshit." A slight gasping sound came from somewhere near Annie. "The responsibility for that oil spill is entirely yours, and it demeans the American public when you even attempt to portray yourselves as anything but culpable. However, I've come up with some ideas that will help improve your image without compromising the truth, and in the long run, I'm convinced this approach will serve you better. I know it's not what you asked for and you'll either like it or you won't. I'm not going to try to persuade you either way; I'm simply going to put it out there for you to consider."

Her colleagues looked dumbfounded but she went on, focusing on slick-head.

"Transatlantic Oil has run amok with the environment for more than seventy years, and it's culminated in the worst oil spill in history. Now you want to convince the public that you're not the bad guy when the truth is, you are. I propose that instead of playing games you take it on the chin, then pull it together by making some real changes. First and foremost, apologize—take full responsibility. Spend your money on tasteful, mostly print ads that let the public know you're sorry and doing what you can to fix things. In the meantime, you want to improve your image. The only way to do that is through change, by doing things differently." She paused for a sip of water.

"I've outlined some recommendations in the presentation folder, and I'll only mention a few. One is to update and make fail-safe your shipping fleet. Another is to stop belching waste into the fragile environment. You have the finances and the capability to far exceed EPA guidelines, so why not do it? You could also designate a percentage of your profits to environmental groups and put effort into reclaiming spent oil fields, turning them into something beautiful and healthy. But whatever changes you decide upon, I advise you to make them discreetly, behind the scenes, without fanfare. Don't go shouting all over the place: Hey, look what we're doing! The public will find out eventually, and it'll come across as sincere, rather than your typical, transparent PR move."

Slick-head began to pound his Montblanc into the folder, but Annie ignored him.

"To summarize, I recommend that you spend the money you would have spent on a farcical ad campaign on something important, lasting, and truly worthwhile. It may be the most intelligent money you've ever laid down, and it'll make you the trendsetter of big business. The world has become a population of oil junkies, and you've been the worst kind of pusher. You've taken full advantage of our addiction. The best thing you can do now is to take yourself out of that role and create a new, enlightened one for yourself. And who knows, while you're at it, you might even save the junkies from themselves."

Rich had begun perspiring with her first sentence. He was now so wet under his jacket that he felt as though he'd just stepped out of a pool. Afraid to look at the faces around the table, he forced himself into a standing position and began to speak.

"Thank you. Now, ladies and gentlemen, I'd like you to consider the other side of that proposal. The agency is perfectly willing to launch whatever campaign you decide upon, and since Ms. d'Inard is leaving us as of today," he fairly hissed out her name, "we do not consider her presentation our own. We'd like to request your indulgence in granting us another week, so that we may strive to fulfill your expectations and present you with several more options."

Annie was still standing, and she smiled when she realized Rich had just fired her. When he finished speaking, she retrieved her things from the conference table. "I want to thank everyone for their patience. As Rich said, this is my last day at Haymaker's and I'll never again waste another minute of your time, or mine for that matter, spouting bullshit or listening to it."

The conference room was hushed, the mouths around the table mostly agape. Annie smiled at everyone, even Rich, whose face had gone the crimson of a shiny apple. Casually and without another word, she left the table and traversed the corridor to her office. Jack was away from his desk so she wrote him a note, simply saying thank you for everything and good-bye. She picked up the box with her things in it, flung her handbag over her shoulder, and then, almost serenely, she drifted out of the office.

She started her car engine but remained in the parking lot, her seat belt on, because she didn't know where to go. The building in front of her was no longer hers to go to. Inside they would be cursing her and swearing that she would never work in advertising again. The road home no longer led there. Overnight, the old stone farmhouse that she and Mike had so lovingly restored had ceased to be her haven. Mike still lived there, her son Marc still lived there, but Annie's bags had been brought down from the attic and were now scattered about her room, half full. The plans they had made for this weekend were canceled, excuses made. The friends they would normally see, the social events they would attend, the lazy Sunday mornings in front of the fire that gave way to relaxed family dinners—all these were gone, no longer hers to enjoy and take for granted. As she contemplated the loss of these things—sitting in her Mercedes, dressed in a pricey designer suit, adorned with the beautiful jewelry her husband had bought her—she was overcome with a fearful anxiety. She took a last look at her office building, put the car in gear, and headed for the river.

She drove on and on, following River Road, the Rolling Stones on the CD player. Her stomach begged her for food, but she took no notice. Her fuel tank was almost empty; she didn't care. Her car phone rang several times, but she didn't answer. After untold miles, she pulled off the road and parked alongside the water. Leaving the car doors open, she blasted "Let It Bleed" into the crisp air.

The lyrics rang out, "We all need someone we can lean on." As she listened, it struck her that she had no one. It wasn't that they were friendless, on the contrary, she and Mike were always on the go, having to turn down as many invitations as they accepted. But none of those friendships were very close, for in their high-powered world, intimacy was inadvisable. There was always this sense of having to guard yourself and your secrets, this fear of giving away something that might come back to haunt you. And with information as personal as this, no one could be trusted; she could never risk the damage it would do to Mike's dignity. No, she would have to manage alone, survive the coming months in isolation, without help or encouragement from anyone.

She wanted to think of something other than that dreadful disease, but it was impossible. The next instant, she recalled Jack telling her about a message from her doctor's office. Very quickly, she had one of Matt's nurses on her car phone.

She tried not to hope for anything when she nervously identified herself. "Yes, it's Annie d'Inard. You have lab results for me?"

"One moment." There was a rustling of paper. "Dr. Bennett said to tell you that our tests verified the ones the Red Cross ran. There's no change."

A sigh escaped. It could have been worse. "Thank you," she responded.

She had paused the music during the call, but now she cranked it up again. It moved into another cut, "Tell me honey, what will I do, when I'm hungry and thirsty, too?"

What will I do, she asked herself. She closed the car doors against the cold and turned the volume down. She was glad that she had decided on Scotland, because it comforted her to think of seeing it again.

When she went there the first time, she was barely a woman but she had already suffered a devastating blow. And in the aftermath, after months of fear and self-doubt, she mustered the courage to embark upon the journey, to undertake the rebuilding of herself. It wasn't the easiest but it was the wisest decision she had ever made, because she had been transformed, and not just by the voyage, but by something wonderful and unexpected—the discovery of love.

After all these years, the memory of Andrew still warmed her. Only twice in her life did she know love like that, and one of those times had been with Mike. She hadn't expected it then, either. Just like before, it had come over her quietly at first, as an overwhelming sense of peace that cocooned her, body and soul, and then, miraculously, transformed itself into a driving passion.

But the warmth faded when she reminded herself that Andrew had turned away from her, just as Mike had. She wondered at that now, at whether it had been her fault in loving them both too much, in wanting and needing more than they could give.

A sigh escaped as she glanced at the clock in her dash. The afternoon was wearing on, and her son would soon be home from school. It's time to go, she told herself, time to move on.

After so many restless nights, fatigue caught up with Annie. She fell asleep before her husband returned home, so she didn't get to tell him what had happened at the agency. On Friday night, she and Lucy went off to Marc's basketball game on their own. She had hoped to hear that Mike was coming too, but nothing was said about it beforehand.

They were in the bleachers, about fifteen minutes into the action, when they spied Mike coming toward them. He meant to sit next to Lucy, but she quickly scooted to her right so as to put him alongside his wife.

"I'm glad you could make it," Annie said to him. "Marc will be so happy you've come."

His mouth moved into something that resembled a smile.

They said nothing to one another until halftime, when Mike asked if she would walk outside with him. She followed demurely.

"Your secretary called me today. He was very worried about you. He'd phoned the house, but Lucy told him you weren't taking any calls."

"He filled you in on what happened, I take it."

"He thought I knew. It was somewhat embarrassing for both of us."

She wasn't sure, but he did appear distressed by the news. "I'm sorry. I was so tired last night, I fell asleep before you got home."

"You might have called me at the office."

"I didn't want to bother you. I don't feel I have the right anymore."

That comment was unexpectedly hurtful. "Do you want to tell me about it now?"

She shrugged. "There isn't much to tell. Rich and I got into it again just before the client meeting. When I told him I wanted a leave, he asked me if I'd lost my mind. That question made something snap, and suddenly everything I was doing seemed like an absurd waste of my time. I just stopped caring then, and when I was sitting in the conference room, waiting to give my presentation, I realized that the one thing I did care about was telling the truth. So that's what I did, and it got me fired."

A couple walked past them, and they waited until they were out of earshot. Mike gazed off into the fallow field that surrounded the private school. "I can understand your need for honesty."

Annie looked at the ground as she spoke. "It felt good. It reminded me of who I used to be."

He might have responded to that, but he recognized that this was neither the time nor the place, so he changed the subject. "I've been thinking. For Marc's sake, you and I should put more effort into our communications. And in that light, I'd like to propose a truce."

He'd caught her off guard. "A truce?"

"When you're away, it'll be even more critical. We can't not speak to one another when I'm caring for your son."

"No, no, of course not," she answered, surprise evident in her voice. "You're willing to do that? You're willing to talk to me while I'm gone, keep me apprised of everything?"

"It's the right thing to do, like my making time to come here tonight was the right thing." He hesitated briefly before adding, "I haven't done it often enough."

She had to contain herself, because the astonishment she felt over his remarks was almost turning into delight. "If you could do more of that, give him more of your time, it wouldn't only be good for him, Mike, I think it would do you some good, too." She watched his face; she might have gone too far.

He bit his lower lip before saying, "I want to make the most of this time we'll have together. He's growing very fast, and it won't be long before he's off to college. I see this as an opportunity I may not have again."

"Yes, yes, it is that." Her arms wanted very badly to wrap themselves around him, and she had to shove her hands into her pockets to keep them still. "By the way, have you heard anything from Matt?"

"Yes, I did, yesterday. I'm negative."

She tilted her head backward and in her mind said to the night sky—thank you, thank you, thank you. "I'm so very grateful for that, I thank God for that," she had to say aloud.

"And you?"

In an emotionless tone, she answered, "No change. That's what the nurse said, no change."

They became silent. Mike appeared to be wrestling with something, and it was another minute or so before he asked, "Have you made your reservations yet, for your flight?"

"Not yet."

"When are you thinking of leaving?"

"Does it matter to you? I mean, do you have plans to be out of town anytime soon?"

He answered, "No, I'll be around."

With discernible sadness, she told him, "Well, then I guess there's no point in waiting. Since I no longer have a job, there's nothing holding me here. I've discussed my plans with Lucy, and Marc and I spoke about it again today. He seems fine with my going next week, if that's OK with you."

He looked away again to answer, "I've no problem with that."

His ready acceptance of that decision dissipated what remained of her earlier burst of happiness. Still, there were things she wished she could have told him, so he would know that she was not giving up on their marriage, like how essential restoring her self-respect had become, and how the choices she was making now were meant to help her in that quest. But she read his pained expression as disdain, so she merely said, "We'd better get back inside" and started away.

Laying a hand on her arm, he halted her, then stammered slightly as he said, "One more thing. Since you've refused my financial support, will you allow me a gesture of goodwill, for Marc's sake?"

Gesture of goodwill—it sounded so detached and impersonal. "What's that?"

"Let me pay your travel expenses. That'll give you a head start and make me feel a little better about sending you off."

She frowned as she responded, "You're not sending me off."

"I know," he answered, then completed to himself: It just feels like it sometimes.

They reentered the gymnasium side by side. They were greeted by several people, fellow parents and others they knew from the community. They nodded and smiled and looked as though everything were normal. But the ache in

Mike's chest grew—the one that had been threatening while they spoke outside—as it occurred to him that unless he could find the courage to do what needed to be done, this could be the last time they presented themselves as a married couple.

As Annie took her seat, the words of one of the songs she had listened to the day before came to her mind: "She was practiced at the art of deception, well I could tell by her blood-stained hands."

She looked down at her lap and the hands that rested there. Her eyes settled on the beautiful rings that her husband had given her, the ones she wore on the third finger of her left hand.

Chapter 6

The housekeeper, Lucy, was an uncomplicated woman, with little education and a penchant for speaking her mind. But she was loved and admired by the family she cared for, because what she lacked in tact and specific knowledge, she made up for tenfold with her keen intuition and uncommon sense.

She was not at all happy with Annie's decision to leave, and she wasn't shy about expressing that. On the day before her departure, she accosted her as she was finishing her packing. "I never knew you to give up without a fight," she blasted out, angrily throwing a pile of freshly laundered clothes on her bed.

Keeping at her task, Annie answered flippantly, "There's a first time for everything."

Lucy scowled and folded her arms in against herself. "I don't see how going away is going to help anything. I've seen you through some bad times, but I've never seen you give up and walk away before." She was making reference to the time before Mike, when Lucy and Annie first met. She'd been employed by someone else then, by the man Annie had been involved with just after her divorce from Marc's father.

Annie stopped what she was doing and turned to face her. "For the record, I'm not giving up. And this isn't like before. There was something I could fight against then."

"Maybe there's nothing to fight against," she countered, "but you certainly have something to fight *for*."

Emphatically, Annie responded, "It's the right thing to do, to go away and give Mike his space. It's the only thing to do." Then she went back to her preparations.

Lucy tilted her head to one side as she said, "So you had an affair, so what? Say you're sorry and take your licks, but don't go running off! Stay here and fix things!"

Annie glanced sideways at the woman, then laughed abruptly. "You're a piece of work, you know that? You don't miss a goddamned thing, do you?"

"No, I don't, and I've known for quite a while what you were up to. What I don't understand is why he didn't see it." She toned down slightly and relaxed her posture. "But maybe he did. Maybe that's what got him in such a huff. He's mad at himself because he saw the signs and did nothing about it."

Annie finished folding the sweater she was holding, then held it to her chest. She sat on the bed as a spark of memory ignited and she recalled the morning when the letter came, when she'd told her husband about Glenn. He'd nodded his head and did not seem surprised; on the contrary, he'd looked as though a question had been answered for him.

"Listen, Lucy, I love you and I appreciate your concern, but I can't talk to you about what's going on in my marriage. I can't do that to Mike."

"OK, fine, I understand that, but you mark my words. Going over there won't make things any easier, it'll only complicate them." She started away but turned back. Pulling an envelope from under the pile of clothing she'd brought, she handed it to Annie. "A woman dropped this off while you were in the shower. She said to tell you it's no mistake, whatever that means."

As Lucy left the room, Annie looked over her airline ticket. It was the same flight she had decided on, but she had made reservations for coach. This was first class to London, connecting to Edinburgh. Information was also included regarding a limousine that would pick her up at the house and take her to the airport. A post-it note from the travel agent said that Mr. Rutledge had made these arrangements, and that he had paid for everything. A single tear rolled down a cheek as she recalled her husband's words—gesture of goodwill.

On the morning of her departure, Marc was relaxed and happy. He treated his mother as though she were leaving for vacation, telling her to take lots of pictures and to have a great time. Lucy was a little tearful and the dog was nonchalant, but an excruciating few minutes passed in the quiet of the morning as Annie said good-bye to her husband.

She had hoped he'd come to her but he didn't, so she waited in the living room while he showered and dressed after his run. She watched him descend the stairs, ready to leave for the office. Her presence startled him slightly.

"I want to thank you for what you did," she simply said.

He took a long breath. "I know how much you hate flying. You'll be more comfortable in first class."

It was risky, but she decided to say it anyway. "You shouldn't feel guilty, Mike. None of this was your doing."

Her comment rankled him. "Who said anything about guilt?"

"I'm sorry, I didn't mean, I just wanted to say thank you."

He went to the closet for his overcoat and yanked it on. "I can afford it. It's no big deal to me." He was at the front door with his hand on the knob, then he turned toward her. His expression had changed, but it was unreadable. "Take care of yourself, and let me know if you need anything."

"I will," she answered. The tears were coming in force, blurring her vision and adding a rasp to her voice. And then, on impulse, she whispered, "I'm not giving up on us."

His voice had changed, too. "I'd appreciate a call when you get there." The handle turned and opened the door, almost against Mike's will.

A rush of cold air quickly filled the space between them, and then it was over, just as rapidly, as the door closed again and caught the lock.

She waited in the first-class lounge with her dark glasses on, a tissue wadded in one hand. She paid little attention to anyone or anything, except to take notice of a distinguished-looking gentleman who was accompanied by an entourage. They sat in a far corner, separated from everyone else, and much activity centered around him, with papers being looked over and signed and cell phones ringing. When it was time to board, two airline attendants came to escort him so that he might be the first.

At the Center City offices of Westfield, Brown, Fleming, and Rutledge, the firm's youngest full partner wrapped up the day with a team meeting. The group of fifteen topnotch corporate specialists that Mike Rutledge led was fully engaged. They were in the early stages of what would likely be a long battle, representing a tobacco company in a civil action suit. The meeting went well but for the preoccupation of the group leader, whose gaze frequently drifted to the windowed wall of the conference room.

When everyone had gone, Mike rose from his chair, then walked to his adjoining office. He stopped before one of the windows and checked his watch. It was almost seven, a clear, cold, March evening. Across the street, his eyes caught the twinkle of lights that adorned the trees along Broad Street. Annie always liked seeing those lights, saying how it made every night seem like a holiday, like Christmas.

He lifted his eyes toward the sky. She would be taking off about now. He pictured her as the British Air 747 roared down the runway, her face tense, moist palms gripping the seat arms. If he were beside her, she would reach for his hand with both of hers. His smile would bring reassurance while the jet climbed into the night. For one brief moment, as he stared off into the night sky, he wished that he were with her, holding her trembling hands.

He became aware of a growing unease. It did not feel at all right letting her go like this, hounded as she was by onerous regrets and the ineludible fear of death. He looked again to the glimmering lights that brightened the street below. Tonight felt nothing like Christmas.

For the beginning of the flight Annie sat still, lost in thought. But when the cabin lights were dimmed and the passengers quieted, the restlessness she'd been trying to control brought her out of her seat to walk the aisles. She paced back and forth a few times with her head down, and in doing so managed to walk full speed into a fellow passenger. It was the gentleman she had seen in the lounge before they boarded.

"I'm so sorry, I wasn't looking where I was going."

She had knocked a partially full glass from his hand when she bumped him, and he bent to recover it. When he straightened up, he was smiling. "It's quite all right, no harm done."

"I didn't hurt you, did I?"

"Not a scratch. Are you all right?"

His refined English accent and manner charmed her and made her smile, too. "Yes, thank you. I'll be more careful next time."

With a deferential arm gesture, he motioned for her to pass him. She turned and watched him go to the galley for another drink, where the flight attendants flirted and fussed over him. When he returned to his seat, Annie was still standing in the aisle, and she noticed his face for the first time. Despite the darkened atmosphere, she could make out that it was marked by a large scar that ran across his left cheek and two smaller ones that broke up his forehead. For a few moments, she forgot her own troubles as she wondered about him and about how it had happened. An injury of that kind seemed out of place in someone of his obvious stature. She looked away when he drew nearer so he wouldn't catch her staring at him.

Sleep was hopeless without some assistance, so Annie consumed two large Cognacs. She stretched her legs across the empty seat next to hers and cuddled under a blanket. Her head rested against the window, and the last thing she saw before closing her eyes was the luminous ocean night.

The dream began as a familiar one. Annie was wandering through her garden at home, stopping now and again to inhale a fragrance, when everything turned white and stiff. The winter came abruptly, cruelly, killing everything within its reach.

Then there was wind, warm and steady and damp, that carried the scent of the ocean. The sky transformed from snow to pewter, and the clouds rumbled in the distance. She felt the approach of a powerful storm but she welcomed it, for she knew it would bring an end to the still life that surrounded her. She waited in the open, unafraid, as the lightning ruptured the heavens and drew ever nearer. When it was almost upon her, it seemed to swallow everything in great, blinding flashes of light, with bone-penetrating shudders and booms—and yet, she remained at its mercy.

Then the vision changed from the readily familiar to the vaguely so. The disturbance had delivered her to the sea, and she lay on her back, stretched upon the sand. Her nose recognized the pungency of a wood fire, and she stood to find it. A bonfire burned toward the west, its smoke trailing along the beach like a giant, beckoning finger. Beyond it she could see what appeared to be a human figure; it called to her in a voice too ethereal for the earth. It took some effort, but she finally discerned its message: "Come back to me," it said, and the words bore into her soul.

The dream left her dazed and disturbed, and the attendant who served her breakfast asked if she was all right. Annie put great store in dreams, especially ones such as this had been, the kind that lingered upon awakening, leaving her to wonder at its meaning. In this distracted state she remained, gazing out the window, when the gentleman she had bumped into stopped at her seat.

The morning light was brilliant, and he was wearing dark glasses. "Travel to London often?" he congenially inquired.

"It's been a while." She was self-conscious and preoccupied, and glanced only briefly at him, then back out of the window.

"Staying on here, then?"

"No, I'm connecting to Edinburgh," she informed him.

"Business, is it?" His accent bespoke breeding and a privileged education.

"No, vacation, sort of."

"In March? You're a brave sort," he teased.

As it surfaced, the sweetness of the memory imparted a smile to her lips. "The last time I was there, I arrived in March. It was the most beautiful spring I'd ever seen."

He leaned slightly so that he might better hear over the droning engines. "If you don't mind my asking, how long ago was that?"

She sighed as she sadly recalled, "Twenty-two years ago." Then she returned her gaze to the window.

Straightening himself abruptly, he commented, "That's a long time." Then, more formally, he offered, "I hope you have a pleasant holiday." He left her without waiting for a reply.

She turned her head to say thank you, but he was already gone.

* * *

The flight to Edinburgh was bumpy and uncomfortable and the approach downright terrifying as they searched for the runway in a fog so thick the pilot referred to it as a "pea-souper."

But the atmosphere inside the airport was relaxed and welcoming, and the people she encountered readily helpful, like the young man at the care hire. Had he not taken the time to go out to the car park with her, she might have spent the remainder of her day looking for the reverse gear.

In all her distraction, she forgot to change her money, and she didn't realize it until she was near the toll plaza on the Forth Road Bridge. She made a sudden, dangerous swerve to pull the car over, then got out and walked to the nearest booth.

Her cheeks bright red, she told the attendant, "I feel terribly silly, but I've just flown in from the States and I forgot to get some pounds. All I've got is American money."

The woman smiled warmly and continued to take tolls from the prepared motorists. "Not to worry," she told her, "let me ring up my supervisor." It took no more than half a minute. "He says it's about equivalent to fifty cents. Can you give us fifty cents?"

Annie handed her a five dollar bill. "This is the smallest I've got. I left all my change at home."

"That's too much," the attendant replied. "You just come on through my booth. I'll put the money in for you."

She was astounded by the gesture. "Out of your own pocket? That's so nice of you!"

"It's nothing," she blushed.

"Please take the five," Annie insisted, "keep it for yourself."

The woman shook her head and patted the hand that held the bill, saying, "Maybe someday I'll come to the States and need some assistance, and someone will help me out."

She knew it was no use trying to persuade the generous woman. "I do hope I'm the one with that opportunity," she told her. "I'd forgotten just how nice people are here. Thank you so much!"

She returned to her car and as she drove past the smiling toll taker, the woman waved to Annie as though they were old friends.

Crossing the bridge was like reliving a dream. Memories washed over her, her destination called to her, scenes from the past played before her. Tears began to cloud her vision, and it was a miracle she didn't have an accident. Her arrival at St. Andrews, however, jolted her out of the dream.

Even though it was early in the season, she found the streets jammed with people and automobiles. Hotels and bed and breakfast establishments had sprung up everywhere, and many of the quaint, local places she once knew had given way to tourist shops. It was horribly upsetting to see the changes because for all these years, Annie had kept her memories of St. Andrews like a sacred relic.

She'd made reservations at the Russell Hotel but didn't go there right away. She drove through the West Port instead, then down South Street to where it ends and curves into Abbey Walk. She parked her car at the pier and followed the path up the cliff. Reaching the top, standing between the sea and the cathedral ruins, her heart began to pound wildly. The bench was still there, the very same bench! Had she not been surrounded by people, she would have fallen to her knees and kissed the earth. She would have embraced the wall, sung to the ruins, laughed with the gulls. She raised her eyes to the top of St. Rule's tower and thanked the gods that this place, so holy in her eyes, had not changed.

Reverently, she entered the cathedral grounds. She reveled in each step she took on the soft, mossy grass. She walked from corner to corner, breathing in the fresh sea air as though she was taking the cure, touching tombstones and bits of wall as though they were alive. When she had drunk her fill, she went out again and made her way to the bench.

A couple had been occupying it, and when they left she rushed in after them. The seat retained their warmth and as she settled herself down, her hand touched the heat. She closed her eyes and imagined that it had been Andrew sitting there. He was wearing his scarlet robe, and he'd just gotten up to hurry off to his lectures.

She remained on the bench for an unknown amount of time as the memories visited her, one after the other, like mourners at a wake coming to pay their respects.

Mike was at his office when she reached him. The sound of her voice was unexpectedly comforting. "How was your flight?" he asked.

"Not bad, thanks to you. I even caught a little sleep."

With an ocean between them now, he found it easier to talk. "What's it like being back?" he wondered.

"It's almost not the same place, it's changed so much. I can't believe how crowded it's gotten, and the tourist shops are everywhere. There's this enormous, brand new hotel on the Old Course, and there are loads more students than there used to be, but I haven't seen a single scarlet robe, not a single one."

"It must be upsetting," he observed.

"It is. It brought tears to my eyes." She could hear the rustle of papers and accurately pictured her husband going through them as they talked. "But then I went to the cathedral. I parked down by the pier and walked up the hill, and thank God—thank God—at least that was the same. Going in that gate was like opening a door and walking into my past."

Mike's secretary interrupted in a soft voice, and he responded that he'd only be a minute. "What'd you do after that?" he asked, when he turned his attention back to Annie.

It occurred to her that he was being nicer than he might otherwise be because someone could hear. Never mind that, she told herself, at least he's talking to you, and that's more than you deserve. "I stayed there for a long while, because it was the only place I felt connected. It seemed to be the only place that hadn't changed. You know, I'd never thought about it before, but while I was sitting there it struck me how sad it is that the cathedral stood for such a short time as it was meant to be, whole and beautiful. It made me think how nothing perfect can last."

Mike shifted uncomfortably in his seat and briefly drummed his fingers on the desk. "Have you checked into your hotel yet?"

"I'm in my room now. How's Marc?"

"I took him out to dinner last night, just the two of us. We had a good talk. He seems fine with your being away. In fact, he's excited about you being in St. Andrews again, because he knows how much it means to you. How's the Russell? Is it like you remembered?"

She was sitting on the bed staring down at the coverlet, but now she lifted her gaze to the bay window that afforded a view of the West Sands. "I was never in any of the rooms before, but they're very nice, very comfortable. But the bar, that's exactly as I remember it, the same burgundy velvet upholstery, the same window seat. It was very weird walking in there after so many years. I expected to see my friends sitting with their pints, waiting for me."

There was silence.

"Mike?"

The paper rustling ceased. "Yes?"

"I know this is hard for you to hear and even harder to believe, but I've never stopped loving you." She kept her focus on the wide, flat beach that lay stretched before her, recalling that it was there that she'd last seen Andrew. "It's just that I've always had this hunger. No, it's not that," she realized now, "it's more like an emptiness."

He said nothing.

With her thoughts a muddle of past and present, she worried that she wasn't making sense, so she explained, "When I was sitting at the cathedral today, I realized that I've always been this way. I keep trying to fill that emptiness and in my efforts, I seem to keep making the same mistakes." She held onto the receiver with both hands.

Her deeply personal reflections threatened the safe distance at which Mike needed to keep his wife. To remove himself, he asked her, "When do you see about a cottage?"

She hadn't expected him to respond to her musings, but she was still sorely disappointed. In a dejected tone of voice, she informed him, "I'm meeting someone tomorrow morning."

"Well, good luck with that. I hope you find what you're looking for."

She wondered if he meant something other than a place to live. "I'll call you in a few days to see how things are going at home, OK?" At home, how painful it had become to say those words.

"That's fine. Try to reach Marc today. He's anxious to talk to you."

"I'll call the house as soon as we hang up." She paused for a moment before she added, "I miss you, Mike."

It was quiet on the other end, then Mike said, "Best of luck with the cottage, and thanks for calling." It was a very business-like voice.

Annie felt stunned and disconnected after the call ended, so she remained where she was, staring out at the West Sands. A vivid image began to take shape in her mind; it was of herself, driving away from Andrew, his solitary figure fading into the mist and smoke. She rose from her seat and walked to the window, when she realized that the disturbing dream she'd had on the flight this morning was about that, about the last time she'd seen him. Standing alone at the hotel window, twenty-two years removed from that night, she experienced the despair all over again, and was consumed by the emptiness it left in its wake.

When he'd replaced the receiver, Mike found himself staring at a painting that hung in his office, a watercolor that had been a gift from Annie for their fifth wedding anniversary. She had commissioned a local artist to paint their farm, and much to her surprise, the artist had included her in a rather melancholy pose standing near the pond. Mike was always intrigued by that image of his wife, and he fancied that the artist had captured an expression of her soul. After studying it for a couple of minutes, he approached the painting, then laid a delicate finger on the long, dark hair.

* * *

When Mike Rutledge announced that he would be marrying the beautiful Annie d'Inard, his prestigious law firm gave the couple an enormous party at the Bellevue Stratford Hotel. With the exception of a few single women who had had dreams of marrying him themselves, everyone was delighted for the firm's youngest partner. They were happy for him because his life had been so cruelly disrupted three years earlier that many of his close friends had begun to wonder if he would ever recover.

He had been devoted to his wife Michele, and they were expecting the birth of their first child in four months. The usually miserable Philadelphia winter was passing happily; the couple had spent a particularly enjoyable holiday together, looking at children's things in the stores and planning for next Christmas with their baby. On her way to work one dark, February morning, Michele impulsively pulled into the empty parking lot of a bank to get some cash. As she completed her transaction at the ATM, she was approached by a man with a gun. Seconds later, she lay on the pavement, bleeding profusely from the abdomen.

When it happened, Mike had already been at work preparing for the day in court. Since her handbag and car had been taken, the police had to wait for the bank to identify Michele through their transaction records. While his wife underwent surgery and lay at death's door, Mike argued his case and went about his business. He was not notified until that afternoon.

She had been resuscitated at the scene and lived twelve days on a ventilator before the decision was made to end life support. No one understood why such a thing should happen to people as happy and in love as they were, and although the surveillance camera caught the criminal and he eventually was sentenced to life in prison, Mike's pain was not eased; he felt as though he'd been given his own life sentence. He took two months off from work, it was not possible for him to return any sooner, and when he did, his colleagues could not believe the transformation. He'd lost twenty pounds, his hair had begun turning gray, his cheeks had fallen in, and there were permanent dark circles under his eyes.

He buried himself in his work, arriving at the office before anyone else and staying until nine or ten o'clock at night. His professional life prospered as a result, and his reputation as a corporate litigator grew and was soon unsurpassed. Just over two years after his wife's death, he won a landmark case representing a tobacco company and was made a full partner. At about the same time and in an effort to please his well-meaning friends, he reluctantly began to date, but it was painfully difficult and he usually saw a woman no more than once.

Annie d'Inard had moved into her Society Hill apartment with her year-old son a year and a half after the death of Michele Rutledge. Her apartment was on Spruce

Street, a couple of blocks away from Mike's townhouse. They never spoke but became familiar with each other's faces because they shopped in the same places, used the same dry cleaner, the same drugstore. He noticed Annie initially because of her son; the little boy appeared to be the same age as his child would have been.

Mike's townhouse was located next to a park where Annie brought her son, and the window in his study overlooked it. At first he paid attention only to the child, but over time he began to notice the boy's mother more and more. Her strikingly pretty face always seemed to wear a sad, stressed look, a look he recognized from his own, the kind that said she struggled with something inside. He noticed too, how devoted she seemed to the child, and how tender and loving she was with him. And they always seemed to be alone; he never saw a man about. He would watch for them on Saturday mornings, sometimes going to sit on a nearby bench when they were there.

The better part of a year went by like this. Then suddenly, they seemed to disappear. Their regular visits to the park stopped, and Mike began to wonder if they had moved away. Time passed, a couple of months or more, before he saw Annie again in the grocery store, but she was without the child. He had never seen her without him and it instantly worried him. He waited for her to come through the checkout before approaching her; he had to know if the boy was all right.

"I beg your pardon, you don't know me but I'm your neighbor."

She smiled, though not broadly. "Yes, I've seen you around."

"I hope you won't think me impertinent, but I wonder if everything is all right with your little boy? Is he well?" He watched her eyes fill with tears and it made his heart skip a beat.

She was always on the verge of tears these days and they came pouring down her cheeks now. "He's fine, really, he's well. It's just that he's been with his father, and I'm having a terrible time getting him to return Marc to me."

Annie was holding a bag of groceries and Mike took it from her. "Would you like to go for some coffee?" he asked softly.

He waited at the door of her apartment while she put away her purchases. Then they walked to a little coffee-house on Headhouse Square, where they were seated at a table in the middle of the crowded room. Everyone around them seemed extraordinarily busy, bustling in with full shopping bags, gulping coffee, and then running off again, as though engaged in a race.

"I've seen you and your son often," he began. "My house is near the park where you bring him on the weekends."

"Oh," she answered and sipped at her steaming café au lait.

His coffee sat before him, untouched. "I hope you don't think I'm being nosy, but I've enjoyed watching him play and watching you with him." After he said that, he felt himself blush.

She set her mug down and allowed herself a minimal smile. "No, I don't think that. It really is like a small town here, isn't it?" she said to put him at ease.

"We all live so close together in the neighborhood, it's hard not to notice one another." He was quiet for a moment, watching her sad, hazel eyes. "I'm a lawyer, you know. If you're having legal problems, I might be able to help."

Annie had been studying his face as they spoke. In the hour or so that they'd been together, she'd felt herself being drawn into his eyes, wondering what it was behind them that made her feel so comfortable with him. "I was the one who was ill, not my son," she said, then waited to see if he reacted. When he didn't, she continued. "I had to go into the hospital for a while, so I asked my ex-husband to take Marc. He lives in San Francisco. Now that I'm ready to take Marc home, he won't return him, and he's threatening me."

He seemed distressed as he asked, "Physically?"

"No, with something personal. He's threatening to go to court and say I'm an unfit mother so he can get custody of him."

He lowered his eyes. "I take it there's something then," he realized, "something he can use against you."

"It has to do with what I was hospitalized for." She dropped her gaze and sighed before adding, "I got into trouble with prescription drugs."

In his most professional tone, he responded, "I see." But the tone quickly changed into one that indicated his concern. "Are you better now? Are you through it?"

"Yes," she answered in a voice quieted by shame. "I'm still battling some depression, but the worst is over. I'm much stronger now." She took a breath before adding, "But the depression, I don't think that's going away until I have my baby home. God, but I miss him." Those last words came out awkwardly through the spasms that were tightening her throat.

He fancied that he could feel her anguish as she spoke, feel it reaching into him, just as he had when he'd been watching her from a distance those many months. But in her presence, the sensation was far more intense; it made him want to take her hands in his, want to say to her "it's all right, I understand," but he fought the urge, reminding himself that they had only just met, though it certainly seemed otherwise to Mike.

"Well, I don't handle this kind of thing myself, but I can refer you to someone who does," he told her instead. "I can find you the best attorney available, if that will help."

He watched her hands, soft and pale and unadorned, as they wrapped gracefully around her mug.

"Attorneys cost money," she frowned. "I don't have money, he does. He's an investment banker with a rich second wife. His funds are limitless, mine are nonexistent. I had to take a leave of absence from my job, and I used up the little savings I had just to pay the rent."

Mike sat pensively before speaking again. "It's terribly unfair that the law favors those with money. I've never liked that about my profession," he admitted with a slight shake of his head. "But maybe there is something I can do. I'm not a family lawyer, you understand, but I wouldn't mind writing letters for you, and I'd do it gratis."

Annie was genuinely surprised. "Why would you do that?" she wondered.

He shrugged as he answered, "Oh, selfish reasons. It'd help me feel better about what I do for a living, for one. And you know, in matters like this, sometimes all it takes is a well-written letter or two." For her sake, he smiled.

When she smiled back at him, the green in her eyes intensified, and all the noise and activity that surrounded them seemed to diminish, making it feel as though the crowded coffeehouse had suddenly emptied out.

"You'd do that for me?" Her voice was childlike and disbelieving. "But we've only just met, and you don't even know the particulars."

For the first time since Michele's death, Mike Rutledge felt something other than aching sadness. Sitting close to Annie, breathing in her perfume, seeing the smile he had brought to her face, he forgot where he'd been the past few minutes. He forgot his surroundings, what it was he was supposed to be doing, and for a few precious moments, he forgot what had happened before.

"Yes," he answered, in a gentle voice, "I'd do that for you." His breathing quickened when their eyes met again. "I was wondering, do you have any plans for dinner tonight?"

Chapter 7

St. Andrews, 13 March, 1994

I parked my car at the foot of the pier and climbed the path up the cliff. My heart beat fast, though not from the effort. I am here, I am back, I said to the stones. There was no music.

So much is familiar, so little is certain, everything trapped in the movement of time. Gulls circle and dive, creating imperceptible spirals of motion, clouds tumble through alleys of wind. A young man and woman sit near me and tenderly speak their hearts. I wait alone and try to listen to mine.

I sat for a while on the bench. I felt disturbed and sad. I returned to my car and drove the winding road to Crail. I went into a pub and ordered a pint of heavy, then sat alone in the corner, listening to the crackle of the fire. It did not taste as I remembered.

After eating breakfast alone in her room, Annie left for her appointment with the land and estate agent on Church Street. She descended the steps of the Russell, paused when she was on the street, and then abruptly turned left. She walked the long way round, down The Scores to Golf Place, and then up North Street and over. She took this detour because had she not, she would have been confronted with something she was unprepared for. Within feet of the hotel there was, or used to be, a small, unassuming cottage that had been very important to her. It wasn't that it brought back unpleasant memories; it was the opposite. But the memory of that special place played such an integral part in the person she was that it unnerved her. She was not ready to see it again: She was afraid to see it again.

Looking through the selection of mostly flats that the real estate agent had prepared for her, Annie disregarded all but one: a furnished, two-bedroom cottage south of St. Andrews that was the tenant house to a farm. The agent made a quick call to the owners, and they were on their way to see it. While they drove along the Kingsbarns Road, he discreetly inquired after the reason she was planning a long stay in St. Andrews.

"Are you with the university?"

"No, I'm not."

"Are you familiar with the area at all?"

"Yes, but from many years ago."

"It couldn't have been that many." He smiled politely. "Were you an exchange student?"

"No, I wasn't," she answered, looking out the window. The fields of rape seed were already growing into a vibrant, deep green. Soon the hills would be draped in a spectacular yellow, so vivid and brilliant it could be rivaled only by the sun.

The young man turned off the road after a few miles, onto a dirt and gravel drive that was riddled with holes. The drive traced a line of woods to the left and edged a large crop of barley on the right. They drove for a quarter of a mile before seeing the little cottage.

It sat alone on a high, flat plain at the top of steep cliffs that dropped straight to the sea. The farmhouse and its outbuildings were within sight, but they were farther down the lane where it curved and followed the coastline. Annie walked around to the rear of the cottage before going in. The rear-facing windows all had this view—fields, cliffs, sea, and in the distance, hard to make out in the mist, the towers of St. Andrews. Grinning, she shook her head in disbelief. It was exactly what she'd hoped to find. Everything about the place seemed right, even familiar, as though it were meant to be.

"I'll take it," she told the agent.

He looked surprised. "Before you've gone in? I should have thought that . . ."

"Is there a problem?"

"Oh no, not at all, it's just that you being an American, if you'll forgive my saying so, I would not have thought this the sort of place you'd be wanting."

"It's exactly what I'm looking for."

He raised one brow slightly. "I see, well you must go in and allow me to point out a few things." He opened the back door and they went into the tiny kitchen. "There are a few saucepans and the cooker works well enough, but as you can see, it's not meant for haute cuisine."

"That's fine. I don't have much of an appetite these days."

"There are two bedrooms off the hall, and the bath is here." He opened the closed door next to the kitchen for a quick peek, then led her into the main room. "And this is the sitting room. Unfortunately, it doesn't have the view."

"That's too bad."

"The furnishings have seen better days, but the beds are new. Mr. and Mrs. McBain are lovely people. I'm certain they'll help if there's anything in particular you need." Anticipating a problem, he grimaced slightly when he informed her, "There's no central heating, you know."

"That's OK," she answered, "there's a fireplace."

He quickly added, "Mr. McBain keeps the coal bunker filled and there's a wood pile. I would imagine you noticed that. There's no telephone either, but you can arrange to have one connected if you'd like. Now then, are you still interested?" he asked.

"It's perfect," she told him. "When can I move in?"

Back at his office when all the papers had been signed and Annie was given the key, the young man recalled, "You didn't say how it was you happened to be here before. Might I ask?"

"I had come here to visit a friend. I didn't stay long, though, to my everlasting regret."

Annie drove back to the cottage to make a list of what she needed. She then spent the rest of the afternoon in and out of the shops, making a few purchases. Among them were a corkscrew, two decent wine glasses, a French coffeepot and mugs large enough for café au lait, and a handblown glass vase. It was a pleasant enough afternoon and the shopkeepers were every bit as charming as she remembered, but her loneliness was difficult to bear. With every step, memories came back to her, recollections of having been in those shops before, walking those streets with Adam, with Susannah and Melville. But the most bittersweet memories were of Andrew. For more than twenty years she had dreamed of being back and doing the very things she did today, but in her dreams she was never alone, she was always with Andrew.

That evening she decided to have her supper in the public room instead of the dining room at the hotel, having noticed an older gentleman enjoying his meal there the night before. He was there again and was almost through his plate of broiled sole when Annie came in. He had a congenial, welcoming smile, and when he saw her tonight he nodded and said "good evening." When she finished her dinner, she walked over and introduced herself; the solitary manner in which she'd spent the afternoon left her hungry for someone to talk to.

"Tom Keegan," he answered, "how do you do? Won't you sit down?"

His table was next to the fire, and she welcomed the opportunity to sit near the warmth. The evening had grown chilly and blustery, and rain had just begun to tap the large window at the end of the room. Gordon, the owner of the Russell, responded to the change in temperature by dropping several lumps of coal on the grate, then stoking it into a blaze. That completed, he asked Annie and Tom if they had enjoyed their dinners.

"Looks like we're in for some rough weather," Tom offered, once Gordon had left them. "Are you on holiday?"

"Of a sort. I'm taking an extended leave from my work."

"Oh? What kind of work do you do?"

"I've been in advertising for the past seven years. Before that it was public relations, which is pretty much the same thing, the same bullshit."

Tom laughed but seemed embarrassed.

"I beg your pardon," she said. "I'm afraid I've offended you."

"I'm not offended, just taken a bit off guard. I see a great many American films, you know."

Now she laughed. "What a public relations fiasco they are! My God, the image we present to the world through our movies. But it's our own damned fault. We've no one to blame but our greed-driven, violence-worshiping selves."

He was pleasantly surprised by her comments and decided he'd like to know her better. "Might I buy you a drink? What are you having?" Their table was next to the bar, and he had only to give a slight nod to the barmaid, whom he knew by name.

"Thank you, that's very kind. I'm drinking Scottish heavy."

"That's an unusual drink for an American woman. How do you know heavy? That's what the locals drink."

Her face softened and she glanced at the window seat before telling him, "I was here many years ago, when I was a young woman. Heavy's what my friends and I would drink because it was the cheapest. I've been waiting all this time to taste it again."

A pretty, dark-haired girl of about six or seven, who'd been sitting in a corner with her schoolbooks, went to the bar to help herself to a soft drink. When she finished, the barmaid gave her the drinks that were meant for Tom and Annie, and as she served them he said, "Thank you Judith, dear, that was very kind of you. Did you finish your schoolwork?"

"Not quite," she answered sweetly, "but mummy says I must go up now."

"Well then, good night to you," he answered, "and sweet dreams."

Through a wide grin that revealed some newly erupting teeth, she responded, "Good night, Mr. Keegan."

"The owner's daughter," he informed Annie as they watched her leave the room. "I live here in the hotel, you know. I'm from the Borders, but I've retired and come to St. Andrews for the sea air."

"You live in the hotel? Wouldn't you be more comfortable in an apartment?" she wondered.

"A flat would be too much for me. I haven't the strength to tidy up and cook, you see. I've only half a lung left, and I've been rather weakened by months of radiation therapy."

Annie lowered her voice. "Oh, I'm so sorry. Lung cancer?"

"I was quite the smoker," he grinned, as he lifted his glass of Scotch. "At least I've not had to give this up."

She clinked her glass on his. "Here's to you, Mr. Keegan!" She almost said "to your health" but then thought better of it.

"Tom, if you please. I prefer Tom." He relished his drink, holding the taste of it for as long as he could. "Were you a student here?"

"No, but my friends were. I was only here for two months. I arrived late in March of 1972 and left in late May." She relaxed and settled back into her chair.

"And you haven't been back since? It must have changed awfully. That's a long time to have been away."

"Oh, that it has. The town's really spread out and turned into something of a tourist mecca. It wasn't like that before."

"No, I imagine not," he realized. "A lot of it has to do with the E.E.C., you know, open borders and all that. And there are the golfers who feel obliged to make a holy pilgrimage here. Do you play?"

"I've only played once in my life." She looked out the window in the direction of the Old Course. "And that was here, on the Jubilee Course."

"Really? Well, I should say, if you were to do it only once, this is quite the place to have done it."

Annie returned his smile. "Are you ready for another drink? It's my turn to buy. I think I'll switch to a single malt, too."

She rose and walked to the front of the bar, then whispered to the barmaid to put all their drinks on her bill.

Back at the table, she tasted the Scotch with some trepidation, then looked into the glass as she said, "You know, the first time I had Scotch was back then. It might have even been in this very room. I drank quite a bit of it while I was here and liked it, but for all the years afterward, it never tasted good to me. I could never drink it. Now I find I'm enjoying it again. Isn't that strange?"

"It's like a great many things, I think, that are influenced by the time and place," he observed. "Like a picnic, when ordinary sandwiches taste marvelous because of the setting."

"I never likened it to that, but of course it's that way." She was beginning to feel a little drunk, and it loosened her tongue. "The taste of it, it reminds me of someone, someone who often tasted like this when we kissed."

Tom chuckled. "From the expression on your face, I'd say it's a nice memory."

Grinning broadly, she asked him, "Do you see that window seat? We always sat there, my friends and I. That was our spot. We came here when we wanted quiet because the other pubs were so crowded and noisy. We'd sit there, all squeezed in together, and there was always room for one more." The recollection, which at first made her happy, filled her now with melancholy as she realized how far removed she was from those wondrously simple days.

Tom observed the sudden change in her expression and saw her eyes moisten.

"Look at me, getting maudlin with a perfect stranger," she said as she wiped away a tear. "I should go up to my room before I ruin your evening completely." The alcohol was getting to her, weakening the meager defenses she'd been holding against the memories.

"There's no need to rush off, and you're not ruining my evening," he wanted her to know. "Stay and have another," he said, nodding to the barmaid again.

They sat in silence while their drinks were served.

"I do apologize, Tom. It's just that returning has been more difficult than I imagined. And now that I'm here again, it's really hit me how that part of my life is over."

She finished off her nearly empty glass and in one seamless motion, traded it for the other.

Tom lifted his fresh drink. "I know that feeling well, especially now."

Understanding the reference, she blushed in embarrassment. "Please forgive me. I don't mean to run on about myself. God, but I'm an idiot tonight."

"Not to worry. It's nice to think about something other than myself."

Attempting a smile, she asked him, "Are you alone here?"

"My wife died four years ago."

"Have you any children?"

"I have a son I haven't seen in years. We had a falling out and he went off very angry. I'm ashamed to say that I don't even know where he lives now."

"Oh my, that's very sad." She began to think of how much she owed Mike for bringing Marc back to her. A dull ache formed in her chest, and she had to look away as she told Tom, "I have a son. I can't imagine how awful it would be to not see him for years."

In a stoic voice, Tom told her, "It's one of those things, you know. Our relationship was never an easy one."

"Does he know about your health?" she asked.

"He left soon after his mother died. I was diagnosed almost exactly one year after that, after Marjorie died."

"Didn't he have any friends that you could contact to find out about him?"

He lifted his glass again and twirled it, keeping his eyes on the honey-colored liquid. "There are a few. When I moved here, I gave them my address and they promised to give it to him should they have the opportunity."

The light in the public room was poor, but as she studied his face, she recognized how sallow his complexion was. "I guess that's all you can do."

His head tilted slightly. "There are a great many things one can do in life, a great many choices to be made as you go along. But as time goes on, those choices become fewer and fewer. You get to a point where you run out of them, and all you're left with are the consequences of the ones you've already made."

"How true that is," she answered, her speech slurring slightly. "And we make those choices so blithely when we're young, thinking we have so much time—time to undo the mistakes, time to right the wrongs. But it slips away from us, doesn't it? It goes speeding on its way, and we never get it back."

Disconsolately, he added, "With each choice, we set things in motion that lead us further and further away until it's virtually impossible to get back." Tom was thinking of his son and also feeling the unbinding effects of the Scotch.

"Impossible," she echoed, "how I despise that word."

Tom's face said that he did, too.

A chatty group of Japanese golfers entered the public room then. They commandeered the window seat and as they settled in, Annie regarded their polite maneuverings with curiosity; they bowed and stiffened and made every attempt not to infringe on anyone else's space. How different it was from the way she used to be with her friends, she mused. They welcomed the warmth and scent of one another, the wonderful intimacy of bodies rubbing and hands touching. She looked past the golfers and into the reflective window; the rain was blowing horizontally from the sea, pounding it with noisy persistence.

She turned again to Tom. "Just up the street from here, there is, or used to be, a little cottage that was named 'The Whaum.' I haven't been able to walk in that direction since I've been here because I'm afraid to see it. I'm afraid it won't be there, or it'll be so different I won't know it, or it'll make me too sad to see it again. It reminds me of things." She sighed before explaining, "There was a time when I had an important choice to make, and it reminds me of that. I've always wondered if I made the right one, and I've always felt in my heart that I didn't."

"It's not easy to look back," he responded, "especially when one's made a mess of one's life, though I speak for myself. Your life is probably not a mess."

Annie swallowed the lump in her throat. "It is a mess."

He waited for her to say something more. When she didn't, he told her, "Well, one thing is certain."

"What's that?" She felt the escape of another tear, and quickly brushed it away.

"Whatever choice you made, whatever the consequences, you have your health and your youth, and you still have time and choices left to you. You should go and see that cottage; face whatever it is you have to about the past and then get on with it. Time is an impatient companion. It never waits for us."

Her throat tightened at the mention of her health, and she had to sit quietly and think of something else before speaking again. "You're a damned good sport to listen to all this rubbish from someone you've just met," she finally said.

With a quiet, understanding smile, Tom observed, "It's easier sometimes, isn't it, talking to strangers?"

She nodded her agreement, then asked him, "I was wondering, if you don't have any plans, would you be my guest for dinner tomorrow? I promise not to break into tears again." She tried to laugh but didn't quite make it.

"I'd be honored."

She turned her head away from her companion and looked once more toward the window. Outside, the sea was rearing in fits of anger, the rain blew harder against the glass, and the taste of Scotch in Annie's mouth was strong.

Chapter 8

Annie spent only four nights at the Russell Hotel because she wanted to get her spending under immediate control. She had a fixed amount of money, the funds Mike had insisted she save from her own salary over the years, and she needed to spread it as far as possible. She had no way of knowing what would become of her, whether she would remain in Scotland indefinitely or whether she would ever be able to return to her home. She could count on nothing and knew she'd best be prepared for anything. And it was important that she not be dependent on Mike.

One expense Annie could not avoid was a telephone. A cell phone was out of the question, but as a mother so far away from her child it was imperative that she be reachable. The young land and estate agent helped her through the bureaucracy, and she had one installed by the end of her first week; she made certain that Lucy and Marc had the number as soon as it was connected.

The car was her biggest problem. It was hired from the airport, the least expensive model the agency had, and it was eating up her budget. But she decided she'd rather go hungry than feel confined, so she tightened her belt and resolved to keep the petrol costs to a minimum. If she stayed on longer than a couple of months, she would have to find another way.

And there was so much to see in Fife; on beautiful days it was hard to stay put. There were so many glorious pastures, carefully tended farms, quaint cottages and country inns. There were castles open to the public, museums to visit, harbors to sit beside, and charming villages to explore. Spring was ready to burst, and she wanted to keep an eye on it, to watch for it and see it happen, little by little, day by day. She had waited many years to see the spring again in Scotland, too many years.

When the weather was bad, she turned her attention to her cottage. It had most certainly seen better days—the furnishings were deplorable, the windows and walls caked with coal smoke and badly in need of paint. Her first efforts were on those walls; she scrubbed them until her arms hurt. She was able to get the windows clean without much trouble, removing and putting away the dingy curtains that hung on them. They afforded little privacy and anyway, as isolated as the house was, she didn't need them. Despite her efforts, it remained a rather pathetic place, but no matter; she had not rented it for what it looked like inside. As thrilled as she'd been when she first saw it, she was even more delighted with her choice when she discovered that it had its own little path that descended the cliffs from the lawn's edge and led directly to the beach.

On the day she moved in, she celebrated with the purchase of some spring flowers and a decent bottle of wine. Flowers were something she was unwilling to do without, no matter how frivolous the expense. She poured the wine and christened the cottage with a toast, then placed the tulips and jonquils in the vase she'd purchased. She smiled to herself as she fiddled with the arrangement, thinking all the while that this was something she'd be doing at home. Then, in the next instant, she chastised herself. She knew she had to stop doing that, to stop thinking of that house as her home. Mike might never want her back, and she needed to be prepared for that. It was no good thinking any other way.

She pondered these things while she was unpacking, settling into self-imposed exile. She thought of this and more as she hung her clothes in the shallow bedroom closet, as she scrubbed the chipped bathtub, and as she arranged her toiletries in the rusting cabinet. With no one to speak to, her mind flooded with thoughts, old ones that had plagued her throughout the past, and a new, unsettling one that had only recently emerged.

Did Mike ever really love me, she wondered now, or was our relationship all about rescue? That would explain the loss of him, she decided, the withdrawal of his attention when she no longer needed saving.

Annie could tell by the way he'd handled her airline ticket that he was feeling inclined to do it again, feeling inclined to take care of her. That's how it had been when they first met and married; he'd come riding in like the cavalry. But Annie and her son had not been the only beneficiaries of his actions; in delivering them, he discovered something that he sorely needed—a way to fill the void that had been left by the loss of his wife and unborn child. Caring for them made him feel his worth as a man again, and better than he had in a long while. But when Annie and Marc were well and strong and standing on their own, he inexplicably began to back away, and as time went by, he managed to construct a wall around himself so thick with reticence and detachment, it proved impossible to breach.

She took a break from her cleaning and unpacking and walked to the kitchen to make some tea. As she stood before the cooker waiting for the kettle's whistle, she attached new importance to the idea of putting distance between them. I can't let that happen again, she told herself. No matter what happens with my health or my finances, I can't let him rescue me again. If he comes to terms with what I've done, if he decides to forgive me and give our marriage a second chance, that's another matter. But to stay with me because he feels sorry for me, I don't want that, I've never wanted that. I want him to love me, really love me, and I want to be allowed to love him.

Although she recognized the necessity of being away, it was still terribly difficult. She missed her son awfully—

the sound of his laughter, the teasing way in which he played with her, the life his youthful spirit imparted to the household. The endless quiet of the cottage made her sometimes long for Lucy's chatter and her running, sardonic commentary on everyone and everything. She missed the dog, too, who shadowed her when she was in the house and never failed to express his delight at seeing her at day's end. As for her husband, missing him was something she was accustomed to, though oddly enough, it was his absence that she felt most keenly.

Still thinking of her family, she stirred her tea, then walked with it to the kitchen window. If I'm here when school's out, she told herself, I'll have Marc come over. In the meantime, I'll make ready for that and have everything as nice as possible for his arrival. As she began making plans in her head, the lawn captured her attention. Though it was a pleasing sight, it was altogether too plain. It occurred to her that it would be nice to see something colorful from the windows and to have a place outside to sit and view the sea. As soon as possible, she resolved, I'll plant a garden. That'll make it more like home. That'll make me feel better, and this, after all, is Scotland. How can I be without a garden?

Scanning the grassy expanse from her vantage point, she decided on the location—the lawn's edge, near the path that led down the cliffs. A bench surrounded by flowers would be lovely there. She donned a warm jacket and walked outside to be certain. The bench could be angled toward the north and west so that she might view the sunset and the bell towers of St. Andrews. As she contemplated her garden, Annie was overcome with a sudden, profound awareness, as though it were only now sinking in, that she was here again, really here. Just up the coast, within her reach, lay the cathedral, the castle, the university—the Whaum. The Whaum—how that place haunted her. Tom Keegan was right, she needed to face it. Tomorrow, she promised herself. I'll go by there in the morning, when the sun fills the rose garden.

In late March in Scotland, the dawn becomes impatient. Like a developing insomniac, it rises earlier and earlier each morning and stays bright later each night. It is such a rapid, significant change from the brevity of the winter day that everyone and everything is affected. In St. Andrews, arrangements of daffodils appear everywhere: on the deep windowsills of homes, on counters in shops, and in the streets, overflowing large buckets as they're offered for sale. Sidewalks are swept clean, windows are made to sparkle, and gardens are cleared and prepared. The rich, mahogany earth of the surrounding fields is tilled and carefully planted to the accompanying cries of scavenging gulls, and the sheep grow fat with their offspring. Everyone comes alive with the lingering light, and everything is purified by the cleansing rains and winds.

On one such bright morning, Annie awakened with a smile; the dream she recalled was so sweet, it helped her forget her troubles for a time. It had been about Andrew, and it had left her in a wistful frame of mind, no longer afraid to do what she must.

She parked on Market Street and did her shopping first. After she stowed her purchases in the car, she headed down Butt's Wynd. She had strolled casually along the streets while she shopped, smiling at whoever caught her eye. But when she reached The Scores and knew she was close, her demeanor changed. With the cottage now in sight, her heart slowed, and it brought the whole world down to its pace. Her feet became heavy, her breathing grew difficult, and her leg muscles weakened. So it was in a dreamlike state that she came upon it and the woman working in the enclosed garden.

Annie ground to a halt and stared at the unfamiliar face.

The woman returned her stare with kindness. "Lovely morning, isn't it?" she offered in an English accent.

The voice roused Annie from the slow-motion stupor. "Yes, yes, it is that."

The woman's face turned quizzical. "Is something wrong?"

Annie stammered slightly. "No, it's just—I knew this house—once—a long while ago. It's very hard—seeing it again."

The woman had been putting some primrose in planters, but she set down the trowel and moved closer to Annie. She removed a gardening glove and offered her hand over the low stone wall that enclosed the entrance. "Eileen Hampton," she said.

"Annie d'Inard, forgive me for staring," she said. She turned her gaze slightly, then asked, "Where's the gate? There used to be an iron gate with a little plaque on it with the cottage name."

"Yes, that's right."

"The Whaum."

The woman smiled and nodded. "We took it to be repaired. It was rusting through in spots."

She had to force a swallow, her throat was that tight. "Really?"

The woman's curiosity was roused. "How long ago did you know the place?"

Her eyes filled with tears as she answered, "A friend of mine lived here in 1972."

Mrs. Hampton assessed her for a moment. "American, are you?"

"Yes."

She smiled again. "First time back since then?"

"That's right."

She gestured toward the front door. "Would you like to come in? I was just about to make myself some tea."

Annie's heart picked up speed. "Oh—I'm—I'm not certain. I don't want to trouble you."

"It's no trouble."

Mrs. Hampton removed her remaining glove and made her way toward the bright blue door. She turned to beckon Annie, then opened it slowly. As she did, Annie experienced a rush of emotion so intense it made her body shudder. Without permission, her feet began to pull her forward, and with a few awkward, trembling steps, she was inside, standing among the spirits.

St. Andrews, 27 March, 1994

 It was more than a week before I could bring myself to go there. I had skillfully avoided it on my walks, turning around before I got close enough to see it. When I could endure it no longer, I chose the quiet late morning to go. I knew the sun would begin to fill the garden, and I walked upon it from the east.

 I slipped through a hole in time, walking through that door and into those rooms. They were different, but so was I. I saw them, though. I saw past the fresh paint and new furnishings; I saw them as they were. I heard the mantel clock that was no longer there, the shrill kettle calling from the kitchen. I felt him come to greet me with that smile, those eyes, so incredibly blue. She was talking, telling me what they'd done to the house, but I didn't hear.

 May I go into the rose garden, I asked. I went through the French doors. They're gone, she said. We've done away with the roses. Are you unwell, she asked. I need to sit down for a moment, if you don't mind. The time came rushing back, and I was there, alone.

Time can move ahead without us. We can lag behind, refusing to let go. But like the wake of a giant ship, time forces change upon us, unsettling all we have put in order, rearranging, sometimes ruining, and there is no escape.

 I came back to myself and stood to take my leave. You must return and meet my husband, she said. I thanked her for her hospitality.

 Though it was no longer there, I pulled the little gate behind me. I could feel him as I walked away. I saw his sapphire eyes darkening, his sandy hair tussling with the wind. He would stand at that gate and wave good-bye, then fold his arms and watch in silence as I was preparing to leave him.

Part II

I am the daughter of Earth and Water,
And the nursling of the Sky;
I pass through the pores of the ocean and shores;
I change, but I cannot die.
For after the rain when with never a stain
The pavilion of Heaven is bare,
And the winds and sunbeams with their convex gleams
Build up the blue dome of air,
I silently laugh at my own cenotaph,
And out of the caverns of rain,
Like a child from the womb, like a ghost from the tomb,
I arise and unbuild it again.

Percy B. Shelley, From *The Cloud*

Chapter 9

March 1972

It was her brother Timmy that Annie held tightest to that day in the airport. It was his embrace and voiced concern, punctuated by his moistening eyes, that meant the most.

"Remember the things I taught you."

"I will."

"Don't try to go fast. You don't know enough to drive fast."

She grinned. "You don't have to worry about that."

The final boarding announcement came through on the loudspeaker.

"Oh, the trucks, did I tell you about the trucks?" A growing anxiety was evident in his face and voice.

"What about them?"

"They generate a kind of wind tunnel when they're moving. If you get behind them, they'll pull you along and help you out, but be very careful about that. Don't follow too closely. If they stop suddenly, you're in trouble."

She had to reach up to kiss her younger brother's cheek. They had both grown into tall, young adults, but Timmy had surpassed her by four inches. "Don't worry about me. I'll be careful and I'll be fine. I'm a fast learner."

"You only had two lessons. I wish we'd had more time," he said with concern, but the worry on his face suddenly gave way to a grin. "When I was talking to Paw-Paw the other day, he reminded me of how determined you were when you wanted your training wheels off. He said that you were the bravest little girl he'd ever seen."

She smiled and answered, "When you talk to him again, tell him how much I love him, will you?"

"Sure."

The tears were coming on, and she dabbed at her nose with a tissue. "I'd better get going. I don't want them to leave without me." She looked to her parents. Her mother's face was red from crying, and her father was holding her securely around the waist. "I'll miss you," she told them.

"Be careful, sugar," her father answered. "Remember how much we love you."

Her mother was too upset to speak. The idea that her young daughter would be gone for months, traveling in foreign countries and mostly unreachable all the while, was more than she could bear to think of. Still, she and her husband knew they had to let her go.

A flight attendant approached Annie. "Excuse me, miss, but if you've got a boarding pass for this flight, you'd better get a move on."

She squeezed Timmy's hand, then released it. Without another word, she turned toward the gangway. The last thing she saw before entering the corridor was the three of them huddled together and waving. Timmy was the only one with a smile on his face.

The flight carried barely more passengers than crew, so Annie sat undisturbed and thoughtful. With the drone of the jet engines as her lullaby, and the hypnotic vision of stars in the ocean night, she fell into a dream. It wasn't a dream as they typically occur, with distortions and vagaries that mingle disparate themes. This was more like a visitation, startling in its clarity, that magically returned her to a specific place and time and seemed to transform her very body to a little girl's again.

It was midsummer in New Orleans, and the heady fragrance of gardenia wafted through the window above Annie's bed. She awakened to the call of a mockingbird and sat bolt upright, her green-brown eyes wide with excitement. The familiar scents of grits and bacon told her that her mother was making breakfast, so Annie ran to the kitchen. She yanked at her mother's apron, and demanded to see her grandfather right away.

As soon as she was dressed, the four-and-a-half-year-old ran from the house, opened the door at the end of their tiny concrete backyard, and entered her grandfather's dry-cleaning business on Oak Street. She went to her grandfather because she was like him, her mother had told her so, and she knew he would understand. Head-strong, just like her grandfather, stubborn, just like him—her father said that, too. It made her happy when they said this, because she wanted to be like him.

Over and over again she'd made her father tell her about the first time her grandfather saw an airplane up close, how he paid the pilot to take him and his two small sons for a ride. They flew through the air like birds that day, her grandfather laughing and clapping and not wanting to come back down, while her frightened grandmother watched from the ground. She thrilled at that story and believed her grandfather to be the bravest person in the world, loving him beyond all reason.

Annie loved her grandmother, too. She was soft and warm and kind, and it felt good and safe to be in her lap.

Love seemed to always pour from her no matter what Annie did—unconditional, cleansing, renewing love. But she was not like her grandmother; she was like her grandfather. She knew she was like him because everyone said so. She wanted to soar above the clouds like her grandfather, like a magnificent bird with big strong wings—not like a frightened one, a weak one, who had to watch the others from the ground.

When she found her grandfather, he was with a customer, but she tugged at his sleeve and insisted he speak with her.

"I dreamed you took the training wheels off my bike and I could ride it, just like that," she said with enormous eyes and tremendous excitement.

"You're not ready," he chuckled. "Your feet barely reach the pedals."

The customer laughed, too.

The excitement fled from her face. But in its place came a look of such ardent determination that it seemed not to belong on a child. "Yes I am," she insisted.

Her grandfather recognized that look, and he quickly changed his mind. "All right then, let me get my toolbox," he said, winking and smiling.

In a couple of minutes, the two were on the cracked pavement in front of Annie's house, and Paw-Paw, as she called him, was removing the training wheels from her blue Schwinn bicycle. The sun broke through the thick morning haze and ignited the streaks of gold in her otherwise dark hair.

As soon as the wheels were off, she climbed onto the bike. Her grandfather helped her steady herself by holding onto the seat and running alongside as she peddled.

"Let me go now!" she shouted with certainty, then wobbled for a few seconds before falling to the ground. She was bitterly disappointed, but she got up and brushed herself off. "Let's do it again," was all she said.

This time he held the bike longer as she peddled furiously up the street.

"OK, let go!"

She managed to stay upright for a few seconds longer before falling again, badly scraping her skin on the concrete this time. But she ignored her bloody knees and knuckles and shouted, "Come on Paw-Paw, I wanna try again."

He helped her back onto the bike that was too big and heavy for her.

The little girl locked eyes with her grandfather. "I'm gonna do it," she said, and without further ado, she set her jaw, trained her eyes on the sidewalk ahead, stood up on the pedals, and put all of the power and energy she could muster into the struggle. This time when her grandfather released his hold on the seat, she surged forward on her own. Suddenly aware that she was doing what she had only dreamed of that morning, she let go a scream of delight. It was in that moment, as she peddled furiously up the sidewalk, that she felt all vestiges of fear slip away, leaving her with the very certain belief that she could do anything.

* * *

The rumble of the breakfast cart and the voices of flight attendants asking, "Would you like tea or coffee?" awakened Annie. But her dreamy state persisted and even while she ate her meal, she stayed with her memories, thinking now of her sixteenth birthday in 1968.

She'd given herself a party. Friends who were in a band had offered to play for free, and hoards of teenagers showed up, invited or not. Some sat in the dark woods near her house, drinking themselves into a stupor, only occasionally coming into the garage for a dance. Among them was Annie's friend Rob Mitchell, who had been drafted that year and was now home on leave. In one short week, he was to be in jungles on the other side of the world.

Annie had grown into a voluptuous young woman well in advance of most of the girls her age. She had round full breasts, a slender but curvaceous body, and long strong legs. She was aware of the attention her figure attracted and in a naive way, she invited it. She flitted around her guests that night as she'd always seen southern hostesses do, wearing a fluorescent pink miniskirt and a tight, low-cut T-shirt.

When Rob arrived, he was already drunk. "Happy Birthday, Annie Fannie," he slurred. "That's a helluva out-fit you're wearin'."

"You don't think it's too short, do you?" she grinned.

"Naw, it's outta sight." He handed her a beer.

She took a long sip and then grabbed him, pulling him into a dance.

"Man, I dig this song," he yelled into her ear as they twisted and shook their bodies to "Gimmie Some Lovin."

Rob's eyes were drawn to her chest. Her nipples had hardened and they protruded invitingly through the thin fabric. When the song ended, he looked into her cleavage. "Let's go in the woods for a while, Annie Fannie," he said as he fought the urge to put his hands on her breasts.

Before she could answer, someone else asked her to dance. They moved away as the band struck up again, and she resumed her twisting and wiggling with her new partner. Rob could not keep his eyes from her. He guzzled another beer and then, in the middle of the song, made his way through the dancers. Without saying a word, he fell to his knees, grabbed her right leg with both hands, and took a horse-size bite out of her thigh. His teeth tore through her pantyhose, and she shrieked in agony.

"Rob! What'd you do that for?"

The band stopped playing and it was suddenly unearthly quiet. Only those nearest Annie knew what had happened, and everyone else stared as though she'd gone crazy. Her tears came instantly, for her leg throbbed with a pain deeper than anything she had ever experienced.

"You go home right now," she railed at Rob. "Get out of here. I can't believe you did this! How could you? I can't believe this is happening!" She limped off to a chair where she could sit and rub her leg, her tears unabated.

Rob followed like a scolded puppy, his head and shoulders drooped. "I'm so sorry, Annie. I don't know why I did that, I don't know what got into me. Please forgive me. I'm an idiot."

People had been staring at her, but now they turned their heads and whispered. Annie couldn't hear what they said, she could only imagine, and that made everything worse.

"No! I'll never forgive you!" she screamed. "Never! Get out of here! Go home! I never want to see you again. You've ruined everything!"

Rob left her then. She watched him disappear into the woods, still carrying his beers, fading into the dark blue, alone. For a moment she wanted to call him back, but when she looked again at the torn stocking and realized that her face must be awash with mascara, she dismissed that desire and rushed to the bathroom to try to make things right again.

The next morning when she awakened, instead of being flooded with happy memories from her party, the ache in her thigh brought on tears. When she pulled the covers off and saw her leg, she was horrified; the resulting bruise extended from her knee almost to her hip, and it hurt so badly she could barely walk. She limped around for days, cursing Rob every time she had to climb stairs or when she inadvertently bumped her leg.

It was less than two weeks later, while Annie was still feeling sorry for herself, that the news came that Rob's helicopter had been shot down and everyone on board killed. Private Mitchell and the others with him hadn't even set foot on Vietnamese soil. When Annie was told, she looked at her leg; white spots in the mottled purple still marked where his teeth had sunk into her. She sat alone in her bedroom all that evening, staring at those marks for hours. The pain returned with a vengeance that day and recurred for months afterward, throbbing and aching every time she thought of Rob.

A stewardess stopped by to retrieve her breakfast tray and announce that they'd be landing in forty-five minutes. When she was gone, Annie brushed at a tear and returned to her private thoughts. As the next memory surfaced, she found herself shaking her head in disapproval, wondering how she could have been so stupid.

The summer that she graduated from high school, at age seventeen, she gave up her virginity, not because she was in love, but because she thought it was time. She felt her inexperience weigh on her; it held her back, kept her a child, so she approached it with her characteristic determination, as though it were her first two-wheeler or something someone had told her she couldn't do.

The man she picked was not a hesitant boy like those she'd dated in high school. The friend of a friend, he was an older man, much older than she, who saw her as a conquest. He had no idea that she was without experience; he felt sorry when he found out.

When it was over, Annie drove herself home. The maturation experience she'd sought had left her feeling neither happy nor triumphant, nor womanly. In the privacy of her bathroom, she mopped her tears and rinsed the blood from her panties, then soaked in the tub for hours. She was quiet and thoughtful for weeks afterward, and she never saw or spoke to him again.

That summer Annie did a lot of reading, with a particular emphasis on her favorite poet, Percy Shelley. By the time she left for college, her spirits were greatly improved, and she was thrilled that she would be going away with her two best friends, Jane Ann and Issie. But when she arrived at the University of Tennessee in Knoxville, she was immediately disappointed.

Although the family's limited finances had kept her from visiting the campus beforehand, her active imagination made up for that. Through her Shelley-induced idealism she envisioned the campus as a nourishing place, an idyllic world of intelligent discourse and meaningful pursuits. What she found was quite unlike that.

The town was depressed, impoverished, and colorless; local people had hollow, lifeless faces. The air smelled of smoke and factories, and some days it was hard to breathe. Classes were enormous, professors rarely knew students by name, and discussion was almost nonexistent.

Students, for the most part, seemed interested only in weekends and football games. She had decided on the school because it was where Jane Ann and Issie were going, and without their consoling presence she might have left. But together the girls were determined to make the best of it.

Her room, located at the end of a long, dark corridor, was positively dismal. Its single window opened into a center area that was little more than an air shaft. The window was covered with soot and hung with dreary, tattered curtains. Everywhere she looked, she saw brown or gray; there were no flowers, precious few bushes, and only sad, neglected, old trees.

But a few days after her arrival, she discovered the university's singular concession to the sublime, and it quickly became her special place. It was an extravagantly conceived bronze fountain of Greek mythological figures, and Annie immediately loved it. Frenzied bursts of water danced around it, drowning out the banality of the environment. It quickly became the place for her to go. Near it, she could dream; listening to it, she could forget. She would go there to read her beloved Shelley, do her course work, or write a letter home. Sitting near the fountain, she felt a kind of energy and an invitation to think, out in the open, away from depressing interiors and closed minds.

Nineteen sixty-nine was an inspiring time. America had watched with pride as the soles of man-made boots left indelible impressions on the moon's delicate skin and looked the other way while napalm burned the tender flesh of Vietnamese children. The economy prospered from factories that fueled the war machine, belching foul waste into a vulnerable environment in the bargain. Previously healthy American boys returned home from Southeast Asia in body bags, and others came back on stretchers and in wheelchairs, hearts and minds as broken and crippled as their limbs. Annie took it all in with wide-open eyes and a fair amount of nausea.

She went with Jane Ann to the November War Moratorium in Washington, in a single chartered bus from a college of 25,000. With thousands of other young Americans, they pleaded for the war to stop. For demonstrating in front of the Justice Department, they were assaulted with tear gas and saw fellow protesters beaten with nightsticks. The girls sobbed as they ran from the scene, terrified by what they witnessed, and unable to reason why their national guard—their own countrymen—assailed them. They found refuge in the basement of a church and slept all night on the cold floor; they could hear people crying in their sleep. Jane Ann sobbed openly and Annie held her, comforting her, trying to be as strong and unafraid as she'd always been.

On the trip back to school, Annie sat with her recently made friend, a senior student from New Jersey in whom she saw great things. He gave her mescaline as the bus raced out of town and, incredibly, she laughed for eight hours.

She admired the young man from New Jersey. His name was Jason, and he was bright, involved, and committed. She attached herself to him and his causes; he was taking risks that thrilled and inspired her. She would spend hours with him in the student union, helping him hand out leaflets, getting petitions signed, listening to him argue for everything from students' rights to the overthrow of the government.

In January, Jason organized a campus protest. Hundreds of students came, most simply to watch, but as the crowd grew larger, the university officials grew nervous. They called in the troops, and because he was the leader, Jason was arrested. From the police wagon, Jason dictated a statement for Annie to read to the crowd.

National guardsmen arrived wearing gas masks and carrying rifles angled across their chests at the ready. Annie stood before the crowd, reading Jason's statement that asked the students to disperse peacefully and not resist the authorities. The following morning, her picture appeared in the local paper with her name and address.

Almost immediately, she began receiving threatening phone calls. At the same time, a female student named Agatha, who'd been active in the protest, was attacked near her off-campus apartment. She was assaulted by several men who pushed her around between them, then onto the pavement, breaking her arm in the fall.

Annie was very shaken by these events, and as soon as he was released from jail, she went to Jason's apartment seeking his advice and reassurance. She found him distracted and unusually quiet.

"It's been awful, Jason, just awful. I've been getting phone calls from these scary rednecks, calling me a commie agitator and all sorts of ridiculous things." She was animated and loud, waving her hands about as she spoke. "One even said he'd kill me to protect his country if he had to. Can you imagine?" she screeched. "I've been afraid to go anywhere. After what happened to Agatha, I've just been hanging out in my room, waiting for you to get out."

"It wasn't nice for me either," he answered solemnly, his eyes focused on the floor.

"I wish they'd arrested me, too," she declared. "Then I wouldn't have had to listen to all that garbage on the phone."

Her thoughtless statement rankled him, and he snapped at her. "I can't believe you said that, Annie. Fuck! Don't ever say that! You have no idea what it's like to be in jail, and it's something you never want to find out, believe me!" His face flushed bright pink.

Surprised by his response, she asked, "Why? Tell me what happened. Did they interrogate you or something?" She had a mental picture that was like a scene from a movie—Jason in a chair, the light shining in his eyes, being asked to name his commie friends.

"No."

"What'd they do?" she insisted.

He raised his voice again. "I don't want to talk about it!"

"Why not?"

Jason's memory played a very different picture from the one Annie was imagining, and he tried to force it from his mind. Toning down now, he said, "Look, I said I don't want to talk about the past few days, OK? I'd just as soon forget they ever happened."

She studied his face for a moment. "What we need is a distraction," she decided. "Why don't we go to a movie? They're running a Bergman film at the student union."

"Bergman's too heavy for me tonight. I've got a better idea." He moved to take something from a drawer. "I copped a couple of hits of acid from a buddy of mine. He said it's really good stuff. You've never dropped acid before, have you?"

Annie's eyes widened. "I don't think I want to do that," she said, and unconsciously backed away from him.

He cocked his head in challenge. "Why not? You afraid or something?"

She folded her arms and stared back at him, trying to face down the dare. "I'm not afraid of anything," she declared, "but people bum out sometimes, don't they? Don't they freak out sometimes?"

"Sometimes," he admitted, "but that's with bad stuff. This is good shit. My buddy's dropped this and he says it's really good. You're not going to freak out. This stuff is clean."

She frowned at him and shook her head again. "I don't know."

He didn't want to do it alone so he continued to prod her. "Come on, don't be a bummer. This'll be far out, you'll see. Remember how much you enjoyed that mescaline? This'll be even better. It really takes you out there." He looked awestruck as he explained, "Man, you see and understand things you just can't otherwise. It's like being on a different plane, on this high spiritual plane. It's really far out, you'll see."

"I haven't had time to think about this," she defended. "Maybe some other time."

Jason seemed brighter now, more like himself than when she'd first arrived. "You're makin' too big of a deal out of it. Come on, don't make me do this alone. I was countin' on droppin' some with you. It's so much better with someone you care about." He moved closer to her, rubbing her shoulder and smiling, while he awaited her answer.

"OK," she finally said quietly, though the debate still raged in her head.

They chased it down with some fermenting grape juice he had in the refrigerator. Annie was determined to enjoy herself and initially, she found herself laughing with Jason. But in the middle of a laugh, something strange happened; the senses she had relied upon all her life suddenly failed her. And what followed was nothing at all like the spiritual experience Jason promised it would be. It was more like a descent into hell.

Her nose betrayed her first, telling her of things that weren't there, then it was her eyes. Familiar objects changed shape and did things they were not supposed to. Her own body became strange and unfamiliar; it seemed to move in ways it never had before, leaving traces of itself like echoes, as it floated in slow motion through liquid space. Frightening images and terrifying thoughts appeared out of nowhere, out of nothingness, chasing her mind into dark corners, into fearful chaos.

She moved agitatedly from place to place within Jason's small apartment, trying to find something that would connect her to reality. She opened the closets, the refrigerator, the cabinets, having to work out each and every time how to turn the knob or use the pull. She stared in wonder at the extraordinary things she found in those places, the pronged pieces of metal in the kitchen drawer, the paper-covered triangles that hooked onto the closet rod, the strange canister with the long elephant-like nose.

As time went on she began to experience brief flashes of lucidity. She grasped hold of those moments, trying with everything in her to keep them going, but for the first time in her life, she was powerless. Despite her most determined efforts, her tenuous hold on sanity would slip away, and she would once again find herself immersed in a sea of monsters and murk.

Jason was in his own world, his hands occasionally moving through the air like an artist at work on canvas. He rose from his chair now and again to put records on the stereo, but mostly he just sat and stared at something, at nothing. And when Annie sat before him and pleaded for his help, he responded by taking her hand and leading her to his bedroom.

And then, while her mind convulsed with the pandemonium, Jason had sex with her. It was only her second time.

Annie could neither fight nor refuse him. She could only cling to the tiny threads of reality that made their way through the agony, like the sound of a radio playing in another room, and wait for it to end. She had wanted Jason to help her, she had pleaded for his help, but he was lost in his own mind, and the act of taking her body without her permission had transformed him into monster and enemy.

The monster penetrated and violated her and seemed oblivious to her anguish as she made pathetic, wailing sounds, so full of pain and fear they frightened her even more as she heard them herself. And he could not get enough of her. He bit her nipples and drove himself hard against her insides, so hard it shot pain into her abdomen and chest as he savagely pumped, bruising her body where he grabbed it and thrusting her head against the wall.

Somehow, it became morning. Slowly, slowly, agonizingly slowly, the confusion lifted, the visions disappeared, and Annie could recognize what she touched and trust what she heard. The monster snored and moaned next to her, the odor of sweat and semen rising from his skin.

Despite the return of a somewhat reliable reality, she found herself still oppressed by something odious and unrelenting. The fear that had come upon her during the night was not gone. It had not left; it had closed over her like a heavy net and enveloped her. Like a creature from a Tolkien story, it had encased her in its web and filled her with its venom, and she could not cast it off.

As soon as he was able to drive, Annie asked Jason to return her to the dorm. He dropped her at the entrance, saying he'd call. She didn't respond. When she walked away from his car, she said aloud, as though swearing an oath, that she would die before she'd ever see or speak to him again. Once inside, she didn't go to her room but to Jane Ann's. When she answered the knock, Jane Ann saw something she had never before seen: She saw Annie, terrified.

She was too panicked to cry. "Janie," she pleaded, "you've got to help me."

"What is it? What's happened?" The look on Annie's face had Jane Ann's heart racing.

"I've had a bad trip, Janie. I'm so afraid. I feel like I'm losing my mind. I can't control my mind. I'm so afraid."

"My God, Annie, my God!" She reached out to her friend and gripped her in a tight embrace.

"Help me, Janie. Can you help me? I need some help." Her arms were limp at her side. "If only someone could help me. I've been asking God to help me. I want to be like I was before. I want yesterday to have never happened. No one's listening, Janie. I don't think God's listening. I'm afraid no one can help me. I'm so alone. Don't leave me alone. If I stay alone, I know I'll go crazy." Her voice trailed off, and she was barely coherent.

Tears filled Jane Ann's eyes. "I won't leave you." She released the hug to look into her friend's face again. She saw so much wild fear in those green-brown eyes that she had to look away.

Annie stayed in Jane Ann's bed for several days, barely able to speak, afraid to fall asleep, afraid to dream, afraid her mind would run wild again and never come back. Jane Ann's roommate took some of her things and went to stay in Annie's room without being asked, then discreetly stayed away. Jane Ann made tea for her, read to her, and played Abbey Road for her on the stereo. The wreck that had been made of her best friend was painful for her to see. But Jane Ann stayed close, talking about things she knew Annie liked, reminding her of brilliant spring days and warm summer nights, lit with stars and lightning bugs, instinctively weaving a rope for Annie to hold onto. Slowly, Annie recovered enough to sleep and return to her own room, but Jane Ann sadly realized that her friend had truly changed.

The Annie who had feared nothing was now afraid of everything. She was afraid to be alone, afraid to be with people. She couldn't drink from a water fountain for fear someone had put LSD in it. She wouldn't speak to strangers; the head-on eyes she was famous for now hid from others, looking away, looking down. She shared a room with Isabella but couldn't speak to her. She couldn't laugh; she felt she had to keep herself in check at all times. Issie suggested she go to the university crisis center, which she did, and they assigned her to see a graduate student in psychology. But it didn't help because talking about what had happened wasn't something Annie wanted to do; more than anything, she wanted to forget.

She was unable to go to class so she dropped most of her courses. Doing the simplest and most ordinary of things, like getting herself something to eat or laundering her dirty clothes, became exceedingly difficult. But strangely, in spite of all this, and even in times when she felt most afraid, Annie frequently made the effort to get dressed and go to the fountain.

She would think of the fountain and feel herself drawn there, and she would have to go. She would sit close enough to feel the mist, the sound of the falling water the only thing she could hear. It was only then, in those solitary moments, absorbed by the magic of the myth, that she would feel better.

Looking at the sculpture, Annie became the woman, and becoming her, she understood. In her face she read defiance, the rejection of things expected, the very type of rebelliousness that Annie had been born with. In the woman's naked form, clad only in a billowing cape, she recognized freedom, the kind she had never known but longed to experience. And the dauntless manner in which she straddled her mount helped Annie understand the conviction with which she met her fate; it showed her how to meet her own. When she left the fountain, she would carry those feelings with her for a time, and with each subsequent visit, they remained longer and longer.

In March, Annie decided to drop out of school entirely. Jane Ann and she tearfully exchanged volumes of the complete works of Shelley and Keats; Isabella cried. Annie said her good-byes and tried not to think about things too much. But before she left college, as she waited for the time to pass and the horror of what had happened to fade, she spent those last days and hours at the fountain, looking into the face of Europa as she rode into the wind, astride the back of the powerful bull.

The announcement that they would be touching down at Heathrow in ten minutes shook her from her reverie. When she came out of it this time, it was easy. In the weeks and months that followed her leaving school, it hadn't been at all easy to forget or to separate herself from that experience. Indeed, there'd been a time in the not-too-distant past when she thought she would never get over the horror, that she'd never be free of the fear. But time can be a friend in certain circumstances, and it certainly had been in this one. With each passing day, her fear had become less acute to the point that two years later here she was, able to think of it without being overcome. In fact, had the fear stayed with her, she never would have been able to make this voyage, to travel across the ocean with the idea of going on and seeing the whole of western Europe. And she never would have contemplated doing it alone, on a motorcycle, as she was planning to do now. I've come very far, she congratulated herself, and I'm going to go even farther. I'm going to resurrect that lost person, bring back that brave little girl, help her grow into the woman I always wanted to be.

The realization that she was about to set foot on exotic, foreign ground, to see and experience wonderful new places and people, made her feel fresh and light and clean. She rifled through her rucksack for her compact mirror so that she could fix her mussed hair and face. In her reflection, she saw evidence of the excitement that filled her insides, and it made her smile. That smile stayed with her as she made her connection to Edinburgh, and by the time she stepped off the plane in Scotland, it was very nearly etched into her face.

Chapter 10

When she spied Adam beyond the customs barrier, she breathed a sigh of relief, then waved happily. Arriving in Scotland felt wonderfully triumphant, but it hadn't been easy getting there.

Soon after she left college, Annie's father's job took the family to the suburbs of Philadelphia. Still suffering the aftereffects of the bad trip, the transition to a new environment slowed her recovery. She spent many hours alone in her room, missing her left-behind family and friends, mourning their loss. It took her several months to gather the strength she needed to face this new world, because she experienced a lingering paranoia and fear of crowds. Even then, when she did start going out and doing things again, it was in increments.

Her brother Timmy was her salvation. He was the only person who could make Annie laugh, and it was he who prodded her to get out and start doing things again. At Timmy's urging, she enrolled in a few classes at Villanova University, and it was there that she met Adam Wilson.

He was a gentle, soft-spoken young man, who had plans to go to Scotland for his junior year. Annie enjoyed his company; he was intelligent and funny, and more importantly, uninterested in her as a woman. She missed him when he departed for St. Andrews University, and they corresponded for many months while Annie continued her part-time studies and worked at her job.

With her only nearby friend gone, she hunkered down at her duties in a nursing home, where she cared for the old and forgotten, feeding them their supper, washing their worn-away bodies, and tucking them into bed. Some seemed oblivious, some decidedly suffered, and the daily encounter with hovering death did something to Annie's psyche. While Jane Ann and Issie went about pursuing their degrees and enjoying their young lives, Annie went back and forth to the nursing home and drifted into a kind of numb detachment.

Jane Ann was still at the University of Tennessee, but Issie had gone to France for a semester. Timmy was getting on with his life, too. In his third year of high school now, he had many friends and an active social life, and the intimacy the siblings had shared as children began to slip away. Since the day he was born, Annie had adored her baby brother, and their time together as children had been her happiest. Watching him now as he roared off on his motorcycle to spend the evening with friends, she found herself longing for simpler times, and it made her heart ache.

Adam's letters were like a gift. They were one of the few things she had to look forward to. He wrote to her of the town of St. Andrews, where everything was clean and neat, people were friendly, the university was challenging, and life in general was blissful. When she wrote back that it seemed to good to be true, he responded that she should come and see for herself.

* * *

On a February night in 1972, as the crowd from a basketball game left the high school next to Annie's house, she and her family were startled by a loud thumping noise. Seconds after, the sounds that followed sent them from their house to see what had happened.

A half-dozen people lay in the street. A car with blood spattered across its windshield was abandoned near them. People had gathered around, some crying, others screaming, many just standing with their hands over their mouths. A few rushed to help the injured. Annie looked to see what she could do, while her mother held pressure on the gushing head wound of a young boy. She spotted a girl lying somewhat distant from the others and rushed to her, then knelt by her side.

Her young face was serene, and it showed no signs of suffering. Annie assumed the girl was unconscious and held one of her pale hands in hers.

"It'll be all right," she said to the girl, and pleaded for someone in the crowd to bring her a blanket.

A nearby man removed his coat on this cold winter night and covered the girl with it. Annie shivered as she tucked it carefully around the motionless body, all the while talking in sweet, reassuring tones.

"Everything will be fine, the ambulances are coming," she heard herself say. She didn't know what else to do, so she held onto her hand and tried to keep the girl warm for what seemed an eternity.

When help finally did arrive, the rescue workers pushed Annie aside and hurriedly lifted the girl to a stretcher. The limp body gave way and her buttocks sank to the ground.

"Be careful with her!" Annie shouted to the attendants.

One turned sharply to her and in a harsh whisper responded, "She's already dead."

Annie felt the blood rush from her head and the force of a sob push its way upward, from her guts to her throat.

Back in their house Annie's parents did their best to reassure her and Timmy, but the bewilderment and pain on their own faces made that impossible. Annie felt herself overcome with a bone-deep cold and went to her bed to cover her shivering body with layers of blankets.

She closed her eyes and tried to quiet her thoughts, but her mind played through image after image, face after face, always returning to the young, still girl. And what Annie discerned in that sweet face frightened her more than anything she had ever encountered. Reflected in the girl's peaceful visage was the imprint of unexpected death, the kind that sneaks up from behind, that arrives while you are busy doing something you always do, something ordinary: the kind that taps you on the shoulder and says it's time to go, and you have to go, ready or not.

Panic threatened her. She looked around the room where she now spent much of her time, in the house where she wanted to believe herself safe. The furniture that she had had as long as she could remember appeared alien, as though it belonged to someone else. She was overcome by a feeling of dread and wondered if she was going to have a flashback. God please, she prayed, don't let it happen again, keep me sane, keep my mind clear. Ever since the LSD, every time she experienced unusual sensations, she worried that it was starting again.

Annie needed calming. Without thinking, she fumbled through her closet for a book she'd kept from high school, a text of English literature. It almost opened itself, showing her the page to which it had most often been turned. She read:

"I am the daughter of Earth and Water,
And the nursling of the Sky;
I pass through the pores of the ocean and shores;
I change, but I cannot die."

It was her favorite poem. It was how she used to feel, before Jason, before that night, but not any longer. She looked across the room at her reflection in a mirror. Her face, once bright and full of light and energy, was colorless and empty. I look more dead than the girl in the street, she thought. The fear inside her made her feel dead, it made her numb. She pulled her arms in around herself and grabbed her nightgown at the waist. Tears came. They felt hot, acidic.

Then, abruptly, the fear was gone, and in its place came revulsion. God, I'm so sick of this, she said aloud, sick of everything, of hiding, of being afraid, of watching life from the sidelines.

The face in the mirror looked back at her. For a moment, only a moment, she saw herself as she once was. Then she blinked and saw herself again as she was now— pale, thin, unable to look herself in the eyes. She shut her lids to force this image out, but she could not escape what was happening inside.

She felt odd, as though she were drifting away on a tide. Something powerful and inexplicable seemed to be pulling her out of the room, away from herself.

And in the next moment, she was back at college at the fountain. Her tears were splashes of water and she was Europa. She wore a flowing gown that covered only one breast. The bull stirred and snorted beneath her. The wind blew her robe and hair, and the exuberant water around her smelled of the sea. She took a deep breath. She felt a profound ache in her chest, but she felt alive.

She opened her eyes and looked again at her reflection. She saw a hint of something, an undeniable energy that was familiar, comforting. She sat very still for several long minutes, watching, waiting to see if it would go away. It didn't.

Closing the book, she began once more to shiver, though not this time from the cold. With trembling hands, she removed the stack of blue envelopes and postcards from her dresser drawer. Late into the night, she read and reread the letters from Scotland. Sometime before morning she stopped shaking, picked up pen and paper, and wrote to Adam. Before she did anything else that day, she took it to the post office so that it would go off at once. She had no time to lose.

She got her passport and airline ticket and bought a few new clothes. She didn't know why, but when she saw a long cotton gown, the fabric painted with flowers in shades of blue and lavender, she had to have it. Then, with only days to go before she left, she decided to ask her brother for a favor.

They were alone and he was sitting at the kitchen table playing at some homework he didn't want to do, while his sister washed the dinner dishes.

She was curiously nonchalant as she inquired, "Hey Timmy, before I leave, will you teach me to drive your motorcycle?"

He scrunched his face at the absurdity of her request. "What do you want to do that for?"

She bent to a lower cabinet to put away the pots and pans, and when she stood again, she calmly answered, "I've saved a fair amount of money, you know, from my job. And I've been thinking that when I get to Scotland, I'd like to buy a motorcycle, because I can't imagine a cooler way to see Europe."

He was stunned. "But you're a girl!" he proclaimed as though that explained everything.

Laying aside the dish towel, she put her hands on her hips and asked, "So what?"

"So what?" he echoed. "Do Mom and Dad know you're doing this?"

"I mentioned it."

Shaking his head in disbelief, he exhaled. "Jesus! Do they think you've really lost it this time?"

With growing impatience, she demanded, "Would you just teach me? If those idiot friends of yours can drive them, why can't I? I mean, come on, they're living proof that it can't be hard."

He was shocked by her request, but he was also delighted at seeing his sister like this. "It isn't," he admitted, trying to keep himself from smiling, "but driving with other cars and trucks can be tricky." He expanded his chest to further explain, "There are assholes who try to run you off the road, and there's rain and trucks and oil slicks. You need physical strength and a little guts."

"I've got guts," she insisted.

His brow knitted. "What's happened to you?" he wanted to know. "You've been acting weird the past couple of weeks."

"I'm not weird," she declared. "I'm just getting back to being myself."

"Is that it?" He affected a stern, fatherly look for a moment, then let it give way to a smile. "You've been such a nervous little homebody for so long now, I almost forgot how you used to be." He sized her up for a moment, then decided to ask the question that had nagged him for two years. "Something really bad happened to you at U.T., didn't it?"

Annie nodded twice, then fixed her eyes on her brother. For some time now she had known that she needed to say this to him, but she'd wanted to wait until he was a little older. With her departure less than a week away, she realized there was no time like the present. "I want you to promise me something. Say you will."

He frowned at her. "I need to know what it is first."

Their parents had gone to a movie and the house was unusually quiet as Annie considered how to say this to her brother. She took a deep breath and leaned backward against the sink, her arms folded in front of her. When she looked at his expectant face again, she realized there was no better way than to come straight out with it.

"Promise me that no matter what, you'll never, never drop acid," she said. "Promise me that no matter how hard somebody tries to talk you into it, you'll never be stupid enough to do it. Promise me, Timmy."

He'd never seen it happen to anyone, but he'd heard enough stories. He swallowed hard as the image formed in his mind. "Was that it? Did you have a bad trip?"

Her face reflected the pain that always accompanied the memory. "That expression can never describe what I went through—never. It's impossible to put into words how horrible it was."

"Do Mom and Dad know what happened?" he asked.

She shook her head. "I only told Jane Ann and Issie. I could never find the courage to tell Mom and Daddy, and I don't want you to tell them, either." She knew she could never bear their reactions, the pain and pity and concern, for it would make it all too real and close again.

"I won't," he answered solemnly, for in truth, he wouldn't know how to say something like that.

She looked as though she might cry any minute. "I've only told you because I love you, and I don't ever want you to go through anything as awful as that."

The mere mention of that night revealed so much residual damage in his sister that Timmy felt himself being touched by it. Wanting very badly to make her pain go away, he quietly answered, "If it means that much to you, OK, I'll promise." He dropped his eyes to the table before he looked at her again. "But you have to promise me that you'll be careful in Europe and come home safe and sound, OK?"

"I'll be careful," she responded and tried to smile.

He didn't return her smile. His expression remained serious. "But the motorcycle thing, if anything bad happens to you, I'll feel like it was my fault because I taught you."

The idea of him wracked with guilt because of something that might happen to her was disquieting. And yet, she knew she needed to push past that concern, because it was becoming increasingly clear to her that this was something she had to do.

She tossed the whole thing over in her mind, then declared, "If anything happens to me, at least I'll have been out in the world living my life again. I hate what's become of me. I hate the way I've been afraid of everything. I've got to change that. Besides," she thought to add, "you never know when it's going to happen, do you? It could happen right here, in front of the house, couldn't it? So if that's the way it is, I might as well get on with it and have some fun, right?"

He grimaced as he recalled that horrific night when three teenagers had been killed by a drunk driver and several others were seriously injured. Anyone who witnessed that scene had to have been altered by it. It had changed him, and he could see in the weeks since it happened that his sister had been changed by it, too.

So despite his misgivings, he said, "OK." Then he sighed before adding, "After school tomorrow, when the parking lot empties out, I'll give you your first lesson."

She walked around the kitchen counter to plant a kiss on his cheek, then she hugged him around the neck. "No one understands me the way you do," she softly said. "I love you so much."

"Yeah, me too," he answered. He was still sitting and while she embraced him, he reached his arms around her waist.

With so much to do in such a short time, there was little occasion for Annie to rethink her plans, and she wanted it that way. She packed everything she was bringing into two bags. Then she phoned Jane Ann to say good-bye and to be certain she had the correct address for Issie in France. On the night before her departure, she lay awake for hours trying to imagine what lay ahead. When she finally fell asleep, she was visited by a prophetic dream.

She was lost in an eerie landscape; she felt afraid and tried to leave as the way out grew smaller and tighter. But panic drove her, and she crawled on her belly in the cold and slime, then found herself on the other side in the daylight. She squinted her eyes to see what she thought was a rock move its head to graze upon the grass, then to look upon her. She recognized it as a bull and ran to chase after it as it bolted away from her, leaping over obstacles and finally out of sight.

Chapter 11

Adam had borrowed an automobile to meet Annie at Edinburgh airport. His face beamed with delight when he caught sight of her. He had been in Scotland since September and thus far had only been able to share this place through letters, so the prospect of sharing it now with someone he cared about was nothing less than intoxicating. He good-humoredly rushed her to the car to begin the hour-long drive to St. Andrews. Annie gripped the door handle tightly as they drove, unable to shake the concern that they were driving on the wrong side and that a steering wheel should be in front of her.

They crossed the bridge that spans the Firth of Forth and entered the Kingdom of Fife; the day was cold but brilliantly blue. They chatted incessantly along the way, and before they knew it, they were driving past the Old Course and entering the town. Adam slowed in the town, turned right on Double Dykes Road, then headed down Hepburn Gardens to Buchanan Gardens. He pulled into the car park at one of the university residences, David Russell Hall.

"I've made arrangements for you to stay here as a visiting student," he explained while they were still driving, "so everything's all set. You'll have breakfast and dinner in the dining hall with the other residents, too. It's all included." He cleared his throat, "Oh, and ah, I paid for the first two weeks."

"Adam," she gasped, "you shouldn't have done that!"

"I wanted to."

"But that's too generous."

"It isn't much really. It's about a pound a day."

"But that's a lot for two weeks! You have to let me reimburse you."

"No," he insisted. "I want to do this."

They entered David Russell Hall at the doors marked "Reception" and were greeted by a cheery older woman who knew Adam.

"Thees must be ye friend from America," she said, smiling at Annie. "We've got her room all ready."

They followed her down a corridor out to a covered path and into a building named Fraser. She unlocked number 28 and handed Annie the key.

Annie looked around the room. It was a good size, with bright, clean walls and a wash basin and mirror centered between two closets at one end. Besides a single bed, the room held a large desk and lamp, a straight-back chair, and a more ample, softer chair for lounging.

"The lavatory's just there," the woman said, pointing to a door close by. "Ye share it wi' the three other students on thees floor and there's washing up powder ta keep it clean. Everyone's expected ta tidy up after themselves. There now, I'll leave ye ta get settled."

She wondered at this statement for a moment, having somewhat understood it despite the woman's heavily accented speech. Knowing students as she did, she fully expected the bathroom to be filthy.

When Adam left to get her bags, her gaze turned to the view from the large window. The residence halls were small by American standards and were far enough apart that the landscape could be viewed between them. And in the spaces between buildings she saw gardens, carefully tilled and planted as though this was someone's home. Beyond the gardens, Annie could see a farm field, and beyond that, woods and a blue horizon.

She was still at the window when Adam returned. "God, it's so pretty here. Everything's so clean and neat. I've never seen anything like it!"

"And you haven't really seen the place yet," he grinned.

"When do I get to see the rest of the town?"

"Soon. I need to head back to Southgait for a bit, so why don't you have a nap or a bath. I won't be long."

Alone now, Annie unpacked her things, carefully unfolding and hanging the long, blue gown. That complete, she decided on a hot bath. She found the bathroom austere but almost immaculate. The porcelain tub was large and had separate hot and cold faucets. She hadn't seen any like them since her grandmother's old house. The bathroom also housed a tiny sink and an odd looking toilet. She was distressed not to find a shower and had to give some thought as to how she would wash her hair. After filling the deep tub, she immersed herself in the warmth, tilting her head back in the water and almost floating. Relaxing now, she thought about the strangeness of the things around her; from light switches to doorknobs to windows, everything seemed different. Back in her room, she noticed that her bed was made with one sheet and a single covering, a fluffy comforter inside a freshly ironed cover. She worried that she would be cold at night.

She settled into the chair by the window to wait for Adam and watched as the students passed on the nearby walkway. It began to occur to Annie that she was very far from home, and it was strangely exciting to realize that in all of this country, she knew only one person.

She sprang from the chair when Adam knocked, telling him, "I missed you!"

He smiled and took her hand. "Did you rest?"

"I'm too excited to rest, but I had a good soak."

"Are you hungry?"

"Famished!"

He continued to grin. "Let's go have supper then, and afterward I can show you a little more of the town."

"It's still so light. What time is it?" she asked. "I need to set my watch."

"It's seven thirty, and in the spring it stays light a lot longer here than at home. Everyone tells me that by May it'll be daylight past ten o'clock, and by June it'll be past eleven."

"Wow, that's cool!"

"The winter was the reverse of that, though. The nights were terribly dark and long. We spent a lot of time in the pubs by the fires."

"That sounds like a nice way to deal with it," she chuckled, "all huddled together with a few beers."

They drove to the town center in the tiny car and dined at the only foreign restaurant in St. Andrews, a place simply named "The Chinese Restaurant."

Annie laughed at Adam's choice. "My first meal in Scotland and I get Chinese food?"

"On Sunday night the only other place that's open is the fish and chips shop," he explained, "and I wanted to do something nicer than that for your arrival."

After dinner, Adam asked if she felt up to walking. "I want to show you something very special," he told her.

They left the car parked on Market Street and walked to where the street narrowed and ended, past beautiful, old stone houses. Gulls seemed to follow them, and the evening air was full of the sea.

As they turned at the end of the street, Adam pointed to a particularly old and charming home. "They say this house was built with stones from the ruined cathedral, after the protestants burned it down."

They turned right at the next corner and had walked only a little farther when in a hushed, reverent voice he said, "There it is" and raised his eyes.

In the lingering dusk, rising up from a moss-velvet cushion of lawn, lay the majestic ruins of a medieval cathedral. They stood outside the surrounding walls for a few moments, then entered the grounds through a gate. The evening was cold and blustery and no one else appeared to have ventured out, so the place had a compelling solitude. Slowly, they traversed the path that led to the larger ruins, then stopped where the portal had been. They said nothing, and Adam watched Annie's face as she surveyed the scene.

The large arch of a clerestory window remained, supported by three smaller arches and flanked by two tall spires. Nearby, a perfectly square tower rose even higher than the spires' peaks. The wall to the right of what had been the structure's main aisle remained largely intact, its chiseled stone weathered but persistent, a solemn reminder that this had been a sacred, protected place. Massive stones that had been the cathedral floor lay buried by gentle grass, more conducive to genuflection now than they once were. The gulls that had followed the two young people perched themselves upon the timeworn stones, some in the window arches, some on the head-stones, watching, waiting, holding their feathers against the wind. They were alone there, standing before the cathedral like pilgrims who had journeyed far, and in the evening color, with the wind and crying gulls sounding more beautiful to her ears than the chants of monks, Annie felt its power.

"I've never seen anything more glorious in my life," she whispered.

He smiled broadly. "I knew you'd love it."

Her eyes widened and she pulled her arms in around her torso. "I feel something. I can't really describe it, but it feels mystical." She looked to the surrounding cemetery. "Maybe it's all the souls that linger here." She took a deep breath of the salt air. "They must be at peace, resting in a place like this. Maybe that's what I feel, their peace."

Adam had been looking away, but he turned again to face Annie. Seeing her now, he recognized that she was different from the person he had known at home, and he had the peculiar sense that the transformation had just happened, right in front of his eyes. He'd only known her briefly, but the girl he'd been acquainted with had always seemed nervous and unsure of herself; this young woman was self-possessed, and her countenance was more serene and lovely than he had ever seen it.

"I'm so happy you came," he said to her in a soft voice.

She reached for one of his hands. "God, this is incredible. Thank you so much for inviting me." Squeezing his hand she added, "You know, ever since I decided to come, I've had the very strong feeling that something extraordinary is going to happen here. I've been feeling this tremendous excitement, like something wonderful is about to happen, and it got even stronger when we walked in here just now." Her eyes returned to the ruins, to the spires, and to St. Rule's tower.

The wind gathered up its strength and rushed between them with a swishing sound that was like the breath of a slumbering giant. It sent a shiver through Annie, and she closed her eyes momentarily.

She was visited then with a vision of herself on a motorcycle, driving away from the cathedral. A human figure stood motionless amid the ruins, obscured by a cloud of smoke. She was filled with a heartfelt, penetrating ache over the sight of that figure, and she opened her eyes again to release the vision and ease the ache.

Adam drove Annie back to David Russell. She dressed for the cold March night in a long flannel gown and socks, and moments after she pulled the comforter to her neck and closed her eyes, she drifted into the deepest and sweetest of sleeps.

Awakening early to the sound of gulls and wind, Annie looked out the window upon a stream of students, most of whom wore red academic gowns, all flowing in the direction of David Russell's main hall. She was surprised at first, but then she recalled Adam telling her that the students followed the centuries-old tradition of wearing their robes to lectures. Glancing at her watch, she realized that she was in danger of missing breakfast. She hurriedly washed her face and brushed her teeth, then threw on jeans and a warm sweater.

Inside the dining hall there was much activity, with students animatedly discussing their plans for the day amid the aroma of cooking bacon and toasting bread. Annie showed her meal pass to a young man at the entrance and stood by awkwardly, wondering what she should do next. Another young man approached her then, and with an enormous grin and obvious pleasure, he held out his hand.

"I'm Melville Lumsdaine," he said. "You must be Adam's friend from America. I've been keeping an eye out for you."

It was impossible not to return his generous smile. "Yes, I'm Annie."

"Would you like me to help you get some breakfast?" he asked, and before she could respond he added, "Of course you would. Here, allow me." He picked up a tray and tableware, then walked into the serving area, motioning for her to follow. "What would you like: eggs, sausage? Don't Americans like big breakfasts?"

"Some do," she continued to smile, "and this morning I'm one of them."

"Good girl, I like a woman with a hearty appetite." Mel helped her fill her tray, then carried it to a table where several other students sat. They were all watching Annie.

"This is Adam Wilson's friend from America," he proclaimed and proceeded to introduce her.

She took a seat next to an attractive young woman named Susannah Barclay. With the self-possession and clipped accent of the English upper class that Annie had only before encountered in movies, Susannah said, "It's absolutely lovely to meet you. Adam's told us so much about you. We've all been terribly excited to see you."

"He wrote so many wonderful things about this place, I decided to come and see for myself," she blushed.

Melville's grin broadened as he declared, "You have such a lovely accent! Southern, is it?"

She nodded as her blush deepened.

"Adam's asked us to help you out until you get your bearings, get you to meals on time, point you in the right direction, that sort of thing," Mel informed her, his accent less formal than Susannah's. "I'm free this morning. I haven't got tutorials until after lunch, so would you like to walk with me into town? I can show you around a bit, if you'd like."

"That'd be great," Annie replied. "I'm supposed to meet Adam at Southgait Hall at eleven. He showed me where it is last night, but I'm not sure I can find it again."

"It'd be my pleasure," he beamed.

"Don't walk her all over creation, Mel. The poor darling's probably tired," Susannah said as she rose from the table and kissed his cheek. "I'm off. See you at lunch. Cheerio all."

"Right you are," Mel answered. "Cheers, luv, half past twelve."

Susannah pulled on the gown that had been draped over her chair. Melville observed her graceful departure with adoring eyes, then turned his attention back to Annie. "Would you care for some coffee?"

"Yes, thanks."

"White or black?" he asked.

"White?"

"You know, with milk."

"Oh, white then, please."

He brought her a large cup of steaming coffee, made very light brown with hot milk. When she had finished her breakfast, Melville, who wore the same long robe as the other students, advised Annie to get a warm coat.

"It's a sunny day but the wind off the sea can be fierce."

It was indeed a cold day, but no one seemed to mind. Their path took them by neatly appointed houses with tiny front yards, where housewives swept walkways and tended to garden areas. Cyclists rode past Annie and Mel in droves, and many other students walked along with them. No one seemed in much of a hurry. Most of them smiled at or greeted the two, and most wore their red gowns though some sported black ones. Annie felt out of place in her brown coat.

"How long are you staying in St. Andrews?" Mel asked her.

"I'm not sure. I haven't decided yet."

"Were you going to go elsewhere or just keep to jolly old Britain?"

"I'd like to see France and Italy and anyplace else I can get to."

"That sounds the thing. I should love to see those places myself."

They had walked a little farther in silence when Annie spoke up again, emboldened by Melville's warmth and interest in her.

"What I was thinking of doing—I'd like to buy a motorcycle, a used one of course, and drive it to France."

Melville looked astonished and didn't respond immediately. "That's an amazing idea: for a woman, especially." He couldn't quite picture this slender girl driving a motorbike.

"I know," Annie smiled.

Melville went quiet as he tried to imagine it. She had noticed a similar reaction in Adam yesterday when she'd told him of her plans. Adam had regarded her suspiciously, wrinkling his brow and squinting his eyes almost as though he were having trouble seeing her.

Sunday evening it had seemed like a ghost town, but this morning the town moved and breathed like a living thing. The streets were noisy and bustling. Merchants displayed abundances of fruit, bushels of potatoes, green vegetables of all sorts, and flowers—flowers were everywhere when Annie and Melville strolled through the West Port.

First they walked up South Street, then down Market, then they sat for a while on a bench. Melville chatted amicably, but Annie was mostly silent, in awe of what was going on around her. She had never seen so many contented faces, so many baby carriages, so much conversation between people in the streets out in the open on a cold, blustery day.

At a few minutes before their meeting time, Adam appeared at the entrance to Southgait Hall, slightly out of breath and wearing his scarlet gown. He embraced Annie warmly.

"Did you sleep well last night? Did you get breakfast? I see Mel found you!"

"Yes, yes, and yes!" she laughed. Mel laughed, too.

"Did Mel show you around? I hope he didn't show you too much. I want to show you everything!"

Mel spoke up, "We've only had a bit of a stroll, up and down a few streets, and I talked so much I doubt she could pay attention to anything else."

"Good, thanks for taking care of her this morning."

"It was my great pleasure, and Mademoiselle Barclay and I are looking forward to dining with you this evening, if you'll allow us," he offered.

She was thoroughly charmed by Mel and smiled every time he spoke to her. "Thank you, that'll be great."

"We'll wait for you in the reception, then. See you about seven? I shouldn't be late if I were you. The food diminishes quickly, or should I say, decays quickly," he teased.

He laughed his wonderful, open laugh, then said "Cheerio," to which Adam answered the same.

Adam asked Annie up to his room, because he wanted to wash up and put his books away before they went to lunch. He left the door open while he organized himself, and two Southgait residents stopped by to introduce themselves to Annie. The first was Patrick Ramsay, a formal and rather forward Englishman who made no attempt to hide his attraction to her. When the second young man happened by, he awkwardly introduced himself as Andrew Gordon, telling her with downcast eyes what a pleasure it was to meet her. He was tall and lean, and there was something compelling about him because of the contradiction between the regal way he held himself and the reticent manner in which he approached her. When she and Adam left his room, Andrew remained standing in the hallway, and as they rounded the corner leaving him behind, Annie felt momentarily anxious, as though she had forgotten something important.

Adam took her to the Central for a pub lunch. They had steak and kidney pies, which he recommended, and afterward took a walk to see the university. They crossed through a little cobblestone side street to North Street to see the university quadrangle and St. Salvator's Tower. The buildings and wall that connected them and formed the quadrangle were all made of a stately gray stone, and the grounds inside the enclosure were meticulously cared for. Adam pointed out initials set in a paving stone that marked the execution site of Patrick Hamilton, who suffered a long and agonizing death for the crime of being a protestant reformer. She was baffled by this account, for it seemed impossible that torture and murder could occur in such a serene and lovely place.

They continued on, down a narrow alley named Butts Wynd, which connected North Street with The Scores. The Scores was a particularly pretty street, with many grand stone houses whose rear yards and windows looked out upon the water. This street marked the northern boundary of the town where it met the North Sea.

Continuing along The Scores, Adam pointed out several university buildings, among them the Philosophy Department where he attended a good many of his lectures. "You'll have to come with me sometime. I've got the most interesting professors, and the classes are really enjoyable."

"I'd like that, because I don't know what I'm going to do with myself while you're in class."

"You don't need to worry about that," he informed her. "Practically everyone I know has offered to spend time with you. Tonight after dinner, we're supposed to meet some people at the Russell Hotel for a drink if you're up to it."

"Oh sure, whatever you want to do."

Adam abruptly stopped walking to give her a tight hug. "It's so good to have you here. It's wonderful being able to share all this with you!" He then pointed to the structure across the road. "This is our famous castle. Isn't it beautiful?"

They were standing in front of the English Department, which was across the road from St. Andrews castle. Like the cathedral, the castle had been reduced to ruins during the Reformation. All that remained were the battlements, which were splendidly situated on the cliffs.

"I can't imagine sitting in a classroom and having things like this to look at," she observed. "I'd be so distracted. How do you keep your mind on your work?"

"It's not always easy, especially when it's a gorgeous day like today."

Annie slipped her arm through Adam's and squeezed it, then she yawned.

"Tired?" he asked.

"Maybe a little."

"Of course you are, your clock's all messed up. Why don't I walk you back to David Russell so you can get a nap before dinner?"

Annie was having a strange dream, the kind where everything is all mixed up, people and places and time, when someone knocked on her door.

"Good evening. Your dinner awaits, mademoiselle."

She sat upright in bed and tried hard to bring her mind into focus.

"Hello in there!" the voice said again.

The confusion cleared, and she realized where she was and whose voice she was hearing.

"Melville! I'll be right there!" She quickly went to the mirror, pulled the brush through her long hair, and then rubbed the sleep from her eyes. When she opened the door, Mel and Susannah greeted her like old friends.

"We met Adam as he was heading back to town," Susannah told her. "He warned us you'd probably be asleep if you didn't turn up for dinner. Peckish, are you?"

She was unfamiliar with the word. "Peckish? I don't understand."

"Hungry, my dear," she smiled. Linking her arm with Annie's, she kept hold of her while they made their way to the dining hall.

The tables were noisier and more active than they had been at breakfast, and strange things were being served, dishes Annie had never before seen.

"What's that?" She pointed to a round ball of something that looked fried.

"You're in luck," Melville proclaimed, chuckling. "They're serving haggis tonight. It must be in your honor."

"What is it?" She couldn't even guess.

"Well," Susannah's pretty face took on a careful look, "it's the leftover bits of a sheep, all ground up and spiced, then cooked in the sheep's stomach. It looks dreadful I know, but it really is quite good."

"Oh my," was all she could think to say. She asked for potatoes and vegetables and was about to refuse the haggis offered her by the server when she suddenly had a change of heart and said, "What the hell, I'll try some."

Mel congratulated her. "That's it, old girl! Marvelous, brave thing aren't you?"

Since they weren't due at the Russell Hotel until nine o'clock, the three went to the common room after dinner. During their meal, Annie hadn't said much, as she found herself watching and listening to her companions in fascination. The slightly rotund Mel was a few inches shorter than the tall and elegant Susannah, and he was considerably more casual. But despite their disparate appearances and manners, he somehow fit with her, for behind Susannah's careful speech and obvious class, she exuded a compelling warmth. She also displayed a confidence in her sexuality that made Annie envious. They were very certainly lovers, she decided, and the affectionate way they treated one another struck her with great poignancy. As she watched Mel stroke her cheek or kiss her hand, she lamented never having known such tenderness and wondered if she ever would.

In the common room, the students were seated facing a television, noiselessly awaiting the start of a program.

Mel seemed anxious to watch and told her, "I think you'll enjoy this."

Annie recognized the opening strains of the "Star Trek" theme as the students let out a cheer. She turned to Susannah to observe, "I didn't know you got American television here."

"It's not," she informed her, "it's the BBC, and this is the most popular series on."

Annie watched the rerun with mild amusement, but she was more interested in the students' reactions to the characters, for whenever "Scottie" had a scene, they roared with laughter. "Why are they laughing?" she asked her friends.

"It's because his accent is so terribly phony. It's really quite funny!"

It had always sounded like the real thing to her.

During the afternoon, the sky had clouded over, the wind had eased up, and now the air was heavy with mist. Instead of walking along the road to town, the threesome followed a path behind David Russell that led to another dormitory. Susannah took the middle position and interlinked their arms. Earlier, when she'd taken Annie's arm as they walked to dinner, it had made her slightly uncomfortable. But this time she experienced a curious warmth with Susannah's touch.

"There now," Susannah said, as she pulled her close, "this is lovely, isn't it?"

"Yes, it is," Annie answered a little timidly.

The path continued past several lecture halls and descended toward the sea. Mel pointed out the golf course, now off to their left. "That's the Old Course. Do you play?"

Nodding, she responded, "In my senior year of high school, it was offered as an elective for physical education." She chuckled when she recalled, "Not that I had any real interest in golf. I had a crush on the boy who was teaching it."

Susannah laughed. "Well, that's as good a reason to learn as any I've ever heard. Then you *must* play while you're here, you simply *must*," she declared. "You can't be in St. Andrews without taking a round on the links. It just isn't done."

They had arrived in town and were walking up The Scores when Mel called out to someone. "Hello, Andrew! Come and meet Annie."

Annie recognized him as one of the young men she had met while she was in Adam's room. He was just about to enter a pub they were passing.

"Hello Annie, it's very nice to see you again." His voice was gentle and reserved, and he was dressed in a sweater and tweed jacket that suited him perfectly, giving him the comfortable appearance of a country gentleman.

"Oh, you've met. Well good. Why don't you join us? We're meeting Adam at the Russell," Mel explained.

Annie suddenly wanted him to know, "It'd be nice if you could."

"Thank you ever so much," he answered, "but Colin Wemyss and some others are expecting me here." He gestured toward the Scores Hotel. "Would it be all right if I popped in later?"

She felt a little embarrassed now and sensed the beginnings of a blush. "Of course, whenever you'd like."

"May I bring my friends?" he asked. "I'm certain they'd like to meet you." His smile was disarming.

She couldn't have said what was causing it, but her cheeks felt as though they'd caught fire. "Of course," she answered, dropping her gaze to the sidewalk.

The public room of the Russell Hotel was warm and glowing. A coal fire burned softly, and the red velvet upholstery seemed to absorb its heat. At one end of the room, a large bay window afforded a view of the sea. A padded seat hugged the window's perimeter, and Adam and several other young men were waiting there. They all rose when Annie and Susannah entered the room. One of them pushed ahead of the others and held out his hand to Annie. When she offered hers, he took it and kissed it softly.

It was Patrick Ramsay. "Lovely Annie, how marvelous to see you again."

Adam appeared a touch uneasy as he took Annie by the arm and began introducing her to the others. When the introductions were complete, Patrick asked if he could get her something to drink.

She was uncertain how to respond and turned to Adam to ask, "What do you think?"

"You're legal here," he informed her, "so you can have whatever you'd like."

Patrick made a suggestion. "How about a lager and lime? That's a nice little drink for a lady."

She cringed from the paternalism in his statement, but in the interest of harmony, decided to let it go. She had, after all, like most of her friends back home, been drinking illegally since high school.

Mel and Patrick went to the bar and returned quickly. Adam's other friends had begun making polite conversation with Annie when Patrick returned with her drink and squeezed in next to her.

Although she was put off by his forwardness, she had to admit he was extraordinarily good-looking, a blond with a rugged complexion and a muscular build. His manners were impeccable but for a tendency toward arrogance, and he looked Annie straight in the eyes as he spoke to her. But his eyes roamed all over her body when she spoke, as though he were sizing up something he wanted to buy.

"You're from the southern part of the Colonies, aren't you?" he inquired. "I've always thought I'd like to go there. It seems to me the most civilized part of your country."

Annie was both amused and irritated by the reference to the Colonies. "Civilized? Yes, in an old-fashioned sort of way, I guess you could say that. People tend to be more polite and formal than in the North, and we do have our traditions." She said this last part with a hint of derision.

"Well, that's what I meant, after all," he responded, missing the sarcasm. "I don't think your country tends to be much on tradition. Tradition is very important to the British, you know."

"Oh, we're big on tradition in the South, all right," she eagerly told him, "and I don't think it's necessarily a good thing."

Adam, feeling a little left out, interjected, "We're thinking of going to the Scottish dance this Friday, Annie. Would you like to come?"

She had always loved to dance, but she could not remember the last time she had. "Sure. What's a Scottish dance?"

Another of Adam's friends, a young Scot named Robin Keay, answered her. "It's called a *ceilidh*, actually. It's held at the town hall and put on by the local people, but many of the students go. They have one almost every weekend this time of year. There's a band and they do the old dances as well as the new. It's a fun evening."

The conversation continued for an hour or more, everyone present chiming in, telling Annie about St. Andrews and asking her questions about America. Once, she made the mistake of referring to the "Scotch" accent and people. She was gently but firmly told that the proper term was *Scots* or *Scottish*.

"Scotch is a drink," Robin laughingly informed her.

Someone bought Annie another lager and lime. By the time Adam suggested it was time to leave, she was feeling quite giddy.

"I hope you'll allow me to escort you on Friday night," Patrick said to her as he helped her with her coat.

The door to the public room opened then, and Andrew Gordon entered with two friends. He approached Annie directly.

"Forgive me for coming so late," he said. Turning to Adam, he politely greeted him.

Patrick suddenly grabbed Annie's arm. "Pity that, Gordon," he said with some impatience, "but we were just on our way out."

Adam suggested to Andrew, "We're going to the ceilidh this Friday if you'd like to join us then."

"Thank you, I would, and I'll look forward to it." He turned back to her and noticed how tightly Patrick gripped her arm. "Perhaps you'll allow me a dance or two, Annie."

The energy from his smile was so powerful it was unsettling. And the way in which he'd said her name—it made her feel odd, almost as though something electric had been turned on in her abdomen. "Yes, yes, of course," she answered. "I'd like that."

Patrick frowned at her response and tightened his hold on her.

Adam insisted upon accompanying Annie back to David Russell. Robin and Patrick asked if they might come along, and the little entourage made its way through the streets with Robin and Adam leading the way, Melville and Susannah hand in hand at the rear. The streets were hushed, very few lights burned in windows, and the mist was like an enormous blanket laid softly upon the slumbering town. Out of respect for the sleeping townspeople, the friends conversed quietly while they walked. Annie listened mostly and drank in the sweetness of the sounds, the muffled laughter, the kindness they showed one another.

Halfway back to the residence hall, the same odd feeling that had come upon Annie at the cathedral ruins returned. By the time she reached her room in Fraser, she recognized what it was. When she was tucked in bed and had closed her eyes, she saw the rolling fields that surrounded St. Andrews laid before her like a banquet, and heard the soft voices of her new friends saying good night.

Peace had settled into her.

Chapter 12

By Friday morning Annie knew names and faces, but when she walked into the dining hall for breakfast, she heard so many "good mornings" that she couldn't possibly respond to them all. The warmth and readiness with which she was welcomed into the enclave of students astounded her; it was the polar opposite of what she'd experienced at her own university. Everyone was kind and polite and helpful, even the townspeople, and by week's end she felt comfortable enough to go just about anywhere on her own.

While Adam attended his lectures, she explored St. Andrews, following the streets wherever they led. Each discovery was a wonder to her, every little alley, church-yard, quaint cottage, or grand house. On one of her early excursions, she stopped in the sweet shop near the end of South Street. It was the first time she used her Scottish pounds and she was somewhat anxious about it, but the shopkeeper was charming, and to demonstrate his honesty he slowly and carefully counted the change into her hand. With an enormous smile she thanked him, then carried her purchase the short distance to the cathedral. Settling in the cold sunshine on the bench overlooking the sea, she bit into the orange-flavored chocolate and marveled that she had never before tasted anything so delicious.

But it was more than just the chocolate, she knew; it was this place, this wondrous ruin of a cathedral. There was something so seductive about it, perched as it was on the edge of everything. Just outside its walls, cliffs dropped straight to the sea. Like the Europa fountain, it was a place that inspired her to dream, to imagine herself across the North Sea, on her motorcycle, wandering through Paris or Rome or some remote, medieval village, feeling the wonder of exploration and the exhilaration of living under her own power, the freedom of following her desires. It was an extraordinary sensation that made her heart beat stronger and made her breathe more deeply the salty ocean air.

During that first week, Annie was introduced to the custom of four o'clock tea. On Tuesday, Adam had tea for her in his room, serving hard cookies he called biscuits along with it, and she noticed with curiosity that most of the other young men in Southgait Hall seemed to be doing the same thing. The following day it was tea with Melville and Susannah, and the day after that Annie and Adam were invited to Patrick Ramsay's room. Patrick put on quite a display for Annie with his matched tea set and the special cakes he'd purchased. But despite the pomposity with which he entertained, she enjoyed herself, for it seemed extraordinary that a man should go to this trouble for her.

After dinner on Friday, Mel brought his guitar to the common room and entertained everyone with songs he had written. One was called "Susannah," and though the lyrics were awkward and his singing voice not the best, it almost made Annie cry. She had instantly developed a fondness for the pair and was continually amazed and heartened by the affectionate respect they showed one another. And she loved the way Mel called Susannah "Mademoiselle Barclay" and had taken to calling her "Mademoiselle d'Inard."

Later that evening, Adam arrived with Patrick, and together the group walked to the ceilidh as they had planned. Patrick nearly pushed Adam off the sidewalk in his effort to be next to Annie, and when he took hold of her arm, she found herself wishing instead to be linked with Susannah, whose touch brought her considerably more warmth and pleasure.

The hall was already packed with people, and a small band consisting of a fiddle, drums, guitar, and accordion warmed up the room. An even mixture of townspeople and students were present, and the locals ranged in age from the very young to the barely-able-to-get-around, but when the music started even the feeble joined in the dancing. The familiar songs they played came across rather silly as adapted to their instruments, and in another circumstance Annie would have found the music beneath her dignity. But it all seemed perfectly wonderful here. The laughter and merriment were contagious, and when Patrick pulled her to the dance floor, she was all smiles.

As the evening wore on the activity changed. When the band took a break, tables and chairs were moved out of the way. Patrick had left her and gone to join the long queue for beers when Andrew Gordon came to sit beside Annie.

"Are you enjoying yourself?" he politely inquired.

She noticed for the first time how brilliantly blue his eyes were. "Very much, I love to dance. How about you? Are you having fun?"

"Yes, I am," he said, "but my favorite part of the evening is yet to come—the reels. May I have the pleasure of dancing one with you?"

"I'm afraid I don't know how," she replied.

He stood and offered his hand. "It's not at all difficult, and I can tell you what to do as we go along."

Despite her misgivings, his smile beckoned and she found it irresistible. She gave him her hand and he held gently to it as he led her to the center of the room.

An introductory sort of music called the dancers to the floor. People rushed forward, gathering in circles of eight. Annie and Andrew joined a circle with Susannah and Mel. Her heart began to pound as she realized she knew nothing of what she was about to do and feared she would make a terrible fool of herself. But Andrew had placed them so they would not have to dance at first and could stand and watch, clapping their hands to the lively music. When it was their turn, he softly gave her instructions, offering encouragement and praise, putting her more at ease with each step. Annie loved the Eight-some Reel and eagerly joined in at the next one, staying on the dance floor with Andrew.

"You do this as though you were born to it," he commented while they waited for the music to begin again.

She blushed as she responded, "You're a great teacher."

Susannah moved close, saying, "You did that very well, darling," before delivering a kiss to her cheek. "You're so lovely. Isn't she lovely, Andrew?"

"Yes, she is," he answered, briefly averting his eyes.

The band struck up again. To begin this reel, each gentleman reached his right arm around his partner's waist, holding the lady's back against him as they grasped left hands. When Andrew took Annie in this embrace, she felt him do it in stages, inching her ever closer to his body until she was pressed against it. When they touched, they both felt the rush of heat that ensued. It was only reluctantly that they separated themselves to continue on with the dance.

Patrick didn't allow anyone else to dance with Annie after Andrew. He took it upon himself to hold her hand between dances and didn't leave her side again. When the dance ended, most of the students went to the Scores Hotel, where they ordered pints of Scottish heavy. Annie decided to try the heavy tonight instead of the lager and found that she liked it.

"It's not at all as bad as it looks," she told Susannah, who laughed and responded, "You'll have to try this some time," referring to the Guinness stout she always drank.

Mel teased Annie about her enthusiasm for the reels, and she wanted to know when the next ceilidh would be. From time to time, she glanced across the crowded pub to catch a glimpse of Andrew, who sat with friends in a far corner. After a while, Patrick noticed this and deftly positioned himself to block her view.

Back in her room, she whirled around as she brushed her teeth and readied herself for bed. When she lay tucked under the down comforter and closed her eyes, she heard again the sound of the band, and while stars lit the early spring night, Annie danced in her dreams.

Her first weekend in St. Andrews was so busy it flew by. On Saturday, she spent most of the morning hours in the village walking with Adam, going in and out of the shops to make a few small purchases for lunch. She loved the courteous way the shopkeepers greeted them, and she especially loved the grocer on South Street with his tall, neatly packed shelves. Clerks wearing starched cotton overcoats climbed ladders to retrieve the items from the high shelves and greeted most customers by name, saying things like "Good morning, Mrs. McKirty, what canna we do fer ye today?"

They purchased cheese and bread, a bit of ham and two oranges, and as the clock towers sounded out the noon hour and the shops closed up for lunch, they went back to Adam's room to enjoy their meal. Whenever she entered Southgait, she found herself hoping to see Andrew, and she was disappointed that he was not around this afternoon. When they had eaten and warmed themselves with hot tea, they went out again, this time for a walk along the Lade Braes.

They followed an alley alongside Southgait Hall to the Lade Braes Walk, which winds its way for several miles to the outskirts of town as a public footpath and park. For much of the way, it forms a boundary between private backyards.

"Why are all the yards so muddy? Don't they plant grass here?" Annie asked as they strolled along.

Adam laughed at her. "They're gardens, all these muddy patches. The Scots prefer gardens to lawns. In a few more weeks, practically everywhere you look you'll see flowers. The whole town will be spectacular with flowers."

They crossed over Bridge Street and rejoined the path, which wound alongside the Botanic Garden. It followed the Kinness Burn, a wonderfully noisy creek with borders that were protected by the public park. Adam explained that *burn* was the Scottish word for stream.

"This is my favorite place to walk," he told her. "I come here when I need to think."

It was indeed a special, quiet place. No cars or bicycles were permitted, and unlike the bustling village streets that were filled with people and activity during the day, it offered abundant peace.

As they walked, they monitored the approach of a young mother, pushing a baby carriage alongside a little girl who looked to be about three years old. The child was asking questions of her mother in a dear little voice, thick with the local accent. The sounds of it drew and held Annie's attention.

Adam looked straight ahead and continued talking. "Patrick's a very good friend of mine. Do you like him?"

"Why, yes," she said, still watching the family. The mother had stopped to tie the little girl's shoe.

"He told me he likes you very much." He paused and looked away so that she couldn't see his face. "He'd like to spend more time with you."

"Really," she responded, and wondered why the two had discussed such a thing between themselves. Laughing slightly, she questioned, "Who does he think you are, my father?"

He didn't see the humor. "No, he's just being polite."

"Well, I'll give him that. He is polite." Patrick was always holding doors for her, helping her with her coat, her chair, fussing over her. "But he bothers me a bit. He's a little too pushy for my taste."

The family was passing alongside now, and they exchanged greetings. Annie peered into the pram for a glimpse of the baby. "What beautiful children," she complimented the woman.

"Aye, they are bonnie and more than a handful." She affected a weary mother's grin as she added, "They've the temperament of their coloring." They both had bright red hair and round, cherry cheeks.

When they were gone, Annie commented to Adam, "I love that accent." They resumed their walk in silence as she considered what he'd told her about Patrick. He hadn't responded to her remark about his aggressiveness, so she decided to change the subject. "Speaking of Scots, how well do you know Andrew Gordon?"

He shrugged. "Not very. He's a nice chap, but he keeps to himself pretty much. Why do you ask?"

"No reason," she grinned, "it's just that he interests me, but he seems so shy. I asked Susannah about him. She said that for the three years they've been at university together, he's been fairly mysterious. Apparently no one knows much about him except that he comes from the West Highlands."

"I didn't even know that," he answered, "but it makes sense. Robin Keay seems to be his closest friend, and he comes from that area, too."

As they continued on, Adam grew increasingly pre-occupied. When they were near the point of leaving the Lade Braes to return Annie to her residence hall, he finally spoke again.

He seemed sullen when he informed her, "I'm not going to be able to spend as much time with you as I have. I'm getting behind in my work."

That distressed her. "I'm sorry," she readily offered. "Has my being here caused you a problem?"

"Nothing that I can't handle," he responded almost curtly.

The sudden change in Adam bewildered her. Although she'd been drawn to him as a friend and had felt comfortable enough to accept his invitation to Scotland, he was still virtually a stranger, and she was keenly aware that he knew next to nothing about her.

Mel and Susannah had invited Annie to accompany them to chapel in the morning, and Adam and Patrick were to meet them there. Just after she'd awakened Sunday morning, Mel knocked on her door.

"How about joining us for breakfast in Susannah's room, Mademoiselle d'Inard?"

"I'd love it!" she answered and kissed his cheek.

Susannah had cleared off her desk to lay out their breakfast. The three sat around the makeshift table drinking coffee and savoring every bite of the bakery rolls Mel had purchased, which they loaded with butter and marmalade. Just before they left for chapel, Susannah pulled an academic robe from her closet.

"Robin Keay has an extra one of these and he's offering it to you to wear while you're here, so you won't feel out of place."

"Oh, how nice, how very sweet of him!" she exclaimed. "But is it OK to do that? I don't want to get anyone in trouble."

"Of course it's all right," Mel replied. "No one will give it a second thought."

Annie excitedly pulled on the heavy wool gown, then looked at herself in the mirror. The image reflected the three of them, each in a gown now, and what Annie saw was that she was no longer an outsider. She smiled broadly at the sight, and her hesitation about wearing it disappeared instantly.

Susannah heartily approved. "It's a marvelous color for you, and I must say, you're looking a sight better than when you arrived."

Annie's cheeks had taken on a pink glow from all the time spent walking outdoors, the hollowness of them had rounded out somewhat, and her eyes were brighter.

"Now, you know the tradition of wearing these things, don't you?" Mel asked her. "If you're first year, you wear it full up on the shoulders, second year drooping back at the neck, third year off a shoulder—one for arts, the other for sciences." He demonstrated as he spoke. "And then fourth year, when you're almost gone, you drop it halfway down the back so that it nearly falls off."

She now understood why she'd seen so many students' gowns hanging off them, hems dragging the ground as they walked. "So how should I wear it?" she wondered.

"If you were a student here, you'd be third year as we are, right?" Susannah asked her.

"If I'd stayed in college I would, but I didn't even finish my first year." Her face and demeanor changed suddenly, as the memory of that horrible night, the reason she'd left school, flashed through her mind.

Susannah observed the change in her. From their earlier conversations, she had already gleaned that Annie's experience at university had not been good, and the alteration in her disposition at the mere mention of that time convinced her now that she was right. "So wear it as a second year would then, no need to revert back to your first year," she instinctively said. "One must move on, after all, and put the past in its place."

As had happened in so many of their encounters, she was heartened by Susannah's acceptance and understanding. The worried, anxious look disappeared, and she leaned to kiss Susannah's cheek in gratitude.

Susannah returned the kiss with one of her own.

The church service was a lovely spectacle, resplendent with gothic beauty and ceremony. The hymns, accompanied by a stirring pipe organ, gave Annie goose bumps and made her eyes fill with tears. Susannah noticed and touched her arm in a gesture meant to comfort, but her sensitivity and sweetness in doing so made the tears flow, and by the time the service was over, her eyes were puffy.

They parted from Adam and Patrick, who had to return to Southgait for their Sunday dinner. Their meal at David Russell was later, so Annie, Melville, and Susannah took their time returning. They stopped for a while in Kinburn Park to sit huddled together on a bench, absorbing the brightness of the late morning.

"The weather's been splendid, hasn't it?" Mel observed. "Before you came it rained for weeks on end, but now we see the sun every day. There's nothing to attribute it to but your arrival," he teased.

Annie smiled at him. "You're so sweet, Mel."

Susannah had been sitting in silence, wondering whether or not she should ask a question that had been nagging her. She finally came to a decision, but she approached it cautiously. "Annie, I've been wondering. Do you still mean to purchase a motorbike for your adventure on the continent?"

She nodded and deepened her smile. "I'm more determined than ever."

Susannah had discerned that, but for someone she now considered a friend, she thought it right to voice her concerns. "Mel and I were talking, and we wondered if you knew about the Eurorail pass," she continued. "They're marvelous, inexpensive things, and I believe you can go almost anywhere with them."

Annie was aware of them. Issie had written from France and told her she'd purchased one. "The problem with them is that you're restricted to places with train stations. I want more independence than that," she informed them. "There are lots of little out-of-the-way places that I'd like to see, and with a motorcycle I can go where I want, when I want."

During the course of this exchange, Mel had stopped smiling and was now also looking concerned. "It sounds very adventurous and romantic, to be sure, but in reality it may be rather dangerous," he said. "Do you know how to drive a motorbike?"

"My brother taught me before I left," she informed them.

Four students approached the trio then, one of them a divinity student in his distinctive black robe, emblazoned with the purple cross of St. Andrew. They were friends of Mel and Susannah and had not as yet met Annie.

They chatted for a few minutes before Mel checked his watch. "We'd better get going," he advised the girls. Missing the only meal served on Sunday was not something he wanted to do.

Susannah linked her arm with Annie's as they rose from the bench, and when they were underway again she told her, "Back to what we were saying before. I hope you don't think I'm interfering where I have no business."

"Absolutely not!" she assured her.

"Good, because I wouldn't be much of a friend if I didn't tell you that I worry about you. But truth be told," she thought to add, "you should also know that I envy your courage and independence."

Her words struck a meaningful cord in Annie, especially when she referred to herself as her friend. "Thank you for saying that. I consider you a friend, too, and it's wonderful to know that you understand, because courage," she paused momentarily, shaking her head slightly, "that's exactly what this whole thing is about."

The growling in Mel's stomach made him impatient. He'd been leading the way, but now he moved between the girls and slipped his arms in theirs, pulling them close and speeding them up. The wind came up suddenly and made whips of their gown hems, tangling up their legs as they walked, yet urging them on ahead.

Chapter 13

Back where Annie used to be, things went on as usual. There was growing racial unrest, worsening crime and violence, and an increasingly disaffected youth, as the nightly news tallied the casualties and cargo planes full of coffins unloaded their burdens of squandered life.

She corresponded with her family and almost regretted it, for every letter reminded her of the past and a place she had been but never wished to be again. But despite a desire to not be reminded of certain things, she sometimes watched the BBC news, finding it at once interesting and shocking, for it showed her things about her country she had not known, from a point of view she hadn't before heard. After one particularly horrific news show in which Vietnamese civilian casualties were explicitly displayed, she found herself in the uncomfortable position of having to defend her country's actions to some angry students, who, out of sheer frustration, turned on her and asked why "she" didn't just get out of there and leave those poor people alone. She heard herself saying something to the effect that she didn't think it was that simple, when Susannah leapt to her rescue by proclaiming that Annie was no more responsible for Vietnam than they were for the mess in Northern Ireland. This quieted the rabble but it did not comfort Annie, who felt disconcertingly guilty that she was not back there trying to stop it. And she couldn't help but think of Timmy; she had left him there alone to face an uncertain future with the draft. Only after a long walk along the Lade Braes, listening to the voice of the burn, did she feel better again.

That was the remarkable thing about this place. Whenever she felt unhappy or worried, all she need do to chase the gloom was look around. Because everywhere she went and everything she saw gave her the greatest of pleasure. Not the kind of pleasure that was mostly excitement, but the kind that had its origins in some mysterious place deep inside, that brought forth such calm and contentment it made her glow from the inside. And glow she did, and smile, too, walking into town to meet her friends or stroll the streets, popping in at Innes Booksellers to buy a postcard or the sweet shop for an ice cream. The shopkeeper at B. Jannetta's now greeted Annie as though he'd known her for years.

In a letter to her friend Jane Ann, she wrote, "How could anyone not feel happy and at peace in a place where mothers feel safe enough to leave their babies outside while they're in the shops, along with all their packages and things! And not only do they not seem to worry or give it a second thought, but if a baby should make a fuss while mummy is busy inside, whatever passing stranger is nearby will stop to give the pram a jiggle. Have you ever heard of such a thing? Can you imagine living like this?"

As she wandered the streets of St. Andrews, attentively watching and listening, Annie couldn't help but be thoughtful, and this thoughtfulness gave birth to a new perspective. In contrast to her drudging existence at home, life in this graceful town seemed purposeful and quietly beautiful. The past flowed into the future, the winter into spring, children played amid the remains of ancient times where lush grass and wildflowers grew. It was like a perfectly executed ballet, without beginning or end, that made her laugh and cry and never let her down, holding her spellbound and wistful, always wanting more.

Despite her misgivings about Patrick, Annie continued to see him. Adam spent less and less time with her, and Patrick, as though it were planned that way, just naturally filled the gap.

A dance was scheduled for the coming weekend at the student union, and Patrick asked Annie to be his date. Before the dance, he invited her to dine with him at Southgait Hall, which, unlike David Russell, was all male and more formal and traditional in atmosphere; the residents wore ties and jackets to dinner and were served their meals at the tables. Annie accepted his invitation eagerly, harboring the secret hope of seeing Andrew.

She shed her usual attire of sweater and jeans and wore a pretty skirt and blouse with a blue shawl wrapped around her shoulders. When she arrived in the hall, she was surprised to find herself the only woman in the room, and she almost gasped in delight as all the young men rose from their seats. She could not have felt more special, for they remained standing as she made her way across the room, escorted by Patrick and Adam, and only sat when she had.

During the meal she noticed Andrew, who was seated two tables away. She caught his eye once or twice, and he returned the glances with a warm smile.

When the pudding was being served, he came to greet her. "How are you getting on? Still enjoying the old gray town?"

Before she could say anything, Patrick answered for her. "She's been enjoying herself immensely, thank you."

She bristled at his effrontery, but Andrew merely smiled, then started away. She wanted to call him back, but Robin Keay, who was sitting with them, did it for her.

"Andrew, stay a moment. Have a seat." Robin brought a chair from a nearby table for his friend, then turned to Annie. "Tomorrow I'm moving out of Southgait into a cottage on The Scores. It was left to the family after the death of an aunt."

"Oh, I'm sorry," she responded.

"Thank you, but it was for the best. She was widowed and quite old and wasn't getting on well. The house has been empty for months now, and tomorrow I'm going over to do some tidying up. I'm mentioning this to you, because I'm not at all sure about things." He was speaking quickly and nervously, as though he were afraid that what he had to say would not be well received. "I've never kept house before and I don't know much about it. I wonder, would you have the time tomorrow to stop in and perhaps give me some direction? I thought, you being a woman, you'd know more about it." This was the most conversation Annie had ever heard out of Robin, and it was punctuated by a bright red blush.

Coming from someone else, the chauvinism in that request might have put her off, but the charmingly awkward way Robin had asked for her help left her chuckling. "I'd be delighted to stop by. I'll even help you clean."

He blushed again as he protested, "Oh no, I couldn't possibly let you do that. I'd only ask for your advice."

She continued to smile. "Don't be silly. I'd love to help. Besides, I'd like to return the kindness of the loan of your extra gown. I've really enjoyed wearing it."

"Have you? I'm very glad of that," he grinned, "though actually, it wasn't my idea." He looked to Andrew, who affected a slight frown.

Seeing his displeasure, Robin quickly returned the conversation to the cottage. By the time they finished the pudding, he had received so many offers of help that he found himself hoping they wouldn't all show at once, because there was no way he'd be able to fit that number of people into the small house.

April was well underway, and the stirrings of spring fever could be felt among those gathered at the student union dance. Annie felt it, too, as the days grew longer and brighter and green sprouts of daffodils emerged from the mud, racing toward the light. Near the end of the evening, when it was time to dance the reels, she could not be kept from the floor. Patrick stayed close, but in these country dances you could not keep the same partner, only begin and end with him, so at times she found herself dancing with Andrew. Whenever they were thrust together, she smiled so much her face hurt, and the smiles she generated in him were wonderful for her to see.

As the band packed up and everyone headed for the pubs, Andrew brushed past her and briefly touched her arm. "Good night, Annie," he said. The flesh that he'd touched tingled with bursts of heat as she watched him walk away.

At the bar the young men ordered drams of Scotch to drink with their pints, and Annie wanted to try that, too. Susannah joined her, and the young women attracted some attention as they knocked back the potent stuff, then quickly chased it with beer. When they walked away from the bar, they were giggling and unsteady and had to hold onto each other for support.

"Annie, I must tell you," Susannah said in a loud whisper, "I'm a bit pissed."

Annie knew that this meant drunk, not angry. "Well, my dear," she said, mocking her accent, "I must say, you're the most elegant drunk I've ever seen, and I love you dearly for it."

At this, Susannah threw her arms around Annie's neck and hugged her, then pushed away so that she might see her face. "I love you, too, you know. It's really quite astounding isn't it? It's as though we've known each other our whole lives."

The two embraced again, holding on solidly and kissing the other's cheeks. The others looked on in astonishment, and only Melville seemed unperturbed.

Patrick had not approved of Annie's decision to drink Scotch, but she had ignored his efforts to stop her. When he saw how drunk she'd become, he scowled, "I think the ladies have had enough to drink."

He insisted on accompanying her back to David Russell, and when Mel and Susannah left them, he took Annie to her room. He invited himself in and ran the tap, then offered a warm cloth for her face.

"I should be very careful with the whisky," he said. "Ladies don't often drink the stuff."

"Ladies, what ladies?" Annie laughingly asked.

"It's none of my concern what Susannah does," he declared, "but I won't have you humiliating yourself in public."

"Susannah is a lady if ever I've seen one," she retorted. "If she can get drunk, then so can I."

"It's not proper behavior," he insisted, "and I won't have others thinking less of you because of it."

With a click of her tongue, she dismissed his concerns. "I don't think anyone thinks less of me."

Her conduct in the pub had put him in a reproachful mood, so he decided now was the time to say this. "There's something else. You keep telling people that you want to buy a motorbike and drive it to France. I've kept my mouth shut about it, but I think it's a bloody awful idea."

And who the hell asked you—she wanted to fire back. But she didn't, because she had stretched out on the bed and the room was spinning.

"People are talking about you and this motorbike thing and frankly, I find the whole matter embarrassing," he continued. "I've a better idea for you. Forget this foolishness and consider spending the summer with me. My parents have a country place, and I've written to ask if you might join us there." He paused now and waited for a response.

It was not the invitation that irked her. "Embarrassing? Why's it embarrassing?"

"You're a lady, that's why. Well-brought-up ladies don't do such things." His voice carried the scolding tone of an angered parent.

She might have flown into a rage had she not been so drunk. With difficulty, she sat up and scowled at him. "It's not embarrassing to me and if it's what I want to do, I'm going to do it. And why are you bothering yourself about this anyway? It's my decision to make, not yours." She swayed a little as she tried to remain upright, then she gave up the effort and lay back again.

He decided that she was too far gone to reason with, and the sight of her on the bed, her long, sensuous hair spilled over the pillow, aroused him suddenly. He sat alongside her and took hold of her face with both hands. He kissed her, rather angrily, forcing his tongue into her mouth and using his weight to pin her down. In the next instant, he slid one hand under her skirt and grabbed her panties; he was about to pull them off when she screamed into his mouth. The intensity of her reaction startled him, and he removed his mouth from hers.

"Don't do that," she shouted, pushing him away.

His face was red and he was panting. "Why?"

His actions had brought vivid memories to the surface, and she found herself angry with him not just for what he'd done, but for what he'd made her remember. "Where'd you get the idea you could do that? You're lecturing me one minute about getting drunk, and the next you're trying to take advantage of me because I am!"

"No, that's not it."

"Yes, you are."

"I'm sorry. I didn't mean to. It's just that you can be so stubborn. I thought I might get past your stubbornness that way."

"By forcing yourself on me?"

"I thought you'd want it, too."

Though he'd intended them to calm her, his words only deepened her outrage. "Not that way, never that way! And while we're at it, since when did I give you permission to answer for me? What the hell did you mean answering Andrew like that? I didn't like that one damn bit, not one damn bit! I can answer my own fucking questions."

"There's no need for vulgarity."

Realizing how much stronger he was than she, she felt increasingly vulnerable and insisted, "You should go, Patrick. I want you to go." She stood quickly and folded her arms. When she did, her head began to throb.

Disappointment and regret filled his face, and though it had been crimson only moments earlier, it was now a little pale. "I'm sorry," he told her. "I truly am. I should never have done that."

Her voice softened slightly. "No, you shouldn't have."

"Let's not part this way. Accept my apology if you can, and let me make it up to you. Let me take you to tea this week, please. I don't want you angry with me, I'm too fond of you." He ended on a pleading note and affected the look of a repentant little boy.

Trying to quell her growing nausea, she exhaled slowly and sat back down on the bed. "All right," she answered, because she wanted him to go and leave her alone. "Let's do that. Tea would be nice."

Finally recognizing that she felt unwell, he kissed her hand and said good night, but not before securing some aspirin from one of her neighbors. On the walk back to Southgait, he went over and over the incident in his head and cursed himself for his rashness. He decided that his best course of action would be to keep his distance for the next few days, given how angry she'd been. *I should give her time to cool down,* he told himself, *and curse that bloody Gordon for having come to our table anyway.* Although no one could see it, the very thought of that arrogant Scot made his blood boil and brought the color to his face again.

Mel and Susannah were spending the day in the library, so Annie slept off her hangover, then walked into town alone. She found Robin Keay's cottage easily. It was only a few houses up from the Russell Hotel on The Scores, and he had described it well. Although she'd passed it many times before, its lack of garden and general disrepair had aroused little attention. It troubled her that she had left something undiscovered in this town that she now knew so well, so before approaching the door, she stood outside for a moment and looked it over.

It was very old and considerably run-down, certainly the most humble-looking home on the street. It had a low tile roof, rather steeply slanted, with two chimneys visible from the front and a stone wall that enclosed its tiny entrance yard. The rusty iron gate that united the two portions of wall was left open, and as Annie passed through it she noticed a small engraved plaque that read "The Whaum." Strangely, she experienced a sense of deja vu when she saw this, and that sensation gave rise to a shudder that originated somewhere in her chest, then radiated to her limbs.

Robin answered her knock happily, welcoming her and inviting her to the parlor. "Do come in. Andrew's here and we've been quite busy already."

Inhaling, she repeated, "Andrew?"

The strong odor of mildew was being chased by the breeze from an open window. Upon entering the parlor, Annie saw him bending to stoke the fire; he heard her voice and turned to her with his smile, the smile that caused her cheeks to blush and her insides to tingle.

"Hullo, I've just put another bit of wood on to warm you. Do come in and sit by the fire." He wiped soft, sand-colored hair from his eyes as he straightened up, hair that he'd allowed to grow to his collar.

Robin hurriedly removed some things from the couch and beckoned her to sit. "I'll just go put the kettle on. I won't be a minute," he said, and scurried off, leaving them alone.

An ornate mantel clock chimed the hour while Andrew cleared a chair near her. As she made herself comfortable on the sofa, she cast her eyes around the old room. It had a quaint loveliness about it, though disordered now and dusty, and the furnishings had clearly seen better days. She found their worn appearance pleasing, however, because it hinted of the life that had been lived around them and seemed to welcome the presence of future life. The mantel was cluttered with various odd pieces, ornaments and souvenirs that had been collected over the years and were placed there, it seemed, to evoke memories. At the far end of the room, beveled glass doors offered a view of the overgrown garden. Andrew sat with his chair across from Annie but turned to the side so as not to block the fire's warmth.

"It's a nice cottage. It's really sweet," she said to him. He was very close and she looked into the deep blue of his eyes, a blue as compelling as the skies over the cathedral.

"It's quite ordinary, really, as far as Scottish houses go," he answered. "It's old and drafty and the facilities are a bit difficult, but with time and some good cleaning, it'll come 'round and be a proper place to live."

They kept their eyes together, and he allowed himself a long, searching look without saying anything more; the look reactivated her tingling. An instant of intense quiet followed when all they heard were the soft beats of the mantel clock measuring out the time. It seemed to Annie that what she heard was her heart and that he could hear it, too. She averted her eyes in embarrassment, but even as she did, she felt him drawing them back. The shrill whistle of the kettle pierced the calm of the parlor, and very soon afterward, Robin entered carrying a rattling tray laden with china cups and saucers and a steaming pot. Andrew cleared a table for him to place it on.

The encounter with Andrew's eyes left her feeling slightly disoriented, as though she'd just awakened from a dream. "Oh, this is so nice of you. Thank you," she fumbled, "but you didn't have to go to all this trouble for me."

"Nonsense, you're our first guest and it's our pleasure."

"*Our* guest?"

"Didn't Andrew tell you? He's moving in, too."

Andrew poured the tea, saying simply, "I've not had the opportunity. Do you take milk and sugar, Annie?"

God, she thought, how I love the way he says my name. It never sounded so pretty. "Yes, thank you."

He stirred, then handed the cup to her. "Robin feels as though he'd be too lonely here on his own, so he's invited me to be his flatmate."

"I'm very glad he said yes," Robin remarked. "I can't think of anyone better suited, though it would be nice if he could cook. Neither of us can cook."

"Oh dear, I think you're in for some trouble then," she laughed. "Remind me not to stay for dinner."

The young men protested that they were fast learners and that with a little instruction and some time, they should be able to handle themselves well enough. But Annie continued to tease them and look skeptical.

When she'd finished her tea, Robin asked, "Would you care to see the rest of the place?"

The kitchen was just off the parlor and they went there first. It had a small electric cooker, as they called it, a tiny refrigerator, a large pantry, and at the center of the room, an old scrub-top table and chairs. The table was littered with newspapers and kitchen utensils. Old cans and various bits of trash were piled in one corner, and dirty dishes seemed to be scattered everywhere. The enormity of the task was beginning to impress her.

"As my aunt grew more feeble," Robin explained, "she couldn't even manage to carry out the rubbish. Most of the family lives at a distance, so no one was nearby to help. And since she passed on, I'm afraid no one's had the time or the inclination to come by and tidy up."

They walked around the house slowly, Annie noting the things she thought should be done first. The dining room was in relatively good shape and the bedrooms even better. The bathroom looked as though they'd already tackled it.

Her mood brightened. "It won't be that bad. I think we should concentrate on the kitchen because that's going to take the most work, and it'll make you feel much better when it's cleaned. The other rooms will just need some airing out and dusting and mopping. I don't suppose there's a washing machine."

"No, I'm afraid not, but if we gather the things that need to be washed, I'll take them to the laundrette," Robin answered.

Back in the kitchen, Annie rolled up her sleeves. She started with the pantry shelves, pulling everything off and wiping them down with dilute bleach. She had Robin at the sink washing the dishes while Andrew dried the things and handed them back to her to be organized on the clean shelves. They chatted happily as they worked, and the time passed quickly. Andrew had a delightful sense of humor, and he made them laugh repeatedly as he adopted a stiffened accent and pretended to be a butler. At one point in the afternoon he began to sing, and Robin joined in now and again for the parts he knew.

It was a traditional ballad, *Annachie Gordon*, that recounted the tragedy of an ill-fated love. Annie was mesmerized as Andrew unfolded the song's tale without the slightest bit of self-consciousness.

The maiden Jeannie loved Annachie, who was away at sea, but while he was gone her father forced her to marry a wealthy lord. She swore that she would never bear the nobleman's children and on her wedding night, Jeannie died of a broken heart. Annachie returned that very day, but too late. He found her laid in her burial chamber, and he kissed her cold lips until his heart turned to stone.

Andrew's voice was true and compelling, and his eyes kept returning to Annie's while he sang. She had stopped what she was doing to listen more intently and when he concluded, she felt herself on the verge of tears.

"That was so beautiful," she whispered, "but too sad."

He was riveted to her misty eyes. "They were doomed from the start, but still, they couldn't help loving one another."

Robin was aware of the tension between them, and it made him a little uncomfortable. Trying to lighten the atmosphere, he teased, "Tell me, Andrew, was Annachie an ancestor of yours, do you think?"

With great reluctance, he tore himself away from Annie. "I don't imagine he had any descendants since he died without consummating his love." He smiled and turned again to his cleaning task, but it was next to impossible to keep his mind on it.

By late afternoon, the little kitchen almost sparkled, and most of the rubbish had been removed from the house and piled in the front yard to await collection.

Mel and Susannah stopped in on their return trip from the library, just as the dinner hour drew near. Annie was hesitant about leaving, but the young men urged her to, saying that she'd already done far too much. Mel was eager for his supper, so he hurried her off. When they were about a block away from the Whaum, Annie looked back to see Andrew, still standing on the sidewalk. He gave her a little wave, then turned and stepped behind the gate. Her heart did something odd at that moment, something it would do repeatedly in the weeks ahead: It slowed and seemed reluctant to beat, giving her the distinct sensation that it was being deprived of something essential.

After dinner on Sunday, as they sat drinking coffee in the common room, Mel brought someone to meet Annie.

"This is Colin Wemyss," he told her. "I thought you two should meet. He's got a motorbike that he's interested in selling."

Her face lit as she asked, "Really? What kind of motorcycle?"

"A Norton, 1963 Jubilee. Would you like to see it? It's just outside."

Mel and Susannah accompanied them to the car park and when Annie saw the old motorcycle for the first time, it scared her. Jesus, she thought, I could never handle this. It was large and heavy looking, not at all like her brother's lightweight machine, and her immediate reaction was to tell Colin that she wasn't interested. But the excited looks on the faces of her friends pushed her to examine it further.

She asked Colin, "How many cc's is it?"

"Two-fifty," he responded.

"That's all?" With its fat tires and heavy steel mudguards, it seemed at least twice that size. "Is it in good shape? Does it run well?"

"I've had it for four years and I've taken quite good care of it," he informed her, "but like all motorbikes, it needs attention now and again. Would you like to drive it?"

Her heart was beating very fast, so fast she was beginning to feel dizzy, but the sound of Susannah's voice saying, "Oh, do drive it. I'd love to see you drive it!" made her move ahead.

Colin quickly showed her the gears and brakes, cautioning her that she might need to put some muscle into them. Then he offered to start it up. The engine roared ferociously and attracted the attention of everyone within earshot. Annie's knees went to jelly, but she somehow managed to mount it. She practiced changing the gears with the clutch held in, and then, with some difficulty, pushed back the kick stand. It was overwhelmingly heavy.

"How much does this thing weigh?" she called to Colin.

"Oh, about 650 pounds," he answered, yelling over the noise.

"Damn," she responded.

A small crowd had gathered behind them, and their expectant faces left her no choice but to go on with the thing. She put it into first gear, pulled back gently on the accelerator, and then eased up on the clutch. The machine responded by surging powerfully ahead.

It was a good thing it was Sunday dinnertime and little traffic was on the roads, for Annie automatically turned into the righthand lane as she pulled into the street. She couldn't hear the warning shouts of her friends over the bike's roar, but once she got through the gears and headed farther up the road, she suddenly realized her mistake and swerved to the left, losing her balance and almost toppling the motorcycle. Miraculously, she recovered her equilibrium and a short distance ahead, she pulled off the road to regain her composure.

As she straddled the idling bike, the roar and vibration made her feel as though she were sitting atop something alive and fiercely strong. The concerns voiced by Mel and Susannah came back to her now, and her jaunt on this powerful and obviously dangerous motorcycle was proving their validity. When I get back, she decided, I'll tell Colin thanks very much, but it's not the kind of bike I'm looking for. I'm crazy, but not this crazy, she laughed to herself.

She turned the bike around with great difficulty and headed back to David Russell with just a little more ease than when she had left. But when she came into sight of her waiting friends, something happened that changed her mind again. The assembled crowd let out such a cheer that she actually heard them over the engine and that sound, that sight ignited something in Annie that had long lain cold and still.

Chapter 14

Never on the face of the earth was a spring more magnificent than that spring in St. Andrews. The sun was never more brilliant, the colors were never more vivid, the delicate aroma of flowers was never more intoxicating. The grass along the Lade Braes burst forth green and lush, adorned with delicate violets and bluebells, sprinkled with the drifting petals of fragrant fruit trees. Snowdrops, crocuses, daffodils, and hyacinths were everywhere in profusion in the parks, around the university, among the ruins. Nature's preeminence was neither to be suppressed nor denied that season. Flowers even blossomed among the rocks of the steep cliffs wherever a bit of earth could take hold.

In the morning, with her friends off to their lectures, Annie eagerly walked to town. She lingered long to take it in—at Kinburn Park, along the streets at the flower seller's stalls, in front of the little cottage gardens, at the manicured patches of the university quadrangle. On occasion, she ventured out of town beyond David Russell along Buchanan Gardens to the little cemetery and beyond, to the fields to watch the lambs. She would return along the Lade Braes, removing her shoes to feel the tender grass on her feet or to dip them in the coolness of the burn's water. Breathing and drinking in the brilliant, long days, she was filled with joy and longing.

On two occasions, Annie went with Adam to his philosophy lecture. The building was located on The Scores, with its rear windows overlooking the sea. The professor welcomed her to join them and was kind enough to ask her opinion in their discussions. The second time she attended was a particularly splendid day, and to fulfill the romantic desires of his students, the professor took them out to the lawn to read Wordsworth aloud. Annie could not believe how wonderful it all was. This is how it should be, she thought, as she twirled a tiny violet in her hand. This is how I want my life to be—filled with small, exquisite moments. The sea breeze played with her hair and the sun lit it as she tilted her head to follow the passage of the racing clouds.

Adam watched her then, blithely reclined near a bed of fragrant double daffodils, the green in her eyes never more intense. He had never felt closer to her, he realized, but at the same time, he had never felt more distant. For things had not happened with her as he had wanted them to, expected them to. When she first arrived he had thought that she would be with him, that together they would love this place and walk through the days. But quietly, and without his being able to do anything about it, he found himself pushed aside as she went about making her own friends, finding her own way. And he now understood that the special connection he had hoped for would never be. He told himself that it was for the best, that she was not the girl he thought she was, that she was not worthy of his affection. But at times like these, when he saw her smiling at him, sweetly oblivious to the pain she had caused him, he would want her in spite of himself, and he hated her for it.

* * *

One warm afternoon, Annie decided to stop in at the Whaum to see how things were progressing. Robin was home and, as usual, happy to see her.

"I've just put the kettle on. Would you care for a cup of tea?"

"If it's not too much trouble."

"Absolutely not. Andrew's off, and I'm happy for the company."

As they sat in the parlor sipping at their tea, she complimented him on how comfortable the cottage had become.

"My next project, if I can find the time, will be the garden," he informed her. "Now that spring is really here, I'd like to do a bit of weeding and whatever I can to help it along. I remember seeing this garden when I was a child. It used to be splendid."

"Really?" she asked. Until now, she'd paid little attention to the rear yard.

When they finished, they went through the French doors to take a look together. The yard had been laid out as a small, formal rose garden, with clusters of bushes in neat rectangles and paths between the spaces for meandering and dreaming. It was surrounded on three sides by high stone walls, with the rear of the house completing the enclosure. A beautifully weathered old bench was situated in the middle of it all, set against a wall and tucked under an arbor.

"It's almost all roses," she exclaimed, "and they're trying to come back!" Many of the bedraggled bushes were colored with the red sprouts of new leaves.

"Yes, but I'm afraid that without some help, it'll soon be a hopeless mess," he sighed.

As the idea took hold, she excitedly told him, "I'd love to fix up this garden! I've got lots of free time and you don't. Why don't you let me see what I can do with it?"

She seemed so genuinely enthusiastic that he could not say no. "All right, you're on. I found a spade and clippers and a few other wee tools when I was tidying up," he said. "Come by whenever you want and help yourself to tea. If the door is locked, there's a key under the flowerpot by the entrance."

She thanked him profusely, then asked if she might get started right away.

"Why not," he told her, "but I've got to be off. Stay as long as you like. I'll catch you up later."

Annie remembered having seen an apron when she'd been there before, and she went in search of it. She took the tools and a bucket out to the garden and got to work immediately, digging up weeds and carefully removing the tangle of wild vines from among the old bushes. She quickly became lost in the work, the sheer pleasure of the spring air and sun, and the scent of the soil. She heard seabirds above her and occasional gusts of wind rush their way around the wall enclosure, looking for a way out. An hour or two had passed when she heard the sounds of someone in the house. She looked in the direction of the cottage and saw Andrew walking toward her.

She was on her knees in the mud, smudges of dirt were on her face, and some of her long hair that she'd secured with a barrette had loosed itself in the breeze. He marveled at her mussed appearance, for it seemed terribly intimate—as though she were revealing a secret part of herself—and it filled his heart and left him unable to speak. He offered both hands to help her up and, without saying a word, pulled a handkerchief from his tweed jacket. His hands seemed to have a will of their own as he placed one under her chin and drew her face upward, then tenderly began wiping the smudges from her cheeks.

She might have been embarrassed by the gesture, but she wasn't, because his touch was more welcome than any she had ever experienced. Instead of the tingling she'd felt on other occasions, it now filled her with warmth and a sense of calm, and she closed her eyes to revel in it.

He'd waited so long, so very long to be this close to her, he slowed his movements so that it might last a few seconds more.

When she opened her eyes again, she softly explained, "I came by earlier to see how things were going, and I persuaded Robin to let me do what I can do with this poor garden."

Andrew's heart was beating so erratically that he needed to sit down. He gave her his smile and then took her hand to lead her to the bench under the arbor. He worked at bringing himself under control before he said, "There's an inordinate amount of work to be done here. Do you think you can manage?"

When they were sitting together side by side, her sense of calm deepened. "Well, I don't know, but I'd like to try. I used to work with my grandmother in her garden. It wasn't much of one though. It was just an alley between their house and ours, where my brother Timmy and I played. We lived in the city then, next to my grandfather's business." For a few seconds, her thoughts drifted back in time. "I was just thinking about her when you came in. She would have loved this place."

"Is your grandmother dead?" he asked.

Nodding slightly, she answered, "She died four years ago, just after my sixteenth birthday. It's very sad that I can't share this with her, because I believe she would have thought St. Andrews the most beautiful place on earth."

His smile had softened. "But maybe you are, sharing it with her I mean. Perhaps she's enjoying it through you."

At first she thought it a peculiar thing for him to say, but then, in the next instant, she knew it to be true.

"I've always believed that we carry on for our ancestors," he offered now, "close and distant, that we carry on their dreams, their spirits."

His smile was as comforting as a fire on a cold day. "Yes," she responded, "I believe you're right. I could feel her in me while I was working. It was almost as though my hands were hers, because I'd never done this sort of thing before, but my hands—they knew what to do." She looked down at them.

He reached to touch one and ran a fingertip over the scratches that crisscrossed her knuckles. "Does it hurt?" he asked her.

"No," she answered him, smiling. Whenever he touched her, it seemed at once miraculous and the most natural thing in the world.

"I'm glad of that," his voice grew more tender, "because I would never want you to suffer for any reason."

Thinking that he was teasing her, she almost laughed at his declaration. After all, they were only thorn pricks. But then she looked into his face. He seemed very concerned about something, and it made her ask, "What's wrong?"

He sighed and shook his head slightly. "It's odd, you know, but whenever I see you, I think of things."

"What things?"

He had to look away as he responded, "Of things that are, and things that can never be." *God, what am I doing?* he asked himself. *Why is it that every time I'm near her, my heart wants to spill out and make a fool of me?*

Softly, she questioned, "Like what?"

He tried to smile. "It's nothing. I'm being silly. Forgive my melancholy."

She reached for his hand and caressed it in hers as she said, "Please tell me. I'd like to know."

The effect she had on him was overpowering, and the profound pleasure her touch evoked made him long for more. "You're so free," he told her. "I envy your freedom." *He wanted her hand to stay with his forever.*

Their eyes followed a gull as it swooped low over the garden before she asked, "Aren't you?"

"I have obligations," was the response he gave, "matters that tie me down and dictate my life to me." *God, if only I were,* he lamented. *I'd lift your hand and put it to my lips and tell you everything I'm feeling, everything I've felt about you since the day we first met.*

Her brow wrinkled slightly. "But you're so young, I mean, you're still in college. How can you be obligated to anything yet?" She recalled Susannah telling her that she'd never seen him with a date, and she thought of a possible reason. "You're not married, are you?"

"No," he responded, though not entirely convincingly. "That's not it. It's more a matter of family duty. Until now I mostly accepted it, but lately I find myself wishing I were someone else." *There it went again, his heart, pouring out in front of her.*

"Why now?"

"Because the person I am keeps me from being who I want to be." He blushed immediately because he knew that what he'd said made no sense.

He was wrong. It made perfect sense to Annie. "Sometimes you just have to push past who you are to get to where you want to be. That's what I've had to do. That's why I've come here," she offered. "Something happened to me a couple of years ago that changed me, turned me into someone I didn't like. When I made the decision to come here, I also made the choice to leave that person behind."

Her revelation touched him and made him think of his own past, of the devastating event that had changed him. He turned on the bench so that he might face her directly. "And now that you've put that behind you, what will you become? Who is it that you want to be?"

It was a good question, one she hadn't yet fully answered for herself. She gazed off toward the house as she carefully considered her response. "Someone that others can love," she told him, "and someone that I can be proud of, that I can love, too."

He wanted very badly to respond to that, to say—oh, but you are that, in my eyes you're that and more, so much more—but he held back.

The French doors had been left open when he came to her, and from the house they could hear the mantel clock begin its chiming. It was quickly followed by the authoritative voices of the church towers.

"My God," she inhaled, "I was supposed to meet Patrick half an hour ago!"

She scampered about retrieving the gardening tools, dropping each of them into the bucket with a clang, then ran inside to wash her hands and face. Andrew calmly followed and brought her a clean towel, watching as she brushed and refastened her hair with the barrette.

"I'm so sorry to break off our discussion like this," she told him breathlessly, "but I'll be back tomorrow if it's all right with you and Robin."

His heart was too full to answer, so he simply smiled and nodded. He helped her into her borrowed gown and she was off, running up The Scores to Butts Wynd, folds of red beating beside her like wings. He stood at the Whaum's gate and shouted "Cheerio!" as she began her flight, but, after she rounded the corner at the wynd and left his sight, the emptiness he felt was insufferable.

Patrick was standing outside the old student union looking anxiously up and down the street. She called out as soon as she spotted him, "I'm so sorry I'm late!"

He puffed his cheeks, then exhaled through pursed lips. "Where on earth were you? I've been waiting for almost an hour!"

"I'm really sorry, I forgot. I lost track of the time. You must have been worried."

"How could you lose track of time? What else have you got to do but meet me?"

Looking at him now, she realized that what she saw in his face was not worry but anger. "It wasn't an hour," she protested, "I'm only half an hour late. I stopped by the Whaum and asked Robin if I might work in his garden for a bit, and I lost track of time."

"The Whaum, what do you mean by going there? You shouldn't go there alone. People will talk!" The barely restrained anger made him clench his teeth.

She made the strategic decision not to mention Andrew. "Robin was home when I got there but he left, so I was alone most of the time."

"Still, you shouldn't go by there on your own. You should know better than that."

She frowned disbelievingly and tilted her head to the side. "You know something, Patrick? I'm getting pretty sick of you telling me what I should and shouldn't do."

"I tell you what to do because you're my girlfriend," he fumed, "and you have a certain responsibility to act properly, and this isn't bloody America!"

That was it. He'd just gone way past anything she would tolerate. "Oh?" she scoffed. "Well, here's a news flash. I'm not your girlfriend and I never was. And no, this isn't America, but at least there most men have the intelligence to respect a woman's independence."

He was utterly appalled, for no woman had ever spoken to him like this. "Are you calling me stupid?"

She might have answered "if the shoe fits," but she didn't want to further inflame this foul-tempered man. They were standing in the middle of North Street and people were passing them, listening to their heated exchange, so she softened her tone now and answered, "Look, I'm sorry I was late. It wasn't intentional, but it won't happen again. It won't happen again because I'm not going to see you anymore."

The shock he was experiencing kept him from giving a full-fledged response. He looked around quickly to see if anyone might have heard her, then he said, "Fine. It's best if we lay off for a while and think things over."

She shook her head again. "You're not hearing me. I don't need to think anything over. It's time to end it, here and now."

His mouth fell open. His hand itched with the desire to slap her face and he might have, had they not been standing in the open with so many people nearby. "Fine. Have it your own bloody way. But don't come to me in a few days saying you're sorry and you want to patch things up, because by then it'll be too late."

Her head lifted back slightly as she abruptly laughed. More than ever, he wanted to smack the brashness out of her, but he kept his balled fists at his sides, then stormed away.

Susannah was cheering Mel's rugby team when she spotted Annie. She gave her American friend a warm hug and kissed her on both cheeks. "They're playing quite well today," she said, "but I do hope Mel doesn't get his head cracked."

Annie's distress suddenly vanished, and she was happy to be near Susannah. Her usually proper demeanor had been cast off today, and as they watched the match together, the girls squealed and applauded whenever Mel's team did something right.

When there was a break in the action, Susannah asked her, "Where's Patrick? I thought you two were meeting for tea."

"I was supposed to, but I was late. He got so pissed off at having to wait for me that he lost it, and then so did I.

But I lost it because I'm sick of him telling me what to do and scolding me like he's my damned father or something."

She knitted her brow. "Really? How'd you end it, then?"

"I told him I don't want to see him anymore." Annie looked toward the playing field as Susannah wrapped an arm around her waist and hugged her.

"Bravo, is what I say to that. He's not the right sort for you, Annie darling, and I've been wondering how long it would take you to see that."

"Too long, apparently," she frowned.

"You're not the first, you know," she thought to tell her now. "Two other girls I know have dated him, and they both found him too controlling." She made an unpleasant face, as though Patrick carried a foul odor. "What you need is a less threatened man," she decided, "someone like my dear Mel, who fancies a woman with a mind of her own." She raised her arm and waved to him.

Mel nodded from his position on the field.

Annie's thoughts turned to Andrew, and when they did, she felt the return of the warmth and calm that had come from their conversation. It led her to ask, "How about Andrew? Is he the right sort?"

She looked puzzled for an instant, then she answered. "As I told you before, no one knows much about him. But he has very fine manners, and he's always impressed me as being of some background, as someone who comes from a good family."

The final whistle blew, and Susannah moaned in disappointment over the team's loss. The field was muddy today, and when Mel came to greet the girls, he was absolutely filthy. But still, he planted a big kiss on Susannah's lips and then one on Annie's.

"I'd embrace you lovely mesdemoiselles, but I'm a frightful mess."

"That you are," Susannah agreed, adding coyly, "Let's get you in the bath and I'll scrub you down." She reached to massage one muscular buttock.

Mel responded to her gesture with his own seductive look, and Annie could picture him in the tub, laughing while Susannah bent over him, her full breasts pouring out of her low-cut sweater, as she tenderly washed his body. She was overcome with a deep ache at that moment and found her thoughts drawn once again to Andrew. What I wouldn't give to have a relationship like theirs, she lamented; I'd give anything to be loved like that.

The version Adam heard of their argument was Patrick's. He was very sympathetic, being fond of Patrick and put out with Annie himself, and he was determined to speak with her about it that very night.

As they were walking into town, Susannah suggested they avoid the usual spots to reduce the likelihood of seeing Patrick, so the threesome chose a small inn near the cathedral. When Adam came in and spotted Annie at the bar, she understood that he had been deliberately searching her out. He asked her to step outside with him in a way that let her know he was itching for a fight. Still, she went with him to stand in the street, in the damp, cold wind that blew up the cliffs from the sea.

He wasted no time in getting to the point. "You've really hurt Patrick, and he doesn't deserve that," he chastised her. "He's been very decent with you, and he feels as though you're taking his feelings for granted. I think you should go to him and apologize and try to make things up."

She shook her head. "I won't do that, because I've nothing to apologize for. I know he's your friend, Adam, but he's got a bad temper, and I told you before, he's too damned pushy. I don't like that. I don't want to be with someone like that."

He looked disgusted and disbelieving. "Well, I don't know what to say to you, because I've known him a lot longer than you have, and I've never once seen him lose his temper."

The implication in that was astonishing. "Are you saying his bad behavior is my fault?"

"I'm saying I don't know anything about his bad behavior, only yours," he declared.

"Mine?" she nearly shrieked. "I can't believe you said that. You really don't know me, do you Adam?"

"I know enough. I know you have a tendency to take people for granted and push them too far. That's why people get angry with you. You bring the anger out in them." He was thinking of himself, not his friend, of how hurt he had been by her not wanting to be with him, how he'd felt pushed aside and taken for granted.

Her expression changed now, from looking annoyed to injured. "Is that what you think, that I bring out the worst in people?"

He toned down a little. "It's something you should think about, that's all I'm trying to say."

For a glorious moment or two, Adam felt triumphant and better than he had in weeks. But the sad, confused look on Annie's face took that triumph away, and now he felt angry with her again for doing that.

As Annie walked away from him, she felt doubt chasing after her, the kind that she might have dismissed but for its nagging little ring of truth. Is he right? she asked herself. Maybe he is, she answered. I never understood why Jason was so cruel. Maybe it was me, something I'd brought out in him. And Patrick, he'd been so gentlemanly at first, but then he changed. Did I do that? Did I bring out the worst in him? Other women don't seem to do that. Look at Susannah. Mel just oozes tenderness when he's around her; that's what she brings out in him.

She joined Susannah and Mel at the bar again, but the rest of the evening she was quiet and thoughtful as she regarded her friends' special chemistry and tried to determine what it was that she was doing wrong.

A dream roused her in the middle of that night. She awoke in a sweat, her heart racing.

She was wearing the long, pretty gown she had brought with her. A heavy snow had fallen on the spring flowers, breaking and burying them so that she could not find them. She knelt in the snow in her beautiful dress and bare feet, digging through the cold with raw, freezing hands, still unable to find them. Her dress clung wet and translucent to the curves of her body, making her feel more vulnerable, more exposed. The snow fell harder, blowing in swirls around her, burying her, too. She sensed that someone was near and called for help. No one came, and her voice echoed back upon itself in the white blindness.

The golden spring mornings would not allow her to feel sad for long; their exquisite freshness wiped away any melancholy that might have taken hold in the blackness of night. The birdsong, the warming breezes, the tumbling clouds and dancing flower heads, all spoke to her of things that were far more important than her trivial concerns. She stayed away from the Whaum for a couple of days, because she didn't want Patrick to see her there or be told of her going there. But she could not get Andrew and their conversation out of her mind, and too, there was the neglected rose garden. They both called to her. So, in spite of her desire to not cause trouble, she made up her mind to go back.

No one answered her knock, so she opened the door and went in. The little cottage was flooded with light and warmth and the feeling of peace. She located the gardening tools and went into the yard to begin her work, leaving the parlor doors ajar. Within a few minutes, she heard a noise and turned to see Andrew standing in the middle of the room, rubbing the sleep from his eyes. She went in to greet him, but he had not seen her.

He was clad only in a wrinkled, unbuttoned shirt and boxer shorts. "Good morning," she smiled, then chuckled, "nice legs!"

"Excuse me!" He turned quickly and went to his room. He reemerged a minute later, this time fully dressed. "Please forgive me, I didn't know you were here, I would never . . . "

She had thought to tease him some more but realized that he was recovering from a blush. "No please, I'm the one who should be sorry. I guess you didn't hear me knock."

"Apparently not." He relaxed and laughed at himself now. "I'm happy to see you though. I didn't know if you'd come back, but I hoped you would."

"Not come back because of Patrick?" she wondered.

"Well, yes," he admitted, "I overheard him speaking with Adam, but never mind them. Would you like coffee?"

"Only if you were going to make some for yourself."

"I most definitely was." He rubbed at his eyes again. "I'll bring it outside so we can have a sit on the bench and enjoy it there."

She went back to work while he busied himself in the kitchen. Some minutes later, he came into the garden carrying a tray that contained two large mugs of milky coffee, two oranges, and some plain tea biscuits. Tucked under his arm was a small parcel, wrapped in brown paper and tied with string. "It's not much of a breakfast," he said, "but it's the company that'll make it special for me." He waited for her to sit, then put the tray on the bench, keeping hold of the package. He handed it to her without an explanation.

Searching his face, she questioned, "What's this about?"

He grinned slightly, saying only, "It's a small gift."

She loved presents and excitedly tore open the paper to find a pair of suede gardening gloves. He was still standing, and she reached for his hand to pull him to the bench beside her. Looking into his cobalt eyes, she sighed, "This is so sweet. What a thoughtful thing to do!"

With their eyes connected, he felt his heart taking off again, and he had to fight to stay grounded. "You'll notice they're quite long, up to your elbows. They're specially made for rose gardeners so they might work without being scratched." He glanced at her hands. "The last time you were here, you looked as though you'd been in a row with a cat."

She tended to feel a little giddy in his presence and she giggled as she said, "Thank you so much. You're so sweet to me. You've no idea how much I appreciate the way you treat me." She followed an impulse then and leaned toward him to deliver a lingering kiss to his cheek.

The sensation of her lips on his skin nearly overwhelmed him. "It's my pleasure," he responded as he handed her a coffee. Keep yourself steady, old man, he reminded himself. All other things aside, she's seeing someone else, isn't she?

Cradling the mug in her hands, she cooed, "It's so nice here. Every time I come to this cottage I feel so contented. It's almost like being home, only better." She tilted her head to gaze into the white and sapphire sky, letting the long silk of her hair fall behind the seat back. "You know, I've never seen such beautiful clouds in my life as I've seen here. And they're always changing and moving. At home the clouds close in and stay for days, very heavy and thick. You feel tied down and trapped on those days. But here they're like dreams that I want to follow, the kind that make me feel as though I can lift up and fly."

Her sensuous voice spilled over him, and Andrew's body warmed with the sound of it. And the picture of her next to him, so free, so open—he longed to caress her, to stroke her hair, to feel again the heat from her lips. He sipped at his coffee to keep himself anchored, but his eyes located her nipples, little peaks forming under her sweater amid the fullness of her bosom. His entire being reacted to their discovery, and he responded in his groin.

For God's sake, he warned himself, keep some control. But what she does to me, what I feel when I'm near her, since the day I first laid eyes on her. No, I can't do this. I can't allow myself to long for something that can never be. I must keep my distance, though God only knows, distance from her is the last thing I want. He needed to move his thoughts elsewhere lest he lose his resolve, so he focused on trying to recall the lines of a poem her words had brought to mind.

He cleared his throat. "Let's see if I can remember how it goes:

> I bring fresh showers for the thirsting flowers,
> From the seas and the streams;
> I bear light shade for the leaves when laid
> In their noonday dreams.
> From my wings are shaken the dews that waken
> The sweet buds every one—"

Annie stared in amazement and then answered:

> "When rocked to rest on their mother's breast,
>   As she dances about the sun."

They looked at each other, both with enormous smiles, and then broke into laughter.

"The Cloud!" she exclaimed. "That's far out that you know that one! That's my most favorite poem! I especially love the last stanza:

> I am the daughter of Earth and Water,
>   And the nursling of the Sky;"

He, too, was stricken with delight as he informed her, "One must know a fair amount of Shelley if one is to attend public school in England, especially mine. He and I attended the same school, you know."

"No! Really? You went to the same school as Shelley?"

"Yes," he grinned, "we were both at Eton College."

"That's unbelievably far out! I never dreamed I'd meet someone who went to the same school as Shelley!"

He laughed at her. "Not at the same time, you know. So you fancy old Percy?"

"Oh yes, everything about him."

Of course she'd love Shelley, he realized. She was the kind of woman he'd write poems about. "He was a remarkably free spirit. He did go his own way, didn't he?"

"He was very passionate about life," she said. "He didn't feel anything lightly or halfheartedly. And he wanted to experience everything. It was as though he knew his life would be short and he'd better get in as much living as possible while he could."

He continued to smile at her.

"And his attitude about love," she went on, "that was really amazing. He once said that for as many women as there were in the world, he thought it possible to love in that many different ways, because he believed that each woman represented something unique and wonderful that he could love and appreciate. When I read that it really impressed me, and it made me wish I could have known him."

He wrinkled his brow as he considered what she'd said. "That's a marvelous recognition of individual worth, I think, and an uncommon attitude."

She liked the way he put that. "It is, isn't it?"

They sat quietly for a moment, drinking their coffee.

She smiled as she questioned, "Do you mind if I ask you something?"

"You can ask me anything you like," he told her.

"You're Scottish, aren't you?"

He nodded and took a bite of biscuit before responding, "They don't come more Scottish than my family." He then grinned mischievously.

She'd been wondering about this for some time. "Then why is it you sound so English? You sound more like Susannah than you do the local people. Where are you from?"

He laughed slightly, then affected a thick Scots accent to answer, "I was born in a wee village in the West Highlands, in mid-Argyll," pronouncing *Argyll* with a strong emphasis on the last syllable.

The sound of him speaking that way made her giggle. "Really? Did you grow up there?"

He resumed his clipped, English way of speaking. "Not exactly. When I was eight, we moved to Cairncurran, which is west of Glasgow. But my grandparents have remained in Argyll, and I've spent at least a part of every summer there."

"Are you close to your grandparents?" she asked.

"Yes, very, though admittedly, I don't see them as much as I'd like." He thought of his grandfather now and made a mental note to ring him at the weekend, for his grandmother had recently written to say he'd been ill.

She remembered her original question and realized she didn't have an answer for it yet. "But why do you sound English?"

With a patient smile, he explained, "At nine I was sent off to public school in England, what Americans call boarding school. That's why you don't notice my accent; they drill it out of you in those places." Now he frowned slightly. "It's the same with Robin. He attended school in England, too." He was peeling an orange as he spoke, and he handed her a section.

She nibbled at it before asking him, "What's Argyll like?"

"Ar-GYLL," he gently corrected. "Very rural, lots of sheep, very sleepy."

"And Cairncurran?"

"Somewhat less sleepy but still rural." He hesitated for a moment, but then, because he knew she would ask, added, "We have a farm called Crofthill and we raise sheep there, just as we did in Argyll."

"It sounds wonderful," she sighed. "I love farms, especially Scottish farms. They seem to be such peaceful places."

"To look at they are, but running a farm is hard work. Some years are good, others brutal, and the work is always there. It never ends." He offered her another section of fruit.

"Thank you," she smiled. "Do you do a lot of work on your farm?"

He cleared his throat before telling her, "We've been fortunate enough to have had help, but at many farms near us—the neighbors, the children I grew up with, for instance—everyone works as soon as they're old enough to hold a pitchfork. It's good work though. It's honest work, and there's nothing wrong with that. There are a lot worse things a man could do."

Something about the way he said that made it sound as though he envied the simplicity of that life. She finished her coffee and set the cup on the bench. "I've also been wanting to ask you, what does *Whaum* mean?"

The happy expression he'd been wearing earlier returned. "It's old Scots dialect. It literally means a 'hollow in the hills,' but a hollow is a protected, safe place, out of the wind, so it's also come to mean 'a cozy, protected place.'"

Her voice expressed her delight as she responded, "It fits this cottage perfectly, doesn't it? It's such a comfortable, cozy place. What a perfect name to give it!"

A glance at his wristwatch gave him a sinking feeling. "Blast, look at the time. I've got to get to my tutorial. I'm in enough hot water as it is. Shall I see you later?"

"If you don't mind, I'd like to keep working in the garden. I've been looking forward to it and anyway, I've really nothing else to do," she wanted him to know, "since I'm not seeing Patrick anymore."

As that settled in, his eyes widened with excitement. "You're not?"

"Nope," she grinned, "we argued the other day and I ended it, but it was going to happen anyway, argument or not."

"Oh?" His heart had jumped into an excited pace at the news, and it quickened his breathing. "Why's that?"

Her smile was tinged with mischief. "Because I'm sure he won't want anything more to do with me when he finds out I've given Colin a down payment on his motorcycle."

The rhythm of his heart changed again, as he suddenly found himself teetering between two potent emotional states, between the exhilaration of realizing that she was now free to be with him, and because he was not free to pursue her, a dreadful foreboding about where it all could lead.

Chapter 15

The spring was putting on weight. Trees were plump with blossoms and the buds of tender new leaves, answering the sun's long calls to awaken. Lambs, no longer wobbly, ran with strong, untiring legs and ventured far from their mothers.

Annie made gardening at the Whaum part of her daily routine because it gave her purpose and made her happy. In the morning after breakfast, when Mel and Susannah had scurried off to their tutorials, she had often felt lonely and left out, but now, with the garden that needed her, her day had purpose. And, not at all the least of it was the glorious bonus of seeing Andrew and spending time with him.

Very quickly, she learned his schedule. Depending on the day, she knew what time he would walk through the French doors to greet her and compliment her progress, and she planned her day around it. As for Andrew, Annie soon knew unmistakably how he felt about her. He would run from his lectures to the cottage, often for just a few stolen moments, frequently forsaking his studies when he should have been hard at work in the library. They both looked forward to their time together more than anyone knew, more than they ever even admitted to themselves, to tea in the little parlor—in front of a fire on the cooler days—to quiet talks and shared amusements, and to the strange, unacknowledged peace they felt when they were alone together in the little cottage.

One particularly lovely afternoon as Annie pruned the old bushes, Andrew observed, "It's almost May."

"I know," she smiled. She was always smiling when he was near.

"Will you come to May Morning at the castle?"

Nodding, she answered, "Susannah and Mel say it's worth getting up for."

"Or staying up for." He retrieved the severed canes for her, then put them in the rubbish can so she wouldn't hurt herself. "There'll be a bonfire on the beach the night before, and many of us will just see the night through there."

"It sounds like fun," she commented.

"Robin and I were thinking to have a little gathering here beforehand. I hope you'll come."

"I wouldn't miss it." She finished what she meant to accomplish, and they went into the cottage together. "Do you have much studying today?" she asked him.

"No more than usual. Why?"

"I thought we might take a walk to the harbor and then along the East Sands. It's such a pretty day."

"That's a fine idea," he agreed. "Let's do that."

They reached their favorite bench outside the cathedral gate and sat for a time, gazing over the water. After a few minutes, Andrew took hold of her hand and brought it to his lips. As his lips caressed her skin, his touch melted her heart; it always did that, and she longed for him to do more. But for all their days together, he had done nothing more than hold her hand or kiss it. When he completed the kiss, he rubbed his cheek along the spot, then let her hand rest with his in his lap. Though she wasn't touching him, she could feel his arousal beneath her hand.

"I have something to tell you," she said softly, looking ahead. "You know that I asked my parents to send some of the money I saved. Well, I got a letter from my mom this morning. She's wiring it to the Royal Bank of Scotland, and it should be through any day now. When it comes, I can settle up with Colin and buy his motorcycle."

His only response was to tighten his grip slightly. He kept his eyes focused somewhere over the water.

She was puzzled by his silence. "Don't you have anything to say?"

Releasing her hand, he sighed heavily. "I shouldn't say anything. I know this is what you want."

She tried to see his eyes, but he wouldn't allow it. "It is, but you can say whatever you like about it, whatever you're feeling."

He stood abruptly and asked, "Shall we go for that walk now? We'd better get to it or you'll miss your supper."

"I don't care about supper," she answered meekly.

"Nonsense, you need to keep up your strength. Handling a motorbike is going to require stamina, and you'd best start building it." He began walking away without waiting for her, something he'd never done before, leaving her to stand alone in her growing bewilderment.

When they were well into the steep cliff path that led southward from the beach, she called to him. "Can we rest a minute? I need to get my breath."

He walked on for a few more yards, then settled into a sandy alcove. He sat with his knees flexed and his arms wrapped around them while he waited for her to catch up.

When she reached him, she remained standing. "You're mad at me, aren't you?"

"No," he answered firmly, "it's not anger I'm feeling."

"Then what is it?" When he didn't respond, she sat next to him, nuzzling her side into his.

The sensation of her body touching his was like witchcraft, like being brought under a spell. He felt his resolve slip away, and he held his breath for a moment as a pained expression overcame his face. "Do you recall our conversation that first day you came to work in the garden?"

She nodded as she answered, "You told me you had obligations that kept you from being who you want to be."

All the way along the path, he'd been waging an internal debate over whether or not he should say this. But now, sitting alone with her in this cove, hidden away from the world, all his arguments against it crumbled. "That's right," he told her. "And part of that, part of what I want, is to be with you."

"But you are with me."

"Not the way I want to be." He turned to meet her eyes, and as he did, his hands reached for her face. It felt precious and fragile, as though he were holding something he was not meant to touch. "May I kiss you?" he heard himself ask.

She said nothing, but her answer transported him. Her lips had been wanting to meet his for so long, they almost devoured him. She drank him into her at first, then she slowed herself so that she might savor the sensation of tasting him for the first time. He could do nothing but yield while his feelings gushed so powerfully from his insides, they seemed to be draining the life from him.

They both weakened, and their bodies reclined on the sand. Their lips separated but as their eyes opened, they found them trapped in the other's. The external world had vanished from their sight, and they were adrift on a miraculous cloud that was formed only of their senses. It consisted of nothing more than the scent of them as the heat of their bodies gave rise to it, the taste of them as their lips perceived the sweetness, and the wondrous sensation that their fingers conveyed as they tenderly explored. And too, there was the torrent of blood that left them lightheaded as it rushed to pulsate distant parts of their bodies, places that wanted connection.

With their eyes still locked, Annie brought his hand to her breast. He touched the hardened nipple, then reeled from the intensity of the pleasure.

"I've wanted to be with you for so long," she whispered.

He closed his eyes. It was happening as he'd feared; his feelings for her were moving into forbidden territory, going beyond his control. God help me, he prayed. Opening his eyes on her, he confessed, "Every night, I dream of you. Sitting in my lectures, I can think of nothing but you. When I return to the Whaum, I hold my breath until I see you. I think I may die if you're not there."

She fell into a rapture from his words; never before had she been spoken to so lovingly, so reverently. She meant to answer him with words of her own, but her lips wanted fusion with his again. This time it was his mouth that devoured hers. His tongue sought a place there and dove after it again and again. He had never kissed like that before.

Her mouth relaxed and received him, even as her legs spread and the pulsations in her vagina deepened. His body pressed, and his hand explored the surface of one thigh, then the inside of it. She moaned so deeply that it vibrated the muscles in his throat. Then she reached for his hand and brought it to the spot where it had stopped short.

"I want you," she murmured. "You don't have to stop."

He was another person. He had left the earth and headed for the stars, and he was floating into ecstasy. He rubbed at the place where he would join with her, become a part of her, and he lingered in the joyous anticipation.

"Just be careful, Andrew," she uttered in the softest of tones. "I could get pregnant."

That voice, that reproachful, righteous voice of conscience, responded to her warning, and it spoke with such authority that it sent him crashing back to earth. *Whatever are you doing?* it demanded of him. *You know this is wrong.* He moved slightly away so that he might sit up as the sensual cloud that had surrounded them dissipated in the salt air. Never before had the reality of his responsibilities hit him so hard.

She rubbed his arm, realizing she should explain. "It's OK, you know, it'll be all right if you pull out before."

He lifted his face to the sky. *God, God,* he pleaded, *why are you doing this to me? Why have you let me love her so when you know that I can't?*

She saw him wavering and fearful, so she suggested, "We could go to the drugstore first if you want."

He couldn't respond; his mind was choked in confusion. *This beautiful young woman that I've loved since the day I saw her, she's offering herself to me—she wants me to make love to her. And God, more than anything I've ever wanted in my life, I want her. I want to be naked with her, I want to be inside of her, and so help me God, I don't care if I make her pregnant. Why have you brought her to me? To make me suffer? Is this the punishment for what*

I did—for that one horrible, unforgivable mistake that I can never undo?

Seeing the distress in his face, she asked him, "Have I done something wrong, Andrew?"

He struggled through the tangle of his thoughts to answer, "Oh no, Annie, God no. You've done nothing wrong, nothing at all."

"Then tell me, please tell me what's bothering you. I don't understand."

He turned to look at her. Reclined on the sand, her hair floating about her head, she seemed to be adrift on a cloudy sea. Her face, soft and dreamy, was like a child's, just awakened, with eyes that conveyed absolute trust and made him long to journey behind them, to take that last step and fall hopelessly, irrevocably in love. "Your eyes," he whispered, "they're like shattered emeralds sealed in amber."

Her lips moved into a slight smile as she responded, "The way you see me, I want to be seen that way forever." She brought one of his hands to her mouth and kissed the tips of his fingers. "I think you're afraid of something. I want you to know that whatever it is, it won't matter, because my feelings for you, they've gone beyond that."

Although he was a novice in the ways of love, these past few weeks with Annie had taught him something fundamental about it; he had come to understand that without complete openness, without honesty and commitment, there could be nothing. He wanted to have everything with her, be everything to her, so in the next instant he decided to tell her, but before he could open his mouth, the voice of his conscience spoke again. She will never understand, it insisted. The truth will only bring her pain, and, it added, it is right to protect those we love from pain.

Once again, his face filled with anguish. "I need time," he said to her. "I need to slow down. This is going a bit too fast for me."

It did not seem that way to Annie; she had already waited too long. "OK," she answered through her own confusion.

"Let's just take our time with this. There's no rush, is there?" He brought one of her hands to his lips and kissed it repeatedly.

She wanted to answer—oh, but there is, time is running out for us, Andrew—but she said, "No, there's none." She worried now that she had lain herself too bare, put too much of herself on the line for someone who was not responding as she'd hoped. She turned her head away from him and, with difficulty, swallowed the tears that were forming in her throat.

Their walk back to David Russell was quiet and solemn, and the emotion that emanated from the pair surrounded them like an aura. Andrew's mind stayed focused on one thing: on what he needed to do so that he could be free to love her as he wanted. Annie's heart was filled with that aching pain that comes of having been close to something so beautifully rare and wonderful—something that would bring its own sort of precious freedom—and then not be allowed to touch it.

* * *

Annie checked her mailbox every day and regularly received letters from home, but she was surprised one morning to finally receive a postcard from Issie, to whom she had written some weeks ago.

Saintes-Maries de la Mer, France
Dear Annie,

If I hadn't recognized the handwriting or been perceptive enough to know that there could be no other Annie who would tour Europe *on a motorcycle,* I'd still be wondering—what person do I know in Scotland? Come down here fast, it shouldn't take more than three or so days if you hitch, or are you going to the big rock festival with the Stones in England? Katie and Flynn are here from UT—did you ever meet them? We went to Morocco and just got back. It was hard to leave, hash only costs 40 cents a gram—and that's the good stuff!

Love,
Issie

That same day, Colin Wemyss met Annie at David Russell after breakfast. When she saw the motorbike that was soon to be hers, it gave her an eerie chill.

"Would you like to drive?" he asked. "It'd be good practice."

Her fear welled up again. "No, you drive us there."

She wrapped her arms tightly around Colin's waist as they roared off on the road to Dundee.

Jack Gow's motorcycle shop was usually filled with men on a Saturday morning, and this day was no exception. Annie drew gap-mouthed stares when she entered the store, and it was not because of her beauty. She brought the bustling activity to a virtual halt when Colin asked for help outfitting her for her motorcycle.

"Beggin' your pardon?"

"She's buying my Norton from me, and we're here to get her outfitted."

"I see," he answered with widened eyes. "Well, Miss, I suppose you'll be needing everything then?"

"Whatever that means," she shrugged. "I've never owned a motorcycle before. I suppose there are some necessities."

"We should start with a jacket," Colin suggested.

The occupants of the shop watched her every move. She tried on several options before deciding on a black, Belstaff oilskin, which zippered and buttoned up tightly to keep out the wind and rain. Colin then helped her find an appropriate helmet and visor, gloves, and waterproof overpants. He suggested other things, too, like a high bar mirror, and he recommended buying an extra chain to carry with her.

"The chain is the part most likely to break," he explained, "and you'll probably be in some remote French village when it happens. Speaking of that, we should set you up with a few tools."

"But I don't know anything about fixing a motorcycle," she protested.

"You'll be amazed at what you can figure out on your own," he assured her. "And if you have a few proper tools, you can manage nicely."

That worried her. "Is this bike prone to breaking down?"

"They all are," he answered, and it made the men around them laugh.

"Shit," she said, almost to herself, "that's something I hadn't thought about."

Someone nearby chuckled at her response, and Colin added, "You know, a lot of continentals own motorcycles. They call them motos. If you've broken down, you should never be far from someone who knows about patching things up."

Their next stop was the Scottish Union and National Insurance Company, from which Annie purchased the required insurance and joined the Automobile Association. After their discussion about breakdowns, Colin decided that would be a wise move, because for only a little extra over the usual dues, the AA would come to her rescue abroad. She breathed a little easier after that, and now, with their errands complete, they headed back to St. Andrews.

She hung the rough-looking motorcycle jacket next to the pretty, long gown she'd brought with her and shook her head as she recalled the day she'd purchased it. Her mother had tried to talk her out of it, saying that it was impractical for the kind of trip she was planning and that she'd likely get no use from it. But Annie could not be dissuaded and now it hung unworn, collecting dust, as proof that she had been right.

* * *

The University of St. Andrews was established in 1410. It was not known how long the May Morning tradition had been followed, but it was thought to be nearly as old as the institution itself. The custom included festivities the night before, generally involving the consumption of large quantities of Scotch. These antics continued until just before dawn when the students would gather in the quadrangle. Dressed in their academic robes, black divinity gowns mixing in with the scarlet, they would form a silent, candlelit procession to the castle on the North Sea. Standing solemnly in the ruins, they would greet the arrival of the first May sun, the symbol of life, youth, and rebirth.

With the Whaum only a block away from the castle, Robin and Andrew decided to invite a few people over on that evening. They served beer to their guests and welcomed them to warm themselves by the fire before going to the beach. It was the first time Annie had seen Adam since that night in the pub, and she made a concerted effort at cordiality.

"It's good to see you. I've missed you," she told him.

He did not return her smile. "I've been busy. I'm a student, you know."

"And that's one of the reasons I've left you alone," she added, "so you could get your work done."

"And what's the other reason?"

"You know what that is," she answered. She could see where this was going and was sorry now for having approached him.

He answered with a smirk. "I'd like to know what you think it is."

She exhaled before saying, "It's Patrick, of course."

"Yes, Patrick," he responded, folding his arms in front of him. "Patrick who would have been here tonight with his friends were it not for you coming between them."

She was in too good of a mood to let him upset her, so she retorted, "From what I can tell, Patrick and Andrew were never friends. Anyway, Robin invited him. He could have come if he'd wanted."

His voice raised slightly. "To watch you cavorting with Andrew?"

"Look," she said, her voice deliberately low, "it was a mistake getting involved with Patrick, but it's not the end of the world." She might have passed along what Susannah had said, how others had also found him too controlling, but she wanted to be kind. "He's a very good-looking, intelligent guy," she said instead "He'll easily find someone else."

"He wanted to be with you," he insisted. He'd had to catch himself because he'd almost said "I wanted to be with you."

She wrinkled her brow in puzzlement. "So what? What about what I want? What is it you think, Adam, that a woman's supposed to let herself be taken over by a guy just because he wants her, even when she realizes he's not right for her, even when he's absolutely wrong for her? Is that what you think?" She waited for a response. When none came, she added, "It's OK. I know the answer to that, even if you don't." With a curt smile and a see-ya-later, she went into the kitchen to find Andrew.

As he watched her walk away, the words he'd spoken played back in his head, and he felt mocked by his own stupidity.

A bright, new moon shone in the sky, the kind that made the water sparkle and look as though it were dressed in a giant, sequined cape. A sea breeze blew briskly enough to keep everyone awake, and an enormous bonfire crackled and spewed pieces of itself into the air. Andrew and Annie sat on the sand with their backs against the high cliffs, their sides touching, looking into the fire. She was glad for the warmth of the gown she wore; its heavy wool and great length had surely comforted many a student from the North Sea winds for many a century, just as it did tonight.

Hours into the evening, Andrew was considerably more drunk than she. "I had a chat with Adam earlier," he said to her. "I told him how very grateful I am that he invited you here."

She smiled at him. "For that, I can never repay him, and I'd like to tell him so. I hope he'll get over being pissed-off so I can do that before I leave."

The reference to her departure sobered him like a cold gust of wind, but he braced himself against it. "When will you go?" he asked.

"Actually, I got a letter from Issie yesterday regarding that very thing," she informed him with some hesitation.

"You know Issie, my friend who's been studying in France this semester."

He drank more whisky and nodded.

"The apartment they've been renting, they have to leave there at the end of the month. So she said if I want to catch up with her, I've got to get there before the thirty-first." The fire's heat was blowing away from them, and it made her shiver.

Knowing how quickly that time would come, Andrew wrapped an arm around her waist and pulled her close. With his lips nearly touching her ear, he whispered, "I need to tell you something. That day on the beach, I didn't want to stop. I had to. I knew that if I didn't, there'd be no going back, and I'm not free to make that kind of commitment."

She turned her face to his. "I don't need a commitment," she told him, her breaths coming a little quicker, "I'm happy to be with you without one. I'm not a virgin, Andrew."

Although he'd been raised in an environment where people never spoke this frankly, especially about sex, his immediate reaction was—my God, how I love her openness. "I know, I sensed that," he told her. "But what does that matter? What matters is how I feel about you." He had to stop himself. He wanted her to understand, but he couldn't go too far. Still, he needed her to know. "I don't think I could be with you without that. I think it would break my heart."

His words filled her with so much emotion that she had to bow her head. "What I wouldn't give to be able to go back," she whispered.

He felt the pain and regret that accompanied her words, and he stroked her cheek to soothe her. "No," he told her, "I wouldn't change you. The way you are, that's what draws me to you. Don't you realize that?" Then he grinned a little as he added, "I am, you know, a virgin. One of us should know what to do, don't you think?"

She'd had her suspicions and hearing him admit that now, she understood that he was bestowing her with the most intimate and precious of gifts. "There's so much I would change if I could," she told him, "and the first thing would be to have you as my first. I think if I had that, I'd be the luckiest woman in the world."

The smile that formed on her lips as she contemplated that, warmed him through. "You know, that's exactly where my thoughts have been. How much more blessed could one man be?"

She rested her head on his shoulder, and they sat looking into the fire.

Quietly, he added now, "Not to change the subject, but have you heard about the Kate Kennedy Ball?"

"I've seen the posters around."

"It's quite the affair. There's dinner followed by dancing, and it ends with breakfast in the morning."

She chuckled softly. "I thought New Orleanians were the party animals of the world, but you all put us to shame. Is it against the law in Scotland to have a party end before dawn?"

He laughed and cleared his throat. Then, somewhat nervously, he asked, "I was wondering if you would, if you'd do me the honor, but I imagine, I mean, I don't imagine you've brought the proper dress with you."

Her mind flashed to that day in the store when she'd seen the gown and been inexplicably drawn to it. The feeling came upon her suddenly that there had been a reason for it that she was only now discovering. She grinned so broadly, she could hardly answer. "You won't believe this, but hanging in my closet, right now, is the perfect thing. I did bring a long dress with me, and yes, I'd love to go to the ball with you. I'd be the honored one!"

He responded with a smile that rivaled hers. "I do believe it. Somehow, in my mind, practically since the day we met, I've seen you there dancing with me."

He reached for her hand, and when they touched the sensation that traveled between them was like sparks jumping from opposite poles.

Mel and Susannah had been otherwise occupied on the beach; he had brought his guitar and joined an impromptu jam session near a smaller fire, while she chatted with friends and tried to keep warm. When it was getting on three, she went in search of Annie and Andrew, who'd staked out a relatively warm spot near the main bonfire.

She greeted the couple with, "My lord, but I don't believe I've ever been so cold. Any chance of a snuggle?" Her nose was cherry red.

"Sit next to me," Annie offered, and she squeezed closer to Andrew to make room.

She wrapped her left arm snugly around Susannah and pulled her close. Susannah responded with a gentle kiss to Annie's lips that made her muscles go limp. Andrew drew Annie in with both arms. When she turned her face to him, he kissed her mouth, letting his lips linger. Susannah rested her head on Annie's shoulder, smiling at what was happening next to her, and Annie suddenly wanted to cry. She kissed Andrew back, holding tightly to Susannah, while in her mind she formed a prayer. She prayed to the stars, to the gods, to whatever powers might hear—please, please, slow the time. I want this night to last forever.

Half-awake and dreamy, the three snuggled into one another. Andrew took Annie's face in his hands and kissed her: on the forehead, on the eyelids, on the nose. She let his tenderness seep into her and wipe away all thoughts of the past, all worry about the future. Safe in the kind of generous affection she had never before experienced, she dozed now and again and dreamed of the approaching ball.

The crowd quieted as it drew closer to dawn. Clusters of blanket-wrapped, huddled students were scattered about the beach, looking like haystacks in a field. Mel had finally stopped playing his guitar and gone looking for Susannah. He found the trio asleep, their bodies resting on one another's like napping puppies.

He touched Susannah's shoulder to awaken her. "We should be on our way," he told them, watching as they yawned and stretched. "It's nearly dawn."

A few groups had already begun ascending the stairway on the cliffs.

The solemnness of the gathering at the quadrangle was a perfect contrast to the party on the beach. An excited hush fell as everyone assembled, as those who'd been up all night were joined by those who had recently risen from warm beds. Everyone was dressed in their robes, and many carried flickering candles as they fell in behind the pipers. Still mostly quiet, they began to move from the center of the quadrangle to emerge more orderly, four or so abreast, on The Scores. The procession crossed over the street and into the castle grounds, where they merged with more waiting students, who were gathered around a maypole.

Four pipers and a single drummer took their places on the battlements, as the sky lightened and giant streamers of color, as red as the field of attending gowns, blew across the darkling sea. Annie stood between Susannah and Andrew, their arms linked and hands clenched together. Robin was nearby. Melville set aside his guitar case to take up Susannah's other hand. Annie realized that she was surrounded by all the people she had come to know since her arrival. Adam was a few feet away and he called to her, managing a smile. Even Patrick had said good morning when he'd seen her in the quadrangle. Now they all stood together expectantly, looking toward the ruined battlement where kilt-clad pipers stood against an awakening sky.

Quiet blanketed the grounds as the dawn grew imminent. Slowly, a single piper opened the air with the awkward, off-key yawning and screeching necessary to fill his bag. The other pipers remained still, and as the crown of the first May sun burned through the wall of the horizon, he began to play.

The voice of the pipe cried out to all in attendance. It reverberated through their bones and sank into their flesh, leaving messages there, each unique in all who listened. There could not have been a soul untouched. To some it spoke of the new, to others the old; in some it tasted sweet and in others quite bitter. For some it told of hope, for others it cried of loss, and for Annie, who felt at that instant as though she were awakening from a dream, it spoke of the moment, the moment that was here and passing and could never come again. She squeezed tight the hands she held and blinked back the burning in her eyes, knowing that from this time forward, she would never again hear a bagpipe without seeing this place, without feeling this wind, without knowing the pain of loss. She turned to look at Andrew. He had been watching her face as she was overcome with tears.

The lament of the solo piper ended once the entire orb had been revealed—now absolute, brilliant, and daunting. The glittering, fantasy night sky was no more. The piper's fading refrains were taken up by his fellows. They quickened the pace with the drummer, whose beat brought out the dancers. Cheers went up among the students, glasses were raised, and mugs and bottles were passed. Several different lines of reels formed along the grounds and a group of girls took up the ribbons of the maypole. Toasts were made to all and sundry, and more of the sacred Scotch was consumed. Andrew handed Annie his bottle. She took a long drink, winced, and then passed it on to Susannah.

Andrew made a low, sweeping bow before her. "May I have the pleasure, lassie?" His tongue rolled the words in an exaggerated accent.

She answered, "Why certainly, kind sir," in a molasses drawl.

"What a marvelous couple they make!" Susannah shouted to Mel before they, too, joined in the dancing.

The musicians played "The Dashing White Sergeant." Annie's head was light and she felt a little dizzy, but that didn't stop her. She swirled and skipped among the ancient ruins, with 200 or so other young people, clapping and laughing while the little band of pipers serenaded the rising sun.

At the end of the second dance, loud cheers went up; on the battlement, about two dozen young men were undressing and revealing bare bums to the crowd. Annie turned to ask Andrew what they were doing but he had gone. She next saw him on the battlement, rapidly undressing. More young men were running forward and joining the group, and Annie went to Susannah.

"What on earth are they doing?" she asked her friend.

"They're going into the sea. It's part of the tradition. My God, but Andrew's endowed!" she exclaimed with delight, jabbing an elbow into her side. "You lucky wench!"

The girls bent with laughter but kept their eyes on the feast of nakedness.

"Aren't you going in, Mel?" Annie asked through her giggles.

"Not on your life. I learned my lesson last year; that water's bloody cold!"

Two dozen or more young men climbed down the rocks while the crowd, now crammed along the battlement, shouted their encouragement. The would-be swimmers rushed because there was honor in being first. Then they were in, screaming with the shock of the cold, uttering curses, splashing one another. The crowd cheered and laughed. In about a minute, a young Englishman named Harry disgraced himself by not swimming the length of the castle rock pool and being the first one out. When the others quit the water, they clambered up the rocks, screaming from the cold. Annie laughed so hard her eyes teared.

They dressed without drying off and were rewarded by the crowd with applause and Scotch, every available bottle passed to the swimmers. Annie averted her eyes from Andrew's splendid body, not wishing to make him self-conscious, while Susannah stared shamelessly.

"I can't believe you went in that water!" she called to him when he came near.

He was now dressed and gulping Scotch. "That was brilliant! Marvelous feeling that, nothing like it!"

She watched a shiver come over him. "I should take you back to the Whaum and build a fire for you before you come down with pneumonia or something."

"Nonsense!" he protested. "A splash in the sea now and again is good for you!"

The pipers struck up another reel, but the crowd was thinning and it was generally quieting down. If thoughts could have been heard aloud at that moment, the castle grounds would have resounded with the din of ruminations over warm beds.

Mel gave Andrew a congratulatory slap on the back. "Well done, old man. Well done." He then turned to Annie. "We're headed home. You coming, my dear?"

She looked to Andrew. With all her heart, she wanted him to invite her back to the Whaum. She imagined going into the bathroom and scrubbing his back while he soaked, maybe even joining him in the tub. Then they would climb into bed and snuggle into one another, falling asleep in each other's arms. They wouldn't have to make love, she told herself, if he still wasn't ready. She prayed for this as she looked to him, but he only smiled and brushed the long, damp locks from his forehead, waiting for her to answer Mel.

Her voice was subdued. "Yes, I suppose I should," she reluctantly said, then kissed Andrew on the cheek. His skin tasted like the sea. "And you'd better get into a hot bath."

"That's a good idea," he responded. "I think I'll do just that. Shall I see you later, then?"

"Sure," she answered, disappointment filling her heart.

The night that she had wanted to last forever had come to a jarring end, like hard, screeching brakes applied at the end of a roller-coaster ride.

Chapter 16

It would be more than an hour's wait before breakfast would be served at David Russell Hall. Annie decided to have a soak herself, but the bathroom in her hall was already occupied so she went to Susannah's room instead. She found her bedroom empty and heard water running in the nearby W.C., so she knocked there.

"Yes?"

"It's Annie. I wanted to talk, but I'll just wait in your room."

"No need. Come in, darling, it's not locked." The steam-filled room smelled of lavender. Susannah lay in the milky water, her head back, her eyes closed, her arms draped over the sides. "My God, this feels good," she declared, making no effort to conceal her body.

"That's exactly what I wanted to do," Annie told her, "but someone beat me to it." She sat on a small stool next to the tub and looked away at first. But curiosity got the better of her, and since Susannah's eyes were closed anyway, she allowed herself a surreptitious glance.

Her friend's body was remarkably like her own. Susannah's breasts were large and very round like hers, but her nipples were much darker and more pronounced. Her underarms were unshaven though, and the tufts of dark brown hair drifted in the water like sea grass rolling on the tide.

She opened her eyes, then held out her washcloth and asked, "Would you be a dear and lather my back?" As she rose from the bathwater, it cascaded over buttocks that were perfect pears, full and firm.

Annie became suddenly anxious and grabbed at the soap with shaky hands. Averting her eyes, she said, "I wanted to talk to you about Andrew." She worked the soap into a lather, then timidly applied the cloth to her friend's back.

Susannah moaned slightly, then asked, "Do it harder, would you? It feels so good."

She had to place her left hand on Susannah's hip to steady her while she scrubbed. She meant to keep to the upper portion of her back, but something compelled her to slide the cloth downward to the bottom of her cheeks, then to the back of her thighs. She realized suddenly that what was driving her was akin to arousal, not unlike what she experienced when she touched Andrew.

"Oooh, that's so nice," she cooed, encouraging Annie to do more. Then she whirled around suddenly. "Mind?"

It took an instant to register, but when Annie realized what she wanted, her mouth fell open.

Susannah smiled a knowing smile. "It's all right. We did this at school. It's harmless enough."

Little beads of perspiration rolled down Annie's bosom as she passed the soapy cloth over the hardened nipples in front of her. Susannah sighed again and closed her eyes. The cloth barely made contact with her skin, and when Annie passed it along her abdomen, Susannah reached and took it in hand herself. "Ta," she said, as she washed between her legs. When she finished, she reimmersed herself in the bath and looked up at her friend. Then, in an abrupt turn, every bit as abrupt as this sudden physical intimacy, she questioned, "Are you in love with Andrew?"

The directness of that shocked Annie out of her self-consciousness. "I think so," she answered, "but I'm not sure I know what it means to be in love."

Susannah had drained the tub and was refilling it now with clean water. "Why is that?" she wondered. "Surely you're not still a virgin."

"Hardly," Annie scoffed.

"How, then, could you not know about love?"

She bit at her lower lip and studied the patterns in the linoleum. "I'm ashamed to say," she told her, then lifted her eyes to watch as Susannah rinsed her hair. Her hands wove through the strands and swished them in the water. "I'm very fond of him, I know that," Annie added. "I feel things for him I've never felt for anyone else."

Susannah blithely observed, "Sounds like the beginnings of love at least."

Annie sighed and looked troubled.

"Then what's got you so distressed?"

"It's what I wanted to talk to you about." She paused and pondered how to say this. "I really want to be with him, but he told me something last night that's made me wonder if I should."

"What's that?"

"It's very personal. I shouldn't say."

She responded quickly, "Don't then."

"What I can tell you," she decided, "is that when I first thought about what he said, it made me want him more. But I've been thinking about it this morning, and now I worry that becoming more intimate would be wrong."

"Why wrong?"

"Because I have to leave."

"We're all leaving." She finished rinsing herself and removed the rubber plug. The gurgling sound of the water as it spiraled through the drain seemed inordinately loud in the small room.

"But when I leave, it'll be for good," she explained. "You all will be back in the fall."

She understood now. "And you're afraid he'll be hurt when you leave."

She nodded. "He's very sensitive, Susannah. When I'm with him, it's hard to explain, but it's like he's trying to protect himself from something, and I'm beginning to think that it's me he feels he needs protection from. But it's so confusing, because he pushes me away one minute, and the next he does something like this morning when he invited me to the Kate Kennedy Ball."

"He did? Oh that's splendid!" she exclaimed. "We can all go together! Oh, we're going to have a lovely, lovely time!" When she stood, she pointed to her towel and asked, "Be a dear, would you?"

Annie retrieved the towel, then tenderly patted her friend's back.

While she did this, Susannah sought to reassure her. "If you want my advice about Andrew, I'd tell you to stop worrying about him. It's obvious to everyone that he's fond of you. Just look how he was with you last night! And it's also quite evident that he's not the kind of man who'd get involved casually." She took the towel from Annie to finish the job herself. "I told you, in the three years I've known him, I've not seen him date anyone at all, only dance with various girls at the gatherings." Dry now, she reached for her lavender bath powder and began dusting herself with it.

Annie coughed slightly as the air in the bathroom thickened with scent and powder. "But that's exactly what worries me. If we do become involved, I know it won't be casual, and that scares me." They were facing each other now, and Annie looked into Susannah's eyes to confide. "I mean, I've never been in a real relationship before, and the men I knew, they didn't care about my feelings. All they cared about was getting me into bed."

Susannah frowned as she commented, "How coarse." She donned her robe and led the way to her room.

Annie followed and waited until they were inside before she said, "To a lot of people I know, having sex doesn't mean that much. They don't need to be emotionally involved, and they don't need promises or anything. It makes things easier that way, less complicated." When she finished saying this, she realized how absurd it sounded.

Susannah's facial expression was a mixture of disgust and disbelief. "Less complicated? Easier? That sounds positively dreadful to me." Standing in front of the mirror, she fluffed her hair with a fresh towel.

Annie sat on the bed, then leaned her back against the wall. "It is dreadful, you're right. I know that firsthand because I used to think like that, or I tried to anyway. I tried to keep my feelings out of it."

"Keep feelings out of sex? How on earth do you do that?" Susannah removed her robe and rummaged through her clothes drawers, totally at ease with her nakedness.

Annie's voice became heavier. "When I'm with Andrew, when he tells me how he feels about me, it makes me realize just how awful that kind of sex is, how it feels like something gets ripped out of you every time."

"Sex shouldn't make you feel like you've lost something, my darling," she told her. "You should feel fuller from it, not less because of it." She finally found the clothing she was looking for and began dressing. "I think you Americans take sex too casually. In my opinion, you're better off taking care of yourself, if you know what I mean, than jumping into the sack with someone you don't love."

Annie's face turned quizzical. "I don't understand."

"Masturbation, my dear," she said, as though it should be perfectly obvious. "It's a great way to keep yourself out of trouble."

"Oh," she responded, and made an odd face.

Susannah thought she discerned the reason for her peculiar look. "Don't you masturbate?"

"Not really, not on purpose, anyway," she admitted.

She gasped. "I'm astonished!"

Awkwardly, Annie confessed to her friend, "I've had dreams, sometimes, where I wake up and I think I'm climaxing, but I'm not sure."

"Well, upon my word, I would never have believed it!"

"Do you—masturbate, I mean?"

"Of course!"

"But you have Mel."

"I didn't always, and sometimes he's not available." She smiled that wicked smile of hers. "And anyway, I learned it a long time ago at public school when I was about thirteen. It was a tradition, if you will." She chuckled to herself. "The older girls taught the younger ones."

It was usually Susannah who was shocked by the things Annie said, but now the tables were turned. "What?"

"You heard me. The older girls taught the younger ones how to do it."

"You mean, to make yourself come?"

"Yes, my dear." It was as though she were explaining something ridiculously basic, like how to use a fork. "They did it in front of you or they did it to you, and that's how you learned."

Annie couldn't help but form the mental picture of a young Susannah, naked, being instructed in masturbation by an older girl, and it reignited the titillation she'd experienced while touching her. "I feel like a complete idiot," she prefaced, "but what did they teach you?"

Sighing, she said, "You poor dear, here you are, twenty years old and you have to ask." She sat on the bed next to Annie and put a hand on her shoulder. In a tone that sounded professional, like a doctor dealing with a patient, she inquired, "Do you know where your clitoris is?"

Her cheeks flushed, and she stammered to answer, "Well, no, not really." Susannah shook her head, then stood in front of Annie, unzipping the pants she had just put on, pulling them and her underwear midway down her thighs. Annie suddenly found herself face to face and only inches away from Susannah's dark pubic hair and the thick folds of skin that hung beneath. She began to feel slightly faint as the warm scent of her friend mingled with lavender oil reached her nostrils.

Then, as though she were an instructor giving a demonstration to a classroom, Susannah spread her vulva between two fingers and pointed to the little protrusion of flesh. When she did, Annie felt a tingling in the correspondent place that drew her to clamp her knees together.

"Right here, that's what you play with," she explained. "You rub it up and down or side to side to make it hard. And it makes it better if you put something in yourself while you're at it," she added.

Annie swallowed before she could ask, "Like what?"

"Like a hairbrush handle," she proposed. "That does a fine job of it. But you should wet it first or lubricate it with something like petroleum jelly before you put it in. Otherwise it hurts. Then you move the hairbrush in and out with one hand and rub the little clitoris with the other, and you think of something naughty, like dancing naked in front of men you don't know. Then you'll see what happens." She left her pants undone and let one hand rest on Annie's shoulder.

Annie was decidedly aroused and her voice was barely audible when she asked, "You come?"

"Unless there's something wrong with you," she answered.

As her breathing deepened, the lavender scent infused Annie's senses. "And girls at school taught you this?"

"That's right," she grinned, fastening her pants again. "There was one in particular. She was a couple of years older than I, a pretty blond with small, pointed breasts. She was very good at it. She would do it in front of us and make herself climax repeatedly. You would see the hairbrush move back and forth on its own when she did." She laughed to herself as she recalled the sight. "It was amazing to watch."

To say that Annie was shocked by these revelations would have been a gross understatement. "My girlfriends and I would never even be naked in front of each other," she told her, "let alone do something like that."

Susannah grinned again and folded her arms. "There were girls who would sneak into bed together after lights out and do it, just for fun."

Annie's eyes widened. "Did you do that?"

"Once with the blond girl. Elizabeth was her name, but everyone called her Bitsy. I'll never forget. It was her last year and there was just a month or so left in the term. She brought her hairbrush with her one night and climbed in next to me. She played with my breasts and did other things to me. I was very sore in the morning, but I didn't ask her to stop because it felt sinfully good. I wonder what ever became of her? I believe she was accepted at Oxford."

Annie's heart skipped a beat or two. "Like what? Like what other things?"

"She licked me."

Annie gasped. "No! Really? Holy shit, Susannah!"

"Really, Annie, your language can be appalling," she teased. "Anyway, it's not a big deal as you Americans say. We seldom saw boys, and when we did we were always chaperoned. We needed to find out about ourselves somehow. Besides, I'd say it was a far sight better doing that than getting it from some ugly brute who didn't give a fig for me."

Putting aside her astonishment, Annie admitted, "I'd have to agree with you there. The only way I've ever had it was with someone who didn't give a fuck about me."

"Well, actually they did, didn't they? Give a fuck, I mean." The droll way Susannah delivered that remark made them both laugh. "You poor thing," she told her now. "The girls were good to each other at least, and no one ever told. It was this wonderful, naughty secret that everyone shared."

Annie looked past Susannah now and out the window, thinking about the extraordinary relationship that had developed between them. One minute she loved and admired Susannah as a friend, and the next minute she found herself drawn to her in a distinctly physical, sexual way. By all rights, she should have been ashamed and guilty about that, but she wasn't, and that was part of Susannah's magic that Annie was only now beginning to comprehend. This very pretty and proper Englishwoman with the exceptionally bright mind was so natural and generous with her own feelings, they spilled over into Annie's, and helped her accept her own.

Susannah had remained standing in front of her, watching as she bandied things about in her mind. She seemed to be considering something herself, but then she abruptly said, "I'm horribly peckish, aren't you? Let's get some breakfast." Annie nodded and stood, and Susannah took her arm. They had started toward the dining hall when she giggled. "We came a bit off the track, didn't we?"

Annie smiled and touched her arm with her free hand.

More seriously now, Susannah said, "But back to Andrew. First off, you must remember that he's British, and we Brits, the men in particular, are uncomfortable with emotion. So if you want my advice on how to handle him, I'd tell you to step back a bit and just let things happen. Things will happen as they're meant to, though I've not the foggiest idea how we can ever know that. I believe it though, don't you?"

"I suppose." Annie's thoughts returned to the sunrise, to the mournful piper on the ruined castle wall, a time that already belonged to the past. It reminded her that her days in St. Andrews were passing quickly and in a few short weeks she'd be leaving. Soon all of it, all the places and people she had grown to love so much, would belong to the past. If that's so, she told herself, if things happen as they're meant to, then I guess I was never meant to stay here.

She sighed deeply as she realized this, and Susannah responded to her perceived melancholy by squeezing and patting her arm.

* * *

A note on Annie's door said that someone from the Royal Bank of Scotland had called concerning her overseas draft. She knew that meant her money had come through.

Dressed in a skirt and sweater, she walked into town. The bank teller was cordial and professional, and after he counted it three times, he wrapped her cash in a special pouch. He held the door when she exited the building, and as she stepped onto Market Street, she was overcome with the urge to turn around and hand it all back to him. Though it was only the equivalent of $300 that she carried, it felt like an enormous burden, a critical decision that she had just made that she instantly wanted to recant. Standing amid the bustle of the midday shopping, she was overcome with anxiety and could think of nothing else to do but head for the cathedral.

She sat on the leeward side of what had been a cloister wall. The May sun was strong, and she was warm in her sweater. Grasping the pouch with two hands, she began wishing that she could go back in time to the day she arrived in St. Andrews. She wanted to recapture the wonder, the thrill she felt seeing everything for the first time, but try as she might, she couldn't. For now, sitting among the mystical ruins, Annie was visited by a creeping dread, the certain knowledge that the time of her departure was fast approaching, that soon she would be the owner of a motorcycle and fully committed to going on with her journey. She was weighed down by these thoughts and felt unable to move when a large gull came in for a landing about three feet away. It perched on a fallen stone and fixed its glassy eyes upon her.

Something about the bird's stare made her uncomfortable, and she told it, "Go away. You're freaking me out."

As though it understood, it slowly began to flap its wings, then it lifted off from the stone, releasing a long, piercing call. Annie watched it settle again in the graveyard, not far from St. Rule's Tower and about 100 yards from where she sat. Without thinking, she got up and made her way to its new location. When she came upon it, it was nestled on the ground on a grave against the wall. The enormous bird allowed her to come very close, close enough to read the names engraved upon the marker.

She was saddened to see that they were children who had died very young, siblings who'd been buried in the same grave. All had second as well as their given names save one, the last one, the youngest one. The last entry on the marker read simply, poignantly: Annie, died 22 October, 1861, age 6 months.

"You poor little thing," she said aloud. "You had no time at all, did you?" Like me, she thought, brought to this beautiful place full of hope and promise, then taken away before you're ready.

With the sound of her voice, the giant bird stirred again, and with great loping wings, it lifted and flew in the direction of the sea, calling and crying, bellowing its complaint over the open water until she could hear it no more. She inhaled deeply as she watched its departure, contemplating its unencumbered existence.

How I envy your thoughtlessness, you silly bird, flying wherever you want, taking whatever you want, never doubting yourself or worrying if you've made the right decision. But I wonder now if freedom is what it truly is, when you belong to nothing, when there is no one to miss or remember you when you're gone, to feel the pain of your absence.

Looking to the grave marker once again, she imagined the small bodies that lay buried there for more than 100 years and how it must have broken the hearts of those who loved them to see them taken away so young.

She realized something then, and with the money pouch tucked under one arm, she left the graveyard through the seaside gate, making for the path along the cliffs, headed for the Whaum.

Robin answered the door. "Hullo. Glad you've popped in. We were hoping you would."

They went into the parlor where he had textbooks and papers scattered everywhere.

"I've interrupted your studying. I'm sorry," she apologized.

"Nothing to it, I was just about to cash it in, anyway," he assured her. "Did you enjoy the May Morning thing?"

"Oh yes, very much," she smiled.

He smiled, too, though not broadly. "You and Andrew seem to be getting on well these days."

She blushed a little. "We've become very good friends."

"He's not here just now," he offered. "Popped up to the Russell to give his mum a jingle and then he was to do some errands." A telephone was a luxury they could not afford at the cottage.

"Oh," she responded.

"We were going to get hold of you, though. Would you be up for some golf this afternoon, do you think? Andrew's booked a foursome on the Jubilee Course at two. Adam's already agreed, and you'll make the fourth."

That surprised her. "Adam? Maybe I'd better not then."

"Nonsense. It was Andrew's idea. He doesn't like seeing the two of you fallen out, and he thought it would be a nice way for you to patch things up."

"Did Adam know you were going to ask me?" she wondered.

He nodded.

"And he agreed to play, anyway?"

"Andrew can be very persuasive." His smile was curious, perhaps a little ironic. "He'll be well suited to politics, don't you think?"

Her brow wrinkled. "I didn't know he was interested in politics. He never said."

With a hint of sarcasm, he remarked, "I expect there's quite a bit he hasn't told you."

It seemed like an odd comment and she waited for him to explain, but he busied himself by getting his papers in order. She pondered the image of the gentle, vulnerable Andrew as politician. Had he ever even alluded to it? She stared at Robin for a moment, then looked at her bare legs. "If I'm going to play golf, I'd better go change into something appropriate," she realized.

"Good thinking. We can count on you, then?"

"Should I meet you there or here?" she questioned.

"Outside the Royal and Ancient, a few minutes before two if that suits you."

* * *

When he made the call to his home, he held his breath as he asked Ambrose if his father was there. His relief at hearing that he wasn't was profound, and he waited with some excitement to speak to his mother instead.

"Why Andrew, what a lovely surprise! How are you, my darling?"

"I'm well, Mother, thank you. And you?"

"Very well, thank you." She understood that he was not calling for a chat. University students rarely did that. "To what do I owe the pleasure?"

Plunging ahead, he told her. "I have two American friends that I'd like to treat to a round of golf, and I was wondering if you might ring the Royal and Ancient for me to see if we can play today."

"Of course, my dear, but why not do it yourself?"

"I'd rather not, Mother, if you don't mind. I like to keep a low profile here, as you know."

"Yes, I remember." She used the universal motherly tone, the one that conveyed disapproval.

"And when you speak with them, will you ask them not to refer to me as anything but Andrew or Mr. Gordon, please? Because I really don't want to get into it with anybody."

"Then I have to wonder why you'd go there," she interjected, "for it's quite likely that someone will know you."

"I've only my set of clubs, so I need to borrow some from the R and A," he explained, "and they can arrange a tee time without the usual fuss. All I want is a quick nine holes with my friends, and then we'll be off. I don't want to make an event out of it; I simply want them to be able to say they played golf here when they go home."

There was silence on the line for a few moments before his mother answered. "All right, my darling. I'll ring there now. Give me the number you've rung me from and I'll get right back to you. It shouldn't take more than a minute or two."

"Thank you." He took a second to gather his courage before he added, "Oh, while we're at it, one of them, one of the Americans, is a young lady. We've become good friends these weeks and I've, ah, I've asked her to the upcoming ball." He braced himself for the response, but it still took him by surprise.

"You have? Oh that's lovely, just lovely. I'm so happy you've done that."

"You are?"

"Why yes, I am. I've told your father repeatedly, it's no good you carrying on as though you've already come into your responsibilities. You should be having fun now, enjoying your young life."

"Really?" The shock he was experiencing rendered him almost speechless.

"Really, and I'm so pleased about it." She interrupted herself with an idea. "How are you to get there? Have you given it any thought?"

"No, not yet."

"Let me send my car. Let me send Angus, so you can take her there in an appropriate style."

"You'd do that?"

She laughed lightheartedly in a way he'd rarely heard. "Just give me the particulars, and I'll take care of it."

"Thank you, Mother. I don't know what to say."

"You needn't say a thing. You're only young once, and I've hated seeing you plodding your youth away as you do. You must take more advantage of this time you have, while nothing's official and before it's all lost to you. It goes so fast, my darling, too fast." Her voice trailed into melancholy.

His heart was so lightened by her words that it felt for a moment as though it were floating about in his ribcage. He knew his mother would do her best with his father to get him to accept the idea, and that was far better than having to approach him himself. It was only a first step, he needed to remind himself, so he didn't want to get too excited. Still, on the brief return walk to the Whaum, he almost skipped along the street. And later on, as he recalled her words and how pleasantly surprised he'd been by them, he returned to the Russell to ring his mother again so that he might say thank you once more.

Chapter 17

He'd made certain he was the first to arrive. He secured the loaner clubs from the R and A, then stood outside the entrance doors to keep an eye out for his friends. He spied Annie first as she made her way down the hill on the walkway that led from Melville Hall. His face moved into its usual expression upon seeing her, the one that said he'd forgotten anyone else existed in the world.

"I'm so happy you could come," he greeted her.

Her heart fluttered in its customary dance. "What a nice idea," she sighed, "and such a beautiful day!"

"When you mentioned that you could play, I knew I had to get you here. It would be a pity to leave St. Andrews without having set foot on the holy ground."

She moved closer and took his hand. "Afterwards, when we've finished, I want to talk, just the two of us. Can we do that?"

It was hard to breathe when she was this near, and at the same time, he seemed to be taking the only real breaths he ever had. "Of course," he whispered. She could have asked him to scale St. Rule's Tower from the outside and he still would have said "of course."

They were talking in soft tones, standing with their hands clasped, when they heard a voice call to Andrew. As they turned around to see who it was, an elegant looking gentleman descended the steps of the club entrance and made his way toward them. Andrew's posture stiffened when he recognized him; he released Annie's hand and assumed a look of defiance.

Dammit, anyway, he thought to himself, of all bloody people to run into. As sure as I'm standing here, he'll be reporting back to my father before the day is done. He thanked God that he'd already broached the subject of Annie with his mother.

"Andrew, my boy," the man greeted him, "how fortuitous! I've just been thinking of you and wondering how you're getting on!" As he approached the couple, he shifted his focus to Annie. "How do you do?" he politely inquired.

The man looked her directly in the eyes, and she experienced a chill from the intensity of it. "Fine," she answered, then averted her eyes to escape his.

He patted Andrew's back. "Yes, most fortunate indeed, my seeing you. Aren't you going to introduce us, old man?"

Andrew seemed annoyed, and he struggled to be cordial. "This is Lord Alfred Cowan, Annie. He's a friend of the family," he explained.

"Charmed, my dear, charmed." His eyes sparkled with excitement as he offered his hand.

When she held out hers, he bent his lips to it, but his touch brought on a disconcerting sense of déjà vu that made her take it back quickly and look to Andrew for reassurance.

Lord Cowan cast his eyes over the golf clubs that were near the couple. "Going or coming?" he asked them.

"We're waiting for friends. We're going to play nine on the Jubilee," Andrew answered him flatly, begrudgingly.

"Lovely day for it, isn't it now?" he commented, moving his eyes in a quick sweep of Annie's body. "Say, I have an idea. Why don't I have you and your friends to tea afterward at the Rusacks Hotel? Give us a chance to catch things up."

Andrew watched him scrutinize Annie. God, he despaired, now I know what he's after. "Thank you, it's kind of you to offer," he told him, "but we have other plans."

Lord Cowan pouted slightly as he looked again to Annie. "Don't let him say no, my dear. They've a nice spot near the fire, and I'm certain you'll welcome that after your round on the links." His smile was so practiced that it seemed artificial. "I'd have you to the R and A if I could," he explained, "but lovely as you are, you wouldn't be able to join us."

She understood what he meant by that, for Andrew had already explained that women were prohibited in the clubhouse.

Robin and Adam came upon them then, and when the introductions were complete, Lord Cowan insisted that the party meet him afterward. "I simply won't take no for an answer, and if you don't show, I'll be sitting there alone with all those delicious cakes and sandwiches going to waste."

That statement aroused a hunger in the others that made them say yes. Andrew sighed rather heavily and looked unhappy, as he, too, reluctantly accepted the invitation.

They had an enormously good time on the links, Andrew saw to that. He pushed Cowan from his mind and concentrated on his purpose, which was to remind Adam and Annie of what good friends they'd been. It worked, and by the time they reached the third hole, they were conversing warmly like they used to. They laughed at each other's shots and antics. Robin got down on his knees at one point and put his hands together in prayer as his putt rolled off the edge of a hole. Annie screamed with joy when she was only three over par on the ninth, and the young men cheered and applauded her. When their play was finished, Adam and Annie walked back to the clubhouse side by side, laughing about the game they'd dubbed Scotland versus America.

Scotland had beaten the pants off America.

As they made the short walk to the Rusacks Hotel, the demeanor of the group changed slightly, because Andrew, who'd been just as relaxed and happy as the other three, went quiet and sullen.

Before going inside, Annie questioned him. "What's the matter?"

"Nothing," he responded.

She grinned as she informed him, "I know you better than that."

The simple truth in her statement struck a warm cord in him. "You do, don't you?" He smiled now and decided to let her know, "I don't care for Lord Cowan."

"Why?" she asked.

"It's nothing in particular, but I've never had a good feeling about him," he confided, "and frankly, I resent his intrusion into our afternoon."

"I understand," she told him. Although Cowan had a charmingly debonair manner, there was something about him—underneath the attractive veneer, perhaps—that made her uneasy, too. She took his arm and squeezed it to say, "We won't stay long."

Chairs had been assembled for the party close to the fire. With exaggerated chivalry, Lord Cowan helped Annie to the seat nearest the hearth, then planted himself next to her. They were served an elaborate tea, which included dainty little sandwiches, beautifully decorated cakes on a tiered server, and a marvelous old sherry. After a couple of glasses of the sherry, Lord Cowan moved even closer to Annie, close enough for her to smell the wine on his breath.

"I've never met a lord before," she told him in an effort at conversation.

"Haven't you?" He shifted his gaze to Andrew and chuckled a little.

"I'm not sure I know what it means," she continued.

Andrew squinted and looked away as though he anticipated something unpleasant about to happen.

Cowan laughed now. "It means duty and obligation, dear girl, and the carrying on of tradition." Observing Andrew's anxiousness, he told him, "Andrew, my boy, I do wish you'd relax and enjoy your tea." He lifted the bottle of sherry and refilled her glass. "Tell me, Annie, are you an exchange student?"

Andrew's comments to her about duty and family obligation flashed through her mind. "No, actually I came here to visit Adam," she responded. Adam was helping himself to sandwiches and as his mouth was full, he merely looked over and smiled at her. "But this is my starting point. I'm just about to buy a Norton motorcycle and head off for the continent."

Cowan had been leaning toward her, but he pulled back and straightened up. Grasping the arms of the chair, he exclaimed, "Gracious, did I hear you correctly?"

Andrew had been sitting in silence with his cup of tea. He set it down as he answered, "You did." Then he reached for her hand as though he were defending her from something.

Cowan's brow lifted when he saw how they looked at one another, how their bodies reacted to the simple, physical connection of their hands. It was something that had become increasingly obvious to their friends of late, and it was not lost on this man, who'd known Andrew all his life. "You've got good taste, old man," he declared, "damned good taste, if you don't mind my saying so."

In spite of herself, Annie's cheeks reddened with the compliment.

Cowan's expression changed then to something that resembled a smirk. "So you won't be taking her home to meet your family, then, at the end of term?"

Andrew kept hold of her hand, and Annie could feel his palm moisten. You bloody bastard, he cursed to himself, you cruel man. Now I know why it is I've never liked you. You're deriving perverse pleasure from tormenting me, aren't you?

When he responded to Cowan, his tone was scolding. "As she's told you, Lord Alfred, she's already made plans for a holiday on the continent."

Undaunted by Andrew's disapproval, Cowan continued his query. "Where will you be going, my dear? The Mediterranean coast, perhaps?"

"Yes, as a matter of fact I am," she answered. "When I leave here I'm going directly to Saintes-Maries de la Mer to meet up with a friend. It's right on the sea, south of Arles. After that, I'm not quite sure."

With his disingenuous grin, he shifted his focus to Andrew. "You should go with her, old man. Damned if I wouldn't. A delightfully romantic spot, that, the south of France."

It was something of a shock to Annie to hear him say that. It was almost as though he'd been reading her thoughts, because that was the idea that had come to her today when she'd been sitting alone in the cathedral ruins. And it was exactly what she meant to discuss with Andrew, but later, when they were alone.

He was still holding her hand when she softly told him, "I've thought of that myself, Andrew. It's what I wanted to talk to you about, actually." She would have preferred that they were alone so no one else heard, but she had to add, "It'd be wonderful being together like that, wouldn't it?"

Her seductive words compelled him to look into her eyes, and his heart soared as he imagined the two of them traveling together in France. He wanted to be swept away by the dream, to say—yes, oh yes, it is a wonderful idea. I'd love to go with you. There's nothing I'd like better. But he couldn't, not here, not now, and especially not in front of this man. "I've already got obligations for the summer, Annie," he responded, his voice carefully toned down, "but we'll talk about this later, all right?"

There was that word again—*obligations*. She wondered why he always used that particular word.

Lord Cowan's cough was difficult to distinguish from a laugh. He cleared his throat before saying, "Well then, my dear, if our Andrew disappoints you, just leave word at the club for me. I wouldn't let you down."

Assuming that he meant that playfully, Annie smiled at him. When he returned the smile, she was overcome with a wave of nausea that was followed by a sense of dread. Once again, she looked to Andrew for reassurance, and when she fixed on the pure blue of his eyes, she felt better.

After two hours of tea and sherry, they left the hotel, Adam excusing himself first to return to his studies. Robin hurried off to the library, but Andrew and Annie walked slowly toward the Whaum.

He still seemed distressed as he told her, "I'm afraid you've missed your supper."

"That's just as well," she answered, "I couldn't possibly eat another thing tonight."

They reached the little iron gate, and his heart lightened as they entered the cottage. It always felt so good and safe here, especially when Annie's spirit filled the place.

After he got it started, Andrew stood in front of the fire in the parlor, repeatedly poking at it. She waited on the couch while he was busy, but when he didn't come to sit beside her, she rose and approached him from behind, wrapping her arms around his waist.

His odd behavior throughout the tea had troubled her. It led her to ask, "How do you know that man? I know next to nothing about your aristocracy, but aren't lords important people?"

He set the poker aside and laid his hands over hers. "Self-important, most of them," he scoffed. "Titles like his are inherited, and it's the luck of the draw to be the first-born son."

"Why do you dislike him so?" she softly questioned.

He chose his words carefully. "He does business with my family, but I don't trust him. I never have."

"What business? Sheep?"

"Wool," he thought to say.

Thinking she understood, she answered, "Oh, your family sells him the wool from your farm."

He didn't want to lie to her, so he let her statement stand with just one additional comment, "Cowan owns some woolen mills."

"Oh," she said again. "Well, I trust your judgment," she wanted him to know, "and he did give me a creepy feeling. Every time he looked in my eyes, it was freaky. It was as though I knew something about him, had a history or something with him. I can't explain it, but it was really creepy."

He turned to her and kissed her forehead, then led her to the couch. "Let's forget about him. You said you wanted to talk," he reminded her.

"My money came today," she said. "I'm ready to settle up with Colin."

He looked at the floor. "I see."

She added quickly, "And it was weird, Lord Cowan mentioning it before I could, but I came up with an idea this morning. Instead of going directly to France, I thought I might hang around Scotland a while, maybe go to the west coast, the Isle of Skye or something, and then I thought, wouldn't it be cool if you and I could go to France together?" The green in her eyes seemed to catch fire as she asked, "Why don't we do that? Why don't we go together? You could go home first and see your family, and after I've made my little tour, I could meet you in Cairncurran, and then we could go to France together." Her face was filled with excitement and anticipation.

His head tilted back and he looked toward the ceiling now. Dear God, he pleaded, you're not letting up, are you? You know that this is what I want more than anything, but you're going to make it as difficult as you possibly can, aren't you?

Be careful how you say this, he warned himself. "Annie, the truth is, there are things that I've committed myself to at home that I simply can't ignore. I'd love to go with you, I really would, but you have to be patient with me while I try to sort out these things, while I try to undo some of those obligations."

She realized now that she was far more taken with the idea than he was, and it dampened her enthusiasm. "Sure," she responded, trying to appear casual, as though she'd be happy either way. "There's no rush. I don't need an answer tonight." Then, despite her valiant attempt at nonchalance, her heart compelled her to add, "I just want you to say you'll consider it. Will you?"

"I will." He didn't want to encourage her too much or give her false hope. "And just so you know, I think it's a brilliant idea. I'd love for you to meet my family—my mother, my two sisters—to show you where I grew up, though admittedly, I didn't spend an awful lot of time there."

"Because they sent you away to school?" she wondered. "You were nine when you left, right?"

He seemed suddenly bitter when he answered, "Right, but my father wanted me off sooner than that. My mother had to fight to keep me around as long as she did."

It was difficult for Annie to comprehend sending a child away from home at that tender age. "I can't imagine having to live away from my brother and the rest of my family. I would've been so miserable. Why do people do that?"

He shrugged as he answered, "Tradition mostly. And like a lot of fathers, mine believes the experience toughens you, prepares you for adulthood."

That confused her even more. It was Andrew's sweetness that she found most appealing. Why on earth would anyone want to change him, to harden him?

"But to tell you the truth, I was miserable," he confided. "Even now, it's painful looking back." His eyes saddened with the recollection. "And although my mother's intentions were good, it actually made things more difficult, going in later than the other boys. They were already formed in their groups and friendships, you see, and they viewed me as an outsider. I spent a lot of time on my own." He sighed and looked into the fire. "But then I went to Eton, and that was somewhat better. I was still regarded as an outsider because I'm Scottish, but in other respects I was on even ground with the rest of the bugs."

"Bugs?"

He smiled a little, but Annie could tell it wasn't genuine. "That's what Etonians call first-year boys. Bugs or tits."

"Sounds like a tough place," she observed.

His grin transformed to a frown. "It wasn't tough in the usual sense of the word, but some of the senior boys were merciless. All bugs had to be servant to a senior boy. It was the tradition."

"Servant?"

"The boy to whom you were servant," he explained, "you had to bring him coffee in the morning and lay out his clothes for the day, then do his bidding, whatever he said. Otherwise, you were punished or fined, or both." He looked into her eyes as he finished. The sadness she had observed in him was gone now, and his usually expressive face seemed oddly blank.

"That's so archaic, so demeaning," she decided.

Shaking his head slightly, he responded, "What it is, is so traditional, so English. Anyway, that's in the past, and as you've said, it needs to be put in its place." He stroked one of her arms as he softly asked, "What is it about yours, Annie, that needs putting away?"

She clicked her tongue against the roof of her mouth, hesitated a moment, then said, "Just the most recent parts. But before that there were very good and happy times that I never want to forget. Times with my brother, my grandparents, especially my grandfather." She chuckled as she thought of one in particular. "My grandfather sneaked me onto the roller coaster at Pontchartrain Beach when I was about six. He lied to the man about my age and then argued with him so that he let me on. You weren't supposed to go on until you were eight, but my grandfather knew I was ready. I was always looking for adventure, and he was the one person who understood that about me." She paused, then qualified her statement with, "Before Timmy grew up, that is. He understands me, too."

He smiled as he pictured the scene with the roller coaster. He had no trouble imagining the young Annie standing on the platform, trembling with anticipation but ready to brave whatever lay ahead. "Is he still living, your grandfather?"

"Yeah, sort of. I say that because after my grandmother died, he changed so much that I'd hardly call it living." She dropped the corners of her mouth. "His spirit seemed to die with her, and he's never been the same."

"I think that frequently happens when two people love deeply," he observed. "I can't imagine that the survivor feels like much of one when his reason for living is gone." Bundling her in his arms now, he added, "I'm beginning to worry about that myself, about how I'll survive when you're gone." It wasn't a declaration, but it was the closest he'd come to telling her how he truly felt.

Annie took in a deep breath, and with it came the scent of him—his sweetness mingled with tweed. "Then you have to think about coming with me," she responded. "You have to do whatever it is you must so we can spend the summer together."

He didn't answer. They wrapped their arms tightly around each other and gazed into the flames.

Annie was awakened by his hand tenderly brushing her cheek.

"Why don't you go have a lie down on my bed?" he offered.

Yawning and stretching, she said, "Maybe I will, just for a bit." Her body felt swollen and heavy, the way a body tends to when much-needed sleep is interrupted.

They went into the bedroom together, and she sat on the high, old bed, yawning repeatedly. Andrew took a quilt from the wardrobe and laid it next to her. He then bent to untie her laces.

The gesture embarrassed her. "You don't need to do that!"

He said nothing as he removed her shoes. He fluffed a pillow and then gently nudged her into lying back, covering her with a quilt that smelled of onions and mothballs.

"I had a wonderful day," she whispered. "That was incredibly thoughtful of you to arrange things the way you did, to get Adam and me back together. I know why I'm sleepy now," she realized. "It's because I feel so peaceful."

Her eyes were soft and trusting, the way he'd seen them that day on the beach, the day they had almost made love. They drew him to kiss her forehead as he observed, "Peace is something you haven't had very much of, is it?"

Yawning again, she said, "Don't let me sleep too long."

He wished her "Sweet dreams," then left the room and closed the door behind him.

Annie was wandering, floating almost. It was dusk and an eerie, distant light shone. The Whaum's garden had grown large and dark; forbidding woods lined its edge. She heard a rustling in the trees and moved toward it.

She came upon an open grave and peered in. Her motorcycle was half buried there under rose cuttings and dirt. Moving to clear away the debris, she pricked her fingers on the thorns. They dripped with blood, and she meant to put them in her mouth when someone snatched them away and put them in his. Andrew, she sighed, and as he sucked on her fingers, she felt it pull on her insides all the way from her toes.

Someone touched her arm.

Her voice was deep and sensual as she rubbed the sleep from her eyes, saying, "Oh, Andrew, I was dreaming."

"Yes, I know," he answered, sitting on the bed next to her. "I watched you before I woke you. Your eyelids were fluttering and you were moaning."

She stared at him for a moment, remembering the dream and the sensation of her fingers in his mouth. "I pricked my fingers on rose cuttings and you were sucking on them." As she finished saying this, he picked up one of her hands and began to do just that. He kept his eyes on hers, pulling his mouth over the slender digits, tasting and licking them as though they were coated in chocolate. Her insides became charged and without thinking she let herself say, "I want to be your lover, Andrew. I want to make love with you." Her heart picked up speed. "But when I think of it actually happening, it scares me."

He released her fingers with a kiss to their tips. "It frightens me, too, Annie," he confessed.

She hadn't expected him to say that, and she propped herself against the headboard as she asked, "Why are you afraid? I mean, I know why I am, but why are you?"

He leaned back a little; his eyes went first to the windows, then to her face, but he dropped them to the quilt as he answered, "Because there's a terrible row going on inside of me, between my feelings and my rational self, and I don't seem able to sort out who the winner should be." He sighed deeply before adding, "The consequences of being rational scare me as much as giving in to my emotions, and the worst thing is, I don't believe there's any common ground."

"What are you being rational about?" she wondered.

"Annie d'Inard," he responded. "She'll be leaving soon. She doesn't even live in the same country I do. I don't know if I'll ever see her again, and I know if I make love with her, I'll never want to let her go." With that admission, he began to feel as though he were falling, plunging through the sky like a dreamer.

The spasms in her throat made it difficult to swallow. "And what if you don't let her go?"

He needed to catch himself; he had to stop the fall. "Ah, but you have to know Annie," he answered. "I could never stop her from doing what she wanted. And I would never want to keep her from pursuing her dreams, from doing what she needed to."

Those words said that he understood her, and the realization of that made her want him even more. She took both of his hands in hers and intertwined their fingers.

The encounter with Alfred Cowan had reminded Andrew of just how difficult it would be to pursue his own dreams, and while she'd slept, he'd been able to think of nothing else. "And beyond all that," he told her now, "there are yet further snags and hitches. Even if we somehow managed to get through the initial ones, there are others, things I don't care to get into. Complications and obstacles lurk out there that might well prove insurmountable." Even as he was trying to pull away from her, he studied the contours of her face, the little bend to her nose, and he marveled at the thick dark lashes that rimmed her soulful eyes.

They sat in silence for a minute before Annie decided to tell him, "Something happened to me a couple of years ago that took away my courage, made me afraid of most everything. I've pretty much gotten over that, but I've got a new fear now, one I never expected to have. I'm afraid of you loving me." She swallowed hard again. "You're not like any man I've ever met before, Andrew. You're deeper than Loch Ness and more mysterious, too."

He laughed at her choice of words, then lowered his head and sighed.

"You're so much finer than I am," she told him, "and I don't know if I'm worthy of you. I have this horrible, nagging fear that if you get to know me better, you won't like me. And I'm worried, too, that I'll hurt you, because I seem to do that to people, and then you'll end up hating me. I think that's what scares me the most, the idea that you could end up hating me."

"My, just that," he quipped, "nothing else?" He was thinking, but couldn't say, that it was he who feared not being worthy of her, and it was he who feared having to hurt her.

She brought his hands to her lips and kissed them one at a time, then rested her cheek on one. "I could never bear it if you hated me. I can't think of anything worse happening to me than you hating me."

"Funny, but I've been thinking rather along those same lines," he admitted. "If I let myself love you and you left me, I think I'd have to hate you to survive it." It almost choked him to say that, and it was with great difficulty that he added, "I couldn't bear that, Annie."

The room was quiet, and they stared at one another for several long moments, each disturbed by what the other had revealed and by what they had finally admitted to themselves. Annie's chest felt tight, as though something were squeezing her heart, and she wanted desperately to ease the discomfort.

She still grasped his hands, hands that were strong and gentle and warm, hands that she longed to feel exploring her body. "Susannah told me I should stop fretting over this, that I should just let things happen with you."

A sad but determined look came over him. "I wish I could afford that luxury." He could not meet her eyes, so he stared at the quilt that covered her legs. "But there's a price to pay for that sort of extravagance, and I don't know if I'm prepared to pay it." Abruptly, he took his hands from hers and stood up.

"OK," she answered. She searched her heart for other words to say, but it seemed to have stolen away, gone into hiding. It cowered now, trembling behind a wall of self-doubt and pain.

He walked her back to David Russell and afterward, instead of going home and to his studies, he went to the pub. When he was good and drunk, he returned to the Whaum. Before undressing, he switched on the lamp next to his bed. In the light he spotted two long, dark hairs on the pillow slip. He carefully plucked them off and wrapped them in a tissue, putting the tissue in a corner of his nightstand drawer. When he lay on the pillow, the scent of her perfume reached him, and it brought burning tears to his eyes. He turned onto his stomach and buried his face in the fragrance, releasing painful, wrenching sobs between deep breaths—breaths meant to take in the aroma of her—until he finally fell into lonely, despairing sleep.

Chapter 18

She had the money in her pocket; dinner was over and she was waiting outside in the David Russell car park with Melville and Susannah. Her friends grew excited when they heard Colin thundering down Buchanan Gardens, but Annie started to tremble.

"Well, here she is," Colin said to her as he halted the bike and set it on its kickstand.

"He," Mel corrected him, "It's now a 'he' and his name is Percy B."

"Why Percy B.?"

"After Percy Shelley," Annie informed him.

"Well, best of luck with him," Colin said, seeming pleased with the wad of money he was holding. "Want to run down to the pub for a congratulatory drink?"

Mel wasn't ashamed to ask, "You treating? You're the one with all the dosh."

"Why not," he answered. "Going to drive Percy down, Annie?"

Susannah grew excited. "Oh, do! You can give me a lift. Mel and Colin can walk and meet us."

"Sure," she told her, because she could not deny her friend.

It took three tries and all of the energy Annie could muster to get the engine running. It didn't help that her knees felt like jelly. And with Susannah sitting behind her and throwing off the balance, she swerved like a drunk as she pulled into the street.

They arrived in front of the Scores Hotel pub with a great roar, attracting the attention of its patrons, some of whom

came out to see her. Annie held court for a time, smiling at
her admirers and answering questions about her planned
odyssey. Susannah stood by to tell anyone who asked how
marvelous and brave she thought her friend was. When the
questions ran out, they went inside for celebratory drinks.

Andrew had been at the bar with Robin, and they'd
witnessed her arrival but had not joined the curious in
the street.

All that afternoon his friend had seemed out of sorts,
so Robin decided to ask about it. "It's Annie, isn't it? What
are you going to do about her?"

He was already peeved, but Robin's impertinence set
him off. "Why do I have to do anything?" he wanted to know.

"I just thought that what with the situation at home,
you might be pondering how to end it."

He responded with uncommon rancor. "End what?"

Warily, Robin explained, "I thought there was something between you."

"There's nothing."

He frowned his disbelief. "Oh, sorry. My mistake, then."

Andrew didn't have to see her to know that she was
entering the public room, but he made no effort to greet her.

It took less than a minute for Annie to spot him. When
she did, she was instantly flooded with anxiety; he couldn't
help but know that she was there, and he was obviously
avoiding her. But besides being hurt, she felt utterly confused because only yesterday he'd indicated that he understood how important this was to her.

She wasted no time in approaching him. "The bike is
mine now. It's all paid up," she said to his back.

He did not turn around. "Congratulations. Can I get
another?" he called to the bartender.

"Are you mad at me, Andrew?" she asked.

"Angry, do you mean? Americans have the most peculiar expressions," he scowled.

"Are you?"

He had still not looked at her. He'd kept his eyes on the
activity behind the bar. "It's a bit difficult," he answered,
more gently now.

With the change in his tone, she understood what only a moment ago had eluded her. "I know it is; it's hard for me, too. Things are moving so fast now, and it's all so confusing. How am I supposed to know if I'm doing the right thing?"

God, he thought, here she is again—going directly into my heart, reading me, telling me what I feel.

When he didn't respond, she asked him, "Do you have any free time tomorrow? I was thinking maybe we could go for a ride in the country. Would you, Andrew, would you go with me so we can be alone and talk?"

When he turned to look at her, he was drawn into her eyes, so soft and sad and pleading, and the distance he'd been trying to put between them was no more. Bloody hell, he cursed himself, you're hopeless, aren't you? "I'll be back at the Whaum by half past twelve," he offered, "if you'd like to come by then."

She had an awful time getting to sleep that night. Percy B. sat outside the entrance to Fraser, under an overhang and out of the rain that was falling. His presence there was like an omen, a disturbing vision that had somehow turned real and was now looming, waiting outside her door. It was the crystal ball on the fortune-teller's table, waiting to be read. It would carry her into her future, into the gray and boundless unknown. What am I doing, she asked herself, but she could not find a comfortable answer.

It was almost dawn before she finally fell asleep.

After breakfast she decided to do some practice driving. If she was ever going to be comfortable handling the enormous bike, she had to have more experience with it.

The sky had broken through the night's rain and it was a bright, miraculous morning, the kind that inspires courage. She left David Russell and turned right onto the Strathkiness Low Road.

She drove slowly because the narrow road curved frequently, and it was difficult for her to adjust her weight and lean properly into the curve. Had she been able to drive on the right side of the road, it would have been much easier, and the experience of many years of balancing a bicycle would have lent itself to the motorbike. But as it was, when she came upon a bend, she had to actively go against her instincts and fight to keep herself in the left lane. More than once she lost her balance, and four times in the morning's brief exercise she terrified herself and had to pull over to recover her composure.

On the last of those occasions, her thoughts were drawn to her childhood and the day she tackled her first two-wheeler. She pictured her grandfather on that steamy summer morning, and saw in his face how especially proud he'd been of her. I wonder what he's doing right now, she thought. If only he could come over, if he or Timmy could somehow magically transport themselves to Scotland, I know they'd help me find the courage I need. But just thinking about them heartened her, and when she took off again, she felt different, stronger.

She caused heads to turn on South Street, just as she'd done last night arriving at the pub. But the noise the machine made embarrassed her. It disturbed the peace of the morning's shopping and drew attention to her in a way she didn't like. She would have preferred to be among the quiet pedestrians, feeling like one of the locals, and she loathed Percy in that instant for having separated her from them.

Patrick was leaving Southgait Hall as she passed, and the sight of her on the motorcycle infuriated him. He stopped in his tracks to glare at her, but she did not see him.

She decided to go to the cathedral for a time. After her driving exercise, she needed her fix of peace. It never failed to come to her here—no matter her state of mind—it seemed to be absorbed through her skin. She parked outside the entrance and went in, carrying her helmet under one arm. In her heavy oilskin jacket, wearing jeans and hiking boots, she felt like a warrior decked out for battle. She located a wind-protected spot and glanced at her watch. She would wait here until it was time to meet Andrew. She wasn't sitting long when Patrick came upon her.

He sounded irritated when he told her, "I saw you passing by and decided to follow you."

She managed a smile but she was thinking, God, what does he want now? "How's things?" she asked him.

"Going well," he answered, with more emphasis than was necessary. "I've been at it, getting ready for the end of term." He looked away from her in the direction of the motorbike. "I see you went through with it."

"Yup." She let out a long breath, as though she'd been holding it for some time. "I've been doing some practice driving this morning. It's a little scary, actually. It'll take some getting used to."

"Yes, I imagine so." It pleased him to know that. He didn't want it to be easy. "When are you leaving?" he wondered.

"I need to be in France before the end of this month, so I'm thinking of leaving on the twenty-third."

He frowned at her now. "You know, you do look a bit rough in that outfit. It's not at all becoming." He wanted that to upset her; he hoped it did.

She was unperturbed by his comment and laughed as she responded, "I can hardly wear a dress and high heels to drive a motorcycle now, can I?"

"No, I guess not," was all he thought to say. He pictured her like that, skirt flying in the wind, slender legs hugging the engine, and he suddenly realized how vulnerable she was. "I'm late for a tutorial," he informed her. "I should be getting on." He began walking away, but that image remained in his mind and it compelled him to turn back to her and add, "You take care driving."

"I will, thanks," she called to him.

Andrew had not arrived yet, so she let herself in and went to the rose garden. Her hard work had paid off. The roses were budding and what had only recently been a neglected mess was now neat and orderly, and pleasing to look at. She left her helmet and jacket in the parlor and waited for Andrew under the old arbor.

When he came outside to greet her, it was not with his usual excitement. "Sorry I'm late. I needed to speak with one of my tutors."

Recognizing the concerned look he wore, she asked him, "Are you doing all right in your courses? You don't seem to spend much time studying."

"No, I don't," he admitted, obviously annoyed with himself. "That's what he wanted to see me about, actually. But I'll rally at the end. I always seem to pull it off when I need to." He smiled at her now and asked, "What do you want to do today?"

"Well, it's such a pretty day. Why don't we get something for lunch and then go have a picnic?"

"That's a brilliant idea," he answered. "I'll just be a minute." He went to his room and changed out of his jacket and tie into more casual clothing. When he came out, he was carrying a blanket. "We'll need this," he told her. "It rained last night, and the ground will be damp."

It was awkward for Annie to drive Andrew on the motorcycle; it was an uncomfortable reversal of roles. But Andrew seemed fine with it, and was rather pleased when people recognized and waved to them. They stopped in at three of the little shops in town: one for meat pies, another for fruit, and the third for a bottle of wine. Andrew clutched the blanket and their purchases between them as they left town on Bridge Street and turned off onto Largo Road.

He squeezed her waist and kissed her neck as they drove. "You're an astounding woman, do you know that?"

They'd been following the winding road for some time when they saw the sign for Dunino church; Andrew pointed to it, so Annie made the turn. They followed the narrow road that was lined on both sides with stone walls, then turned left to find a small chapel sitting in the middle of nowhere, surrounded by pastures and grazing sheep.

"This is perfect," she told him, "just what I'd hoped we find."

He seemed excited when he asked, "Do you know what this place is? This church was built on the site of a Celtic ritual ground to sanctify the place where Druids held their pagan ceremonies. Amazing little spot, this."

They found the chapel unlocked and ventured inside. No one was around, but it was obviously visited and tended to as evidenced by the burning votives and fresh flowers on the altar. They explored it quietly, Andrew taking Annie's hand as they wandered the aisles. When they went outside again, they briefly had to shield their eyes from the sunlight.

"There's a footpath that leads into the woods," he observed. "Let's follow it."

He closed the farm gate behind them, then took hold of Annie's hand again as they walked alongside the grave-yard wall and into the woods. They descended into a ravine and were plunged into an unsettling darkness that was not unlike the experience of a solar eclipse. The sound of rushing water beckoned from below, and the path had brought them to a rocky plateau that jutted some twenty feet above the streambed. A curious basin was carved into the enormous, cylindrical boulder.

He excitedly told her, "This is it! This is where they made their sacrifices!"

"What kind of sacrifices? Not human?"

"Sometimes," he said, "but most of the time it was lambs."

She imagined the basin at her feet filled with blood instead of the rainwater it now held. "My God," she gasped, "they sacrificed human beings? People?"

"Yes," he calmly answered. "Didn't you know that?"

"I thought Druids worshiped trees."

"They were fond of oaks and mistletoe, actually," he informed her, "and they believed that spirits inhabited the forests, but they also engaged in some brutal rituals."

The darkness of the woods and the precariousness of their location was already spooking her, but this informa-tion intensified her feelings of dread.

Aware of her discomfort, he asked, "You all right?"

"This place is giving me the creeps," she whispered, as though someone might be listening.

He put an arm around her waist. "It wasn't yesterday," he teasingly assured her. "The practice ended 1,600 years ago. And anyway, when you stand outside the university chapel, you're standing where people were murdered, you know, and much more recently. What's the difference between torturing and slaughtering those labeled heretics by the Holy Church and slitting an innocent's throat to ensure a good crop or a mild winter?"

"I guess the throat slitting makes more sense." She laughed nervously. "At least it has a purpose."

"I couldn't agree more," he responded.

They descended the steps that had been chiseled out of the stone and reached the streambed. A smile came to Andrew's lips as he touched the carving in the rock that was just to their left.

"Isn't this glorious?" he asked her, tracing the ogham with his finger. "It's got to be 1,500 years old if it's a day. You know, where I was born, where my family comes from in Argyll, we've hundreds of prehistoric sites, many dating back 4,000 years and more. You're familiar with Stonehenge, aren't you?"

"Sure," she answered.

"Well, in—" he had to catch himself because he'd almost said Kilmartin. He didn't want to identify that location, because it was too intimately involved with his family. "In the area around my grandfather's house, on his land actually, there are several standing stones similar to the ones at Stonehenge, and there are burial cairns and ritual sites."

"Wow, that must be cool. It must have been a great place to play when you were a kid," she realized.

"It was, actually." The recollection brought a warm smile to his face. "I used to pretend to be a Celtic king who lived in those times. My grandparents gave me a pony and I'd gallop her through the fields, wielding a toy sword, fighting off the Norse invaders." He chuckled slightly as he added, "And there was even a fair maiden I'd rescue— the neighbor's daughter, Fiona, with her long, flame hair.

She'd be tied up at this site called the Temple Wood and about to be scarified when I'd come riding in."

She loved the picture that created for her. "I wish I could have been that maiden," she told him, sighing slightly. She wanted to hear more about his childhood, but the quiet of the woods was suddenly pierced by a shrill call. "What was that?"

"Just a hawk," he explained. "It's all right. He's merely hunting his supper."

Looking around nervously, she told him, "This place is eerie. What you said about the spirits in the woods, I can almost feel them." Reaching for his arm she urged, "Let's get out of here and back into the sunlight."

He took her hand again and led her up the steep path. Pointing to the meadow across from the church, he said, "That's the perfect spot for our picnic."

The location they chose was on a gentle hill with a magnificent vista that sloped toward the sea. Andrew removed his jumper and sat cross-legged on the moth-eaten blanket. Annie pulled off her hiking boots and settled herself next to him. The smile on her face broadened as she absorbed the pastoral beauty of the Fife countryside.

The valley they overlooked was a patchwork quilt of tended fields—some in golden bloom, some the rich, silky brown of freshly tilled soil, others the deep jade of new crops—all sparkling and moving in the sunlight. The lambs in the next pasture played noisy games with one other, bleating and calling as though engaged in a game of hide-and-seek. The emerald grass where they sat was exquisite; spread throughout with tiny violets and bugleweed, it looked like purple crystals sprinkled on green icing.

"You're very lucky, Andrew Gordon," she declared.

He had begun opening the wine with his Swiss Army knife. "Lucky?"

"To live in such a beautiful country."

"Aye, it is that," he agreed.

"Is it like this on the west coast, too?" she wondered.

"The terrain is more rugged there, and the lochs make for more isolation, but it has its own special beauty. And the islands are majestic. Each of them is unique." He passed the bottle to Annie, and they took turns drinking from it. As he was closing his knife, he asked her, "Handy little tool, this. Do you have one to take with you on holiday?"

"No."

"Well then, you must have this one," he decided and held it out to her.

"Oh Andrew, that's very sweet, but I can't take your knife." From her grandfather and brother, she understood how important a pocketknife is to a man.

"Nonsense, I insist." He lowered his voice when he added, "Perhaps you'll think of me when you use it."

"I'm going to think of you all the time," she said, "with or without the knife."

Andrew drank more wine and looked toward the neighboring pasture. "I hadn't realized the lambs had grown so. Time certainly does have its way with us," he mused, attempting a smile.

She laid a hand on his. "Have you given anymore thought to France, to coming with me?"

He sighed. "In all honesty, I've thought of little else. But I've got to go home as soon as the term ends. I didn't mention it the other day, but the family goes on holiday immediately after."

"Oh," she said, then she had a thought. "How about meeting me in France then, after your vacation?"

"How could we do that?" he wondered. "You don't even know where you'll be after your friend leaves."

That worried her, but then she remembered, "I could write to you. I could figure out a good place for us to meet and write to you. Issie says you can get mail at American Express offices, so you could send a letter there."

He mulled that over while he unwrapped their meat pies. That might work, he realized, but only if my father doesn't put up too much resistance. At any rate, it's more realistic than her original idea of coming to Crofthill and picking me up.

"What keeps me from saying yes to you," he decided to tell her, "aside from the holiday, is that I'm supposed to be working with my father this summer, learning the family business. I gave him my word on this, so I can't just up and announce that I'm not going to do it. I've got to ask his permission." When he concluded, he stared off into the distance.

She saw how the idea of that troubled him, so she decided not to press him.

They finished their meal in silence, then lay on the blanket watching the clouds race over them as though they had someplace important to go.

Her voice came softly to him, like a melody carried on the breeze. "So many times lately, especially when I'm with you, I feel as though I've died and gone to heaven. I can't imagine paradise is any nicer than Scotland, and I can't imagine any angel more wonderful than you."

Her words and voice aroused him, and when he turned his head to look at her, it was all he could do to keep from kissing her. Steady on, old man, he warned himself, but this girl is becoming everything to me. "Forgive me, Annie," he tenderly whispered. "You're so open with me and I'm—" he hesitated. "Talking about things like this, about feelings, it's much more difficult for me."

She kept her gaze skyward. "It doesn't matter, Andrew, because I know your heart. I feel what's in it."

That simple answer sealed his fate. If he'd had doubts before, he could no longer remember what they were. He turned to his side and pulled her body to his. When their lips connected, it felt as though they were flowing into one another.

They stopped long enough to look into each other's eyes. She asked a silent question and when she saw the answer, she moved her hand to his penis. She stroked it through his pants, rubbing and squeezing, and then moved down to massage his scrotum. He began to breathe deeply, audibly.

She brought her lips to his ear. "I won't ask you to do what you're not ready for, but we can touch each other. We can be together without going all the way."

His heart was pounding so wildly, his breaths now came in gasps. She locked her eyes with his as she unbuttoned his shirt, then ran her fingers through the sandy, curled hair. She rolled on top of him and rubbed herself against his thigh, again kissing and stroking him. He reached his hand between her legs and began to rub her. She responded by thrusting her pelvis against him, rhythmically and determinedly. Their kiss grew deeper and they were all alone there, in the middle of that spring meadow, with no one else in the world.

Breaking away from his mouth, she straddled him with her legs, then pulled off the turtleneck sweater she was wearing. Deftly, she reached around and unhooked her bra.

He took hold of her arms to keep her still so that he might admire her. The sun was behind her back and it shone through her hair, like light through a prism. The breeze blew it across her face and shoulders, and he reached to clear the strands from her eyes, whispering, "God, you're so beautiful. I'm almost afraid to touch you."

She took his hand and put it to one breast. He grasped it, then tugged on the nipple. She sighed a deep, erotic sigh, and taking hold of the breast with both her hands, she lowered herself to his face, guiding the nipple to his mouth. He moaned with the exquisite pleasure of it—the intoxicating taste and aroma of her flesh, the tickle of her hair on his skin—and he sucked her nipple as though there were milk to be had from it. She tossed her head and arched her back. Never had she felt so much pleasure. She was reminded of the dream she'd had when she'd felt him sucking her fingers, and the sensation carried all the way from her toes.

He began slow, rhythmic thrusts, pressing his erection against her. She continued to hold her breast to him. His sucking grew more intense and he tried to take the whole of it into his mouth. It caused her a little pain, but she did not take herself away because she understood what was happening to him. He thrust himself more forcefully and let loose an explosion inside his pants like none he'd ever known before, beyond all description. He released in seemingly end-less waves the semen he so desperately wanted to put in her, feeling the warm, sticky fluid collect on his abdomen.

His body shuddered with the last waves of expulsion. She kissed him with her tongue now, deep into his mouth. He sucked on her tongue like he had on her nipple, trying to take something from her, trying to be quenched. With all the restraint he could muster, he kept himself from saying aloud what his whole being wanted him to say, what every quivering, excited cell in his body begged him to say—I love you, Annie, God, how I love you.

She ended the kiss gently and then lay on the blanket next to him. She took him into her arms. She understood his vulnerability and wanted to protect him. Fearing that he might feel foolish and embarrassed now, she sighed to him, "I'm so glad that happened."

All his intellectual faculties seemed to have been lost. His eyes were blank, open spaces when he looked at her.

"We're closer now," she whispered.

"Yes," was all he could say. He felt heavy, as though he were drugged or under a spell; whatever she might ask of him, he was powerless to resist.

"Do the same for me, Andrew."

With that she unzipped her jeans and pulled them below her knees, her underpants with them. The sight of that most private and intimate place roused him from the stupor he was experiencing. She took his hand again and this time brought it to the dark tangle of hair.

Her voice was deeply sensual when she told him, "I want you inside of me."

His fingers slid into her so easily he was shocked. Her lips were warm, moist silk and he was astounded, touch-ing this part of a woman for the first time, by the miracu-lous sensation of it. And then he became aware of the delicate aroma that drifted up from her, earthy and exotic at the same time, that treated his nostrils to the same acute pleasure his fingers now knew. Instinctively, he moved two fingers into her, letting them do what his penis ached to do, as the walls of her vagina opened and closed on them. He watched her—naked down to her knees, beautiful and free and open, reacting to his touch—and realized that he'd become stone hard again. With every ounce of strength he had, he fought to keep his hands from undoing his trousers. Entering her now would have been easier than taking his next breath. But connecting with her was essential, he felt he would die if he didn't, so he put his mouth to hers and thrust his fingers deeper, his pelvis mimicking their motion.

His thrusts were like a plea, and she answered by doing what he wouldn't, by reaching for the button on his trousers, then slipping her hand inside. He felt strong and hot and damp, and the throbbing in her hand made her feel as though she held his heart.

With her other hand she unzipped his trousers now, and when she did, they were flooded with the scent of his semen. Their bodies reacted to this discovery with an impassioned, rhythmic dance.

All at once in that meadow, two young people from very different worlds shared something rare and wonderful, and previously unknown to either of them. With his fingers inside of her and her hands stroking him, they climaxed together, a moment so natural and perfect it seemed mystical—an exchange of electricity and fire that burned forever, like a brand, the other on each of their hearts.

They lay together, breathing in the air they shared, clinging, listening, waiting, neither one wanting to break the spell. The white clouds of earlier had been chased by heavy, blue ones, and the sun was lost for a time. When Annie began to shiver, he secured his trousers and helped as she dressed herself again. Then he wrapped her in the blanket with him, pulling her body to his as close as physically possible. No words were spoken, but a connection had been made that allowed them entrance to the other's soul.

They watched the sky, they heard the wind, the world around them seemed at perfect peace. Time passed and they were unaware, unconcerned—it raced over them in dark, billowing clouds, and it moved the sun lower in the sky.

They were so close, Andrew's voice seemed to come from inside of her when he asked, "Tell me about the boy you loved. Tell me what happened."

It took a moment, but she understood. "I wasn't in love, and it wasn't a boy. It was a grown man that I barely knew." She moved her head so that she could see his eyes. "It happened only once, and I never saw him again." She watched him sigh and look away.

"I'm sorry," he murmured.

"I wanted it that way," she admitted, as the memory of it brought an ache to her heart. "I was attracted to him and I didn't think being in love was necessary. I couldn't have been more wrong."

He shook his head. "I can't imagine that. I can't see you being like that."

The sadness that revelation so obviously brought him deepened her own heartache, but as difficult as it was, she had to tell him the rest. "And there was a second time, with another guy. That happened only once, too, but it was a completely different circumstance."

He was holding her in his arms, but he changed his position slightly so that he could see her more directly. "Were you in love then?"

He asked that question so poignantly it almost made her cry. "Oh, Andrew, it's so hard to talk about. I've never been able to. It's been too awful to even think of."

His face filled with concern. "Why?"

She pulled away from him and sat up, then hid her face with her hands. "I wish it had never happened. If there were anything I could change, it would be that."

His anxiety grew. "Why, Annie? Tell me."

"Because it was the most horrible night of my life. Because it was the worst thing that's ever happened to me in my life."

He swallowed hard before he asked, "Did he force himself on you?" He was waiting to know for certain but had already felt it in his gut.

"It was worse than that. He gave me acid. Almost right away, I started to bum out. I had a bad trip. I freaked out." The familiar dread and nausea filled her insides. "And then he had sex with me. I didn't want him to, but there was nothing I could do to stop it. I couldn't stop what was happening in my mind and I couldn't stop him." The tears that flowed from her were as heavy as beads of mercury.

He reached to touch those tears, then he kissed them, catching the droplets as they made their way down her cheeks. The sensation it conveyed to Annie was like the lifting of a burden, the sharing of an oppressive, crippling weight.

"That's what coming to Scotland and buying Percy is about," she told him through the tears. "It's about getting past that night, getting over it. That night filled me with terror. It made me afraid to live. I need to get beyond that and back to living, back to being myself. I need to stop being afraid."

He took her in his arms again as it all came together in his mind, falling into place like the last few pieces of a puzzle. The reason he'd felt so drawn to her from the start, the sense he always got that she carried the key deep within her that gave her access to his heart, to that place in his soul where he hid his own pain and regret. And it was now perfectly clear that despite his doubts and fears, they were bound for each other like clouds that merge with the wind, like stars that collide in the far-off universe. It would happen in silence and the world would go on spinning, unaware, but a cosmic, fundamental difference in the core of his being would alter everything.

"I want to take that away from you," he whispered. "I want to lift that pain and fear from you." He had never meant anything so sincerely in his life.

"You do, Andrew," she answered him, "you do."

He pressed her head into his chest. If ever he'd given thought to stopping her, to keeping her from going on with her journey, he understood now how wrong that would be.

And in the same moment, he knew with certainty that he was right in holding back that last bit, in postponing the lovemaking he longed to share with her. She deserved so much more than that. He would not be just another man to her, just another night of regret. He would wait until he was free to give himself fully so that he might shower her with his love, without the encumbrance of guilt. How horrible would it be, he pondered, for both of us, to find what we've hungered for, only to have it eaten away by remorse?

With that realization, he made up his mind to tell her, "I'm going to do everything I can, Annie, to come to you, to be with you in France. I want you to know that. I'm going to do everything in my power to be with you this summer." For a moment, he allowed himself a look into the future, and he envisioned them in a hotel room somewhere on the Mediterranean. The shutters were flung open to the warm stars, and their tanned, naked bodies were locked in embrace, sweaty and spent from hours of lovemaking.

"Will you?" she questioned. "Will you really try?" For days now she had dreamed of nothing but that, and her vision of what it could be like was nearly identical to his.

He stroked her arm and held onto the dream. "I will. But I need you to trust me and be patient a while longer."

"I do trust you. I trust you completely," she answered.

Her declaration brought on the guilt. I need to make myself worthy of that trust, he reminded himself. I must find the courage to tell her the truth, all of it, because I owe her that—but God knows, it won't be easy. It may hurt her terribly, and Christ, how could I ever hurt her? It would kill me to have to hurt her.

As the sun settled lower in the sky, they packed up their things and headed for Crail. They went into a harbor pub that offered a large, crackling fire and cuddled into a corner near it. A radio played behind the bar, and when the first strains of the Van Morrison song reached their ears, they were driven to stand before the flames and dance to it.

Softly, he sang to her, "I want to rock your gypsy soul." Her whole being responded to him, melted into him. Seeing this, the barkeeper turned up the volume, and the few patrons in the place went thoughtfully quiet in acknowledgement of the journey the young lovers were embarking upon, as they sailed into the mystic.

Chapter 19

Andrew slammed the public telephone to the receiver, then left the Russell Hotel brimming over with anger and frustration. He found Robin in the crowded Scores pub and pulled him aside to talk.

Robin guessed at the cause of his friend's upset. "Reached your father, did you?"

He nodded.

"Now, how'd I know that?" He grinned slightly. "Perhaps it's that look you're wearing that says you'd like to throttle someone."

Andrew clicked his tongue in disgust. "My mother had already clued him in, so I didn't have to say much. He began by encouraging me to withdraw a few pounds from the bank to spend on her. Go ahead, have some fun, he said. Have a fling with her, nothing's official yet. She's an American of no consequence, no background. Have your way with her if you like. It'll be good for you, make a man of you. But that's to be the end of it, no more than a fling, understand? You can't be serious about wanting more from someone like that. You know what your responsibilities are, and on and on he went and he wouldn't hear another word from me."

Robin arched his brow. He knew his roommate well enough to understand that this would not be the end of it. "So what now?"

"If only I knew." He paused a second, then exclaimed, "God!" Picking up his glass of whisky, he knocked it back in one swallow.

"So what about France? Will you tell her you can't go?"

"No way in hell will I do that!" he declared adamantly.

Robin merely stared at him, waiting to see what he would do. In recent weeks, he'd frequently been surprised by his friend's behavior, watching him swing from one mood to another, seemingly filled with joy one moment, then consumed with despair in the next.

"But I tell you what I will do," Andrew continued, "the only thing I can do at the moment. I'll get pissed and try to put the whole damned, bloody mess out of my mind."

"That'll be a bit difficult," Robin said, glancing toward the door, "because she's just come in."

Annie spotted Andrew almost immediately, but Colin drew her aside to ask how the motorbike was running. Andrew watched from a distance for a few minutes before going to her, pondering what he would tell her.

As he approached her, he reached for one of her hands and squeezed it, saying only, "I've missed you."

Something unusual in his face and voice, instantly troubled Annie. "Everything all right with your classes? Are you catching up on your work?"

He frowned slightly. "Let's not talk about that." A table had just been vacated in a far corner, and he nodded in that direction. "Grab those seats and I'll get us some drinks."

He was back quickly. Sitting beside her now he told her, "I've been trying to speak with my father and I've finally just reached him. I wanted to broach the subject of France."

Suddenly fearing the answer, she asked with some trepidation, "And did you?"

Andrew sat looking at her tensed face for a moment; he could not bring himself to disappoint her, so he made a quick decision. "We didn't get that far. But the good thing is we've begun a dialogue and I'm very hopeful that in time, I'll be able to bring him 'round." He smiled but not very well.

Annie heard the insincerity in his voice. She heard it and knew what it meant. But time was running out for them and she did not want to spend what little they had left fretting over things she couldn't control. "I'm so glad to hear it," she told him. "So where do we go from here?"

Still with his affected grin, he answered, "We go to the Kate Kennedy Ball tomorrow and we have the most splendid time that's ever been had so they'll be talking about us years hence. And we start making plans to meet somewhere this summer, say, late June or early in July. What do you say to that?"

"I think that sounds wonderful," she answered and returned his smile as best she could.

At breakfast Susannah asked her, "Can I see the frock you're wearing tonight?"

Back in her room, Annie pulled the blue gown from the closet and held it to her chest. It was a floor-length cotton print with flowers in all shades of blue and lavender, and it had a deep, squared-off neckline that was bordered with lace. The elbow-length sleeves were gathered at the top and trimmed in lace, and the waist was fitted and pulled in by a bow that tied at the back.

"Oh Annie, it's so lovely! How ever did you know to bring something like that with you? Did Adam tell you about the balls?"

She chuckled. "Nope, he didn't. I bought it on a whim just before I left, and now I know why."

"Oh?"

Her expression turned serious as she told her friend, "It was because of Andrew, because I was destined to meet Andrew."

Susannah smiled and took a seat in the chair by the window. At first she thought Annie was joking, but when she looked at her again, she realized how sincerely she meant that. "I'm intrigued," she said. "Tell me more."

Annie returned the gown to the closet, then settled cross-legged on her bed. "I think I love him, Susannah. I believe I'm in love with him."

Her immediate reaction was a warm smile, but she didn't keep it long. "And what about him? Is he in love with you?"

"He hasn't said, but then neither have I." She pulled her lips in and bit the lower one. "He's given me the impression that he is. But there are complications, things he keeps alluding to, things he says he has to sort out first."

Andrew, with his fine speech and manners and rather secretive nature, had always intrigued Susannah. So the chance to learn something about him now was too good to pass up. "What things?"

"It's something about working for his father this summer," she explained, "and commitments he's already made."

"Why should that have anything to do with you?" she wondered.

"Because I want him to meet me in France. I want to spend the summer with him, and he says he wants that, too."

Susannah adjusted her position in the chair and looked at the floor as she asked, "Has he told you anything about himself, about his background or anything?" She was dying to know if the conclusions she'd drawn about him were correct.

"Sure."

"Like what?"

Annie recognized some time ago that Susannah had a tendency toward nosiness, and she liked to tease her about it. "Well, let's see," she responded, holding up a hand to count with her fingers. "He's twenty-one years old. He has a mother and father. He was born in Argyll. He lives on a sheep farm called Crofthill. He has two younger sisters, oh, and he went to boarding school, to Eton."

Susannah's eyes went as wide as saucers. "Did you say Eton?"

Annie nodded.

"Good lord, how'd that come up?"

"We were talking about Shelley. He told me they went to the same school."

Settling back into the chair, Susannah seemed pleased with herself. "Well, I'll be. I knew it! I told Mel, quite a long while ago mind you, that he belonged to the upper class! Damned if I wasn't right!"

Annie found the idea laughable. "Upper class? He's just as strapped for cash as the rest of us! Anyway, they're farmers, my dear," she mocked her friend, "sheep farmers."

"Sheep farmers don't send their sons to Eton, Annie," she scoffed. "Do you know the first thing about it? It's only the most elite public school there is. Most of our aristocracy were educated there, you know. You don't just waltz in because you feel like it. They have a few scholarship students but for the most part you need money to get in and plenty of it."

That didn't seem right. She'd never gotten the impression that Andrew was rich. But then something occurred to her that she thought to tell Susannah. "I met someone the other day, this friend of his father's, Lord Cowan. Andrew told me his father does business with him."

Grasping the arms of the chair, Susannah screeched, "Jesus! Lord Alfred Cowan?"

"That's right."

"He's one of the richest men in Britain, Annie!" she told her. "Lord bloody Cowan," she uttered under her breath now. "Well I must say, young Mr. Gordon intrigues me more every day. What else did he tell you? Anything else?"

If she were to be honest, Annie would have to admit that she was curious about his connection to Lord Cowan, but after telling Susannah that she loved Andrew, she felt more than a little embarrassed to add that she found his explanations wanting. She continued in a playful vein. "Nothing that's any of your business, Miss Nib-nose. And anyway, if you're so damned eager to know more about him, why don't you just ask him yourself?"

"Damned if I won't," she responded. Her grinning face was colored with mischief.

She gave herself plenty of time to get ready, knowing she'd have to compete with the other girls on her level for the bath. But she was still primping when someone knocked on her door.

"Your young man's in the reception," a familiar voice called.

She took a last look in the mirror, fussed with her hair for the tenth or so time, and snatched up her shawl.

The lobby was filled with ebullient young people, all decked out in their finery. Annie spied Susannah first, standing to the side with Mel and some others, dressed in a simple violet gown that was adorned with a pale lavender orchid. She moved toward her and in doing so almost walked into Andrew. She had not recognized him.

Like a soldier in full dress uniform, he wore the kilt and tartan of his ancestors. He stood tall and proud among the throng of students, his sandy hair neatly combed, his blue eyes ablaze, holding the bouquet of flowers he'd brought for her. He was so elegant and regal, for a second Annie felt as though she should curtsy.

When he spoke, his voice seemed to be the only one in the room. "My beautiful Annie. How lovely you are!"

"Andrew! I can't believe you! I didn't know you'd wear your kilt. It's so wonderful! You look like a Highland prince!"

His expression changed and Annie wondered if she'd said something wrong. The noise returned and she began to notice that about half the young men in the room also wore the traditional Scottish dress. Many of the young women were dressed that way, too, in long skirts and fancy blouses draped with a tartan sash.

"This is so cool!" she exclaimed. "I love this!"

Andrew smiled again as he declared, "My God, but I'm the luckiest man in the room." He couldn't take his eyes from her.

She felt soft hands touching her shoulders and whirled around to receive a kiss from Susannah. "Stunning, simply stunning you are!" Susannah said as she embraced her.

"You're the gorgeous one, Mademoiselle Barclay. And Mr. Lumsdaine! What a handsome gentleman you are!"

Blushing, Mel brushed at the lapels of his rented tuxedo. "I'd say it's Lord Andrew here that looks every bit the gentleman, not me. I wish I could wear one of those things."

Susannah had been giving Andrew the once-over, so she witnessed his discomfort at being called Lord Andrew.

Self-consciously, he asked, "Are you ladies ready? The car's just outside, and Robin and Carol are waiting."

"Carol MacDonald?" Mel questioned, chuckling. "I didn't think the old boy had it in him!"

Andrew led them to a large, fancy car, the make of which Annie could not identify. A chauffeur, smartly dressed in a gray suit and cap, opened the doors for them.

"How'd you manage this, old boy?" Mel wondered.

"It's a gift from my mother for tonight, her treat to all of us," Andrew answered.

Susannah's comment was accompanied by a curious, wry grin. "A Bentley, what a lovely gesture," she said.

Annie had never ridden in a chauffeured car and excitedly asked him, "Will you thank her for me? This is really great."

He took her hand in his and held it as they drove.

Mount Melville House was a few miles out of St. Andrews, an old estate and manor house that had once been the property of a prominent family. It now belonged to the Fife County Council and was used mainly for this purpose: as an elegant backdrop for the many formal affairs held by the university throughout the year. They joined the queue of taxis and automobiles that lined the long drive, and when they finally reached the entrance, Andrew offered Annie his arm. He escorted her up the steps as though she were the most honored guest there.

Once inside, Robin and Carol were swept away by other friends. Andrew and Mel made their way to the bar, returning to the girls with glasses of champagne.

Andrew held his high to offer the first toast. "To Annie d'Inard. Thank you for accompanying me this evening and making me the proudest, happiest man here."

"Here, here!" Mel said, before rejoining, "But I must say that the lovely Mademoiselle Barclay has made me the proudest man in the room."

They sipped at their drinks, and Annie felt her throat tighten. In recent days, especially in these utterly blissful moments, she'd begun to be plagued by a creeping melancholy. It came upon her because her days in St. Andrews were quickly nearing an end, and she was beginning to feel the loss.

Somberly, she looked to her friends to say, "I'd like to toast the gods, the fates, whatever winds blew me here, and say thank you for bringing me to this place, to make the dearest friends of my life, friends that I will never forget as long as I live, no matter where I go, no matter what I do."

Neither Susannah, nor Mel, nor Andrew responded. They all looked into their glasses and drank, then they each in turn reached out to her. Susannah hugged and kissed her, Mel put an arm around her waist, and Andrew tenderly brushed a wisp of hair from her cheek.

The cocktail reception lasted about an hour. At nine o'clock, the doors to the banquet hall were opened to reveal long tables, dressed in white linen and lit with candelabra. Andrew held Annie's chair as he always did, and she smiled to herself as she realized how comfortable she'd become with being treated this way.

As they began to eat Mel teased her. "I see you still haven't mastered the fine art of British table manners."

Regarding her American habits, she'd been the brunt of more than a few jokes during David Russell dinners, but she'd learned to accept it with humor. "And what, pray tell, am I doing wrong now? I'm not cutting my meat into little pieces. I'm eating soup."

Susannah responded with deliberate exaggeration of her clipped speech. "One may not tilt the bowl towards oneself, only away. This terribly important custom emanates from the captain's tables in the Royal Navy, my dear, when it was considered better to have the soup splash on the officers seated across from you, than on one's own waistcoat."

Dinner lasted a luxurious three hours, longer than Annie had ever sat at one meal, and while they dined they were entertained by a classical quartet. But when the cheese was served, the genteel atmosphere that had accompanied the earlier courses dissipated. In an adjacent hall a local band began playing reels, and Annie and Andrew were among the first on the dance floor.

Standing across from her and bowing as was done to begin this dance, Andrew seemed like someone from a bygone era. The line of men beside him were mostly in kilts too, and the picture it created—the ladies in their long gowns, the tapestry-draped walls, the parquet floors reflecting the firelight—was like something from a Jane Austen novel. It made Annie feel like Miss Elizabeth dancing with Mr. Darcy.

They whirled around to an Eight-some Reel, a Strip-the-Willow, and then the Dashing White Sergeant. After the fourth dance, they returned to their seats for a rest and their pudding.

A little breathlessly, Andrew asked her, "Are you having fun?"

Her cheeks flushed hot and bright pink as she answered, "I'm having the most wonderful night of my life." The room was warm and she fanned herself as she looked to the throng of dancers, wondering aloud, "Why can't it always be like this? Why can't life be nothing but dances and balls and times spent with our friends?"

He responded thoughtfully, "I imagine if we had this every day, we'd neither appreciate nor enjoy it as much. Perhaps that's why I treasure you so much," he ventured, "because I know I have you for such a short time."

With a skeptical, sideways glance, she asked him, "Do you really think that? I do believe I'd treasure you still—no, I'd treasure you more, if I had you with me every day."

He might have responded to that in a typically British way, with embarrassment and self-conscious humor, but something about her directness demanded an equally direct response from him. "The truth is," he said, briefly averting his eyes, "in truth I cherish every precious minute I have with you, Annie, and I know I'd continue to, no matter how few or plentiful they were."

Her cheeks filled with heat again, as she daringly proposed, "Well then, let's give that a test, shall we? Spend the summer with me and we'll see how you feel at the end."

He only smiled in response, but his heart was answering her, saying unashamedly—I know how I'd feel; there'd be no end. I'd never be able to say good-bye to you, and I'd want to spend the rest of my life with you.

"Shall we take some fresh air?" he asked her now. He helped her with her chair and they walked to the terrace, where they secured fresh drinks and seats that afforded them a view of the gardens. "What day exactly are you leaving?" he softly questioned.

"A week from Monday," she answered.

"That's so close."

"Too close."

He could not meet her eyes. "Are you looking forward to it?"

"You know I'm not." She tenderly rubbed his arm. "When do you think you could come to France?"

With his gaze still fixed somewhere in the distance, he answered, "I need at least two or three weeks at home. We have that family holiday."

"Are you going away somewhere?" she wondered.

"We have a place on the Isle of Mull," he explained. "My parents take us there when everyone is home from school. My mother looks forward to it because it's usually the only time save Christmas that we're all together. And my father takes the time to do some fishing with me, and a bit of sailing."

"I'd like to meet your family someday," she told him.

He seemed uncomfortable again, as he stood and straightened his sporran. "I'd like that, too, but we're off the subject. I'm thinking the last week of June would be a good time to shoot for. We'll have all of July that way, and we can celebrate Bastille Day together. How does that sound?"

She loved the idea. "Perfect, that's how! Bastille Day in France! The end of June is good because it'll give me time to get my bearings and figure out where we can meet. And it'll give us time to get letters back and forth."

The band had been taking a break while they spoke, but now the music struck up again.

He held out his hand, asking sweetly, "May I have the pleasure, lassie?"

When she was standing, she bent her knees and pulled at the sides of her skirt, answering, "I'm honored, my lord!"

His tone turned slightly scolding, and he dropped the corners of his mouth. "Why do you call me that?"

She was baffled by his response and readily assured him, "I'm just teasing you."

He took a deep breath and smiled again, then led her into the large hall.

The band stopped playing at two o'clock, but the party was still in full swing. A disc jockey had set up next to the band and as they packed up their instruments, he began to blare rock and roll to the dancers. No one appeared the slightest bit tired; in fact, the crowd seemed infused with new enthusiasm by the sounds of the Rolling Stones. With the cranked-up opening to "Brown Sugar," Annie grabbed Andrew's hand and ran with him to the floor. She began to dance but stopped a moment to kick off her shoes so she could really get into it, as only an unrestrained American would at such an event. She drew the attention of all those who witnessed, including Mel and Susannah, who came from across the room to dance next to her.

She bent to the floor and came up again in rhythm with the music, singing the lyrics, and was so contagious in her enjoyment that she had everyone around her doing it, too. Kilts, tuxedos, and evening gowns went down to the floor when she did, then came up again with her, shouting, "How come you dance so good?" The DJ delighted in the enthusiasm of the crowd so much he couldn't bring himself to end it, so to the screaming approval of the dancers, he started the music over again. This time the entire room engaged in the "Annie dance."

Near the end of the second playing, the dancers swayed their arms in the air for "I say yeah, yeah, yeah" and went down to the floor again for "whoo!" repeating that action until the lyrics ended. As the music finished, Andrew drew Annie to his arms and kissed her while the room swirled around them and their fellow dancers sheltered them from the outside world.

Recognizing that everyone needed a rest, the DJ's next selection was "Wild Horses." Andrew and Annie retained their embrace but ended their kiss. He slowly shifted his arms and nudged her into dancing. Savoring the taste of her, he buried his face in her hair to inhale her sweaty scent. Consumed by the sensuousness of the moment, his muscles went limp with her warmth, as though she were a hot bath he was lowering himself into.

Doors had been opened on the terrace, and some of the couples moved outside to refresh themselves. Andrew maneuvered her toward the cooling breeze and eventually into the night air. The damp chill roused them from their reverie and made them alert enough to focus on the lyrics of the song. "I have my freedom but I don't have much time—faith has been broken, tears must be cried." It seemed like a warning to Andrew, and he felt a sudden shock as a jolt of reality passed through him.

And as she listened to the lyrics, feeling his body grow rigid, Annie was visited by a profound disquietude that left her doubting she would ever see him again. With a few prophetic words from Mick Jagger, all her hopes and dreams for their summer together, the fantasies she'd invented for them—they all came hurtling out of the night sky, disintegrating like meteors that burned through the atmosphere.

They stopped their dance and looked into each other's eyes.

She fought her intuition and said to him, "Promise me, Andrew, please promise me you'll come to France."

He swallowed hard before answering. "I promise I'll try my best."

That was not the right answer, but it was typically Andrew, typically evasive. She insisted as she never had before: "I want your promise to come—not to try."

His heart wanted to give her what she wanted, but his honor demanded that he answer truthfully. "I can't give you that," he was compelled to say.

"Why not?" she demanded to know.

"Oh Annie." In stark contrast to the warmth he was experiencing only moments earlier, he now felt bitterly cold, as though he was standing naked against a harsh, winter wind. "We've been through this so many times."

Angrily now, she said, "And I still don't understand."

"I know you don't, you can't," he realized, "that's the problem."

"I understand what happens between us," she said, choking with pain, "when you let it."

Seeing the hurt in her eyes, her fierce disappointment, he despised himself utterly and completely. But the only response he could muster was, "You have to trust me."

Her heart was sinking, falling into a hole—a long, seemingly endless tunnel. She captured his eyes with hers, trying to stop the fall, but the words she uttered reflected her despair. "You're not going to come, are you?"

His heart felt strange too, as though it pumped air, not blood.

The strong legs she'd been dancing with seemed suddenly as fragile as a bird's. "You're not going to meet me in France, are you? Just tell me the truth."

"The truth." He had to think for an instant what that was; he'd held it from her for so long, it had become obscure, even to him. "All right," he exhaled, "the truth is, I'm engaged, Annie."

The words did not ring true. Instantly she decided that she'd misinterpreted them—a result of the loud music, it distorted her hearing, that had to be it.

He waited a moment, and knowing she was trying to explain away what she'd heard, he determined not to prolong the torture. Every muscle in his body tensed again as he uttered the words he knew would crush her, "I'm engaged to be married. It's not announced yet, but the intention is to do that this summer. We're to be married when I finish at university. Everything is all planned and set."

"That's not true," she insisted. "It can't be true."

God, how he wished it weren't. "It is," he forced himself to say. "It's why I've held back from you, why I couldn't be with you."

Her voice raised and broke in mid-sentence. "But if you love someone else, you should have told me!" Disbelief was slowly shifting to outrage.

"I'm a coward, Annie," he answered. "I'm such a coward that I'm going to marry someone I don't love."

Outrage quickly gave way to bewilderment. Her mouth lifted in one corner and she made a hissing sound before asking, "Do you expect me to understand that?"

Her pain and confusion overwhelmed his own, and he lowered his head to answer, "No, I know you can't."

She raised one hand and faced him with the palm of it. "Stop. I can't listen to any more," she said, then spun around and walked briskly away.

Watching her leave him, he felt suddenly paralyzed, riveted to the spot where he stood.

Annie found her shawl scrunched into her dining chair and snatched it up, wrapping it around her chest in embarrassed awareness of her exposed cleavage. Making her way through the crowd at the entrance hall, she went out through the front door, then walked quickly onto the unlit grounds. Her stride was purposeful, as though she was making for David Russell, but when she was some distance from the manor house she halted, realizing that it was a long walk in her dress shoes. And anyway, it was too dark to manage. She looked back to see the building ablaze with light and heard the sounds of laughter coming from the terrace. It seemed a cruel mocking of her despair. She felt suddenly like the outsider, and walked deeper into the darkness toward an enormous old beech, skulking behind its trunk like a prowler.

Shivering now, she grasped the shawl tightly and longed for a warm coat. But in the midst of this wish, the tears came, silently at first, and uncontrollably. The wrenching sobs soon followed, buckling her bird legs with them and bringing her to the ground. She huddled into her knees and tried to muffle the noise.

In the distance, a tall, proud Scotsman remained alone on the terrace, watching a dark figure make its way across the lawn, then disappear into the woods. He stood apart from the animated group of people near him, unmoving. His heart felt still and bruised. When the first strains of morning birdsong reached Andrew's ears, he looked toward the east. The night was passing quickly. Soon, buffet tables would be set inside with breakfast. He went to the bar and gave the keeper a five-pound note for a half-full bottle of brandy and two glasses, then followed Annie into the darkness.

He found her still crouched behind the tree. He set the bottle and glasses down, then quietly removed his jacket. "Here," he gently offered, "put this beneath you."

The moisture from the ground was seeping through the thin fabric of her dress, but she shook her head in refusal, then turned away from him.

The need to comfort her was like a powerful craving, but he kept his hunger at bay, knowing more anguish was to come. Solemnly, he told her, "I have to finish what I started." He draped the jacket over her shoulders.

Through the blur of her tears, she lifted her gaze to him. "You've said enough," she told him.

He poured a brandy for her, then a larger one for himself. He gulped about half of it before settling next to her. "Please listen to me," he quietly pleaded. "It's the only way you'll understand."

She didn't respond but set her glass aside as she nervously straightened the folds of her dress, lamenting the purchase of it. If only I hadn't bought the damn thing, she thought now. If only I'd listened to my mother. I wouldn't be here, sitting under a tree in the dark, so full of hurt I could die.

Having upended his drink, Andrew forced himself to begin. His only preface was, "I told you about Eton. I was just twelve when I arrived there." The emotional tone was gone, and he droned with the detachment of a lecturer speaking about something that had long ago ceased to interest him. "I told you that they called the first-year boys bugs or tits, but some us us were given other names. A few of us were labeled pretty boys. That's what they called me, pretty boy. And they gave that label to the boys," he hesitated before explaining, "to the ones that some of the upperclassmen were interested in." Fleetingly, he glanced at Annie, then he looked away again. "I didn't understand or know how to handle that kind of attention, and one of the older boys came to my rescue. He befriended me. He was kind and sympathetic, but most importantly, he kept the others away from me."

Annie was experiencing a growing unease, as she asked, "Why are you telling me this?"

He closed his eyes. "Because I've never told anyone. Because you need to know. I want you to know. Please listen to me and let me finish."

Even in the darkness, she could make out the grave expression he wore. "All right," she reluctantly said, "go ahead."

When he exhaled, it felt like the escape of old, stale air, air that he'd been holding in for years. "He kept the others away by saying that I was his, and it was a great joke between us, because I wasn't. But to keep up appearances, he'd have me to his room and we'd spend time alone together, talking, looking at magazines. He had nude magazines that he hid under a floorboard." He shook his head in despair, saying, "I was so young, Annie. I was so naive." He picked up the bottle and poured himself another glass, then held to the neck of it with one hand.

As her anxiety grew, she lifted her glass and sipped at it, hoping to settle her queasy stomach.

Although he'd had to force himself to tell her the things he just had, the rest of it came spilling out now, like so much putrid fluid from a lanced wound. "On one of those occasions he touched me, he fondled me. I was looking at a centerfold and he said he'd just wanted to see if it made me hard. It had, of course, and he explained that he was checking to see if I was aroused by women. It confused me to be sure, but I didn't respond negatively. He was my best friend and I trusted him." His cheeks flushed with heat, but he stifled his embarrassment to continue, realizing there was no turning back now. "It happened again on another occasion. He touched me when I was aroused then smiled approvingly, and that was the end of it. But one day, just before a holiday when most everyone had gone home, we found ourselves among the few left at school. He was waiting with me for my father to arrive, and we were alone in his room." He fought to maintain some emotional distance, and with that effort it sounded as though he were telling the story about someone else. "He gave me a new magazine to look at, but this time he suggested we go into the lavatory so we wouldn't be caught. I can't remember what I was thinking at the time, even if I was thinking, but I was very aroused looking at those pictures," he recalled, "which were of something I'd never seen before—a woman performing oral sex on a man." He fingered the peeling bottle label and searched his empty glass before he could continue. "While I was engrossed in the photos, he knelt before me and undid my trousers, and before I knew what was happening, he had his mouth on me."

Annie had been looking at him while he spoke, but now she turned away. "Oh God," he heard her say softly, despairingly.

Her disappointment stabbed him, and his heart wanted to rupture and spill the life from him so he wouldn't have to endure the pain of her knowing. But it stubbornly went on beating, perhaps because there was relief in having it out at last, in sharing it with someone for the first time in his life. "My father had arrived and the housemaster was looking for me," he continued. "He'd come into the room and we didn't hear him. He opened the door to the lavatory and saw us."

"Jesus," she whispered, barely audibly.

The ensuing silence left his words hovering ominously as he waited for her reaction to his confession, fully expecting her disappointment to turn to revulsion. It was several long moments before he found the courage to add, "My father was told. Because I was so young, they decided that I wasn't to blame and they expelled him." His detachment fled and the pain welled up as he recalled, "On the drive home, my father cried. I'd never seen him cry before. He told me that I'd humiliated and disappointed him in a way he'd never dreamed possible. My shame was unbearable."

Although she could not look at him, the anguish she felt from him was like a punch in the heart. She began to cry again, but her tears were no longer for herself.

Seeing her tears, he longed to reach out to her, to make some physical connection. But he still feared her rejection, so he kept his distance. With all the strength he could muster, he finished telling his story. "My father secured assurance from the school that only those directly involved would ever know. It was a long time before he could even look at me again, let alone be close to me in any fashion. He took it upon himself to watch me carefully and to direct me in everything I did after that, although I sensed he felt nothing but contempt for me." The bottle label tore from his fidgeting, and he stared at it for a moment, as though contemplating how to fix it. "Over the years, things have become somewhat better, but it's made our relationship horridly awkward. I don't believe I'm a homosexual, and I've tried to convince him of that—not that what happened hasn't caused me to doubt myself," he admitted, "but I've never been aroused by any other men. It was truly an isolated incident, though I think that's very hard for my father to believe."

The trees poured out birdsong in the faint but growing light as Annie turned to search his eyes. "I'm so sorry," she started, but she couldn't go on. Words were frustratingly useless, pathetically inadequate to convey what she felt.

Although he meant to sound positive about it, she could sense some desperation as he went on. "About the engagement, my father arranged it. She's a lovely girl I've known all my life, and it's a strategic alliance of sorts. Our families share similar interests. He truly believes he's doing the right thing in making this commitment for me, in focusing me on this," he defended. "He doesn't trust me to do the proper thing on my own, you see."

"Oh," she answered, leaving his eyes and lowering her head.

"It's very important to me to not let him down in any way. I've disappointed him too much already."

Andrew's binding guilt, guilt that had forced him to sacrifice himself in payment, made her profoundly heartsick. "I understand," she whispered as she contemplated the years he'd lost suffocating in that guilt, his innocence strangled by it, unbearably alone in that suffering.

"It's just that," he paused and sighed, "I'm not in love with her, not the way I should be. Meeting you, being with you, has made me see that. I'd accepted my fate before, but now—" He halted abruptly, deciding he should not finish that. "I had to tell you these things because I couldn't allow you to think that I was rejecting you. I want you to understand why I can't go against my father." His voice changed suddenly, taking on a childlike quality. "I want him to trust me again. I need my father to love me again."

With those poignant words, she saw the grown man sitting beside her as he was then, a weeping young boy who believed he'd been bad and lost his father's love forever. Thinking of that boy, she was overcome by a ferocious melancholy, but in the next moment, she was filled with self-loathing as it occurred to her how difficult she'd made things for him by wanting him, by trying to pry him away from the responsibilities he'd so often referred to. "I feel absolutely horrible," she managed through her tears, "because I know I've made things worse for you."

He understood where she was taking that, and it made him immediately protest, "But you haven't!" Like a flash of brilliant sky after the gloom of a storm, it came upon him now that she was not revulsed but sympathetic. He was infused with courage by this realization, and he reached for her hands. "Annie d'Inard, for the first time in my life I've felt like a man, and that's because of you. It's all because of you. How can you feel bad about that? I can never thank you enough for that—never."

Struggling to control her grief, she found his eyes again.

When he recognized forgiveness in hers, his face cleared of pain, and he lifted her hands to kiss them. "I shut myself down," he told her. "I locked myself up after that day. But you brought me out of that. You made me feel things for you that I've never felt before. You unlocked me; you freed me from my prison." The love he felt for her all but dissolved his heartache. "Even with all the complications it's brought, I've never felt better or more alive, and that's because of you. You've got to know that. If you don't understand anything else about all of this, please understand that and know how grateful I am to you."

Day was delivered around them, but they sat shrouded in the mist that clung to the lawn.

His sapphire eyes drew her into his heart. "When I think that I might never have met you, that our paths would never have crossed but for you coming here, when I think of how you've haunted me from the beginning, of how you became a part of my life, how you changed that life, when I think of all these things—" He was too choked with emotion to continue.

She reached her arms for him, and they embraced in a way they hadn't before.

Her lips touching his ear, she whispered, "You've got to get out from under this. You've got to put it behind you." She knew she'd never said anything more true or important in her life.

He nodded slightly and moved his arms to deepen their embrace.

"Whatever I can do," she wanted him to know, "whatever will make it easier, just tell me." Then she had a thought, which she added with resignation. "I won't put anymore pressure on you about France."

He understood something about their relationship that she didn't, and loosening his embrace so that he might see her face again, he told her, "I think the best thing is for you to continue to be yourself with me. You're like a tonic to me, Annie."

They sat quietly in the brightening light, their arms wrapped around one another; the world they looked upon seemed made of green dew. Inside Mount Melville House, breakfast was being consumed by the revelers. Soon its rooms would be empty again and everything that had happened in the night would pass into memory.

As they clung to one another, Annie waded through the muddle of her thoughts, desperately trying to find something to say that might comfort him. She was coming up blank when she realized that he hadn't really finished the story. "Andrew," she asked softly, "whatever became of your friend?"

The sadness returned to his eyes as he answered, "Philip, his name was Philip."

"Do you know what happened to him after he was expelled?"

He released her now and looked away, focusing somewhere in the distant woods. He took two deep breaths before he answered, "He went home." He would have liked to leave it there, to let that be the end of it, but he couldn't because he needed her to understand him completely, to forgive him completely. With the anguish the recollection brought no less intense than the day he was told, he voiced what he was most loathe to remember: "He went home and hung himself."

As that image and all it carried with it took shape in her consciousness, she closed her eyes and forced the air from her lungs. When the pressing need for oxygen compelled her to take it in again, it was wretchedly, excruciatingly painful.

Chapter 20

It was eight in the morning, and Annie had been up for more than twenty-four hours. She should have fallen asleep the moment her head hit the pillow, but she didn't; she lay awake with eyes burning and wide and a heart filled with aching. She heard Andrew's words, felt the enormity of their impact, and saw the disturbing resignation in his eyes as she contemplated the shame and self-doubt that had plagued him throughout his adolescence. And then there was the bomb, the dream-shattering words—"I'm engaged to be married." It all flashed on and off in her mind like a glaring neon sign, making sense one moment and none the next. After twisting from side to side untold numbers of times, she finally fell asleep, but the experience was far from restful.

A dream carried her home. Her brother Timmy was confined to his darkened room with the measles, and the utter loneliness of it broke her heart. She sneaked in to be with him, and when their mother came by she hid under the bed. Crawling out again, she was now with her friend Jane Ann; they were in the midst of a protest and surrounded by hordes of screaming people, their faces contorted with anger. It sickened and terrified Annie, and she began to run, leaping into the fountain that surrounded Europa and the Bull. Wet and shivering, she felt bewildered and alone. Then the sculpture transformed into the cathedral ruins.

The plaintive sounds of a bagpipe poured from St. Rule's Tower, showering her with a melancholy peace.

Gentle hands touched her shoulders, and something warm enveloped her body. She knew it was Andrew, and with closed eyes she put her lips to his. But the kiss was strange and when she looked to see why, it was Susannah who was holding her with her mischievous smile.

When Susannah grasped her breasts, she realized she was naked, but the feeling of warmth returned when Andrew embraced her from behind. She nestled into him and felt his erection press into her flesh. Susannah was still in front of her, and she reached to touch Annie's bottom. Andrew's penis grew harder, pushing toward her opening, and Susannah's hand guided him to it. She felt him pulsate inside of her as their four hands explored her body and their two mouths sought the taste of her. The wild, forbidden pleasure of their intimacy was more compelling than anything she had ever experienced, and she gave herself over to it completely.

It was early evening when she awakened to a knock. Susannah and Mel were at her door ready to leave for the Whaum because Robin had invited them for dinner.

"Ready, my beauty?" Mel asked her.

"Not really," she answered, as she rubbed the sleep from her eyes. "I need a bath first. Why don't you go on ahead? I'll just be a half hour behind you."

Susannah caught a glimpse of something in her face and it made her ask, "Too much of the bubbly last evening?" though she knew that wasn't it.

"Yeah," she answered, then looked away.

"Want some company?" she offered. "Mel can go ahead. He and Robin can get the fish and chips."

Annie tried to smile but couldn't. "Really, I'd just as soon not keep you. I won't be long."

Understanding now that her friend wanted time alone, Susannah told her, "Take your time, darling. We'll see you when we see you."

As Annie slipped into the hot water, she felt happy for the solitude because she needed more time to think. In the span of one hour last night, her entire world had changed.

And seeing Andrew today—she knew that wasn't going to be easy. The young man she'd grown to love, to trust so explicitly, now seemed like someone else. Or did he?

The water cradled her as she sank into it, and she tilted her head backward and closed her eyes. In the enveloping warmth, she recalled her dream and remembered how aroused she'd been by it.

Her thoughts began to race. Susannah would have stayed with me if I'd let her, she realized. She would have come into the bath and sat at my side and scrubbed my back as I'd done for her. And then what? Would we have done more? That day we were together, when she showed me how to masturbate, would I have stopped her if she'd reached to touch me? Would I have pushed her away if she'd done as Philip had done to Andrew?

When the answer came to her, she sat up abruptly, splashing the bathwater onto the linoleum. No, she knew the answer was no. And why is that? she wondered. This sort of thing has never happened before—not to me! There's never even been the slightest spark with another woman. No, it's Susannah who brings this out in me; it's very particularly Susannah. But why? Because she's so damned attractive, she answered herself, so intelligent and funny, so pretty and self-confident—and she cares about me. She reaches out to me as a friend, and that makes me feel good. It makes me feel safe and protected. And I trust her.

As she realized these things about herself, she understood with perfect clarity what had happened to Andrew. He'd been young and vulnerable—isolated in his early years at school, then befriended at Eton by someone he admired: an older boy who cared about him, protected him, made him feel safe, but then made overtures he didn't understand. And in his desire to go on trusting, he'd set aside his confusion and given in, yielding to emotions he'd had no experience with.

She ached for him as she contemplated the pain it had wrought, but she couldn't fault him. How could she? She knew firsthand how powerful and compelling those feelings were.

Quickly she shampooed her hair, then rinsed it with fresh water. As the water gurgled its way through the drain, she dried herself, then wrung her dripping locks. In front of the mirror now, she used a forearm to wipe away the fog. Seeing that aspect of her arm made her recall the night when Jason had left her with so many bruises. She'd stood in front of a mirror then, too, staring at the marks, wondering if she'd ever be the same.

How I wish that night had never happened, she lamented, but in the next moment she recognized that if it hadn't, she never would have come to Scotland. In all probability, she would have stayed in college and gone on with her life without ever seeing St. Andrews, without ever walking its beautiful streets scented with flowers and salt air, without ever standing amid the windy, mystical ruins. She never would have met Susannah and Mel, whose friendship had enriched her so, never sat by the fire in a 400-year-old pub, planning her journey on Percy B. She never would have known the joy of dancing to bagpipes in celebration of the first May sunrise, nor experienced the pleasure of working in the garden at the Whaum, nor enjoyed the perfect peace of tea in its little parlor with Andrew. Andrew, most tragically of all, she never would have known Andrew.

If I could go back and change it, she now questioned, if I could erase that one, horrible night—knowing it would also remove these people and places from my life—would I? She looked hard into her reflection, without blinking, until she knew the answer.

Percy B. sat waiting outside Fraser as usual; as usual, she shunned him. She might have started him up and gotten to the Whaum more quickly, but she was in no hurry. She took the long way, following Buchanan Gardens at a careful pace, stopping now and again to admire a particular garden. It was only a week, that's all she had left, and she wanted to savor every waking minute.

As she drew near the cottage, her heart moved into its customary dance, and she had to give herself a talking to. He's engaged, she told herself. He's going to marry someone else. You can't carry on like this anymore. But engagements can be broken, her heart argued back, and anyway, he doesn't love her: He admitted that.

The old gate moaned as she pushed it open, but she halted when she heard the sound of footfalls on the gravel.

Andrew's voice carried from a corner of the entrance garden. "Annie, don't go in yet."

They stood for a moment, looking silently into one another.

"Walk with me?" he asked.

She nodded, and he held the gate for her.

They were almost to the castle before he spoke again. "I meant to say this last night. I need to ask your forgiveness. I should have told you straight off what my situation was; it's just, I didn't want to. I wanted to be with you, and that would have been impossible if you knew. I deliberately deceived you and that was wrong, but I did it because—" he stammered slightly, "because I wanted to be with you so much, so very much."

She responded the only way she could; she reached for his hand and tenderly embraced it with hers. The burden his heart was carrying lifted then, enough that he was able to take her in his arms and press her to his chest.

They returned to the Whaum so they wouldn't hold up dinner, but after a few hours of eating and drinking and quiet conversation, Mel and Susannah headed back to David Russell. Carol MacDonald was there, Robin's date for the ball, and it seemed right to give them some time alone, so Annie and Andrew went walking again. This time they settled on their favorite bench just outside the cathedral grounds. It was past ten on a Sunday night, and most of the town had gone to bed.

Their view over the sea was almost directly north, and they gazed off into the sky, still colored with dusk.

"I'll miss this," she said. "I'll miss these long days."

He took hold of her hand. "Is that the only thing you'll miss?"

The question irritated her, and she snapped at him, "How can you ask that?"

His head drooped slightly. "Please forgive me."

Still bristling impatience, she told him, "And you don't need to keep asking that. You already have my forgiveness!"

Knitting his brow, he questioned, "I do?"

"Of course, you do! Do you think that after everything we've meant to each other, I'm going to hold things against you that you can't help, that you can't change? Do you hold what happened to me against me?"

His response was impassioned. "Of course, I don't! What I feel about that, what I didn't say the other night—I could kill him for what he did to you! I could wrap my hands around his throat and choke the life out of him." He had to work at regaining his composure, his ire had risen that much.

She had not meant to inflame him. "I'd never want that. It wouldn't help me. It would only break my heart," she said, then softened her tone to add, "and anyway, what we need, both of us, is to move on."

Briefly, he looked into her eyes.

"It's more difficult for you," she realized, "because you're the kind of person who keeps things bottled up, but that's no good. That only makes things worse."

He seemed annoyed with himself when he responded, "I know."

"I can help you with that." Pausing for a moment to collect her thoughts, she leaned forward and looked toward the sea. "Since last night, I've been doing a lot of thinking, trying to put things into perspective." Her face had been tensed, but as she turned toward him, it relaxed. "The reason I came to St. Andrews in the first place was because of what happened with Jason. And today I asked myself, if I could go back and change things so that night would never have happened—knowing it would also change my future, take away my chance to come here and meet you—would I do it? Would I change it?" Her brow wrinkled as she looked into his perfect eyes. "And guess what answer I came up with?"

He shook his head to say he didn't know, but his heart was picking up the pace, his breaths coming more quickly.

"I don't think I would, and do you know why? It's because I'm better for it, Andrew. Because I'm alive and well and somehow a better person because of it. I'm stronger and happier and much more realistic, and I've learned to love and appreciate life in a way I never did before." She smiled at him now. "And I know the same is true for you. You've come away from that experience a kind, sensitive, strong person, and you've got your whole incredible life ahead of you to do whatever you choose with."

He seemed embarrassed by what she said. "Annie, you give me too much credit."

"I do not!" she interrupted. "You may not know it yet, but you're all those things and more." Some of her smile fell away. "But there's something else I want to say to you. I want you to know that I understand what went on with Philip because of something that's happened to me—with Susannah."

He began to feel anxious, and he turned to the side so that he might better see her face.

"I've found myself in circumstances with her where I've been attracted to her—sexually—" she bravely declared, "and that's never happened to me before with a woman. We haven't been together," she wanted him to know, "but the feelings are there for both of us, I think."

He shifted his focus to the ground around his feet and tried to keep his emotions from coloring what he had heard.

"Until today it's confused me, but because of what you told me, I think I understand it now. I haven't been attracted to her because she's a woman, Andrew, but rather in spite of it. What's appealed to me is the person—the warm, generous person who's reached out and been my friend," she explained. "The fact that she's the wrong sex isn't my choice. It's just the way it is. She's an extraordinary human being and that's very sexy, I think, no matter what package it comes in." Smiling again, she went on to say, "And I believe that's exactly what happened with Philip. He was kind and protective. You were lonely and hungry for affection, and he offered it to you." She reached for his hand, and he squeezed hers in response. "And besides that," she thought to add, "Susannah told me what happens in your same-sex boarding schools. It's not natural being kept apart like that. That's the time you discover your sexuality and it's damned hard doing it alone. There needs to be someone to explore it with." Her voice had a lightness to it now, a little ring of laughter.

His head lifted back suddenly as he expelled the air from his lungs.

It was hard to tell what he was feeling just now. "Have I upset you?" she worried.

Slowly and deliberately he closed this eyes, then he opened them on her. "Your acceptance of me, your trust, you've given me the greatest gift I've ever received, and as long as I live, I swear I'll never forget you, Annie d'Inard."

The way he said that sounded like a good-bye. She let go of his hand, then pulled in her legs to put her feet on the bench, wrapping her arms around her knees. Resting her chin between her knees, she cast her eyes downward when she said, "Last night, I told you I'd stop pressuring you about France and I will, but there's one more thing I need to say about it, because I want you to know how I feel."

"Never be afraid to say what's in your heart, whatever it is," he assured her.

As though she might find the right words scattered there, her eyes kept searching the ground beneath them. Then she put her legs down abruptly and turned toward him. With conviction enough for both of them, she said, "I want you to come. I don't care about your engagement, and I don't need a commitment. I just want to be with you. I've never felt this way about anyone before, but it's so strong and important to me, I think I'd do anything to hold onto it, even if it's just for a little while—even if a month or so is all we'll ever have."

My God, my dearest God, he cried in his heart, I love her so much, so very much. Help me not to hurt her; help me do the right thing. "Oh Annie, there are so many things I want to say to you. But you must understand something about me. I can't, I won't break promises. I won't say things to you I can't support with every inch of my being, and I won't walk away from commitments I've already made." A solid mass seemed to have formed in his throat, and it imparted a tone of uncertainty. "I'm going to do my damnedest to be with you this summer, but if I can't, promise me you'll never think it was because I didn't care about you. Promise me that." He reached to stroke her dark, silky hair and tenderly tucked some of it behind one ear.

It wasn't the response she'd hoped for, but it was the one she expected. She swallowed her pride and tried to cover her heartache as she whispered, "I promise," then laid her hand over his as it caressed her dampened cheek.

The approaching night hovered above the sea; their minds saw it as the future and their thoughts wandered into it as the wind gathered its evening pace. High above the horizon, strange colors began to emerge, like dawn in the wrong place. At the same time they heard a peculiar, far-off sound that was reminiscent of radio static. The colors grew brighter and more distinct, with waves of red and flashes of green that rippled into gold, then melded to orange.

It took a moment to register, but Andrew grew excited when he realized what they were witnessing. "Annie! Look, do you see? It's the northern lights—the aurora!"

"Oh, my God!" she exclaimed. "Is it really?"

"It is!"

"It's so beautiful!"

"It's breathtaking!" he agreed.

The worry that had clouded her heart and mind was suddenly lifted, and she gasped when she realized why. "It's a sign! It's a sign from the gods, Andrew—a cosmic message!"

He chuckled, "You sound like a hippie."

"Well, I am, you know, pretty much. But really, it is a sign! I know it is!"

Bending first to kiss her forehead, he went back to stroking her hair.

She confidently proclaimed, "It's to remind us that there are things far more important than the silly details we worry over, things beyond our control."

Oddly enough, her explanation made a strange kind of sense to Andrew.

"They approve of us," she decided, "and they're telling us not to give up." The lights were diminishing now, folding in upon themselves like lowered sails. But as they faded, she was left with the very certain knowledge that she and Andrew were destined for one another, and it filled her with hope. "Even if you don't make it this summer," she told him, "we're going to be together again. I know that. I can feel it."

As quickly as it had begun, the aurora was ending, and Annie knew it was because the message had been delivered. She nestled herself back into Andrew's arms, and he took tight hold of her. Far from easing his anguish about their parting, the sight they had just witnessed distressed him further and gave him the disquieting sense that something ominous was looming ahead of them, that was going to tear them apart.

* * *

On their return trip to David Russell, Susannah seemed pensive, and Mel questioned her about it.

"Tired, Mademoiselle Barclay?"

"No, not really," she responded.

"You were awfully quiet this evening, not a bit yourself," he teased.

"I was observing," she answered, a tad flippantly.

He already knew the answer, but he asked anyway, "And just whom were you observing?"

"Andrew, of course."

He laughed at her. "See anything, did you?"

"The usual," she quipped, "and then some."

"Oh? And what, pray tell, was that?"

Although no one was nearby, she quickly scanned their immediate vicinity before asking, "Does the family name Stuart-Gordon mean anything to you?"

He raised his eyes skyward, then shook his head. "Can't say it does."

"I'm not surprised," she responded. "But if you knew the first thing about the aristocracy, it would."

He continued to tease her. "Do enlighten me then, Mademoiselle, for obviously it means something to you."

Her facial expression was pure annoyance. "It's only the oldest, bluest bloodline in all of Britain, you imbecile, and some say the family with the true right to the throne— truer than the Hanoverians."

Now it struck a familiar cord. "You mean the Earl of Kilmartin, that chap?"

She sighed exasperation. "The same."

He scratched his head. "Isn't he the university chancellor?"

That was one thing she hadn't thought of. "Oh right! He is! I'd forgotten."

"So what's that to do with the price of eggs?" he wondered.

Not wanting to be overheard, she lowered her voice to a whisper. "I did a bit of snooping this evening in Andrew's bedroom."

"Susannah!"

"I know."

"I'm ashamed of you!"

Sheepishly, she responded, "I couldn't help myself. But you know I've always been curious about him, and that Bentley last evening—Annie may have thought it was, but that was no hired car, and you know that as well as I do."

"So? That doesn't give you the right to go nosing about in the man's personal things."

"Hush!" Someone was approaching them, following the path from David Russell to Melville Hall. When he was out of earshot, she whispered again, "I found letters in his dresser drawer, all addressed to an A.J.A. Stuart-Gordon! And when I was shuffling through them, I noticed one in particular that bore a noble coat of arms and the return address of Crinan Castle, Kilmartin, Argyll."

In spite of himself, Mel's eyes grew wide. "So you think?"

She nodded eagerly as she told him, "I didn't have chance to read it, but it began 'Dearest Grandson.'" Her face settled into smugness.

"Holy mother!"

"My thoughts exactly," she grinned.

He was coming to the same conclusion as Susannah, but the reaction was his own and typically Mel. "He might have bought our rounds a time or two more, the tight bugger!"

She frowned at him. "Do be serious."

"I am!"

They were almost to his room now. They remained quiet as they mounted the stairs and didn't speak again until they had closed the door.

"So what do you mean to do?" he questioned her.

Susannah shrugged, then folded her arms. "I don't know. Maybe I'll ask him. I may just come straight out and ask him who the blazes he is."

"And how are you to do that," he wondered, "without letting him know you were snooping?"

Her eyes darted to one side of the room, then the other. "*Burke's Peerage and Baronetage,*" she proposed.

He wasn't following her. "What about it?"

"I'll research the family tomorrow," she decided, "in the library. If I find what I'm looking for, I'll say I came across it by accident." Once again, she appeared quite pleased with herself.

Mel smiled seductively before he began unbuttoning her blouse. "Regular little Miss Marple, aren't you, my dear?" he teased, then ran his tongue along the side of her neck.

She giggled in response and reached for his crotch.

Susannah had ample time between her morning labs, but she practically ran to the library anyway. She went straight to the reference section. When she located a copy of *Burke's Peerage*, she carried it to a quiet corner. She gasped slightly when she recognized the coat of arms and the crest from the letter. Able to study it now, she saw that it was a wild boar amid heather, hovered over by an eagle with a thistle in his beak. Beneath it read: The 22nd Earl of Kilmartin (Alexander Malcolm Andrew Stuart-Gordon), Viscount Rannoch,

Baron Kilmartin of Mull, and Lord High Constable of Scotland—Seat: Crinan Castle, Kilmartin, Argyll.

She understood that as Lord High Constable he was the first subject in Scotland after the Blood Royal, and if that weren't enough, the entry revealed that he was married to Lady Catherine Victoria Marguerite Bowes-Lyon, who was first cousin to the Queen Mother. Reading on, she discovered that their only issue—the heir presumptive—was Donald Malcolm Duncan, who carried the courtesy title of Viscount Rannoch and a birth date that would make him the right age to be Andrew's father. He was married to Lady Mary Elizabeth Louise Maclean, the youngest daughter of the Marquess of Kintyre, and of their three children, the only son was Andrew James Alexander—A.J.A.—the same initials she'd seen on the envelope! When she recognized that the birth date was the right age for Andrew and that he, too, carried a courtesy title, the Baron Kilmartin of Mull, she declared aloud, "The sly bastard!" This drew an insistent "Shhh!" from a nearby librarian.

Annie slept late that morning and missed breakfast, so she didn't arrive at the Whaum until nearly lunchtime. No one was home so she let herself in, then retrieved her gloves and tools from the small utility room. Only a few weeds had sprouted and not much else needed to be done in the garden, so she finished quickly, then walked slowly around her domain, noticing every bud that had newly appeared and wondering if she would see any of them open before she left. When she went inside again, the little cottage was unearthly still, and the quiet exaggerated the persistent ticking of the mantel clock.

A loneliness came upon her suddenly, and it drew her to Andrew's bedroom. It was also quiet there, but his presence made it less so. She could feel the haste with which he'd prepared himself this morning, leaving his clothes strewn about, his pajamas in a heap on the floor. The bedclothes were left unstraightened, too, and she impulsively lifted a pillow, then brought it to her face. The scent of him was strong, intoxicating, and she sank to the bed with it. A thought came to her mind as she clung to his pillow, a thought she didn't want to have. I wonder what she looks like. I wonder what her name is. I wonder if she feels electricity jumping through her insides when he smiles at her—as I do. After several long minutes, she finally, reluctantly, replaced the pillow and left his room, closing the door behind her.

Andrew was not at the pub that night, but Robin was there chatting with some friends when Annie approached him.

After exchanging greetings, she asked him, "Where's Andrew?"

Robin had a tendency toward distance, but tonight it seemed more marked than usual. He smiled rather oddly, then sipped his pint before answering, "Didn't he tell you? He borrowed a car and went to Edinburgh to see his father."

She was instantly overcome with dread and worry. "Oh, and no, he didn't say. Is he coming back tonight?"

"I expect so," he answered dryly, "but I couldn't say when."

* * *

Andrew sat quietly in his father's hotel suite, watching him take first one telephone call and then another. When the phone rang the third time, Andrew finally spoke up. "I've got to get back tonight, Father. Couldn't they hold your calls for the next half hour?"

The tall, handsome heir apparent to the Earldom of Kilmartin, whose only son was his mirror image, rang up the desk. Andrew could picture the groveling on the other end. "Yes, your lordship. Of course, your lordship. Is there anything else we might do for you, your lordship?"

Donald, Viscount Rannoch, held his distinguished face expressionless as he took a seat across the room from his son and asked, "All right. What's so important?"

Knowing that his father frowned upon emotional displays, he was trying to play it cool. But the anxiety Andrew always felt in his presence made him stammer slightly as he began, "I, umm, I didn't like the way we left things after our conversation regarding the American girl."

"Oh?"

He was doing it again—what he always did, pushing in that quietly aggressive way he had. Deciding to try a different approach, Andrew asked him, "How's Mother?"

"She's well. I understand she sent her car for you the other night so you could take the girl to a ball."

"That's right." As if you didn't know, he said to himself. And I know you only approved it because you wanted the driver to report on me.

"She must have been impressed," his father ventured. "I don't imagine she'd ridden in a Bentley before."

He shrugged the leading question off. "She didn't make much of it. She only asked me to convey her thanks to Mother."

"Hmm," was all Donald answered, looking away.

Andrew suddenly experienced a surge of courage that led him to say, "Listen, Father, since you insist on keeping her in the conversation, I'd like to assure you of something."

As he folded his arms, he responded, "I'm listening."

"I don't want you fretting over this thing," he told him, then paused to remember what he'd rehearsed on the drive to Edinburgh. "You needn't, because in the time I've spent with her recently, I've come to realize that she's not someone I could stay involved with. She's attractive, to be sure, and I enjoy her company, but aside from the physical, there isn't much else between us. So you needn't concern yourself, because I'm certain whatever there is between us will burn itself out quickly." For emphasis, he affected what he thought was a knowing grin.

"I see," Donald smiled. "Well, that is reassuring. When is she leaving for France?"

Nonchalantly, as though it didn't at all matter, he answered, "The end of the week." In truth, every time he thought of that it tore at his heart and ripped at his gut.

"I'm happy to hear it," Donald let him know. "Your idea about a rendezvous with her must seem fairly ridiculous to you now. Am I right?"

In spite of himself, he stuttered again. "Well—well, not entirely. It hasn't quite burned itself out yet, and you know what you'd suggested about having a fling with her," he reminded his father. "I was thinking, France would be as good a place as any for that. I'm not likely to run into anyone we know there—not in the places I'd be with her, am I? And when I'm through with her, I can just be on my way and she can go back to America—end of story, right?" Saying those words left him with a sick feeling and the sense that they had been uttered by someone else.

"Right," his father responded. They sat quietly together over the next few moments while Donald scrutinized his son. He broke the silence with, "You'd like me to give you permission to go to France, I expect, now that I'm reassured."

Though he feared what was coming, Andrew bravely attempted a smile. "I'd hoped you would when you understood that the situation is not as serious as you'd first thought."

With decided sarcasm and his firmest, most authoritative tone, his father told him, "Well, let me assure you of something, Andrew." He uncrossed his legs and zeroed in on his son as though he were a target, then fired in rapid succession, "You haven't fooled me, not for a moment. I see now that this thing is even more dangerous than I'd originally thought. You've never lied to me before. After all we've been through, you've never lied to me. If she can make you lie to me—well, I can see that I was right about her. You put your mind back to your work and then you come straight home. I take this thing very seriously. If the King can abdicate for a woman like that repulsive Mrs. Simpson, well it's plain that this can cause someone as young and foolish as you to make the worst mistake of his life. Say good-bye to her and come home. I'll keep you busy enough that you'll soon forget her, but rest assured, I'm not going to let you make another mistake greater than the one you've already made. You've a particular destiny you must hold to, and you know what it is I mean by that. Do we understand each other?" While delivering his edict, he'd hardly taken a breath.

Andrew glared at him; he abhorred the reference made to his destiny because his father always used it to exert control. "I understand you, Father. I've always understood you," he found the courage to say. "I wish that just once in your life you'd try to understand me." His eyes filled with tears at that, and he struggled to keep them from spilling over.

Recognizing how upset his son was, Donald almost softened. "But I do understand you," he said, thinking suddenly of the young woman he'd loved and almost left Andrew's mother for. He reflected for a moment on how important she'd been to him, how he'd count the minutes until he could be with her again. "Look, Andrew, you've a lovely fiancée who's expecting to see more of you this summer, and you've other responsibilities, as well. You need to start learning the family business. And your grandfather is in poor health, you know. You should go and see him—be with the family if the worst happens. You can't afford to let a distraction like this keep you from your duties, your family." The viscount tried to smile. "I know you think I'm interfering, but as your father I feel I must, because you've no experience with women. When you're older, you'll be able to handle these matters on your own. I've learned to keep distractions like her in their place," he confided, albeit a little too proudly, "but that comes with maturity. Right now, you don't have that maturity and you need a firm hand to guide you. Am I making myself clear?"

Andrew spat the words, "Perfectly, Father, perfectly," his face plainly displaying the revulsion he felt over what his father had said. And in the next moment, he was even more sickened by what he'd done, attempting to win his father's approval through deception, through lies, and the denigration of his feelings for Annie. The extravagant hotel suite in which they sat seemed suddenly rank, filled with the odor of betrayal. He snatched up his jacket and went directly to the door to escape the stench, but before opening it, he turned back to his father for one more volley. "Just for the record, I don't consider philandering a sign of maturity, nor is it anything to be the slightest bit proud of."

Although that insult struck home and tapped into the regret he harbored, Donald responded with cool detachment, "I'll see you at Crofthill, Andrew." Then he walked back to his desk and the telephone.

Chapter 21

Tuesday after breakfast, Annie got the clothes together that she would be mailing home. She folded the blue gown carefully, wrapping it in some tissue paper she'd saved. Then she wrote a note to her mother that she included in the box, asking her to be especially careful of the dress. It said, "I wore it to a ball in a castle. My date came for me in a chauffeur-driven car, wearing a kilt and looking like a prince. I want to save this dress so I can remember that night forever and ever."

She used the bungee cords Colin had given her to strap the package onto the luggage carrier, then drove Percy B. into town wearing neither jacket nor helmet. It was a particularly warm and beautiful day, and her long hair flowed behind her like a dark veil. She drove up Buchanan Gardens, past scores of students she now knew, many of whom shouted and waved to her as she passed. She went through the West Port and up South Street, then pulled into a parking space in front of the post office. As she secured the bike on its stand, Colin Wemyss walked over to greet her; he was accompanied by a young man Annie had never seen before.

"We heard you coming. I told John, that's my old bike; there's no mistaking the sound of her."

"He's a loud one, all right," she grinned.

"Oh, right, it's now a 'he,' " he laughed. "May I introduce you to my good friend? He's come to visit me from Oxford. Annie d'Inard, this is John Millar-Graham."

"It's nice to meet you," she said quietly.

He was a good-looking young man with a warm but devilish smile. "It's a great pleasure to meet you," he answered. "Colin wrote that he'd sold his bike to an American girl. He said you were amazingly competent on the thing, but I must admit, seeing you driving into town just now was more than amazing. I feel a little in awe of you."

"You're making me blush," she said, casting her eyes downward. "It's not a big deal. It's just unusual, that's all."

His smile deepened as he said, "Well, I'm still in awe."

"Posting something this morning?" Colin inquired, glancing at the package.

"Yeah, I'm lightening up for the trip. Sending home some things I won't be needing."

"Good idea. May I help you?"

"Thanks, Colin, but it's not heavy," she answered, releasing the cords from around the box.

"Please allow me." John gently pried the package from her hands and gestured for her to lead the way into the building.

When they came out, Colin asked if she might join them for lunch.

"Oh, thanks, but I've eaten already," she responded.

"Will you be at the Scores, then, tonight?" he asked.

She nodded.

John was still gaping at her. "Perhaps you'll let me buy you a drink."

She smiled and blushed again, as she answered, "That'd be nice."

Susannah knew Andrew had tutorials during the afternoon in St. Salvator's College, and she waited for him in the quadrangle. When she saw him emerge from the building, she quickly approached him.

"I say, Andrew, can we talk?" she asked with uncharacteristic abruptness.

Something showed in her face that he read as concern. "I take it it's important," he observed.

"I think it is. I'll stand you a pint at the Central."

"All right," he answered, then let her lead the way.

It was tea time, and they were the only ones in the pub. They settled onto a banquette at the back of the room and sipped at their beers without speaking, each of them looking straight ahead, their eyes on the young man who polished the oak bar.

Andrew was the one who broke the silence. "You wanted to talk?"

Although she was hoping to have gotten to the bottom of her glass before broaching the subject, halfway through her Guinness was going to have to do. "There's no use beating about the bush," she said. "Is your grandfather the Earl of Kilmartin?" There, I've done it, she congratulated herself, lifting her pint again.

Andrew released the breath he'd been holding but didn't otherwise respond.

"Annie has no idea who you are, does she?"

For a moment he considered asking how she found out, then he dropped the idea, realizing it didn't matter. It was pointless to deny it now, and anyway, he didn't want to. "No, she doesn't. And yes, he is."

Susannah gasped, and her voice went up an octave as she questioned, "Are you going to tell her?"

Gently, he asked, "Could you lower your voice, please?" The young man doing the polishing was near them now, tackling the tables.

She nodded and brought a hand to her mouth.

"I hadn't planned on it," he answered.

"Why?" she asked in a whisper. "Don't you think someone that close to you has a right to know?"

He drank more beer before saying, "Under ordinary circumstances, but these are not ordinary circumstances."

"Is it because you've kept it a secret from everyone? I don't understand that. Why have you done that?"

With a hint of irritation, he informed her, "Because I've wanted to be a student, Susannah, just a student—like you, like everyone else—not the grandson of a peer, who also happens to be the university's chancellor. I didn't want the attention. Surely you can understand that."

As she considered it, she recognized how his identity would set him apart and attract the wrong sort of friends—the kind that weren't really friends at all. "That's quite a reasonable thing, actually," she admitted. "But how have you managed? Surely there are people around who know you."

He sighed before explaining. "Before I arrived, my grandfather dispatched a letter. It explained my desire for privacy, and it went to all the important staff and faculty at the university, requesting their help in maintaining that. And, of course, any friends or relatives who might be around—they were told of my wishes, too."

Susannah merely nodded, realizing that the esteem in which the earl was held would assure their cooperation. "But you've lied to Annie," she protested. "You've told her you live on a sheep farm, that your people are sheep farmers, for God's sake!"

He couldn't meet her eyes as he answered. "It's not an outright lie, though I admit I've deliberately misled her. We do live at our estate in Renfrewshire, and it is a sheep farm. My grandparents are at Crinan Castle."

She pursed her lips and slowly shook her head. "It's still not right."

"No, it isn't, but I'm trying to protect her," he defended, "truly, I am."

"From what, Andrew?"

The young man seemed to be listening to their conversation, because he slowed his movements and turned an interested ear toward their table. Having observed this, Andrew stood and pulled fifty pence from his pocket and laid it near their glasses. "Let's finish this outside," he said to Susannah.

They headed down Market Street toward the cathedral. Once they'd turned onto Castle Street, he revisited her question. "I'm protecting Annie from my father," he told her. "He's upset enough about the situation because he thinks he knows how I feel about her, but he doesn't really. He doesn't know the true depth of it. If he did, he'd call on his friends at Whitehall and have her deported."

A kind of burning sincerity always showed in Andrew's expression, but he looked more earnest and concerned than Susannah had ever seen him. It made her feel oddly nervous, perhaps a little frightened. When they had turned onto North Street, she stopped walking to say, "I'm worried about Annie."

He had taken a few steps ahead of her, but he turned around now, slipping his hands into the pockets of his Harris tweed. "That's two of us, then, but that sounds so trite," he realized. "You know I feel much more than that."

The sun was high and brilliant, and the cathedral ruins were visible behind Andrew as they stood on the windy street. Susannah observed his tall, regal form as it was framed by the towering spires, thinking what an appropriate backdrop that was for the heir to so much Scottish history, a young man whose ancestors had led the Scots for more than 1,000 years. "So what's to be done?" she wondered, thinking of Annie again.

"I hadn't planned on telling her before she leaves, and I haven't changed my mind about that," he informed her. He let that sink in before asking, "And you? What do you plan to do now that you know?"

She looked into his eyes now, and she imagined that she saw what Annie must see: unfathomable depth that drew you in, made you want to dive headlong into it. "I don't know," she told him. "I don't know what the right thing is. I need to think."

Softly, he beseeched her, "May I ask a favor? Before you do anything, will you please hear me out?"

Susannah was becoming mesmerized; in the span of one short hour, Andrew had undergone a transformation, allowing his aristocratic bearing to show through, and his charm and elegance were having their way with her. She nodded her agreement to his request without even realizing she'd done it.

"I'd like you to consider something," he proposed, then paused to take a deliberate breath. "Although I'm going to try to convince my father to let me meet her in France, he may not, and then I'll have to make a choice. He won't make that easy." He looked into her eyes again, and when he did, she nearly swooned from their intensity. "If I want to be with her and he's against it, he'll make it the most difficult choice of my life. I don't know how I'll fall when that time comes; I can't say. But it is fair to say that I may never see Annie again after she leaves here." Thinking of how that would affect her friend, Susannah suddenly wanted to cry.

He removed his hands from his pockets and clasped them together, almost as though he were praying. Casting his eyes downward, he continued, "If it comes to that, it may be less painful for her if she doesn't have to deal with the idea that it was my duty and family that I chose over her." Lifting his gaze again, he asked, "Do you see what I mean, Susannah? Do you see why I've chosen to keep this from her?"

It was becoming very clear; some mature practicality was showing through Andrew's sincerity, and she could not argue with the logic of it. She was not a member of that privileged class, but she knew enough about it to understand that it was a tight-knit group, one that rarely admits outsiders. And she knew from Annie that he'd already warned her about his so-called obligations. She had seemed to accept that he might not be able to join her. "Yes, I'm afraid I do," she solemnly responded.

Attempting a smile, he told her, "You're a good friend to her. Her feelings for you run very deep, you know." He experienced a momentary twinge of jealousy regarding that very thing. "I know you'll decide to act in her best interest."

As the realization struck her, she looked him square in the eyes. "You're going to break her heart, Andrew. You're not going to meet her and it'll break her heart."

He held his breath, then released it in a heavy, dejected sigh. "I wish that weren't so. You don't know how much I wish that weren't so." Looking off into the distance, he added in a quiet voice, "Sometimes I think I'd give anything to keep that from happening."

Susannah stared at him in silence, not knowing what to say. When the tolling church bells made her realize that she was late for an important tutorial, she bid him a hasty goodbye and began walking away. She felt suddenly anxious for him and turned back to see if he was all right; he hadn't moved, and his eyes were filled with pain. A chill ran through her in that moment, and it was then that she recognized how very deeply he loved Annie.

When they'd packed in their studies for the evening, Mel and Susannah accompanied Annie to the Scores. Susannah seemed a little sullen as they walked, and Annie took her arm.

"What's wrong?" she asked her friend.

"A bit under the weather, that's all," Susannah answered, though in truth she was deeply troubled by the decision she'd made to keep what she knew about Andrew from her.

"We don't have to go out tonight," Annie offered. "Mel and I could take you back to your room and make you some tea."

"Right you are," he chimed in. "Whatever would make Mademoiselle Barclay feel better. I know she's had a tough day." She'd already told him about her conversation with Andrew, so Mel understood the origins of her mood.

"No, thanks," she responded. "What I need is a pint or two, then I'll be up to speed."

They went directly to the bar and ordered their drinks. The pub was especially crowded, and Colin and John had to maneuver their way through the crowd to them. When Colin introduced John, Susannah brightened somewhat, perhaps from the prospect of engaging in one of her favorite pastimes.

"What are you studying at Oxford, John?" she asked, her curiosity in high gear.

"I'm an art student at Trinity College," he answered.

"And how long are you staying in St. Andrews?"

"Just until Sunday," he informed her. "Then I head back to finish the term."

Annie had been quietly searching the room for Andrew, and John made an effort to bring her into the conversation. "Colin tells me you're planning an expedition to the continent."

"Yes, I am." It was hard to keep her eyes from the door.

"When are you off?" he wondered.

"I'm leaving Monday."

He grinned when he asked, "Monday, really? And you're going alone?"

"I'm leaving alone, yes, but a friend may join me later in France," she informed him, still watching the door.

"That's nice," he commented, briefly turning his head to see what it was that interested her so. "It's a pity you're leaving Monday. If it were Sunday, I might have asked you for a lift to Oxford."

"Oh, well, that's too bad," she responded absentmindedly. She was growing worried about Andrew and paying little attention to their conversation.

"I don't know if it's possible, but if you could change your departure date and give me a lift on Sunday," he ventured, "I'd be happy to show you my hospitality in Oxford. I could show you 'round the colleges and the points of interest."

Andrew came in at that moment.

"Thank you, John. I'll think about it," she answered, only half hearing what he'd said. Then she made her way toward Andrew.

Susannah had been listening to their conversation, and when Annie walked away, she said, "Do tell me more about yourself, John."

Andrew had been drinking already; she tasted it in his kiss.

"You were supposed to be studying," Annie scolded as she took her mouth away.

"I tried. I couldn't keep my mind on the bloody thing." He'd been too absorbed with the idea that Susannah might tell what she knew, but he could see now that she hadn't. He breathed a sigh of relief as he asked, "Want a drink?"

His demeanor distressed her. "You're upset about something."

"It's nothing," he answered. "Just the same old shit, the same sodding thing."

It was now obvious to her that he was quite drunk, because he'd never spoken that way in front of her before. "Have you had dinner?" she asked.

"Yes, no, I don't remember."

"Why don't we go to the Whaum and I'll fix you something?" she offered.

"I'd rather have a drink," he told her. Finding an opening next to Susannah, he leaned in to catch the bartender's attention. "Buy you a drink, old girl?" he asked, when he noticed her. "How about a real drink for a change? Something other than that bloody Irish piss."

Looking down her nose at him, she declared, "You're rather rude tonight, and a bit blotter, too, I see."

As though itching for a fight, he sharply retorted, "What of it?"

Susannah merely smiled, thinking to herself, so you want to go at it, do you? "Of course, I'll have a drink," she answered. "I'll have a single malt, and make it that twenty-year-old stuff, will you? You know the one I want—that expensive swill, made by that aristocratic family. What's their name? I've forgotten, Stuart something or other?" Unhappy though she was about keeping his secret, she realized now that there was perverse pleasure to be had from tormenting him with it.

He responded with disdain, "What do you want to drink that rot for? I wouldn't touch that piss myself."

She wanted to laugh, but instead she sneered, "Well, doesn't that take the biscuit? Then I'll have whatever you're having. After all, you're the whisky expert, aren't you?"

He turned to her now, and she saw anguish in his eyes as he implored, "Give me a bloody break, will you?"

Annie stood behind them while this conversation went on, feeling confused and left out.

John was still there, too, and once again he made the effort to speak with her. "That your friend?"

She nodded.

"Seems vexed about something, doesn't he? Well, I imagine it's something important that's set him off."

Andrew turned around to them and handed Annie a Scotch. "Who's this, then?"

"John Millar-Graham," Susannah informed him. "He's a friend of Colin's come from Oxford for a visit."

"Want a drink, old man? My treat this evening."

"Why not," John answered. "Thanks."

"Andrew bloody Gordon's the name," he declared, then with an American-style handshake, squeezed John's hand to the point of pain.

Susannah couldn't help giggling at his behavior.

But John was not amused; he was decidedly put off. Still, he made an attempt at changing the tone of the conversation. "I've enjoyed speaking with Annie. Splendid adventure, this idea of hers," he commented, smiling at her. "Takes a bit of courage, wouldn't you say?"

Looking at Annie, Andrew softened. "She's one of the bravest people I know, and I tell her that all the time."

Emboldened now, John continued. "I'm trying to convince her to leave a day early and give me a lift back to Oxford. She might stay a few days, if she'd like, and I'd show her around in return." He looked to Susannah first, then Andrew, as he asked, "Don't you think she'd enjoy that?"

Annie thought she saw Andrew's complexion grow red, but it was hard to tell in the dark pub. "I think she can do as she bloody well pleases," he muttered before finishing off his Scotch. Then he turned back to the bar and his glass of heavy. He remained that way, back to them, drinking his pint.

Annie tapped him on his shoulder, but he didn't move. "All right, Andrew," she said as she squeezed in next to him. "You're pissing me off, you know. What the hell is the problem?"

"Have your drink, would you?" was his response.

"I'll have my drink if you tell me what's wrong," she insisted. "Have I done something to upset you?" She was grateful it was so noisy because it kept others from hearing them.

"No," he answered, unconvincingly. "Look, why do you always want to know everything? Why do you always ask questions I can't answer? Sometimes I just get ticked off, that's all." Then, with more vehemence, he added, "You, of all people, should understand that." The bartender set three more glasses of Scotch in front of him.

"I know you went to see your father," she informed him, "and I can guess it went badly, but all this alcohol isn't going to change that or make it go away."

"Leave it alone, would you?" His voice was less angry now, more plaintive. "Just stay here with me and have your drink and leave things. I just want to get tight tonight, all right?" The pain he was trying to hide was suddenly very evident.

Having recognized how extraordinarily upset he was, she decided there was nothing else to do but what he asked. She finished her whisky and picked up one of the full glasses in front of Andrew. Looking at it for a moment, she took a deep breath, then tilted the glass all the way back. She came up coughing from the experience, and it made Andrew laugh his first real laugh in many days.

In the brogue of Argyll that he knew she loved, he congratulated her, "There's a good lassie." Then he handed her his beer. "You'll be wanting this." The sound of him speaking that way set Susannah to giggling again, and he nudged her with an elbow, coaxing, "And you, old girl, you need to keep up."

They stayed until last call. Colin lived in a small flat just up the street from the Scores Hotel, a block away from the Whaum, and he and John saw an unsteady Andrew home. Mel, who was fortunately rather sober, had the dubious honor of seeing the ladies safely to their beds.

Mel walked between them, holding them up, directing them when they reached an intersection, waiting discreetly off to the side while they urinated behind some bushes. Annie and Susannah were laughing so hard and loudly that he frequently had to hush them up, afraid they'd disturb the sleep of those whose houses they walked past.

"That Andrew," Susannah giggled. "He was a perfect cad tonight. I had no idea he could be so vulgar. He was positively rude!" she declared, then doubled over with laughter.

"Downright impudent, that's what he was. Did you hear him, Mel?" Annie asked through her giggling bursts.

"No, I'm afraid I missed it," he answered, shaking his head at the silliness of their conversation.

"Lord Andrew was absolutely coarse," Susannah shouted. "I had no idea he possessed such a mouth!"

Mel was holding to her arm and he squeezed it until she said "ouch!" before admonishing, "Mind your own mouth, Lady Susannah."

"Insolent young man!" Annie added.

Susannah burst out again. Then she stopped laughing abruptly and twisted her legs together, crying out, "I'm going to pee myself!" She tried to keep herself in check, but the laughs still jumped out like hiccups she was trying to suppress.

Annie fell to her knees, holding her stomach against the laughter.

Mel didn't know whether to laugh or be appalled, as he scolded, "Good lord ladies! Get hold of yourselves!"

Susannah was able to pull herself together somewhat, and trying very hard to be sober and ladylike for a moment, she said, "You know, my dears, I'm pisitively possed."

Now the three of them lost control, and it was Annie's turn to squeeze her legs together to stop from wetting herself.

Mel had to sit on a low wall and put his head between his knees, he was laughing that hard. "Did you hear yourself, Susannah—'pisitively possed,' you said!"

Lights went on in the house they were near, and they could hear the sound of a door latch being lifted. They quickly hushed themselves and hurried on to David Russell, still giggling but trying their best to muffle their outbursts.

The ladies slept through breakfast, and Susannah missed one of her lectures. Annie got up around noon and drove Percy B. into town, looking for Andrew. He was not at the Whaum, and she waited there for more than an hour before leaving. She then went to sit in the quadrangle, hoping to see him between lectures, but she didn't. The afternoon passed quickly, and she eventually went back to David Russell for dinner.

The first part of their conversation in the dining hall was about how sick they were that morning, to which Mel righteously proclaimed, "You deserved it—both of you."

After a look that clearly communicated her scorn, Susannah determined to move on to a new topic. She'd been thinking about this on and off throughout the day, and the more she contemplated Annie's predicament with Andrew, the more certain she became that she should do this. She broached the subject with, "You know, I like this Millar-Graham chap, Annie. Do you?"

Tonight's dinner wasn't very appetizing, and Annie pushed her boiled meat and mushy potatoes around her plate as she answered. "He seems nice."

"I should take him up on his offer if I were you," Susannah ventured.

"What offer?"

Susannah smiled encouragement. "To give him a lift to Oxford, of course. You'll love Oxford. It's quite a lovely place—very different from here, you know."

Mel interrupted them. "Don't you want that?" he asked Annie. She responded by sliding her plate toward him.

"But I'd have to leave on Sunday," she remembered. "I think that's what he said. He needs to leave on Sunday."

"Well, it's one less day here, true," Susannah acknowledged, "but I should think it would actually be easier to leave with him on Sunday than to stay one more day and leave on your own. Going off on your own—it won't be easy."

"I know," Annie realized, "but I don't like the idea of losing a day." That lump rose again, the one that formed in her throat every time she thought of leaving.

Susannah patted her arm and swallowed at her own tightening throat. "I understand, but you can't make the journey to the ferry in one day. You'll need a place to sleep over, and Oxford would be a good choice for that."

"It would?"

"It's close enough to the ferry at Southampton that you could get there in a couple of hours, I should imagine. Right, Mel?"

With jowls full of overly tough meat, he mumbled, "It's pretty close. I'm not certain how close, though."

Although she'd asked him a question, Susannah scowled at him once again, this time for speaking with his mouth full.

Starting into her rhubarb pudding now, Annie considered the idea more earnestly. "Maybe I'll talk to him tonight," she said.

"Why don't you?" Susannah coaxed. "Ask him about the ferry and everything. You've nothing to lose."

Nothing to lose. She questioned that. Only one day with you and Mel—with Andrew. It was far from nothing, she knew; it was everything.

When they were alone later, Mel questioned Susannah about why she was pushing so hard about Oxford.

Bristling with impatience, she asked, "Isn't it obvious? It's because of Andrew. Because I'm afraid she'll never see him again, and I don't want her leaving here all alone, thinking of him, putting all her hopes into their reunion. And who knows? John's a nice enough person. Maybe something will happen between them that'll distract her and make it easier for her if Andrew doesn't show."

Mel didn't look convinced, but to appease her he said, "I suppose so." From his own decidedly male point of view, however, he saw it as a recipe for trouble.

Chapter 22

Andrew was chatting with two young women at the bar when she came in. He was smiling and looking to be in much better spirits than he had the day before. She had to think for a moment if she'd ever seen him talking to other women in that relaxed and comfortable a fashion. He had a different, more confident air about him, she realized— very different from the way he was when they first met. Wondering at that, his words came back to her—words he'd uttered the night of the Kate Kennedy Ball: You've made me feel like a man for the first time in my life, Annie. It made her smile to know it.

She approached him from behind and waited for a break in the conversation to make her presence known. "How was your day?" she asked, still grinning.

"Not bad," he answered, "though I missed seeing you at the Whaum. What did you do this afternoon?"

"I was there but late because I slept in," she informed him, "and when I realized I'd missed you, I walked around town. I went to all my favorite places, kind of saying good-bye. Then I walked on the Lade Braes for a while. It was very sad, actually."

The smile left his face, and he put an arm around her waist. "I keep hoping that some miracle will happen," he told her softly.

"And I keep focusing on the possibility of France. If I didn't have that . . . "

He interrupted her with a kiss to her forehead. "There's a ceilidh Friday night. Want to go?"

"I'd love it," she responded, then tenderly kissed him back. "Can we go sit at a table?" she asked him. "There's something I need to talk to you about."

They found an empty spot in a far corner, then sat close and leaned their heads toward one another.

Before she said anything, he told her, "I owe you and Susannah an apology. I was an insufferable ass last night."

She chuckled before responding, "Actually, we got a kick out of you. It was fun seeing you act like one of us." She caught herself. "Not that you aren't; you are, of course, it's just that your manners are always so perfect." Her face was growing redder by the moment.

He seemed hurt. "I'm far from perfect, Annie."

"I didn't mean—"

He shook his head. "Never mind."

"Now I'm the ass."

"Forget it." For her sake, he smiled. "What was it you wanted to talk about?"

She cleared her throat before beginning. "Do you remember that friend of Colin's offering to show me around Oxford if I gave him a lift there?"

Andrew seemed to know this was coming. "You've decided to go with him, have you?"

Averting her eyes momentarily, she said, "Yeah, do you mind?"

"It's the sensible thing to do," he recognized.

She searched his face, wondering if he really meant that, but it revealed nothing. "All right then, that's settled. It means I'll be leaving on Sunday, you know."

"I know," he responded, then briefly bit his lower lip.

"You're all right with this?"

"I have to be practical," he sighed, "and I'd rather not have you on your own."

What she would have liked him to say was "No, I'm not all right with it. Don't go with him, stay here with me, then we'll leave together." But since he didn't, she merely whispered, "Thank you." Then she reminded herself that there was still time for a miracle.

He walked her back to David Russell that night. An earlier rain had left the streets glistening, and the air smelled like laundry freshly hung on the line.

"I'm afraid I've rather a full one tomorrow," he said when they reached her room. "But will you come to the Whaum at midday? I could rush back for a quick lunch."

"I'll be there waiting for you," she said as she kissed him good night.

He turned to leave, but she called him back, then pulled him inside her door.

When they were alone in her room, her heart began to race. "Would you want to stay the night?" she asked softly. "I know what you've said, but we could just lie with one another. We don't have to . . . "

He took up her hand and brought it to his heart, then leaned against her door. "Of all that's happened between us these past weeks, I'm certain of one thing—one thing only." His reason was fighting to keep him from saying this, but in this moment—with her trusting, expectant face so close to his, her breath, so sweet upon the air—his heart won out. "I've never wanted anything more in my life than I want for us to be lovers, but once that happens, there's no going back for me. I have to be able to give you everything, Annie. I can't be with you any other way." He lowered his head and his voice as he added, "I know this is hurting you because it's killing me. But if you can find it in your heart, please forgive me."

The ache that came upon her was like an explosion. With all the times she'd tried, with each offer of herself that she'd made, it didn't get any easier, it didn't hurt any less. The only thing saving her from utter dejection was the knowledge that this wasn't bullshit, that he was struggling with it every bit as much as she was. She knew that with absolute certainty, because in the innermost recesses of her heart, she felt it.

"There's nothing to forgive," she told him, then brought the hand that held hers to her lips, kissing it with the words, "I'll see you tomorrow."

* * *

It rained all day on Thursday, but the evening passed peacefully by the pub fireside. The sun made an appearance again on Friday, and Annie worked for what would be the last time in the Whaum's garden. She pulled every weed she could find, clipped every bit of woody bush, and plucked one by one the insect-eaten leaves she found. By the time Andrew arrived for lunch, she'd gotten everything as near perfect as possible and had replaced the gardening tools in the mudroom. She carefully laid the gloves he'd given her alongside the other things, as though she'd be back again to use them. She thought of taking them with her but she knew she couldn't. It was too final, too definitive, and she couldn't make that statement—neither to herself nor to Andrew.

"I'm so happy Robin's staying here this summer," she told Andrew when he arrived. "I'm glad there'll be someone to look after things."

"It's a pity none of the roses have opened yet. If only there were another week," he said. But he was thinking— if only there were another month, another year, another lifetime. If only I were someone else.

Trying to chase her creeping melancholy, she smiled and asked him, "Are you hungry?"

"Famished."

"I bought some sandwiches for us. Want to eat under the arbor?"

"That'd be lovely," he smiled, "but unfortunately, I can't stay long."

Annie was on her own again that afternoon; with her friends engrossed in their end-of-term assignments, they had little free time. So in the waning hours of her stay in St. Andrews, she found herself abandoned. After seeing Andrew to the Modern Languages building on Union Street, she walked around the town, listening to the Scottish voices, soaking in the flavor and aroma of the place she'd come to love so much, trying to fill her memory to the brim as though it might somehow be an antidote to her loss.

She sat on a bench near the church on South Street, watching the mothers go past, pushing their little ones in prams. They were not much older than she, many of them, and she began to fantasize about being one of them. She imagined herself married to Andrew, living in the Whaum, putting the baby in the pram to walk out and do the day's shopping. The fantasy made her smile broadly, and she was doing that when she heard a distinctly English, "Hullo! Brilliant day, isn't it?"

Looking up, she raised a hand to shield her eyes from the sun. "Oh, hi, John. Yeah, fantastic day."

Gesturing toward the billowy, blowing clouds, he commented, "I thought Scotland was supposed to be wet and gloomy."

"It's the wind," she explained. "It never lets anything stay around for long." Including me, she mused, including me.

"On your own today?" he wondered.

"Yup," she sighed, "everyone's busy with some paper or other, turning in all the work they've put off."

"Colin, too," he informed her. "Mind if I sit?"

"No, I'd love the company. It'll help get my mind off things." As she moved to one side of the bench, the clock towers began to toll the quarter hour. They sat listening together until the brief chorus was complete.

"Sad about leaving, are you?" he observed.

"Very."

The smile he offered her was kind and understanding, and perhaps a tad too familiar. "Well, I'll do my part," he wanted her to know. "I'll see to it that you enjoy yourself in Oxford."

She smiled back at him, then turned her head away.

"We need to leave bright and early Sunday if we're going to make it by evening," he informed her.

"How early?"

"Six, half past, that neighborhood."

"I'll need to settle up what I owe at David Russell tomorrow then, and get everything ready."

He had an idea now, which he shared with her. "You might consider staying at Colin's flat tomorrow night—you know, get yourself all cleared out of your present abode, so you're ready to leave straight away once you're up."

Exhaling, she responded, "I guess I should do that, but maybe I could stay at the Whaum. It's only a block away from Colin, and maybe Susannah and Mel could stay too, so we'd all be together."

"That's an idea," he acknowledged, with a concerned look. "It would be a bit tougher, though, I imagine."

"Why do you say that?" she wondered.

"Saying good-bye and all that. I should think it would be easier to do the night before. Awfully tough, that, seeing your friends standing there as you pull away."

Like the last scenes of a tear-jerker movie, it played out in her mind. She saw herself hugging Susannah and Mel, kissing Andrew for the last time, climbing onto the bike and driving away, her eyes so full of tears she couldn't see, her heart so filled with aching she'd want to die. She suddenly knew John was right, because even imagining it made her feel ill all over.

"I'll have to think about it," she told him. "I don't want to impose on Colin."

"I'm sure he wouldn't mind. Going to the ceilidh tonight?"

"Yeah, we are."

The towers of St. Andrews announced that it was four o'clock, which led John to ask, "Would you care to go for a spot of tea? I saw a sweet little place just up from here."

She knew and liked the place, and had been thinking of going there alone. "Thanks, that'd be nice," she answered and smiled.

* * *

Annie and Andrew were the first ones on the dance floor when the reels began. They danced and drank and laughed and talked as if there were no tomorrow. When slow dances played, they held on as tightly as they could, breathing in the other's scent, tasting the other's skin, letting their hands explore as much as they publicly dared.

Patrick Ramsay was there with a date, and as the evening wore on with more and more drink, Annie often found him staring at her. It finally became so annoying that she decided to approach him, and she did so with Andrew by her side.

She attempted to make a joke of it. "Is my head on backwards or something?"

"No," he snorted. "Just thinking of coming over to say good-bye, that's all. I hear you're leaving Sunday."

"I am."

He glanced at Andrew before he asked her, "Going to Oxford first, are you?"

"That's right, with Colin's friend," she answered.

He grinned. "That'll be nice for you." He should have left it at that; he was already going a little too far. But with that arrogant Scot towering over him, smugly standing beside Annie, he couldn't help himself. "It'll be a nice change for you," he told her, glancing again at Andrew, "and I know how you like change."

Annie watched the color drain from Andrew's face. "Ramsay," he seethed through a clenched jaw, "one of these times I'm going to give you what you deserve, and I hope it's soon, because I'm going to enjoy the hell out of it." He then turned away abruptly, knowing that if Ramsay said one more flippant thing, he'd have to knock the bastard on his ass.

Before following Andrew, Annie moved a tad closer to his smirking face to say, "Gee, Patrick, I wish I had your way with people. You sure know how to bring out the best in them, don't you?"

As for watching the couple that evening, Patrick wasn't the only one. Robin had trouble keeping his eyes from them, too, but it was Susannah who noticed that. When a break occurred in the dancing, she left Mel's side and went to have a chat with him, her curiosity once again in high gear.

She wasted no time in getting to the point. "What bothers you about them?"

Robin was caught off guard. "What do you mean?"

"Annie and Andrew. You seem as though you disapprove or something."

He shook his head slightly. Andrew had warned him that Susannah knew, but having held the secret for so long, the thought of revealing it made him uncomfortable. "I don't know what you're talking about."

She smiled that wicked smile of hers. "Sure you do, and so do I."

He affected some irritation, insisting, "I'm not going to discuss this with you."

"Come on, Robin," she coaxed, "you're not betraying a confidence because I already know. But it's fairly obvious that something's worrying you. If it has anything to do with Annie, you should tell me. Maybe I can help."

It was weak to start, but Susannah's plea melted his resolve. "I think they're beyond help; that's what worries me. I think they're headed for disaster."

"Why do you say that?"

"Because there's no way for them to win in this situation, no matter what they decide to do." He swallowed several gulps of the beer he was holding. "That car and driver were sent to spy on them, you know. His father's been worried about what's going on between them, so he asked the chauffeur to report back to him. He admitted as much to Andrew."

"Oh, my," she responded.

The floodgates had been opened for Robin. For three years now he'd had to keep what he knew about Andrew Stuart-Gordon to himself. It felt good, for once, to not have to do that. "He's engaged, you know, to the granddaughter of the Duke of Argyll—Lady Janet Campbell. They have plans for an enormous affair this September to announce it and make it official. Everyone who's anyone will be invited."

"Holy shit!" She'd never used the expression before, but having heard it so much from Annie these past weeks allowed it to roll off her tongue. "Is her father Lord Campbell, the Home Secretary?"

"The same," he answered, closing his eyes in a long blink for emphasis.

"Damn," she said now. My poor Annie, she bemoaned—my poor friend. She's so in love, she thinks they're destined for one other! And that Andrew, that cad! I could throttle him!

Since he'd already said more than he should, Robin didn't see the point in holding back the details. "The duke is solidly behind this. He sees it as an opportunity to align the generally disliked Campbells with the well-loved Stuart-Gordons." Feeling the need for more privacy, he pulled her backward nearer the wall. "After Janet's father, there are no male heirs, you know, and Janet's his eldest, so she could well succeed to the dukedom." He let that sink in for a moment as he watched her mouth fall open. "They keep talking about meeting in France this summer, but you see now why that will never happen. The families have too much invested in this union to let it fall apart, no matter how Andrew feels and no matter what he wants. His father's already given him a dressing down over it."

Quickly, she recalled the things Andrew had told her. Dammit all, why didn't he mention this? He'd been so absolutely sincere, she hadn't doubted that. He was going to do everything he could, he said, to be with Annie this summer. And she believed him. How could she have been so gullible? She began to question her decision about not telling Annie. Maybe she should after all; maybe that was the best way to protect her.

"You need to keep this to yourself," Robin admonished. "He still wants it that way, you know."

It was suddenly all too much, and Susannah felt sick inside. As uncharacteristic as it was and try as she might, she could find nothing more to say at the moment, so she merely nodded at Robin, then walked away in something of a daze to look for Mel.

"My word," Mel said as he listened, "my word."

"The Campbells have never been forgiven for the massacre at Glencoe," she explained, "and in contrast to that, the Stuart-Gordons are so revered by the Scots, they'd be forgiven for anything. And many believe they should carry the Argyll dukedom, not the Campbells. Andrew's marriage to the granddaughter gives them a very real chance at that. That kind of alliance is made in heaven," she scoffed. "Even if Andrew wanted out, which I have to doubt now, do you think his father and grandfather would stand for that?" She answered her own question with an exaggerated twist of her head. "If he doesn't marry her, someone else would claim that right. How could they let that happen?"

"My word," he said again. "All this time, drinking with him in the pubs, chatting over whatever. He'll likely be one of the most influential men in Britain when he comes into his own." He wasn't thinking of Annie just now, but of the incredulity of his friendship with Andrew.

"Tell me what to do, Mel," Susannah pleaded, "because for the life of me, I can't think what the right thing is."

He easily read his girlfriend's face. "Don't tell me you're thinking of spilling the beans. Why in God's name would you do that?"

She responded impatiently, "Because she's pinning her hopes on meeting him again, that's why, and the likelihood of that happening is about the same as you getting engaged to Princess Anne." Her remark was punctuated with a sarcastic frown.

He feigned hurt as he protested, "That's not such an improbability. I might woo her if I set my mind to it."

She grimaced at the idea of that. "Do be serious. Won't it be better if she knows the truth—if she knows why he never shows instead of wondering about it, thinking it was somehow her fault, as she likely will?"

He shook his head. "I don't agree. Say you tell her now—right now. You pull her aside and say, 'Annie, Andrew here has been lying to you. This chap that you're besotted with, he's been playing you for a fool and he's no intention of meeting you this summer. In fact, he's about to announce his engagement to someone else.' How do you imagine that'll make things better?"

She squinted at him when she realized how much sense he was making.

He went on to speculate, "And how would she feel about you, do you think, for telling her? How would you explain why you waited until the last minute to do this, making her departure even more difficult and leaving her no time to sort through anything?"

"All right," she begrudgingly acknowledged, "you've made your point. You needn't beat me over the head with it."

The band leader announced that the song they were about to play was the last number of the evening. Susannah's eyes searched the dance floor and caught the couple in deep embrace as the music began. A sad, sympathetic sigh escaped from her as she realized that this would likely be their last dance.

After the ceilidh, the group of friends went to the Russell Hotel and commandeered the window seat.

In her distressed state, worrying over what to do about Annie, Susannah had once again taken to drinking more than she should. When the alcohol kicked in, she snuggled next to Annie and linked her arm with hers. "Do you remember when you first arrived? You'd drink a pint of lager and lime and get blotter, now you're up to five pints and you're just a tiny bit tight. Whatever would your parents say?"

When their outburst of giggling quieted, Andrew asked them, "Want a wee whisky, ladies?" and it restarted their laughter.

"Why not?" Susannah slurred as she reached to hug Annie. "My friend and I are drinking to each other tonight, and it's time to raise another."

Andrew handed them each a glass, "To what are we drinking now?" he asked.

"We're drinking to Miss Annie," she declared. "You and I, Andrew, we'll drink to her together because you and I share a secret regarding her, don't we?"

"And what's that?" Annie chuckled.

Andrew grew anxious suddenly. "Susannah, don't you think . . ."

Mel added, "Careful, old girl," as he pinched at her thigh.

Susannah ignored Andrew and brushed Mel's hand away. Then looking around to see who might hear her, she whispered, "We share something—something that has to do with you. Do you know what that is?"

"I haven't the foggiest," she giggled.

"Susannah," Andrew pleaded now, "be careful. You've had a lot to drink."

"Be careful about what?" Annie asked playfully.

"He doesn't know what I'm going to say. He thinks he does, but he doesn't. But then again, maybe he does," she said, then laughed wickedly.

Whatever she wanted to say, Andrew could see she was determined, so he braced himself against it.

Susannah lowered her voice again. "The secret is, we both love Annie, don't we Andrew? Both of us, we love Annie so much we're willing to lie to protect her."

She didn't take it seriously, but she asked anyway, "Lie to me?"

"Yes, that's what I said. We'd lie to protect you from being hurt."

With his heart running at a full gallop, Andrew sat in fearful silence.

Annie now thought she understood. "Well, I'd lie to protect either of you if I had to, because I love you both, don't I?"

Susannah chuckled as she proclaimed, "Good, then that makes us even!"

"Ladies," Andrew said, when he was able to take a breath again, "want to go to the Whaum for some coffee? You'll both need it if you're going to be able to walk home."

It was after three in the morning when Annie climbed into her bed in Fraser 28. She lay staring at the ceiling for a few minutes before she started to cry. Andrew, she called out in the darkness—Andrew—over and over, hoping against hope that he might turn around and come back to her.

In the little cottage on The Scores, a light burned in the back bedroom, the one that overlooked the roses. Andrew hadn't bothered to undress when he returned from David Russell, because he knew there'd be no use to it. Instead, he sat fully upright on the bed and stared into the darkness of the garden, waiting for the sunrise, wondering how he would find the strength to make it through this day.

Chapter 23

Susannah awakened her for breakfast. Annie threw her arms around her when she opened the door. They didn't speak. They stood in the doorway hugging like that for some time before walking arm in arm to the dining hall.

Mel and Susannah went with her to the matron's office to pay what she owed and then back to her room to pack up her things.

"Will you stay with us tonight?" Susannah asked. "We can stay all together, the three of us in Mel's room, or you can sleep alone in my room if you prefer."

"I think it's better if I stay at Colin's," she answered, as she packed and repacked her bags.

Susannah seemed incredulous. "Colin's? Why there?"

"Because we've got to leave at six," she explained, "and I don't want to disturb any of you that early. But that's not the only reason."

Noticeably upset, Susannah had taken hold of Mel and was hugging him tightly.

"John made me think of it." Her throat, so easily irritated these days, was starting to spasm again. "It's going to be hard enough leaving, but with you all standing there—it'd be that much worse. Do you understand?"

"So we've got to say good-bye tonight? This is too much," Susannah protested, "first we had until Monday and then it was Sunday and now it's tonight. Oh Mel!" she cried, hugging him even tighter.

Annie halted her packing and moved toward the couple, then put a hand on each of their arms. "Please understand. I'm trying to figure a way to do this so it won't be too awful."

"She's right, my love," Mel agreed, stroking his girlfriend's hair. "It's going to be better that way. We'll have our drinks and a marvelous time like we always do, then we'll say good night just like we always do. It'll be easier for all of us that way."

"And what then?" Susannah pouted, like a disappointed child.

"I'll see you in London at the end of the summer," Annie consoled. "August probably, whenever I run out of money. I'll wire you and let you know when I'm coming, and then we'll be together again—the three of us—before I go home."

"Do you promise?" Susannah questioned.

"I promise, of course I promise! I love you two and I can't not see you again. I just can't," she said, then joined the couple in their embrace.

When Annie knocked on the door of the Whaum, Percy B. was parked just out front. Her bags were strapped onto the luggage rack, and Andrew did a double take when he noticed. "What's this?"

"I'm out of my room," she explained. "I settled the bill, and I won't be staying there tonight." She handed him the package she was holding to her chest. "This is the gown Robin loaned me. I wanted to thank him again for it. He probably has no idea how much I've enjoyed wearing it and feeling like one of you, like one of the students."

"I'll tell him," he said, taking it from her. "Staying with Susannah tonight?"

"No, actually I was going to ask if I could stay here, but then I thought better of it, because I know you wouldn't want that." She waited now, clinging to the hope that he would refute her statement. But when he didn't, she informed him, "I'm staying at Colin's. We can leave bright and early that way."

He stared at her as though he hadn't understood a word she'd said. He looked at the bike again, and then he stammered, "Whatever you think best. Would you like to come in?"

They sat in the parlor. Andrew was overly polite when he spoke, as though she were an infrequent guest that he was entertaining. "Would you care for some tea?" he asked her.

"I'd rather have a drink of your whisky."

"Of course, I'll just be a moment." He went into the kitchen and closed the door behind him. It was several minutes before he came out again.

When he sat across the room instead of next to her, she pointedly questioned him, "Do you want to go on pretending, or should we really talk?"

It didn't even sound like him, his voice was that strained. "I think everything's been said, hasn't it?"

The way he was addressing her, anyone listening would have thought they barely knew one another. "Has it?" she asked, through her bewilderment.

"I believe so," he answered, crossing his legs.

That desperate, sinking feeling—the one she always experienced when he rejected her—pulled at her insides. "All right, then," she decided, feeling her anger rise, "if that's how you want it."

And then, as though it had slipped his mind, he casually offered, "A group of us are organizing a party on the West Sands tonight. You should stop by."

"Stop by?" She winced, then repeated, "Stop by?"

He knew how much he was hurting her, and he loathed himself for it. Still, he forced himself to say, "And bring Mel and Susannah, of course. A lot of the people you'll want to say good-bye to will be there."

Her hands began to tremble, and she had to set the glass of whisky down. "I'd thought we'd be together today. I'd thought we'd spend this time together."

He couldn't allow her to finish. "I've rather a lot to do today. I have work at the library, and then I've promised to help get things out to the beach. We're doing a keg and food, then there's the wood we'll need for the bonfire."

"Couldn't I help?" she asked, her voice faltering.

Standing now, in a gesture that said it was time for her to go, he told her, "That's awfully kind of you, but I'm certain you've other things you need to do today." The pain shooting through him was unlike any he'd ever known. "I'll see you later, then?"

She stood too, and her voice cracked as she demanded to know, "Why are you doing this? Why are you treating me like this?"

Robin came into the cottage then, carrying bags of food.

Ignoring her question, Andrew moved to help him. "Got everything we need?" he asked in a peculiar voice.

"Yes, got it all, I think. How are you, Annie?"

Before she could answer Robin, Andrew informed him, "She was just leaving."

With her mouth agape, she stared at him in disbelief. Then she abruptly spun on her heels and left the cottage.

"What was that about?" Robin asked as she slammed the door.

In the next instant, Andrew's knees gave out and he sank into a chair. He leaned his head to the seat back and spoke to the ceiling. "She told me she's staying at Colin's flat with that Oxford chap she's leaving with tomorrow. I had to get her out of here before I said or did something I'd regret." He shifted his gaze to the garden. "I was miserably cold to her. It was the only thing I could think of at the time." He stared at the roses for several long moments before speaking again. "I don't know how I'm going to do it. I don't know how I'm going to make it through this day."

"With a little help from your friends," Robin answered him, hoping it would bring a smile to his friend's troubled face.

It didn't.

Percy B. remained parked in front of the Whaum, but Annie's bags were gone. She sat with them next to her on the steps leading up to Colin's flat at Eden Court. She sat there for quite some time—she didn't know how long—

before Colin and John came back from wherever they'd been. In contrast to the way she'd been treated at the Whaum, they greeted her with warmth.

"All set then?" John asked, lifting her bags from the step.

"Yeah, pretty much."

"Care for something?" Colin offered when they were inside.

"No, thanks," she answered. "I just wanted to leave my things here. I want to try to catch up with Adam to say my good-byes, and then I'm meeting Mel and Susannah when they're finished at the library."

"Going to the party on the West Sands?" John asked.

"I suppose," she sighed.

He smiled as though he understood a secret. "Come by later if you want. We can go together."

Adam wasn't in his room at Southgait, so she borrowed some paper to leave him a note. She had written it and slipped it under his door when she saw Patrick. He didn't see her; he was at the end of a corridor talking to someone she barely knew.

"Gordon's getting what's coming to him, isn't he?" she heard him say. "But if you ask me, he'll be happy for it later, as I am, when he realizes what a bloody whore she is. That's her style, isn't it? Going from bed to bed—bloody tart."

She felt the heat rush to her cheeks. Part of her wanted to confront him, to get right in his face and tell him the hell off, but another part of her was shamed by his comment and understood how he might feel that way. The remorseful part of Annie won out in this awkward moment and led her to steal away and head for the library.

In the note she left for Adam, she said she'd be waiting outside the library. About a half an hour after she arrived, she saw him walking toward her.

He wore a serious expression. "Well, it's time, isn't it?"

"I'm afraid so," she answered. "How about you? When are you going home?"

"A week from Monday," he informed her.

"But you'll be back next fall, you lucky dog."

"I am, aren't I?" he gloated. "I'm really looking forward to next year. It should be great." He felt some triumph in lording that over her.

In a gesture meant to convey her sincerity, she moved to touch his hand; he yanked it away abruptly, and it took courage for her to say what she said next. "I know things got difficult between us, but I've loved being here, and I have you to thank for that. I do thank you Adam. I thank you from the bottom of my heart."

"Well, I'm glad you enjoyed yourself," he answered, frowning slightly. "I just wish you'd been more careful about people's feelings." And to himself he added—about my feelings.

As it had in Southgait Hall when she overheard Patrick, the blood rushed to her cheeks, only now she lost her tenuous composure. "You mean Patrick's? Really, Adam, he's got problems that have nothing to do with me. I know he's your friend, but he's got an awful mean streak in him."

"As I told you before, I'd never seen that side of him until you came along."

She was growing more upset by the minute. "That doesn't mean it wasn't there!"

With a smug, superior expression, he informed her, "It's not just Patrick you've upset. Poor Andrew, Robin is really worried about him."

She looked at the ground now and lowered her voice to implore, "Please don't talk about Andrew. You've got no idea about Andrew and me."

He was not going to let it rest. "Robin says he'll be lucky if he passes this term. He's focused so much attention on you he's hardly done any work."

Her stomach was becoming queasy. "Adam, let's not talk about him, OK? You don't understand about us."

"Well, it's good you're leaving," he decided. "It's time for you to leave, though it would have been better done sooner. Hopefully, Andrew can get back on track and pull things out in the end."

Time for you to leave—what a terrible blow those words struck. Leave this place that she had grown to feel such a part of, that she wanted so very much to belong to—she felt as though he'd kicked her in the gut.

"Anyway, I've got to be off. Have a safe trip on your motorcycle," he casually offered as he walked away.

"Thank you," she called to his back, valiantly fighting her tears. But when she turned away from him to see Susannah and Mel approaching her, she gave up the fight.

"What's the matter?" Mel asked. "Wasn't that Adam?"

Nodding, she sniveled, "He made me feel terrible about Andrew, just terrible."

"There, there," Susannah consoled, putting her arms around her.

"It's not just what he said," she nearly sobbed. "I went to see Andrew earlier and he was awful to me. He treated me so coldly, like we barely knew one another! It's my last day here and he told me he was too busy to spend time with me! You know how I feel about him, Susannah. I need to be with him now."

"Annie, dear, let's have a sit down," she told her, drawing her over to a bench.

Susannah sat on one side of Annie, Mel on the other. Susannah pulled some tissues from her handbag and offered them to her. While Annie blew her nose and composed herself, Susannah gathered her thoughts.

After all her ruminations over what to do, it had been Susannah's intuition about Andrew that had helped her reach the decision she had—to keep his secret. In the end, it had come down to one simple thing; she had decided to trust him because whenever she looked into his eyes, she clearly saw his misery.

"This day is very tough for Andrew," she began. "It's tough for all of us, but it's especially tough for him. You yourself said how deeply he feels things. You've got to see that your leaving is going to be the hardest on him. Mel and I have each other, you have your adventure ahead of you, he has to go home to deal with his father."

Annie's distress was replaced by surprise. "He's told you about his father?"

Oops—she thought—I hadn't meant to say that. "We had a chat a few days ago," she decided to tell her, "when we ran into each other. His father may be difficult, but he's still his father and Andrew has to find a way to manage with him."

She had regained some composure, but tears were still streaking her cheeks. "I know," she said.

"I think he's doing what he must just now, so it won't be too bloody awful when you leave. Can you see that?"

"I suppose," she answered, then blew her nose again.

"Then, if you care for him as much as I think you do, you'll let him deal with this in his own way," she encouraged. "He's worried that he may not see you again and having a devil of a time coming to terms with that."

Annie viewed her friend with some suspicion now. "I suspect you had more than a little chat with him."

Knitting her brow, she answered, "He told me some things, yes, about his circumstances."

Mel was watching her, waiting to see how she would handle this.

"Nothing intimate of course," she continued, "but enough so that I understand. When I think of it now, I believe he confided in me so I might help you when the time came. He cares that deeply about you, you know."

Mel gave his girlfriend a smile of approval. "You should be comforted by that," he told Annie.

"I am, a little, but I want to be with him. He's trying to keep from loving me, but it's too late for me. I love him so much I feel it in every pore. Every fucking inch of me hurts at the thought of leaving him."

Like Andrew, Susannah had grown fond of Annie's unorthodox style, her directness most especially. "Goodness, I am going to miss that tongue of yours!" she chuckled, but then she turned serious again. "Then you're going to have to be brave and buck up, aren't you? And to do that you're going to have to focus on what's ahead of you, not on what you're leaving behind." She put both arms around her and kissed her forehead before telling her, "And I probably shouldn't say this, but I have such a strong feeling about it."

"About what?"

"I think, I feel this, really—that although this may not be the right time for you and Andrew, there is something so strong between you that somehow, someday, you'll come together again."

While Susannah imagined this happening in the far-off future, Annie pictured their reunion only weeks from now in France. "Really? You feel that? I do, too, Susannah. I feel that, too." Something vaguely familiar, like a dream remembered, brought her a much-needed smile.

* * *

The friends had dinner together in a little café on Market Street, then they walked to the Whaum. Finding no one at home, they went to Colin's flat and he invited them in for a drink. John seemed happy to see Annie, and the five of them talked for about an hour before deciding to go to the party on the West Sands. From the front windows of Colin's flat, they could see the enormous, blazing bonfire and the growing crowd.

It was after ten and the daylight lingered, but the smoke-filled beach took on an eerie quality. The air was very still and a mist rolled off the sea to mix with the fire's exhaust, causing it to drift across the sand like a thick fog, like a low, enveloping cloud. As they moved through they disturbed it, and it swirled round and round the feet of all who walked on the beach that evening.

Annie saw Andrew appear out of the haze; behind him there were only gray-white swirls of air, dense and reflective. He walked toward her with a gravity, with a weight upon him, it seemed, his face more somber than she had ever seen it. He carried a bottle of Scotch and a paper cup, and he offered the cup to Annie.

"Have a drink with me?" he asked quietly.

She walked with him to the water's edge. They sat together on the damp sand, apart from the crowd. She took drinks from the cup, he from the bottle, and they said nothing for a time.

When she finally spoke, her voice was muted by the heavy, moist air. "Andrew," she softly questioned, "will you forgive me?"

"For what, Annie?"

"For leaving," she explained. "I hope someday you'll forgive me for leaving."

A little sound emanated from his throat, and he coughed to cover it.

"I think somehow I've made a mistake in buying Percy and going ahead with this craziness. I think I should have been more open to other things—to doing something else."

He dug the bottle into the sand and dropped his head onto his knees. The depth with which he took his next breaths was disturbing, almost frightening.

Plaintively, she asked, "Won't you talk to me? Won't you tell me what you're feeling?"

When he lifted his head, she saw anguish burning through his eyes. "I, I can't put it into words," he muttered.

"Then let me feel it." She reached her arms around him and held on as tightly as she could. His head fell heavily on her shoulder; his breath warmed her neck, and his despair bore into her bones. They stayed that way in the still night air, in the smoke and mist, exploring the agony together.

"I need to tell you something," she whispered after a time. "I know it might make things harder, but I need to say it because it's important. I love you, Andrew. I love you more than I've ever loved anyone in my life. No matter what happens, don't ever forget that and don't ever doubt it. Whatever lies ahead for us, never doubt that I love you."

In this moment, he prayed for understanding—dear God, why have you been so cruel? Why have you given me this precious gift, my precious Annie, only to take her away?

His need to connect with her made him reach for her face, and he cradled it in his hands. With the utmost tenderness, he kissed her cheeks, her chin, her eyes and nose, saying nothing. But in his heart he was answering her, telling her the truth—that not a single breath came from him that didn't find its origins in his love for her. His touch confessed that there was not one waking moment, and precious few unconscious ones, when his mind wasn't consumed with her—the image of her hair blowing about her face, the dreamily recalled perfume of her skin, the melody of her voice. With every kiss, he told her these things, though his throat refused to give form to the words, refused to allow them to be heard in the open making them more real than they already were. The need to say them choked him, though, and when he could no longer tolerate the strain, he pulled away from her.

His emotions were overpowering him. He needed to anchor himself to something tangible, so he reached into his pocket for his knife. Offering it to her, he said, "I want you to take this and have it with you and think of me when you use it." He had to give her something of himself, if only his Swiss Army knife.

Once again, the disappointment ambushed her. Why don't you say it, her heart pleaded. Why don't you tell me that you love me? Couldn't you give me that one blessed gift before I leave?

But even as she was despairing, she could hear Susannah telling her to let him handle this in his own way. With that in mind, she responded now, "Thank you, Andrew, I will." Stroking the knife as though it were alive, she began searching her mind, running through her sparse inventory, wondering if there were anything of hers she might give him. "I'd like to give you something, too. Would you take my earrings?" she asked, touching one of the gold hoops she always wore.

He was moved by the gesture, but he protested. "Oh no, I can't take those. They're from your brother! I know how much they mean to you. No, you must keep them."

Timmy had given Annie those earrings for her eighteenth birthday, so she reluctantly agreed. "I'll think of something else before I leave," she promised.

They resumed their embrace and tried to forget the time.

It was well past midnight when Mel and Susannah approached the couple. For some time now they had watched them from a distance, not wishing to disturb their last moments together, and most of that time they had been deep in conversation with Robin, John, and Colin.

"Sorry to interrupt, darlings," Susannah apologized, "but it's getting late, and we need to be heading back."

Annie's eyes filled immediately. "Shall I walk with you?"

"I think we'd better go on alone," Mel said. He seemed to be holding Susannah up.

John was standing behind them. "I hate to mention this," he added timidly, "but you and I need to get up rather early tomorrow, Annie."

Andrew rose and began walking away. Annie spoke briefly to her friends, then ran after him.

"I'm going to walk with them as far as the path and then I'll be back. Will you be here?"

"Yes."

"I won't be long." She kissed him quickly, then ran back to her friends.

When they reached the point where the path to David Russell began, they stopped and looked at one another. It was Susannah who spoke first.

"We're going to say good night, and that's all there is to it. I won't say that other thing," she insisted.

"OK, but can I say I'll see you in August? Is that all right?"

"Yes, that's good. See you in August, my darling." Susannah's voice caught on itself.

The embrace that followed, the three of them tightly pulled together, said the rest.

Annie and John went to Colin's flat. Annie fumbled through her bags until she found something.

"I've got to go back and give this to Andrew," she explained, as she headed out the door.

"You should take the bike to save time," he told her. "I'll drive you if you'd like."

"All right, but I can go alone."

"As you wish, but I think you might need me to drive back."

She didn't understand why he'd said that. She stared at him for a moment before answering, "OK, let's go."

Andrew heard the sound of the motorcycle and moved toward it. John left them immediately and made his way to the bonfire where Colin and Robin were still huddled.

When they were standing face to face again, Annie lifted her hand and unfolded it. "It's not a gift like your knife is, because it's certainly not something you can use, is it?" She smiled at him and he managed one, too. "But it's all I could think to give you that was in some way personal, that would make you think of me when you saw it."

"I'll treasure it," he said, grasping the barrette that she used to twist up her hair. "Can you stay a bit longer?"

It was now after one, and she answered with great reluctance, "It's late. I'd better be going soon. John says it'll be a long day on the bike, and you can't take naps on a motorcycle."

"No, of course you can't," he responded, and dropped his head.

She had promised not to do this, but she couldn't help herself; it was the hope she had to cling to, to keep her heart beating on this impossible night. "We have to do what we can about France, Andrew. I'll write you as soon as I know anything. I'll understand if you can't make it, but I'm going to be praying that you can."

His shoulders drooped and his head seemed unbearably heavy. "I'll try. I'll do what I can," he told her.

"We need to think that way. We can't think that this is really good-bye."

"No, we can't," he agreed.

"Remember the northern lights—the sign from the gods. I know we're meant to be together."

"Yes," he answered, his voice faltering.

"I said good night to Mel and Susannah, and that's what I'm going to say to you, OK?"

"Yes, all right. Good night, Annie." He turned away from her and walked into the smoke. He didn't look back. He continued on until he was about thirty feet away, then he stopped dead in his tracks, overcome by trembling.

She knew he was beginning to cry. "Andrew!" came out of her—from her guts or her bones, she couldn't tell where—but it didn't sound like a voice. "Andrew!" sounded again. She started to go to him when a strong hand on her shoulder halted her.

"Annie," John said, into her ear, "don't make it harder for him."

When she turned around, she saw the faces of Colin, John, and Robin, all gaping at her as though she were about to do something foolish.

"I can't leave him like that!" she protested. Something was wrong with her ears. Everything, including her own voice, was sounding hollow and distant.

"It's better this way," she heard, as though from very far away. "Just go now. I'll see to him." Robin's voice was strange, too, like he was talking into a box.

John gently took her arm and began leading her away. "It's time, Annie. You need rest before tomorrow."

She knew she was walking, but she couldn't feel the ground beneath her. Her mind was slipping, falling into a void, a place where it couldn't grasp anything. Percy B. roared suddenly and a hand reached out, pulling her onto his seat. She felt the kickstand go up and heard the acceleration as the wheels began to roll.

Her heart seized and wrested as though it were caught on something. She turned to look back as Percy lunged forward. In the smoke and firelight, the solitary figure remained, still with his back to her, still trembling. The burning light faded as the bike moved off, while the beach behind them turned to black and fell away, into the cold and unforgiving sea.

Chapter 24

Demons clawed and scratched at the windows, blowing frightful, howling sounds through the cracks as they fought to get in. They chased the stillness and pounded upon the glass, making certain Annie heard them, causing her to awaken—because they wanted her to know what she'd done.

Her mind was coming back. It settled into the disquiet of her head, a head that resounded from too much Scotch and warily observed the queasiness crawling through her stomach. She remembered bathing and drinking—drinking far too much—soaking in the hot, soapy water and weeping into it endlessly until all her strength seemed spent. Now she lay naked in a bed, in a dark room she did not recognize, while she listened to the fierce squall that blew outside. She gradually became aware of the wetness between her legs.

Arms enfolded her and a warm body pulled her back to it. The unmistakable prodding and poking of an erect penis made her gasp, and she closed her eyes tightly as memory forced itself upon her. The penis continued its probing, its seeking, making its way through the puddle that she cradled between her thighs. It found its way into her, and she felt the soreness it had left behind earlier as it began to stroke her insides. Her head throbbed and her stomach felt as though it would burst up through her throat, but that was not the worst of it. A sickness like none she had ever known overcame her as she realized that this was not the man she wanted it to be, the man whose name she had called out repeatedly through the night. This was not Andrew.

John remained inside of her despite the internal war he was waging, alternately overcome by guilt and the driving aggression of sexual desire. He kissed the back of her neck and spoke softly, saying, "It's all right," as he gave into his need. He had felt her need, too—a need that was not for him but for the man she loved—and he had let it carry him past the wrongness of it all.

The sickness was rising up to smother her, and she had to get away from it. "John, John, please," she begged, "please stop."

He removed himself but retained his embrace of her. "I'm sorry," was all he could find to say.

Cautiously, she brought herself to a sitting position, then wrapped her arms around her torso. "Could you get me something—something for my head and stomach, please! I'm going to be sick!" she warned.

He rose and went quickly into the bathroom, then returned with a trash bin and a glass of some seltzer-like medicine. She drank it down and then sat very still, waiting to see if it would come up again as she stared into the empty bin.

He was naked and standing in front of her. "Is there anything else I can do for you?"

She looked up at him now, crying, "Oh God! Oh Jesus, tell me this didn't happen!" She began to weep.

He sat next to her and put a hand on her shoulder. "It's my fault," he told her. "I let you have too much to drink."

"Oh, God—oh, God!" she cried again, tilting her head toward the ceiling.

"Please, Annie, I'm dreadfully sorry, but you were so sad, so very sad. I'd never seen anyone so sad. I wanted to comfort you. I was trying to comfort you."

She lay back carefully, trying not to further disturb her sick head or stomach. "Cover me," she whispered, as her exposed body began to shiver.

"Are you cold?" he asked, as he pulled the bedclothes to her neck.

"Terribly, horribly."

He lay next to and facing her, vigorously rubbing her arms to generate some heat. "Is that better? Shall I get another blanket?"

She couldn't answer. She could only cry and crouch into a ball, holding onto herself as her face went all twisted and ugly. The already puffy eyes yielded yet more tears, and John felt her torment reaching out to him. He brushed the hair from her cheek and barely touched her skin with his kiss. The gentleness of his caress allowed her to release some of the anguish, just as it had before, so he went ahead, hoping to see more of it go.

He moved his hands over her strong shoulders, then reached around to her back. Her muscles relaxed with his stroking, and she brought her legs down from their fetal position. Her tension was easing, her tears abating, and as he looked into her eyes, she seemed to be asking for something, something he was all too willing to give. He rubbed the outside of one thigh now, then the inside, parting her legs slightly. When she didn't protest, he took hold of his stiffened penis and guided it into her once more.

Why she didn't resist she couldn't have said; what she felt she didn't know. John hadn't forced himself on her, that was certain. He had tenderly offered. And he'd been so sweet, so sympathetic and understanding, even though in her drunken state she had called him Andrew. What was happening now wasn't love; that was certain, too. But whatever it was, it was working against the suffering somehow, against the loss and despair, against the agony of Andrew's rejection. Somehow, in the realm of fantasy or dreamy wishfulness or pure lust—whatever it was—it worked to keep the most desperate pain she'd ever experienced from killing her in that awful night, in that long and terrible night. And that was all that could be said about it, because that was all she knew.

With the light of day, the demons were no longer at the window. They left chaos behind them, though. The wet streets were filled with wasted blossoms that would never bear fruit, with broken limbs and newly born leaves that had been severed from their branches. And many of the flowers in the gardens along The Scores had not survived, their petals beaten off, their stems bent and broken.

Annie had difficulty opening her eyes because they were almost swollen shut. Before he did anything else, John brought her another glass of medicine and a cool cloth for her eyes.

"Want some tea?" he asked, after she'd swallowed the seltzer.

"Let me just lie here for a few minutes first," she told him. "I'm feeling better but I don't want to push it."

She dozed off and John let her sleep for another hour. When he awakened her this time she was physically better, but when she heard Colin's voice in the other room, it made her feel ill all over again.

She could hardly get the words out, as she asked, "Was he here last night?"

He shook his head. "No, don't you remember? He slept at a friend's."

She gasped slightly. "Why'd he do that? Does he know?"

He touched her arm. "Relax, I told him I took the couch. That's why he slept elsewhere, so one of us could have the bed and the other the couch."

In an anxious whisper, she admonished, "He can't know, John. No one can know! If Andrew ever found out, it would kill him, really kill him!" Her face was pathetic, her eyes pleading even through the puffiness.

"No one is going to know anything," he answered emphatically. "Do you think you can get up now? It's late. It's half past seven."

Slowly, she moved to dangle her legs from the bed. When she was standing, she saw the unmistakable stains on the sheet. "Oh no, oh God," came out of her again. "What are we going to do about that?"

John thought for a moment. "I have an idea. We'll put it to soak in the tub. We'll tell Colin that you've had your period come unexpectedly in the night."

My period—my God, she worried now. She remembered thinking about that last night when John said he didn't have any rubbers. But it should be all right. It's due in two days. "Good, that's good," she whispered. "That's what we'll do. We'll say I've scrubbed it clean and left it to soak. I'll just do that now," she decided, then practically ripped the sheet from the bed.

Colin looked away in embarrassment when he saw Annie's eyes. She took a seat at the table where John had set her cup of tea and quietly began drinking it, staring into the cup.

John tried to relieve some of the tension by informing Colin, "She's had an awful night. Leaving her friends is turning out to be much more difficult than she'd imagined."

"Andrew's had a night of it, too," he responded.

Annie looked up for the first time. "What's happened?" she asked.

"Nothing's happened," he answered. "It's just that after you left—well, we were all very concerned about him. The storm was coming, and no one could get him to leave the beach."

The cup in her hand began to shake and spill suddenly, so she set it down.

"Had enough?" John questioned softly.

She nodded.

"We'd better be on our way, then."

Colin and John took a towel with them and went outside to dry Percy. Then they secured the bags to the bike before coming back to the flat for Annie. She descended the steps to the street warily. John grasped her arm because she seemed so unsteady. When she took her first deep breath outside, she noticed that strange, faraway scent in the air, the kind that comes only after a powerful storm has moved out. As she surveyed the carnage that surrounded her, her thoughts were drawn to the Whaum's garden. Although it was barely beating now, her heart slowed even more when she realized how badly it must have been damaged.

The engine started up easily, and John let it run for a few minutes while he bade his friend good-bye.

"I hope Percy is as good to you as he's been to me," Colin told Annie. "Have a wonderful time on your trip."

"Thanks," was all she could manage.

It had already been decided that John would drive. In her present state it was quite impossible for her to do anything but ride along, but there was a second's hesitation as John handed Annie her helmet.

"What about you?" she asked. "You're driving."

"I have dark glasses," he answered.

"But wouldn't the visor be easier to drive with?"

"Yes," he admitted, "but it's your helmet."

"Then you wear it," she decided. "Whoever's driving should wear it."

"All right, but you should take my scarf," he told her. He unwound the woolen scarf he had around his neck, an item of apparel Annie had never seen him without, save last night in bed. He laid it gently on her shoulders before securing it inside the collar of her jacket. "We'll tuck your hair under to keep it from flying about."

Thinking of that, Annie automatically reached into her pocket for her barrette; her hand grasped air and her heart stood still for a moment.

John mounted the bike and revved it up. He reached for her, and she straddled the seat. As she sat, the sore feeling in her vagina flooded her consciousness and renewed her shame.

"Please don't go past the Whaum," she asked, because she knew she could never bear it.

John nodded his understanding and rubbed her arm to convey that.

"But take me by the cathedral," she said now. "I want to see it once more."

They started off. At the end of North Street, he parked and shut off the engine. Annie got off the bike and walked into the grounds alone. She drank in as much of the scene as she could, etching the details into her memory: the bench where she and Andrew would sit, St. Rule's Tower, the crumbling gravestones, and the ruined walls. Her last look was through the window arches at clouds the high wind was chasing across the sea.

"Good-bye," she said aloud. "Thank you, I'll never forget."

They left the village by way of Hepburn Gardens, passing David Russell Hall still in its Sunday morning slumber. In Melville Lumsdaine's room, however, the occupants were not asleep.

"Listen," Susannah said, when she recognized the rumble. "I think I hear Percy."

"Must be," Mel answered.

They were lying in each other's arms, and they tightened their embrace.

Just at the edge of town, John felt the bike beginning to vibrate. He pulled off the road onto a cemetery entrance. But when he stopped, he realized that the vibrations had not been coming from the bike but from the sobs of his passenger. He turned off the engine, removed the helmet, and twisted around to ask, "Will you be all right?"

Through her tears she asked, "Why does it have to be this way? Why are there always endings?"

He shook his head as he set the kickstand. "I don't know. I expect it's just the nature of things." In her overly emotional state, he'd been debating the wisdom of this, but he thought now that it might be comforting in some way. So reaching into his jacket pocket, he pulled the envelope from it. "This was on the seat when I went out to dry the bike."

The handwriting was recognizably Andrew's, though it simply read—*Annie.* With some trepidation, she took it from him, then walked a short distance away to read it in privacy. Realizing that he must have put it there after the rain stopped made her fearful of its contents, made her wonder if he somehow knew what had happened with John. Still, she found the courage to open it.

They were not his words, but she could feel the depth of sadness with which he had written:

The flower that smiles to-day
To-morrow dies;
All that we wish to stay
Tempts and then flies.
What is this world's delight?
Lightning that mocks the night,
Brief even as bright.

Virtue, how frail it is!
Friendship how rare!
Love, how it sells poor bliss
For proud despair!
But we, though soon they fall,
survive their joy, and all
Which ours we call.

Whilst skies are blue and bright,
Whilst flowers are gay,
Whilst eyes that change ere night
Make glad the day;
Whilst yet the calm hours creep,
Dream thou—and from thy sleep
Then wake to weep.

It was signed "Percy Bysshe Shelley."

An old man with white hair was in the cemetery. He opened the wrought iron gates to come to them. "Canna be o' some help?" he asked in a thick Fife accent.

"Ta, but we're just stopping a moment," John informed him.

He noticed Annie's eyes and the stricken expression she wore as she clutched the letter to her chest. "Is the young lass all right, then?"

John answered for her. "She was visiting St. Andrews, and now she's quite distressed to be leaving."

Ignoring them both, Annie kissed the paper, then carefully folded the letter. She put it in the inside pocket of her jacket where she'd also put the knife and patted them as though they were alive.

The old man raised a single brow. "Oh, tha' is a sad thing, now. I feel for ya, lassie. I've been here all my life, and I'll be spending the rest of eternity here, too." He motioned toward the headstones. "But I belong here, and if ya don't, then I s'pose ya'd better be getting on ta wherever 'tis ya do belong."

John smiled at him, then restarted the bike. The man turned and went back into the graveyard, pulling the gates after him. The noise of their closing was hard. It was solid and conclusive, and loud enough to be heard over the roar from the motorbike.

He hadn't meant them to, but the old man's parting words pierced her. And with the clang of the gates behind him, it came to her with perfect clarity, more clear than anything she'd ever known in her life, that there was finality in that tone. She knew she'd heard the thunder of judgment, the booming voice of prophesy. She knew she'd heard the sound of the Gates of Paradise closing behind her.

* * *

Before the rain started there was wind. It came first as a gentle breeze, tossing the smoke upward in puffs and clearing the air, but then stronger and stronger it blew until the fire was laid horizontal and the sand was lifted off the beach. The partygoers quickly packed up their things and sought shelter from what they knew was coming—all but one that is, who remained where he was, sitting at the edge of the water with an almost empty bottle of Scotch.

Andrew could not leave. He felt anchored to the place where he had last seen Annie, though now an hour or two had passed, because here he could continue to feel her presence and imagine her sitting with him on the sand. He could not get up and walk to the Whaum; he would not pass near Colin's flat where he knew she was, where walls and doors separated them, where Percy B. sat outside waiting to take her away. The rain beat down on him, stinging and cold, drenching him to the bone, and still he did not move. It blew against him ever harder, blinding him, making it difficult at times to breathe, yet his only action was to clasp more tightly the barrette she had given him.

Sometime in that night he did move, though he didn't remember doing it. He walked into the Whaum, and the sloppy sound of his shoes awakened Robin.

Aghast at the disheveled sight of his roommate, he exclaimed, "What the bloody hell? Why didn't you come in?"

There was no answer.

"Please go and change out of those things," he implored. "You're going to catch your death!"

Andrew walked into the bath, and after a time, Robin heard the sound of the tap and the tub being filled. He returned to his bed but not to sleep, because something he'd seen in Andrew's eyes left him feeling too uneasy to rest.

The morning light found Andrew sitting in the parlor, staring out at the battered rose garden. Ruts had formed in the ground from the runoff, large branches from surrounding trees had crushed the bushes, and part of the arbor had come down. He stared at the scene for some time before going to his room for a jacket.

He had laid Annie's barrette on the table next to his bed when he'd come in, and seeing it there now, without its owner, was more difficult than he ever could have imagined. He opened the drawer to put it away, out of his sight, and noticed the folded tissue that he had put there some weeks ago. He reached for it and tucked it into his pocket.

He left the Whaum with an envelope in his hand, looking for Percy. On the street, he witnessed more of the same havoc that had been wreaked on the rose garden, though, oddly, he wasn't bothered by any of it. To his mind, the devastation he saw everywhere was nothing less than appropriate.

He found the motorbike drenched like everything else and parked just in front of Colin's flat at Eden Court. He wiped the seat with his sleeve before leaving the envelope there, anchored under a stone. Then he crossed the street and walked to the Catholic church that bordered the little park across from the Russell Hotel. He let himself inside the garden and stood behind some bushes along the wall, where he would not be visible, and waited. He had to see her one more time.

From his hiding place, Andrew watched Colin return to the flat, a pillow and blanket wedged under one arm, and it was obvious he'd spent the night elsewhere. He saw John and Colin come out to dry the motorbike, watched John put the letter in his pocket. He followed Annie's every gesture as she emerged from the building aided by John, her eyes so puffy he could make it out even at his distance. He noticed how carefully she walked, as though she were wounded or ill. He held his breath as John removed his scarf and tenderly wrapped it around her neck. He noticed how gingerly Annie straddled the bike when she sat, how weak she seemed when she reached her arms around John's waist. He watched her speak to John's ear, then his squeeze and rub of her arm in response, in an overly familiar way. He witnessed all of this, hiding behind the bushes, clutching a small piece of tissue in one hand, and he suddenly knew something he didn't want to know.

He couldn't have said exactly how—if anyone had asked, if he'd been able to speak—but the truth was he knew because he could see in her what others couldn't. And he saw her that morning, wearing her shame like a cloak.

Andrew watched them drive off together. He heard the bike double back and move in the direction of the cathedral, its roar the only sound on this quiet Sunday morning. He listened as it left the town headed for David Russell, fading off, leaving him to stand like a thief in the bushes, still clutching the tissue. When he could hear it no more, he walked out of the walled enclosure, across the park, and onto the jetty.

He stood alone in the morning air, watching the sea carry on its pretense of calm, imagining where they were at that moment, thinking they'd probably reached the little cemetery at the edge of town. He looked down at his hand and then opened his fist to unfold the tissue. There was no breeze to do what he wanted, so he brought the tissue to his mouth and blew on the two long, dark hairs, sending them to fly over the water.

Chapter 25

Percy B. tackled the hilly country roads, great and lumbering, like some mighty workhorse unharnessed and out of the pasture. He made a fuss as he carried his passengers, bursting through the morning quiet with the strain of it, his clamor bouncing against the stone walls and falling back on them. They raced on as the sun rose on the horizon, turning the yellow fields to brilliant gold, the dew-pale green to deep jade. Sheep regarded their passing, cattle momentarily lifted their heads from the grass, and a farmer or shepherd here and there noticed their flight. They moved farther and farther away from the place Annie wanted to be, wished to be, and deeper into the future, into the unknown. And with every mile put behind them, the ache in her heart grew that much deeper.

When they reached the Forth Road Bridge, Annie turned and looked behind her. The past was already there, in the distance—Andrew part of it, Susannah and Mel, too—and it tore at what was left of her heart. When they were on the span, a gust of wind caught them from behind, pushing Percy ahead faster, more recklessly, and John had to fight for control. The cold waters of the firth beckoned them from below, and for an instant it seemed as though they might plunge over the edge. But John managed to counteract the crosswinds and bring them safely to the other side. They both breathed a sigh of relief when they were on solid ground again.

They stopped once after Edinburgh to warm up with hot coffee and were quickly on their way again, John obviously feeling pressed for time. While they drank, he told Annie that they would stop for lunch when they reached Newcastle upon Tyne, and they made it to the outskirts by half past eleven. They left the motorway and drove into the city, parking in front of a large, busy pub.

"I thought you might like to see this. It's a bit of local color," he said, as he led the way inside.

The pub looked as though it could have been a movie set. It was a classic from early in the previous century with a long, oak bar, well worn by the rubbing of countless bodies and untold numbers of polishings. The large room was filled with the working class of Newcastle, all with glasses in hand, talking and eating their way through the midday. The clientele was almost exclusively male; a few women were about—sturdy, weathered looking women who served the customers—but there were no female patrons to be seen. John ordered two pints of the local brown ale and then found a seat for them on a long bench.

She frowned into the glass. "I don't think I can manage this."

"Nonsense, it's exactly what you need. Couple pints of this and you'll be right as rain."

She sipped at the ale and although it tasted good, the face she made was like a child's when forced to swallow nasty medicine.

"What do you think of the place?" he asked her.

"I feel like an extra in a film about British miners," she whispered.

He laughed, then said, "That's it exactly. Finish your pint and I'll get us something to eat."

She watched him walk away toward the bar. Sitting alone in this alien environment, she had to ask herself what on earth she was doing here, in Newcastle, with John. Her stomach turned again, and she had great difficulty swallowing the beer that was in her mouth.

With prodding from John, they finished their meal quickly and were on the M-1 motorway in no time. The highway seemed mean and ugly to Annie, almost American, and it deepened her sadness over leaving the gentle, Scottish countryside.

The road was mostly flat now, and John was finally able to get some speed out of Percy. Annie clung to his body as they maneuvered in and out of traffic, her bottom still uncomfortably sore from their nighttime encounter.

They were driving through a wood, part of the Sherwood Forest actually, when Annie tapped John on the shoulder and asked if they might stop; her bladder was uncomfortably full. He located an appropriate place, a lay-by for traveler's picnics; they pulled into it and parked under the cover of an old tree. Annie walked into the deep shade, far from the road, and relieved herself behind a fallen trunk. She then sat on the trunk and buried her head in her lap.

Eventually, he came looking for her. When he found her, he realized she'd been crying again.

He asked softly, "May I sit with you?"

Her response was unconvincing. "If you like."

"Would you like to talk?"

"No," she answered. "I just need to think."

"About Andrew?" he wondered.

Her eyes had begun to swell again, and she sighed heavily. "What I've done. I don't know why I did it. I just hurt so much. But it's more than that," she had begun to realize. "I'm angry, too, angry that he turned away from me, that he let me leave with you without ever saying . . ." She stopped herself, because she didn't want him to know those details.

As he debated telling her this, he picked up a nearby branch and began drawing circles in the moist soil. Finally deciding it might help her, he carefully said, "When you were with him on the beach last night, Robin and Susannah wanted a word with me. They asked me to take you away from him, to help do that, anyway. I thought it a peculiar request, so I pressed them for the reason. They said it was important that he make a clean break from you—something to do with his family situation. And the way they put things, it seemed terribly so, important, I mean."

As it dawned on her, she brought a hand to her mouth. Of course, Susannah knows he's engaged. Andrew must have told her in that conversation she mentioned! And Robin, he had to have known all along; that's why he was always a little distant, a little odd with me, she realized. They both knew, and they saw the hopelessness of it. Why didn't I? she asked herself. Why have I let myself believe and hope against hope, only to be shot down in the end? But I was so sure of him, she lamented, so very sure that he loved me.

"I didn't say this to hurt you," he wanted her to understand. "But I thought you should know. There's no use feeling guilty when . . ."

She resented his thinking that he knew something she didn't, and she interjected, "I know what's going on. Why do you think I slept with you?"

That was surprisingly hurtful to John, and he retorted, "If he wanted to be with you, he would have, you know. He'd be with you now."

She snapped her head toward him, then stood abruptly, her eyes glaring hatred. "What do you know about us, anyway? You don't know a damned thing about us!"

Her indignation irked him; he also stood, and just as he met her face, she slapped his. One of his hands went to soothe the sting it left, while the other grabbed her wrist. They stayed locked in confrontation for a moment before he seethed, "The truth hurts, doesn't it?"

"Like the truth of my wanting to be with Andrew and not you?" she lashed back.

He squeezed her wrist. "You can close your eyes and call me his name and pretend all you like. But I know the truth that you refuse to see."

She bristled. "What truth?"

With a malicious grin, he answered, "That you wanted to be with me last night as much as I wanted you."

She scoffed and turned her head away.

He laughed. "And it's happening again, isn't it? You want me right now, don't you?"

"Bullshit," she declared. "I want Andrew."

Her stubborn refusal only ignited his desire. He let go of her wrist and grasped her upper arms as he demanded, "Admit you want me."

She shook her head defiantly.

With her slap to his face, the tenor of their relationship had suddenly changed; a door had been opened that let something dangerous in, something that impelled John to tighten his grip on her arms and shove her backward against a tree trunk as he insisted, "Say it!"

The aggressiveness of his action infuriated her, but instead of pushing him away, she seized him tightly and pulled him to herself. With emotions that were a tangle of anger and lust, of hurt and loss, she grasped his buttocks and pulled his pelvis to hers. "So what if I do?"

His organ stiffened in response. "I want to hear you say it," he demanded as he pinned her against the tree.

Once more, she shook her head.

"Tell me!"

She could see how irate he'd become but that only made her more defiant. "It's Andrew I want."

His erection hardening against her, he responded, "Andrew's not here. I am!"

She dug her fingers into his flesh and glared at him. "I fucking know that!"

John received the message, and what she was saying to him was clear: I can't willingly, consciously betray him, so we have to do this in anger, with contentious passion.

In softer tones, he told her now, "I know what you want, even if you can't admit it." Then he abruptly unzipped her jeans and yanked them from her hips. He was breathing deeply, and in the next instant he found himself overcome by the strong scent of her. It was his scent mixed with hers, and it drove him a little crazy.

With her bottom exposed, Annie experienced a powerful rush of excitement. And just as it had last night, it rapidly overtook her, dulling her heartache as it chased everything else from her mind. She closed her eyes and spread her legs to his intrusion. The act was not so much an invitation as it was a giving over, like a junkie in the grips of a craving, extending her arm for the needle.

John could not get into her quickly enough. "Open your eyes and say it to me. Tell me you want me!" he demanded as his penis throbbed inside of her.

Her juices poured over him as she confessed, "I do."

He kissed her neck and felt the goose pimples rise to his lips. His powerful thrusts lifted her off the ground. "Tell me again!"

Slowly, she opened her eyes to his. "I want you."

The feelings that were exploding in him were unlike any he'd ever experienced; they were savage and forbidden and more than a little frightening, but he willingly, shamelessly abandoned himself to them. "What do you want me to do to you?" he demanded over his thumping heart, then watched as her eyes ignited into green fire.

The rush intensified and burned through her flesh. "I want you to take me," her voice answered, even as her heart was filling with guilt.

He kissed her as she finished saying that, pushing his tongue to the back of her mouth, wanting to hurt her, to make her scream out in pain. With one more powerful thrust and a great grunt, he released himself inside of her. "Oh, my God!" he called, and it echoed through the forest.

She felt his strength go and strained to hold him up.

For the next minute, John didn't stir save to moan into Annie's neck, his body pinning hers.

She could feel him pulsing inside of her as she asked, "Are you all right?"

"Oooh," he exhaled. "Don't move." The overly acute sensitivity of his organ made him squeeze her arms to keep her still.

When he reluctantly withdrew himself, she saw how red and swollen he had become. "Does it hurt?" she asked.

He winced to answer. "It's bloody sore. Are you?"

"I'm beyond sore," she told him.

She had not pulled her jeans up yet, and seeing her standing in front of him that way, in her ravaged, vulnerable state, sent him off again. He exhaled as he said, "I know it's crazy, but I think I'm going to be hard again." Then he swallowed before asking, "Do you want me to stop?"

She knew what she should answer—yes, we have to stop. We shouldn't be doing this. But she didn't. She couldn't, because in the span of the last twelve hours, she had discovered that the need for sex can arise as an essential, consuming thirst, and it didn't matter that it had been Andrew who'd left her parched and suffering for the want of it. It was John who offered her a drink.

She looked into his eyes, then uttered, "No."

He was slightly breathless as he responded, "Good, because I want you so much, I don't think I can."

He coaxed her into sitting on a cushion of leaves and removed her hiking boots. Her jeans came off next, then he removed his own boots and trousers. Kneeling now, he nudged her legs apart and slowly, very carefully, reentered her.

Before he began to move, he softly asked into her ear, "All right?"

She answered by taking his head in her hands and pulling his mouth to hers.

John had meant to take this one slowly and tenderly, but Annie's kiss told him that was not what she wanted. She attacked him with her mouth, swallowing his tongue so violently it pulled on the lining of his mouth. But he was undeterred; his desire plugged into hers and fired up like a generator. Together they let the wild feelings carry them, transport them to that place where sex and lust exist purely on their own, without the complication of love.

They made animal sounds there in the shaded wood, grunting, moaning, biting into one another, reacting to the pain and the pleasure at once. His hips drove hers and rolled her in the leaves. She sat on top of him, sliding herself up and down, causing him to pound the ground with his fists and call out in anguish. He coaxed her into lying belly down while he massaged her ass and listened to her groans. Then he raised her by the hips, bringing her up on all fours, and reentered her body. He reached under her sweater and unhooked her bra so that he might take her breasts in his hands. Although he knew he should be gentle, he could not refrain from pulling and pinching her nipples. They screamed together as he pounded her more severely now, as though some external force was driving them beyond their human endurance. They wailed and sighed and writhed and forgot that they were part of the civilized world, as John thrust ever harder and ejaculated yet again.

Sometime earlier, when John had gone to find her, a truck driver stopped at the lay-by for the same purpose as Annie. He heard the couple before he saw them and hid away to watch, as John pulled Annie's jeans down and drilled her against the tree. They were unaware of his presence though he was very close, close enough to capture every detail.

Breathlessly, he watched their first encounter. He could see how red and swollen they both were; he even fancied he could smell them. He couldn't take his eyes away as they played out the passion again, Annie lying on the ground now, her legs spread toward the voyeur, inviting him to her tumid lips. He heard the smacking of their flesh, watched as John's scrotum slapped against her, the driving muscles of his buttocks taut and prominent. Propelled by his own need, the man unzipped his trousers and stroked himself as they wrestled in the leaves. He imagined that it was his engorged organ that Annie slid herself on, torturing him with the exquisite pain of it, leaving it glistening from her moisture with every stroke. He was even thinking that he would roll her onto her belly and mount her from behind when John did exactly that, both of them screaming like savages, wilder and more frenzied now than mating animals.

The stranger stayed with them through it all, watching every move, imagining every touch, hearing every sound. He delighted in their obvious pain, and when the time came, he fell to his knees with penis in hand as he frantically joined John's climax and aimed it toward Annie's baleful face.

Annie thought she heard footsteps but was too weak to be concerned. She lay on the forest floor, half naked, semen dripping from her like sap from a felled tree. John rolled away and onto his abdomen, falling almost immediately into a deep sleep. She drifted off, too, without any attempt to cover herself. Her legs still slightly spread, she sank into the decaying, pungent leaves and fell asleep to the sound of creaking boughs, rubbed together by the wind.

Crazy, scattered images whirled around in her head in that place where nothing makes sense just before sleep comes. She heard jumbled voices and floated through different, unrelated scenes before entering nothingness. She lingered for a few restful minutes in that nowhere place before coming back out of it into a full-blown dream. She stood outside the cemetery gates and watched the old man caring for the graves, pulling weeds, polishing the headstones. From time to time, he looked up and smiled. She clung to the wrought iron with clenched fists and waited for him to open them, but he would not.

Then she was back in the gloom of the wood, outstretched upon the leaves, juices trickling from her vagina. Something cold grasped her leg and drew it away from the other, separating her swollen labia. She wanted to sit up, but when she tried to move, her hands seemed shackled to the ground, her body encumbered by an enormous weight. She felt the cold climb up one thigh, wrapping itself around and around, until it reached the moisture it sought and slid into it, wriggling its large, hooded head against the bruised walls. She struggled to awaken, to bring herself out of the blackness, but she couldn't. The head danced to a frenzied, pulsing rhythm inside her, punching every bruise, tearing further the already battered membranes. With one last violent leap—as though it were trying to burst through—it halted, then slithered out, biting her as it left. Her cry tore through the darkness.

Startled and disoriented, John sat bolt upright, but he quickly realized that Annie had had a nightmare. He reached for her and pulled her to him. "Shhh, it's all right. You were dreaming."

"I was? It was so real." Her eyes were wide and wild looking.

"What was?"

She looked around frantically. "A snake, a snake climbed up my leg and slid into me. It bit me. It was horrible!"

"My word, that is horrible!" He looked around, too. "I don't see anything. Maybe an insect was crawling on you."

She glanced at her throbbing bottom and touched it warily. "It seemed so real, but it must have been a dream." Her hand came away extraordinarily wet, and the scent it carried with it was powerful. "I guess I'm not bitten, just sore. I'm so sore." Tears began to drop onto her cheeks.

He kissed her forehead. "When we get to my flat, I'll run you a nice hot bath. You'll feel much better after that."

"How much longer 'till we're there?" she sniveled.

"We're about halfway."

"Oh John," the flow of tears increased. "I don't know if I can manage sitting on Percy again."

"I've a pullover in my sack," he offered. "We'll put it under you to make the seat softer, and I'll stop more often to give you a rest, all right?"

The lorry driver had waited for them to return to the motorbike. He smiled at the couple as they walked past his cab and watched every move that Annie made, the picture of her naked bottom still fresh in his mind. His right hand clutched his now relaxed organ and he stroked it gently, tugging on the foreskin. His leering, black-toothed grin spooked her, and she whispered into John's ear to hurry and get them out of there.

The stranger laughed as Annie carefully straddled Percy's seat, and John tucked the sweater under her. When they drove away, he closed his eyes and conjured up the memory, one that he would happily recall for the rest of his days. He could feel again the engorgement, the slipperiness, hear again the slurping sound that came from penetrating her depths. He brought his hand away from his penis and to his nose, to breathe deeply of her aroma.

* * *

They weren't on the road long, getting close to Nottingham, when John began losing control of the bike. He managed to pull it over safely and out of traffic near an exit ramp.

"Bloody hell. We have a puncture!"

"What'll we do?" she asked.

"Nothing for it but to go down the road and hope we find a garage."

They walked Percy B. a couple hundred yards or more and miraculously found an open garage. Two dirty, mean looking men were at work in the rear with an acetylene torch.

John approached them cautiously. "Excuse me, could you repair a puncture for us?"

They looked up briefly, scowled, then went back to their work.

He wasn't certain what that meant, so he asked again. "I say, would it be possible?" Then he thought to add, "We can wait while you finish that."

In a gruff voice, one of them answered, "We'll get to it," while keeping at his task.

John raised his eyebrows and glanced sideways at Annie. "Well, looks as though you've got your rest sooner than expected."

Annie noticed a small, filthy boy, about three years old, playing very near the men. Sparks from the torch were flying everywhere as he fiddled with his broken toy, his eyes unprotected. When some of the sparks landed on his dirty head, she went over to him and put her hands on his shoulders with the intent of coaxing him away from the danger. As she touched him, a fierce sound and a great rustling came from under the automobile he sat next to, and before she had any idea what was happening, her right thigh was clamped by the mouth of a German shepherd, who meant to bring her down. In her helplessness, she let out a low, animal-like scream herself, as the beast tried to tear the muscle from her femur.

The two men were there in an instant to restrain the dog, and it took both of them, big brutes that they were, to pull the bitch off Annie. John approached her with trepidation, fearing for himself. He kept his eyes on the animal, as she bit at the air and fought against her restrainers. The little boy stood by, wordlessly clutching his toy.

"She shouldn't ha' touched the boy. She's protectin' the boy," one managed to say.

Annie cried out, "I only meant to get him away from the sparks. I didn't want him burned by the sparks!" and rubbed her leg.

They stared at her. "Ye from America?"

She answered, "Yes, dammit!" through her sobs.

"We'll fix th' puncture now, and ye can be on yer way."

"How is it?" John asked her.

"I need to take my jeans down to see," she sniveled. The cloth had several holes from the dog's teeth, but the jeans were not torn open.

"Go over ther'," one said, pointing to a room filled with greasy automobile parts.

John supported her as she limped across the garage. He helped her undo her pants and gently pulled them down. She winced as he accidentally rubbed against the bite with his hand. The skin was not broken, but the injured area of her thigh was already swelling to the size of a cantaloupe.

"Lord, that's dreadful!" he declared.

Tears poured down her cheeks. "Could you get me some ice for it?"

"No ice." One of the creatures was standing in the doorway, gaping at Annie in her underwear.

"Then how about a clean cloth and some cool water?" John asked him.

"Can do tha'," he answered, before turning and walking away.

The man returned with a reasonably clean cloth and a pot of water. John had sat Annie down and elevated her leg on some crates. He laid the dampened cloth carefully over her swelling thigh.

"That'll teach me," she tried to laugh. "No more good deeds for me."

"That Alsatian came from out of nowhere. I hadn't even seen her, had you?"

"Obviously not!"

"Fiercely protective, anyway," he decided, as he refreshed the cloth and laid it on her leg again. The skin was beginning to discolor.

"God, it hurts!"

"Should I take you to a doctor? That's looking very nasty now, very nasty indeed."

After a few minutes, a woman approached them. She carried a steaming bowl and another cloth, and was every bit as dirty and sullen as the others.

She dipped the cloth in the strange smelling mixture and handed it to John. "Here, put t'on her."

"What is it?"

"Poultice. Hyssop and shepherd's purse."

It was warm and soothing, and Annie looked up and smiled. "Ta," she said, "that feels good."

The woman smiled back and revealed that her front teeth were missing.

It didn't take long for the men to be finished with the tire. They came to get John who, along with the woman, had continued to nurse Annie's wound.

"Half a quid," one of them said, and nothing else—no apology, no concern over the injury.

"Can you ride, do you think?" John asked Annie.

"Do I have any choice?" she responded.

"I guess there's nothing for it but to try," he told her. "We can always stay over in a B and B if you can't go on."

Annie nodded, but her face assumed a peculiar expression as the memory dawned on her.

"What is it?" John asked.

"It's really bizarre."

"What is?"

"I had a bite like this once—in the same place, on this very thigh. A friend of mine bit me."

John thought he'd heard her incorrectly. "What? What kind of friend would do something like that?"

"He didn't mean to hurt me," she explained. "It was at my sixteenth birthday party. He was drunk and I don't think he realized what he was doing."

It was still baffling. "But why on earth would he do something like that at all?"

Seeing the bewilderment on his face, she realized she needed to explain. "He was on his way to Vietnam, John. It was his last party with his friends, and I think he must have been feeling desperate." Her voice trailed off. "Very desperate."

"To say the least!" he declared.

Her face relaxed as she sighed. "I've only just now realized why he did it. After all this time, I've just figured it out. It's as though he was sinking his teeth into the moment, trying to hold onto it, to keep it from passing."

Shaking his head in confusion, he impatiently inquired, "Are you ready?"

"Yes," she answered quietly, her thoughts obviously elsewhere. They were wandering into the past, to the time when she last saw Rob Mitchell, when she sent him away and watched him disappear into the darkness. If only I could do it over, she wished now. I'd run after him. I'd ask him to come back. I'd let him stay.

John started up Percy, "We've got to be on our way. We've lost too much time already."

She tucked the sweater under herself as she sat, then rested her weary head on his shoulder. In the next instant, Percy roared and leapt forward, firing gravel pellets against the garage doors.

* * *

As the day drew to an end in St. Andrews, Andrew Stuart-Gordon lost count of how many drinks he'd had. He'd been standing at the bar for hours, saying nothing to anyone, seemingly unaware of what was happening around him. Susannah and Melville had come and gone, unnoticed. Robin had tried several times to get him to leave and go for something to eat, but to no avail. The bartender had even tried to get him to slow down, but he would not respond to anyone's overtures. It wasn't until Patrick Ramsay came into the Scores that he stirred.

It didn't take much, just the utterance of her name. He didn't hear the context in which it was mentioned. What was said may even have been complimentary, but it didn't matter. He'd said her name and he'd had no right. Patrick only saw Andrew's fist. He saw the fist just before he hit the bar with the side of his head, then crumpled to the floor.

Chapter 26

When Patrick Ramsay hit the floor of the pub, he lay motionless for a few, terrifying moments, while everyone around him stood frozen—everyone but his attacker, who turned back to the bar and his drink. Patrick did get up, though, and rather quickly, all things considered. And though his friends tried to convince him to sit down, he would not.

He had not seen who hit him, but he hadn't needed to. Steadying himself against the railing, he grabbed a bottle from the hand of the bartender, and in the next instant he brought it crashing down on the back of Andrew's head. Andrew calmly turned, looking at Patrick as though he'd expected it, and with his hair soaked by the liquor and blood streaming from his scalp, he landed another punch square in Ramsay's face. Patrick whirled for a moment as blood spurted from his nose, but he had the advantage, being the sober one of the two, and came quickly back with a blasting blow to Andrew's abdomen. Patrick then picked up a nearby chair, and while Andrew's back was bent, he struck with all the power he had and broke it across him, sending him to the ground in a heap of splintered wood. The blood from his scalp wound poured across the pub floor.

They were positively wretched-looking the next morning, but both managed to make it to their tutorials, and both were called afterward to see the dean. They were severely reprimanded, told that letters would be sent home immediately, and advised that they had better not become involved in another such episode or they would be expelled without recourse.

* * *

When they finally reached John's flat just outside of Oxford, Annie and he were exhausted, but she was not too tired to get into the tub to soak. And soak she did, until the water turned icy. And in the morning when John went off to sit for an examination, she got into the tub again.

John returned in the early afternoon to take Annie to lunch. They drove along the river Thames to a pub he'd told her about, the Trout. They parked Percy B. and walked across the Port Meadow to reach the old inn. Near the water's edge, two swans were engaged in mortal combat, and they had to give them a wide berth as they made their way past.

"They're such beautiful creatures. How can they be so violent?" Annie questioned.

"They've probably a dispute over the rights to a female," John glibly responded. "They have a great pub lunch here. I think you'll enjoy it."

In the center of the main room, a prettily decorated table overflowed with all sorts of English pub foods—pies, pasties, meats and cheeses, Scotch eggs, and the like. They piled their plates high and then went back again, both feeling as though they hadn't eaten for days. When they were finally satiated, they went outside again to stroll the grounds and take in the scenery.

"You seem to be in somewhat better spirits," John observed.

"Somewhat," she answered. She did feel a little better, because instead of dwelling on her separation from Andrew as she had been, she was now focusing on the possibility of their reunion.

"Your leg still looks dreadful. Does it hurt much?"

"Not as much as yesterday. The soaking has helped. How was the exam?"

"Went well, I think. It was on the Renaissance, and if I don't know about the bloody Renaissance by now, I'm never going to," he laughed. "We'll go for a drive after we leave here, and I'll show you the different colleges if you're up to it."

"Riding Percy isn't the most comfortable thing for me, but I'd like to see what I can."

"Tomorrow I'll take you to tea at a place called the Nosebag when I've finished up. And we can pop in the tourist bureau and collect ferry information for you, too. I expect you'll want to leave on Wednesday."

"Or Thursday," she shrugged. "I have time to meet my friend."

Nervously now, he told her, "Wednesday would probably be better."

"I'm not certain my leg is ready for that," she informed him. But his anxiety was not lost on her. "Why would Wednesday be better?"

He stammered as he began, "W-well, of course, I wouldn't want you to push yourself. It's just that if you stay after Wednesday, things could get somewhat complicated."

They were standing on the bridge, looking down at some punters on the Thames, but she turned to him to ask, "How do you mean?"

He'd been searching for a discreet way to tell her this, but with the moment at hand, he simply blurted, "My girlfriend's due back then."

"Your girlfriend?" she repeated, then left her mouth agape, trying to remember if there had even been a hint of her before. "I don't recall you mentioning her," she finally said.

"No, I don't believe I have," he readily agreed.

They'd been leaning on the bridge railing, but John straightened up and began shuffling around. She looked away from him and toward the rival swans, who now drifted lazily along the river. She wondered if they'd given up because they decided the lady swan in question wasn't worth it, or was it was because she'd gone off with someone else?

"There wasn't a good time," he thought to add.

"Wasn't a good time?" She would have liked to scream this, but because they were within earshot of others, she whispered in as nasty a tone as she could manage. "How about Saturday night in St. Andrews, before we slept together? That would have been a good time. That would have been a hell of a lot better time than now, John."

"I didn't think it mattered," he defended.

"To whom? To me or to you?" she demanded to know.

"To either of us."

"And why wouldn't it matter?"

He stammered again. "B-because, it was just—well, it wasn't anything important. You and I, we aren't in love."

Annie almost smiled now, thinking about what they'd done together, how she'd betrayed herself, betrayed her love for Andrew, and possibly ruined her chances with him. She repeated the words to herself—*wasn't anything important.*

Awkwardly touching her back, he added, "We're fond of each other, to be sure, but it's not the same as love."

She caught him in the eyes before saying, "To be sure."

"I've known from the start how you feel about Andrew," he explained. "And I've made a commitment, you see. We've been together for several years now." He blinked and looked away from Annie. "What happened between us—I didn't mean for it to interfere with that, with my relationship, you understand. At least, I hope you can."

"Can I?" She raised her eyebrows but kept her face relaxed.

Blushing now, he admitted, "I'm in love with her, Annie."

She frowned as she pondered the absurdity of his having sex with her while being in love with someone else. Then she laughed at herself for being critical of him. After all, hadn't she done the same—and worse? "You needn't worry, John," she assured him. "I'll be on my way before she returns." Then she sarcastically added, "I wouldn't want to stand in the way of love."

The intensity of her gaze was difficult to tolerate, so he averted his eyes. "I appreciate that very much, Annie.

You're a sport," he declared, then instantly regretted his choice of phrase.

Annie was quiet during her tour of Oxford but politely appreciative. Late in the afternoon, they stopped in to visit a friend of John's at University College, a chap named George. As they entered the grand old residence hall where he lived, Annie noticed a plaque that contained some reference to Percy Shelley. She stopped to read it.

Excitedly, she exclaimed, "This is where he lived! This is where Percy lived when he was a student!"

"He was only here two terms," John informed her, "before he was sent down."

"That's something we have in common, then," she grinned, still focused on the bronze plaque. "I was only at college two terms."

"Were you expelled?" he asked.

"No, I dropped out."

"Why?"

She dismissed the inquiry. "It's a long story, and I wouldn't want to bore you."

As they went into the building, she ran her hand along the wall, wondering if Shelley had touched there, too.

They went out that night to a club of sorts, a hangout for students. John chatted with his friends, and although he introduced Annie to most everyone, she couldn't help but feel like the outsider. Throughout the evening, she kept mostly to herself, nursing her loneliness with drink after drink. When they returned to his flat, she undressed to a T-shirt and underpants and climbed into bed. She turned her back to John. When he tried to touch her breasts, she covered them with folded arms and said curtly, "No, thank you."

By Tuesday afternoon, her leg was feeling considerably better, so Annie drove Percy into Oxford. A few of the people she'd met the night before recognized her as she roared up to the quadrangle at Trinity College, and they seemed to regard her with some suspicion as she walked across the lawn to meet John.

"All finished?" she asked him.

He nodded.

"How do you think you did?"

"Well, hopefully. Ready for some tea? I certainly am."

They headed off toward the Nosebag under the watchful eyes of his well-meaning friends.

After they'd been served, John reached for her hand. She tried to take it away, but he gripped it tightly. "I want to tell you something, while I have the chance," he said. "I'm sorry for the way I told you about my girlfriend, about Lena. It was very insensitive of me."

"Well," she blinked slowly, "considering the circumstances, considering what we'd already done, I don't suppose there was a nice way to say it."

"I really am quite fond of you, you know. I'm going to miss you. And—"

She regarded him suspiciously. "And what?"

He lowered his voice. "We've had an awfully good time in bed, and out of it, like in the wood."

Annie blushed and looked into her tea.

"You really turn me on, you know, despite how I feel about Lena. I can't help feeling very excited when I'm near you."

She kept her eyes lowered and didn't respond.

"I almost wish Lena could meet you. I think she'd like you."

She looked up now. "Are you crazy?"

"No, I'm serious. I think she'd like you."

Frowning, she told him, "Let's not take that chance, John. Are we going to get the ferry information after we leave here?"

"Yes, and you can make a reservation from the tourist office so you're assured of a space. We should also pop in at a bank and get your pounds changed into francs," he suggested. "And fill your tank with petrol, too."

"I'll do that. I want to be all set to leave, and I don't want to miss the boat now, do I?"

They went out again that night to the same club they had been to the evening before. Annie felt a little lighter. Her mood was brightened by the idea of leaving for France and getting closer to the place where she might rendezvous with Andrew. And adding to that, her period had begun that day, which brought her incalculable relief.

She danced several times with John and others and enjoyed herself somewhat, but she had to work at keeping the memories at bay. Her mind kept flashing pictures of herself, dancing reels with Andrew, whirling and laughing until they were both exhausted, until they collapsed gratefully into slow dances, rubbing their bodies together as though there was some deep itch inside, that only the touch of the other could relieve.

Back in the flat when she was lying next to John, close to falling asleep, he reached a hand toward her, and though she thought he was trying to make another move, he merely grasped one of hers and kept hold of it as they both drifted off.

John had nothing to do the next morning, so while Annie packed her belongings and took a bath, he went to the market. When she emerged dressed and ready, he had an enormous English breakfast waiting.

Out on the street, he started to secure her things, but she stopped him. "I need to learn how to do this on my own, don't I?"

While she worked at it, he timidly offered, "I think I've hurt you, and I want you to know that I'm sorry. I never meant to."

The day had been rainy to start, but now it was clearing and a warming southerly breeze was blowing. Contemplating his apology, she lifted her head to the sky and watched the clouds, realizing they were blowing northward, toward Scotland. She wished she could just lift up and hitch a ride on one, to be carried over the cathedral ruins, then dropped into the Whaum's garden.

When she looked at him again, she said, "You got me through the second worst night of my life, John, and I'm grateful for that. The only thing," she hesitated before continuing, "I guess I persuaded myself that you loved me a little, and in my mind that made what we did less terrible. But now . . ."

"But I do love you," he protested, then quickly qualified, "in a way."

"Sure you care about me," she agreed, frowning a little, "but not the way people who sleep together should care about one another."

John lowered his eyes. "Do you feel that way about me?"

Smiling slightly, she shook her head. "It's so ironic, isn't it? I mean, we both love other people, yet that didn't stop us from doing what we did. I don't get it, I don't understand how that happens." She vividly recalled what Susannah had told her—that she should feel fuller from sex, not less because of it. "I'm just hoping that something starts to make sense soon, so I can figure out what the hell's going on, why we make the choices we do, why things get so screwed up." She finally got the bags the way she wanted them, nice and tight so they wouldn't shift about.

"Good job," John recognized.

Looking at the ready and waiting motorcycle, her thigh began to throb, but instead of making her think about how hard it would be to drive with her injury, the ache led her to remember Rob Mitchell. In the next moment, she found herself saying to John, "You know that friend I told you about, the one who bit me just before he left for Vietnam?"

He winced slightly and nodded.

Unconsciously, she rubbed at her leg. "He never even made it there. His helicopter was shot down before they could even land."

He closed his eyes to exclaim, "God! That's terrible!"

Her forehead furrowed. "Is it? I mean, I've thought about this, and who knows what was waiting for him if he hadn't been killed right away? He might have been captured and tortured, or wounded and left lying in the jungle, suffering alone for days before he died."

Shaking his head at the brutal reality in that, he answered, "But then again, he might have made it home safely."

After learning of Rob's death, she'd consoled herself with this cynical notion, but something dawned on her now that she hadn't before considered. "Maybe. But if he'd been given the choice, he'd probably have taken life at any cost— no matter how awful." The muscles in her face relaxed with this understanding, which came not just in relation to Rob, but also to herself. "It felt like death the other night, parting from Andrew, like separating from him was killing me—really."

His expression turned quizzical, and he wasn't sure he was following her.

She reflected for a moment on how the agonizing pain had made everything gray and hazy and distant, how she'd felt herself shutting down, disconnecting. "I guess that's why I reached out for you," she told John, letting her eyes find his. "Having sex with you kept me feeling something. It kept me alive. Maybe what I was doing was choosing life at any cost." Her gaze lowered, and she went quietly into her thoughts.

Touched by her words but unable to find his own, John removed the woolen scarf from his neck, the one he always wore, that seemed to be his trademark. Holding it out to her, he said, "Take this with you," and before she could reach for it, he began wrapping it around her neck and tucking the tails inside her jacket. "You're an astounding woman," he told her tenderly. "I'll never forget you."

It was time to go, she knew, so she gave the kick start a jump with her good leg; the tears were threatening, but she managed a smile as she pulled on her helmet. With Percy roaring, she carefully straddled him, released the balance stand, then looked back to shout, "Who knows? Maybe we'll meet again!"

"I hope so!" he answered.

She was about to put the bike in gear when she decided to leave him with something to grin about. "Next time you're in the Sherwood Forest, think of me!"

Over the clamor of the motorbike, he called back, "It's fair to say I'll never pass through there again without thinking of you." Then he smiled broadly.

She reached one hand for him. He squeezed hers back, then she was off.

He heaved a heavy sigh as he watched her inept rounding of the corner, and as she disappeared from his sight, he said aloud, "God keep her safe."

Annie was shaking as she began her drive. Her legs were weak and her heart felt that way, too, but she made it to the ferry following the directions John had written out for her. The ship hands secured Percy B. to the bulkhead, all the while watching Annie as though she were some sort of oddity. One finally spoke to her and offered that he'd never seen a girl drive a motorbike before. Annie grinned and answered that only an American woman would be crazy enough to undertake it, but that remark only added to the young man's bewilderment.

As she waited on deck for departure, she unconsciously assumed her warrior stance; in her black oilskin jacket, jeans, and hiking boots, her helmet tucked under an arm, she resembled a soldier on the deck of a warship, about to be sent into battle.

She tried to keep her thoughts on what lay ahead, but it was hard not to dwell on what she was leaving behind. She wondered where Andrew was at that moment. She wished there'd been a phone at the Whaum, so she might have called him before she left. She pictured him packing and leaving for home about now, and she prayed that he would somehow be able to work things out and come to her.

The only thing that does make sense, she began to realize, is my love for him, my need to be with him. He's brought me more peace and joy than I've ever known, and I know I bring him those things, too. That's why he'll forgive me, she told herself. That's why he'll find it in himself to forgive me for turning to John. He'll understand that it was because I hurt so much. He'll understand, because he'll have felt that pain, too.

While a handful of people on the dock waved good-bye, the ferry began to slowly pull away. Watching the coastline pass into memory, her mind reached again for Andrew. As the vessel gathered speed, she imagined him standing by her side, his arm securely around her waist, anchoring her to him as they lunged into the perilous currents of the English Channel.

* * *

Andrew finished his remaining days without further incident, staying away from the pubs so he wouldn't run into Patrick Ramsay. On Wednesday, the day Annie left for France, he returned from his last tutorial to find his mother's chauffeur and Bentley parked in front of the Whaum.

The driver had to put some effort into covering his shock at seeing the young man's battered face. "Good afternoon, Lord Andrew," he greeted him, tipping his cap.

He was a little annoyed at the man's punctuality and he responded bluntly, "I'm not ready, Angus."

"Take your time, young master," he told him.

Robin was inside the cottage, making ready for a visit home where he would stay for only two weeks, because he'd managed to get a job in St. Andrews for the summer.

While Andrew was putting the last few things in his steamer trunk, Robin came into his bedroom. Sighing, Andrew told him, "I wish I could change places with you. I wish you could carry on for me at Crofthill, so I could stay on here."

The last two days had seen a decided shift in the way Robin related to his house mate, and it was partly due to Andrew's physical appearance in the aftermath of the fight, which diminished his sometimes intimidating good looks. But it was also because it had been Robin who sat with him in the doctor's surgery while his scalp wound was sutured and his injuries tended to, which cast the young aristocrat in a less imposing, more ordinary light. These things, combined with the statement Andrew just made, emboldened him to speak his mind now. "It's good you're going home. It'll refocus you, being there. You need to get back to your life and responsibilities, because you've come off track."

He halted his search of the dresser drawers to ask his friend, "Have I?"

"Indeed, I think you have," he answered. "There's been such a change in you."

He smiled momentarily, then walked to a window to gaze off into the garden. "I'll miss you, Robin," he told him, "and this place. I've such wonderful memories here." Taking his leave of the Whaum today was almost like saying good-bye to Annie again.

"I'll miss you, too," he responded. "But you'll have a wonderful summer—going around with your fiancée, having your holiday on Mull. It'll be lovely, you'll see."

Still looking into the garden, he answered, "I will have a wonderful summer, you're right, but not because I'll spend it with Janet. It'll be because I'm going to France to meet Annie, and as soon as I hear from her and where she is, I'll be on my way."

Early on in their friendship, when Andrew entrusted him with his secret, Robin began to feel a special responsibility toward him. And that was never more true than now, as he watched him take one precarious step after another, moving closer and closer toward what he feared would be his undoing. "Please don't speak like that," he pleaded. "You told me yourself what will happen, how your father will react. Don't do that to yourself."

He grinned slightly. "If that is to be, then let it. I can't do this any other way. I couldn't live with myself if I gave up now."

Deciding to try a different tack, Robin offered, "I understand how attached you became to her. She is quite a pretty and remarkable girl. But you'll get over it if you give yourself time. You need to give yourself time, because you're not thinking clearly just now."

His eyes once again drawn toward the rose garden, he conjured the image of Annie as she was the first time she came to work in it: on her knees in the mud, the wind blowing her hair about her face. He remembered how terribly intimate that moment had been, how he'd looked into her eyes as he tenderly wiped the smudges from her cheeks, feeling the profound connection that would only deepen in the days and weeks ahead.

"You needn't concern yourself," Andrew assured his friend, "because I'm thinking more clearly now than I have in a long while." He turned toward him to add, "I watched her leave on Sunday, you know. I stood in the bushes and watched her leave with someone else, as though I had no right to approach her, to speak to her again." He swallowed the bitter tears that accompanied the memory. "When she was gone, I walked out onto the jetty. I stood there and told myself that I'd never see her again, and I tried to say goodbye to her in my heart. I tried with everything in me, but it just wouldn't happen. It wouldn't happen because it can't—because the truth is, I can't live without her."

Obviously distressed by what he was telling him, Robin implored, "Then think! Think what will happen if you go on like this."

Calmly, he answered, "I have, and I'm prepared to deal with it. I'm prepared to give up everything for her, if need be."

Stunned by this revelation, he questioned, "Are you thinking with your head and not your heart? Because that's where a decision as important as this should be made. No," he corrected himself, "must be made!"

He dismissed that with an exaggerated frown and a twist of his head. "That's where you're wrong, but I wouldn't expect you to understand, because you've never been in love like this." Having said it aloud for the first time, having put it out there as an indisputable fact, brought him a rush of excitement.

Robin hesitated a moment, then looked directly into Andrew's eyes; he hadn't wanted to say this because he hadn't wanted to hurt him, but he now felt he must take the risk. "What if, what if you don't hear from her? What if she's changed her mind about things? What I mean to say is, since she left with John, she could well decide to stay on with him, couldn't she?"

He laughed at the absurdity of the idea. "That won't happen."

"Are you so certain?" he wondered. "Look, I didn't want to tell you this, but I know that Colin slept at Michael Chapman's flat that night." Then pointedly, to make certain he got it, he added, "They were alone. Annie and John were alone in his flat."

Andrew's demeanor did not change. "I know."

Obviously befuddled, he questioned, "You do?"

He smiled again. "Yes, I do, and it doesn't matter. In fact, it helps make things clearer for me." His smile deepened. "I know they were alone. I saw Colin return that morning. It angered me at first, but when I was standing on the jetty, I realized something. I realized that even if she'd slept with him it didn't matter, because what is between us is stronger than anything else. It makes everything else insignificant. I don't expect you to understand, but that's the way it is." He moved away from the window and sat on one of the straight-back chairs in his room, then folded his arms.

For some reason, seeing him this smug and self-assured made Robin resentful. His nostrils flared slightly, something they tended to do when he was upset, as he admitted, "You're right. I don't understand." He took a breath before adding, "I grew up in awe of your family, you know. Never in my wildest imaginings did I think that you and I would become friends. My family has always lived comfortably, but you—you're the descendant of Scotland's finest, the heir to a legend. People all over this country look to the Stuart-Gordons for direction, for leadership and example. That gives you a certain responsibility, you know, to more than yourself."

"But I don't want that responsibility," he calmly explained. "You know that. I never have. It's blasted bad luck to have been born who I was."

"It's your lot," Robin countered. "We all get dealt our lot, like it or not."

Andrew rose and moved across the room so that he might put a hand on Robin's shoulder. In a congenial, conciliatory tone, he said, "Let's not speak of this anymore. There's no point, and I don't want to say good-bye like this. I want to thank you for asking me to live here with you, and for your friendship. You're the best I've ever had, you know."

The sincerity with which Andrew had uttered those words placated him somewhat, but Robin still felt compelled to say, "You can thank me by going on and doing the right thing."

A certain serenity filled Andrew's countenance as he responded, "Then rest easy, Robin, because that's exactly what I intend to do."

* * *

Going home to Crofthill was not pleasant. He was instantly beset with questions regarding his appearance by his mother and sisters, but before he could adequately answer, Ambrose advised him that his father was awaiting him in his library.

The viscount was on the telephone as usual and he didn't even suspend his conversation long enough to acknowledge his son's presence. Andrew sat quietly waiting for more than ten deliberate minutes.

"I've had the dean ring me up," Donald finally said, still not looking at him. The fiscal year was coming to an end, and he'd had a trying week with the business comptroller. The call regarding his son's bad behavior had been the icing on the cake.

"I expected he would," he casually responded.

"What started it?" he demanded to know.

He was in no mood to appease his father, and he answered glibly, "I did."

Donald glared at him, his seething anger barely constrained. "I didn't ask you who, did I?"

"No, you didn't," he acknowledged.

Donald took hold of a paperweight and tried to squeeze down on the heavy glass it was made of. "I can guess, though, can't I? It was that bloody American whore." He had no reason to call her that, he knew, save a desire to lash out at his son.

With that remark, Andrew's restraint dissolved. "You've no right to speak of her in that way. I swear, Father, take back what you've said or I'll . . ."

The conversation with Andrew's dean had opened old wounds and made him recall the humiliation of what had happened at Eton. "You'll what, you bloody fool?"

An intimidatory move followed as father and son both rose and approached one other, like dogs, hackles rising for a fight. The tension in the room was oppressive.

"You'll what?" the older man repeated.

Andrew clenched his fists but held them at his side, knowing he could never raise a hand to his father. "Nothing Father, nothing," he finally uttered, backing off slightly. Then, in a decided change of attitude, he implored him, "Leave me alone about this, will you?"

"Leave you alone?" he railed. "When you've disgraced the earl and the family name with your behavior—again!" He said that last word with particular vehemence, meaning it to pierce its target.

Now Andrew moved closer to his father. Taking hold of his lapels, he could barely get the words through his clenched teeth. "You listen to me. I'm sick to death of your bringing that up—sick to bloody death of it, do you understand? As if you've never in your life made a mistake, as if you're some kind of perfect specimen for me to model myself after. You, with all your bloody whoring and God knows what else."

Donald freed himself from his son's grip and stepped back far enough to deliver a powerful slap to his already bruised face.

His head was twisted to the side with the force of it, but he jerked it back to look his father square on and grin. "Nicely done, old man, nicely done. You make things easier for me every day," he hissed, before turning away.

"Where do you think you're going?" Donald demanded of him. "I'm not finished with you!"

As he strode briskly from the library, his only response was an unsettling laugh.

It was late and his mother had held dinner for him, so he should have gone to his room to dress and ready for it. But he didn't. Instead, he went directly to the garage and asked the footman for the keys to his Austin Healey, then drove like a madman toward Kilmacolm and his favorite pub.

Chapter 27

She understood why they secured Percy to the bulkhead when the ferry began to roll in the channel and people came out of the lounges to lean over the railings. And as they picked up speed and moved farther from shore, the rolling changed to pitching. Annie sat quietly in the passenger cabin, however. While others held hands over their mouths and turned green, she remained relaxed, as though all this were expected—as though she'd known that it would be this way, that it had to be this way.

The crossing took all night, and the pitching of the ship finally eased toward dawn. Few of the passengers slept, but Annie dozed on the bench she occupied—fifteen minutes here, a half an hour there. As they drew nearer the mainland, she went on deck to follow their approach to France. The morning sun was somehow different here, more brilliant and warm, and the colors of the nearing coast were also distinct. The greens were softer, and there were muted browns and pale pinks washing through the picture.

She was excited to leave the ship, but when she did, she was suddenly struck with the realization that she hadn't the foggiest idea where to go. She spied a post office close to the dock and went in. Using her high school French, she asked the clerk where she might buy a map. Then she inquired how much a telegram would cost, decided she could afford it, and sent one to Issie to let her know she'd arrived. After studying her map and drinking the best café au lait she'd ever tasted, she determined that she would head straight for Paris. She had in her possession a book of European youth hostels that Mel had given her as a parting gift, and she planned to find one in Paris and spend the night there. It was with that idea in mind that she headed toward the City of Lights, confident that all would be well.

It was heartening to be driving on the right side of the road again, and she was energized as she began. She saw the towering cathedral of Rouen off to her right and for a moment wanted to go visit it, but in the interest of time she decided to keep moving. The terrain was flat and therefore easy to drive, and she was glad for that. Percy B. was a happier motorbike when he didn't have to strain over the hills. She made reasonably good time, considering she never drove faster than fifty miles an hour, and arrived at the outskirts of Paris just as evening rush hour began.

The easy driving she'd experienced on the highway ended abruptly, as car upon car crowded in around her, annoyed with her slowness and eager to pass. What had seemed like fun suddenly became anxiety producing and difficult. She managed though, and kept straight on, following the signs that read *Centre Ville*. She drove deeper and deeper into the incredible city, people and traffic streaming in and out of it like the occupants of a giant anthill.

Annie began to worry. The avenues she was seeking were nowhere to be seen, and as the number of streets she passed increased, so did her distress. At each traffic light she searched frantically, desperate to see something that might help her find her way.

As she scanned one particularly busy intersection, Annie was astounded to discover that the motorcycle driver next to her was a strikingly beautiful woman. She was dressed in white leather from head to toe, and the seemingly brand new motorbike she sat astride was entirely white, too. She wore no visor with her helmet, and her perfectly made-up face was there for everyone to see, gorgeous and composed, with just the hint of a pout on her painted mouth. Annie couldn't take her eyes off the woman, and she was momentarily ashamed of Percy, who was old and worn, his maroon paint chipped in places, his fenders dented. And she wasn't much better, with her dirty face, faded jeans, and well-worn hiking boots.

The magnificent Parisienne glanced only briefly at Annie, then lifted her bobbed nose. When the light changed to green, she seemed very deliberately to leave her American counterpart in the dust. As Annie watched the white apparition disappear, expertly weaving in and out of the maze of traffic, she had to declare aloud, "Far out. Far fucking out."

The tangle of tiny streets and traffic soon became unnavigable, and Annie noticed how the drivers of motorized bicycles and mopeds popped them up onto the sidewalks to get around things. She decided to do that, too, but after driving a few blocks along the old walkways, she had to question why she was bothering when she didn't know where she was going. Finally admitting to herself that she was utterly lost, she stopped Percy and parked him alongside the wall of a corner building, taking careful notice of his location. Then she pulled out her hostel book and searched for some clue against the street map of Paris. She walked several blocks in one direction, then in another, trying to see what main streets she was near, but that was hopeless, too. Despairingly, she returned to Percy. It was then that she noticed a young man passing nearby, who was smiling at her.

He was about her age and altogether nonthreatening, so she decided to approach him. *"Pardonnez-moi, parlez-vous anglais, Monsieur?"*

"Yes, a little," he answered, very sweetly.

"Oh, thank goodness!" she sighed. "I wonder if you can help me. I'm lost. I'm looking for a youth hostel," she explained, pointing to the listing. "This one, do you know where this street is?"

His brow raised. "Oh, this is very far from here, in another *arrondissement.*" Then, putting his index finger to his chin, he told her, "Let me see if I can explain how to get there."

"Well, that's OK," she said. "I mean, if it's far, then I'd rather not go looking for it. Maybe you know of another hostel or even an inexpensive hotel nearby?" she thought to ask.

"Inexpensive?" he chuckled. "Not in this *quartier,* but perhaps you could go away from here."

"Oh no," she shook her head, "I'd rather not go anywhere right now. The traffic is awful. There must be something around."

"Are you American?"

She pursed her lips and exhaled as she answered, "Yup."

"Is that your moto?" he wondered.

"It is."

"Well, if you want to give me a lift, I can take you to a small hotel I know, and I can help you through the traffic."

That sounded good. "Really? Do you mind?"

"Not at all. It would be my pleasure."

She had a better idea. "Can you drive a motorcycle?"

He made an odd face and looked as though he'd been insulted. "Of course."

"Well then, you drive and I'll ride," she decided. "My name's Annie. What's yours?"

"Phillipe," he grinned. "It's a pleasure, Annie."

He maneuvered the tangled Parisian streets with ease, hopping up onto the sidewalks when necessary, weaving in and out of the chaos with skill, then deftly arriving at a small hotel several blocks away. They went in and inquired about the rates, then came out again.

"Sorry, Phillipe, but I can't afford it," she told him. "I have to be careful with my money, or I'll run out of it fast. Do you know of any other?"

They inquired at two more that were within walking distance, only to find similar prices.

Annie's anxiety was growing again. "Lord, are they all like this?"

"I have an idea," he offered. "I have a friend who lives near here. Let's go see him and ask if he knows of anything."

They left the sheltered streets and drove onto a boulevard that followed the river. Annie looked ahead and across the water, where she saw the Eiffel Tower for the first time.

"The Eiffel Tower!" she exclaimed, shouting into his ear. "The damned Eiffel Tower. I can't believe it!"

"It's normal," he shouted back.

They arrived at an elegant apartment building and rang the bell. They were buzzed in and reached the apartment using an antique elevator fashioned of wrought iron. A well-dressed young man met them at the door.

Phillipe began conversing in French, and Annie could not follow at all. The speed with which they spoke was astounding, so she stood by in silence. After a minute, the young man greeted her in very polished English.

"How do you do?" he asked, as he offered his hand.

"Fine, thanks. It's nice to meet you. What a beautiful apartment!" The large windows of the flat afforded a view of the River Seine and the Eiffel Tower.

"It's my parents' place, of course, but thank you. Would you care for some tea?" he asked her.

"Your English is fantastic," she observed, "and thank you. Tea would be great."

"I attended school in England," he explained, before heading toward the kitchen.

As Annie sat with her tea, the animated French conversation continued.

"I'm afraid I can't help you with a place for tonight," the young man said after a time. "Phillipe thought that I might be able to offer you our guest room, but my parents are not at home, you see, and I don't feel that would be appropriate."

"No, of course not," she said, astonished that Phillipe would do that for her. "I couldn't follow what you two were saying, but thanks anyway. I'm sure I'll find a place."

"Well, if you would like," Phillipe suggested now, "you can stay with me tonight, although my place is very small, and I fear you won't be comfortable there."

The efforts he'd made on her behalf encouraged her to accept the offer, although it had certainly never been her intention to spend the night with a stranger. "I don't mind if it's small," she responded, "but are you sure you want a guest?"

"I'd be honored," he answered. "But I warn you, it's a very tiny place."

Assuming he was comparing it to the luxurious quarters they were in, she responded, "I'm sure it'll be fine."

They finished their tea and bid good-bye to Phillipe's friend. It was growing dark outside, and Annie yawned and stretched before climbing onto Percy.

"Are you hungry?" Phillipe asked her.

"Actually, I am. I just realized I haven't eaten all day."

"There are some little shops near where I live," he informed her. "It's not very expensive there, and we can get something nice."

"OK," she agreed, "but let me treat you, since you're letting me crash at your place."

"Crash?"

"Yeah, crash," she chuckled. "It means sleep."

"Oh," he said, though he remained confused. "Thank you very much. I'll accept your kind offer, since I'm completely out of money at the moment."

They left Percy in a park at the center of an area filled with shops and cafés. They purchased pâté and cheese in one of the shops, bread in another, and an inexpensive red wine in still another. The total cost of their meal amounted to little more than three dollars. Then they went to sit on a bench near where Percy rested. Phillipe took a large, skeleton-type key from his pocket and used it to spread the pâté on his chunk of bread. Annie watched him, somewhat appalled, before remembering that she had Andrew's knife in her jacket pocket.

She grasped it as though it were his hand, reluctant to let someone else touch it, knowing that the last person other than herself to have done so was Andrew. It warmed her hand to hold it, and she was instantly comforted by its presence, but seeing Phillipe struggle with his key to slice the cheese, she felt compelled to offer it.

"I have a knife, Phillipe. Would you like to use it?"

"Yes, thank you," he said, then added, "I'm sorry for my manners. I haven't eaten in a while and I'm rather hungry."

Phillipe wiped the knife with his grimy handkerchief before returning it to Annie, who carefully tucked it away again. He finished eating quickly, but she took her time because something had happened to her appetite.

"I apologize for not offering to take you to a café," he told her. "It would have been nice for you, this being your first time in Paris."

"You've been very kind, and you've done more than enough for me," she answered.

"One needs money to enjoy Paris, I'm afraid."

"So it seems," she agreed. "I only came here because I thought it would be easy to find a hostel, and when I looked at the map, I saw that it's where I can get on the *auto route du soleil.*"

"Where are you headed?" he inquired.

"The Mediterranean coast, Saintes Maries de la Mer," she informed him. "My friend told me to take that highway, because it would be the quickest way to get there."

"Saintes Maries," he mused. "It should be lovely there. I should like to see it sometime. I've never been to the coast." Then he added, "Van Gogh painted there, you know."

She was aware of that, but sensing that he might be trying to wrangle an invitation, Annie smiled at him and said nothing. A nearby clock tower struck the hour ten, and she yawned again.

"Are you getting tired?" he wondered.

"Not getting, I am—dead tired," she emphasized. "I was on the ferry last night and hardly slept."

"We can go to my little place now, if you'd like."

"Yeah, I would like," she answered. "I don't think I can keep my eyes open much longer."

They checked on Percy to make certain he was secure, before walking the two short blocks to the apartment building in which Phillipe lived.

It was one of those grand old Parisian buildings, six stories high, that had been built in the middle of the nineteenth century. They entered through a side door where

Phillipe triggered the timed lights. He carried the heavier of her bags as they began mounting the stairs.

"I'm all the way at the top," he warned her, "so pace yourself."

They climbed and climbed, and Annie was out of breath by the time they reached his floor. The lights had gone out before they got there. They traversed a long, narrow corridor and could hear conversations and radios coming from the apartments they passed. When they arrived at his room, he unlocked the door with the key he'd used on the pâté.

"After you," he said, then he reached to switch on the light.

When she saw where she would be spending the night, Annie felt ill. It was more of a closet than a room, about six by ten, with one window and a sink the size of a small pot. A table was situated next to it that displayed a few cooking implements, a hot plate, and a box of sugar cubes. A narrow bed was pressed against the wall opposite the window, leaving room for a single chair, which lay buried under a mound of soiled clothing. He had no dresser, only some hooks on one wall, which supported a tattered winter coat, a well-worn shirt, and two questionable towels. Between the bed and the windowed wall was a rug that looked as though it had been rescued from the trash and just enough space to spread her sleeping bag. She sighed loudly as she looked around and tried to decide what she could do about the situation, realizing that at this late hour she had few if any options.

Phillipe discerned her disappointment. "I warned you that it was tiny," he apologized.

"Where's the bathroom?" she asked. She wasn't sure if it was the cheap wine she'd drunk or the staleness of the room, but she was definitely nauseated.

He attempted a smile. "I'll show you."

It was a communal affair used by all the occupants of this floor, and it made her even sicker when she encountered it. She'd never seen anything like it: a ceramic hole in the floor with two raised foot pedals flanking the hole, a water tank and pull chain above it. Remnants of human waste were scattered all over the white ceramic, and flies buzzed excitedly when the light came on.

"I'll just be a minute," she told him, and got in and out as quickly as possible. I will not be sick, she told herself as she suppressed her desire to vomit. Back in the room with Phillipe, she found herself chatting nervously. "How long have you lived here?"

"Two years."

Two years spent in this cramped space, no bigger than a jail cell, would have been like serving a prison term. "Is it cold in the winter? I don't see any heat."

"Yes, and hot in the summer," he told her, "but it's the best I can do."

"Don't you have a job?" she asked.

"Not now," he answered. "I'm looking for one, though."

"What about your family? Don't you have family?"

"They don't live in Paris."

"But couldn't they help you, I mean, with some money until you get a job?"

He lowered his eyes. "They have barely enough for themselves."

She scanned the room, and her gaze rested on the box of sugar cubes. "How do you eat?"

He saw what she was looking at and he reached into the box and popped one into his mouth. "Sometimes I don't, but these give you energy," he grinned.

She watched his face for a minute as she tried to bring her anxiety under control. "I guess I should try to get to sleep," she mumbled, though what she really wanted was to pick up her things and leave. But at the same time, she was overcome with pity for this young man who'd gone to so much trouble for her.

"You take the bed," he told her.

The filthy bedclothes might be inhabited by creatures she'd rather not encounter, so she blurted out, "Oh no, I couldn't," and quickly began unrolling her sleeping bag.

"But you're my guest," he insisted, "it wouldn't be right."

She avoided looking at him now, because every time she did, her anxiety grew. "Phillipe, you're very sweet to offer, but I can't put you out of your own bed. I'll be perfectly fine on the floor, really."

He sat on his bed and watched as she readied herself for sleep. She did not change her clothing; she merely removed her jacket and boots. She wanted to get Andrew's knife out of her pocket and hold onto it as she slept, but she was under the scrutiny of her host and worried that the gesture might insult him. Instead, she folded her jacket and used it as a pillow, though it was hardly the sort of thing she would have preferred to have under her head.

"All set?" he asked, when she finally settled down.

"Yup. You going to sleep, too?" It occurred to her that it might be too early for him, so she offered, "If you want to go out or something, go ahead. I'll be fine here," hoping he'd do just that.

"No, I've nothing else to do. Want the light out?"

"OK." Although the room was very warm, she zipped the bag around her; it was more a protective, instinctual move than anything else. "Good night, Phillipe," she said awkwardly. "Thanks for letting me sleep here. I'll probably be up early. I hope I won't disturb you."

"Don't worry about me," he responded.

She turned on her side, her back to him, and began to pray.

She awakened sometime later, it couldn't have been much later, and she opened her eyes to see her host staring at her. He was wide awake, lying on his side, propped up on an elbow and looking intently at Annie. Her anxiety was such that she couldn't keep quiet.

"Is anything wrong?" she asked him.

The light that filtered through the window illuminated his face and made it appear ashen. "I can't sleep," he said.

"Is my being here disturbing you?" she asked nervously.

"No, actually it's nice to have company. I do get rather lonely here."

That response broke her heart. Desperately trying to think of something to say, she offered, "I'll buy you breakfast in the morning before I leave."

"I'd like that," he answered.

She wanted to cry now, and she wasn't certain if it was compassion or fear that was making her feel that way. "I'm going to try to get back to sleep, OK? I've got a lot of driving ahead of me tomorrow."

"Don't let me keep you up," he responded.

Uttering, "Good night, again," she went back to her prayers, her pleas to the gods to keep her safe and get her through to the morning.

Morning did come and safely, but not before Annie had awakened at least four more times to assess her situation. When the sun was up and the day well underway, she rose and went to the deplorable toilet. She returned to the tiny space to find Phillipe washing at the sink.

"Did you sleep well?" he politely inquired.

"Well enough," she answered, "and you? I'm afraid my presence here disturbed you."

"Oh, no, it wasn't that. It's just that it's been so long since I've slept near anyone. I'm afraid I'm not used to it."

The utter loneliness of his existence was deeply disturbing. "Can I use the sink to brush my teeth?" she asked, wanting desperately to change the subject.

"Of course. I'm sorry I have no coffee to offer you."

"I'm going to buy you some, remember?" she told him, as she fumbled through her bag. "It's the least I can do to repay you."

His eyes following her every move, he offered, "Would you like to leave your things here while we have our breakfast?"

She interpreted that as an invitation to stay longer, and she quickly answered, "No thanks. I'd just as soon take them and be on my way right after, if you don't mind." Then, afraid she may have hurt his feelings, she explained, "It's a lot of steps to get back up here."

"Yes, it is that," he agreed.

They sat at the bar of a little café near where Percy had spent the night. Fresh croissants were piled high on a platter, and Phillipe eyed them hungrily.

"Let's have some of those," she suggested, and he nodded eagerly. Her heart ached as she watched him struggle with the brief wait before they were served.

They didn't say much as they ate, Annie only having half of her croissant before offering the rest to Phillipe. When it was time to pay, she handed the change from her fifty franc note to him.

Avoiding his eyes, she said, "Take this for me, will you, as payment for the room."

"No! I couldn't!" he protested. "You were my guest!"

"Please," she insisted, "you'll make me feel much better if you do. You went to a lot of trouble for me yesterday, and I owe you."

"It was no trouble," he blushed.

Softening her tone now, she asked, "Please take it, please, for me."

Embarrassment forced him to lower his eyes as he sighed and closed his hand around the money.

Merchants were setting up their stalls in the park where Percy awaited her, and when they approached the motorcycle, they were accosted by an irate man. He shouted obscenities at Phillipe, flailing his hands in the air to illustrate whatever it was he was saying.

"What's the matter?" Annie asked her companion.

"We parked your moto where he sets up his stall," he explained. "He's very angry."

"Tell him I'm sorry, will you? Tell him I didn't know."

"I already did that," he informed her.

The merchant continued to curse and complain, and his vehement demonstration was raising her ire. "Well then," she decided, "tell him to fuck off."

He must have understood the word *fuck,* because after she said it the man exploded. He began pushing Phillipe on the chest and shoulders, trying to incite a fight, all the while railing at him, his face bright red. Phillipe raised his voice and pushed back as a crowd quickly gathered around them. Annie realized that her remark had made a bad situation worse, and she was now fearful for the smaller and thinner Phillipe, who was pathetically outnumbered and encircled by the merchant's fellows.

"Please! *Si vous plait!* Stop!" she shouted, as she tried to squeeze herself between them.

The merchant began to vent his anger on Annie. Seeing this, some of his comrades decided that he'd gone too far. As Phillipe pulled her away, the man also was pulled off by three of his friends, and they held him back as he struggled to get free. Phillipe seized the opportunity and took Annie's arm, walking her quickly toward Percy B.

"Get on your bike and go," he advised. "Get out of this mess!"

"But what about you?" she asked, as she frantically secured her bags. "I can't leave you here like this!"

"I can handle this," he answered, though unconvincingly. "But you'd better get out of here while you can."

"Get on the bike with me," she decided. "I'll ride you up the street and away from here."

"No, it's better that I stay and settle this, because I'm likely to see him again. Go on," he encouraged, "now, before he gets loose from his friends."

Her heart was pounding wildly as she finished with her luggage, then jumped on the starter to make Percy roar. She reached her arms around Phillipe and kissed him on the cheek before she climbed onto the bike. He smiled and blushed ever so slightly, then motioned to her to get going.

"I wish I could take you with me!" she shouted over the noise.

"Don't worry about it," he called back to her, trying to smile. *"Bonne route!"*

She pulled up the kickstand and started off. Phillipe stood watching for a moment before going back to face what he must. When she paused before merging into the manic Parisian traffic, Annie turned to glance again at the young man. The sight of him, standing alone against that raucous group, brought on an overwhelming sadness, an all-consuming pity. Never in her life had she seen anyone more isolated, more alienated. She popped the clutch and lunged forward, heading for her escape route, the auto route du soleil, hardly able to see where she was going because the tears blurred her vision so.

The quarter in which she had spent the night was thankfully close to the highway entrance, and she found it in no time. With a fairly clear road ahead of her, she yanked the accelerator all the way back and let Percy B. have his head. She wanted to put thoughts of Phillipe from her mind, but as hard as she tried not to think about him—and all the things that had happened since she'd left Scotland—the scenes kept playing over like clips from a movie, worrying and distracting her, making her question—my God, what have I gotten myself into?

Phillipe's loneliness ate away at her and made her feel her own that much more acutely. More than ever she longed for the protection of St. Andrews, the peace that comes of belonging, of being known. She craved the comfort of the Whaum and the shelter of friendship, and most of all, she hungered for the love of Andrew—the giving and receiving of it—that assured her in a way she'd never before experienced of her value as a human being.

But there was no way back; she understood that. Everyone would be gone by now, the streets devoid of scarlet robes, the lecture halls and halls of residence abandoned. The Whaum would be empty, too, its roses blooming unseen, its mantel clock unwound and silent. Andrew's things would have disappeared from his room, his bed stripped, the mattress left to air. The only hope of seeing him again lay before her, in places yet to be discovered, so she put her energy into getting herself there, to that place and time when they would come together.

But even as she conjured that dream, her conscience shattered it. Do I deserve to be with him when I've forsaken my feelings for him and given myself to someone else? Maybe this is my penance, it occurred to her—to be alone and cast out into an unkind world, left to wonder if it will ever happen again, if I'll ever know again the simple joy of being near him.

These thoughts tormented her and made her keep a steady wrist on the accelerator. Faster and faster she drove, and to ease the strain on old Percy, she let herself be swept along in the funnel of wind behind a large truck. Racing toward the Mediterranean that morning, Annie was certainly also running—away from Paris, away from loneliness and anonymity—like someone who'd committed a heinous crime and was now being pursued by the relentless hounds of justice.

* * *

Andrew's mother, the Viscountess Rannoch, was totally confused about what was happening. After having only a glimpse of her battered son the night before, she'd heard raised voices coming from the library. She'd seen the servants whispering, and she didn't at all understand how Andrew could be so rude as to leave without a word when he was expected at dinner. Her husband had refused to discuss it, and this morning there was more shouting accompanied by slamming doors. When she could tolerate it no longer, she took it upon herself to get some answers.

She listened while they went at it in the library, then called to her son as he stormed past her open door. "Andrew, come here! Come here and sit down and talk to me!"

He halted in the hallway, sighed, then entered the morning room where Mary sat with her correspondence. "I'm sorry, Mother," he told her. "I should have spoken to you yesterday."

"The entire household is in an uproar since you've returned!" she scolded. "Close the door behind you. The servants have heard enough."

He answered demurely, "I know. I'm sorry, but it can't be helped."

"And why is that?" she demanded. "And for God's sake, what on earth happened to your face?"

Finding solace in the cushion of an overstuffed chair, he answered, "I was in a fight."

"A fight? You mean with fists, with another person?"

"Yes," he answered, with a certain amount of pride.

"I'm ashamed of you!" she declared. "How utterly vulgar!"

In his other lifetime, he would likely have agreed with her. But he was not the timid, awkward adolescent he used to be, and it was a self-assured young man who informed her, "If ever anyone needed a sock in the jaw, it was this bloke. If you knew all the circumstances . . ."

"So this is what you and your father are arguing about?"

"Partly, but there's much more to it."

Impatiently now, she asked, "Would you be so good as to enlighten me?"

He braced himself. "I'm not going with you to Mull."

"What did you say?"

"I'm not going, Mother. I refuse to spend two weeks trapped there with the viscount."

Mary was well aware that her son only referred to his father in this way when he was angry with him. "I can't believe what I'm hearing."

"I don't mean to hurt you," he wanted her to know.

The usually placid woman was uncharacteristically agitated. "What's happening to this family? What are you doing to it?"

"I'm not doing anything to this family," he asserted. "I'm trying to be myself, and Father is refusing to see that I'm an adult with the right to make my own decisions, my own choices. He's the one causing the turmoil, not I."

"Some choices are not yours to make," she reminded him.

"Right," he scoffed. "Like whom I'm to love. I'm to let Father make that choice for me, right?"

She thought she was beginning to understand. "So this is about Janet, about your engagement?"

"Not entirely."

Increasingly frustrated, she asked, "Then what is it about?"

"It's about Father and me. It's that simple," he realized now. "It's about his not trusting me to make my own decisions."

"You're young, Andrew. You need guidance."

"Guidance? I'd hardly call it guidance. It's tyranny, it's a damned bloody dictatorship, it's . . . "

Appalled by his attitude, she declared, "I can't understand what's happening to you! Something has gotten into you; something has changed you."

In calm contrast now, he answered, "I've grown up, Mother."

"No, that's not it," she insisted, shaking her head. "Something's changed you."

"Believe what you want," he told her, "but the problem is that I've grown up and Donald still wants to treat me as a child."

"Brawling and deciding not to go with us to Mull—is this an example of your maturity?" she mocked.

Somewhat chastened, he beseeched, "We always spend a good bit of that time sailing, and I can't tolerate two weeks in close quarters with him, Mother. I just can't. Please don't ask me to."

When Mary looked into her son's face, it stirred an uneasiness in her gut, and it was not the cuts and bruises she saw that disturbed her. A tension hung in the air about him, evidence of emotions she'd never before witnessed in him, and it frightened her. She'd seen something in her husband, too, something equally upsetting though all too familiar, and she understood now that the two were headed for a terrible collision.

Realizing this, she came to a quick decision. "All right, if you'd rather not come, I'll speak to your father on your behalf."

Uncertain he'd heard correctly, he asked, "You will?"

"Yes, I will. If you're so set against it, you're better off staying here on your own. It's clear no good will come of you joining us."

His face relaxed a little. "That's what I've tried to tell him."

"I'll help him see the wisdom in that," she offered, though she knew it would not be easy.

"Thank you, Mother, thank you very much."

"But you must do something for me in return," she added.

He winced in anticipation. "What's that?"

"I want you to apologize to your father."

Exasperated now, he pleaded, "But I'm not the one who needs to apologize!"

"Nevertheless, you're the one who must," she insisted, "if you want me to act on your behalf, that is. There'll be no convincing him to allow you to stay, otherwise."

He lifted his eyes to the ceiling to exclaim, "Christ!"

"Andrew!"

"All right," he answered.

"Thank you," she said softly. "You know your father. Someone must take the initiative and it won't be Donald. Now come here and kiss your mother."

* * *

They were standing face to face in the upstairs sitting room that provided neutral ground between their bedrooms.

"No!" he insisted. "Stay out of this, Mary! Dammit anyway, but it was your interference that brought this about. I never should have let you talk me into sending him to Eton. He should have gone to Gordonstoun as I did, and my father before me. He'd have learned discipline and respect for duty if he had."

A tad impatiently, Mary replied, "That place would have destroyed him and you know that as well as I. He has far too gentle a nature to be abandoned in a harsh environment like that."

"That environment was exactly what he needed," he declared, shaking his head in frustration. "He'd have learned to control his impulses!" He had never discussed it with her, because the fact that she was his mother didn't make it any less humiliating. But he was thinking now, as he had many times since then, that what had happened at Eton never would have happened at Gordonstoun.

She kept her voice low, her tone nonthreatening. "Listen to me, Donald, please. He's every bit as stubborn as you. Forbidding him will do no good. It'll only makes matters worse."

"He's disrespectful and willful," he nearly shouted.

In spite of herself, the viscountess laughed.

"I can't see anything funny in this," her husband scowled.

"I recall your father saying something quite similar about you. It doesn't seem that long ago, either."

"That was different," he knew absolutely.

"How?"

"He was simply trying to control me, to exercise his control over me."

Wary of saying anything at this point, Mary merely smiled and took a seat.

Her quiet smugness irritated him. "That's not what I'm doing. I'm trying to save him from himself. A girl is involved in this, a most unsuitable girl. Did he tell you that?"

"No."

"The one he took to that ball," he informed her. "He thinks he's in love with her, and he wants to break things off with Janet."

Instantly, Mary's face changed. "I hadn't realized." She took a moment to contemplate the idea. "Well, who is she? What kind of family does she come from?"

"She's an American with no money, no connections. She wasn't even a student at the university. She's here on some dubious personal journey. She purchased a motorbike so she could drive off to the continent, and she wants to take our son with her!"

"Oh, dear." She looked away. "I hadn't realized."

"Do you see why I'm so upset? He could throw away his whole future because of this girl, because of his impetuous urge to pursue her."

She had difficulty picturing it. "A girl alone on a motorbike traveling through the continent?"

"Exactly. Can you imagine?"

Bewildered, Mary answered, "No I can't. What on earth do you think he sees in someone like that?"

He shrugged and fleetingly recalled another young woman he knew long ago. "I suppose there's appeal in the freedom someone like that represents," he said, thinking of her, "and she's reputedly attractive."

"How do you know that?"

Calmer now, he responded, "Alfred Cowan told me. They were on the links and he happened upon them. He invited them to tea afterward. According to him, she's charming and pretty, and reasonably intelligent. He had no trouble seeing what Andrew sees, but you know what a rake he is."

"Yes, of course," she answered, feeling increasingly distressed, because for Alfred to have said those things, the girl must have considerable allure. "But Alfred's a man," she reminded her husband, "and like it or not, your son is now a man, too."

He sharply disagreed. "If Andrew were a man, he'd see this for what it is! I gave him my permission at first. I told him to go ahead and have a bit of fun, sow some wild oats if he's a mind to, but he's not content with that. He wants to be free of his engagement, free of his responsibilities, free to go to her. He expects me to give my blessing and wave good-bye to him with a smile on my face, but I can't do that, Mary. I won't do that!"

She sat quietly as her husband moved to light up his pipe, then watched as he generated clouds of smoke that drifted between them. "No, of course not," she finally said to him. "You can't let him ruin his life over a simple infatuation. But you have to let him stay at Crofthill, Donald. You can't force him to come with us to Mull. You understand that, don't you?"

Albeit reluctantly, he saw her point and responded gruffly, "Yes."

"Keeping on this way will only drive him further from you," she went on to say, "so you must stop arguing with him before you make matters worse."

Donald nodded, because he understood that his son was too much like him to be dissuaded.

"Let him stay here by himself," she proposed, "but try to make things up before we go. Hopefully he'll calm down in a few days and come to his senses. He'll be quite lonely on his own. Perhaps he'll even want to join us after a time."

He laid his pipe aside. "But what about the girl? What if he doesn't come to his senses and goes off to meet her? Cowan ventured an opinion on this. He fears Andrew has already gone over the edge."

"Where and when are they supposed to meet?" she wondered.

"In France, at the end of the month."

"Well, we've time, then, don't we? Let's see if we can't handle this another way than by arguing and forbidding."

"All right, you're right," he grumbled, then went back to furiously sucking his pipe. But when the idea came to him, he held it motionless in midair, and his frown transformed to something that resembled a smile. "We'll let him stay here and see what comes of it, but in the meantime I'm going to take out some insurance."

The look on his face reminded her of Alfred Cowan just then, and that was not reassuring. "What are you going to do?"

He'd been standing during the course of their conversation, but he settled into a chair. "I'm going to lock his passport and birth certificate in my safe."

A few moments earlier, as Mary saw the possibility of restoring peace to her family, she had begun to relax. But upon hearing her husband's words, she was overcome by an icy chill that made her shiver suddenly, and left her with a sense of foreboding.

Chapter 28

It was called the "Highway of the Sun" because it led to the normally sun-drenched south of France, but today the sun shone only in the Paris environs; Annie was on the road no more than an hour when it started to rain. She pulled into a rest stop and donned the waterproof pants Colin had wisely recommended she buy, then set off again.

The rain had begun as a drizzle, but it quickly grew steady and hard. As it did, the trucks that passed her splashed more and more dirty water her way. Before long, she was coated with an oily slime that made it difficult to see through her visor, and it became necessary to pull over at every available location and clean it as best she could. At the third such stop, she went into the restroom and discovered that despite the waterproof quality of her jacket and over pants, the rain was getting through to her clothing. John's scarf was the only dry thing on her body. She ordered a coffee in the restaurant and sat for a while to warm herself.

The weather had already slowed her progress, so she didn't stay long. As the morning progressed, she found it necessary to stay longer at each stop, trying to recover from the cold she now felt in her bones. At about noon, she afforded herself the luxury of a hearty soup and a longer rest, toying with the idea of changing her wet things. But she decided against it, knowing that the dry clothes she would put on would quickly become wet, too, and what would she do with them, anyway? Where would she put them?

She dreaded the return to the highway. Despite her helmet, the spray from the passing vehicles had begun to feel like so many slaps to her face. As she drove she sang for distraction, but the only song she could think of at the time, though appropriate, didn't raise her spirits. She recalled Eric Clapton's, "Lonesome and a Long Way from Home." Throughout the day, it continued to play in her head even when she'd stopped singing it.

The day went on like this, the rain unrelenting and punishing, the trucks merciless, the distance between rest stops longer and longer. But Annie persevered, knowing that somewhere at the end of this road she would find friends and sunshine, and the promise of seeing Andrew again.

She had started early, at around seven, and as the evening came on her strength began to wane. Heeding the ferocious growling of her stomach, she stopped for another bowl of soup and discovered, as she made the short walk to the café from her parking space, that her entire body ached. From her forehead to her toes, she could feel the growing soreness, the reaction of her muscles to having been taut and cold for so many hours. She swallowed a couple of aspirin from the bottle she carried, and when she finished her soup and went back to Percy, she found it incredibly difficult to jump his starter and climb onto him again.

The rain tapered off as she drew closer to Lyons. She began seeing signs for something called a *péage,* and when she recognized the unmistakable lines of vehicles queued up at the tiny booths, she understood. She slowed and pulled into one of the longer lines, worrying about the transaction that would surely be difficult for her in French.

As the queue she was in slowed to a stop, she put her weary legs to the pavement to support Percy. They were cramped and weakened and didn't want to be asked to hold up the heavy bike, so they simply gave way. Percy fell over on his side, taking Annie with him, crushing her with his enormous weight. It all happened without her being able to stop any of it, in a sort of slow motion. The next thing she knew, she was lying helplessly on the pavement of France's busiest highway.

In a matter of seconds, people were hovering around her, calling to her as she lay motionless—*Ca va? Ca va?* A couple of men lifted Percy off and walked him away from the traffic, and a couple more lifted Annie and helped her away, too. Trembling and disoriented, she sank to the curb when she reached it. An official from the tollbooths came to investigate and spoke to her in English.

Noticing the "GB" sticker on Percy, he asked her, "Are you British?"

"No, American," she mumbled.

Her pallor made him ask, "Have you eaten today?"

She recalled the two bowls of soup she'd consumed, and she answered, "Yes, thank you," although her stomach nagged at her as though she hadn't. "It's just that I've been driving all day in the rain, since Paris, and I'm very tired."

"Want some coffee?" He smiled at her.

"Thanks, that'd be nice," she responded, though more caffeine was not what she needed.

He helped her inside the building they were near and offered her a chair. As he prepared a cup for her, he inquired, "Where are you going from here?"

"Saintes Maries de la Mer," she informed him.

His expression turned serious. "Not today, surely!"

"I was hoping," she ventured.

"Oh, no, not today!" he insisted, noticing the dark circles under her eyes and how her hands shook when she reached for the mug. "You'd better stay somewhere for the night and start again in the morning. It's too far for today."

Warily, she asked, "How far is it from here?"

"About 300 kilometers."

Upon hearing that, she almost cried. "No! That far?"

"Yes, about. So you see, it's quite impossible for you to make it today."

What am I to do? she wondered. I suppose I can go a bit farther, a couple of hours more, maybe. But I want so badly to be where I know someone. God forbid I spend another night like the last one. "I am pretty tired," she admitted to the man, "but I've got to get as far as I can today."

Shaking his head, he advised, "Better have a good meal and some rest. Get yourself some dinner at the restaurant." He pointed to the rest stop café he could see from his window.

"I'll do that," she decided. "Can I pay you for the toll or do I have to drive through?"

"I'll take you through, no charge."

"That's very kind of you, thanks."

"It's normal," he answered, smiling again.

Buoyed by a decent meal and more caffeine, Annie resumed her journey. The terrain had changed from green and lush to a sandy soil with pine woods, and the temperature had risen noticeably. With the rain behind her, she pulled over after a time and changed out of her wet top into a dry and cooler one. It was warm and humid here, and without Percy's roar covering it, she could hear the sounds of crickets coming from the pine forest. It reminded her of her childhood in Louisiana, of times spent with Timmy and her grandfather. It fortified her and gave her the courage to move on once again.

But it wasn't long before she realized she could go no farther. Night was falling and she had pushed herself to such an extent that she literally could not continue. With her eyelids refusing to stay open, the possibility of getting off the highway and into a hotel no longer existed. Like an airplane that had run out of fuel in midair, she was coming down quickly, and she needed to find a spot to land.

She had traveled into sparsely populated country, almost two hours past Lyons. The land was rugged and wild, complete with mountain crags and vast, barren expanses. She spied the signs for another rest area and quickly determined that she must stop there. She was happy she had, when even the effort of putting Percy B. onto his kickstand proved to be too much for her.

She looked around and thought to herself that it could be worse. A parking lot somewhat distant from the small restaurant seemed designed for motorists to spend the night, so with a determined effort, she drove Percy toward it.

Beyond the lot, she saw nothing but woods and she went into them, deftly maneuvering the maze of trees. Because the ground was soft, she left the kickstand up when she turned off the engine and leaned the bike against a tree.

Then she surveyed the area, looking to see if anyone was watching her. When she was satisfied that she was unobserved, she removed her bags and sleeping sack from Percy.

After locating the hammer and screwdriver she carried for emergency repairs, she laid the down-filled bag on some pine straw and put the softer piece of luggage at her head for a pillow. She removed Andrew's knife from her jacket and then, because it contained her money and passport, stuffed it into the foot of the sleeping bag. When she had secured her belongings as best she could, she got into the bag. With the hammer in her right hand, the screwdriver in her left, and Andrew's knife tucked into her jeans pocket, she fell asleep quickly. The last thing she remembered doing was praying it wouldn't rain.

Amazingly, she didn't awaken until daylight, when traffic and activity picked up at the rest stop. When she opened her eyes and realized that she'd made it safely through the night, she clasped her hands together and said out loud—thank you! The woods were filled with birdsong and the scent of pines warming in the sunlight, and as she breathed in the new day, she felt happy to be alive.

She sang a Beatles song as she rolled up her bag and secured her things on Percy again, a much happier tune than she'd sung yesterday. "Here comes the sun, do do do do, here comes the sun, it's all right." She went into the restaurant bathroom to wash up and brush her teeth, and when she emerged she felt infused with new energy. Her appetite returned with a vengeance and after a hearty breakfast, she was speeding on her way again.

The sun shone brilliantly, traffic was considerably lighter, and the fields of red poppies that Annie saw everywhere were downright inspiring. She smiled to herself as she realized that she'd found the France she'd come to see. Driving Percy became fun again, and in less than two hours she was entering the town of Saintes Maries de la Mer.

It was a small, medieval town with narrow streets and tiny alleyways, and it was extremely crowded and busy this morning, filled with colorfully dressed, exotic looking people. Annie didn't know it, but she'd arrived on the day that gypsies from all over Europe converged on this place in an annual pilgrimage to Sarah, their patron saint. It was slow going through the crowds, but after a time she found the apartment that she was looking for. She knocked at the door excitedly, and when it opened, Issie threw her arms around her before she could say a word.

"My God," she cried, "I can't believe you made it!" She released her to look toward the street. "Where's this famous motorcycle?"

"Over there, a bit muddied and tired," she answered, pointing at Percy.

"I can't believe you!" she said again. "What on earth possessed you?"

"You know me," she chuckled. "I like doing things the hard way."

The girls wrapped their arms around each other's waists as they made their way to the motorcycle, so Annie could retrieve her bags.

Back at the flat, she asked Issie, "Before I do anything else, do you think I could take a bath? I haven't had one for three days, and . . ."

"Say no more," she answered. "Let me just heat up the water. It won't take long. My roommates have gone to the market so you go right ahead and take your time." She started toward the bath but turned back. "Man, it's great to see you!"

Annie was still reveling in the warm water and soap when Katie and Flynn returned, laden with fresh bread and vegetables. Like Issie, they were students from the University of Tennessee studying in France for one semester. They'd been eager to meet Annie, and after introductions and a couple of glasses of wine, they set about preparing lunch.

The meal was wonderful. It consisted of roasted chicken, a ratatouille that Flynn had prepared, fresh tomato salad with olives, pungent cheeses, and crusty bread. Of course there was also plenty of strong, local wine. As hungry as they all were, they had so much to talk about between mouthfuls that it took them better than two hours to eat.

"So, the plan is for you to meet Andrew if he can get away," Katie summed up.

"Yeah, and I need your help to figure out a way for him to reach me."

"He can always write you care of '*Poste Restante*' here in Saintes Maries," Flynn offered.

"What's that?"

"General delivery mail," Katie explained.

"I've got a better idea," Issie said. "Why can't she use Brigitte's address? I'll bet that Brigitte would let them use the apartment as a place to meet, too."

"Who's Brigitte?"

"A friend of ours," Issie explained. "You'll meet her tonight. She and some other people are coming over and we're all going to the gypsy fete. Brigitte's not an exchange student; she's French and lives here. She has an apartment that she's not giving up, and she'll be away the entire summer in Greece—Corfu, actually. She's told the three of us that we can use it since we have to vacate ours. We won't have keys, but she hides one near the door."

Excitedly, Annie told her, "That sounds perfect! Do you think she'll mind?"

"I don't think she'll mind at all," she smiled. "I'll introduce you tonight and then we can talk about it before everyone gets drunk and we forget."

The next day, as soon as she was up, Annie borrowed some stationery and a stamp from Issie so that she might send the letter without delay.

13 Rue des Deux Maries
Saintes Maries de la Mer
30 May, 1972

My Andrew,

I arrived yesterday morning. Getting here was not quite the happy adventure I'd hoped for, but never mind that. It's done and behind me. I have the very strong feeling that what's ahead will be wonderful, though, because last night the full moon rose out of the Mediterranean, and just like the aurora we witnessed, I knew it was a sign!

The gypsies are here, converged on Saintes Maries from all over Europe in a pilgrimage. I went with my friends to the place where they danced last night. I watched their dancing and got swept away by their passionate guitars, and it made my imagination run wild. I saw us together on Percy, riding off to wherever we choose, like two gypsies ourselves, not worried about money or time or responsibilities to anyone but ourselves. My heart felt like it would thump out of my chest with the thought of it!

Andrew, you must come! Here's how we'll work it: Issie has a friend here she introduced me to, Brigitte, who'll be in Greece all summer. She's leaving the key to her flat hidden near the entrance, and she's said that you and I are welcome to use it as we like. The address that I've written at the top of this letter is hers. The place is very easy to find. It's the street that runs along the sea and the building in which her flat is located is across from a café—La Camargue. You can't miss it. The key is hidden behind a loose stone near the door, four feet to the left of it and one foot from the ground. I talked to Brigitte for quite some time last night, and she said if you were to arrive before I returned, it would be perfectly all right for you to go in and make yourself at home. Of course you can write me there, but wouldn't it be oh so wonderful to send yourself instead of a letter?

Issie and I are leaving day after tomorrow and we'll be gone for about two weeks. I know you'll be with your family during that time, so I thought it'd be good to see some sights with her while I wait for you. We plan to go to Paris first, then to Brussels and Amsterdam. We'll return by driving through Germany and Switzerland to end up at Brigitte's flat. Issie wants to go to Italy after that, but I intend to stay in Saintes Maries until I hear from you.

I'm going to wait until you arrive to see the French countryside, because I want to share that with you. When you come and if you have the time, I was thinking we might go to Italy, too, and see Florence and Venice—maybe even Rome. How does that sound?

I send this letter with the greatest hope that it'll incite you to join me, because, the truth is, my soul longs to be reunited with yours. I know it'll be difficult with your father and all, and in light of your engagement, it may not be the "right" thing to do, but in my heart I know that if we don't at least try to be together again, we'll regret it for the rest of our lives. And, Andrew, I know that Shelley would agree and approve, don't you?

I'll send some postcards from my travels over the next couple of weeks and pray to the gods who turned on the northern lights for us that you'll be waiting for me in Saintes Maries when I return!

With all my love,
Annie

She gave some thought to mentioning what had happened with John, in case he already knew, then decided against it. It would be better done in person, she realized. Besides, her instincts told her that it wouldn't matter, that even if he were already aware, he would still come to her, still want to be with her. Her heart told her that.

* * *

His family had gone to their castle on the Isle of Mull, and Andrew was alone at Crofthill with only minimal staff when the letter arrived. He read it over at least ten times before sitting down to pen his reply.

7 June, 1972
Crofthill
Cairncurran, Scotland

My Annie,
What joy I know! What utter joy! I thank the gods that you made it safely to Saintes Maries, and I plead with them to keep you safe on your upcoming journey!

After you left St. Andrews, my confusion cleared and I realized that I could never be without you. When I returned home, I told my father that I'd be joining you in France. He reacted as I expected but never mind that. I am determined that I will find a way to come to you.

I managed to fail two of my exams, which means I'll have to do re-sits before next term. Father has not as yet heard this news, because I'm at Crofthill on my own while the family are away. There will be hell to pay and some matters to tend to before I can depart, but I optimistically predict that I should be ready to leave for the continent in less than a week. I have committed the directions to Brigitte's flat to memory and hope to be there soon, to either meet or await you. I don't think I'll be able to sleep or eat until then.

I don't know why it's taken so long, but I do finally see what is important and necessary, and I want with all my heart and soul to come to you.

Enough of this slush. You know how I feel.

Everything I have,
Andrew

He brought the letter directly to the post in Cairncurran and waited in the town square until he saw the Royal Mail lorry arrive. He breathed an audible sigh of relief as he watched the truck drive off from the village, bound for Glasgow, then went into the pub to knock back some courage before he would ring up his father.

Andrew closed the door to the library, walked to the viscount's desk, and dialed the phone standing up. He would not sit in his father's chair.

His mother was reluctant to call his father to the phone. "He's spoken with the dean. He knows about your exams, Andrew. I think it best if you wait a few days before you talk."

"It can't wait, Mother."

"What's so pressing?" she insisted.

Inhaling first, he told her, "I've decided to go to Janet and break things off. After that, I'll be leaving for France."

"Oh dear," Mary murmured, "oh dear."

"It'll be all right, really it will," he tried to assure her. "I don't love Janet, Mother. I love someone else."

Plaintively, she asked her son, "Please, Andrew, don't do anything you'll regret. Take some time before you act. Why don't you pack a bag and come here? I promise to keep your father calm. We can sit down together and discuss this rationally before you make any final decisions."

"That would take too much time, and I don't have time to waste. Besides, it's not going to do any good. Father's going to be angry about this no matter how we handle it, and I'm going to go to her no matter what he says."

"Please," she implored, "I beg you to reconsider."

Sounding more mature than he ever had, he gently told her, "Just let me speak with him, Mother. I need to get this over with."

It was several long minutes before Donald picked up the receiver. "Your mother's told me of your intentions," he said without emotion. "I expected as much from you."

Ignoring the put-down, he remained civil. "I didn't want to leave without speaking to you. It wouldn't be right."

There was no response.

"I hope in time you'll come to see that it's not the life-shattering event you think it is." The silence on the other end of the line was unsettling. "Please, Father, I want you to understand. I don't want to go away with all this anger between us."

In his most authoritative, intimidating voice, Donald finally responded. "All right Andrew, I've listened to what you've had to say. Now you listen to me and listen well. As your father, I cannot allow you to do this. There's too much at stake here, and if I were to sit back and allow you to undo all that's been done to bring about this union, I'd not only be failing in my duty to you but to your descendants, as well."

Though his emotions wanted to be in control, Andrew fought hard to stay logical. "But we don't even like Campbells; we never have! From the beginning I've not understood why you've pushed this. We've far more respect and importance than they. Binding our family with theirs is not only unnecessary, it demeans us. It taints us with their ignominy!"

"They've moved beyond that," Donald graciously declared, "and it's not about Glencoe anyway. It's about finally bestowing that title rightfully, upon true Scots—your own sons and grandsons, for Christ's sake—and not the English fops who would pursue Janet to claim it!"

With righteous indignation, Andrew asked, "So you'd have me pursue her for reasons no more lofty than theirs and condemn myself to a loveless marriage in the bargain? Is this what you'd have me do?"

Without hesitation, his father responded, "I'd have you act responsibly, with the good of your family and heirs in mind, and stop wallowing in self-indulgence."

As much as he would have liked to accomplish this through rational argument, Andrew could see that it was futile. So, with as much calm as he could muster, he informed his father, "I'm going to France."

"Fine," Donald snapped at him, "but you'll have to swim the channel to get there."

"I don't need your money," he told him. "I'll manage to get passage somehow."

There was a detectable bit of exuberance in his tone as he responded, "That's not what I meant."

In fearful anticipation of what his father was about to say, his heart began to race.

"You're not going to get very far without your passport," he casually informed his son.

Andrew's face went white, and he gripped the telephone so tightly he could feel the plastic give way. "What have you done with it?" he demanded to know.

"It's locked away in my safe, and in case you've a mind to claim it was lost and apply for a replacement, I've stowed your birth certificate there, as well." The viscount's voice was clearly triumphant now.

In this moment, it was all he could do to keep breathing, so saying anything to his father was out of the question. He did, however, raise his eyes to the painting that hid his father's safe, a 200-year-old oil of Leda and the Swan. Leda nuzzled the swan's head in her full, round breasts, and her dark hair and loving eyes reminded him of Annie.

His father's voice came back to him. "Get your things together and come here and we'll talk."

In the ominous quiet of his father's study, Andrew continued to stare at the painting. After a moment, Donald said something else to him, but he didn't hear it because he was hanging up the telephone.

He went to the carriage house and asked the footman for a hammer, the largest one he could find. His demeanor frightened the young man, who couldn't have been more than sixteen. He ran toward the workroom and came out with two heavy hammers: one a mallet type, the other a sledgehammer.

Despite his fear, the footman followed his young master at a safe distance as Andrew quickly traversed the drive to the main house. Inside the library, he swung the painting so violently away from the wall that he managed to loosen a hinge, leaving it to hang haphazardly to the side. Then he stood on a chair and delivered the sledgehammer to the dial, over and over, with great grunts and tremendous effort, battering and finally breaking it. He put down the tool and tried to open the door, but it would not budge. He picked up the hammer again and went at the metal with more vehemence than before, hitting every bit of the door now, not just the dial. He swung with such force that he lost his balance and almost fell from the chair. When he still could not open the safe, he screamed for the footman who was waiting, trembling outside the study door.

"Bring me more tools! Anything you can find that might work to pry this bloody thing open!" The young man could not seem to get his feet to move. "Now! Do it now!"

As he rounded a curve in the hallway, the footman collided with Ambrose.

With the family away, Ambrose had been reading and enjoying the peace of the mostly empty household when he'd been disturbed by the unusual sounds.

"What's all this, now?" he asked the flustered young man.

"I'm sorry, sir! It's just that young master wants me to rush!"

"What's all the racket about?"

"Lord Andrew is hammering at his father's safe!"

His face filled with concern. "What did you say?"

"He's trying to break into his father's safe!" he declared, just as other servants were gathering nearby.

As it sank in, Ambrose's first thought was to protect the family from embarrassment. "You go about what you were doing; I'll take care of this," he said to him. He lifted his eyes to the others and added, "And that goes for all of you! On your way now!"

"Yes sir, thank you, sir!" the boy answered with audible relief before he fled the house.

When he entered the study and saw Andrew having at the safe, Ambrose felt ill. The sight of the usually reserved and well-mannered young man, out of control with anger and frustration as he was, made the older man sick with dread. Ambrose couldn't think what to say, so he walked over and stood in anxious silence as Andrew swung the hammer with decreasing enthusiasm. His energy waned as he began to realize that his efforts were futile.

As he stepped down from the chair, Andrew looked hard at his father's valet. "Did you have anything to do with this?" he demanded.

"To do with what, sir?" he quietly questioned.

Frowning with annoyance, he asked, "Why do you do that? Why do you call me *sir* when you've known me since I was born?"

"I know my place, sir."

He was breathing heavily as he railed, "Blast! Blast it all! Damn it all to hell!" Then he composed himself enough to wonder, "Were you privy to his plot? Did you know about this? You should have warned me, Ambrose."

Still at a loss, he responded, "I'm afraid I don't know what you're referring to, sir."

"I'm referring to locking my passport in this damned safe so that I can't leave, that's what!"

With a barely noticeable shake of his head, he answered honestly, "No, sir, I wasn't aware that his lordship had done that." He finally understood what was happening to the young man. He'd have to have been blind and deaf these past several days to be unaware of the conflict between father and son, and the reason for it.

Andrew dropped the hammer, then let his body fall heavily upon the couch. His ears resounded with the echo of the hammer's clang, and his hands throbbed from the repeated impacts; he rubbed them against his thighs while his mind went in clamorous search of options. There must be a way—there must be some way that I can get into it. His eyes lit when it came to him. "Do we have any dynamite about?"

Ambrose gasped. "You're not serious!"

"I've never been more serious in my life! Do we have any?"

"No, sir, I'm certain we don't. We've no call for anything like that."

"Then I'll get some. I'll go into Glasgow and get some."

As a servant, Ambrose knew it was not his place to interfere. But the young man's state was more than frightening, and in his father's absence, he felt it his duty to do what he could to stop him from making a terrible, irrevocable mistake. "Sir, surely there is something else you can do. Let me take you up to Mull. Let me take you to see your father. There must be some compromise that can be reached. There must be . . ."

Andrew shook his head adamantly. "No, there's nothing more to be said between my father and me. In fact, I never want to see the bloody bastard again—never!" He straightened in his seat as a new, less radical idea emerged. "I know what I'll do! I've got it! I'll go into Glasgow, all right. I'll go there and I'll find someone to sell me a false passport. Surely there are people about who do that sort of thing. People get false documents all the time, don't they?"

Ambrose's eyes were incredulous. "Yes, I'm certain there are ways to obtain a false passport. But sir, that's an imprisonable offense! You could be arrested for merely attempting to secure one, my lord. Think what could happen."

Andrew's smile was unsettling. "What would be different? I'm a bloody prisoner here, aren't I?" He stood and walked toward the door, but he stopped when he reached it to look back at Ambrose. "What does it matter? What does anything matter if I can't be with her, if I can't make my own choices and love whom I choose? Am I to let my life be ruled by my tyrant father? Am I never to know what it is to live my own life, my own way?"

"Let me help you, Andrew," the older man pleaded. "Let me speak to your father on your behalf."

The distress washed from his face suddenly, and he looked more like himself. "Thank you for calling me by my name, Ambrose. But I'm too fond of you to allow you to be put in that position. I'll manage this on my own. I'll find some way to get to her." He started away.

"Sir! Andrew! Please, come back!" he called, even as he heard the sound of the enormous entrance door being pulled shut.

The still quivering young footman handed Andrew the keys to his Austin Healey. He had no suitcase and no toothbrush, but he had about 200 pounds in his pocket. If the cost of the false passport was more than he had, he told himself, he could sell the car. He sped up as he left the estate, going rapidly through the gears and hardly slowing for the curves. All he could think about was getting to Glasgow as quickly as humanly possible and finding some way out of Britain before his father had time to call on his powerful friends and alert the police.

The faster he drove, the more his mind raced, running through possibilities and alternatives: how he would start, where he would go in the city to get some information. He would have to work fast and get out of the country quickly, he knew that. He lamented the fact that there'd be no time to break things off with Janet in person. He'd have to write to her from France. The idea offended his sense of honor and he deeply regretted that, but there was nothing else he could do now. His father had seen to that.

He wouldn't sleep, he told himself. He would keep at it until he got out, until he got what he wanted. He could sleep in France when he got to Annie. He allowed his mind to rest on that awhile—on the image of himself lying with her, each of them naked, wrapped in the other's arms, spent from their lovemaking. Beyond that he couldn't see, he wouldn't look, not to the morning after or the next day or week, or to the time when she had to return to America. He focused on his desire for her, his need to express his love as a man for the first time, and to do it over and over again until he collapsed with exhaustion. He kept this image foremost in his mind as he drove faster and faster on the narrow curving road that led from Crofthill to Kilmacolm, where he would follow the Bridge of Weir Road into Glasgow.

The dilapidated lorry lumbered along, taking up most of the roadway and maneuvering the curves awkwardly, carrying a full load of hay. Ian, the man who drove it, was a neighbor to Crofthill, a weathered, bent fellow who looked older than his years, who had raised six children without a mother for the last eight. He'd seen more difficult times than easy ones. He'd struggled through sick sheep and children, years when there was precious little to put on the table and nothing but worn shoes on his young ones' feet, but he'd always managed somehow. The family at Crofthill had helped. They'd sent food from their larder and the outgrown clothing of their own children, and had always had Ian's children as their Christmas guests, delighting them with presents and delicious treats. When most of the children were ill with the measles, the viscountess brought the doctor, then came every day with food and to help nurse them. Andrew and his sisters had passed many a happy summer afternoon together, playing games in the fields with Ian's children, chasing sheep and climbing trees. His first kiss had been with Ian's eldest daughter.

They were well-known to one another, this man and Andrew, after many years of being neighbors and friends, and so it was that they recognized each other and looked into each other's eyes in that split second before the impact.

In the undisturbed peace of the Renfrewshire countryside, it was more than ten minutes before someone happened upon them, and it took that person another fifteen minutes to return with help from Kilmacolm. Among those who had come from the village were the constable, several shopkeepers who doubled as emergency help, the rector, and a woman who had had nurse's training.

The rescue party gasped at the sight of the red sports car they immediately recognized, horribly crushed, with its driver still behind the wheel. His face was cut and bloodied almost beyond recognition; his barely breathing body was discolored and limp, with one leg contorted and wedged against the dash, its splintered femur protruding through the muscle. They stood frozen, staring at the mangle of steel and human flesh for one, long awful moment.

When they looked toward the lorry, they couldn't see its driver at first—not until they'd walked over and searched alongside the overturned vehicle. It was then that they'd spotted his body, pale and lifeless, lying among the scattered and broken bales of hay. It was clear that nothing could be done for him—nothing, that is, but for the rector to kneel beside the stillness that was once a father and friend, and clasp his hands in prayer.

The constable laid a hand on the pastor's shoulder. "Better not waste time. We canna do nothin' for poor Ian now, but someone needs to go up to the house and tell the lad's family while there's still breath in him."

MacDougal, the grocer, was nearby, and he anxiously informed them, "The family's gone on holiday. Their cook told me. Lord Andrew's the only one home!"

"Well then, you go up to Crofthill and tell the cook or whoever's there, and be quick about it, now!"

"Aye!" came the answer.

As his anger threatened to overwhelm him, the Viscount Rannoch had taken a rifle and his deerhounds and gone to the moor, for it would not do to have others see him in this emotional state. A consummate aristocrat, schooled at severe Gordonstoun no less, he was always conscious of the need to control his Scottish temperament—that passionate, not so deeply buried part of himself that he seemed to have passed on to his son. He'd told his wife that he would return when he would and that he was not to be disturbed while he hunted, so when he heard the sound of a horn and his name called after, he let go his last remaining restraint, emerging from the hide with a beet-red face and violent intentions.

The estate manager had come looking for his employer with several hands, not knowing how difficult it might be to locate him. After nearly an hour, they found him perched menacingly atop a rise. While the overseer spoke softly to the Kilmartin heir, the search party remained at a distance, alongside the wagon path that led downward through the glen. They understood the gravity of the situation and watched in sympathy as the color fled Donald's face and he laid aside his gun and sank to his knees, his arms pulled in as though he'd suffered a blow to the stomach. But they turned away in embarrassment when they heard the sound that came from him: that chilling, guttural, animal sound of a grown man's anguish.

Part III

We meet not as we parted,
We feel more than all may see;
My bosom is heavy-hearted,
And thine full of doubt for me:—
One moment has bound the free.

That moment is gone forever,
Like lightning that flashed and died—
Like a snowflake upon the river—
Like a sunbeam upon the tide,
Which the dark shadows hide.

Percy B. Shelley,
"We Meet Not As We Parted"

Chapter 29

St. Andrews, 14 April, 1994
It has been a mystery to me for most of my life, and the years have not made it less so. It hangs on me like a curse, follows me like a blessing, troubles me like an undecipherable dream. So far along the road now, it still compels me to examine it, to wonder about it, to feel again the longing— the aching, sweet torment.

Annie had invited Tom Keegan out for dinner, but he didn't feel up to leaving the hotel. So they sat together for the third time now, having a light supper in the Russell public room. The hotel was half full and the bar rather quiet, and as the wine worked its magic, the conversation turned to the recounting of Annie's prior visit to St. Andrews. She withheld the more intimate details from her companion, but there was no mistaking the impact that Andrew had had on her life.

Tom was captured by her story and prodded her with questions. "So that was it? You never saw or heard from him again?"

"I never saw his face again, but I heard from him once," she sighed. "It was the response to my initial letter. I received it in October, weeks after I'd returned home." Her brow wrinkled as she explained, "That girl, Brigitte, the one whose apartment we were supposed to meet at—she forwarded it to me. Apparently, her neighbor had been taking in her mail and holding it for her while she was away."

His curiosity was roused. "What did it say—that he couldn't make it?"

"You would have thought that," she softly responded, "but it was the opposite. He was thrilled to have heard from me and said he'd be on his way to France in a few days." Her eyes fell to the table. "It sounded as though he'd made up his mind to be with me no matter what."

With a quizzical face, he commented, "That's odd. I wonder what happened."

"I corresponded with Susannah and Mel, you know," she informed him now, "and when I asked them about Andrew, the response was simply that he hadn't returned to the university and no one seemed to know why."

With increased emphasis, he declared, "That's very odd. So what did you do? Did you keep writing? Did you try to ring him?" He poured the last of the wine into her glass.

"After I got the letter, I wrote immediately to explain— so he'd know how long it took to get to me. He didn't respond, but I kept on writing anyway. I did try to phone once, a couple of months after that. It was around Christmas," she recalled. "Wherever he'd been, I figured he'd be home for the holidays."

"Didn't you reach him?"

"The number he gave me—they said there was no one there by that name. I remember very clearly that the man who answered the phone had a very stiff and proper English accent. He said in no uncertain terms that there was no one there by that name and then suggested that I'd been given the wrong number."

Tom seemed disappointed. "That's rather sad, isn't it? And more than a bit mysterious."

"I never called again, because phoning overseas was ridiculously expensive then."

"So you gave up?"

"Not at first, but I'd gone back to college and was busy with that, and there were other things, things that happened in my family." She hesitated, then decided not to get into that, because even after all this time, it was still too difficult. "I wrote less and less often but for more than a year."

"And your other friends? They heard nothing?"

Shrugging, she answered, "If they did, they never said. I even wrote to Robin at the Whaum, but he didn't respond. Susannah did her best to find out what had happened but didn't come up with anything." Her tone turned slightly cynical when she added, "At least that's what she said."

He tugged at his chin and shook his head slightly. "That's odd."

"You seem skeptical," she observed.

"I am," he admitted. "People don't simply vanish in Scotland. South America it's not." He grinned now as he looked at her.

She smiled, too, but briefly.

"Perhaps something untoward happened," he offered, "an accident or some such thing."

"I think Susannah would have heard if it had been something like that," she answered. Her brow furrowed as she added, "The irony of the damned thing—if I'd gotten that letter while I was in France as I should have, I could have come back to Scotland and gone in search of him myself."

"Would you have?" he questioned.

She nodded emphatically to say, "I would have thought something terrible had happened to keep him from me. I was so sure of him, Tom, of his feelings for me. I've never been that sure of anyone." An uncomfortable burning arose in her throat and she lifted her glass to drink. "And that letter, reading it only made me more certain, more certain and more confused."

His eyes conveyed sympathy. "Will you try to find him while you're here?"

"I already have—no luck. It was a four-digit phone number I had, and everything's changed since then, of course." She frowned. "And as for finding Andrew Gordon in Scotland's directory assistance—there are so many of them, I don't know where to begin."

"It is rather a common name, I'm afraid, and of course there's the possibility that he's in England or elsewhere." He signaled to the barmaid. "Shall we order another bottle?"

"Better not. I've got to drive home, you know," she answered, pushing her glass away. "I'm considering going over to Cairncurran one of these days to see if I can locate Crofthill. Whoever lives there now might know of the family."

"That's an idea," he told her, "and it might even be his family. People tend to stay put around here." With the barmaid at their table, Tom asked for a glass of Scotch and a coffee for Annie. He watched the young woman walk away, then turned back to his dinner companion. "The night we met you told me that you'd had an important decision to make and that you'd always wondered if it was the right one. Was it the decision to go on without him?"

She looked into Tom's face momentarily, nodded slightly, then focused on the vacant window seat. She smiled ironically as she said, "I thought I was acting unselfishly by giving him space to make his decision freely." *Just as I've done now,* she realized, *just as I've done with Mike.*

They sat in silence for a few moments, both of them lost in thought as Tom sipped at his Scotch and she her coffee.

He tilted his head to the side. "You must have a theory. What do you think happened to him?"

She sighed. "I think he sent that letter, then had a change of heart and was too embarrassed to say so. I believe he was ashamed to confront me, even by mail."

"But you kept writing. Why did you if you believed that?"

"Because I wanted him to know he could tell me, that he could tell me anything, because that's how we were with each other. I kept hoping he'd remember that and get in touch with me, because he meant so much to me, Tom— so very much." She swallowed hard. "Losing him was one of the worst things that ever happened to me."

For a moment, as Tom watched her eyes fill with tears, he felt an urge to reach out and touch her hand. But he was far too British for displays of that kind, so instead he smiled softly and looked away when she brought her napkin to her cheek.

When they said good night, Annie stepped out of the hotel into the mist and quiet along The Scores. She had parked her car near the golf museum but didn't go to it immediately; instead, she walked in the opposite direction to the Whaum. Going there was easier now, since her initial visit, but no less disturbing.

She returned tonight because something so remarkable had happened on her first visit that it affected her still. Standing inside the thick, protective walls of the Whaum, she was overcome with the awareness that she was not alone and certain that the presence she felt had nothing to do with the current owners. It had come to her with the whistle of the kettle as Mrs. Hampton bustled about the kitchen putting together their tea. And she had been certain that it was Andrew's spirit she felt, for with its arrival came a feeling of peace, a very particular peace that she knew only then, only with him.

As she stood peering through the darkened windows tonight, she experienced it again—that same, eerie feeling that another living being was near her, though clearly she was alone on this foggy night. She wondered now if that ghostly apparition had been the source, the inexplicable power that had drawn her back to St. Andrews.

When she finally turned away from the Whaum and toward her car, something hauntingly familiar happened inside of her, and it delivered her with a profound sense of déjà vu. Her heart grew heavy and sank, and felt as though it were caught on something, or—more likely— that it was being deprived of something it sorely needed, something essential.

* * *

Since his wife's departure for Scotland, Mike Rutledge seemed to be putting in even more time at the office, though he did yield some concessions to a personal life, making certain to have at least one weeknight meal at home with his stepson. But for the rest of the week, it was business as usual as he deftly juggled clients and cases that would bring lesser attorneys to their knees.

This morning, however, for reasons he could not quite put his finger on, it was all getting to him. His head was down, his eyes scanning the papers beneath them, but the focus was not there and the interruptive voice of his secretary didn't help.

"I have two personal messages for you, and both callers claim that it's important," Vicky said as she handed the slips of pink paper to her boss. "Shall I get them for you now?" she asked, viewing him with the same deep concern she had so often shown these past weeks.

As he read them, he clicked his tongue in disgust, then exhaled loudly. "All right. Get this one first and close the door." While he waited for the connection, he stared at the watercolor that hung across from him, the one that featured Annie standing near their pond.

Without enthusiasm, Mike said, "Hello Jack. How are you?"

Jack sounded relieved. "Mr. Rutledge! I'm so glad you called back! I hated to bother you. I know how busy you are, but I've been unsuccessful in reaching Annie at your home. Your Lucy should be working for the CIA, you know, for all the information I get out of her!" He laughed agreeably before continuing. "Anyway, I wonder if I might leave a message for Annie with you?"

Mike grinned to himself over the comment about Lucy. "Of course."

"How is she, by the way? I'd hoped she'd keep in touch with me at least. I can understand her not wanting to call the office, but she can always reach me at home."

"She's been out of the country, Jack. Otherwise, I'm sure she would have phoned."

"She's traveling? Oh marvelous, that's just the thing I would have recommended," he cooed. "I do miss her, though. She was wonderful to work for—the best boss I ever had."

"I'll tell her you said so." He cleared his throat. "I don't mean to be rude, but I'm in something of a rush."

"Oh sure, sorry. I do tend to go on, don't I?" he chuckled, then lowered his voice. "They'd kill me here if they knew I was passing this on, but the major, and I do mean major, British ad firm of Lynch and Collings is looking for her. They want her as a consultant on what they deem an enormously important account. They've called several times, Mr. Rutledge. They seem set on hiring her. It sounds like a great opportunity, but I was reluctant to give them your home number. I know it's unlisted."

Mike sharpened his attention. "British, you said?"

"That's right. They're in Oxford. Want the information?"

Quickly, he scribbled the number. "I appreciate the call, Jack, and I know she will, too. But I've got to run. I'm due in court."

"I understand." He inhaled abruptly. "Oh, one more thing! You have to tell her this. After she left, Transatlantic pulled their account, then went back to their own PR department with instructions to do exactly what Annie had proposed! Now Rich is crying foul. Can you believe that?"

He responded with a cynical burst of air. "I can."

Mike glanced at his watch, then began gathering his things when Vicky's voice came through on the intercom.

He could not hide his irritation. "What now?"

Timidly, she informed him, "Sorry Mr. Rutledge, but that other number. He's on the line; he's just called again."

"Shit," he hissed. "All right then, put him through." He'd been seated while he spoke to Jack, but for this call he stood behind his desk.

"Mike Rutledge?"

In an icy voice, he responded, "Speaking." Then he let a deliberate, tension-building silence follow.

"This is Glenn Winters. I'm . . ."

"I know who you are," Mike answered sharply. Though no one else could see it, his face assumed the expression he was famous for, the one that struck fear in the heart of his adversaries.

Glen stammered slightly. "I wonder if we could meet? I think it'd be better than speaking over the phone."

Mike's tone was pure business now. "Where and when?"

"Harry's. Tomorrow, say five-thirty?"

"I'll be there." As he hung up the telephone, Mike's eyes unwittingly returned to the watercolor. When they settled on the melancholy image of his wife, the pain that burned through them made him turn away.

He'd put it off until the end of the day, but before he left for home he made the call to Scotland.

The ring of the phone had startled her, but she was happy to hear his voice. "Mike!"

"Did I wake you? I know it's late, but it's the first chance I had to phone."

Although it was past midnight, she was nestled in front of the hearth, soaking up the only heat the small cottage afforded. "It's OK," she responded. "I wasn't sleeping. I was reading." She often fell asleep in this location because the adjustment to the cold bedroom was just too hard to make.

He felt awkward suddenly, and he offhandedly inquired, "Oh? Something interesting?"

"Mildly, a novel I picked up the other day. But it's so wonderful to hear your voice. I miss . . ."

The awkwardness passed, and the reality of their situation settled in. As it did, he cut her off in mid sentence. "I got a call from your secretary, Jack. He had some news he wanted to pass on to you."

"What's that? Haymaker's burned down?" she scoffed.

"Ever hear of a British ad firm called Lynch and Collings?"

"Sure," she answered. "They're the cream of the cream. They're so good and in such demand they can handpick their clients."

"They're trying to get hold of you," he told her. "It seems they want you as a consultant."

The words leapt from her mouth. "No shit?"

In spite of himself, Mike smiled on the other end of the line. When she spoke like this, it always brought to mind a picture of the wild-child that used to be—the jeans-clad spirit with the flowing hair, who had wandered around Europe on a motorcycle. He felt strangely affectionate toward that young woman he never knew.

"Is that what Jack said? Really, no shit?" An excitement arose in her voice that had long been absent.

"According to Jack, they've been fairly persistent. And when I mentioned it to Lucy, she told me that someone with a British accent has called the house looking for you, though Jack swears he didn't give them our number."

Hearing him utter those simple words, *our number,* brought on a rush of warmth. "It's a gift from the gods if it's true!" she told him. "I don't mind saying I've been more than a little lonely and trying to think what to do with myself. A gig as a consultant would be great!" For a few seconds she was quiet as the idea fully formed in her head, but on its heels another came to supplant it. "You know, Mike, I've been thinking," she began. "I was wondering, actually, if you might consider coming over and meeting me someplace?" She gave it a moment to settle in. "We need to talk, and it might be good to meet someplace neutral, you know, not in our house. You could use a vacation, and I'd go wherever you'd like—you pick it. We don't have to stay in the same room," she added, to make sure he didn't feel pressured, "or even at the same hotel if you'd rather not. We could just spend some undisturbed time together."

He didn't want her to finish, because he knew it would be difficult to resist her pleas. "I'm up to my neck, Annie, and anyway, Marc needs me around." Pausing momentarily, he recalled something else he needed to tell her. "By the way, his father's cooking up elaborate plans for the summer. You'd better talk with him before they get too far along." He understood the impact those words would have on her, and in a slightly sadistic way, he enjoyed delivering them.

"Sure." As she contemplated having to deal with her difficult ex-husband, it darkened her mood. "Are you still at the office?" she questioned.

"I am. Lucy's with Marc, of course, and I just spoke with him. They've had dinner and he's got a friend over. They're studying for a math test tonight."

She almost didn't want to ask but she had to. "Does he miss me much?"

"Of course he misses you, but he's a teenager remember, and his world right now revolves around his friends. And this time of year, the weather's getting nicer and he's out and about more. If you were home, you'd see very little of him."

"I feel so guilty about being away from him."

"I wish you wouldn't," he told her. "He's perfectly fine, and he's looking forward to going to Scotland to see you."

Going to Scotland to see you—the way he said that, it sounded as though he'd accepted her living there as something permanent. She scanned her small sitting room, comparing it to the comfortable home she shared with Mike and her son, then heaved a heavy sigh. A rush of wind rattled the frail windows, and forced the escaping clouds of chimney smoke into hasty retreat, back into the room.

Across the ocean that separated them, she softly called, "Mike?"

"I'm here," he answered with noticeable reluctance.

"Have you had any more blood work?"

The reluctance shifted into annoyance. "Matt says there's no point in doing it any more frequently than every six weeks, but he did repeat it once, just to be certain."

She swallowed hard before asking, "And?"

When he was reminded that she might be ill, he found it difficult to stay angry. "And it remains negative."

In her heart she gave thanks, then she asked, "Can you ever forgive me, Mike?"

He almost said—perhaps, someday—but instead he answered, "It's too soon to be talking about forgiveness." In the same moment, one of the cleaning people knocked on his door, and he was exceedingly grateful for the distraction. "I need to get going. It's late."

Annie could hear the fatigue and stress in her husband's voice, and in her need to reach out to him, she pictured herself at home when he arrived. She would have a glass of wine with him while he ate his supper, she imagined, then take him up the stairs, leading him by the hand to their bedroom. She would undo his tie and remove his shirt, then sit behind him on the bed, straddling his back. Massaging his neck and broad, strong shoulders, she would coax him into lying back. Then she would raise her nightgown over her naked hips and lower herself onto his erection to rock him into peaceful release. He would fall asleep in her arms, breathing deep, exhausted breaths, nuzzled against her breasts.

But that image faded quickly when the reality of her current predicament reminded her that having sex with anyone was impossible just now, let alone the man she'd so grievously betrayed. "Please call me again soon," she whispered to him.

She couldn't have known it, but he'd been indulging in his own fantasies about her, and for a moment he wanted to say something to his wife. He wanted to tell her that what she had done ripped his gut out, and that with each passing day, the wound grew more putrid. Then, in the next instant, he wanted to say that he wished he'd been a better husband, that he wished he could go back and do it all over again. But in the midst of these jumbled thoughts, the memory of his earlier conversation with Glenn surfaced, and it shut out everything but his anger.

"Tell Marc I'll call him on Sunday, as usual," she said.

"I will," he answered, then abruptly replaced the receiver.

She sat with the telephone in her lap for what seemed a long while after that, staring into the hearth. The fire was dying, but she could not move to stoke it.

* * *

Harry's Bar and Grill was filled with the well-suited clientele that normally poured in at that time of day—the stockbrokers, the lawyers, the stressed-out corporate people who needed a drink before taking the train home. They all crowded in at the bar and couldn't get that first drink down fast enough. Mike Rutledge was known there, as he was at every important gathering place in the city, and he asked Christian, the mâitre d', if he knew Glenn Winters.

"Not really, but I think he's waiting for you at a table in the corner. That gentleman asked for you when he arrived." He made a discreet nod toward the far side of the room.

Mike approached Glenn with the self-possession of a matador striding toward a bull, though inside he felt considerable dread. As Glenn rose to greet him, he was overcome by the man's presence. He had expected Mike to be handsome, but he was not prepared for and was somewhat intimidated by his composed sophistication and natural elegance.

"Glenn," Mike said without inflection. He shook his hand.

Worried that his palms were wet, Glenn took his hand away quickly. "Can I get you a drink?"

Mike's polite response came as effortlessly as taking his seat. "Christian's bringing me my usual, thanks."

In the first few minutes after he had entered the bar, the esteem in which Mike Rutledge was held became glaringly evident to Glenn, when about a dozen people went out of their way to greet him and the staff practically groveled before him. When Annie first married Mike, Glenn's curiosity had led him to ask the hospital's lawyers about him. He discovered that his winning streak as a corporate litigator was unsurpassed. To add to that, he had impeccable manners and style, an Ivy League education, and the restraint and bearing of the well-bred wealthy. And if all these attributes were not enough, Mike Rutledge was beyond reproach for another reason—one that he himself was always uncomfortably aware of. The tragic, senseless murder of his first wife had set him apart and made him immune to criticism.

Because of his position in this delicate situation, Glenn had expected to have the upper hand. He was, after all, the other man, the man Mike's wife had been unfaithful with.

And he, too, was a man of consequence and achievement. In addition to his position as CEO at one of the premier medical centers in the country, he had a major stake in the fastest-growing health care organization in the country, and from it he was accumulating great wealth. But although Glenn had come to Harry's feeling confident that he would control their meeting, it rapidly became clear that Mike was the man in charge.

When his drink had been served, Mike instructed Glenn, "We need to speak discreetly."

"Of course. Would you rather go someplace else," he asked, "one of the hotel bars, maybe?"

"I'd know just as many people wherever I went," Mike answered. "At least this place is noisy." He sipped on his drink, a Maker's Mark and soda, which was mostly soda; he liked to keep his edge.

Glenn was on his second Scotch rocks. "I don't have to say how awkward this is." He waited for Mike to take the ball, but that was not his style. "You should know that we never wanted to hurt anyone," he added clumsily.

Mike asked harshly, "What did you want to see me about?" He would not give him the opportunity to make excuses, and he did not want to hear him refer to Annie and himself as "we."

"You're right. It's pointless for me to try to explain," he said, then decided he might gain some leverage by being more assertive. "Anyway, I'm not here for absolution."

Mike's expression was unreadable, but the set of his jaw was worrisome.

"I've had every test I could," Glenn informed him now. "I've been thoroughly examined, and I have no trace of the virus or antibodies to it. I appear to be in perfect health. I would have told Annie this myself, but I've no way of contacting her except through you."

Mike was taken off guard. He had prepared himself for everything or so he thought, but he had only prepared himself for the worst, and the unexpected nature of this news set him off balance. Something seemed to break loose in him, and he almost smiled. It was only with difficulty that he remembered where he was and who was seated at the table with him.

Glenn made a quick sweep of the room with his eyes, then dropped his voice. "So you see, she couldn't have gotten it from me."

The accusatory tone in those words caught Mike on a nerve, and in a split second he went from wanting to smile to wanting to kill the man in front of him. With every ounce of restraint he could muster, he responded, "I had hoped, at the very least, that I would find you a man worthy of her affection. I'm afraid you've sorely disappointed me." He glared at Glenn as he took a breath. "Had you been the friend she thought you were and had you known her truly, you could never have implied what you just did."

"Well, I suppose there are other explanations," he muttered, beads of perspiration forming on his upper lip. Then he impulsively blurted, "Have you been tested?" He had not wanted to go in that direction, he had not planned on it, but it was too late now.

Mike exhaled slowly, then focused on Glenn from beneath his furrowed brow. "Do you think me such an insufferable ass that I would not be completely forthcoming in a situation like this?" His detachment had slipped away, and he made no attempt to recover it. "To set the record straight, I, too, am healthy." He would not tell this person that he had been absolutely faithful to his wife, that he had never even looked at another woman since the day he'd met her. It was none of his damn business, and he would not give him that satisfaction. "But unlike you, I believe Annie when she says there have only been the two of us and now, unlike you, I look to other reasons for the results turning out as they did. Other possibilities exist, you know, or did you take the trouble to delve into any of that?"

"Well, yes," Glenn stammered. "I'm told that certain types of viral illness can cause a false positive." For one ludicrous moment, he wished for an earthquake to level the building, a fire to leap from the kitchen, a car to come crashing through the street window—anything that might give him reason to jump and run.

"With all the resources available to you at Quaker, I would have imagined that, at the very least, you would have done a literature search on the subject."

"Well, to be honest, I haven't," he heard himself apologize, feeling pinned to the chair by Mike's eyes. "But I did speak with an expert in that area."

"He should have informed you, then," he seethed, "that there has been a fairly high incidence of false positives among those who've been vaccinated against influenza, and that there are several documented cases with results just like hers, with no disease and no obvious explanation for the false results."

Never in his life had Glenn wanted so badly to be out of a place. He'd accomplished what he'd set out to, but he was painfully aware that in the process he'd also made a bad situation worse. The ever-increasing tension between the two made him squirm in his seat, then suck on the ice cubes that were left in his glass.

Fortunately for him, Mike wanted very much to be rid of Glenn Winters. He observed his growing unease and enjoyed it, glaring in silence before saying, "You can go now, Glenn." He made no effort to hide his disgust. Then, for maximum effect, he added, "I've already taken care of the bill."

Glenn stood and left the restaurant as quickly as he could without running. He did not look back, and he went directly home to have dinner with his unsuspecting wife and children.

As Glenn left Harry's, Mike kept his eyes focused on the table, specifically on the glass vase that held several stalks of white freesia. It reminded him that spring was here, that time was passing, and that Annie had been gone for nearly six weeks. Realizing this disquieted him, and he rose abruptly to leave.

On his way home, Mike stopped by the cemetery where Michele Rutledge was interred with their tiny child. He sat on a bench near their crypt for more than an hour without stirring, his heart and mind so full he felt unable to move. When he finally returned to his car, he walked like a man who'd suffered a beating. Before he started the engine, he searched his planner for a phone number. He left a message with Dr. Robert Weiss's service, asking him to return the call as soon as possible. Dr. Weiss was the psychiatrist Mike had seen in the months following Michele's murder.

Chapter 30

"Good morning, Lynch and Collings," a pleasant voice offered. "How may I help you?"

"Good morning. My name is Annie d'Inard. I understand someone there has been trying to get hold of me regarding work as a consultant."

"May I have a number where we can reach you, Miss d'Inard? I'll have one of our associates return your call."

"Yes, I'm in Scotland. The best time to reach me is the morning. I don't have an answering machine."

When she hung up, she didn't think anyone would call back.

* * *

Mike Rutledge sat uncomfortably in the same upholstered chair he'd sat in some fourteen years ago. It had been redone, some things in the office had been changed, and the psychiatrist in front of him had lost a considerable amount of hair. But as he sat collecting his thoughts, he realized, to his distress, that since he'd first come here, little had changed inside of him.

Dr. Weiss opened the conversation. "It's been a very long time, Mike. I was quite surprised to get your message."

"Yes," Mike answered, as his gaze fell to the floor. This was not going to be easy, he realized. It hadn't been before, and there was no reason for it to be now. But something had to be done. Another week of sleepless nights and he might start to go mad.

"Where would you like to begin?"

Though he'd already given it careful thought, he took several more moments to sort and organize what he would say. He began awkwardly. "I married again. I've been married now for almost ten years."

Dr. Weiss allowed himself that minimal smile so characteristic of those in his profession. "I remember reading about it in the paper, and I see you and your wife mentioned in the society column from time to time."

"We were happy," jumped out of him. "I loved her. We had a good life."

"You're using the past tense," he observed.

He crossed his legs, then uncrossed them, then folded his arms. "She's living in Scotland now. She's been there for more than a month."

"Why is that?"

He went through the same set of movements again, then ran a hand through his hair. "We decided to separate."

The therapist allowed a few seconds to pass. "What happened, Mike?"

He balled his fists, then rested them on the arms of the chair. "She'd been having an affair, and she had to tell me about it because—" he struggled with the disclosure of something he considered so private, "because she got a letter from the Red Cross. They were advising her that she could no longer be a blood donor and that she should see a doctor."

"Why?"

Saying it was like divulging a deep, dark secret, and the words stung as they were spoken. "Because she tested positive twice in a row in their HIV screening."

Sounding as though he'd just taken a sip of something overly hot, Dr. Weiss inhaled through pursed lips. "I see."

With that revelation behind him, the rest of it came with more ease. "My life, our life, it went from being relatively calm and peaceful to—it was suddenly like we were caught in the middle of a hurricane."

"Go on," he told him.

"I couldn't see how I could continue to live with her, so I said I would move out. She said that it was more appropriate for her to leave, because she was the one who'd ruined things. So I stayed at home with her son and she left. She couldn't think of anyplace else to go besides Scotland, so she went there."

"And I sense you're having difficulty with this," the therapist prodded.

"Yes," he admitted.

"Why is that?"

"It's so hard to say." He searched for less committed words but couldn't find them. "Because I love her. I've never stopped. I love her and I want her back, but I can't bring myself to tell her so."

"Why do you think that is?" he questioned, though he already knew the answer. It had been the stumbling block in Mike's therapy those many years ago, the reason he'd given up and walked away before there'd been any real breakthroughs.

The question was as expected as it was annoying. "I have trouble with that to begin with, and you know it. Even when things are going well, it's difficult for me. It was even difficult with Michele." He stopped speaking abruptly and looked as though something were stuck in his throat.

Dr. Weiss kept his eyes on his patient. "What is it you want to say?"

His head shook slightly. "I failed them."

"Whom did you fail?"

"I failed them both."

"Your wives?" he asked, emphasizing the plural.

"Yes, my wives," he admitted, angrily. "They both loved me and I failed them. I let them down." His voice cracked, and he struggled to keep some composure. "I've always held it together. It was hard after Michele's death, but I pulled it together. I did the right things and I kept going. And when I married Annie, I pulled her together, too. I stabilized her life and gave her and her son a wonderful home. I gave them everything they needed." He stopped abruptly as he recognized the fallacy in that.

"What made you stop what you were saying?" he wondered.

"That's not true."

"What's not true?"

"I didn't give them everything. Annie wanted another child, and I didn't give her that."

"Why not?"

"You know why not. I couldn't bring myself to." He raised his voice and let the anger come into his face. "When that bastard, that rotten filth of a human being shot my Michele . . ." he choked and had to force the words out, "he shot her in the abdomen. He blasted her uterus apart. He shattered my child and he left my wife bleeding to death on the pavement, all for a fucking car and $200." Tears that had been damned up for years washed his pain-stricken face. "I couldn't help them, Bob. They needed me and I was busy. I didn't even sense that something was wrong. I should have sensed something, shouldn't I have? What kind of a fucking man am I?" The emotions he was experiencing were so powerful, they seemed to be disconnecting him from his physical self; his limbs were tingling and he felt slightly dizzy.

Dr. Weiss saw his patient's tenuous control slipping, and he knew he needed to help. "You're a human being, Mike, a good human being. But humans aren't gods. We're fragile and vulnerable, and we're limited in what we can do."

"What good are you if you can't help the people you love when they need you?" he demanded. "I couldn't help Michele. I couldn't help our baby, I'm not helping Annie; she could be dying now and I can't even tell her how I feel about her. What the fuck good am I, then?"

There was so much to latch onto—too much for one session—so Dr. Weiss echoed, "You said she could be dying now," in an effort to ascertain all the facts.

Mike exuded frustration as he explained, "They haven't found the virus in any of her blood tests, but they did find antibodies. They think she could prove to be all right, but they caution us because that damned virus is so clever that no one completely understands how it works. That man, her *lover*," he spat the word, "he claims he's completely negative, but I don't know if he can be trusted. And her doctor is noncommittal. He wants to see six months of negative tests before he'll say with certainty that she doesn't have it." The thought rekindled his anger. "Half a goddamn year to worry about losing her."

"How does that make you feel?"

Mike deplored these rote inquiries. "How the hell do you think it makes me feel? Helpless, totally helpless, just as helpless as I felt over Michele, and—" he paused, then blurted out, "and I feel responsible."

That seemed an odd turn, and it made Bob Weiss wonder aloud, "How's that, Mike?"

"If I'd given her what she needed, if I'd been more open, Annie would never have turned to another man. I knew she needed more. I knew it and still I withheld. It's my own goddamn fault she went to him. If she dies, I'll be responsible, every bit as responsible as I was for Michele's death."

He expressed puzzlement, "I don't understand why you feel responsible for what happened to Michele."

Mike put one elbow on the chair's arm and rested his head in that hand. He rubbed at his forehead, breathing in and out loudly. "I could never bring myself to tell you this before. I've never told anyone." He grimaced suddenly as he experienced a sharp pain tearing through his head.

"Do you have a headache?" Dr. Weiss asked him.

"I always have a goddamned headache," he railed. "It's because I'm always so fucking busy, so damned preoccupied. Nothing's changed. When Michele and I were together, I never did anything but work. She took care of everything: the house, our meals, all the errands, her job, too, and she never complained. I never had to do anything, not even something as simple as getting cash when I needed it." The physical pain eased up and as it did, his eyes filled with tears. "I took money out of her wallet that morning, Bob. I took her cash like I always did because I was too busy to get some for myself. I left her a note. I told her I'd taken her last sixty dollars. I left her a note because I knew she'd want to know." The emotions had exhausted him and his voice was giving out now. "She was pregnant and she was always hungry—we joked about it. She'd wake up in the morning and immediately start thinking about what she would eat that day." He almost smiled with that memory, but the next one sent him crashing again. "I could have taken half of it, but I didn't. I took it all. I left her a note because she was in the shower and I was in too much of a hurry to wait. And when I came home two days later, when I came home from the hospital to shower and change my clothes, the note was still there, next to her teacup." His eyes closed as the anguish washed over him. "Her cup was half empty and her lipstick was on the rim. She probably didn't finish because she wanted to have enough time to stop at the ATM." His tears had dried up, but now his face was contorted with pain.

Bob Weiss sat in empathetic silence with his patient, watching his visage change again, its tormented appearance giving way to the kind of troubled, lost look that said he did not know where to go from here. He felt an overriding need to offer him something, some help or solace, so after a few moments he told him, "It's a profoundly human trait to hold oneself somehow responsible for meaningless, senseless acts like Michele's murder. It's a way of explaining the unexplainable and, sometimes, I think, of punishing oneself for being the survivor."

"I am responsible," he insisted.

The older man sighed as he contemplated the struggle his patient had before him. "You've been holding this in for a very long time Mike, and I expect that the guilt you now feel over your present wife's predicament is due partially to your unresolved feelings about Michele and your unborn child, and to an increasing awareness on your part of the difficulty you have with intimacy." He paused to let his words sink in, then he added, "We have a lot of work to do." He reached for his appointment book. "I think we should begin as soon as possible. When can you come again? How about next Tuesday?"

He furrowed his brow, then rubbed at it again. "I'm so goddamn busy, I don't know if I can come back."

Dr. Weiss responded sternly, "You're going to have to make a choice, Mike. You're going to have to decide which is more important to you: your career or your relationships, your work or your well-being."

* * *

St. Andrews, April 1994

There is neither evidence nor records, and no way to tell if memory deceives us. We ate, we drank, we moved about and touched things—we felt things—but there is no mark, no trace, no fossil left behind. Yet we believe and struggle against it all—against the lack of evidence, against the emptiness, trying to prove to ourselves that it really was.

I am alone now, and the time between us is as wide as the universe. I stand at the window finishing my tea, without a sound, without a word to speak, watching the rain wash everything away.

Annie was in the bath and the phone was ringing. She started to go after it and changed her mind, but it would not cease ringing. She stood dripping on the old carpet with only a towel against her chest as the caller identified himself. He was Jeremy Whitman, from Lynch and Collings.

"Ms. d'Inard? How happy I am to have finally reached you! It's been several weeks since we set out to locate you."

"So I understand," she answered, the water from her hair trickling onto the receiver. "I've been away, well here, actually."

"How extremely fortunate for us that you're in Britain!" he declared. "We were prepared to bring you over on the *Concorde,* if necessary."

"My, my. What could you possibly need me for that would justify going to that expense?" She was excited but skeptical.

"Our creative director is quite taken with your work," he told her. "He's inviting you to come and meet us to see if you'd like to work with our group on an important, upcoming project. Do you think you'd be interested?"

"As a matter of fact, I'm very interested," she allowed herself to say.

"That's super! He'll be so pleased. When can you come to Oxford?"

"Whenever you say."

"Is the day after tomorrow too soon?"

"No, that's fine."

"We'll handle your accommodations and travel. Would you like to fly or do you prefer a car? We could send a driver for you if you'd like."

"That won't be necessary, thank you. I've got a car here and I'll drive myself. You can book me a hotel, though, if you don't mind."

"It'll be our pleasure. I'll have the secretary ring you back with the particulars and of course, we'll take care of all your expenses."

"Thank you, I appreciate that." Jeremy was about to ring off when Annie abruptly asked, "Oh, by the way, who is your creative director?"

He took a second to clear something from his throat. "Why, Michael Collings, of course."

She racked her brain trying to recall if they'd ever met.

She left late the next day and stayed overnight at a small inn somewhere in South Yorkshire. In the morning she drove on again. She had followed this route before on Percy B., but she hardly remembered it. What she did remember was her shame; she remembered her shame, the sound of the gates, and her brief though unforgettable encounter with John Millar-Graham.

Oxford was more crowded and bustling than it had been on her first visit, and upon entering the city confines, she quickly regretted having chosen to drive. It was jammed with people—locals, students, and of course, hoards of tourists. But it was still wonderful, with its buildings that looked like something out of Dickens, and its artful and enticing shop windows. Her distress over the traffic and confusion was soon relieved by her almost royal greeting at the Old Parsonage Hotel. The staff went out of their way to see that she had everything she needed, and she was discreetly informed that there was to be no charge to her for anything she required, from manicures to apparel.

Her suite was charming, and she was in it an appropriate—not too long, not too soon—half hour, when the phone rang.

"Is everything to your liking?" It was polite, oh so English, Jeremy Whitman. "Is the room comfortable enough? If there is anything that displeases you, we can remedy it."

"It's lovely, Jeremy." She caught herself. "May I call you that?"

"Please do," he responded.

It was sinful pleasure to be immersed in such luxury after weeks of roughing it in her spartan cottage, and she was especially looking forward to a long and leisurely soak in the deep tub. "Everything seems perfect," she told him, "or as damn close to it as I'm likely to come."

He laughed, slightly and nervously. "Our creative director would be honored if you'd dine with him this evening. The hotel restaurant is excellent," he suggested.

"That's a good way for us to meet," she agreed. "What time?"

"What time would you be comfortable with?"

She smiled to herself, thinking that when it comes to good manners, no one can hold a candle to the English. "Eight, eight-thirty."

"He'll meet you in the main dining room at quarter past eight, then. Thank you, Ms. d'Inard."

Every seat in the small dining room appeared to be taken, and as she waited at the entrance, she marveled at how quiet so many people could be. The interior space was lit only with candles, making it difficult to see, but she stood under recessed lighting that made her feel as though she were onstage. A few diners turned their heads to look at her, tall and sleek in her green silk dress, and she began to feel self-conscious. But it was only a moment before the maître d' approached and addressed her by name.

"May I escort you to your table, Ms. d'Inard? Your host has already arrived."

When the man at the table stood to greet her, Annie experienced an odd, uncomfortable sensation.

"I'd have known you anywhere!" he said and kissed her hand. "Your hair is different, but you've hardly aged a day!"

Her heart pounded and she didn't know why. "Have we met before?"

"John," he said, "from Trinity College." He locked his eyes with hers, waiting for the recognition.

"Oh, my God!" Rather inelegantly, she plopped herself down in the seat. "John Millar-Graham from Oxford, from twenty-two years ago. My God, John, you were the one looking for me?"

"I hope you'll forgive the little ruse. I hadn't wanted to spoil the surprise."

Her eyes were wide and incredulous. "But why? After all this time, why?"

"I read the profile in *Ad Week*," he explained. "I thought it would be great fun working together."

She put her hand to her chest, unconsciously asking her heart to slow down. "This is such a surprise."

His smile turned warmer. "It's absolutely delightful seeing you again. It's hard to believe so much time has passed."

"You look well and prosperous," she commented, still gaping at him. He was dressed in an expensive, stylish suit; his hairstyle was current; and he had the confident air of success about him. She would never have known him, never have recognized him as the slightly Bohemian art student from Oxford with whom she'd shared the wildest sex in her life. Trying to stay focused, she asked him, "So you're with Lynch and Collings?"

With detectable pride and a lift of his brow, he answered, "I am."

Thankfully, her heart had regained its normal pace. "Is this really about business, or were you merely following a whim?"

"A little of both." He signaled to the waiter. "It was a good business move, and it was also somewhat personal—a way to pay back a debt."

"A debt?"

"Yes, a debt." The waiter was standing by. "May I order you a drink? We have all evening to discuss this."

"Newcastle Brown Ale," she grinned.

"You remember! Splendid! Do you remember it as well as I do, I wonder?" Although he'd been planning this for some time, he was finding it a little hard to believe that the woman he'd fantasized about for so many years was sitting across the table from him.

Dropping her smile now, she said, "Actually, I'd prefer Jack Daniels. Make it a double."

"Come now, it can't be as bad as that!" he protested. He marveled at how gracefully she wore her age, at how the years had deepened her character and made her more richly beautiful.

They sat quietly while they were served.

"I was just thinking about you, driving here," she said, as she lifted her glass.

"Oh? Why?" He kept his eyes on her while he drank.

She was recognizing him now, recognizing the mischief in his eyes. "You must know where I was when you found me—St. Andrews! How could I have not thought about you, driving down here from there. How could you have not been on my mind?"

He regarded her with a kind of sweetness, a nostalgic sweetness. "And how could I have not thought to get in touch with you after I read about you?"

"But that was well over a year ago," she reminded him.

"True, but I didn't have a reason to call you then. I do now, and I've always wanted to know what happened to you after you left here." He seemed as though he wanted to say something more, but he didn't.

"It's unbelievably ironic that you should have been look-ing for me now, at this time," she said. When I'm so preoc-cupied with the past—she told herself—when I've hardly been able to think of anything else. And of all people to meet again, why couldn't it have been Andrew?

"Why is that?" he wondered.

She was uncomfortable saying this, and it came out a tad awkwardly. "I'm here because I'm separated from my husband, and I'm at loose ends. I need something to do with myself."

"I'm sorry to hear about your marriage," he told her, sensing her discomfort. "Perhaps it'll work itself out, what-ever the problem is."

"Only time will tell that," she responded. "Are you married?"

"Yes, and actually, she's the same girl I was dating when you were here. Lena and I married in '74 and we have three children, two girls and a boy. My son's gone up to Cambridge, of all places." He grimaced with mock dis-taste. "Do you have children?"

"Only one, a boy. He's almost fourteen and from my first marriage." She wrinkled her brow to indicate her unwill-ingness to talk about herself. "How long have you been with Lynch and Collings?"

He pouted slightly, seemingly disappointed that she wanted to talk about him. "Let's see, about sixteen years. Lena's father brought me in because I wasn't making much of a living as an artist," he chuckled. "Her father's Michael Collings, you know, and seven years ago I bought his half of the business from old Marcus Lynch when he wanted out. My father-in-law helped engineer that, of course."

"So you're a partner. My, I am impressed. Now it makes more sense, how you could ask for me, I mean. You must know that your firm has the reputation of being the best in the U.K. It just wasn't logical that you should need someone like me. You already have the best ad talent in Britain."

"True, we do," he proudly agreed. "But you don't stay on top by maintaining the status quo. It's good to add some fresh blood to the mix, especially when you're striking out on something as important as this account."

"What's the account?"

Grinning again, he answered, "Nether Largie, Incorporated—among other things, the largest producer and exporter of Scotch whisky in the world. Their other interests include wool and Scottish products of all kinds, everything from shortbread to kilts. If it's a Scottish export, it's probably theirs."

"Who or what runs them?" she asked.

"An old, titled family who's been in control since they built their first distillery in the seventeenth century."

"Sounds stuffy," she commented.

Laughing, he answered, "They're not your typical polo-playing, fortune-squandering aristos, if that's what you're imagining. They're savvy businessmen who've made clever use of their money and built themselves a fortune instead of spending one. They've married strategically, planned and acquired, and kept it all under tight control for several hundred years. In fact, they've only recently gone public." He twirled his glass, then took a long drink before qualifying, "They went public with the big stuff, that is, the mass production distilleries and the Scottish specialty exports, but they've maintained private ownership of the small, exclusive distilleries—my pricey single malt here being from one of those."

"What are you going to do for them?" she asked. "It doesn't sound as though they need much help with anything."

He settled deeper into his chair and tilted his head slightly. "We're already handling the routine stuff, but this is a special project, that done well, could be a tremendous coup for the firm. A few years back, the CEO founded something called the Highland Land Trust." He reached now for his attaché and removed a folder, which he handed to her. "The details are in there. It's been funded with family money in an effort to preserve a way of life that's being threatened. As you're probably aware, the wool business has been in decline for years, and farm after farm has gone under because of it. The Highland Land Trust buys the land from a farmer on the brink, then leases it back to him so he can keep going. They've also convinced many of these farmers to switch all or part of their herds to milk-producing ewes and set up regional co-ops for making and distributing cheeses. In addition, they have contractual relationships with almost all the preexisting sheep dairies in Scotland and northern England through the Scottish Cheese Producer's Association." He paused long enough to take a sip of water and signal to the waiter for another drink. "The market for Scottish cheeses is virtually untapped. They're practically unheard of outside of the U.K., and the plan is to introduce them first to the continent, then to the U.S. and Canada. With the wool market in the doldrums, this could provide viable alternatives for struggling farmers. And the exciting thing is, we've been given carte blanche. We have no ridiculous budget restrictions for the campaign."

She raised her brow at that. "Have they done the necessary research?"

"Yes," he responded quickly. "There's tremendous potential there, and they're ready to move ahead. Are you interested?"

"What are we talking about, multiple-language TV spots for the E.U., print, radio—the whole nine yards?"

"Exactly. And don't forget America. He wants the Canadian and American markets, as well."

"Who's he?"

He looked at her first, waited a moment, and then, as though it would mean something to her, he answered, "The chairman and CEO, the twenty-fourth Earl of Kilmartin."

Grimacing at the idea of working for such a person, she questioned, "Is he the one we work with, or do we deal with an underling?"

He seemed somewhat disappointed at her lack of recognition. "We work with his lordship. He makes the decisions: He runs the show."

Her expression still slightly pained, she questioned, "Is that what we have to call him—his lordship? Is he reasonable, open-minded, and easy to deal with?" She knew it was an absurd question. Clients never were those things, and she imagined it far less likely that one addressed as "your lordship" would be so.

"At times," he answered, with a good-natured chuckle.

The prospect of doing something meaningful for a change, that would actually help people, was quite seductive. And the fact that it had to do with Scotland, a country she'd always loved and wanted to be a part of, made it irresistible. "OK," she told him, "I'm interested. How are we going to work this?"

"You name your price and I'll pass it along to Lord Kilmartin. I've already told him I'm trying to bring you onboard."

That surprised her, because it implied that she had something of a reputation here. "And strictly as a consultant, right? I don't want to run the thing. I don't want that much work. And I won't put in more than five days a week, OK?"

"Fine," he said, nodding. "Whatever you say. You call the shots."

She didn't want to be perceived as too demanding, so she added, "Not that I won't put forth my best effort, but I've been having some health problems, and I don't want to get overly tired just now."

He seemed genuinely concerned. "Nothing serious, I hope."

Trying to smile, she answered, "I'm handling it." Knowing that now was the time to address these matters, she continued, "And one other thing—I'm expecting my son to visit next month as soon as school lets out. I don't want to do much at all while he's here because I want to spend time with him, all right?"

"That's fine," he grinned. "Can you stay on for the rest of the week?"

"I don't see why not."

"I'll send a car 'round for you in the morning and we can go over the contract at my office. Will you be needing a solicitor to look at it for you?"

The question made her think of Mike, and it brought on deep pangs of sadness, realizing that with the signing of that contract, she'd be committing herself to an even longer separation. "My husband's a lawyer," she told John. "I can fax it to him if I have any questions." Better do that anyway, she thought, and keep Mike apprised.

"Right," he answered. "Jeremy Whitman can spend the next few days bringing you up to speed. Have you a laptop with you?"

She shook her head.

"I'll have him get you one, then, and a fax machine so you can work from St. Andrews." He seemed quite pleased. "Any questions?"

Furrowing her brow, she said, "It sounds like a great opportunity, John, but I have to ask you, are you really sure you want me? I walked out on my job at Haymaker's," she wanted him to know, "because I hated having to wade waist deep through bullshit every day. That attitude makes me a pain to work with. If you spoke with my former boss, I'm sure he'd warn you away from me." She stared him down for a moment and he looked right back at her without blinking.

"I have spoken with him," he informed her, "and I know all about how you left Haymaker's. I also made it my business to know your work, and I found that I like and respect it. This isn't going to be one of those horrid little campaigns you despise. I don't do those." While he said this, his eyes never left hers.

"OK," she answered, grinning slightly and offering her hand across the table. "As long as we can agree on the terms, you've got yourself a consultant."

"Excellent!" he beamed, squeezing her hand. "And when you're in Oxford, you can either stay at the hotel or with Lena and me. We have a little guest cottage, and I think you'd be very comfortable there. You'd have your privacy and I know it would please Lena. She's looking forward to meeting you."

She hadn't expected that. "Oh dear," was all she could think to say.

"Is there a problem?" he asked.

She frowned at him. "Let's not get carried away with this. Stay with you and Lena? Do you think that's wise?"

He scanned their immediate vicinity first, then in a lowered voice, said, "That day you left, you weren't gone twenty minutes when Lena walked into my flat. I thought it was you coming back for something you'd forgotten, and I called your name from the kitchen. Imagine my surprise when Lena came in and asked—Who's Annie?"

Annie shook her head despairingly, then finished off her drink.

"I felt so guilty I confessed the whole thing then and there," he whispered, "and it was a damned good thing, too, because when I finished, she calmly informed me that she already knew, that my good friend George had rung her at her parents' country house and told her." After all this time, it still pissed him off, and he looked away as he muttered, "Bloody, jealous bastard."

Great, she thought, look what I've gotten myself into. Maybe I should back out, here and now. "Listen John, on second thought, I don't think we should do this."

"Because of Lena? But I told you she's looking forward to meeting you."

"I've got enough problems," she interrupted, "and I certainly don't want to cause you any."

He chuckled first, then with a confident grin, told her, "Trust me, it won't cause problems. We've got a great marriage and a happy life, and the fact that you and I work together won't affect that."

She wasn't convinced. "But it'll be damned awkward, won't it?"

"Not for me," he said, "and I think I can speak for Lena and say she's fine with it, too."

She searched his face, which appeared sincere and relaxed, thinking how much she would like to have the work, the reason to get up in the morning. And, too, she could use the money, because if she was to maintain her independence, she was going to need it. So, against her better judgment, she decided to say, "OK. But if it doesn't work out for whatever reason, you have to release me from my contract. Will you agree to that?"

"Of course," he told her, signaling to the waiter again. "But it won't come to that. Let's have some bubbly, shall we, to celebrate. And let's order something wonderful. I'm ravenous."

With champagne flutes in hand, they toasted their collaboration, and when their appetizers were served, Annie thought to tell him something. "I still have the scarf, you know."

It took a moment, but then he remembered. "I wrapped it around your neck as I sent you off to the ferry at Southampton, didn't I?"

The recollection was bittersweet, and she sighed as she answered, "You did."

Observing her melancholy, he decided to ask, "Tell me, didn't you keep in touch with any of your friends from St. Andrews?"

She nodded. "I kept in touch with Melville Lumsdaine and Susannah Barclay. We wrote for years afterward. Mel's correspondence dropped off first, but Susannah and I kept it up for about fourteen years. The last I heard from her, she'd given birth to twins and they were both very ill. I kept writing to her but I never heard back. I think something terrible must have happened, because she was always very good about keeping up."

He looked thoughtful. "Have you tried to reach her since you've been here?"

"Yes, using the last address and phone number I had, but without luck."

"Perhaps I could help," he offered. "Would you like me to try to locate her?"

She smiled again. "I'd love it if I could see her. She was very, very dear to me."

"I'll see what I can do, then." He hesitated before asking, "Didn't you keep in touch with that Scottish chap? What was his name?"

"Andrew," she said softly, reverently. "I wrote, but he never answered my letters. Well, actually, I did get one letter from him, but that was all. We were supposed to meet in France, if you remember, but he never showed."

"Pity," he observed, "you two seemed very close. What happened, do you know?"

"We were more than close and I don't know what happened. I thought—well, never mind. It turned out to be a rather short story."

"Would you like to see him again, if you could?" he wondered.

She looked off into the distance, and when she spoke, her voice carried the undertones of regret. "I can answer that best by saying that in the past twenty-two years, there's hardly been a day gone by that I haven't thought of him."

The mischief was there again, this time in his smile, as John lifted his glass to hide behind it.

Chapter 31

When she was back in St. Andrews, Annie phoned her housekeeper.

"How are you, Lucy? How's everything?"

"Annie! Everything's fine. We're all fine, but we miss you. It's damned quiet around here. I miss the commotion you always cause. Are you coming home?" she asked. "Is that why you're calling?"

"I'm actually calling to ask you to send me more clothing," she told her, "because I'm going to be here a bit longer than I had planned. I've agreed to consult for an agency in England, and I need working clothes. Do you mind getting some things together and shipping them to me?"

Decidedly disappointed, she answered, "I'd rather you shipped yourself back here, but I'll send you what you want." She hesitated for a moment before asking, "Aren't you and Mike even trying? Have you thrown in the towel?"

She responded softly, "I haven't Lucy, but Mike's still too hurt. He needs more time to decide what he wants to do. And I'm not going to rush him. I'm going to give him all the time he needs."

"Let me ask you something," she blurted out. "Is it over? Is the other thing over?"

"It's over," she answered solemnly.

"Good. Then it's only a matter of time," she responded confidently. "You'll be back together before long."

Lucy's declaration roused Annie's curiosity, because the woman's intuition was so frequently on target. "Why do you say that?"

"Because I can see what's going on inside of him."

"What can you see?"

Her response was swift and certain. "I can see how much he loves you," she told her, "but I don't know if he's seen it yet."

"I wish I could believe that."

Grinning to herself, Lucy said, "Like you said, give it time. Now, what clothes do you want me to send you?"

As they were discussing Annie's wardrobe, Marc came in from school.

"Mom! I was going to call you. Did you get my letter?"

"Yes, how are you, sweetheart?"

"I'm fine, great really."

"That's nice, I'm happy to hear it." She was overcome suddenly by a powerful urge to hug him, to kiss his forehead and inhale the scent of his skin, her grown-up baby's skin. "I know Lucy has been taking good care of you," she said, more to console herself than anything. "Did Mike tell you that I got hired as a consultant here?"

"Yeah, he did. That's great. What do you think about Dad's idea for the summer?" Marc had already written to her of his father's plans.

"Is that what you want to do? Stay in Barcelona with his family?"

"Yeah, I think it'll be cool. I can get to know my cousins better and spend more time with Grandma and get really good at Spanish. It should be awesome."

She laughed slightly, pleased with his enthusiasm and happy that he sounded so well. "If that's what you want, then that's what I want. But will you come to Scotland first so we can spend time together?"

"Sure, but Dad says if I want to go to Spain I should only stay for ten days with you. He's going to meet me in Barcelona, and we're going to travel together for a while before he goes back to San Francisco. Is that OK?"

Her disappointment was clearly evident when she responded, "I was hoping to have more time than that, honey."

"Dad says we need to travel early in June or forget it," he explained. "It gets too hot after that."

It infuriated Annie that her ex-husband still carried on as though her wants and needs were irrelevant. She had to calm herself before she spoke again. "Perhaps your father will be good enough to allow me to visit you in Barcelona after he's gone." She heard the bitterness in her voice; so did her son, and she instantly regretted it. "Hey, wait a minute, I've got an idea. After your dad's gone back home, maybe you could take the train to Pau and meet me there. It's been a few years since we've seen my cousins, and I know they'd love a visit from us. What do you think about that?" She wouldn't fight about it. She couldn't, because since the divorce, Marc's summers had always belonged to Carlos.

"Sure, that sounds great! I could come for a week in July—maybe Bastille Day."

His reference to meeting her in France for Bastille Day turned something on, something buried, and her mind wandered back in time for a moment.

"Mom?"

"I'm here. I'll call them, then, and see if we can work it out." She paused again before asking, "How's Mike, honey? Does he seem all right?"

"He seems OK. I think he's kind of lonely, though. It's pretty quiet around here on the weekends 'cause I usually go to a friend's house or something. I think it's going to be tough on him this summer when both of us are gone."

Annie's voice grew huskier. "I'm trying to talk him into taking some time off and coming to Scotland. I thought we might go to the Highlands or the Isle of Skye or something. I think a break would be good for him, don't you?"

"I think he could use a vacation. All he ever seems to do anymore is work. "

"Mention that to him, will you?"

"Sure, Mom, I will. But I've gotta go. I've got spring soccer and I need to get something to eat first."

"OK, honey, but let me talk to Lucy again for a minute. I love you."

"Love you, too."

* * *

To celebrate her employment, Annie invited Tom Keegan out to dinner. When she arrived at the Russell, he was dressed in a suit and was waiting outside on the landing, looking very frail. Gordon, the hotel owner, was watching for her, and when he saw her car, he came out to help Tom down the steps.

Once he was buckled in, Tom told her, "This is a nice treat. I haven't been anywhere but the doctor's surgery in quite some time."

"I'm so glad you could join me. Are you sure you're up to this?" The way he looked worried her.

"We're just going from the car to the restaurant, right?"

"Right," she answered, as she headed the car down North Street toward the cathedral. "No walking or anything strenuous."

"What a marvelous bit of rubble this is," he commented, as they came upon it. "There's something rather mystical about it."

"There is, isn't there?" She pulled the car over so they could both have a good look.

They headed out of town on Grange Road, following it for about ten miles before turning onto a narrow road.

"How ever did you find this place, this inn we're headed for?"

"On one of my excursions. I went in for a drink, and some great aromas were coming from the kitchen."

They continued on for a few more miles before spotting the inn ahead of them. It sat at a "T" intersection, quite alone, with nothing but pasture to be seen in any direction.

Tom seemed pleased. "What a marvelous find."

Upon entering The Peat Inn, they were greeted by the proprietor. In his thick, Fife accent he welcomed the pair, then led them into the drawing room. It was a large, dark room with low ceilings and furnishings that bore the patina of age. A small fire burned in the corner fireplace—more for atmosphere than for warmth—and as Annie and Tom settled back into their seats, drinks in hand, they felt cozy and content.

"It's wonderful in here, isn't it?" Annie asked her companion.

"Yes, marvelous. There's something to be said for preserving the old. Do you think I might be preserved as well?" he laughed.

"How old are you, Tom?" She watched his hands tremble every time he lifted his drink.

"Sixty-two. I'll be sixty-three next month, if I make it that long."

She worried about that, too, and although she knew it was a delicate subject, seeing him tonight incited her to ask, "I was wondering if there might be something I could do to help you find your son?" Hiding behind her glass, she awaited his response.

He released a small sigh. "In the past, my pride would not have allowed me to even consider that. But as my health fails, that pride is stripped away, and I find myself wanting to say yes. Let me think about it, will you? And let's not speak of it again tonight. I'd rather hear about your position."

When they were seated in the dining room, Annie ordered champagne to accompany their soup course. The waiter served her *powsowdie,* a broth made from sheep's head, and Tom the traditional *cullen skink,* as they enjoyed the first icy glass of bubbly.

"Is that the smoked haddock soup?" she asked him.

"Yes, and quite delicious it is." He raised his glass. "I'd like to offer a toast to you and your new position. Best of luck with it!"

"Thank you!" she smiled. "You know, I didn't get to tell you, but it's the damnedest thing. The person who hired me, he's an old friend of mine, someone I met here when I was young."

He almost choked on his soup. "You're joking?"

"I wish I were," she answered, shaking her head.

"Which one, Melville?" He knew it couldn't be Andrew. She'd be jumping for joy if it were.

"No, John. The Oxford student that I left with."

"Well, I'll be. What a small world! Was it coincidence?" he asked.

"No. He read an article about me in a trade publication, so he knew I was in the business."

He was trying to read her face and was confused by her lack of excitement. "You don't seem happy about it."

"Actually, I'm not unhappy, it's just that, of all the people I'd like to see again, he was last on my list," she admitted.

"Oh? Why's that?" he wondered.

She looked off toward the hearth, then back to her companion. She thought about telling him the truth, saying that John was a bitter reminder of her pain and loss, and, most importantly, of her betrayal. But instead she explained, "Because he's connected with the least pleasant part of that experience—the leaving, the saying goodbye to Andrew." She hesitated briefly before adding, "And everything that happened after that."

Despite their frequent meals together, Tom had shared very little of a personal nature with Annie. Tonight, however, he was more open, perhaps because he'd been feeling so unwell in recent days. He laid aside his spoon and focused on her. "I get the sense that the past connected with this place, with St. Andrews, serves as some sort of departure point for you, that you feel as though your life took a wrong turn after you left."

He was so spot on target that it made her smile. "You know, Tom, you remind me of one of my most favorite people in the world—of Lucy, my housekeeper. She has an amazing ability to cut through the crap and get right to the heart of things."

"Before I came to St. Andrews," he told her, holding the stem of the champagne flute, "I spent several months in a hospital, a last resort cancer center. It was the most tragic of places, and it wasn't because of all the disease. The real tragedy was seeing so many people with so many regrets and no time left to undo them." He paused while their main course was served, and because the plates were too hot to approach, he polished off his champagne. "But it was also a free place," he continued, "and I mean free in the sense that when people are under the gun like that, there's nothing left to lose, so they're finally free to be themselves. They release themselves from the bullshit that you so often refer to. They tend to focus on the essentials."

With the threat of death hanging over her in recent weeks, Annie had been feeling that way herself. "What do you see as essential, Tom?"

He propped his elbows on the table edge, then clasped his hands together. "First and foremost, you must be true to yourself; you must be honest about who you are. And you must love yourself and let yourself be loved. It sounds simplistic, I know, but although they're fundamental matters, they're very difficult for most people. I think if you can manage these things, all the rest follows—the fulfilling relationships, the success, the peace of mind—it all follows." Casually, he lifted his cutlery to taste his salmon. "This is quite good, you know. How's your venison stew?"

"Delicious," she answered, smiling somewhat. The waiter brought the half bottle of Haut-Medoc that Annie had requested, and she paused to taste it. When he was gone again, she said to Tom, "You know, what you said doesn't sound simple at all, not at all." She looked away from him for a moment, then settled back into her chair, wine glass in hand, musing, "I think loving yourself must be the hardest part, don't you?"

"For some people," he agreed, "but it doesn't matter really. They're all connected; without one, the others will elude you. You can't love yourself if you aren't true to yourself, and you can't let others love you if you don't love yourself. If no one loves you, it's hard to accept yourself. It's all interconnected."

Annie shifted her gaze to the fire.

"Penny for your thoughts," Tom said after a few moments.

When she looked back at him, her eyes were misty. "You know I went to the Whaum."

"Yes, you told me."

"What I didn't mention was the weird experience I had there. I felt a presence, a very strong presence, like spirits." She hadn't told him this before, because she imagined he'd think her crazy.

"Whose spirits?"

She was emboldened by the fact that he wasn't laughing or giving her that look—the one that asked: Have you taken leave of your senses? So she answered forthrightly, "At first I thought it was just one, but then I realized there were two, and I think they were his and mine, Andrew's and mine. It was as though they'd been there all along. Mine was very clearly left behind, I already knew that. I realized it when I first arrived here. But I didn't know until I stepped into that house that he'd left his here, too."

"Really?" he asked, displaying neither judgment nor sarcasm.

With slightly widened eyes, she added, "And it wasn't just some passing whim. It was something I felt deeply, and I felt it again the other night when I stood outside the Whaum after leaving you. And that second time, I realized how far I've drifted from that part of myself, from my essence, if you will—my spirit."

They sat in quiet contemplation for more than a minute. "But it's coming back to you. I can see that, I can see the change in you," Tom said.

"Really? What do you see?"

"I see you more at ease with yourself, more at peace than when you first arrived."

That was true, and she grinned slightly as she recognized it. "And now I need to make peace with the people I love, the people I've hurt. If I can do that, it'll set me free," she said.

He had no trouble relating to that; after all, his fondest hope was to make peace with his son before he died. "I'd like to offer another glass," he said now. "Let's toast the freeing of the spirits!"

"Here, here," she agreed, then cautiously added, "but how about your own? Let me help you find your son," she implored. "Let's set your spirit free, too."

His smile was filled with warm gratitude. "Thank you, Annie," he said sincerely.

That heartened her, and as she lifted her drink to her lips, she offered up another private toast, though in truth it was more a wish than a toast. She made it first to Mike, with the fervent desire that he would someday be able to forgive her. Then she toasted Andrew, wherever he might be, in the hope that she would find him again, if only for a single meeting, so they might somehow reunite and rekindle their disavowed spirits.

When she returned to her little cottage on Anstruther Road, Annie changed her clothes, donning jeans, sneakers, and a warm sweater. Then she went out again and headed for the path that led from the cliff tops to the sea. The tide was out, and there was plenty of beach to meander along in the moonlight. She walked with a lightness of spirit, an openness of heart and receptiveness of mind, as she had not done in many long years. Her journey took her toward the bell towers, all the way to the East Sands and back. It was only to the crow of the farmer's rooster at the first streaks of dewy, pink light that she returned home again.

As she made her way along the last mile of beach, the dawn broke, and the exquisiteness of it brought her to tears. It made her recall the May morning that she had shared with Andrew when they'd sat all night on the sand, in one long, beautiful embrace, waiting for the sunrise. It reminded her, too, of that vastly different spring morning: the day she bid good-bye to St. Andrews, when she left on Percy B.—with John.

Pain always accompanied these recollections, and she hurried up the cliff side path and into her cottage in an effort to escape it. She changed into her nightgown and climbed into bed, hoping for a dreamless sleep. But in the empty silence of the house, her thoughts overflowed, and she had no recourse save to pull out her journal and explore them.

St. Andrews, April 1994
 There is absolution in the spring morning. There is compassion in the breeze, a kindness about its misty caress. It is all understanding and forgiveness.

Spring reprieves what has been condemned by winter; it exonerates autumn's wastefulness and pardons the sins of opulent summer, all in one magnificent gesture. It knows death and is not afraid to acknowledge it—seeing full well that its very existence depends upon death's thievery. It looks the thief square in the eyes and says, go ahead, do your worst. I will triumph again, no matter your ravages.

We are partners in that dance—we are part of nature.

Nature brought a storm that night, a fierce, howling storm the night we were last together. It washed away hope and beat back generous spring, leaving the streets scattered with her infant corpses. Disrespectfully, I drove over the bodies as I left. I added to the horror of the scene and wasted the quiet with my ugly roar. I imagined that spring wept at my harshness, at my irreconcilable choice, and I have always wondered what became of my poor abandoned roses.

Chapter 32

Her computer and fax machine arrived the day after she returned from Oxford, and Annie got to work immediately; it felt good to have purpose again. After three days in Oxford with Jeremy Whitman, she'd gone back to Scotland with a box full of sketchy proposals, and she dove into it. By the end of the week, she knew that the entire campaign Lynch and Collings had been planning needed to be scrapped.

The idea for the new campaign came to her while working in the garden. With her landlady's blessing, she had located it at the end of the lawn that spread behind the cottage to the cliff's edge, for it was this vista that she looked upon most frequently, whether indoors or out. She purchased a teak bench, the kind that would weather to a misty gray, and made it the focal point of her design, placing it at the easternmost point facing the sea, on a little outcropping of earth about thirty feet square. The fringe of that outcropping, the last yard's width of it, became the flower border and here she planted heather. She placed the more tender perennials in front of the border, facing the bench and lawn so that they might be offered some protection from the wind and salt spray.

Gardening time was good thinking time, an opportunity to let her thoughts wander undirected and easy. On one magnificent spring morning as she worked at her little project, she saw the image of what would become the nucleus of the new campaign. She put her gardening things away and got right to it. Forty-eight hours later, she was faxing her proposal to John Millar-Graham.

John wasted no time in getting back to her and barely said hello when he rang her up. "I've gone over everything with Jeremy and the others, and we want you to come down as soon as you can so we can get to work. Can you be here tomorrow?"

"If I can get a flight," she answered, then timidly asked, "Do you like it, John?"

"It's inspired, Annie, brilliant! It's just what's needed to grab the attention of our intended audience."

"Do you think his lordship will like it?" She laughed nervously, because it was an awkward thing for her to say.

"I'm going to see if he can meet with us by the end of next week. Do you think we can have a decent presentation together by then?"

That was almost funny. "With your staff? No problem."

"Super! I'll set things up. You staying with us this time? It's up to you but we'd love to have you."

She had been feeling increasingly lonely in recent weeks, and it led her to respond, "Thank you, I'd like that. Are you sure I won't be in the way?"

"Lena will love the company. She lives to entertain."

"Tell her I'm looking forward to it, then."

"I'll transfer you over to my secretary to make your travel arrangements, and I'll have my driver waiting for you at the airport. Cheerio!" His excitement made him sound young and full of life, like the John she knew long ago. For a moment, it made her feel that way, too.

* * *

Twice a week Mike Rutledge went to see Bob Weiss. He would sit quietly in the chair at the beginning of the hour, never sure what to say, waiting for something to happen inside of him—something that was always difficult and never seemed to get any easier.

"Why do I always struggle with this?" he asked at the beginning of this session.

"You're the only one who can answer that."

"I want it to be easier."

"That's good; that's positive, Mike. Is this the only time it's difficult," he questioned, "when you come here?"

"No," he admitted.

"Tell me about the other times."

"It's almost the same thing when I'm in bed with my wife," he said as he dropped his gaze to the carpet.

"Can you explain that a little better? I don't understand."

He wanted to be angry about the way Bob asked that, but he fought the desire. "I want it to be easier to be close. I want to be able to say things, to feel things, but it's so hard for me. There's always something in me that I can't reach through or tear down." His voice saddened as he went on. "I feel her reaching out to me and I shut down; I go away. I feel her needing me, wanting something from me, and it scares me."

"Why do you think that is, Mike?"

"I don't know."

"I think you do. You've said it to me before."

"I don't know what you're talking about," he said, while inside he fumed. Wasn't it enough that I admitted the things I did? What the hell does this man want from me?

"Do you feel completely adequate as a man, Mike?"

He was teetering on the edge of anger, and that question pushed him over. "What the fuck kind of question is that? Christ, I don't know why I waste my time coming here! Yes, I'm adequate. I'm more than adequate. Over the years we'd have sex several times a week, and I was almost always able to bring her to climax."

"You said 'have sex with,'" he observed, "not 'make love with.'"

"That's what I meant," he seethed.

He blinked slowly. "I think you said exactly what you meant."

He'd had enough, and he stood abruptly. "You know, this psycho horseshit is too much. They say lawyers are the masters of double-talk, but you guys make us look like amateurs."

"You're right," Bob conceded, "so I'm going to cut the crap and be straight with you, because I think it's time for that." He gestured with his hand for Mike to sit again and waited while he settled in. "You told me in our first session that you felt you'd failed Michele and your child, that you'd failed in your manly duty to protect them. Their loss damaged you in a way from which you've been unable to recover. In your fear of being hurt again, you've constructed a wall around your emotions that's become impossible to let down. Even when you want to, you can't."

Mike disagreed. "I'm not afraid. I'm not afraid of anything."

"Yes, you are," he countered. "You just said it a few moments ago. You said you're afraid of your wife wanting you, needing you."

"That's not the same thing."

"It's not? How isn't it?"

"Because that's not real fear," he protested. "Real fear is being afraid of the world—of things in the world. I'm not afraid of an opponent or a challenge or even a murderous creep I might run into on the street."

"But you're afraid of being loved," he interjected.

"That's not the same thing, not the same at all."

"I think you're right about that." Dr. Weiss paused and softened his tone. "I think it's much worse."

"Well, at last! At last an honest opinion and a straight answer. Is that permitted?" he sneered.

"Occasionally," the psychiatrist smiled.

"Well, don't worry, I won't tell anyone."

In an effort to regain control, Dr. Weiss said, "Let's talk more about your feelings for Annie, and let's continue to be very straight with one another, all right?"

"All right." Mike wasn't certain he wanted this, but he was getting tired of dancing around the thing.

"When you first came to see me, you said you still love her. Today you've said that you're afraid of her wanting and needing you, but I get a strong feeling that there's more to your feelings than that. I sense a lot of anger when we talk, but you never express it. Aren't you angry with her, Mike?"

"Of course I'm angry! Who wouldn't be? She betrayed me. She slept with another man and put us both at risk, and she lied to me. She humiliated and deceived me, all the while saying she loved me. Who wouldn't be angry with a wife like that?" Mike grasped the arms of his chair when he added, "There've been times when I felt as though I could choke the life out of her!"

"But that's not all you feel."

"No, of course not." He relaxed his grip on the chair. "It never lasts, that feeling, that anger—it's fleeting."

"What happens to make it go away?"

He had to consider this, reach deep for this. "I think about her. I remember who she is and what she's been through, and I can't be angry anymore. And I think about myself."

"What about yourself?"

He wasn't going to say it; he didn't want to admit this to him, to anyone, but it came out of his mouth anyway. "About the fact that I'm not enough for her."

"How's that?"

He'd done it. He'd made the admission Weiss was after and the world hadn't ended, so he might as well say the rest. "She needs so much, so much love. I feel sometimes like there's this enormous void, this emptiness in her that's impossible to fill. I try, but it seems impossible. It saddens me, because I wish I could, but I just can't."

Dr. Weiss questioned softly, "And does it leave you feeling inadequate?"

Mike clicked his tongue and exhaled loudly. "All right. Yeah, if that makes you feel better."

After a few moments of silence, the therapist asked, "When was the last time you spoke with her?"

"About a week ago. We spoke about a week ago."

"How was that?"

"The same—the same as it's been. She wanted to talk about us, but I wouldn't let her. I cut her off."

He had to give some thought to this. "I'd like you to play a little game with me, Mike. Imagine you were able to be with her and give her everything she needs, that you were able to fill the void and love her completely. How do you imagine that would feel?"

Mike looked away before answering. "I know I should say good—great, but if I'm to be honest, I'd have to say frightening."

Bob was pleasantly surprised to find him so forthcoming. "Why frightening?"

"Because it would be like going into unknown territory. I wouldn't know what to expect next, what to do next, where we would go from there."

Wow, Bob thought to himself, that's quite an insight. Since that had worked, he decided to go a little further. "Let's talk about your needs instead of hers. What would it feel like if she were able to give you what you need, to fill the void inside of you?"

Mike spoke softly when he answered. "I don't know."

"Why is that?"

He looked at the floor as he responded. "Because I don't know what it is I need."

Mike's response was less than he'd hoped for; still, it was better recognized than not. "And I think that's something we need to explore," Bob said. "I think we need to find that out, don't you?"

"I suppose," he mumbled, then fell silent.

Bob Weiss waited several long moments before offering, "One of the most common causes of marital breakdowns is the lack of awareness of emotional needs, and I don't refer only to being aware of the other's needs, but also to an awareness of one's own."

Mike looked out the window and sighed deeply. "There were times," he said, then halted.

"Go on."

He sighed again, then looked at the doctor. "There were times when we were together that I'd want to let it all out, to show her what's going on inside of me, so she'd understand."

"And what would happen on those occasions?"

"I'd get scared. I'd shut down and go away. And then I'd feel the void, the emptiness that left in her."

Bob Weiss knew that what he was about to say, he should probably let Mike discover for himself. But often with patients like him it took too long, or it never happened at all, so he decided to run the risk. "Mike, has it ever occurred to you that every time that happens, that void gets bigger, that emptiness grows? And not just in her, but in yourself—until all there is between you is the emptiness?"

An unnatural stillness filled the room before he answered, "Yes, it has."

Dr. Weiss folded his hands and sat back in his seat, waiting an appropriate minute or two before saying, "I think that's enough for today. See you Thursday?"

Mike remained seated for another minute, saying nothing, then rose slowly and left the office.

* * *

Thankfully, the clothes Annie had asked Lucy to send arrived in time for her return to Oxford. She packed enough for a week and then, at the last moment, decided to bring a cocktail dress. As she carefully folded and laid it in the suitcase, she was reminded of the blue gown she'd worn to the ball with Andrew—of the day she'd folded it up and sent it home to the States. For many years, it had remained in her attic, untouched and unseen, tucked away with the other relics from that time and the only letter she'd ever received from him.

John's driver took her directly to the Millar-Graham house, and she was more than a little impressed when they turned into the long drive. The structure was a magnificent old Georgian manor, fashioned of gray stone, the kind the BBC was fond of using in its dramatic presentations. Although it was not one of those enormous places that belonged to the extremely wealthy, it must have held at least twenty rooms, making it considerably larger than her own. The elegance of the gardens and rolling green lawns, the ivy-covered walls and the graceful old trees, all made for nothing less than utter charm. As they pulled up before the house, she saw

Lena cutting flowers in a garden just off a terrace. Annie marveled at her appearance, which reminded her of a portrait—one that would have been done at the time her house was built, with her blond, curly hair and flowing skirt, standing amid the perennials.

She put aside her cutting basket and descended the steps to meet the car. "Welcome to Fargate!" she offered, as Annie emerged from the vehicle.

Lena possessed the impeccable speech and perfect manners that mark certain well-bred English women, and Annie was instantly reminded of Susannah Barclay. Her apprehension about meeting John's wife fled with that association, but she blushed as she answered, "Thank you so much for inviting me. I hope I won't be in the way."

"Nonsense! We're thrilled to be able to spend the time with you. I never dreamed I'd meet you, but I'd hoped." She wanted to get this out of the way, and she took a breath as she explained, "When John told me about your adventure on your motorbike, I fancied you a sort of folk heroine, and I wished then that we could have met."

Now Annie's cheeks flushed with heat. "A heroine? Oh God, hardly!"

Lena reproached herself for broaching the subject so rapidly and offhandedly, but knew that anxiety had driven her to it. "I didn't mean to embarrass you," she apologized. "Do forgive me. Ronald?" she called to the driver, "Will you take Ms. d'Inard's things to the guest cottage, please?"

When they entered the house, Annie had to sigh. It was every bit as lovely inside as it was outside, and the antiques she saw everywhere made her a little envious.

"This is a perfectly beautiful place, Lena, perfectly beautiful."

"You're very kind to say. John and I feel most fortunate to live here, we do so love it."

"It's easy to see why."

Lena led her to a sunny sitting room, decorated with rose chintz and filled with family photographs, that Annie correctly guessed to be her special place of retreat. "Would you care for some tea?" Lena asked her.

"That would be nice," Annie answered, as she settled into a chair.

When they finished their tea, Annie asked if she might have a tour of the house. They quietly made their way from room to room on the ground floor, and she fussed over a couple of pieces of furniture that she recognized as sixteenth century.

"You have a very good eye," Lena complimented her.

"My husband and I collect," she explained. "Our little farmhouse is filled with lovely old things, but none nearly as old or wonderful as these." She flashed back to the many times she and Mike had gone off on summer weekends, wandering the countryside in search of that special piece.

As they ventured onto the south terrace and through the garden, Lena linked their arms. Just ahead of her, tucked into the woods, Annie spied the guest cottage.

"We both thought you'd prefer the privacy you'll have out here, but if you find you'd rather be in the main house, you may have your pick of the guest rooms."

The cottage appeared larger than the one she rented in St. Andrews, though it was actually about the same size. It was roomier, though, because the interior had been opened up; the walls that had once divided it into several small rooms were removed, and the ceiling lifted to the rafters. The fireplace was much larger than the one at her cottage, made of old, pointed stone, and the kitchen was modern with a well-stocked bar. A stereo system complete with a collection of record albums and CDs was tucked into shelving that covered an entire wall, and the remainder of the shelves were packed with books.

Annie was instantly glad of her decision. "I'm going to be very comfortable here, Lena. Thank you so much for inviting me."

"The bed and bath are just here," Lena said, as she opened the one closed door and led her through it. The room was tastefully decorated, with a large bed that faced the windows for a view of the woods. The bath was pristine and well-appointed, and it smelled of sandalwood soap.

"I've rented a place in St. Andrews, you know," she told her hostess. "It has a great location right on the sea, but the interior leaves a lot to be desired. Staying here will be such a nice treat."

"Yes," she answered, "John mentioned you were living there. Well you know, as long as you're working with him, you should feel free to make this place your own. You can leave your things here and come and go as you like. If we have other guests, they can always stay at the house. We have plenty of room."

She was astounded by her generosity. "You're too kind, really."

"Nonsense," she smiled. "By the way, I'm giving a dinner party next week. John said the earl will be coming to hear your presentation, and I've invited him to stay at the house. Dinner's to be just us and the top few at the firm. He hasn't accepted yet. I hope he's not put off. I'm certain my little Fargate is considerably different than what he's used to. I'm sure it's nothing compared to the grandeur of Crinan Castle."

"He lives in a castle?" Annie asked. Oh God, she thought, he's going to be impossible—insufferably pompous. "Have you been there?"

"No, but I've seen it on the television," Lena informed her. "The BBC ran a documentary on the family, and the countess took the cameras on a tour of the castle. It's perfectly magnificent," she sighed, "with a breathtaking setting in the West Highlands, right on the coast. And that's just their seat. They have three other estates, located in some of the most wonderful, romantic places in Scotland."

Admittedly, her focus had been on the business at hand, not on the man who ran it. But Lena's remarks now sparked an interest. "John says they're an old family."

"The oldest and most important in Scotland," Lena assured her. "He's a direct descendant of the Celtic kings."

Insufferably pompous, she thought again, the kind who look down their noses at everyone, especially Americans. "Well, I've never met him, of course, but how could he not be charmed by this place? It's so very lovely."

Lena appreciated the compliment and responded with a warm smile.

John wasted no time in getting everyone to work. They put in long, hard hours, and by the end of the following week, poor Jeremy was as jittery as one who expected the arrival of the queen. Everyone was keenly aware of the importance this account held for the firm, and they all felt the anxiety that comes of trying to achieve perfection. Everyone that is, but Annie, who seemed to be thriving in the stressful environment.

The earl was coming the next evening and the pressure was on. As John drove Annie home that night, she found him unusually talkative.

"Are you satisfied with things?" he asked nervously.

"You know I am. Relax, John, everything's going to be fine."

"You know, whatever happens, I'm hoping you'll stay on with me," he told her.

Something was amiss about that statement. "You say that as though you expect him to hate the idea."

"He's an aristocrat," he responded, "and they tend to be temperamental and unpredictable, don't they? Who knows how he'll react?"

"So?" she shrugged. "If he doesn't like it I'll change it, I'm not going to force it down his throat. He's the boss, after all."

Still anxious, he answered with a short, "Right. We're dressing up tomorrow night. Did Lena tell you?"

"She did. I've got something to wear."

Glancing sideways at her, he asked, "Is it sexy?"

She frowned at him. "You know, if we were in the States, I could sue you for asking me that question."

They both laughed, though John more than Annie.

"What's he like, John?" she wondered. "You've never really said anything about him." Since her conversation with Lena, she'd been imagining all sorts of things, none of them pleasant, and she thought she should be prepared.

He cast another sideways glance at her, grinned oddly, then said, "He's intense and intelligent, though approachable for the most part. But for all his importance and money, I'd say he's rather brooding. Lena's never met him, but she can't stop going on about him. He suffered some disfigurement from an accident years ago, but listening to her," he shook his head, "you'd think he was Adonis."

"What kind of disfigurement?" she wondered.

"Some facial scars," he answered.

That sparked her memory, and in the next instant she recalled the gentleman she'd encountered on the flight to London—the one with the scars on his face that the flight attendants were making such a fuss about. She wondered whether he could possibly be the client. "Lena said he's married," she commented.

He looked at her again. "Yes, he is," he answered, as though that would somehow affect her.

Sighing, she teased, "Too bad. Is his wife coming with him?"

"I'm not certain," he answered, rather too seriously. "Lena did invite her, of course."

She'd been wanting to bring this up before, but there hadn't been a good time. "Speaking of Lena, she's been wonderful to me, absolutely wonderful. She's the most generous person."

"And why wouldn't she be?"

Annie might have been sarcastic in her response to that, but instead she asked, "You said you told her everything about our relationship. Did you really do that?"

Nodding, he answered. "From how much you loved Andrew and how distraught you were over leaving him, to the fact that I didn't tell you about my relationship with her until we were in Oxford."

"And everything in between?"

He answered carefully. "She knows we slept together. Of course I told her that, but I didn't give her details," he admitted. "She didn't ask and what would have been the point, anyway?" He changed the subject abruptly. "Oh, by the way, we've been so busy I keep forgetting to mention this. My secretary's trying but as yet hasn't located Susannah Barclay."

"I appreciate the effort, John," she said sincerely. "Might I ask another favor?"

He thought he knew what was coming, and he grinned. "You want me to find Andrew."

She had contemplated that very thing, asking for his help, but she quickly dismissed the idea, knowing it wouldn't do to have John connected with Andrew in any way. "No, I need to do that on my own," she answered. She turned her head to gaze out the window. I've got to make that trip to Cairncurran, she reminded herself. I've got to set aside time to do that, to see if I can locate Crofthill and find out what became of him.

They were almost to the house, and as they made the turn onto the drive, she regained her focus. "What I was going to ask is this. I met a gentleman in St. Andrews who's been estranged from his son for quite some time. Tom Keegan is his name." Recalling how ill he'd looked at their last meeting saddened her. "He's dying, John, and I don't believe the son knows it. I'd like to help if I can. I'd like to find the son and let him know about his father. It's a tragic situation. Tom has no one in the world but him."

He could see how concerned she was about this man, and it led him to pat her hand tenderly. "When everything settles down, after the presentation," he told her, "give me the information and I'll see what I can do."

"Thanks, John," she answered, just as they were drawing to a stop.

As tired as she was, Annie had a hard time getting to sleep that night. She went to bed but was up again, pouring herself a glass of wine before nestling on one of the couches. The quiet got to her before long, so she decided to listen to some music. As she fingered through the assortment of music, she came to the conclusion that John kept his collection out here deliberately so he could crank up the volume when he listened.

The selection was much the same as she had at home—some classical, some jazz, many groups from the sixties and seventies. She was delighted to find plenty of Rolling Stones, but she chose a Van Morrison CD to listen to. Sitting back in a chair, her wine in hand, she closed her eyes as the music began. She had cued it directly to the "Into the Mystic" cut, and as the first strains of it reached her ears, she was carried back in time.

It returned her to that spring afternoon when she and Andrew had packed a picnic and driven Percy into the country. Lying in a field of blowing grass and wildflowers, they had very nearly made love. It was the closest they were ever to be physically. She remembered how he had sucked at her nipples as though he was dying of thirst, how healing his fingers inside of her had felt, his touch more gentle than any she had known.

She would never forget the joy of lying with him, their bodies intertwined and aching for connection, and it would color and influence all her sexual encounters to come. Afterward, they had danced in that smoky little pub in Crail to the tinny sounds of a radio behind the bar. Holding her as though he would never let her go, he breathed in the scent of her hair, singing into her ear, "I want to rock your gypsy soul." "Let your soul and spirit fly"—were lyrics her heart would have written.

When the song ended, she cued it up again. This time, she let the tears flow with it. Our souls, our spirits, she asked herself, where ever did they fly to? Thinking of the Whaum and the strange experience she had had there, she wondered if she now knew the answer.

Oxford, April 1994
I thought I caught a glimpse of it once. It was cleansing and pure, like I'd always heard, and it lifted the spirit to godly heights, to breathe the finer air. I found it altogether

too ephemeral, though, more fragile than a finch's egg, and not at all the sort of thing that one could manage over time. We all say we seek it, that we'd treasure it, give our lives for it if need be—and certainly, some do. But I think there is about it a deeper, shameful truth that few are willing to admit.

I believe in truth we run from it, gorging ourselves on the other so that we won't feel the hunger, spending our days in hiding, living out our lives in mortal fear of its touch.

Chapter 33

The private jet belonging to the twenty-fourth Earl of Kilmartin raced across the channel from Brussels and landed precisely on time. At the landing field, the earl was whisked away in a silver Rolls Royce and driven directly to Fargate in the Blenheim Woods section of Oxford.

Lena could hardly contain her excitement when his car pulled up to her house, but she managed to rein it in as she greeted him and apologized for her husband's absence. She'd seen photos of him before, of course, but she was taken aback by how strikingly attractive he was in person.

Blushing like a schoolgirl, she explained, "John is still at the office, your lordship, though I expect him home within the hour." Encountering him face to face like this, in all his regal posture and bearing, she felt a little intimidated. But when he spoke, his warmth and gentle manners entranced her.

"It's quite all right, Mrs. Millar-Graham, and just as well. I confess to some fatigue," he told her, "We've been involved in difficult negotiations this past week and I've gotten little sleep out of it. I'd appreciate a rest before this evening, if you don't mind."

"Oh, of course," she answered softly, "and please call me Lena." She had meant to welcome him with tea in the drawing room, but in light of what he just told her, she made the strategic decision to send it to his room. "I'll just show you to your rooms, then." She looked past him to the Rolls, expecting to see his valet arise from it. When she realized he had no one with him, she felt a moment's panic.

Men like him, she assumed, couldn't possibly know how to care for themselves. "I've no butler," she thought it best to advise him, "only my daily help. Will you be needing someone to lay out your things for you?"

He observed her distress and understood its origins. "I can manage on my own, thank you, though my wife might dispute that. As a matter of fact, I'm looking forward to the solitude. We've been on the road for more than a month without a break, you see, and too much together. That's why I've sent everyone home from Brussels." He punctuated that with a look of relief.

She appreciated his effort to put her at ease and was astonished by the gesture. "John and I are very honored that you consented to stay with us tonight," she told him as they ascended the stairs. "Your long absences must be very difficult for Lady Kilmartin. She and the children must miss you terribly."

"They're all quite busy, I'm afraid, and hardly know I'm gone," he answered. "Janet especially, with her horses and various committees. I may need to schedule an appointment to be certain to see her when I'm at home."

He smiled congenially, and Lena felt the warmth of it.

"I'm sorry she wasn't able to join us," she said. She had not expected someone of his stature to be so open and natural with her, and she was growing more impressed with him by the minute. "Will you be going directly home from here?" she asked.

"Yes, and I'm looking forward to it. I intend to put my feet up and do nothing," he told her, then qualified, "at least for a day."

They laughed together.

"Dinner is at eight and we're dressing. Shall I have some tea sent up in the meantime?" she asked him.

"That would be lovely."

When he smiled again, Lena responded with a blatant blush.

His room housed a large window seat with a view of the rear lawn and garden, and it was there that Mrs. Edgar,

Lena's daily housekeeper, placed his tea tray. The warmth and fragrance of the tea relaxed him. As it did, his thoughts began to drift, carrying him to another place and time. His face took on a dreamy quality, and the hint of a smile surfaced on his lips as he recalled something especially sweet. It was in this state of mind that he saw Annie just returning from the office. She was wearing a black suit with a tight skirt and high heels, and she was walking through the garden and across the lawn to the cottage.

Annie took her time getting ready and didn't walk to the house until quarter past eight. She went in through the kitchen and found Lena flitting about in an elegant long, blue gown, fussing over the hors d'oeuvres that were about to be brought in to her guests.

"You look absolutely gorgeous!" Annie told her, as she kissed Lena's cheeks.

"Thank you, but you're the smart looking one! You have the most beautiful clothes, Annie, and you wear them so very well."

She was wearing a dress that she had purchased with Mike on one of their weekend jaunts to New York. Its silk taffeta fell off her shoulders and graced her cleavage before pulling in at the waist, the soft pink color providing dramatic contrast to the darkness of her hair, which she wore up tonight, but for small wisps that fell defiantly down her neck. She was so strikingly pretty that even the sophisticated caterers turned to admire her.

"Have a glass," Lena told her, as she handed Annie a champagne flute.

"Is everyone here?" Annie wondered.

Lena was decidedly excited, perhaps even a little breathless as she answered, "Yes, they're all in the drawing room hovering around the earl."

"Did he bring the countess, that's what she is, right? I'm not quite clear on these titles."

"No, he came quite alone. No wife, no manservant, quite alone. And yes, she is a countess. An earl is the British equivalent of a European count, so his wife is a countess."

Before she embarrassed herself in front of him, she thought she'd better make certain she understood. "And what's a viscount?"

"The male heir to the earldom, but it can also be a title in its own right. The earl was a viscount while his father was earl, as his eldest son is now. It's somewhat complicated with these inherited titles. It's simpler with the bestowed knighthoods; they're not passed on."

"Why do you call him a lord, then?"

"Marquesses, earls, viscounts, and barons are all addressed that way. Only a duke is referred to as 'your grace' and a knight as 'sir,' but the rest are lords."

"It's all very confusing to me," she admitted.

"You needn't worry about it. People don't expect Americans to know these things." She adjusted the decorative elements of a tray that was just about to leave the kitchen, and the server scowled at her. "And I doubt he'll mind, should you slip up," she added, ignoring the rebuke. "He's remarkably pleasant and down to earth. Wait until you meet him." Lena leaned close so the others in the kitchen wouldn't hear. "He has such presence. I very nearly swooned when we met."

Annie laughed at her. "Have another champagne, Lena."

"Come along, I'm going to introduce you."

When Lena led Annie into the elegant room, she saw a circle of people at its center: Lena's parents the Collings's, John, Jeremy Whitman and his wife, and the other top executives from the agency. Annie couldn't see the guest of honor at first. Lena had to break into the circle, and when she did, the man's back was to them. In spite of herself, Annie's heart took a little leap when she saw that he wore his dress kilt, for it evoked precious memories.

John was talking to the earl when he spotted his wife and Annie coming toward them. "Excuse me, your lordship, Annie's just arrived," he said, nodding his head in a gesture meant to turn the earl toward her.

Annie already had her hand out and was saying "How do you do?" when she saw the scars and recognized him. "You're the gentleman I bumped into on the plane! What a small world!"

He looked back at her and said nothing. He did not offer his hand. A moment of uncomfortable silence followed as everyone around them remained still. When he spoke, his voice was stern and commanding, almost scolding. "Yes," he said, "but we've met before that, Annie."

The way he said her name was strange; it was eerie and familiar. Chills began to form in her spine and run through her limbs. He continued to look hard at her, and she looked past the scars for the first time, into the blue eyes that seemed to know her so well.

The recognition took place inside of her on several levels at once, and she gasped and put her hand to her heart. "Andrew—my God, Andrew—it's you!" Her mind was suddenly devoid of thought, and she was left with little awareness of what was happening around her. What remained was pure emotion. Instinctively, her hand moved to his cheek to touch the deepest scar. "Andrew," she sighed.

His eyes pierced hers, and he jerked his face sharply away from the hand that meant to caress it. He turned his back on her and walked toward a nearby server, who was holding a tray of champagne. John spoke up and said something Annie couldn't make out, but she was aware that the crowd around them was moving away, too. Her hand smarted as though it had been injured, and she let it fall by her side. Something happened to her breathing, and she found herself having to take conscious control of it.

Between breaths, she managed a thought and got some words out, "But you're not the earl. I don't understand. You're Andrew. I don't understand." He'd already walked away, though. In the next instant, she realized that she wasn't getting enough oxygen. She needed a chair; she looked to her right, then to her left, and spied one not too distant. She moved toward it, not knowing if she'd make it. Her legs refused to comply, and she was about to go down when she felt arms around her waist.

John's voice was eerily familiar, too. "It's all right," he told her. "Lena's bringing you something." He helped her into the chair, and she put her head between her knees.

"Here, darling." Lena handed her a glass of water. After a moment, she took it. As she sipped, she heard Lena whisper harshly to her husband, "What the bloody hell is going on here? Would someone like to tell me?"

Lena's father, Michael Collings, tactfully reengaged the earl in conversation, and the protective circle formed around him again. Their voices sounded muffled and distant to Annie. All she could make out was the ring of Andrew's laughter.

"Do you think you can make it to the library?" John asked her.

She stood carefully, and Lena took the glass from her hand. The three left the drawing room as the Millar-Graham's guests cast furtive glances in their direction.

As she closed the door behind them, Lena demanded of her husband, "John, I repeat, what the bloody hell?"

John encouraged Annie to lie back on the couch, telling her, "I'm so sorry. He didn't want me to say. He wanted to surprise you. I had no idea it would be like this."

"But he was bloody rude!" Lena screeched. "He knew her before? You know him, Annie?" She didn't know from whom she should get the story first.

"Yeah," was all Annie could get out. The scars on his face burned in her mind's eye, lingering like the after-effects of a camera flash.

John struggled to explain. "They were friends at St. Andrews, Lena, very close friends."

Lena suddenly understood, for she and John had only recently revisited this topic. "You don't mean to tell me—he's not the one she was so upset about leaving? No, it can't be! He's the blasted Earl of Kilmartin, for Christ's sake!"

John's voice was heavy and sad. "He's the one."

Annie was listening, hearing them talk about her and Andrew, but it was as though she didn't know the people in question. She was trying to get her mind around the idea that she had bumped into him on the plane and didn't even know him. Had he known it was she? And Andrew wasn't an earl—not her Andrew!

Lena's voice grew more tense and shrill. "I don't believe this! And you didn't say a bloody thing to me about it? You let this happen here, tonight, in front of everyone, while he's a guest in my home? I can't believe any of this! Tell me this isn't happening!"

John seemed truly bewildered. "I don't know why he's behaving like this. I engineered this because it was what he wanted. He asked me to do this for him and I did. He didn't want me to talk to anyone about it, Lena. That's why I didn't tell you. He said he wanted to surprise her. I had no idea he'd carry on like this."

"You keep saying that! What did he plan to do, humiliate her in front of everyone? Because that's what he's done, you know! And she's got the bloody presentation tomorrow. What about that? This is the agency's most important account, John!"

His mood shifted into anger as he responded, "Dammit, Lena! Don't you think I know that?"

"I think I should go back to the cottage," Annie told them.

"I think that's wise," John agreed, and he went to the library bar to pour himself a whisky.

Lena grabbed her husband's glass and drank from it. "Why?" she asked. "The damage is done, isn't it?"

"Maybe not," John answered softly.

Lena hadn't quite heard him. "What?"

Though she comprehended little else, Annie understood what John was getting at. "He knows, Lena," she said, though barely audibly. "I saw it in his eyes." Straightening from her semi-reclined position, she looked at him to ask, "He knows, doesn't he, John?"

"Knows what?" Lena demanded, her heart beginning to race.

"Yes, he does," John answered, before looking at Lena. "He knows what happened between us."

Annie wrapped her arms around herself, murmuring, "Jesus Christ."

Watching the faces of both women go pale, he protested, "He said it was ancient history. He said it didn't matter!"

"Ancient history," Annie echoed.

Lena needed it spelled out. "What does he know?"

Annie sounded hoarse when she answered, "That John and I slept together. That's what he knows." She felt something akin to nausea just then, but it was in her head.

Lena uttered the words, "Good lord," as she collapsed into a chair, the pieces coming together in her mind.

"He brought it up," John explained to his wife. "The way it happened—it was right after he took things over, after his father's death, when he and I started working together. We were talking, having drinks at the Connaught one night, when he said something about having been at St. Andrews. I realized that we were the same age and told him my best friend had been a student there, too. I said his name, Colin Wemyss. He looked at me strangely, then he asked if I knew Annie. In an instant it had clicked. He figured out who I was, then and there."

Annie's eyes burned intolerably. She had heard the comment about Andrew's father's death, but she was having trouble assimilating it. Lena could say and do nothing, only stare gap-mouthed at her husband.

"He was angry at first, and he walked out. I was dumbfounded. I didn't know what to do, so I simply sat there and waited. He came back after a while. He'd composed himself and apologized for acting rudely. He smiled and said that it shouldn't get between us and the business at hand; it was, after all, ancient history. Those were his words. I thought he meant them." Even as he was explaining it to them, he was also justifying it to himself.

"Twenty-two years—ancient history," Annie said, shaking her head in despair.

"Maybe he did mean it, at the time," Lena decided, seeming to find something there. Glancing at Annie, she added, "Maybe that was how he felt—until he saw her tonight."

Stirring into the stew of Annie's mind was a growing anger with John. "But how'd he find out we slept together, John? Did you blurt that out, too?" she asked, remembering the circumstances of his confession to Lena.

He frowned. "Of course not. And he didn't say how, only that he knew. I wasn't about to ask him, was I? Things were bloody uncomfortable enough." His expression softened. "I'm sorry it happened this way, but it was his doing, not mine. And anyway, you told me how much he meant to you, how you'd love to see him again," he reminded her. "I thought I was doing good, bringing you two together. Really I did."

Quiet filled the library as each of its occupants tried to decide what to do next.

Annie took a fortifying breath, then stood up. "I'm going to the cottage. Please make my excuses to the others. Tell them I've had a migraine. Jeremy can give the presentation tomorrow. I don't even need to be there. He knows it well enough and he'll do a fine job. I'll pack my things and leave in the morning."

Lena had been deep in thought the last few minutes, but when she heard Annie say she was leaving, she stood abruptly and blocked her exit. "You're not walking out of this, not on your life!" she told her. "What you're going to do is pull it together and sit next to him at the table, just as I'd planned. He's been the rude one tonight. You've done nothing wrong."

"But I have, Lena!" she protested. She'd been holding back the tears, but it was no use now, and she nearly sobbed. "What I did to him—it's obviously not ancient history—not for either one of us!"

The sideways glance she cast in her husband's direction made him wince, as Lena countered, "But you didn't do it alone, did you?"

"No," she sniveled, "and that's why I won't go out there with John and rub salt in his wound. It's best if I just leave quietly."

"I thought there was more to you than that!" Lena exclaimed. "I thought you were strong enough and brave enough to take on the world from a motorcycle! Surely an encounter with an old flame, even one that looks as though he wants to throttle you, surely that's a walk in the park for someone with courage like yours!"

Composing herself now, Annie responded. "It was never courage; it was fear that drove me to do what I did."

"So what?" Lena asked. "You still did it, didn't you? You faced your fear head-on. Why not do that now? Why not go out there and face him, take whatever he has to dish out, then get on with the business of things? A lot is riding on this account, you know, and John had enough faith in you to put the responsibility squarely on your shoulders. Would you disregard all that and tuck tail and run?"

"But what do I say to him?" Annie questioned. "What can I possibly say that won't make things worse?"

"I can think of plenty," Lena answered. "For one, he knows you slept with John, but does he know you never loved him? Does he understand why you did it? I do; I understand why. I know that you loved Andrew so much it was killing you to have to leave him, and you did what you had to do to get through it." Unshakeable determination was evident in Lena's face. "Do you want Andrew to go on thinking the worst of you, that you were wanton and selfish, and not know the truth of it?"

Neither Annie nor John could hide their surprise at hearing what Lena had just said. In addition, Annie was astonished by the way John had communicated that to Lena, which indicated to her his level of understanding.

"And besides that," she continued, "am I missing something, or did you not know who he was? That earldom didn't happen last week. He was born to that title! How could he keep something like that from you? It seems to me there's betrayal on his part, too. Don't you want to get to the bottom of that?"

Annie had to smile at Lena's moxie, and she shook her head when she responded, "I don't want to walk away. If it were just me—well, I know what I would do. But I'm concerned about what this will do to the agency, and to you and John personally."

"I wouldn't worry about that," John told her, as he upended his drink. "It was his blasted idea after all. He put this whole thing in motion. He had me contact and hire you, and I don't intend to let him forget that, no matter how bloody important he is."

"Well, then," Lena said, "are you coming or aren't you? I've got to get back to my guests." With folded arms she stared at Annie, impatiently awaiting her answer.

Annie exhaled forcefully, then grimaced. "All right, I'll do it for you, Lena. But do I have to sit next to him?"

"Right bloody next to him," she ordered. Then with increasing resolve she added, "I'd put you on his blue-blooded lap if I could."

Annie made a stop in the powder room first to repair her makeup and hair. When she returned to the drawing room, the others looked discreetly away. She approached Andrew directly and zeroed in on the deep blue eyes; he smiled rather curtly and spoke first.

"Forgive me for before, Ms. d'Inard. It's been such a very long time. Your familiarity took me off guard."

My familiarity? She bristled at that remark but was all politeness on the surface. "Your reaction was quite understandable, your lordship. I had no right to act so. Please forgive me. And John's just mentioned your father's death. I'm terribly sorry to hear of it. Please accept my condolences."

"Yes, thank you." The expression on his face was unreadable.

A server sounded an ominous gong as the doors to the dining room opened and Lena called her guests to dinner.

There was no shortage of small talk at the table, and there was, of course, tremendous interest in the earl and his family. Annie said very little during dinner, except to compliment her hosts on the food and wine, because she was overwhelmed with the idea that she was sitting next to Andrew—Andrew! After twenty-two years of memory and regret, after hoping and praying that she would someday see him again, she was sitting next to the man who had never left her heart and mind, and he was treating her with something just above contempt.

He smiled and made eye contact with everyone at the table, paying each a bit of special attention—everyone, that is, but Annie—at whom he never looked once.

She heard about his five children, the eldest of whom was a boy about to enter St. Andrews, and it wrenched her heart to think of it. She heard about the Countess of Kilmartin and what a lovely, distinguished woman she was, and a marvelous mother, as well. She listened intently to all of it while saying nothing, feeling more and more the outsider, more and more distant from the young man she knew. The man beside her seemed little more than the stranger she had collided with on the plane. She drank a lot of wine, it was a fine Lynch-Bages, and she barely touched her food. She was getting to the point of saturation with all of it—the wine, the talk of Andrew and his perfect wife and family—when someone asked her a question. It was Jeremy Whitman's wife, Eleanor, who was a little blotter.

"Annie, how are you acquainted with the earl? We're all dying to know!"

Annie recognized the look Jeremy gave his wife—that look that passes between spouses to communicate disapproval. She grinned at Eleanor as she responded, "I think his lordship would be the better one to tell that story." Then she folded her arms and relaxed into her chair.

For an instant he scowled at her. "Ms. d'Inard visited St. Andrews while I was in my third year. Yes, I believe it was my third year. A friend of hers from America was studying there and she came to visit him. That's how we met, isn't it?" He turned to Annie for the first time since they'd been seated.

I believe it was my third year. That's how we met, isn't it? What a load of crap, she told herself. I'd bet my life that you recall every detail, just as I do. "You flatter me by remembering," she told him.

"The university was less than half the size it is now," he continued, ignoring the dig and looking away from her again. "Everyone knew everyone else. It was a very small town and we all gathered in the same pubs, went to the same dances. One knew every face in those days."

"What was he like then?" Eleanor asked eagerly. If Jeremy had been within reach, he would have kicked his wife under the table.

Two can play at this game, Annie decided. "Very handsome, as he is now, and tremendously kind and sweet." She put a hand to her mouth. "Oh, I hope I haven't offended you, your lordship. I'm being familiar again. I do beg your pardon."

When Andrew looked at her, it seemed for a moment as though he might smile.

Lena chuckled under her breath and covered it with a delicate cough. "Shall we have our coffee and brandy on the terrace? It's a lovely evening, and John has some Cubans for those who might enjoy one."

Candles in glass hurricanes lit the tables and flower arrangements graced the enclosure walls of the terrace. A large table was set at one end with coffee and various liqueurs. Annie asked the server for an Armagnac before walking to the far end of the flagstone, away from the group. She stood alone, gazing into the darkness, listening to but not hearing the conversation behind her.

After a few minutes, Lena came to her to say, "On behalf of my blundering husband, I apologize for this evening. I know how difficult it's been for you."

"It gets more so by the moment," Annie confessed, "the more it sinks in. In fact, right about now, I feel as though I've had all I can take."

"I'll release you then," she grinned, "if you'd like to go on to the cottage. You've done a splendid job of recovering the evening, and I thank you for it. I know this mess wasn't your doing."

"Wasn't it?" she questioned, as a single tear rolled down one cheek.

Lena took hold of her hand and stroked it briefly before they returned to the group.

Annie bid good night to the other guests, then offered her hand to Andrew for the second time that evening. This time he accepted it, and when she felt the warmth of his flesh, she very nearly cried. "Please accept my apology for any embarrassment I caused you, and for everything—for everything else." She didn't wait for a reply. She turned and walked into the garden, then disappeared along the path to the cottage.

She left her high heels at the door when she went in. She curled up on one of the couches with another Armagnac, then sat in the darkness in her pink party dress, looking at nothing. She finished the drink and went to pour herself another, when she remembered that she had an important day ahead. Setting aside the glass, she lit a perfumed candle in lieu of the lights. Her mind was so full of thought and worry she couldn't sleep, and an hour or more must have passed when she heard a tentative knock on the door.

Andrew stood in front of her. He had changed out of his kilt and into khaki slacks and a navy turtleneck. He waited on the doorstep with his hands in his pockets, looking at her, saying nothing. For a moment, she felt as though it were long ago. In the darkness, he looked so much like the Andrew she once knew that it gave her chills.

Stepping beside the open door, she bowed low and swept an arm in the direction of the seats. He frowned at her and went in, still without a word, then sat in one of the chairs.

"Yes, your lordship?" she flippantly inquired. "What can I do for you, your lordship? Surely you haven't come here to be familiar!"

"I came to talk to you about tomorrow," he said without emotion. "I understand that what I will see tomorrow is mostly your work. I want you to know that I respect your professional ability and will not allow any past feelings or relationship we might have had interfere with my decision." It all sounded very rehearsed.

"Might have had," she echoed, emphasizing the *might*. "That's very decent of you, your lordship."

He frowned again, and far more vehemently. "Drop that crap, will you? Call me Andrew when we're alone."

"Of course, whatever you say." She cast off her resolve to not have more drink and went for the Armagnac again. Standing at the bar, she asked him, "Would you care for one? It's not yours, but it's good."

"Let me see the label," he commanded.

With her glass in hand, she brought him the bottle, then bowed again.

"No, it's not mine," he told her, "but I am buying an Armagnac chateau."

For the first time that night, Annie laughed, spraying the drink she had just taken out of her nose and onto Andrew. "Oh, dear! Oh, dear me! Do forgive me," she giggled, "you can't take me anywhere, can you?"

Ever so slightly, he smiled. "You always were, well, what shall I say? Different."

"That's the second time I've done that in recent weeks. I just did that to a gentleman I was having dinner with in St. Andrews. He said something so funny."

He lost his smile as he thought of her in St. Andrews, keeping company with someone else. He stood abruptly and made his way to the door. "I'd better get back to the house."

She stopped laughing and put the bottle down, then stepped in front of him as Lena had done with her. "So soon? Please don't go yet, please!"

"It's better if I do," he insisted, avoiding her eyes.

He started to move past her but she moved, too, and continued to block his exit. "Why'd you come, Andrew?" she asked.

"I told you," he said, mustering his irritation, "to make it clear that I would treat you and your proposal with respect tomorrow so you wouldn't fret over it."

"I was fretting," she readily admitted. "I'm worried that whatever it is that you mean to do with me will spill over into John and Lena's lives. They don't deserve any payback. They're not to blame. I am."

"I know who did what," he told her in no uncertain terms. "Now will you let me pass?"

She had so many questions. "Why did you want me here? Why did you bring me here?"

"I don't know. I thought I had a reason, but now I don't know," he insisted angrily.

"I can't get over the fact that we were on the same plane, that we bumped into each other like that!" she exclaimed. "What were you doing on a commercial flight, anyway?"

He'd had a feeling about that, a very strong feeling that they were brought together for a reason, but he wasn't going to share that with her. "My jet was grounded in Philadelphia with engine trouble. I needed to be in London for an important meeting, so I took the first flight out. It happened to be yours. It was pure coincidence."

He'd been in Philadelphia—so close to her—it was almost too much to contemplate. "Did you recognize me right away?" she asked.

"Not at first." He was struggling now, trying hard to keep his distance. "But there was something so familiar about you. That's why I went back to speak with you before we landed. That's when I knew."

Thinking of it made her chest tight. "Why didn't you say something then?"

"I couldn't," he answered, his resolve collapsing. "People on the flight knew me and anyway, I didn't know what to say to you."

It still seemed incredulous. "So instead you worked out this elaborate scheme with John?"

He was beginning to feel embarrassed over the whole thing. "It wasn't an elaborate scheme. He'd shown me the article about you last year, the one in that trade magazine."

"You couldn't contact me directly?"

"No," he responded bluntly.

The muscles in her chest were squeezing the air out of her. "Oh Andrew! If only you knew."

He could feel her strong emotions, feel them influencing his own. He needed to protect himself from them, from her, and he pulled away with a contentious, "Knew what?"

"How I've longed for this, to see you again, to be with you again."

"Don't say those things," he commanded her.

"Why?" she asked timidly.

He answered brusquely, "Because you don't mean them. You never did."

"That's not true!"

"It is true—it's the truest thing about you," he told her. "All those things you said to me, you never meant them." He hadn't wanted to say that, but once he had, it opened a floodgate of bitterness.

"No, Andrew. You're wrong."

His face was growing more and more tense, and it made the scars seem deeper. "You don't know the meaning of love. You only love when it's easy, when it's convenient. When things grow difficult, you withdraw it."

"That's not true!" she repeated. She was beginning to feel again, as though there weren't enough oxygen in the room.

"Of course, it is!" he scoffed. "What happened to all the promises, all the declarations, all the intentions when we were in St. Andrews? As soon as I was out of sight . . ." His voice cracked.

"Please Andrew, don't," she begged, sinking into the chair that was behind her. She was overcome with exhaustion suddenly, and mercifully, it slowed the pace of her breathing. "That was the most shameful night of my life," she told him, her voice deepened by remorse. "And time hasn't been kind. It takes so much from us, but it hasn't taken this. Here I am with you, with John, having to face it all again, to pick up where I left off as though it were yesterday. I feel the shame of it now every bit as much as I did then." The muscles in her neck began to smart and twist, and she reached to rub them.

"Sounds like a kind of natural justice, doesn't it?" he quipped.

When it occurred to her that justice was exactly what he'd sought in seeing her again, it crushed her soul. For twenty-two years, she had longed for the opportunity to tell him how much he'd meant to her; for those same number of years, he had harbored a bitter hatred and a desire for revenge.

Detectable cords of anguish filled his voice when he spoke again. "You didn't even write to me, only the one letter, and then nothing. I waited for your letters, and you didn't even write."

"I wrote to you!" she protested, sounding like a small child.

His face contorted with pain. "Once, you wrote me one letter from Saintes-Maries and then—nothing. You didn't even have the decency to answer the letter that said I was coming to meet you."

"Andrew, please believe me," she pleaded, "I didn't get your letter until months later. It never got to me in France. It was forwarded months later by the girl who owned the apartment, and I wrote to you! I wrote letter after letter. You didn't respond."

"Why do you sit there and lie?" he railed, looming over her as she cowered in the chair. "What's the point? I didn't get any letter other than the one, and you know that!"

"I wrote to you. I swear on my life I did!"

He glared at her in anger and disbelief.

Silence came between them suddenly, almost like a truce. It took words away from them and made them be still, so that they might listen to the calls of an owl coming from the woods. It made them aware of the flickering light and the sensual aroma of the candle. It forced them to share something again, however simple, after so long apart, after so much gone between. It made the two people in the little cottage feel what it was like to be near each other again.

Warily, she encroached upon the silence. "Andrew, please tell me, how did the scars happen?"

He scowled indignation. Why did she have to go there? Why couldn't she leave that alone? "You tell me something," he insisted. "What are you doing here on your own? Don't you have a husband and son to take care of?"

She wanted to stand but was too depleted of energy to move. "I'm separated from my husband. Surely John told you."

"He didn't know why you'd separated."

She would be nothing but honest; she owed him that. "I was having an affair," she answered, as she lowered her head in shame.

His cheeks flushed with heat, and he released that spitting sound that comes from disgust. "I should have known! Christ! You haven't changed, have you?"

"No, I guess I haven't." She gave him that, and lifted her head to meet his eyes. Then, with heartfelt regret, she added, "But you have."

In their repressed intensity, his next breaths conveyed his reaction to what she had said. He bristled and carried on within himself—how dare you! How dare you reproach me for changing when you're the one who changed me!

She could barely see his face in the candlelight, but she was searching it for signs. There was so much she needed to know, longed to know, and why he hadn't told her his true identity, was not the least of it. But the scars worried her the most at the moment, for they seemed evidence of something violent, something tragic. "What about the scars," she said. "Please tell me what happened to you."

He shook his head in frustration, then made his way toward the door. He turned when he reached it and looked back at her. It was too dark to see them, but she could feel what was in his eyes.

"They're the legacy of Annie d'Inard," he told her, then went out.

Chapter 34

Sleep was fitful and long in coming, and when it finally overtook Annie, it carried her through a disturbing collage of past and present.

She was awakened by a gentle knock on her open bedroom door. She looked at the clock first, then turned toward the door to see John standing there with a bed tray.

"I've slept too long," she realized.

"That was my doing," he explained, offering the tray like a room service waiter anticipating a tip. "I've pushed the presentation back to one, because I thought we could all use the extra sleep."

She propped herself against the headboard. "And Andrew, that's all right with him?"

He nodded first, then commented, "It's so odd to hear you call him Andrew. Nobody dares call him that."

Pulling the bedclothes to cover her chest, she assured him, "I won't do it in front of anyone."

She was now sitting upright, so he placed the tray over her legs, then perched on the edge of the bed. "He came to see you last night."

She nodded and rubbed the sleep from her eyes.

"Did you have a good talk?" he asked.

"No," she answered bluntly. The tray was loaded to the brim: scrambled eggs, bangers, toast and fruit, even a sweet bun. As she looked it over, she said, "You shouldn't have brought me all this. I'll never eat it."

"Lena thought you could use some fortification," he responded, "and anyway, she thinks you're losing weight."

She dismissed the observation. "My appetite is off. Have you had a chance to speak with him?"

Casually, as though it were his own breakfast, he helped himself to a slice of toast. "Yes, actually," he answered, slathering it with soft butter, then apricot preserves. "When he came in from seeing you last night. Lena and I had been talking, and she convinced me to do it." He bit into it now and made short work of it.

"Do what?" she asked anxiously.

He washed the toast down with some of her juice. "I didn't think I'd have the courage, but it needed to be said. Lena made me realize that. So I invited him to my library," he informed her, "and we talked about what happened that last night in St. Andrews."

Her heart was picking up the pace. "What'd you tell him?"

"The truth."

"All of it?"

He returned the juice glass to the tray, then stared at it. "I told him how you cried to break your heart, that you were positively inconsolable. I said that I gave you a lot to drink, because I didn't know what else to do, and that I ran a hot bath and told you to get into it. And when it occurred to me that as blotter as you were you might drown, I went to check on you. I told him that when I saw your naked body, that was when it happened, and that it was all my fault, that you didn't initiate it." It took courage to meet her eyes, as much courage as it had taken for him to say these things to Andrew. "I took advantage of the state you were in; I admitted that. I rationalized my behavior by telling myself that there was no commitment between you two. If there were, you'd have been together. I didn't let myself think about how much I was hurting you—both of you."

Annie searched his eyes. "You said all that to him?"

Nodding, he continued. "And more. I told him that you called his name repeatedly that night, that you cried it out as though he might somehow hear and come running to you. I said it was one of the saddest things I'd ever witnessed in my life." John grasped the juice glass again and stared into it for a moment. Then, as though he'd forgotten what it was he wanted to do, he returned it to her tray.

When he'd set it down again, she touched his hand. "Thank you, John. Thank you for doing that."

"I've always felt bad about what happened, Annie," he added. "I convinced myself that what I was doing was comforting you, but I was really just hurting you more."

She sighed as she let that settle out of the air. "What did he say? How did he react?"

"He stared at the floor for a long while," he told her, "I imagine while he ran things over in his mind. Then he asked me a question."

"What question?"

He hesitated, then lowered his voice. "He asked if it continued after that night."

She gasped slightly. "What'd you say?"

"More of the truth."

Annie lifted her coffee cup now, but she didn't drink from it. Instead, she held it suspended. "Did he say anything else?"

"He thanked me for being so open and honest with him. I told him that I hoped knowing what really happened would help him to feel less angry with you. But he said . . ." he hesitated again.

She put the cup back down. "I have to know."

He avoided her eyes when he responded. "He said it doesn't absolve you of your guilt."

As she heard those words from John, it seemed to her that it was Andrew's voice saying them, not his. "He's right," she said, barely audibly.

"You two need to have a sit-down," he ventured.

She shook her head. "He's so angry with me, John. I don't think he wants that."

"I disagree," he told her. "As a matter of fact, I believe that's what he's wanted all along. I think that's the very reason he wanted me to bring you here. And after our conversation last night, I'm even more certain of that." He frowned. "I could see how hurt he was, Annie, and I could tell what a terrible burden it's been for him. He needs to do something about that."

When they were alone in the cottage, she'd seen that, too. She'd felt it every time she'd taken a breath. It was so powerful, so deep, it seemed to permeate the air. Perhaps that was why it was so difficult to breathe when he was near.

John looked increasingly thoughtful. "I don't know, but I think you'll see a different man at the presentation. I think he'll be viewing you differently." He moved closer to her now and reached to stroke her hand. "You seem full of sadness, too. Is it Andrew?"

"It's always been Andrew," she sighed. "He's never left me, but there are other things, too, my marriage for one. My heart is filled with regret, John."

"And I'm certain I'm part of that."

She didn't answer.

John lowered his eyes again. He'd been wanting to say this since their first meeting at the Old Parsonage Hotel, but he didn't dare. Now with all the soul-searching and honest talk that had gone on in the past twelve hours, it seemed quite innocuous. "You know, for years I dreamed about making love to you. You were always a wild, sexual fantasy for me. I've never made love like that with anyone else. It was incredible, really."

"It was frantic and desperate," she said, woefully adding, "and I've never gotten past that feeling of desperation. When I think of it now, it seems that encounter set the tone for me, for all my sexual relationships to follow." She would never have shared something this personal with him had she not been feeling raw, ripped open by her confrontation with Andrew.

"Has there ever been anyone you weren't that way with?" he wondered.

"No," she answered.

"Not even Andrew?"

"We never made love, John."

"That's right. I'd forgotten. Christ!" He rose from the bed and walked to the window. "I remember now. You wanted to go back to him, to make love with him, even if that would be your one and only night together. You wanted to be with him, but I stopped you. I told you it would hurt him much more if you did that. I said it might make you feel better, but it would make it worse for him."

"That's right, that's what you said, and I shouldn't have listened to you." She lifted the tray from her lap and pushed it to the foot of the bed. "Maybe if we'd been together that night, he wouldn't have let me leave. I've always thought that, and it's always been my biggest, deepest regret." She felt anxious suddenly and wanted to get up, but she didn't want to parade around in her nightgown in front of John.

"But it seemed impossible, didn't it? I mean, there even appeared to be some sort of conspiracy among your friends to separate you," he reminded her.

"It did seem impossible," she agreed, recalling her frustration then. "It's all so absurd, isn't it? I mean, we were closer to each other than to anyone else in the world, but I never knew who he was, that he was Lord Andrew, for Christ's sake! Other people had to have known who he was—Susannah probably, Robin certainly. But I was in love with him. How could he keep that from me?"

"Actually, he was more than that," he informed her. "At the time, he carried a courtesy title from his grand-father; he was the Baron Kilmartin of Mull. His second-oldest son carries that title now, and his eldest is the Viscount Rannoch."

The whole thing seemed preposterous, and she stared at him in disbelief. "It would almost be funny, wouldn't it, if it weren't so fucking tragic."

He chuckled. "You know, the last thing Lena said to me as we went to bed last night was, 'Bloody hell, John, did you have to sleep with the Earl of Kilmartin's girlfriend?'"

They both laughed, but for Annie it wasn't amusement that sparked it; it was nervous release.

"Thank God for Lena," she said. "She's been astoundingly generous and understanding."

"And the voice of reason," he added. "She's got everything under control at the house. She's giving him lunch, and he's using my library to do some business this morning. We'll see him at the office at one." He was poised to take the bed tray away, but before doing that, he leaned to kiss her forehead, then changed his mind and kissed her lips instead. He had meant it to be gentle, barely touching, but he pressed his mouth to hers and thrust his tongue between her lips.

She pushed him away immediately. "Jesus, John," she shouted. "What the hell are you doing? God! Things are complicated enough for Christ's sake!"

He backed off and blushed in embarrassment. "I don't know why I did that. It was just an impulse. I was remembering. I'm sorry, it won't happen again."

"You're damned right, it won't!" she vehemently assured him.

As he left the cottage carrying her tray, she vividly recalled that he had ambushed her exactly that way twenty-two years ago, as she sat weeping in the bath in Colin's flat.

* * *

In her pale yellow Valentino suit, she appeared calm and composed, listening as John began the presentation. Jeremy and the others were fidgety and anxious, but Annie and John were the picture of cool professionalism. When it was time for her to speak, she rose from her seat at the conference table with the self-possession of an experienced stage actress. But that composure only came after some serious soul-searching.

After John left her, she went directly to the shower where she would remain for nearly a half hour, trying to squelch her desire to cut and run. Knowing that the pompous client she had expected would instead be Andrew, and that he would be scrutinizing her every move, judging her every nuance, made her question if she was up to it. And she puzzled over whether or not she should tender her resignation. Was it right to go on working with John? Would it be rubbing it in Andrew's face, every time he saw them together?

With her skin shriveled from the hot water, she finally decided that she would not resign. She wanted and needed this job; it was making her happy and giving purpose to her life. And anyway, she knew it would be next to impossible to walk away from Andrew, to look into those blue, compelling eyes and say good-bye again, when so much remained unsaid, so much had yet to be resolved. By the time her hair was dry and her makeup done, she determined that she should go into that conference room with her head held high and give it her damned best effort, no matter the outcome.

With that in mind, she smiled confidently as she began her presentation. "Thank you for your graciousness, your lordship, in allowing us to delay the start of the meeting."

He nodded his head and folded his arms, his eyes following her every move.

She dimmed the lights and triggered the audio-visual system. The sound of wind filled the darkened room. A man called through the wind, then thrilling Spanish guitars serenaded them before an orchestra filled in the drama. Breathtaking photographs of the high Pyrénées were projected on the screen as the music played on. Annie let the show run for a couple of minutes before turning down the sound and stepping in front of the screen to deliver her script.

She was very good at this when she wanted to be—when she was on—and today she was on. As she pitched the concept, everyone in the room was spellbound, especially Andrew, who recognized as she spoke, someone he hadn't seen for many years.

Jeremy finished things off with the technical details. The earl sat quietly, almost expressionless. After John thanked everyone, he asked Andrew if he had any questions.

"We have these gypsies in writing?" He'd said the word *gypsies* as though he'd never used it before.

Annie pulled in her lower lip to keep from smiling.

"Preliminary, binding contracts, your lordship," he answered.

"When can we begin the shoot?"

"Two weeks, more or less, depending on the availability of all involved, of course."

"The sooner the better," he told him. "I have a light schedule for the next month, and I want to be present for the filming."

Annie's heart leapt into her throat at hearing that, for it was her intention to be there, too.

"We'll make it our number one priority," John told him, "and once we have your OK, Jeremy can set the wheels in motion."

"Fine," he answered, almost curtly. "You've got it."

A collective sigh of relief was heard around the table and faces brightened.

John looked relieved, too. "Is there anything you'd like to add to the meeting?"

His response seemed to be an afterthought. "It's very good, it's excellent, this concept. I congratulate you all," he offered, then smiled slightly.

"Thank you, your lordship. We consider Nether Largie our most important client, and we've had our very best people on this."

Andrew was sitting alone at the far end of the large conference table, and the serious way in which he said this, his eyes focused on the writing pad in front of him, his pen pressed into it, made it sound ominous. "If the presentation is over, I'd like a few moments with Ms. d'Inard."

Glancing at Annie, John answered, "Of course," although some concern was detectable in his voice.

Before he did anything that morning, Jeremy made certain the entire office knew what had transpired at the dinner party. As a result, everyone stiffened with Andrew's request, anticipating the worst, then hustled out of the room as though there'd been a bomb threat.

When the door closed and they were alone, Andrew stood and walked to the window. He looked out at the street. "I'm prepared to pay you very handsomely for your work and release you from your contract."

Her heart had begun fluttering the moment they were alone, but now it took a nosedive. "Have I done something to displease you?" she worried.

"No, on the contrary, I'm very pleased with what you've done," he had to admit, turning toward her again. "More than pleased."

"Then why do you want to get rid of me? I was looking forward to working on this project." Her voice weakened, and she stopped speaking to recover it.

He tried to sound rational and unemotional when he responded, "I should think you miss your son, and if there's any hope for your marriage, you'd do better to return to the States to try to work things out, rather than stay on here." It was the excuse he'd come up with in the night as he lay staring at the ceiling, wondering how best to deal with her.

She did not try to hide her distress. "My husband grows more and more distant every day, Andrew. As for my son, he'll be here to visit me soon, and then he plans to spend the summer in Barcelona with his father's family. So you see, I've no reason and nothing to return home to. Having this project to work on has been wonderful for me. It's given me purpose." Her voice trailed off. "I'd hate to give it up now. I don't know what I'd do with myself, going back to that empty cottage." She decided not to finish that thought, because she didn't want to whine.

He lifted his chin and shoulders defensively, as though something was threatening him. "In that case, I'm certain John can find you another account to work on."

"But I gave birth to this," she protested. "I'd like to see it through!"

Her pleading voice and eyes were melting away his resolve. His knees seemed suddenly weak, and he moved away from the window to sit again, directly across from her. It was not a good place to be, he instantly discovered, because he was close enough to smell her perfume.

He glared at her first, then shook his head while the internal debate raged. Then, in a startling change of demeanor, he said, "I don't know if I can do this." His voice had changed dramatically, going from pure business to barely restrained emotion.

She swallowed hard. "Work with me, do you mean?"

Closing his eyes in a sustained blink, he answered, "Yes." He then straightened his back against the chair so that he might feel its support.

As the pain welled up, she lowered her eyes. "Do you hate me so much, Andrew?"

"I don't know what I feel about you," he told her, though that was not entirely true.

She caught something familiar in the way he said that, and she experienced a surge of courage from it, enough courage to tell him, "It would help me so much— it would mean so much—if you could somehow find it in your heart, if you could somehow forgive me."

He didn't want to, but he couldn't help looking into her eyes, to the shards of green that he had so often lost himself in as a young man. "It's so much more complicated than that. I'd need to forgive myself first, and that's much more difficult."

For the first time since they'd met again, he was seeming like the Andrew she knew, and it was transporting her, lifting her. "For not telling me who you were?" she asked softly.

"Yes, that," he admitted, "and other things." Something was happening to him, and it was beyond his control.

Her eyes had captured him, and her voice was seducing him. "What other things?"

Although he hadn't wanted this, he was compelled by his heart to give in, for it felt much better to be speaking it than trying to protect it. "So much happened after you left. There's so much you don't know."

A quivering, nervous feeling overtook her now. "Why don't we get out of here? Let's go someplace for a drink."

"In public?" he questioned. "I can't do that, Annie. I'm too well-known. We might find our picture in tomorrow's tabloids."

"Then let's go to the cottage at Fargate," she suggested. "We can be alone there. We can talk undisturbed. John and Lena will protect your privacy."

He was already feeling and saying too much, and he couldn't trust himself to be alone with her. "I don't think that's a good idea."

"Why? Somehow, we've got to talk. We've got to say the things that need to be said. Keeping them inside, it's like a cancer eating away at us. Time is passing and it's running out, Andrew. It's running out." She swallowed hard again as her throat filled with tears.

"I know that," he told her. He leaned forward to put an elbow on the table, then rested his forehead in his hand. "It sickens me, really sickens me, to think what we let get away from us."

She wanted to respond, but she couldn't. Hearing what he just said filled her with such emotion, she knew if she opened her mouth now, the sobs churning inside would come spilling out.

In a forlorn, plaintive voice, he continued, "I can almost understand that night, that last night, when we said goodbye. I can almost understand why you slept with him, why you needed to be with someone. What I can't understand is why it went on." He caught her eyes again. "Why did you go on sleeping with him?"

She gathered her courage and kept her eyes with his. "I learned something that night, something I've practiced ever since. I had sex with him because of the pain, Andrew. I used sex to get away from the pain. I could never stand it; I still can't." She said this with absolute certainty, as though it was a fact she had long ago come to terms with. But in truth, it was only in recent weeks, alone and confronted with the mistakes of her past, that she'd come to understand this about herself.

She searched the lines of his face, looking for evidence of the young man she'd loved. "The first time I felt that pain—it was on the West Sands, by the bonfire," she said. "You know what I'm talking about, because you felt it, too."

They looked directly into each other again. He experienced a sudden, powerful urge to reach for her, but he fought it with all his strength.

Her instincts told her what to say next. "And you? How have you dealt with it, Andrew?"

Gathering the last vestiges of his strength to keep from touching her had depleted it. As it waned, all his defenses came tumbling down. He sighed as he told her, "I have the businesses, my family, the responsibilities of my title. And there've been others, other women," he confessed, adding with bitterness, "I've kept up the discreet practice of my forebearers, you see." He focused on the table now. "My father was killed five years ago in a small plane crash in the Highlands."

She was momentarily confused but waited for him to explain.

It was not a subject he had ever discussed, but something in him wanted her to know. "He was flying his mistress up to a shooting lodge for the weekend. The investigators say the pilot was killed instantly, but my father and the woman survived initially. A shepherd witnessed it. He said my father was trying to pull her from the wreckage when it exploded."

Annie closed her eyes on the image. "Oh God, that's dreadful. I'm so sorry. That must have been horrible for you and your mother."

"My mother knew; she always knew," he said, "though she never acknowledged it. It must have been a relief, I should think, having it out in the open for once."

Knowing the impertinent nature of what she was about to ask, she braced herself for his reaction. "And your wife, does she know about your affairs?"

"Yes. We've always been better friends than lovers."

His simple answer surprised her. "Friendship is very important in a marriage."

"It's the sustaining factor, I think."

She felt inexplicable pangs of jealousy when she thought of it. "Is she the one—the girl you were engaged to then?"

He nodded.

"Are there other women now? Are you involved now?" It was not idle curiosity; it was a burning desire to know everything she could about him, to fill in as many blanks as possible.

"There's been a woman, a lovely Parisian woman," he said a little sadly. "We're very fond of one another, and we were together on and off for many years. But no longer.

My father's death made me see myself in a different light. I realized that I'd become like him, and I didn't like knowing that." He poured a glass of water from the pitcher in front of him and let the room become quiet.

Her jealousy eased, but in its place came heartache. "I'm sorry for you," she told him. "It saddens me to think of you like that—you, of all people." She remembered too well how ardently the young Andrew had revered commitment.

Her pity might have insulted and angered him, but strangely, it didn't. He set the glass down but continued to hold onto it. "What about the man you were involved with?" He, too, needed to know everything he could about her.

"I turned to him when my husband grew distant, but it stopped when . . ." She didn't want to finish that thought, so she said, "I had myself convinced that I loved him, but it wasn't love; it was need."

He'd heard the despair in her voice. "What happened?"

She winced as she answered, "Something horrible."

"What?"

"I wish you'd come with me to the cottage," she said again. "I don't want to talk about this here."

"No one can hear us," he insisted. "What happened?"

"It's so hard to say."

He tilted his head to one side. "I've felt it, you know. It doesn't make sense, but I've felt that there was something terribly wrong. Tell me what it is."

The intensity of his gaze burned away her reluctance. "I didn't want to get into this, not now, but I—I found out," she struggled for nicer words, but there were none, "it's possible he's infected me with HIV." She closed her eyes, because she didn't want to see his face.

"My God!" He stood abruptly, then repeated, "My God!" He walked to the other side of the room and then back again. He bent to sit in his chair but didn't. Instead, he straightened and paced behind it, back and forth several times. "AIDS? Do you have AIDS?" he finally asked.

"No, not AIDS, not yet, anyway." His agitation distressed her, and she wished she hadn't told him. "I had two positive antibody tests," she explained, "the last two times I donated blood to the Red Cross. They contacted me and told me to see a doctor and that I couldn't donate anymore. That's how it works."

He stopped pacing and sat down. "I don't understand."

She tried to keep herself calm, for his sake as well as hers. "I didn't have the actual virus. They couldn't find it anyway, but the antibody thing is a red flag. It could mean that it's in there, hiding, not yet out to where it can be detected."

He was trying to comprehend how this could happen. "Is he infected?"

"I don't know."

That astounded him. "You don't know? Didn't he get tested?"

"I'm sure he has, but I left right after I told him, and I haven't been in touch with him since."

"Why not?"

"I'm afraid to know," she admitted. "Not knowing buys me time. It's limbo, but at least it's not a death sentence."

His thoughts were racing, jumping from one possibility to the next. "And your husband? Is he all right?"

"So far."

Something occurred to him now, and it made him ask, "When did all this happen?"

"At the end of February, right before I came here. A couple of weeks before you saw me on the plane."

That was it, he realized. That was what he'd felt from her, that intuition that something was terribly wrong. "I can't believe you haven't called this man! You've got to speak to him. He could be healthy, too!"

"What if he's not?"

"Then you'll deal with it! There must be something you can do in the meantime to keep yourself from getting sick. You should be aware at least, and taking care of yourself. But you don't know that yet, and you've got to know first!"

A badly timed knock on the door interrupted them. Andrew shouted, "Not now!" The knock repeated and he pushed his chair from the table with such force that it fell to the floor. "What is it?" he railed, as he flung open the door.

John was red faced and apologetic as he hurried to explain, "I do beg your pardon, your lordship, but it's Crinan Castle on the telephone for you, and they say it's urgent."

Andrew remembered that he had turned off his mobile for the meeting, and he closed his eyes in embarrassment. "Sorry I snapped at you, John. Put it through in here."

Annie had stooped to recover his chair. Straightening now, she told Andrew, "I'll leave you alone."

But as she walked past him, he reached and grabbed her wrist, ordering, "No, stay here," just as John exited and closed the door.

The phone's ring was startling to them both. Andrew let go of her to answer. His face went pale as he listened.

When he responded to the caller, she could hear the anxiety in his voice. "The pilot is waiting for me at the airport. Tell him we need clearance for immediate departure. I'll be there as soon as I can, and tell Lady Kilmartin—tell her I'm on my way." He replaced the receiver and stiffened to his full height. "There's been an accident—two of the children, in the car with their nanny. Cathy seems fine but my youngest, Malcolm—he's only four. He's been hurt. They've been taken to hospital. I've got to go to them."

The look on his face made her ill. It made her want to embrace and comfort him, to tell him it would be all right. "Of course. Oh Andrew, I'm so sorry," she offered, keeping her distance with tremendous difficulty. "Is there anything I can do? Do you know how badly he's injured?"

"No, only that he lost consciousness. It's only just happened in the last half hour."

"I'm so terribly sorry," she said again. "Please let me know."

"Yes, of course." He seemed dazed and disconnected as he retrieved his attaché and walked toward the door. "We'll talk another time," was the last thing he said to her.

John saw Andrew out to the Rolls. Before getting in, Andrew turned and looked to the second-story window of the conference room. He saw Annie standing there in her pale yellow suit, her hand touching the glass. Seeing her like that, he was suddenly visited with a familiar ache— the one that he used to feel when he'd say good night to her in St. Andrews, when he knew that another day had passed, that he was one day closer to having to say good-bye. It came upon him abruptly, unexpectedly, standing there in the street looking up at her, and it did not leave him, even when he boarded the jet to return home to his family.

Chapter 35

The phone in the jet rang just as they were beginning their descent into Glasgow. It was Nigel, the earl's personal secretary.

"All's well, your lordship. Your daughter and Nanny are doing well, but young Lord Malcolm did have a concussion, and he required a bit of stitching. He's perfectly alert, though, with a slight headache, and he was remarkably brave throughout. The Oban doctors suggested he stay overnight for observation, but with Dr. Maclaulin just down the road and able to stop in, Lady Kilmartin's arranged for a nurse here instead. They're on their way home now, with Lady Kilmartin."

"Thank you, Nigel. I'm very relieved. Are you certain everyone's all right?" He needed to hear it again.

"Absolutely, sir," he assured him. "They were all checked thoroughly."

"And my wife?" he wondered.

"Holding up nicely, too."

"We're landing now. Tell her I'll be there within the hour."

"Very good, your lordship. Is there anything else?"

He thought of Annie and the concern she had evidenced. "Ring up Millar-Graham at Lynch and Collings and tell him all's well." He knew John would communicate the news to her.

"Right away, sir. Anything else?"

With matters under control, he remembered something he'd been determined to do today. "As a matter of fact, Nigel, do you think you might get hold of Ambrose for me?"

"Ambrose, sir? Your father's man?"

"Yes, the same. Old Ambrose."

It was a curious request, but he answered, "Of course. I believe he's retired to Arran, hasn't he?"

"Yes, his address and phone number will be in my files. Tell him I'd like to speak with him," he said, then thought better of it. "Actually, I'd like to visit him, if that's possible."

"I'll be on it right away, your lordship."

The helicopter approached from the northern shore of Loch Crinan, then landed on the south lawn at Crinan Castle. It was a cold, rainy day in Argyll, and the Dowager Countess of Kilmartin, the mother of the present earl, watched the landing from the tropical warmth of the conservatory.

"I've always hated that business," she told Nigel Bain, who waited with her. "You know I never wanted that thing put on the lawn," she added, referring to the helipad.

"Yes, Lady Mary, I remember," he answered, "but the helicopter does get the earl home sooner. We are a distance from the airport in Glasgow."

Impatiently, she responded, "Yes, yes, I understand all that, but it's so very noisy, isn't it, and it makes such a fuss with the flowers."

He suppressed a smile. "That it does, your ladyship."

They watched Andrew climb into the Range Rover to be driven to the house.

Although she could not see him from her distance, she was imagining her son's face, which now, with the tiny crow's feet at his eyes and the grays that were working into his hairline, resembled his father's even more. "I never get over how handsome he is," she said, almost to herself. "It broke my heart—that dreadful car crash, what it did to him. But he's still so devilishly good-looking, isn't he?"

Nigel cleared his throat. "He'll be arriving now, your ladyship. Shall we meet him?"

"Of course. He'll want to know about the children immediately."

Andrew entered his ancestral home with a flourish. As always, the servants were gathered in the entrance hall, curtsying and bowing as they had for centuries.

He disliked these antiquated customs and since he'd been earl, he'd toned down the ritual considerably. Kissing his mother, he declared, "I wish we would put an end to this foolishness once and for all."

"You've never had enough respect for tradition, Andrew," she scolded, once the servants had left their vicinity. "There's always been a wild streak in you. I never understood where it came from."

"Where are they?" he asked.

"Janet's with them upstairs. They're fine."

"Excuse me," he told her, then hurried up the massive stone staircase.

A nurse was bending over Malcolm and holding a glass of something for him to drink. "Daddy! Come see my bandage!" Malcolm called when he saw Andrew.

The nurse stepped away as Andrew took his youngest child into his arms. She had to smile when she saw the two of them together, for although Malcolm bore the silky, white-blond hair of a child, he was a miniature of his father, with the same gentle face and captivating blue eyes.

At dinner in the small, family dining room, Andrew sat with his wife, mother, and two daughters. The older boys were at school and Malcolm was upstairs, being watched over by the nurse. It was a very different scene from when Andrew was a child. There was animated conversation, laughter, teasing, even some joking with the servants. None of that had been allowed when Andrew and his sisters were growing up. The only time they had any relief from the suffocating decorum was when his father was away, but even then, his mother demanded some adherence to custom.

"Malcolm thinks this is the greatest thing that's ever happened to him," Maggie, the oldest girl, informed them.

"Yes, well, he'll be properly spoiled from it, I'm sure," her mother answered, then turned her attention to her husband. "Are you unwell, Andrew? You've barely touched your dinner."

"It's been a difficult day."

"How did the thing go at Lynch and Collings?" Janet wondered, taking a sip of wine. "Nigel said they hired an American consultant, a woman I believe," she added casually.

He avoided looking at her. "Yes, they did, and it went very well. They did a splendid job."

"So she's working out," she prodded, "the American?"

"Yes, she's doing most of the creative work."

His mother, Lady Mary, joined the conversation. "It won't be tacky, will it, like so many of those American things?"

He glanced at her. "She doesn't do work like that. Her work is of a much higher quality."

"That's reassuring," Lady Mary responded.

Janet regarded her husband with curiosity, aware of his avoidance tactics. "Are you certain nothing's wrong?"

"I'm exhausted," he admitted. "This was a particularly long trip, and it took a lot out of me today waiting to hear if everyone was all right."

He seemed so distracted, she thought it best to remind him, "You haven't forgotten we have the AIDS benefit ball tomorrow night in Glasgow, have you? The Princess of Wales is coming. She's breaking her resolve to stay out of public life and attending for you, you know."

He seemed distressed. "Is that tomorrow?"

"Is there a problem?"

"No," he answered, then bit his lower lip. "But I was thinking of popping over to Arran to see old Ambrose for a couple of hours."

This didn't come as a surprise, because Nigel had already informed her of his plans. "Well, I imagine you can still do that, if you think you're up to it. He's not well, you know."

Andrew finally looked directly at his wife. "No, I didn't know."

"His health is failing rapidly, I'm told. It's probably a good thing you're going. You may not have another opportunity."

"Yes," his mother added, "I've heard that, too. It's his heart, I believe."

"Then I will go," he decided, "first thing in the morning, if you don't mind. I know I said I'd stay put for a bit. Would it be a terrible imposition?"

Janet answered, "Not at all. Would you like me to go with you?"

He smiled as casually as he could. "Thank you, it's very good of you to offer, but I'd rather go on my own." Thinking now, that his mother might want to tag along, too, he added, "If he is unwell, best not tax him with too many visitors."

Ambrose had been born at Crinan Castle, the son of the valet to the twenty-second earl. He was ten years old when Andrew's father Donald was born, and there was never any question but that he would carry on the tradition and be the gentleman's gentleman to him. They grew up together, essentially, though one below stairs, the other with all the privilege and clout imaginable, and they became very close, despite their differences in station. Ambrose knew more about the twenty-third earl than anyone else in the world. He kept his confidences, helped arrange his trysts, listened and advised in times of need. There was no request that Ambrose would refuse, nothing that he would not do for Donald, and Andrew knew that.

For Ambrose's sixty-fifth birthday, Andrew's father made a gift to him of the cottage he now occupied with his wife. He retired there after Donald's death and now, seventy-seven years old with a frail heart and still sharp mind, he lived contentedly with his wife, Sarah, puttering around the garden when he was able, happily receiving visits from children and grandchildren.

Andrew found him dressed but reclined on a sitting room couch. He was covered with a light quilt on this relatively warm day.

When he greeted his visitor, his breathing was somewhat labored. "Your lordship, I'm so honored you've come! Please forgive me for not getting up."

Andrew clasped the old man's hands in his. "It's I who need ask your forgiveness. I should have come sooner. I've been very lax in not keeping up with you, Ambrose."

"Not at all!" he protested. "I know your responsibilities, and you've your children—so many fine children! You're a good father, your lordship. I know you devote a great deal of time to them."

As he took a seat near him, Andrew inquired, "Is there anything you need—anything at all? You've only to ask."

"Your father left me very well off and I'm perfectly content, thank you, your lordship."

"Your children and grandchildren, are they well?"

Ambrose's children had broken with tradition and not gone into service. "All thriving, I'm happy to report, your lordship."

"Do they need any assistance—with schooling or anything?"

"I've invested the funds your father left me, and they're helping all of us," he assured him. "You're most generous to offer, but there's nothing we require at present."

Andrew seemed almost disappointed. "Very well, but I want your promise that if there ever is anything, you'll allow me the honor of assisting you."

"You have it, sir," he smiled.

Andrew felt awkward suddenly and drew his chair closer to the couch. "Do you feel up to talking? There's something very important I need to speak with you about, but I don't want to tire you."

"Certainly, I do," he readily responded. "It's such an unexpected pleasure to see you, it's given me quite the boost."

Andrew smiled nervously, albeit briefly. "Ambrose, do you remember that summer, that awful summer?"

His eyes closed in a sustained blink before he answered. "Yes, your lordship, the summer of your accident."

"The summer I spent laid up in hospital and then at Crofthill, held prisoner by my father," Andrew cheerlessly recalled.

His choice of words distressed the old man. "It pains me to hear you speak of it that way, of him that way."

The tiniest crack was audible in his voice when Andrew responded, "I'm sorry if it upsets you, but I'm speaking from the heart, Ambrose. I've not spoken of it for many years but something's happened; like it or not, it's got to be brought out, and I must know the truth. Do you understand? Can you help me?"

Ambrose suddenly looked worried. "May I inquire what that something is?"

He sighed now. "That girl, the American I was so fond of—I've just seen her. It's raised so many questions, and I must have answers. I need answers."

With some effort, Ambrose sat a little straighter on the couch, cursing his infirmity, wishing he could face the young earl with more strength. "I understand, your lordship," he finally said, "and I believe I can help you." He reached to tinkle the small bell that was always near him, then awaited his wife.

Sarah was there without delay. "Would you be wanting your tea now?"

Ambrose shook his head. "Sarah, my dear, would you hold off on the tea a bit? I'd rather you bring me the rosewood chest. You know the one."

She seemed surprised and stared at her husband for a moment. "Whatever you wish, dearest."

As she left them and went upstairs, Andrew affected a look of puzzlement. "What's in the chest?"

"What you've come here for," Ambrose answered plainly, straightforwardly.

Andrew felt as though he'd had the wind knocked out of him, and he formed the words with difficulty: "My letters?"

"Yours and hers," Ambrose answered, nodding slightly. "Yours, never posted—hers, never opened."

He'd said that so easily, so factually, and yet it seemed unreal. "You've kept them all these years?" he questioned, his puzzlement giving way to bewilderment.

"It's the one act of disobedience I ever committed toward your father," he said. The pained confusion he saw in Andrew was so like what he'd witnessed then, that all the traumatic memories from that time came crashing back. "He wanted them intercepted and burned, but I didn't have the heart," he explained. "You see, I was the one you'd ask about the post. I was the one who'd see your face—your crushing disappointment when I'd tell you there was nothing." The vivid recollection brought tears to his eyes. "It was the one time I ever wished I'd done something other than serve him. That summer I wished I'd been a shopkeeper."

In spite of what the old man just admitted, it still seemed implausible. "Good God, Ambrose, I hadn't thought! When I came here, I only thought that you might know what happened to them!"

It was in that moment that Sarah returned with the chest. Ambrose's hands trembled when he reached for it, and he held it in his lap while he waited for his wife to leave them again. Its presence in the room immediately affected Andrew, and he could not take his eyes from it. "How could you, Ambrose?"

"As hard as it was to watch you suffer," he somehow found the courage to respond, "in truth I must say I did share your father's concerns. You appeared perfectly willing to abandon your duty for her, sir."

That reference to his duty was so reminiscent of his father that he was immediately incensed by it. "Curse my bloody duty," he declared. "Damn it to hell!"

Ambrose lowered his chin and shook his head despairingly. "You can't mean that, my lord."

His pulse pounding in his ears, he railed, "I swear by God I do! I was young and in love, for the first time in my life, and my damned, bloody duty kept me from it, from love, from something I needed more than anything else on this earth!" Thinking of it now, he was revisited by the agony, the pain that grew with each passing day, every disappointing visit from the postman. "I didn't care who she was," he said, anguish now blunting the sharpness of his anger, "or what loving her would do to me. I only wanted to go to her, to be with her that summer."

"Your father knew that, sir—exactly. We spoke many times about the matter." For Ambrose, Andrew had ceased to be the grown man the world knew him as today. In the last few moments, he'd regressed to that grievously injured twenty-one-year-old, who, when he was told there was no letter today, would turn his head to the window and stare out at the drive, praying to see an old Norton motorcycle making its way to the house. Compassion for that young, broken man compelled him to say, "After the accident, your father did consider finding her and bringing her to you. He thought that he might keep control of things that way, and that seeing her out of her element, at Crofthill, you'd eventually realize that the match would never work."

As insane as it was, he felt an instant's hope over something that was long ago done and impossible to change. "And why didn't he do that? By God, I wish he'd done that!"

"He thought it too risky," Ambrose quickly explained. "He told me he'd never seen anyone so much in love as you. He called it dangerous love, deadly love. It frightened him."

"It was deadly," Andrew knew absolutely. "It was killing me to be kept from her!"

"I beg you to forgive me for my part in this. I beg you for your forgiveness," Ambrose pleaded.

His sigh was monumental. "I know you acted out of loyalty to my father," he told the frail old man, reminding himself that he was not the villain in this. But even as he said this, his head began to throb with a peculiar pain that was unlike any he'd ever experienced, a pain fueled by the outrage he'd held just below the boiling point for years and for which there was no venting. For the man who'd done this to him, whose willful premeditation had changed the course of his life, lay beyond his reach in the cold, irreproachable grave. He was rubbing at his throbbing forehead, trying hard to quell his growing frustration, when something occurred to him that he had to know. "Did Mother know? Was she party to this?"

"She only knew what your father told her," he readily recalled, "that you were infatuated with an American who was after your wealth. He painted her as responsible for everything that had happened: the fight in the pub, your failing the term, the accident itself. He told her that it was all the girl's fault. He kept her ladyship from interfering that way," he said, all the while thinking—please don't let him ask me about Janet. Please don't let him wonder if she was involved. Because if he knew the truth . . .

The claim that Annie was a gold digger was utterly ludicrous. "After my wealth! She didn't even know who I was, Ambrose. I never told her! She loved me thinking that I was the son of a sheep farmer!"

He was genuinely upset to learn this. "Is that so, sir? I didn't know."

"Father knew that I'd kept my identity hidden at university," he reminded him. "He and grandfather even helped with that!"

"Oh yes, I do recall that now."

Mercifully, the pain in his head was easing, so to distract himself from it, Andrew stood and walked to the window. He remained there for several long moments, staring out at the Irish sea, his back to Ambrose. When he turned around again, his face was pale, his brow deeply furrowed. "Yesterday," he said quietly, "my two youngest, Catherine and Malcolm, were in a car crash with their nanny—head-on around a curve. God, but it brought back memories, and God, it frightened me. I was in Oxford when it happened, and I couldn't get to them fast enough. Cathy was fine, but Malcolm suffered a head injury, and he needed sutures."

"I didn't know, your lordship. I'm so terribly sorry. It must have been dreadful for you," he realized. "Will he be all right?"

He was calmer now but more forlorn. "He'll have a scar but close to the hairline. It won't be visible like mine are."

He understood now why things were churning so inside of him. A profound sadness overcame the old man, as he told Andrew, "You carry scars much deeper than those on your face." He glanced downward at the box, still resting on his lap, then moved it forward a little, toward Andrew. "Before I give the letters to you," he said soberly, "I feel compelled to add one more thing if you'll allow me the liberty. I could have given them to you after your father died, but I thought better of it, you see. I worried what it would do to you, to your memory of him. I knew, though, that when the day came and you asked about them, the only right thing would be to turn them over to you. I did know that."

It seemed indelicate, but Andrew asked anyway, "And if you'd died before then, what then Ambrose?"

"I don't know," he answered honestly. "I suppose Sarah would have given them to you. I couldn't decide, you see, if I would be doing you harm or good by turning them over. It's so very difficult to know."

Once again, Andrew fixed his eyes on the box.

"I don't know what's in them, of course," he went on to say, "but it's bound to be painful to read them now, after all this time, knowing there's no going back."

The very idea that Annie's letters were within his reach left Andrew so overcome by emotion that it was difficult to think. "She told me she wrote and I called her a liar," he murmured. "I said there were never any letters, but how could I have possibly imagined it? I would never have believed him so cold-blooded. It's inconceivable that a father would do that to his son."

"Forgive me, sir, please, for my part in it," a wearied Ambrose said.

He was so obviously remorseful that Andrew couldn't carry on being angry. "I do, Ambrose, I forgive you. I'm grateful to you for not having burned them. It's evidence of your compassion." He tried to smile but gave the effort up quickly. "But I must know, did my father ever show so much as an ounce of compassion toward me in my suffering?"

His pleading, confused face once again reminded Ambrose of his youthful self, of the boy who'd returned from university so in love, so determined to fulfill that love, yet so mercilessly thwarted by his father. He readily pictured him on the morning of the accident, savagely battering his father's safe, then plotting his escape even as he was losing hope.

"Oh, my young earl, my young master, that you should ask that!" His voice quavered with sentiment. "Do you recall coming home to Crofthill after the car crash?"

"Somewhat," he muttered.

"You were miserable at hospital," he reminded him. "You wanted to be home, so your father went against doctor's advice and brought you to Crofthill. You were still in tremendous pain, with your internal injuries and your broken leg, but he had a private doctor attend you every day, and he hired two excellent nurses to take care of you. You needed constant supervision and plenty of morphine at that time, you see."

He grimaced to say, "That, I remember."

Ambrose sighed. "On your first night home, we were late in your father's library, he and I, when we heard you scream. Your father ran to you and I followed. We found you with your nurses. They were only turning you to wash your back, but the pain was excruciating for you." He shook his head in despair. "They gave you more morphine and your father stayed to comfort you. I left him with you and in the morning I found him still at your side, asleep in a chair, both of his hands clutching yours. When I awakened him, I realized he'd been crying, his eyes were that swollen, you see." He looked off into the distance as though he were hearing something from far away. "Ambrose, he said to me, I've been praying more earnestly than I've ever prayed in my life, pleading with God to take my son's pain away."

That image struck Andrew, and he softened his voice. "I don't recall him staying with me."

"Oh he did, many a time, many a night, for you were inconsolable and so long recovering." His memory was sparked by another recollection. "There was another time, you'd developed an infection and were delirious with fever. Your father came to me after spending the night with you. He said you'd been crying out her name, calling for her, asking her not to leave you. He told me that with tears in his eyes and then he asked me, 'Ambrose, do you think I've done the right thing?' I worried about that, too, but I answered that only time would tell."

It sickened him to think of himself that way, so injured and desperate, and so in need of Annie. "Time." Andrew spat the word as though it were some vile curse.

"Time," Ambrose said softly, as though he revered it.

They sat in silence together, as both men stared at the box.

After some moments, Ambrose told him, "God forgive me if it's not the right thing to say, but there may never be another opportunity for us to speak."

Taking his seat again, Andrew responded. "Go ahead, Ambrose. There's no use holding anything back now."

He spoke slowly. "The last Christmas your father was with us, may God rest his soul, he was watching you with your children, and he spoke of the matter for the first time in many, many years."

Andrew braced himself for more anguish. "What did he say?"

"He was so pleased with you, with all you'd accomplished. He was that proud of you, my lord. He said what a good father you were—much better than he'd ever been to you. He saw how well young Donald took to his role, how lovely the young ladies were, what a fine young man Duncan was growing to be, and he was excited that the viscountess was expecting again. But in spite of all that, he said something odd to me, something I didn't expect him to say." Ambrose adjusted his position on the couch so that he might breathe a little easier. "He said that time had told, and I didn't know what he was referring to at first."

"What had it told?" he asked, then held his breath.

"It told him that he had robbed you of something very precious—those were his words," he recalled, "and your father said he regretted what he'd done. I asked why he felt that way now, after everything, and he said it was because he'd never seen it again in you—that passion that you'd shown for her—and it broke his heart to realize that he'd been the cause of your losing it. Despite your successes, your wonderful family, your apparent contentment—he understood that something very important had been taken from you, something irrecoverable, and he wished with all his heart that it had not had to be so."

Andrew looked off into space, into the past, trying to conjure his father's face as it had been that last Christmas. "Why did he never say those things to me?" he wondered aloud.

"I imagine for the same reason that I worry about you having these letters," he answered, looking increasingly thoughtful. "And now that you've seen her again, I believe that makes my concern even more valid." He held the box out for him to take, and as it passed from his hands, he added, "They belong to you, they're yours to do with as you please, but for your own sake and for the sake of your family, give yourself time to decide if you should read them. Whatever you learn from them, it may upset many things. It may be very difficult for you afterward."

As he reached for the chest, Andrew's hands shook more violently than the old man's. He stared at it in disbelief, his thoughts chasing after one another. After all this time, to possess the letters that I'd longed so fervently for, that I had prayed for, bargained with God for, why now? Why not then— he asked himself—when it would have meant everything to me, when it would have changed the course of my life?

He shuddered with this realization, but at the same time he experienced a rush of excitement—anticipation tinged with fear—when the awareness came, when he understood that the simple wooden chest now in his grasp not only held his past, but possibly, also his future.

Chapter 36

St. Andrews, May 1994

I often think about what is left, when it's all done, when everything has been said, everything tried, and time has run out. It seems very little considering, what with all the effort, the expended heart, the worn out soul.

I have seen him again and now I know what remains. I felt it cry out from under the wreckage as it rekindled hope, like a nearly extinct ember roused by a warm wind. It burns in me still, on invisible fuel, without reason, beyond belief and in spite of truth—its flames hot and bright and reaching—as though Prometheus himself had breathed them into me.

The team at Lynch and Collings went directly into a planning and strategy session after Lord Kilmartin left, and as difficult as it was to recover herself, Annie had to participate and contribute. When the call came from his secretary that Andrew's children were fine, she breathed a sigh of relief so audible that everyone at the conference table turned to look at her.

The meeting seemed endless although it only lasted two hours, and as soon as they wrapped up, she went into the office she was using to phone Mike.

She reached his secretary. "Vicky, it's Annie. How are you?"

"Annie, hi! Everything's fine, but we're so busy. And you? How's everything in England? How's the consulting?"

"That's all going well," she answered. "The client is happy and we're moving ahead."

After responding, "That's great," she went quiet. Normally, she would have asked if she'd like to be put through to her husband, but she didn't.

Annie waited for it, and when it didn't come, she asked, "Is Mike there?"

She sounded a tad uncomfortable when she responded, "He is, but he's with the RJR people."

In a slightly dejected tone, she said, "Oh, I guess it's impossible to disturb him, then."

Vicky was relieved that Annie wasn't forcing the issue. "Better not, unless it's an emergency."

She didn't want to risk annoying him, so she told her, "No, it's not an emergency. I just need to speak with him, and I've left messages but he hasn't gotten back to me."

Vicky knew that, after all, she was the one taking his messages and returning his calls. "He's been running here and there for depositions," she explained awkwardly, "and this appeal they're working on has everyone stretched to the limit. People around here barely have time to eat, let alone sleep or do anything else."

"I'll try him at home, then," she told her. It would be difficult because of the late hour for her, but she was determined to reach him. "What time is he leaving in the evening?"

When she realized Annie didn't know, she cringed. "He hasn't been going home lately. He's, ah, he's been staying at the Bellevue."

She'd assumed he was home with Marc, so that came as a total shock. "The Bellevue?"

"That's right," she answered, then reminded her, "he's done that before when things heat up like this." With the long drive home, it was sometimes the most practical thing to do.

"Yeah," Annie said, "but I'm surprised neither Lucy nor Marc said anything to me."

Vicky had heard the rumors, but when they started up in the coffee room, she usually walked away. She wished she could do that now, and she handled it by changing the subject. "Your housekeeper is wonderful with your son. I talk to her twice a day, and all seems fine on the home front," she assured her.

Annie sighed. "When you tell Mike I called, please ask him to make an effort to get back to me. I really need to speak with him."

"I will," she answered, feeling rather guilty now. Her attention was drawn to the flashing lights on her telephone. "I've got four calls on hold, so let me get going, Annie. You take care, and good luck with your project."

"Thanks, Vicky."

Annie went directly to John's office after she hung up. She found him standing at his conference table, looking over some papers.

She wasted no time in getting to the point. "Do you mind if I go back to St. Andrews day after tomorrow? We should be pretty set with things by then."

"No," he answered, "not if that's what you want. I told you when I hired you that you could come and go as you pleased."

"But that was before," she frowned, "before I knew about the plot with Andrew. I've been wondering now if all bets aren't off."

"Not as far as I'm concerned," he told her. "Sit down, will you?" He motioned her toward a chair and closed his office door, then sat behind his desk. Once he was in his chair, he opened a desk drawer and removed a bottle of Oban single malt. He poured two fingers into a glass and handed it to her. "Yes, I did conspire with him to bring you here, but I was never unhappy about it, and now that we've been working together I'm actually very pleased about it. And as I said before, no matter what happens with him, I want you here with me."

She didn't really want the drink, but she took it nonetheless, then answered without conviction, "I guess that's comforting."

He poured himself a glass and sipped at it. "Can I ask what you two were talking about when I interrupted?"

He, like everyone else, got the impression that Andrew was set to sack her.

She drank some of the Scotch, then sighed, "We were just beginning to break through a barrier."

He was relieved to hear that, but he was also confused by her lack of enthusiasm. "Well, that's good, isn't it?"

"I thought so," she answered, "but I watched his face, John—when he got the phone call. He's so committed to his family, to his life, it may not be a good thing at all."

"But what's that commitment got to do with you?" he questioned. "You're just trying to get over something that's been painful for both of you. I should think it'll make both your lives better if you can do that."

"I don't know about that." She shook her head slightly. "It might actually be easier for everyone if he were to go on hating me."

He regarded her with curiosity. "Why do you think that?"

She considered her response, then decided it best to simply say, "Never mind, John."

He scrutinized her face until he saw something there, then he took in a short breath. "Oh, I understand." He smiled. "It's still there, isn't it?"

She would not answer that, but she pointedly told him, "I need to go home."

"Go ahead," he responded. "You can be in St. Andrews tomorrow night."

"No," she said, shaking her head, "to the States, I mean. I need to see my husband."

That surprised him. "Well, if you want to do that, I think you should."

She didn't owe John an explanation, she knew, but she felt a sudden need to voice her thoughts. "I walked out on things," she told him. "I left so much unsaid, so much unsettled, and seeing Andrew again, it's just added to the confusion. I need very much to clear things up, to settle things." She stopped now, because she worried that she was revealing too much.

"But would you come back, do you think, afterward?"

"I don't know," she answered honestly.

"I see." He rose from his chair and walked to where she sat, then put a hand on her shoulder. "I'm very sorry about this morning. I hope what I did—well, I'd really like to go on working with you."

That little blip was nothing compared to the bomb blast she'd been through with Andrew, so she responded, "Me, too. Going home doesn't mean I'm walking out on you."

He smiled his relief. "Good. Well, go on then, and don't worry about this end of things. We'll hold them up without you, if need be. It's not as though there aren't telephones and fax machines and the Concorde. You do whatever it is you need to, all right?"

She nodded. "Thanks, John. I appreciate that." Then she took another sip of Scotch, Andrew's Scotch. She looked into the glass and smiled slightly when she realized how much she was enjoying the taste.

* * *

Andrew bid farewell to Ambrose and left the Isle of Aaran as he'd arrived, by helicopter, speeding north over Loch Fyne to Lochgilphead, then overflying the Crinan canal and Dunadd Fort, to set down on the ancient estate of the Earls of Kilmartin. He left in the same manner as he'd arrived, but the journey was not the same. The twenty-fourth earl was encumbered with a small, rosewood box, not particularly fine in its style and not at all heavy to carry. Nonetheless, it weighed him down in such a way that he felt it made the helicopter strain to carry it.

When they'd touched down on the helipad, Andrew waved off the footman who'd been sent to fetch him and walked the couple of hundred yards distance to the family cemetery. He went directly to the twenty-third earl's grave site and placed the chest alongside the monument.

It had been forty-eight hours since he'd slept or eaten much, and his mind was light in the way of sense and cognition. He had no anchoring thoughts to focus him, no concrete perceptions to ground him, nothing to stop the flights of fancy and memory in his head. He sat on the marble bench at the foot of his father's grave and watched them both, the headstone and the box. He watched them intently, with unblinking eyes, through a troubled heart and an unfettered mind. He watched until he began to think that the chest itself was a tiny coffin. Or was it a cradle? It was hard to tell. It seemed to keep changing—unearthed, exposed, not at all where it should be, better off buried and unseen—no, better brought to the nursery and cared for. He was floating from thought to thought, drifting through the past—hearing his father's voice argue with him, hearing himself ask Ambrose if the post had arrived, remembering the relentless pain, the unending nights, the impossible longing for her—when Nigel touched him on the shoulder.

"Your lordship, sorry to disturb. Her ladyship sent me for you." When he saw the expression on Andrew's face, he asked, "Are you all right, sir?"

When Andrew looked at his secretary, he didn't seem to recognize him.

Nigel was sincerely concerned. "Is there anything I can do?"

"I've come from seeing Ambrose," he muttered, returning his gaze to his father's monument.

Glancing at the rosewood chest, he asked, "May I inquire as to his health?"

"He's not well, and I'm afraid I've taxed him more than I should have."

"Surely he enjoyed seeing you, sir," Nigel ventured.

"It's difficult to say," Andrew responded, still with his eyes on the monument. "I asked him some hard questions about things I needed to know—and I needed to know now, before it was too late," he defended. "I had no other choice."

"I'm afraid I don't understand, your lordship."

"No, no you wouldn't," he recognized. "Please leave me. Tell my wife I'll be in soon."

"She's asked me to remind you about this evening. You're to leave in two hours, sir."

"I'll be in," he answered in a strangely flat voice.

"Shall I take the box in for you?" Nigel asked, as he moved toward the small chest.

The response was immediate and startling. "No, leave it. It's mine!" he shouted, sounding like a child whose possession was threatened by another.

Nigel was embarrassed for him, and now even more concerned. "I hadn't meant—I'm terribly sorry, your lordship. Do forgive the intrusion." He turned on his heels and walked quickly toward the castle.

His retreat was witnessed by the Countess of Kilmartin, who had sent Nigel to her husband, then watched from her bedroom window.

After a time Andrew went into his library and opened the safe that had held the secrets of the Kilmartin earls for 200 years. The rosewood chest took its place there, alongside a small package wrapped in aged, brown paper and tied with string.

* * *

As they disembarked in Glasgow, Andrew saw the copilot hand their bags to the chauffeur.

"Why the luggage?" he wondered.

"We'll be staying in town," Janet informed her husband, as he helped her into the Rolls.

"Must we?"

"Yes, we must," she answered, her tone somewhat scolding. "We're invited to a breakfast the Princess of Wales is hosting for the National AIDS Trust, don't you remember? I say, Andrew, what on earth is bothering you? You're awfully out of sorts."

"My meeting with Ambrose. It was very upsetting," he admitted.

"We'll have to discuss it later," she told him, knowing this was not the time to get into something serious. "Do buck up, dearest, this is supposed to be an enjoyable evening."

"I'm sorry," he told her, then tried to smile. "I'll be better after a couple of drinks."

"I do hope the damned paparazzi aren't all over everyone," she commented. "It would be nice for once to have a pleasant, civilized evening without their insinuating presence. It's all this ridiculous fascination with Diana and Charles and the state of their marriage—that's what causes it," she observed. "I do think she's made an awful mess of things."

"Why do you blame her?" he wondered. It was, after all, the public disclosure of his infidelity that had broken up their marriage.

"She's very immature," she said, "going on about love and all that rubbish about his betrayal."

He was not surprised by her attitude; after all, she had looked the other way in their marriage for nearly twenty years. Still, he wanted to know, "Doesn't love have a place in marriage?"

"Of course, it does. What a silly thing to ask!" she scoffed. "But it's not everything and it doesn't last, or at least, it changes. She has her lovely boys, her charity work. She should content herself with those things. Those are the things that last."

Although he was not shocked by them, he found her comments tonight unexpectedly distressing. "Is that what you've done? Settled for those things?"

"We're talking about Diana," she reminded him, "but since you've asked, yes, that's what I've done, and I don't regret it."

When he looked at her, it seemed as though he was seeing her for the first time in a long while. It afforded a certain detachment and allowed him to ask a question that had plagued him throughout the years. "Why did you marry me, Janet?"

She frowned. "Do keep your voice down. The driver might hear you."

The privacy screen was in place, so he was unconcerned. "He can't hear us. Answer me—tell me why."

"For the same reason that you married me," she whispered, "because it was what our families wanted."

"But we weren't in love," he reminded her. "Didn't that matter to you?"

Her expression conveyed her irritation. "Your memory is somewhat faulty, Andrew. I was in love with you. It was you who wasn't in love—well, not with me, anyway." She looked away from him and out the window.

"I find it hard to believe that you really loved me. How could you after what I'd told you?"

She was beginning to lose patience with him, and she raised her voice to respond, "Really, I don't know how you can ask that question! Who has stayed by your side and supported you through thick and thin, through all your wanderings—not to mention giving birth to your five children? It took more than determination to do those things, Andrew, it took love. Yes, I loved you, even when I knew that when you made love to me it wasn't me in your mind or your heart." That had not been easy to say, and it took something out of her.

"That's a very sad commentary on our marriage," he declared, exhaling a sigh.

She recovered herself quickly. "But we got past all of that. We moved beyond it and became good friends, and we've even become better lovers over the years, haven't we?"

"Yes, that's true," he admitted. "But it troubles me when I think that I've kept you from possibly finding something more wonderful and fulfilling for yourself."

"Don't be silly. You've not kept me from anything!" she insisted. "I'm here because I want to be—with you, by your side, raising our children, and it's my choice." She turned to face him directly. "And I've no illusions about what might have been. Have you?"

With her pointed question, he decided to broach the subject, though in a tentative way. "Janet, there's something we need to talk about. It has to do with the reason I went to see Ambrose. I've got to think it through first, but then we must have a sit-down, and I'll tell you everything." He reached for her hand and squeezed it.

She'd been wondering when he would tell her—if he would tell her—and she experienced some relief now, knowing that he would. "Please don't fret over it, whatever it is," she told him. "We'll get past it, as we always have. Now, do cheer up. We're here and damn, if they aren't all over the place like flies on dung!"

As they pulled up to the entrance, the incessant winding and clicking of automatic cameras greeted them like muted applause.

It was supposed to be a ball, but these things never seemed like parties. First, there was the tedious receiving line. Andrew, as the highest-ranking lord in attendance, stood alongside the Princess of Wales. Then there was the dinner, an unadventurous menu complimented by equally dull conversation. Finally, there was the dancing, which didn't seem like dancing. It was more like everyone moving out to the floor for a bit of a stroll after a meal. Janet didn't care much for dancing, so Andrew was free to ask others, rather, obliged to ask others, politely going through the motions with the important wives, wives whose husbands were more interested in the bar than in them. He did dance twice with the princess that evening, one slow and one a little more lively. But Diana's days of whooping it up in public were over, and even though she always enjoyed the earl's company, she kept herself low key.

Breakfast the next morning was slightly more enjoyable. It was a much smaller gathering, only forty or so, and once again Andrew was seated next to the princess.

"How is that marvelous brood of yours?" she asked him.

"Well, thank you, all growing and happy and well."

"How old is the viscount? I've forgotten."

"Donald is just eighteen, and he'll be at St. Andrews come October."

"Wouldn't dare send him to university in England now, would we?" she teased.

"Well, he has put in his time at Eton—that's enough of that, don't you think?"

They laughed together, and the others at the table strained to hear what they found so amusing.

"Actually," Andrew said, growing more serious, "I would break with tradition and allow him to attend whatever university he chose, but St. Andrews was his choice."

"I've always liked that about you," she told him. "It's a very refreshing attitude you have. You attended St. Andrews, I believe."

"Yes, I did, and very happily."

"It's such a lovely place, isn't it?"

"Quite beautiful," he responded.

"I imagine it was more so when you were there," she ventured.

"Yes, it was smaller and more intimate, and a happy place to be. I have wonderful memories." When he remembered being there, he rarely thought of anything but Annie.

She smiled warmly. "I'm certain your son will make wonderful memories for himself, too."

"Yes, I'm certain he will."

A distinguished looking gentleman rose from his seat and approached them.

"Have you met Dr. Coupau?" Diana asked Andrew.

Andrew stood to greet him. "No, I've not had the pleasure."

"He's at the Pasteur Institute," she explained, "and one of the world's experts on HIV. Doctor, this is Andrew, Earl of Kilmartin."

"I'm honored, your lordship," he said, in heavily accented English.

"Lord Kilmartin's an extremely generous supporter of our cause," Diana informed him, "and also a very dear friend."

He bowed his head deferentially. "Then I'm doubly honored, sir. I do beg your pardon for interrupting your royal highness, but I'll be unable to stay for the morning. I'd like a word with you before I leave, if possible."

"Of course, would you excuse us, Andrew?"

The earl helped the princess with her chair.

Andrew kept an eye on Dr. Coupau, and when he saw him about to leave, he hurried over and pulled him aside.

In something of a whisper, he asked, "May I have one of your cards, doctor?"

He observed the look of concern on his face. "Yes, of course, your lordship."

"I might be in touch with you in a few days, if that's all right."

Dr. Coupau thought he understood. "I should be in Lyons for the next week or so. Is there something I can help you with now?"

"No, not now." He lowered his voice even more. "But there is someone I'm very concerned about, and I'd like to speak with you about her." Andrew handed the doctor one of his cards.

"I'll be available to you at any time," he responded. "Let me give you my home number." He scribbled it on the back of his card.

"Thank you, doctor."

"It's nothing, your lordship. I'll be expecting your call."

Chapter 37

Annie arrived in St. Andrews at about the same time that Andrew and his wife returned to Crinan Castle. She knew the milk would be sour and that she was out of coffee, so she made a brief stop at the supermarket before going home. She was in line at the checkout when she spotted a tabloid boasting a large cover photo of Andrew dancing with the Princess of Wales. The headline read "Di steps out with Earl of Scotch!" and it made her burst into laughter. She pointed to the paper and said to the woman near her, who thought she was standing next to a lunatic, "I'm sorry, it's just so funny!"

"Aye, 'tis that," the woman agreed. "The earl's very happily married and completely devoted to his family. Everyone in Scotland knows that."

With that comment, Annie checked her smile and answered soberly, "Yes, I'm sure he is."

She purchased her few things in silence, then went home to her empty cottage.

It was too quiet in the house, and her first thought was to invite Tom Keegan to dinner. She phoned the Russell Hotel, and the young woman at the desk hesitated when she asked for him.

"He's not here," she told Annie. "Ah, he checked out, I mean."

That didn't make sense. "Checked out? But where would he go? He lives there!"

"Ah, well, yes," she responded. "I don't know if I can say. Hold just a moment."

"This is the manager. Can I help you with something?"

"Yes, Gordon, this is Annie d'Inard. I'm a friend of Tom Keegan—you know me. I stayed there and I come to have dinner with him every so often."

"Yes, of course, Ms. d'Inard."

"The young lady said he checked out. Can you tell me where he went?"

"Mr. Keegan has gone to hospital," he informed her.

Her heart sank as she asked, "When?"

"Day before yesterday."

"Is he very ill?"

"I'm afraid so," he answered.

"What hospital?"

"The Fife Hospital in Craigtoun Park."

"Thank you for telling me," she said. "I'll go and see him right away."

Gordon responded, "Not at all. And please give him our best when you do. Tell him my daughter Judith misses him."

She knew where Craigtoun Park was. She'd driven past it many times, but she hadn't realized what is was until she turned onto the drive. Following the long, tree-lined lane, she realized that she was seeing the country house in which the Kate Kennedy Ball had been held. It was Mount Melville House, now converted to the Fife Hospital. When she walked into the entrance hall, her heartbeat slowed as she saw what had happened to the grand old house, as she saw that her memories had been stripped to their bare bones and painted white.

Tom was asleep and attached to a morphine drip. Annie sat in a chair next to his bed and watched him breathe shallow, crackling breaths, recognizing that even in his heavily sedated state, he fought for each one. It was ten minutes or more before he awakened and looked at her.

"It's kind of you to come," he whispered.

She lifted one of his yellow hands and stroked it. "What can I do to help you?"

"You're sweet, but there's nothing," he said. "I'm fine."

"My friend is working on trying to locate your son," she told him.

"Never mind about that. It's too late."

"Maybe not," she answered.

He tried to smile as he asked, "How'd it go in Oxford?"

"It went well—but, oh Tom, you'll never believe what happened! Do you feel up to listening? I don't want to tire you."

"Please do talk," he told her. "I love to hear your voice. It soothes me."

She pulled her chair closer. "The client, the earl—it's so hard to believe—but he's the one, Tom, my one, the young man from here. He's Andrew, from twenty-two years ago!"

The news seemed to perk him up. "No! How could that be?"

She tried to tone down her excitement. "It's incredible really. It was something he never told me—who he was. And it wasn't an accident that I came to work for him. He planned it with the director of the agency—you know, the man I also knew from before. Isn't it incredible? It's like some unbelievable plot in a bad novel!"

He attempted a laugh, but it came out as a gurgling cough. "What happened when you saw him?"

She'd been smiling, but she lost it now. "That part wasn't good. He was angry with me, but I don't want to get into that. Then the next day, after our presentation, he asked to speak to me alone and things got a little better. Oh, Tom, I can't tell you how good it was to see him again! I never dreamed!"

"That's a marvelous story," he said. "How'd you leave it?"

"Well, up in the air, actually," she answered. "Something happened and he had to leave immediately, but he said we'd talk again."

"Your face is different," he commented.

"Is it?"

"It's all lit up," he told her.

She sighed now. "It was so wonderful to see him—to be in the same room with someone I've carried around inside me but without hope of ever seeing again."

"Like my son."

The way he said that tore at her heart. "Oh, Tom! Let me go make a phone call and see if John's located him yet."

"No." He squeezed her hand. "Stay here with me. I don't want to be alone."

"But it'll only take five minutes. Look, John may have already found him but he can't reach me because I'm here."

"Stay with me," he insisted, "at least until I fall asleep again."

"OK, but let me stop talking so you can sleep."

He moved his head ever so slightly, trying to shake it. "No," he told her emphatically. "I want to hear your voice. All there's ever going to be after this is silence."

Those words deepened her heartache.

Tom didn't want to spend his remaining time in maudlin musings, so he said to her, "Tell me about the earl. He's a very famous, important man. I've drunk quite a lot of his Scotch."

As difficult as it was for her, she understood his need to forget. "Isn't it hard to comprehend? I mean, he was my boyfriend. I went to dances with him. He taught me to dance the reel!"

That amused him. "Did he?"

"The first time I ever danced a reel was with him. I'll never forget that as long as I live. We loved to dance together. We danced together right here in this very building. You didn't know that, did you?"

"No!"

"This was where they held the Kate Kennedy Ball," she explained, "before it was a hospital, of course. We danced all night, Tom, literally, all night, until the sun came up. And at sunrise we sat out on the lawn and talked. He shared things with me then, things he'd never told anyone. That's when I knew that I loved him, deeply, even hopelessly, more than I had anyone in my life." Those words came out so naturally, so easily, it surprised her. In a tender, melancholy tone, she added, "I would have done anything for him, gone anywhere to be with him then."

Tom coughed again, although he meant to laugh. "She's back," he said.

"Who's back, Tom?"

He waited until his breathing eased. "Your spirit," he finally told her, "that part of you that you've tried to keep under wraps all these years. I can hear her and I can see her. She's got your face all lit and bright."

"Uh oh, better run for cover!" Annie laughed.

"Rubbish," he said. "I like her."

"You know something?" she ventured. "I like her, too. I always have, even though she's gotten me into more than a little trouble."

"Ah, but life is trouble, isn't it?" he rejoined. "Only the dead have no trouble."

His statement blunted her joy, and she fidgeted as she asked, "Would you like some water?"

"Some water would be nice. Some Scotch would be better."

She held his glass and straw while he sipped. "Can you have Scotch?" she wondered.

"I don't know why not," he said. "That's not what's going to kill me."

That was sadly true. "Shall I get you some?" she offered.

"Later," he answered, "you can get me some of the earl's best stuff, but later. Just stay with me now."

"How about if I stop talking and let you drift off for a while?"

He was feeling the need for some sleep. "All right, you win, but only for a half hour or so. I don't want to sleep longer than that."

It was morning when she left, and the aromas of breakfast drifted along the white halls. Outside the dew glistened, like diamond dust someone had scattered on the lawn, while the birds performed in chorus, as full and resounding as a symphony. It was much like that morning in May so long ago when she'd seen the dawn there, with Andrew. That morning, too, had been heavy and bittersweet, and overladen with sorrow.

Slowly, solemnly, she walked to her car, then stood near it for many long minutes, gazing over the scene. But although she searched, she saw very little of what was near her, because a cacophony of voices filled her heart—the voices of the dead. They spoke of the countless dreams never reached, the prayers unanswered and hopes unfulfilled, the squandered and unrealized love that seemed to linger like a fog, enveloping the earth.

* * *

After he and his wife returned from Glasgow, Andrew spent what remained of the day with his children. The two oldest boys were home on a bank holiday, both of them now living away at Eton, so it was unusual for all of them to be together. He played tennis with his sons, then went riding with his daughters, who, like their mother, were both fine equestriennes. They shared a protracted family dinner, then sat together in an upstairs drawing room watching a Sean Connery film. Andrew carried Malcolm to his bed after he'd fallen asleep in his lap.

When the children had all gone to their rooms, Andrew retired to his private study. His wife went in search of him and found him sitting at his desk in the dark, his back turned to it, gazing into the gardens. The moon was nearly full, and it cast soft, gray shadows about the lawn that created the illusion of ghosts, hovering above them.

Before going in, Janet had stopped before a hallway mirror, smoothing the lines of her boyish hairstyle and pinching at her alabaster cheeks. Her habitually disinterested expression changed momentarily to one of dismay, when she realized that with age, her face was becoming more stern and angular, less soft and feminine. It was disheartening to be sure, for although she was never the kind of woman others would refer to as a beauty, twenty years ago—even ten—she had been considered pretty. But her dismay quickly passed, for she could no more change that about herself than she could the color of her eyes, which were a dull, grayish-blue that no man had ever seemed eager to lose himself in—not even her husband.

She announced herself by switching on a lamp. Andrew turned to face her with his smile—that tender, disarmingly simple movement of his mouth that always managed to weaken her resolve. Self-consciously, she returned it, then settled herself on the couch. After pulling at the edges of her sweater, she casually crossed her legs and asked, "Would you like to talk now about what happened with Ambrose?"

As he rose from his chair, his drooped shoulders and slow movements bespoke exhaustion. When he was sitting next to her, she caught a whiff of the aftershave he wore, and it heartened her somewhat, for it was one she'd chosen. He began by saying, "He told me something, Janet, about what my father did to keep me apart from the American girl. It was very upsetting to learn."

Her comment was dry and noncommittal. "The girl you were in love with when you married me."

"Yes," he answered.

"And does it make a difference to you, now," she wondered, "after all this time?"

"I'm afraid it does," he admitted.

"Why?"

His brow knitted. "Because he had no right to do what he did. It hurt me very much. It still hurts to think of it."

She knew well that there was more to it, that something else had happened, and in her anxiousness to have it over, she blurted out, "I've been waiting for you to tell me that you've seen her."

He held back while he overcame his surprise. "How did you know?"

"I heard you speak of her," she said flatly, "on the telephone, with the man who runs Lynch and Collings." She frowned. "I remember her name. How could I ever forget her name?"

Guilt forced him to look away. "I'm sorry, Janet," he muttered.

She would not beat around the bush with this. She wanted it out and dealt with. "You deliberately brought her here because you wanted to see her."

He may have lied to himself about it, but he would not lie to her. He answered simply, "I did."

"And now what? What happens now?"

He responded earnestly, "I don't know. I've yet to decide."

"Decide what?" she demanded, anger creeping into her tone. "Whether to go to her or not? Whether to leave me or not?"

He hadn't expected it and the question shocked him. "Leaving you has never even crossed my mind!" he protested.

She exhaled. "I see." She stood and walked to the drinks cabinet. Silence followed her, then the creak of the cabinet doors opening and closing, the Scotch pouring into the crystal glass. She drank some of it before asking her husband, "Would you like one?"

He looked up but was having trouble meeting her eyes. "No, thank you," he said.

She stared at him, wondering what he would say next if she said nothing. She let as much time pass as she could bear before asking, "And what am I to do while you go about deciding?"

He searched himself but could find only one response. "Whatever it is you need to do."

"Whatever it is I've always done," she quipped, "when you've been with other women—while I've waited for you to tire of them and come back to me. Is that what you mean?"

Her remark pierced him with shame and regret, and yet he mustered the courage to tell her, "That's not what I meant."

"Why?" she demanded to know.

He had to say it. "Because, this is different. This is very different."

She took a long drink, keeping her eyes on her husband. It came into her mind at that moment that in a few short months, they would be celebrating their twentieth wedding anniversary. Twenty years, she marveled, all the while living with the specter of this woman. What I wouldn't give to be able chase her ghost, to put it to rest once and for all.

Since his conversation with Ambrose, Andrew had thought of little else, trying to decide, trying to know what it was he should do, if anything. The conclusion he had finally reached did not leave him feeling easy. He braced himself now to say the words he knew he must. "I need to see her again, and we need to talk. I have to tell her about the accident and what my father did afterward so she understands what happened. I need to say these things, and I need to hear what she has to say to me. I'm awfully, horribly sorry. I can't tell you that enough, but I have no other choice than to follow my heart in this. And that's what it is I'm doing, Janet, I'm following my heart."

She experienced a sudden, powerful urge to be near him. "It's no good talking across the room like this," she said, as she made her way back to the couch. As she sat, she laid a hand on his thigh, then whispered, "My insides feel like jelly, Andrew."

He didn't see this side of her often, but when she softened and allowed herself to be vulnerable, it reminded him of why he loved her. "God, I hate that I'm doing this to you," he told her. "I wish with all my heart that there were some other way. But this is too important to be kept from you. I love and respect you too much to keep you in the dark about this."

Pouting slightly, she questioned, "Do you, Andrew, do you really love me?"

He reached for the hand that caressed his thigh and brought it to his lips. He delivered a tender kiss to the open palm of it, then answered, "You know I do, Janet. You've been so much to me, such a good mother to the children, such a supportive wife."

She knew the rest of what he would say. It was the way he always spoke of her, of his feelings for her. "Stop," she told him, as she stiffened and moved away slightly. "Please, don't say any more."

He seemed puzzled. "Why?"

She answered scornfully, "Because that's not what I want to hear."

"I'm sorry," he said, although he was still bewildered.

Standing now, she raised her voice. "And don't say that. It's ridiculous to say that!"

"I don't know what else to say to you."

The anger had returned, and with it the Janet that Andrew most often dealt with. "Then don't say anything!" she ordered. "Just do what you have to, but don't say any more to me about it."

Rising from the couch, he replied, "I can't carry on behind your back with this. It's wrong to do that."

"Even if I want you to?" she snapped.

In an effort to calm her, he gently touched her arms, then coaxed her into sitting with him again. "Janet, listen to me," he implored, his eyes searching hers, "and try not to be angry. I want you to understand. I feel as though I've gone back in time, as if I'm being forced to revisit my past, and I have little if any control over it. It's happening because there was so much left unsettled, and now that I know it wasn't her fault, that she didn't just abandon me, I feel compelled to try to resolve things. At the very least, I need to get everything out in the open, once and for all, so I can put it to rest and get on with my life."

Janet could not keep her eyes with his, and she listened to her husband with a distracted mind, remembering that past and recalling her part in it, praying that any knowledge of her role would stay buried with the man who had convinced her to play it. While she thought of this, her eyes focused on the pattern in the Oriental rug under her feet. She traced the lines of it, following them until they led into other lines, only half aware of what was happening to her.

When she didn't respond to him, Andrew pleaded, "I need your help, Janet, because I swear, with God as my witness, I'm every bit as mixed-up and hurt now as I was then." The muscles in his neck twisted in spasm, and he reached to rub them.

Janet's eyes stayed focused on the floor. Something about the pattern in the rug, the meticulous weaving, the orderly motif, the way each individual design complemented the other—it all made perfect sense to her. It was like her life, all carefully planned, patiently executed, neat and organized and beautiful. It was like her life, but it was not like her husband's. His life had always been ruled by his heart, and order and design had no part in the running of it.

It dawned on her suddenly that there was only one way to rid herself of the ghost that had haunted her marriage. It was what he'd said, the words he used—*every bit as mixed-up and hurt now as I was then.* It was a risk to be sure, but she would take that risk because she had to, because it was her best chance of holding onto him. Let him go to her, she told herself. She's hurt him before, and chances are she'll do it again. And when she does, he'll come back to me, and both of us will finally be rid of her.

When she answered, "I will help you," she lifted her eyes to meet his. "I see very clearly now what it is you must do. You must do as you said, follow your heart, because you were never able to do that before. You were prevented from it." Her voice was calmer now. "That twenty-one-year-old is still in you. He's still hurt and angry and hungry to be with her, wanting what he could never have. Until you've satisfied him, until you've sorted things out for him, you can never be settled."

It was a complete change in attitude, and Andrew was astonished by it. Still, he wanted it to be real, so he believed. He reached to stroke her ginger hair.

His touch warmed her and gave her the courage to continue. "It's going to be difficult, but I can't see any other way. I can't hold you here and keep you from her. I won't become what your father was to you. I won't be your jailer."

As she said these things to him, his heart began to beat faster. "Can you let me go to her when you know that I can't make promises to you—that I can't say what will happen if I do?"

"I have no other choice," she replied, as though the logic was perfectly obvious. "You asked me if I loved you when we married. I told you I did. But it's nothing at all like what I feel for you now, after all these years together, after five children, the tragedy with your father, and everything else we've been through. I could never keep you from doing this, Andrew, because the truth is, I love you too much to stop you."

He reproached himself for the anguish he'd caused her. "I'm not worthy of your love," he told her. "I never have been. How can you love someone who hurts you so much?"

She regarded her husband with a look of amazement. "And how can you ask me that question? The answer should be very evident to you, Andrew, because no matter the pain she's caused you, you still love her, don't you?"

He sat alone in the moonlight on one of the terraces under the clear Argyll sky. The household was asleep, and Andrew imagined each of his children as they were in their beds, sweet faces half covered with comforters, dreams animating their repose. He pictured his wife alone in her bed, and his heart ached for her. But he could not go to her, not, at least, until he had seen this thing out, until he had done whatever it was he would do—exorcise the demon or embrace it—until he could return to reason and to his life again. He filled his lungs with the night air, sharp and cold and fortifying. Then he went into his library and opened the safe.

He removed the small bundle wrapped in brown paper and untied the decaying string for the first time in nearly twenty years. He touched the worn gardening gloves and took the barrette into his hand. He held it there, palm open for a moment, then closed his fingers around it and murmured the words—dear God, help me to do the right thing—before setting it aside. Then he reached for the rosewood box.

The phone awakened Lena and she was startled at first, but she recognized the voice immediately. "Is something wrong?" she asked.

"No, Lena, forgive me for ringing at this hour. Is John there?"

"Yes, of course, just a minute."

John propped himself up in the bed and rubbed his eyes before taking the telephone.

"Where is she, John?"

"Annie, your lordship?"

"Please don't do that. Please call me Andrew," he insisted, almost angrily. "Is she there?"

"No, she's gone back to St. Andrews. Do you want the number?"

"Yes, and the address; do you have that?"

"I believe I do. Hold a moment, I need to go to my study."

John was back on the telephone within a couple of minutes. "I have it. Uh, I said she's in St. Andrews. I think she's still there. She said something to me about going back to America."

Andrew raised his voice. "Back to America?"

"Yes, I don't know when, though. I don't imagine she could have made arrangements to leave this quickly. She only returned to Scotland yesterday."

He heaved a sigh of relief. "Thank you, John. Make my apologies to Lena, will you?"

"That was odd," Lena commented, when John returned to their bed.

"It was that," he answered, shaking his head.

"I don't imagine he said what was so important it couldn't wait until morning."

"No. He was obviously very anxious to get in touch with her, but I couldn't tell what was behind it, whether it was anger or what. He did sound that odd."

"Do you think we should ring her up to warn her?"

John shook his head adamantly. "No, I don't. I've been too much in this thing from the start, and this time, I think I should stay bloody well out of it."

From the look on Lena's face, he could tell she agreed.

Andrew crept into Malcolm's room and kissed his youngest son's forehead as he slept. Then he went to the carriage house and started up his Aston Martin. In a very short time he was on the A-83 headed east, toward the rising sun and the Kingdom of Fife.

Chapter 38

The drive from Kilmartin to St. Andrews afforded Andrew plenty of time: time to remember the betrayal, the anger, the loss, and even the longing. The sun rose brilliantly, triumphantly, cruelly across his path, making it impossible to see anything else at times. He cursed its authority. He drove the powerful sports car dangerously fast at times, unconcerned about consequences, as full of emotion and confusion as he had been twenty-two years earlier. He seemed to be traveling back in time as the miles ticked away, as he left behind his sane and predictable life in Argyll, headed for the ruins and uncertainty of St. Andrews.

When Annie returned to her cottage from the bedside of Tom Keegan, it was solidly morning. It was the middle of the night in Philadelphia and she was well aware that she would awaken him, but she had to speak with her husband.

The switchboard at the Hotel Bellevue connected her immediately. Mike answered the phone in that husky, sleepy voice she'd always loved.

"Yes, hello," he mumbled.

"It's me," she said. "I'm sorry to wake you, but I need to talk."

He cleared his throat before asking, "Is there a problem? Are you all right?"

She could tell that he was sitting up in bed, and she could hear the rustle of the sheets. "I'm all right. It's just so long since we've talked, and I needed to hear your voice."

He was clearly worried, as he asked, "Has something happened?"

"Well, yes. Do you remember me telling you about Tom Keegan?"

"Uh, yeah, I think so, the man with the lung cancer?"

She sighed. "I got back from Oxford yesterday and learned that he was in the hospital. He was very ill, so I went to see him right away." She paused and listened as she became aware of a considerable amount of background noise, much more than there should have been.

He seemed nervous. "He's in the hospital? I'm sorry. How's he doing?"

She couldn't respond just now; she continued to listen, but her heart began to beat faster and stronger, making it more difficult to interpret the sounds. She thought she heard a door close.

"Is he all right?" he asked. "Are you there, Annie?"

It came upon her swiftly, like an unanticipated blow to the abdomen, and the impact of it made the words jump right out. "You're not alone, are you?"

Now the line was very quiet. A dreadful, malignant silence followed before she broke it. "I'm sorry to have disturbed you. I didn't think you'd have company."

Her voice trailed off, and Mike couldn't make out her last couple of words. He held his breath for a few seconds before he answered, "I won't lie to you."

"No, don't, please don't," she implored.

He exhaled abruptly. "She's gone into the bathroom. She realized it was you."

A wave of nausea washed through her. "I see," she said.

"We can talk privately now," he added.

She didn't answer.

He couldn't think what to say next, so he asked, "What were you telling me about your friend?"

She replied, "It's not important."

"Of course it is. Why else would you call now?"

The air around her was growing heavy, and it was difficult to breathe. "We'll talk another time. I shouldn't have called."

"It's my fault for not getting back to you," he said. "I should have taken the initiative on this thing. I shouldn't have let it happen like this."

She felt like she was in a dream and falling, falling through that endless dream tunnel. She had to get hold of herself and stop the fall.

"You don't owe me anything," she heard herself respond. "No explanations, no apologies, nothing. You have a perfect right to do as you please. I gave you that right when I did the things I did."

"We have to talk," he said. "A lot's happened and we need to talk. I'm going to be in D.C. with this appeal for a while, but when it's over—it shouldn't take too long—I thought I'd meet you somewhere, London maybe, or Edinburgh. Can we do that? Can we put this off until we can meet, face to face?"

She'd pulled her mind out, but her heart was still in the tunnel. "OK," she managed to answer, hearing the word *divorce* although no one said it.

He could tell how upset she was, so he did his best to distract her. "Marc will be there in a week. He's really looking forward to seeing you. He doesn't like to say, but I know he misses you."

Her son, she'd almost forgotten about her son. That was what she needed to grab onto. It would keep her from falling too far. "I miss him, too. I wish he could stay longer."

"He really tried, but you know how his father is. He told me he's hoping to see you at least once more this summer. He said something about meeting at your cousin's in Pau."

She had so many complicated thoughts that it was hard to get things together in her mind. "Yes, we're going to try to do that."

"That'll be nice," he said, but it sounded forced and artificial.

Annie heard background sounds again and imagined that his companion was growing impatient with her exile to the toilet. She suddenly had a thought that rang like an alarm. "You're using protection, aren't you Mike?"

Sounding slightly irritated, he responded, "Of course, I am!"

"That's good. I'm glad. You've got to take care of yourself."

He softened his voice now. "And you, Annie, are you well?"

"I'm fine, just fine," she lied. "Nothing to worry about with me."

"I do worry. Have you heard from him—from Glenn?" He had yet to tell her about his meeting with him.

"No."

"You should call him," was all he could say, because the woman was at his side again.

"I will," she lied again. "Look, you get back to sleep. I'll wait for you to call me. I won't bother you again."

"You haven't bothered me."

"Good night, Mike." She almost said "I love you," but she stopped herself and used two hands to put the receiver down.

The air in the little cottage was getting heavier; she knew what was coming, so she located her inhaler and took a couple of puffs, then waited on the threadbare couch while it took effect. When she felt better, she went into the kitchen, where she retrieved her gardening tools from their place behind the door. She didn't change her clothes as she should have, but walked across the lawn to her garden, then sat on the bench, gazing over the sea, which today was heartbreakingly blue.

After a time, she began digging with the small shovel. When the hole began to grow, she went to her knees to continue her task. She had pinned up her hair in a French twist the day before, and through the terrible night with Tom, it had come undone in spots, giving her a wild, disheveled look. The more she dug, the more it came down around her face, loosening with the gusts of wind.

Her hands were muddy, but she didn't notice or care. She shoved the sleeves of her sweater to the elbows, smudging them brown, then wiped the hair from her eyes,

leaving smears on her face that looked like old bruises—
like the remnants of old, powerful blows. Her pretty skirt
had become filthy, too, but she kept right on digging, still
kneeling between the bench and the flower border. She
frantically tossed the dirt around her as she dug, crushing
and burying some of the delicate flowers she'd taken such
care to plant.

When Andrew reached the town, it was not the first time
he'd been there since Annie left, but it certainly felt like it.
The car crash and the long convalescence that followed
had kept him from returning as a student, but a year later,
in the summer of 1973, he'd come back to sit alone for his
examinations, then, unceremoniously, to be awarded his
degree. He'd been there many times since to play golf and
always had to work at keeping the memories from his
mind. It was inordinately difficult at first and had gotten
less so over time, but today it felt like a fresh wound, open
and smarting, like there'd been no time to quell the bleeding—let alone to heal. He needed to do something about
that, about the feelings and memories that were threatening to overtake him. He needed to regain some control.

As he made his way along the road that followed the
Old Course, he deliberately kept his eyes from the West
Sands. He got as far as the bus station but turned back to
the Old Course Hotel, where he went in to ask for a room.
He wanted to slow down, to do something ordinary and
reconnect with reality.

The hotel manager was behind the desk, and he recognized the earl immediately. He nudged his clerks aside
to attend to this important person himself. "Is your luggage in the boot, your lordship?"

"No, I haven't any," he told him. "It's an unexpected
stop I'm making."

"May we assist you, then, with some toiletries and such?"

"Yes, do that. Send out for a shirt and socks, too, if you
would, and whatever else."

He ran his eyes quickly over the lean, tall aristocrat,
who was casually dressed in faded jeans, an oxford cloth

shirt, and a tweed jacket. As he handed him the room key, he made the strategic decision to not ask his size or inquire any further.

"I'm not going up now," Andrew told him. "I have something to do first. Just leave the things in the room for me." He started away from the desk but turned back and pulled a business card from his wallet. "My private secretary, Nigel Bain—would you ring him and let him know I'll be staying here? Tell him I've not brought a mobile with me, so he'll have to contact me through the hotel."

He bowed his head in deferential fashion. "Of course, your lordship. My name is Howard Connell, if I may be of further assistance." Watching as he made quick strides of the lobby, he wondered what could have sent Lord Kilmartin off in such haste, without a suitcase or cell phone, or notice to his secretary.

His Aston Martin had remained parked at the entrance, and it was drawing attention. Andrew donned his dark glasses and jumped into the driver's seat, then sped away from the hotel.

He turned onto The Scores. At the corner just before the Whaum, it was now necessary to turn right, and he thanked the powers-that-be for small favors. He turned left onto North Street and followed it to the cathedral, where he pulled over for a moment, engine running. He offered a prayer of sorts, along the lines of "God help me," then tightened his grip on the steering wheel and headed for Kingsbarns. In less than ten minutes, he would be at her cottage.

Annie continued to dig. Her mind was a confused jumble of memory and regret and who could tell what else, but she continued to dig, hearing the calls from the tunnel— Timmy, Timmy, Timmy, over and over—it must be her heart. The air was growing heavy out here, too.

The sound of a car on the drive was unmistakable, the popping and cracking of the stone. She could hear it over the wind, over the calls from inside, the cries from the tunnel.

Andrew might have gone to the cottage, but he'd already seen her, a flash of yellow and white on the green lawn. He strode toward her with purpose, though he knew not what it was. He knew only that there was a churning swarm inside of him, of things that he hadn't dared think about for years, of feelings he'd refused to let himself have.

She had heard the car and stopped her digging. She stood and turned to him, shovel in hand, and the piece of her that was in the tunnel saw him, too, and it smiled.

He had traversed the lawn quickly and was in front of her. He could not smile. He plainly saw hers, but he could not return it. There was too much weight, too many letters read in one night, too much happened in a short time—such a long time gone.

Her smile was beyond her control. "You don't know how happy I am to see you," her heart burst out.

He did not respond. He was a tall mass of tense muscle in front of her, and the severity of his countenance hit her hard.

That piece of her in the tunnel began to fall again. For a moment it had felt as though it might be coming out, but it was falling again. "What is it? What's wrong?"

It was hard to get it out from behind the tension. "Your letters."

The smile had gone into the tunnel, too. "I did write to you, Andrew. I don't know how to prove it."

The response was cold and meant to hurt. "I know. I have them now. I've read them."

She frowned bewilderment. "I don't understand."

Saying the words aloud did not make it seem more real. "My father kept them from me, but I have them now. I've read them."

Her face twisted in confusion. "How?"

His expression was unreadable. "Ambrose, his valet. He's kept them all these years. He was supposed to have burned them but he couldn't." He reached to the inside pocket of his jacket for the small bundle, then handed it to her. "These are yours."

Annie put the shovel down, then held both hands palm open as he laid the bundle of letters on them. The one on top was addressed to her in Saintes Maries de la Mer, France, and had the return address of Crofthill, Cairncurran, Scotland. The dozen or so letters she held felt very heavy, and she sank to the ground with them. A little cry sounded from her deepest recesses.

"Don't do that," he said, still very stiff in front of her.

She clutched the letters to her chest in an effort to stop the cry and bowed her head.

"Why?" he demanded, and she didn't know what he was asking. "Why?" he asked again, emotion creeping into his tone.

She looked up at him with her dirty face, and he could see her bewilderment.

Her lack of understanding infuriated him. "Why didn't you know they weren't getting to me? Why didn't you know that and do something about it—ring me or something, anything? Why didn't you? You should have felt something was wrong. You should have felt it and done something!"

She couldn't think how to respond but clutched the letters more tightly, her gaze falling to the ground.

As he looked down upon her, he felt pangs of sympathy. He wanted to get away from that, so he railed, "Look at you—why are you so filthy? What are you doing out here?"

She answered meekly, "I had a bad night. I was up all night. I came out here to take my mind off things."

He found more to be angry about in that. "You've had a bad night? What do you think I've had? What do you think it's done to me to read these bloody letters after all these years? How do you think it feels to know I can't go back, that I can't undo what's been done?"

She looked up and barely whispered, "I'm sorry," then lowered her head again.

His tone grew louder, more cruel. "You're sorry? Is that all you have to say? Jesus Christ!"

"I'm sorry, Andrew," she repeated, tears streaming down her cheeks.

"Christ!" he hissed. "You have no idea what I went through because of it, none at all. I went through hell, Annie, through hell because I was trying to get to you."

"What happened?" she asked in a whisper.

He reached and grabbed her shoulders. He pulled her to her feet and squeezed her arms while she still clutched the letters. "What happened? I killed a man trying to get to you. I went crazy trying to get to you! I killed a man in a car crash, and I've had to live with that ever since."

Annie's eyes filled with terror as she searched his. "I had no idea. How could I have known?" She looked at the letters in her hands. "Is it in here?"

He ripped his letters from her hands and threw them to the ground. "Yes, it's in there, but what bloody good does it do to read them now?" She bent to pick them up again, but he grabbed her and held her upper arms. "Every fucking day since then I've had to remember. Do you see these bloody scars? I've had to look at them every fucking day and remember!" Reason had left him, and he was operating on pure emotion; his hands moved up to her throat and wrapped around it.

Annie was already struggling to breathe, but as Andrew tightened his hands around her neck, she gasped for air.

"Do you see them?" he shouted, "Answer me!"

She locked her eyes with his and nodded her head. He relaxed his grip slightly.

He was fighting off tears. "Bloody whore, I could almost kill you!"

He had loosened his grip enough for her to speak. Tears came with her hoarse words, "Go ahead, go ahead and kill me if it'll help you. I have nothing to live for."

She had reminded him of something he'd almost forgotten, something he'd wanted to forget. "Bloody hell! Curse you! You come back into my life when you might be dying—curse you, Annie d'Inard!" He moved his hands away from her throat and back to her shoulders, then gripped the tops of her arms and shook her. "What am I supposed to do? How am I supposed to handle this? Can you answer me that?"

"No," she barely got out.

He was breathing with deliberate slowness and depth. "You've upset everything it's taken me twenty years to put together. I hate you for that; I really do."

"Please don't hate me, Andrew," she said between sobs. "I can stand anything but your hating me. Please don't hate me!"

There was renewed anger, but it was restrained and more deadly. "I told you once that I'd have to hate you to survive. Do you remember that?"

"I remember," she said, then dropped her head and sobbed to break his heart.

"Don't do that!" he screamed at her. "Don't do that!"

He shook her so violently that he forced her backwards into the hole she'd been digging. It was more than a foot deep, and when he pushed the downward momentum took him with her. They stood in the hole on the edge of the cliff, and he shook her again.

"Stop it!" he insisted. "Stop crying! I can't take it!"

"I'm sorry, I'm sorry!" She had to scream to get it out. "I can't stop! I don't feel like I can ever stop. I can't bear that you hate me!"

"Stop it!" His voice cracked and he let go of her shoulders. He backed away and out of the hole, as he felt his own sobs coming on.

Annie dropped to her knees when he released her, and as she did, she felt the ground give way. She realized in an instant what was happening and looked up at Andrew— not for help, but as if to say good-bye. He realized it, too, and should have stepped back to save himself, but he didn't.

He dropped to the ground instantly. On his abdomen now, he reached both hands out for her as the edge of the cliff broke free and slipped away toward the sea. She didn't reach for him but he caught her, by one wrist and one forearm—just in time. In a great thundering shudder, all the lovely flowers she'd planted, the shoes on her feet, the letters from the past, all fell away with the cliff face.

He pulled her toward him and onto the lawn, just as the bench and more soil fell away. Then he wrapped himself around her and began to roll them uphill, away from the tumbling earth. They could hear the crashing sound of the bench as it smashed on the rocks below. They rolled over and over, several times very rapidly, until he felt they were at a safe distance. He was on top of Annie when they stopped, and he realized that she was struggling to get her breath. He moved off and helped her into a sitting position, then positioned himself alongside.

He was a little breathless, too. "Are you all right? Shall I go ring for an ambulance?"

"No—I'll be all—right," she struggled to say.

"Are you certain? You seem very ill. What can I do?"

"Nothing."

"There must be something. Let me take you to a doctor."

"No—I don't need a doctor—when I get upset—when I remember—Timmy—I can't get my breath—"

"Timmy, your brother? I don't understand."

She realized that he must not have had all the letters. "Never mind."

He watched with concern as she worked hard to bring her breathing under control. After one long, frightening minute, she quieted some, looking at him with the saddest eyes he'd ever seen.

Sanity was returning to Andrew, and with it the realization of what had just transpired. "You could have died," he told her, in a much calmer voice.

"It wouldn't—have mattered—not if . . ."

"Not have mattered? Of course, it would have! My God! I can't believe what just happened—what might have happened."

She could only say a few words together before taking a breath. "There are so few—things worth caring—about, so few—really, but it's—important to me—how you feel about me—if you really hate me . . ."

The despair in her voice and the forlorn expression on her face were getting to him. "I didn't mean all those things, all those ugly things I said. It wasn't how I really feel. It's just that it's all been so bloody difficult." He lowered his head but kept his eyes on her. "I'm sorry I called you those horrid names. God forgive me, I sounded just like my father."

The muscles in her chest were relaxing, and she was getting more air in now. "Tell me—you don't—hate me," she pleaded, and her eyes pulled him in.

He threw his head backward and clutched his knees. "Christ Almighty! You know I don't hate you! I've tried to, God knows I've tried to! I wish I could hate you! Hating you has never been the problem!"

It took tremendous effort and determination but her breathing was getting easier, and she could hear the cries from the tunnel again. She reached out a hand and traced the scars on his face with a gentle fingertip. He meant to push her away, but something in him prevented it.

Tears began to flow again and wash more of the dirt from her already streaked face. She reached for his cheek with her other hand and caressed it, then she leaned forward and began kissing the scars. His eyes burned and filled, as he felt her breath on his skin, the healing sensation of her lips on the old scars.

As she kissed, she whispered, "My poor Andrew."

"Don't," he said, although it wasn't what he wanted to say. "Don't do that."

She ignored his words and responded to his body, which was growing soft and yielding. He relaxed his head and let it move with her, with her kisses and caresses, his breathing slow and deep. She rested her cheek on his, next to the largest wound, and held his face with her hands.

Her words came without a struggle now. "It breaks my heart to know that you needed me and I wasn't there. Whatever happened, I should have been there. You're right, I should have known something was wrong and come to find you."

His response was a small sigh.

Her voice was like a warm glass of brandy, and he was intoxicated by it. "It's the worst pain there is, when you look back and see things you wish you could change." She pulled away so that she might look into the endless blue of his eyes. "There's nothing that hurts more," she added.

He sighed again and shrugged his shoulders. "It's all etched in stone now."

"Is it? Is all of it?"

"There's nothing we can change about it."

"True—some things are lost to us," she agreed, picturing herself standing alone by a bronze coffin. "But something has already changed, Andrew. When I felt the ground giving way, I was ready to just let it happen, to let it all go and have done with it. But you reached out for me, and that changed everything."

His expression turned serious again. "God knows what would have happened if I hadn't caught you. I'm glad you weren't hurt, Annie, but I'm afraid that doesn't change anything about the past."

She shook her head. "I disagree. What you did, it gave me hope—hope that we might somehow make the past easier to live with."

Hope—it was such an archaic word. He'd given that up long ago. "I don't see how that's possible."

She watched his face carefully, trying to read the lines of it. "Right here in St. Andrews, I told you I loved you, and I meant it with all my heart and soul. And when I said it, I felt something I've never known again—not ever. It felt as though my heart came right out of me. It felt like it went into yours, like our hearts actually touched."

There may have been the slightest trace of a smile on his lips, but he turned away so she wouldn't see it.

"We experienced that, you and I," she said to him. "I know you felt it, too. But you never said it. You never told me how you felt."

He still avoided her eyes, but he answered from his heart. "I couldn't."

She was thinking of their youthful selves—their spirits, abandoned to grief and loss. "The past has made prisoners of us, Andrew, and it won't release us until we make our peace with it. When we do that, we'll be free again."

"We can't go back," he said, although in this moment he wanted that as much as she did.

She rose to her knees and gathered up his hands in hers. "Yes we can. You can bring us both back when you tell me what you never said."

He pulled his hands away. "No," he said, the pain clearly evident. "It's too difficult. There's too much that's gone between."

Her thoughts returned to the dawn and the death of her friend. Although Tom had known her but a short time, his need for an emotional connection with someone as he lay dying overrode everything else. That powerful need helped her understand that of all the comforts that can be offered to a suffering human being—dying or not—only one truly makes a difference.

Still kneeling in front of him, she touched Andrew's face and turned it toward her own. "I know it's difficult, but I also know that when all is said and done, it's the only thing that's worth anything. In the end, love is the only thing that can bring us peace."

What she said struck him hard, and he stared back at her. What if she was near her end? What if she had but little time left? The thought of losing her again burned in him like a fire, and it melted away his last bit of resolve.

Time seemed suddenly suspended. The wind continued to blow, there were birds, more and more of them gathering overhead, and waves that called in from the depths of the sea. But to these two people, each waiting for a sign from the other, the external world seemed paralyzed, disabled.

In his deepest, most protected places, Andrew boiled and churned with emotions he had long ago decided to smother. They proved themselves alive now, alive and gasping for air. He looked at the woman who knelt before him, her dirty, tear-streaked face, so full of need, so pleading. He turned his head away, but then he had to look again. She was pulling it out of him, reaching where only she could.

It took a lot to get it out, buried so deep, so long. It took more effort than it had taken to pull Annie up the collapsing cliff edge. He struggled and hurt and turned away from her, and then he struggled some more. When he turned to her again, he saw the disheveled woman who only minutes ago had almost tumbled to her death—not at all upset by her brush with death, but desperate and sorrowful over the loss of his affection. He was overwhelmed when he realized this, and when his eyes caught that familiar sparkle of green in hers, he could see that she still loved him, and it moved him more than he had been moved in many, many years.

Then, from underneath the rubble of time, almost of its own volition, "I love you," finally came out. After he heard himself say it, he dropped his head to her bosom and sobbed.

She wrapped herself around him. "I love you, too, so much, so very, very much! It's never gone away, never! You've always been here," she told him, and put a hand over her heart.

When she touched her chest, her heart did something strange, like a somersault, and Annie knew what it wanted. She moved her hand to his heart and asked a question with her eyes. He understood and rose to his knees, and they leaned in and pressed their chests together in an embrace that almost forced the air from their lungs, trying to let the two touch, the hearts that had never been the same since they'd separated them that night on the West Sands.

The wind blew up the cliff face and embraced the couple as they pressed their bodies together, breathing in peaceful unison for the first time in twenty-two years. When he finally released her, he took the face of the woman he had never forgotten into his hands, then bent his lips to hers. He kissed them with more profound, overwhelming sadness than he had ever felt, than he had ever realized he carried within him. His anguish gushed from him, from the very cells within him, as he lamented the loss of her, the agony of his denied feelings, the unendurable misery of their separation. And she felt it all.

Lifting his lips away—just far enough to speak—he put words to the feelings he'd never dared express. "I've loved you since the day I first met you, in Southgait Hall. I could barely look at you that day, my heart filled so at the sight of you."

"Really?" She sounded small and disbelieving, like a child.

"When I saw you again that night and realized that Patrick Ramsay had already laid claim to you, I felt such unbearable loss. In one day, with no more than a dozen words between us, I was hopelessly, terrifyingly in love with you. It took every bit of my strength to pull myself together and stand back."

"I had feelings for you right away, too," she told him, "but you seemed so shy, so very shy. Every time I looked at you, you looked away."

He responded simply. "I had to."

She leaned into him and rested her head on his chest. "But we came together, didn't we?"

Rubbing her arms, he answered, "It wasn't long before I realized there was nothing I could do but love you. In spite of everything, I had to love you."

The words *in spite of everything* brought reality to Annie's mind. "There's so much I need to know. Will you tell me everything? Will you tell me about the accident?" She suddenly remembered his letters, and sitting abruptly, she scanned the lawn for them. "Your letters! Where are they?"

Andrew looked around, too. "They must have gone over the side with everything else."

"Oh no!" In an instant, she was overcome with panic. "I've got to go find them. I can't lose them now, not after all this time! I only had them for a moment. Help me find them, Andrew!"

In a gesture meant to calm her, he touched her cheek. "Perhaps it's better for them to be lost. It wasn't easy for me to read yours, Annie. It was actually very painful."

"Painful or not," she said, "I've got to read them! You wrote to me. I didn't even know you wrote to me!"

He took up her hand. "Let me take you to your cottage, then I'll go down and look for them myself."

"No," she insisted, "we'll go together!"

"You need to get some shoes on first."

She stood abruptly. "No, I'm fine." Then she dashed toward the path.

The sight of the debris pile was daunting. A shudder of fear passed through Andrew when he saw it and realized how close Annie had come to being buried beneath it.

"God! Look at that!" He surveyed the rock face to the newly formed edge. "I don't think it's safe to be standing here."

"I have to find them," she told him. "I need them!"

She knelt next to the pieces of teak that were all that remained of her bench and took up one of the larger ones to use as a shovel. She began digging through the dirt and rock, more agitated than she'd been when she shoveled the hole that had precipitated the slide. Despite his apprehensions, Andrew understood the emotions that were driving her, so he began to help. In less than a minute, he had uncovered one of her shoes.

"Good," she shouted, "then they've got to be here, too!"

He lifted away large, heavy pieces of rock, sifted through the soil and broken flowers with his fingers, and glanced frequently upward to check the unstable ledge overhanging them.

"I really don't think we should be here now," he warned. "It would be better to wait until tomorrow. There may be more slides today."

"But what if it rains? What if it rains and ruins them? They'll be wet and cold. It's so cold and dark down there, it's so horribly lonely and cold! I can't leave them all alone! I left him. He's all alone and I'll never see him again! Oh Andrew, help me!" She began to cry and was having difficulty breathing again.

He stopped what he was doing and pressed down on her shoulders to make her quit digging. "Never see who again? What's the matter? What's happening to you?"

She struggled against him. "Nothing, let me go! Let me keep digging!"

"No," he calmly responded. "Something's terribly wrong and I need to know what it is." He tried to take her in an embrace. "What is it? Is it Timmy again?"

She broke free of him, then grasped the stick of wood with two hands to once again plow the mound of debris. Her agitation was increasing, and it was frightening him.

He had a sudden intuition about what was causing it. "What's happened to Timmy, Annie? Is he dead?"

She dropped her makeshift shovel and shivered as her breathing worsened.

"He's dead, isn't he? How'd it happen?"

She put her hands to her throat and stood abruptly. "I—can't—I can't—get my—breath!" She was rapidly losing her color, her complexion at first blanching, then turning bluish-gray.

He laid his hands on her shoulders again. "Listen to me. You can get your breath. There's plenty of air out here and you can breathe. Look at me. Look into my eyes."

Her eyes were wide and panic-stricken, and she made frightening noises as she struggled for oxygen.

"Look into my eyes and breathe with me. Make your breathing follow mine."

He took one of her hands and put it to his chest. "Feel my heart, my heart that needs you, Annie. Feel my breathing and do it with me."

"Help—me!" she gasped.

"I am going to help you. Breathe with me and try to calm yourself. Everything will be all right. I'm here with you, and I won't let anything bad happen to you." He didn't like the way she looked, but there was no way to leave her and get help, and in the state she was in, no way to get her to help.

"I can't, I can't!"

"Yes, you can. You must. Come on, breathe with me."

He exaggerated his own breathing and by gripping her shoulders, he moved them upward as he inhaled and then pushed them downward as he exhaled. Slowly she responded and joined his rhythm, and after a couple of terrifying minutes, he had her breathing relatively normally again and her color much improved. When he felt that she was able, he walked her away from the overhanging ledge to a nearby boulder. He put his jacket around her and they sat together quietly, looking off into the sea. Andrew continued to have her follow the rhythm of his breaths.

He noticed her feet, which were pale blue. "Can you make it up to the cottage now, do you think?"

She nodded.

"Then let's go. I want you to lie down and warm up. I'll carry you if it's too much for you."

"I can make it," she said, although in the wake of the panic attack, her depleted body hurt all over.

They ascended the path slowly, Andrew leading her and not letting go of her hand. When they entered the cottage, he spotted her bedroom and took her directly to it. He turned his back while she removed her filthy clothing and slipped into a nightgown. She began to shiver, so he nudged her into lying down and covered her with two quilts, tucking them carefully around her feet.

"I'll just be a moment," he told her. "I want to put the kettle on. Is there some medicine you can take?"

She pointed to her dresser. "Top drawer."

He returned from the kitchen with a glass of water and handed her the bottle of tablets. "Will this help you?"

She nodded and took two pills, though the directions said to take one.

He went into the bathroom and returned with a cloth for her face, then he sat on the bed and rubbed her icy feet. "Have you a hot water bottle or something?"

"No."

"Never mind then, I'll soon have them warm enough. Where are your socks?"

She pointed to the dresser again.

The kettle whistled and Annie listened as Andrew rattled around her tiny kitchen, searching things out. It brought her back in time, made her feel for a moment as though they were together at the Whaum.

"I'll just be a minute!" he called to her, and in no time he was at her side again with a cup of chamomile tea. "Where's the thermostat?" he asked. "It's bloody cold in here."

"There is none, just the fireplace." She sipped her tea, grateful for the trail of warmth that it left along her throat.

He shook his head and looked baffled. "What on earth are you doing living in a place like this? Isn't John paying you enough? I told him to give you whatever you wanted."

"John's paying me very well. I'm staying here because I like it. It reminds me of the Whaum."

That struck him with great poignancy. "But there's no heat! Did you expect to be gone by the end of the summer?"

"I wasn't thinking ahead. I couldn't let myself."

"Well, surely you can make better arrangements for yourself now."

"I could, I'm just not certain what those arrangements should be."

"And what about your husband? Shouldn't your plans include him in some way?"

His mention of Mike made her recall their earlier conversation, and it brought back the ache. She set her teacup on the bedside table. "Mike's making his own plans," she informed him, then fell back on the bed and closed her eyes.

"Are you getting sleepy?" he asked. "What was that you took?"

"Tranquilizers."

"Should you have taken two?"

She nodded, then turned her head away.

He went back to rubbing her feet. "Can you talk to me now? Can you tell me what's bothering you so?"

The medication was having its way with her. "I was up all night with someone I know. He was my only friend here, and he was dying of cancer. He didn't want to be alone when he died."

Andrew reached for her hand. "I'm sorry." He waited for her to go on.

"It was very hard. It wasn't something I would have chosen to do, not that I didn't care, but the only other time I was with someone like that . . ." Her voice trailed off and she closed her eyes again.

He squeezed and caressed her hand.

"He had no one," she continued, "no family or close friends. The staff was very kind, but it's not the same."

"No, it isn't, but being with him must have brought back terrible memories."

She turned on her side and pulled the covers to her ears. "I can't talk about it, not now."

He massaged her back. "Why don't you try to sleep for a bit? I'll lay a fire and see about getting us something to eat, all right?"

From underneath the bedclothes, she called to him, "You're not going to leave me, are you?"

He leaned over and kissed her forehead. "No," he answered. "You sleep. I'll be right here." Then he pulled a chair close to the bed.

"Aren't you tired?" she whispered to him.

"I am, a bit. I didn't sleep last night either."

She longed to feel his touch again. "Why don't you lie down beside me?"

He rose from the chair and walked to the other side of the bed. He removed his jacket and shoes, then lay next to Annie and embraced her back. She could feel his breath on her neck, and it warmed her entire body.

"I was beastly with you this morning," he whispered to her. "I said horrid, ugly things that I didn't mean."

"It was just your hurt talking, I know that."

"I was cursing you, almost choking you, but all the while," he hesitated a moment, "what I really wanted was to take you in my arms and make love to you."

She thought they had stopped but there they were again—stinging hot, huge tears, tears that filled up her throat and made it difficult to speak. In her altered, tranquilized state, she could not fend them off.

"I want to make love to you, Annie," he murmured, and he kissed the back of her neck.

"They're too cruel!" she cried out through the erupting tears. "Too cruel! I can't take it!"

Bewildered by her response, he questioned, "Who's too cruel?"

She was close to hysteria. "The gods! The bloody, fucking gods—the same ones from before who tricked us into believing we did the right thing when we made the worst decisions of our lives!" She tried to sit up, but fell back on the pillow.

"Shhh," he told her, as he slipped both arms around her waist. "Please don't do this to yourself."

"I can't help it. It's one fucking cruel joke after another, isn't it? I'm tired of it, sick and tired of it! They bring us together again just so they can play one more horrible, mean trick—the cruelest one of all!"

"Help me to understand," he implored. "I don't understand—"

"So many years, we've waited so many years. It's taken so much to bring us together again. Here we are now and finally, we should be able to be together, but I can't allow it, and they know that. The cruel bastards know that I love you too much to allow it! I can't possibly expose you to that God-forsaken virus—that evil, horrible virus. I could never, never do that to you! Never!"

She was a mixture of rage and despair, and she sobbed into the pillow as Andrew did his best to comfort her. "We'll use protection. We'll be very careful. There'll be very little risk to me."

"No!" she cried out. "I can't risk hurting you again." Her face was contorted with pain and her soul-felt cries could be heard through the cottage windows. They pierced the thin panes of glass and were caught up in the wind, swirled round and round on the cliff tops, then dropped over the edge and scattered into nothingness.

He knew that she was beyond reasoning and solace, but he held her against his chest, stroking her hair and saying, "It'll be all right. We'll find a way and we'll make it all right."

She wished with all her heart that she could believe that.

She felt the drug pulling her away from him, back into the tunnel, and her emotions were draining her strength so that she was unable to fight it. Everything was falling, tumbling, like the garden, like the cliff edge, like the letters from Andrew. She heard him say, "I love you, Annie. I'm not going to lose you again," and she felt his touch. She tried to hold onto that, to take that with her as she slipped into the tunnel and toward the purgatory of sleep.

Chapter 39

She was surrounded by them—white, billowy, tumbling things. Every time she reached to touch one, it changed or moved or dissipated. She kept trying to find one that would stay, one that would let her hold onto it, and she thought that she had for a moment: until she felt herself beginning to change, to re-form, to float off like all the rest of them.

The aroma of food broke through the veil of sleep, rousing her partially, then the sound of voices and furniture being moved, muffled though it was. She realized that she'd been dreaming, and when she turned to find no one beside her, she decided that it had all been a dream. But when her eyes began to focus, she noticed the firm indentation left in the pillow and a man's tweed jacket hung on the back of the chair. She touched the spot where his head had been.

The bedroom door creaked as he opened it. "Did I wake you?"

She yawned and stretched. "What time is it?"

"It's going on three. Did you get enough rest?"

"I'm a little fuzzy still, but that's because of the pills."

He sat on the bed and brushed the hair from her eyes. "When was the last time you had a proper meal?"

She smiled and touched his arm. "I don't remember exactly. Yesterday lunchtime, I think."

"I thought as much. I could hear your poor stomach growling as you slept."

"How embarrassing."

"Yes, quite," he laughed. "How about some soup?"

She reached for his hand and brought it to her lips, then she kissed his fingertips. "Something smells wonderful. What is it?"

"I had a meal delivered. I thought I'd serve you a bit of soup first, then run a bath for you."

He rose and went into the kitchen, then returned with a linen-draped tray that contained a large bowl of fish chowder, some crusty bread and butter, and a small bottle of mineral water. The tray was even adorned with a crystal drinking glass and good silverware.

"Where'd you get all this stuff?" she asked, as she propped herself against the headboard.

"Before I came here, I'd checked into the Old Course Hotel," he informed her. "I rang them while you were sleeping and had them send lunch over. I hope you don't mind, but there wasn't much of anything in your kitchen."

"How could I mind?" she smiled. "Aren't you going to join me?"

"After I get you set." He positioned the tray on her lap, then spread the napkin across her chest.

She looked up and grinned. "You're very sweet, you know, but you're treating me like an invalid."

"Am I? Sorry, didn't mean to. I'll just get myself a bowl. I am peckish."

She watched him go into the kitchen, then return carrying a bowl in one hand, and a bud vase with a lovely pink rose in the other. He set the vase on her tray and his bowl on her bedside table.

"Forgot this," he mumbled, as he settled next to her.

A tear came running out and she wiped it away. "You thought of everything, I see."

His emotions felt ready to burst again. He had to tuck into the soup to keep them from getting the better of him, and it was only after several spoonfuls that he found himself able to speak again. "Roses have always reminded me of you."

She touched his hand. "Were they lovely when they bloomed?"

He seemed reticent when he responded. "After you left, I'm afraid I kept away from the garden. Every time I looked out there I fancied I saw you, so I kept out of it."

"That's very sad," she lamented. "All that work and you hardly looked at them. I did it for you, Andrew. I made that garden as beautiful as I could because I wanted to leave something wonderful that would remind you of me."

"You did that, Annie, and you left me more of yourself than you know." The soup he had just swallowed lodged in his throat.

"I've been in it again, you know," she told him softly.

That surprised him. "The Whaum? Really? How?"

"I was walking by one day and the owner was in the front yard. I told her how special the place had been to me, and she was kind enough to invite me in."

"What was it like going in there again?" he wondered.

"It's been remodeled, but the old house is still there behind everything." She almost told him about the spirits, but then she thought better of it.

"It would be difficult, I should think, seeing it again. I know it would be for me."

She nodded slightly. "The hardest part was seeing what they'd done to the garden. It's been newly landscaped. The roses are gone."

He pictured a troop of gardeners hacking away at his memories, and the image plunged him into melancholy. He cleared his throat before asking, "Would you care for a glass of wine?"

"Not just yet," she answered. His forlorn expression left her wondering what he was thinking, and although she didn't like bringing it up, she needed to know. "When do you have to leave?"

"Not today." He couldn't think what to say beyond that, so he asked, "Would you care for more chowder? There's more in the kitchen."

"No, thanks, this is plenty." She took several spoonfuls before asking him, "Your being here with me—is it all right?"

He finished his soup and set the bowl aside. "My wife knows where I am, and my secretary knows that he can reach me through the hotel."

"She knows you're with me?"

"We had a discussion about it before I left."

"Oh," she said, obviously distressed. "Forgive me. I don't mean to pry, but I worry about causing trouble for you."

Despite his best efforts, she could see that he struggled with this. "I'm doing what it is I need to, and Janet understands that."

When he reached for her hand, she drew it to her cheek and held it there.

"Have you finished?" he asked.

"Yes, thanks. It's delicious, but my stomach is in knots."

He set the tray on the dresser, then positioned himself next to her again. "I know why you have those knots. You can't go on ignoring things. You've got to take action and get some answers," he said tenderly.

To avoid his eyes, she looked down at the bedclothes. "I know, I've just been afraid."

He put a hand under her chin, and gently lifted her face to his. "And I know what it is you're afraid of. It would be God-awful to get bad news and be all alone when you did."

That was it exactly, and knowing that he understood brought on tears of relief.

He stroked her damp cheek as he continued. "When I was lying next to you, I couldn't sleep. I kept thinking about your predicament—our predicament—to have found you again after so long . . ." He looked away momentarily and reconsidered what he was about to say. "I want to help you, to do what I can for you."

Like a gentle rain falling on parched earth, his words nourished her. "There's nothing anyone can do," she answered, her voice quiet and resigned. "It's a matter of time—of being tested again and time."

What he was about to say frightened him a little, but he had to speak his heart. "If you are ill, being with someone who cares about you—someone who'll take care of you—it could make all the difference. What I'm trying to say is, what I've meant to ask—will you let me take care of you?"

Her heart took a flying leap, as though it had just been released from some odious dungeon, and she struggled to keep it under control. "Andrew, you're so sweet to want that, to care that much, but I don't see how that's possible. You have your family, your work."

"I'll make it possible. I'll make the time to be with you." He reached for her hand again.

For one fleeting moment, she allowed her heart to soar, but even as it did, her mind stayed anchored to reality. "I just don't see how that could work," she insisted, shaking her head, "or how I could live with myself if I took you away from your family."

"It can work because it has to." His eyes were pleading. "Don't you understand how much I need to do this?"

She tried to be honest with herself, even as she was praying that it could be so. "You've helped me so much already. Hearing you say that you love me has brought me more happiness than I've known in a very long while. But that's the best we can do, Andrew. We can't do any better than that."

He thought back to that moment on the cliffs when, for one of the few times in his life, he'd allowed his heart to speak for him. It had been terrifying at first, but once it was done, he'd recognized that nothing he'd ever said before had felt that right, that good. "We can do better," he said. "We can admit how important we are to each other, and that we need one another."

"But I don't want to hurt you," she told him, choking on her words. "I don't want to do anything that might hurt you or your family."

He sighed. "I know. But at this point it's ludicrous to think in terms of hurt and taking me away from my family. We're so far beyond that it's almost a bloody joke."

"But how'd we get that far? We were so long apart. How'd we pick up like it was yesterday?" She looked into his scarred and tired face. The answer was there, but she refused to let herself believe it.

"Listen to me," he told her, grasping her hand more firmly. "I want to take you to Lyons, to the Pasteur Institute, to see this Dr. Coupau. He's one of the world's experts on HIV, and I can arrange an appointment for you. You need to know, and I want to know what it is we're dealing with. Will you go there with me?"

Her mouth went dry immediately. "When?"

"I thought the middle of next week."

Thank God, she had an excuse. "My son will be here then."

"When does he leave?"

"He's only here for a week," she said, "then I'm taking him to Barcelona. Then we have the commercial shoot in the Pyrénées."

He thought for a moment. "Let's do this. Let me take care of your travel. I'll send my jet to Edinburgh for you and your son. From Barcelona, they can fly you to Lyons and I'll arrange to meet you there."

She couldn't let him do that; it wasn't right, and she was sure his wife wouldn't like it. "That's very thoughtful, but you really needn't. I'll be OK on my own. I know how busy you are."

He wasn't going to argue about this anymore. He stood abruptly. "I want to be there, I will be there, and that's that. Now, I'm going to run a bath for you," he said.

He was already in the bathroom when she called to him, "You have to heat the water first." Then she reached for a tissue to blow her nose.

"I have already," he called back. As he reset the manual hot water heater he grumbled, "My God, but this place is primitive."

She rose from the bed, pulled off her nightgown, and slipped into her robe. "Wasn't the Whaum like that? I remember having to boil water to do the dishes."

"You remember correctly," he answered, as he came back to her bedroom. "And half the time when you wanted a bath, the bloody thing didn't work at all."

He was standing in front of her now, and he pulled her to his chest. They remained in that embrace until the sound of water overflowing the tub startled them.

He ran to the bathroom and opened the drain, calling, "Are you coming?"

Before she got in he stepped outside, then spoke to her through the door. "I'm going to make some phone calls, if you don't mind. I want to check on the children and then touch base with my secretary. I didn't bring a mobile."

"Take your time," she told him as she immersed herself in the warmth.

Margaret, the eldest girl, came to the phone after a servant answered. "Where are you, Daddy? I thought you were to be home with us."

"I'm sorry, Maggie, but something important came up. How's everyone? How's your sister?"

"Fine. She's having her riding lesson."

"And Malcolm?"

"Completely back to normal, I should say, running around and getting into trouble, as usual."

"What trouble?"

"His usual mischief. He hid a silver bowl and got one of the servants scolded for it, so Mummy had to confine him to his room for the afternoon."

Andrew chuckled. "And Mummy, how's she?"

"She's had an awful headache, and she's been lying down quite a bit."

He was instantly worried. "Would you get her for me? I'd like to speak with her."

"Hold on, she's in her room."

Maggie came back after a bit. "She doesn't feel up to talking, Daddy, sorry. Is there a message you want me to give her?"

My poor Janet, he thought. God, how I wish there were another way. "Only that I'm concerned about her, and I'll try to reach her later. Now tell me, how are you and what are you up to?"

Maggie brought the phone to poor Malcolm, who was still confined to his room and who felt very strongly that he was being treated unfairly. When everything was sorted out as much as possible, Andrew said good-bye to the children and rang up his secretary.

Nigel was more than a little put out that he had to be told of the earl's whereabouts by a stranger. "This trip to St. Andrews was unexpected, your lordship. You said nothing about it beforehand."

"This is something personal," Andrew answered. "That's why you weren't consulted. Lady Kilmartin was the only one I discussed it with beforehand."

He sounded a tad petulant as he responded, "I see. Well then, would you care for a briefing on the day's events?"

"Is there anything pressing?"

He knew there wasn't, but to make Andrew wait, he slowly scanned the memos in front of him. "No, nothing out of the ordinary," he finally said, "but you do have that meeting in London tomorrow."

"Damn! I'd forgotten! You're going to have to postpone that."

"Postpone it, sir? You've got people coming in from all over the continent."

"Well then, you'd better get on it right away, hadn't you?" His authoritative tone told Nigel to back down.

"Very well. When would you like to reschedule?"

"You know my schedule better than I do, but for the next two or three days I'll be unavailable, so clear everything through then."

"Three days, sir?"

"You heard me." Andrew changed his tone slightly. "I know you think you're entitled to an explanation, but you're not going to get one. I've said this is personal, and I'm going to leave it at that."

Nigel didn't know whether to be angry or hurt. "Whatever you say, your lordship."

"The world will not end, and things will not go to hell in three days, Nigel."

"I suppose not. I just hope you don't return to a mess."

"Nigel."

"Yes, sir?"

"Leave it alone." It was a direct order.

Annie had gone into the bedroom to dress and do her hair, and the blow dryer drowned out the sound of the telephone.

Andrew didn't want to disturb her, so he answered.

"Sorry, I must have the wrong number," a man's voice said.

The accent was definitely American, and Andrew responded, "Perhaps not. Are you ringing Annie?"

"Why yes, I am. Who's this?" His first thought was that he was speaking with someone from the advertising agency.

"Andrew Stuart-Gordon. With whom am I speaking?"

"Mike Rutledge, Annie's husband. I hope I'm not calling at a bad time."

"Not at all. Hold on, I'll get her for you."

Something clicked in Mike's memory. "Wait, Andrew, you wouldn't be the same Andrew—her friend from years ago?"

"I am."

"Well, what a surprise! How on earth did she find you?"

"I found her, actually."

"That's amazing! How?"

"I'll let her tell you, if you don't mind. It's rather a long story. Shall I get her for you now?"

"Yeah, thanks."

"Nice chatting with you," he said, and he put the phone down. He knocked at Annie's door. "Your husband's ringing."

Annie opened the door and noticed the receiver off the hook. She pulled Andrew into the bedroom and closed the door behind him. "Tell him I can't come to the phone," she whispered.

"Why?"

"Because I don't want to speak with him."

"Because I'm here?"

"It has nothing to do with you. I just don't feel up to talking to him. Please tell him to call another time. Please, Andrew!"

He went back to the phone. "Mike, she's asking if you could call another time. She's a bit indisposed at the moment."

"That's too bad," he said. "Can you ask her when a good time would be? Tell her I'm thinking about coming to London day after tomorrow, because there's been a postponement in the trial."

"Just a moment, let me see if she can come to the phone now." He went into the bedroom and grabbed her by the hand, then practically dragged her to the phone. "Here she is," he said, as he put the receiver to her ear.

She scowled at him for his effrontery, but then she noticed the room. Her little parlor had been transformed. The table had been prettily set by the fire, and everywhere she looked she saw vases overflowing with roses. She wanted to put the phone down and hug him, but she heard Mike saying *hello* several times.

"Yes, Mike, hello. How are you?"

"Annie, I've had a break today and I wanted to say—" he searched for the right words, "I should have spoken with you beforehand. You shouldn't have found out that way."

"It doesn't matter. You have every right to do as you please." She noticed Andrew slipping out the cottage door. "Andrew, don't go," she called.

Obligingly, he returned and settled himself on the couch.

Mike wondered why she'd done that. Didn't she want privacy? "How on earth did you and he get together?" he asked her now, his curiosity getting the better of him.

"It's a long story."

"It must be great seeing him after all these years," he ventured.

"It's been wonderful and upsetting at the same time."

That seemed an odd response. "Why upsetting?"

"Never mind." She wasn't going to get into it with him—not now, not after what happened.

"What's he like? Has he changed much?"

"A lot and hardly at all," she answered.

"You're being very cryptic."

"I'm sorry, I can't help it. It's a strange day I'm having."

"What was it you called me about last night? You never said."

She debated as to whether or not she should bother, but then she said it anyway. "I'd just come home from the hospital. I'd been with Tom Keegan all night. He died early this morning."

"Oh, I'm so sorry. You should have told me."

"Why?" she snapped. "With that woman in bed with you, what would you have done?"

Andrew had been gazing out the window, but he turned now and looked at Annie, his mouth slightly agape.

To say the least, Mike was shocked to hear her mention that in front of a stranger, but what could he do? The damage was done. "You still should have told me," he said. "I know how hard it must have been for you. It must have reminded you of being with your brother."

How dare he mention that! "Let's not talk about this now," she said, her tone somewhat scolding.

"I want you to know that I'm very sorry about the way you found out," he persisted. "It's just that I've been so damned busy."

She would have liked to respond—too busy to phone your wife, but not too busy to get laid. "Look Mike," she said instead, "I know I've no right to be the slightest bit upset, but the fact is I am. For weeks I've been trying to talk to you. I've been doing my damnedest to keep the lines of communication open with no help from you. I had hoped that with time and effort we'd find a way to fix this thing—this mess of my own making," she admitted, "but I see now that it was just a pipe dream."

This was not the way he wanted things to go. "The phone is no place for these kinds of discussions," he responded, thinking, too, of Andrew's proximity. "We need to talk, face to face, and I want to do that soon. There's been a postponement in this tobacco trial, and I was thinking of coming to London for a couple of days."

She looked at Andrew but answered her husband. "It's not a good time."

He was somewhat peeved. "Why?"

"Andrew's visiting and besides, I've got to get ready for Marc's visit. I haven't had time to do that yet. I've been too busy with work."

"When would a good time be?"

"I can't say right now."

Andrew watched and listened intently.

"Why can't you say?" her husband asked, "Is it because you have company?"

"It's because I don't know when I'll have a free day. Right after Marc leaves, I'm going to Lyons and then to a shoot in the Pyrenees, and I've no idea how long I'll be tied up with that." She wanted to ask him—How does it feel, Mr. Rutledge, when your wife puts her work ahead of you?

"What's in Lyons?" he wanted to know.

"Andrew's taking me there."

"Andrew? What for?"

"He's taking me to see a doctor, an AIDS specialist."

That caught him completely off guard. "You told him?"

"Yes."

"I can't believe you'd tell someone that, especially someone you barely know! I don't think that was wise, Annie," he scolded.

That irritated her no end. "Don't worry, Mike. He's not going to tell anyone else. You'll be safe."

"You insult me. It's not myself I'm worried about!" A thought occurred to him, and after he voiced it, he held his breath as he awaited her answer. "Have you had bad news?"

"No, in fact, I've not seen a doctor since I left home. That's why Andrew's taking me to see someone. He thinks it's time to get answers."

He breathed an audible sigh of relief. "Well, I agree and I'm grateful to him for that." This might have been a good time to mention his meeting with Glenn, but this conversation was already uncomfortable enough. Besides, he told himself, I don't know if Glenn can be trusted, and I don't want to hold out false hope. Better to get her news from a doctor, he decided, than from that eel of a man.

A long, uncomfortable silence followed.

"Look Mike, I've got to go, all right?"

"I had hoped for a better talk," he admitted, sounding more conciliatory now.

"I told you, there's a lot going on. We'll talk again after Marc leaves. I'll try to call you then."

"Do that, and let me know when you get news." He waited to see if she would add anything. When she didn't, he offered, "I hope you and Marc have a great visit, and I hope everything goes well for you in Lyons. Say good-bye to Andrew for me, and tell him I said thanks for getting you to the doctor."

Still with the phone to her ear, she told Andrew, "My husband says good-bye and thanks for taking me to the doctor."

"No trouble at all. Cheerio, Mike!" he called, and Mike heard him.

Annie plopped herself on the couch. "I'm telling you, Andrew, you don't want to get involved in this. If I were you, I'd say—it was nice seeing you again, Annie—and be on your way after lunch."

He raised one eyebrow. "I take it you rang your husband this morning to tell him about your friend's death and found he wasn't alone."

"That's right."

"Was this the first you knew of it?"

"Yup," she answered as she blew the air from her lungs.

He frowned slightly as he put it together. "So you came from your friend's deathbed this morning and phoned your husband, only to find him sleeping with another woman. Then I showed up and nearly threw you from the cliff." It wasn't funny, but then again, maybe it was. He shook his head. "My, you have had a bad day."

She wanted to laugh, but she also wanted to cry. Instead, she made a funny face as she responded, "To put it mildly."

He couldn't help but see the irony. "Well, there's an upside to this," he offered. "It should be less sticky with Mike from here on in."

"How's that?"

"You're even now, aren't you?"

"Not really. He, at least, did it after our separation."

He slapped her thigh playfully. "No matter. Go on now. Finish putting yourself together so we can have lunch."

She noticed the room again. "Oh, I didn't say! Everything looks so lovely—all these wonderful roses!" She walked over to one vase and inhaled the spicy scent. "Thank you so much. This is really wonderful!"

"It's very little, really," he said, "but I'm happy it pleases you."

She kissed him softly on the cheek, then scooted off to her bedroom. He stood outside the door and spoke to her.

"While I was waiting for the hotel to bring lunch, I went to see your landlord, McBain. Nice chap."

"What for?" she asked.

"I wanted to see if he might have a tarp to cover the spot where the letters are buried."

"And did he?"

"He did," he answered, "and he went down there with me to do the job. The fellow was distressed to see what had happened. He told me that he'd worried about how closely to the edge you'd planted things. He's offered to help me dig it up tomorrow. He's got the right tools for it, if you still want me to, that is." He softened his tone. "There's a lot of anger in those letters, Annie. I really wonder if they might be better left buried." He was glad for the door between them, because it made it a little easier to talk. "When I brought them to you this morning, I wanted you to read them because I wanted to hurt you. I wanted you to feel as hurt as I did. But I don't feel that way any longer, and now I wish I could spare you that."

The response came straight from her heart. "I don't want to be spared of anything that has to do with you, good or bad. I was cheated of so much. I need to get back what I can of it," she told him, then left it at that.

She was at it again, he realized, giving voice to what was in his own heart, just as she used to.

When she emerged from the bedroom, he beamed, "You're so lovely! You've become more lovely over the years, you know."

"Have I?" she asked, blushing a little. "That's a very sweet thing to say, especially in light of what all the crying has done to my face."

"How about a little wine?" he offered, as he held her chair.

"Sounds wonderful," she responded.

He was setting her plate in front of her. "And after we eat, let's go for a drive. It would do you good to get out, I think." Before taking his place at the table, he bent and kissed her forehead. "Tuck in, now. I want to see you clean the plate."

As they started off down the long driveway, Andrew turned to her. "Do you mind if we go into town first? I'd like to stop at the hotel and have a shower and a change of shirt. I won't be an hour."

"Of course, I don't mind," she answered, "but I won't come with you. You can leave me at the cathedral. I'll wait for you there."

"Why do that?" he questioned.

A slight frown surfaced. "Last week you were afraid to go to a pub with me. Do you want to be seen going into a hotel together?"

He shifted gears and kept his eyes on the road, because it was unnecessary to answer her question.

They entered town via Abbey Walk. When they drove past the community hall, Annie exclaimed, "That was where you taught me to dance the Eight-some Reel!"

"I remember," he said, smiling broadly. "Ramsay wouldn't leave your side after that. His bladder must have been ready to burst because he wouldn't even go to the bathroom for fear I'd have you on the dance floor again."

They laughed together thinking of it, though inside they were both visited by the melancholy that always accompanied the memories.

They arrived at South Street, and he let her out in front of B. Jannetta's Sweet Shop. She watched him drive off, feeling instantly alone and not a little desperate as he left her sight. It disconcerted her to feel that way. This is not good, she told herself, not good at all, even as she checked her watch to time his return. It's only an hour, she reminded herself. He'll be back in an hour.

Andrew found an assortment of shirts and underwear and even a fresh pair of trousers in his suite, along with a note from the manager saying that anything he couldn't use would be returned. Everything he might need in the bathroom had been neatly ordered on the vanity, and he was shaved and out of the shower quickly. He checked his watch and saw that he was ahead of time, so he picked up the telephone and rang Crinan Castle again. This time, he was able to get his wife on the phone.

"Yes, Andrew."

"How are you?" he inquired timidly. "Maggie says you've a terrible headache."

"It's better, almost gone."

"I'm glad to hear it." He looked out the window as he spoke. The rooms had a view of the West Sands, the beach on which he'd said good-bye to Annie that night—that miserable night that forever changed his life.

"Why are you calling?" his wife asked.

He kept himself calm, his voice gentle. "Because I feel bloody awful about leaving you as I did. I need to know that you're all right."

"And what if I'm not? Would it make any difference to you? Would you come home?" she questioned.

He braced himself with a deep breath. "Are you asking me to come home?"

"Would you if I did?"

"You need to ask me first. I can't answer hypothetically." He wasn't being obstinate; he needed to be straightforward, and he wanted her to be, too. "Are you asking me?" he repeated.

A pregnant silence preceded her caustic response. "No, I'm not. I won't demean myself by doing that. Do you feel better now?"

"No, I don't feel better. I don't feel good about any of this, and neither does she, for that matter."

That comment inflamed her. "Well, isn't that generous! But she can afford to be generous, can't she, now that she has you. Tell me, how does it feel to have finally done what you were never able to before?" Since he'd left in the early morning hours, she could think of nothing but the two of them in bed.

He heard the pain and humiliation in his wife's voice and it tore at his heart, but he had no recourse save to keep up the honesty. "We haven't. I wanted to, but she wouldn't."

She had prepared herself to hear that they were lovers now, and his answer astonished her. "And why not?"

"She has her reasons, and I couldn't persuade her otherwise."

It was a relief, a painful relief that her husband was being so open with her. It afforded her an ironic sense of security, knowing that she would be told everything—that she would be the first to know, not the last.

He listened to her breathing for a few seconds. "You need to know what else has happened. I've told her I love her." The words were spoken without remorse.

But for a single sigh, his wife was silent.

He kept his gaze fixed upon the West Sands. "I'm sorry. I'm dreadfully sorry, but I need to have my feelings out. I know what I'm doing is horribly selfish and unbearably painful for you, but I've no other choice in the matter. Somehow, I hope you can understand that I'm not setting out to hurt you or the children. That's not at all what I want." He felt himself on the verge of tears.

She could hear his agony and she let it touch her, distracting her from her own. "What do you want?" she asked him softly. "Do you know?"

The afternoon sunlight was angled through the clouds so that streaks of it appeared to be reaching to the beach. "I can't see beyond today," he told her, as he watched the sand catch a silver fire.

Janet sighed again. "When do you think you might come home? What can I tell the children?"

So much had happened in the last seventy-two hours that it was a struggle to remember what day it was. "It's Monday, isn't it?"

"Yes." She found herself disturbed by that question, for it was not at all like him.

"Before the weekend," he said. "Sometime before . . ."

"The boys will be home again," she reminded him. "Do try to be here for them." Amazingly, all her bitterness was gone.

"Yes, of course. I should be home well before then." He reflected for a moment. "You probably don't want to hear me say this, and you probably don't believe it at this point, but I do love you, Janet."

A long silence followed before his wife answered him. "Of all the things you've said, that's the only thing I wanted to hear, and strangely enough, I do believe it."

He felt as though he'd just received a blessing. "Thank you, Janet."

She experienced a strong urge in this moment to reach out to her husband, to do something—anything—to ease his suffering, for once again she was hearing and seeing the young man who'd been so gravely wounded, so grievously injured. But she let the urge pass and hung up the phone without saying good-bye when it came to her, quite plainly and painfully, that it was not her help that he needed.

Andrew didn't remember leaving the hotel. The streets were crowded, and he had to park his car on The Scores, just up from the Russell Hotel. As he began walking to meet Annie, he still reeled with pain from the conversation with his wife. He berated himself, going over and over what he'd said to her, feeling her anguish as well as his own. He cursed his emotions, his heart, his infernal need. On top of it all, he questioned his sanity.

But something happened to him, in him, as he passed before the Whaum, then made his way along that street— the one he had traversed so many times as a young man. His steps became lighter, his stride longer and surer, and his torment seemed to melt away. It was as though he'd been imbued with new spirit, or, perhaps, revisited by an old one.

The clock towers began to toll the hour as he passed the castle ruins and turned toward North Street, walking among students and townspeople. They tolled, one follow-ing the other, sounding and echoing, seeking to remind and restrain—as they always did—but he was unaffected by them. He continued on his way, and the people he passed on the streets had no idea that the distinguished gentle-man in their midst was no longer living in their time but in a memory, and that he was floating, untethered, toward the cathedral.

Annie was sitting on a fallen pillar watching a young couple—obviously students, obviously in love—when An-drew came through the main gate. There was no earthly way that she could describe her joy at seeing him, coming to meet her, sailing through the emerald grass with the sun behind him, through the weathered ruins, through time itself. She was so full of emotion that she could barely breathe, and he forgot all about everything and everyone when she reached out her arms and embraced him, there, in that sacred place, like she was embracing life itself.

Chapter 40

They sat amid the ruins and clasped hands.

After a few minutes of silence, she whispered, "Tell me everything. I need to know everything."

He kissed her hands. "When you left, I thought I would die from heartache. I sat up all night in that storm and contemplated leaving with you, chucking everything and going away with you. When I went out in the morning, I didn't know what I would do, so I hid in the bushes to watch you. I saw you come out with John. It was then I knew you'd been lovers. I could see it all over you, even from a distance."

Stung by shame, Annie bowed her head.

"I watched you drive off," he remembered. "I tried to say good-bye to you in my heart, to force you from it, but it was impossible. More than ever, no matter what you'd done, I needed to be with you. I went home and told my father how I felt, what I wanted. We fought. We said unforgivable things to one another, then the family left for Mull. I waited for your letter, and when it arrived the joy I felt was indescribable. I wrote and told you that I would come, then drove into town to post the letter straight away. Afterward, I went into a pub and had a couple of drinks for courage, because I needed courage to break things off with Janet and to tell my father. But he had anticipated me and locked my passport in his safe. When I found out, I went insane trying to get at it. I left Crofthill in a rage. I got into my car and drove too fast. I crashed head-on into a neighbor. He was a good man, Annie—a father, a hard-working, honorable man—and I ended his life. I killed him."

She had lifted up her head to watch his eyes while he spoke; she saw them fill with so much hurt and regret that they became impossible to see through. He closed his eyelids when he finished telling her, trying to soothe the burn, to stop the scorching flow.

She kissed the tightly closed lids, letting her lips linger on them, breathing soft air onto them. He felt their cool caress, the healing touch of the woman whose love was behind all the suffering.

Their faces were very close, and Andrew went far into her eyes when he spoke again. "There's not been a morning since that I haven't looked in the mirror and cursed myself—for the rashness of my actions, for all the damage done. And most of those mornings, I've cursed you for coming into my life and setting it all in motion." He pulled himself out of her eyes and turned away.

She allowed him his distance and spoke to the grass beneath their feet. "Somewhere along the way, I got the idea that love was good, that it was a fine thing to be in search of and give to others. But it's never seemed to work that way, not for me anyway. Loving someone always seems to open the door to hell."

He looked back at her.

"I never meant to hurt you with my love," she said.

Sounding more conciliatory, he responded, "I know that, my heart knows that. It's just that it was so unbearably difficult without you. It was impossible to understand why I had to be without you, why so much suffering had to come of our meeting. I was very badly injured in that accident. I spent four weeks in hospital, four weeks I have little or no recollection of, and then the rest of the summer at home in bed, tended to by nurses. Most of it's a blur, the early part of it at least. But Ambrose, my father's valet, he tells me that when I was delirious with fever, I called for you. I begged you not to leave me."

She thought back to that time, to where she was and what she was doing, and she condemned herself for not being aware, for not somehow knowing that he needed her. Her heart, her limbs, her head, everywhere there was a pulse throbbed with his misery.

"When I was better and there were no letters from you, no word . . ." He couldn't go on.

They sat quietly and watched the young couple near them, listening to their intimate laughter. A gull with a damaged wing landed near them and pecked uselessly at his wound.

"I can't imagine how horrible it must have been," she told him.

"Horrible can't possibly describe it," he responded. "My father told me no letters had come, and I believed that you'd forgotten me."

"But I didn't, Andrew!" she protested. "I thought of you every day. I worried that you'd forgotten me, at first, but then I thought better of it. I decided that something had happened to keep you from me, but I imagined that it had to do with your obligations. I didn't receive your letter until I was home. I told you that. It came to me in October sometime, more than a month after I'd gotten home. If I'd gotten it while I was still in Europe . . ."

"If," he angrily interjected. "I do so despise that word. It's another way to torture ourselves, setting things up like that. If this had happened, if that hadn't happened. It's pure torment to think that way."

In an apologetic voice, she responded, "I don't want to torment you anymore." She looked off into the distance. "I want to hear everything you have to tell me, but if it causes you too much pain . . ."

Trying to compose himself, he took a deep breath. "There's not much more to say of it. My father managed to place some of the blame for the accident on Ian, the man I killed, so that I was never prosecuted for my part in it. The official report holds us equally responsible, but I know the truth."

"You said he was a father."

The self-loathing darkened his face. "Yes, with a whole brood of motherless children. His wife had died giving birth to the last one, and he raised them on his own for the most part. He was a very good man, Annie, a far better person than I."

"It would be hard for anyone to be a better person than you," she said.

He shook his head. "There's a lot you don't know about me." He looked to the young man and woman near them. "I went on with things. I pulled myself together and became the dutiful son, the responsible heir. My family undertook the care of Ian's children so that they never went without. My father even paid off the debt on his farm. They all seemed to manage nicely, considering. I guess that was because they had each other." He pushed himself to continue. "His children, they'd been my friends throughout childhood, but I had to keep my distance from them after that. I felt they knew. I still feel that."

"Did you never talk to them," she wondered, "tell them how sorry you are?"

"I did, once. I went to see them when I could walk on my own again."

"You couldn't walk after the accident?"

"My right leg was broken."

Upon hearing that, she buried her face in her hands.

"What is it?" he asked her.

"Nothing," she said, still with her face covered. "Go on, would you?"

"Anyway, I did tell them. I said I wished it'd been me instead, and then I broke down and sobbed like a baby. The oldest girl comforted me like she was my mother."

"I'm so glad it wasn't you," she whispered from behind her hands. "I'm so very glad it wasn't you."

"I spent a lot of years wishing it had been," he told her. "But I carried on, though most of the time feeling numb—indifferent, I guess you'd say—to everything and everyone."

She looked up at him again. "Even toward your wife?"

"Most of all toward Janet," he recognized. "She could never ignite in me the kind of passion I felt for you, and I resented her for that. For the first months of our marriage, I couldn't bring myself to have sex with her. And it wasn't until she became pregnant with Donald that I began to feel any warmth toward her, anything close to love." The self-loathing returned to his face, as he confessed, "I sought my pleasure—if you can call it that— elsewhere. Early on I spent my time with a reckless group of friends, Etonians with more money than sense. I'd disappear for a couple of days, then come home smelling of whores. A model husband, I was."

She tried not to let it, but her face revealed her disappointment.

"You're right to look at me that way," he told her with a bitter grin. "My behavior was deplorable and pathetically self-pitying." The air in his lungs felt stale and sour, and he exhaled the disgust. "I wallowed in that muck for a while, until I got so sick of myself I had to give it up. Then I went about throwing myself into the family business. I decided that I'd take revenge on life by becoming a ruthless businessman."

She desperately wanted to say something positive. "I know it was you who took the business global and made it into the success it is."

"Aye, I did that," he agreed, "and who knows how many alcoholics I'm personally responsible for adding to the world by making more whisky available to more people?"

Her face went sad again. "I think you're very hard on yourself. You can never forgive yourself for being human, can you?" She halted as though someone had interrupted her. "Do you know what I just remembered? I remember sitting here together, not this very spot, but over there a little," she said, pointing toward the wall, "that night we saw the northern lights. We'd come here to be alone, and we saw the lights. It seemed like it was meant just for us, didn't it?"

"It did. It was one of those moments," he started, but his voice dropped off. He was remembering now that it was one of the many times he had wanted to tell her he loved her. If only I had, he lamented, if only I had.

"We'd shared our deepest, darkest secrets, you and I, and we were never closer. You'd told me about what had happened at Eton, and I told you that you needed to forgive yourself for being human. Do you recall that?"

He looked up at the sky. "I do," he answered, and his face seemed somehow less worn.

Annie suddenly shivered.

"Are you cold?" he asked her.

"No, not cold. I just had such a strange feeling run through me. I'm a little spooked."

"What kind of feeling?"

"Like everything was falling into place, like it was all happening as it was meant to. Don't you feel it?"

A strong gust of wind blew through the grounds, and people who'd been wandering about took notice. They buttoned up their jackets, pulled their collars to their necks, and hurried about their business. Andrew had been looking at the sky, watching it race through the framework of the tower windows, and now he trembled slightly. He reached for Annie and embraced her again.

"You do feel it, don't you?" she asked him.

"I do," he admitted. "The weather's about to change."

"It's not the weather."

He looked to the racing clouds again. "I know," he said, "it's being here. It's us being together like this."

"They're playing with us again, Andrew."

"Who, Annie, your gods?" He might have laughed at her, but he recognized how earnestly she believed this.

"Yes," she answered soberly, "exactly."

The young couple near them had also decided to leave, and Andrew and Annie watched in silence as they left the cathedral grounds hand in hand.

"I wonder what's in store for them?" she mused.

"It makes me feel dreadfully sad, watching them," he answered her.

Her thoughts returned to the morning and the letters he had brought her. "Your letters, Andrew, what do they say?"

He sighed before responding. "How very hurt I felt, though not the first few. Those tell you of the accident, about how I tried to get to you and how much I wanted to be with you. I waited and prayed for a response. I fancied that once you'd gotten the first letter, you'd come to me straight away. When you didn't, I told myself it was because you'd gone to Italy or something, and that eventually you'd come back to

Saintes-Maries. So I wrote again and again, and when September came, I wrote to your home in America. I even wrote to Susannah once," he recalled, "but I don't suppose she got her letter either. My father would have been too clever to let that one get by." Andrew rubbed the back of his neck as the muscles in it tensed. They tended to do that whenever he thought of that time. "By September, I began to be very angry with you, and I let you know it. I wrote only a few more times after that, and then I gave up. I had come to believe what my father said about you by then."

A caretaker had moved to the main gate and closed it. Then he stood by, holding the keys, waiting for the few remaining visitors to leave.

"They lock everything up now," Annie informed him.

"Yes, I know," he answered, "the castle grounds, too. One has to pay to get in there. Shall we walk?" he asked her.

They were the last to leave the grounds, and the caretaker clanged the iron gates behind them. When she heard that sound, another cold shiver and a strong sense of déjà vu passed through Annie.

They walked up North Street, and as they turned onto Market, she asked him, "Aren't you worried that someone will recognize you?"

"That usually happens when I'm sitting still somewhere," he explained, "like in a restaurant when people have time to study my face and think about where they've seen me."

"You knew you were in for this kind of life. That's why you guarded your privacy when you were a student."

He nodded. "Exactly, and I wanted my life to be as normal as possible then. I didn't want to have to put up with arrogant asses like Patrick Ramsay, who'd feign friendship because of my family. Are you angry with me for not telling you?"

She answered honestly, "No, I'm really not. You could have trusted me, though. I wouldn't have told anyone."

"Susannah Barclay figured it out, you know."

"That sly dog," she chuckled. "She never said a word. I suppose Mel knew, too."

Her attitude was not what he'd expected, and he was pleasantly surprised by it. "You're an awfully good sport about this," he said.

"It's funny, but it's not a big deal to me," she realized. "What was more important, and still is, is how close we were."

"You're right," he agreed. "Other things were far more important."

They walked for more than an hour as the town went about closing the day businesses and readying itself for the night. They reminisced as they walked, stopping now and again to peer into shop windows. They eavesdropped on the conversations of passing tourists and got a good laugh over a group of boisterous Americans, who were all decked out in newly purchased plaids and Tam o' Shanters.

Their wandering eventually took them through Butts Wynd to The Scores and along that street to the Whaum. When they reached the cottage, they stood transfixed across the road, as though it were some mysterious natural phenomenon or a work of art they were trying to interpret. They lingered there for several minutes before Annie spoke and brought them back to the present.

"I know you'll think I'm nuts for believing this, but I felt it so strongly."

"Felt what?" he asked.

She studied his face. "I arrived in March—you know that—the same time of year that I first came here. I don't believe that was a coincidence any more than our being brought together on that flight was."

While he listened, he stared at the Whaum. What he was thinking and didn't tell her was that he, too, had been struck with that feeling when he recognized her on the plane.

"When I walked in the Whaum," she told him, "that was when I felt it. That was when I understood. I think I was called here by my own spirit. I was suffering for the loss of it, and it called me back to rediscover it." He was smiling at her now, but he wasn't laughing. "And it wasn't just my spirit that I felt in that house; yours was there, too. Even though you and I separated, I think they remained here where they could be together. Do you think I'm crazy for believing that?"

He chuckled slightly. "A little out there, but not crazy."

Her voice threatened to give out on her when she uttered her next words. "When my brother was killed . . ."

He reached for her hand. "You don't have to talk about this if you're not ready."

She looked to the Whaum again. "That's when I lost my spirit. That's when it left me. I thought it had died with Timmy, but it hadn't. It came back here to be with yours, where it could be safe."

He wanted to understand what she meant by that, but first he had to know one thing. "How was he killed, Annie?"

"On his motorcycle," she answered. "It was a year after I came home from Europe. He was going to a local college, and he'd gotten a job and bought himself a brand new motorcycle. He was so proud of that bike," she remembered. "He'd bring it in the garage at night and polish it till it sparkled." Picturing him doing that made her smile. "He was on his way to classes one morning. He'd only gone a couple of blocks from our house. Our dad was at work, and I'd already left for my classes, but our mother was home." All traces of her smile disappeared. "She was sitting in the kitchen, drinking coffee, and she heard the sirens." Annie had to stop now, because it was getting too difficult.

He lifted her hand and kissed it repeatedly.

She kept her eyes on the cottage. "That doesn't seem fair, does it, to be sitting in your kitchen, minding your own business, and then to hear something like that and not know that it's meant for you, that your whole life is being turned upside-down." She went thoughtfully quiet again. After several moments, she asked him, "Do you know what I'd like?"

"No, my darling, tell me," he whispered.

"I'd like to go sit in the Russell and have a pint of heavy with you for old time's sake. Do you think we could do that?"

He was still holding her hand. Without saying anything, he led her the short distance to the hotel. She took the window seat, and he went to the bar for their pints.

They drank their beers in silence. When they were nearly finished, she told him, "He wasn't killed in the accident itself. His right leg was very badly broken. They were considering amputating it."

"That's why you looked at me strangely when I told you I'd broken my leg," he said.

She made every effort to keep the emotion from her voice. "I didn't want to leave him that first night. I told everybody else to go home and get some rest—my parents, and his girlfriend Maryann; they were all so exhausted and upset. I told them I'd take care of him. He was in intensive care, and I sat in a chair next to his bed. He was full of drugs, and he was hallucinating from them. He asked me about white rabbits and things crawling on the walls. He wanted me to kill the things on the walls. It reminded me of that bad trip I had, so I knew how to comfort him. I kept telling him it that would be all right, kept putting cool cloths on his forehead and stroking his hand, trying to keep him anchored to me."

Andrew had been trying to keep his eyes with hers as she spoke, but the misery he discerned there was so distressing that he had to look away frequently.

"They'd told us that if he made it through the night, he'd probably be all right, and I was determined to help him get through it. I wouldn't leave him, not for a minute, not even to go to the bathroom."

He couldn't help but picture himself in his own hospital bed and think what a difference it would have made to have had Annie beside him.

"As the night went on," she continued, "he seemed to be doing better, and I drifted off. Then I was awakened by his breathing. He was having trouble breathing. He grabbed my hand; he grabbed it so tightly that I yelled for the nurses. He looked at me. His eyes were so big, so terrified, they were asking me to help him, to help him breathe. But I couldn't," she bemoaned. "I couldn't do anything. I kept telling him it was going to be OK, then they were there trying to help him. But he kept looking at me. It was me that he needed, me that he trusted." Her voice was pure emotion now. "He was gasping for air. He couldn't get his breath, and there was nothing I could do. I felt his grip on my hand loosen and he closed his eyes, then they pushed me out of the room. They worked and screamed and yelled for things. They knocked over his IV bottle; I could hear it crashing to the floor. Doctors were yelling orders, and more people were running into the room. I kept seeing his eyes; I kept seeing Timmy's eyes pleading with me. I never saw those eyes again, Andrew. I never saw the eyes of my little brother again." Her body stiffened suddenly, as though she was shutting off inside, as though the intensity of the feeling was overloading her circuits.

Andrew didn't care that they were in a public place. He pulled her into his chest and held her against his heart. His own tears were irrepressible as he ran the scene over in his mind, seeing her, seeing her brother, and remembering Annie on the beach, struggling to get her breath, realizing now why she did this. His own heartache grew, as he imagined the suffering she'd endured, carrying that horrible moment with her, reliving it in times of stress.

He retained that tight embrace, and her words were muffled as she spoke into his shoulder. "I promised everyone I'd take care of him. I promised Timmy that everything would be all right, but I couldn't keep those promises. Timmy needed my help and I let him down. I let him go: He was holding onto me and I let him go. I'll never forget the sounds he made, trying to get air, trying just to breathe. That's all he wanted; he just wanted to be able to take a breath. That's not very much to ask, is it? There's so much of it, so much air, and all he wanted was a little bit, just a little bit. Why couldn't he have that?"

She sounded very weak and small, and he moved her away slightly to see her face again. "No, darling," he answered tenderly, "it isn't much to ask. It's impossible to understand why he couldn't have that."

She seemed confused and lost and terribly fragile, and it frightened him to see her that way. He knew that he was watching her slip into something dangerous, into a place she'd been before—a place where she remembered everything, felt everything, as though it were happening now.

Her confusion only deepened, when she explained, "They said it was a fat embolus, some complication of long bone fractures. A tiny amount of fat had gotten into his circulation and ended up in his lung. It choked the life out of him. Such a small thing, really, such an insignificant thing anyplace else. They found it when they did the autopsy."

He shook his head and wiped the tears from his cheeks.

Her voice had a strange, detached quality to it now. "I've never been able to make any sense of it. All these years I've tried, but I just can't. And now I'm trying to make sense of what happened to you, but I can't understand that either."

"Annie," he said, as he watched her face grow more and more troubled. "Let me take you back to the cottage. I'll fix you something to eat, and we'll sit together by the fire. We can talk there."

She looked up at him. "The miserable bastards weren't content to take you from me. They had to take my Timmy, too."

What Andrew saw in her made him realize that she had neither heard nor understood what he'd told her. Gently, he pulled her from the window seat. "Come on, we're leaving," he said.

She seemed bewildered. "We are? Why?"

"Because it's time to go."

"Where are we going?"

"To the cottage."

"The Whaum?" she wondered.

"No, Annie," he responded, "to your cottage."

"But I don't have one," she answered, as though he should know that. In that moment, with her mind a disordered jumble of past and present, she thought she lived in David Russell Hall.

He was very concerned now; he put his arm around her shoulder and led her to the car.

The ride to Kingsbarns was quiet. He held onto her hand between changing gears, turning his head frequently to see if she was all right. She kept her eyes fixed on the road and said nothing, showed nothing of what she was feeling or thinking. When they reached her cottage and he had stopped the car, she finally spoke.

Her voice still had a distant quality to it. "Do we have to go in there? It's dark and lonely in there."

"Where would you like to go?"

"Someplace, anyplace," she answered, "but I hate to go in there at night by myself."

"You're not by yourself," he told her. "I'm with you."

"You are? How can you be?"

He wasn't sure about how to respond to that. "I'm here with you. It's 1994, and Timmy has been dead for a long time, Annie."

She found that statement perplexing and looked at him as though he'd taken leave of his senses. "I know that," she told him. "It's just that you have a family and a home to go to, and I can't go there with you, can I?"

He shook his head now, relieved to see that she was thinking clearly again. "I'm not going to leave you; you need to understand that. We've found each other again and I'm not going to leave you."

"But you'll have to sometime. You'll have to."

He started up the engine again.

"Where are we going?" she asked.

"To Crail," he answered. "We'll find a restaurant and have a bit of supper, and if you want, we'll get a room for the night."

"But you can't do that," she understood. "It's too risky for you."

"I can do whatever I bloody well please," he told her, "and it pleases me to be with you."

"No, turn off the car," she decided, sounding more like herself again. "We'll stay here."

When they opened the door, the fragrance of roses enveloped them. It reassured both of them—Annie especially—that this was where they were supposed to be. While Andrew laid the fire, she remained near the doorway, motionless, like a polite guest waiting for an invitation to sit. He asked if there was anything he could do for her and she shook her head no, so once the fire was ablaze he went into the kitchen and began bustling about to prepare something to eat. He was at the sink doing a bit of washing up first when he felt her arms close around his waist.

"Thank you," she told him. "Thank you for caring so much about me."

He dried his hands before turning to embrace her. "I've never loved anyone the way I love you, Annie." His breath was warm on her neck, as he whispered, "I don't know how to ask your forgiveness though, and I need to beg you for that."

The bewildered look returned to her face, and he led her into the parlor to sit in front of the hearth.

"I made very stupid and selfish assumptions," he said "and I've been angry with you for years because of them. I came here this morning and unleashed that anger on you, and I had no right, no right at all. I was so busy being sorry for myself that I didn't even give a thought to what you might have been going through. Now that I know, I don't think I can ever forgive myself, though I need to ask for yours." He lifted her hands and kissed them.

She kissed his before she answered. "There's no need for that. I understand, because I hurt, too. What's happened between us today, that's made up for everything." She crouched down and rested her head in his lap.

The firelight flickered on the walls, and the wind was the only sound they heard as it wrapped itself around the little house. Andrew stroked her hair as she lay in his lap, then scooped it up and combed his fingers through it, marveling at the array of colors it cast, even in the dim light. After all the time that had gone by, it seemed perfectly miraculous that he was holding her again, touching the hair that had always seduced him with its sensuousness.

His need to nurture her made him ask, "Are you hungry? There are leftovers from lunch. I could warm something."

"No thanks," she answered. "I'm more tired than anything, and those pills haven't completely worn off yet."

That would explain some of her behavior, he realized. "Shall I put you to bed?"

Her voice grew soft, and she rubbed at his thigh as she rallied the courage to ask, "Can you stay with me tonight? There's my son's bedroom but . . ."

He looked into her eyes. "But what?"

She straightened herself on the couch. "If you'd like, what I mean to say is, I'd like it if you'd sleep with me." Feeling suddenly foolish, she looked away in embarrassment and wished she could take it back. But the trouble was, in spite of everything, she longed to lie with him, to feel his body next to hers throughout the night.

"We never did that. We never spent the night together," he recalled sadly.

"It wasn't for lack of trying on my part," she reminded him, then smiled fleetingly.

He smiled, too, then rose from the sofa and held out his hand. She looked into his palm for a moment, then gave hers to him so that he might lead her to the bedroom.

She stood near the bed and began unbuttoning her blouse. He watched her for a few seconds, then he asked, "Would you let me do that?"

Her hands fell to her sides as he moved closer. With the touch of the first button, her heart began to dance. But when he leaned in to kiss her, she moved away.

She settled herself on the edge of the bed, pushing her hands into the mattress, then looked up at him. "I think we need some ground rules."

"All right," he answered, though it was difficult to speak from behind his pounding heart.

She sighed. "I think it's reasonably safe to kiss, from what I've read and been told, as long as it's not deep and prolonged. We probably shouldn't have kissed the way we did this morning."

"I could start kissing you and not stop for the next year," he told her.

Her breathing quickened. "I want to sleep with you, Andrew. I want to be naked with you; I want to feel what it's like to hold you." She lowered her voice, "But I'm not going to let you inside of me, not even with a condom, because I don't trust them to protect you."

He brushed some hair from her cheek and tucked it behind her ear. "It'll be inordinately difficult," he wanted her to know, "but leaving you tonight, that would be far worse."

She hesitated for a moment, then conquered her reluctance. "I've been giving it some thought, and if you can promise me that you'll respect my wishes—my desire to protect you—I was thinking that it'd be safe for us to make love with our hands." A rush of heat inflamed her cheeks.

He tenderly lifted her chin. "The way we did when we were young."

She kept repeating inside—God, how I want you. "Yes," she answered, "like that." Steady on, she told herself, you need to keep some control. She asked him now, "You don't have any cuts on your hands, do you?"

He displayed them to her, palms up first, then down, and the simple action seemed wildly erotic. They were strong and tanned, and knowing that in a few moments they could be exploring her body was making her giddy with desire.

She blushed again. "They say the virus dies as soon as it comes in contact with the air, but you should probably wash them afterward, just in case."

"All right," he answered, capturing her eyes. "But I want to tell you something. I want you to know that I'm well. Because of the affairs that I've had, I've been tested at my physical exams, and I'm perfectly well."

She didn't say anything, but as she pondered the irony, she frowned.

He understood that frown. "It's important for you to know, because you could be, too. It wouldn't be fair of me, would it, to recklessly endanger you? You don't know anything for certain yet."

"No, you're right," she realized. "Thank you for telling me." She was still sitting on the edge of the bed, and she looked down at her lap as she recalled how careless she'd been with her husband's health. She regretted that most of all.

Reaching his hands out, he pulled her to him. Ever so gently, he kissed her lips, then he began removing her clothing.

She remained perfectly still with her eyes closed, treasuring each tender movement, every brush on her skin from his fingertips. When she was completely undressed, he nudged her onto the bed, and remained standing for a moment, taking in the sight of her reclined body. Modesty made her bring her knees together and fold her arms across her breasts, though one hardened nipple peeked through.

"I remember the first time I saw you naked," he reverently told her, "and you're every bit as beautiful now as you were then."

Now he began to undress, revealing his lean, muscular body and an erection that Annie thought magnificent. She smiled broadly. "I remember the first time I saw you, going into the sea on May Morning."

He smiled, too. "I don't know if I did that to show off or if a plunge into the cold water had become a necessity after kissing and fondling you all night." He bent and kissed her lips again, then her face and throat. He lay beside her and moved to her abdomen, his mouth traveling over her belly with licking strokes. Then he took one of her nipples into his mouth and suckled it while he massaged the other, all the while rubbing his hardness against her. She threw her head back and moaned, a rich, visceral moan that aroused him all the more.

She coaxed him into lying on his back so she could take her turn. She kissed the scars on his face, slowly tracing them with her tongue as though she meant to dissolve them away. When he shut his eyes in a tight squint and wrinkled his forehead, she said, "Don't, Andrew, don't keep your feelings locked away from me. Let me know them."

He opened his eyes and released perfect, round tears to her, tears that she put her lips to and drank. He tasted them when he kissed her mouth again.

She spoke with her lips touching his. "We need to share everything, you and I. We can't be any other way."

He understood that, but still he told her, "I've kept it to myself for so long."

"I know," she said, kissing him again and lapping up the flowing tears. "Let me take it from you. Let me take the sadness from you."

He closed his eyes again. "I don't know if I can. I don't know if I can be that open."

"My Andrew, my love." She took his hand and placed it over her heart. "It's me, your Annie. I'm here with you now."

"I'm afraid to let these feelings out." And as he said that, he realized why. "Because I'm terrified of losing you again."

"Shhh, my darling," she tenderly whispered, "not tonight. Let's not talk of that now. Just feel my love, Andrew. Let me give it to you."

She could feel his muscles relax as she went back to the exploration of his body, kissing every inch of his throat, his hairy chest and belly, moving downward to his penis. She touched it gingerly with her lips, a little afraid that it was not a safe thing to do, and the sensation it conveyed made him sigh deeply. With one hand she began to stroke him, caressing and massaging his scrotum with the other.

Breathlessly, he asked her, "Where do you want me to come?"

She released him with another tender kiss, then lay on her back. "Here," she answered as she cupped her breasts.

He straddled her and she welcomed him into the space between them, her hands supporting her fullness while he thrust. He tried to hold back, but it was impossible. When it happened, it felt as though his insides were spewing out of him, as though it would never stop. When it was finally over, he was utterly weak.

She sat up to support him and pressed her body to his, rubbing the warm fluid into their flesh. They embraced then rolled together on the bed, Andrew moaning and sighing, calling, "Oh Annie, my Annie."

When they relaxed their embrace, he kissed her repeatedly on the face and throat, reverently massaging the full breasts he'd given himself to. His hands, lubricated by his semen, moved downward to caress her abdomen. His fingers found her tangled hair. They lingered there for a moment, then glided into her. As he thrust them more deeply, he whispered into her ear, "I never forgot how you felt, never." She had been the first woman he'd ever touched there.

She, too, had never forgotten his touch. His presence inside of her had been so welcome, so healing—just as it was now. She reveled in the sensation and took his face in her hands so that she might kiss it over and over.

He delivered some of her own, copious moisture to her hardened clitoris, then with his other hand, rubbed it with increasing intensity, sending her to a place where all she knew was need and pleasure. She pointed her toes and arched her back, then groaned into his mouth as the spasms began. In this moment, entering her would have been easier than breathing, and it took superhuman effort to keep himself from doing that.

The bedclothes were sticky and wet and heavy with their scents as they went into the night, as they embraced and pressed their flesh together, unable to be close enough. Exhaustion finally carried them into sleep, their arms holding tightly, her cheek pressed to his chest so that she might hear his heartbeat. Their breaths came in unison— the long, deep breaths of satisfaction. A waft of roses drifted through the doorway and crept over them, covering them like the most delicate of sheets.

The sea and its wind-child grew still and quiet, and the farm fields and pastures that surrounded them were mute, shadowy witnesses. The coal fire burned through the night and illuminated the windows of the little house, providing the only light in the consuming darkness. From the outside, the panes of glass seemed to flicker like distant stars that no one saw, in the East Neuk of Fife, in a humble cottage on the cliffs, that had broken free from the world.

Chapter 41

The inhabitants of St. Andrews noticed nothing unusual about the morning. Housewives swept sidewalks and puttered in gardens, university students hurried to their classes, shopkeepers washed windows and prepared to open for the day. As the morning progressed, the traffic grew heavy and the streets full, while groundskeepers tended to the Old Course and hotels fed breakfast to ravenous tourists. Life went on as usual in the old gray town, but several miles down the coast, two people awakened and looked at one another, recognizing that their entire world had changed.

He'd been watching her as she slept. He whispered "Good morning," just as her eyes opened.

Her face lit with an enormous smile, but it lessened when she asked, "Are you real? Is this real?"

He'd been asking himself that same question, pondering how the dream that he'd given up so long ago could finally materialize. It seemed wrong somehow to attach words to such a miracle, so he answered by putting his lips to hers.

She felt his erection press into her flesh and teased, "My, but you are the randy one."

"I haven't felt this way for years," he admitted as he positioned himself on top of her.

She brought her thighs together to hold him there. "You're wonderful, you know, to show such restraint. Thank you for that."

"My Annie," he answered, kissing her throat and chest, "don't you know I'd do anything for you?"

They had drifted off to sleep again when they were awakened by a knock on the front door.

Startled, Andrew sat abruptly and rubbed his eyes. "Bloody hell, the hotel! I'd forgotten."

"The hotel?"

"I'd arranged for them to come this morning." He hastily pulled on his jeans and shirt. "I'll just be a minute," he said as he closed the bedroom door.

He returned before long, carrying two glasses of freshly squeezed orange juice.

She giggled when she saw him. "Room service?"

He bowed playfully. "At your service, madam."

"How'd you know you'd be here this morning?" she chuckled. "Awfully sure of yourself, aren't you, your lordship?"

"They needed to collect their things from yesterday," he grinned. "Hungry?"

"Dying of it!"

He lifted her robe from the chair and helped her into it.

"What do you want to do today?" he asked, as they took their seats at the little table.

"Be with you," she said.

He unfolded the napkin in the bread basket, then offered it to her. "I have an idea for us."

"It sounds wonderful," she told him, helping herself to a sweet roll.

He laughed slightly. "You don't even know what it is yet."

She eagerly bit into the crisp roll, which was flavored with tiny currants. Her mouth still full, she answered, "It doesn't matter. I love it, whatever it is."

He pointed to the picnic basket behind her.

"I do so love you," she declared. "Where are we going?"

He answered simply, "You'll see."

They took a long, sensual bath together, gently rubbing one another with soapy hands, exploring, caressing, massaging, lingering so long that the water turned frigid. There was no shower, so Annie kept a large enamel pitcher at the ready for pouring clean rinse water; they took turns doing this to one another and had to keep restarting the water heater. Once again, Andrew cursed the outmoded contraption.

"I don't mind it," she told him, "because it takes me back to the Whaum. If we'd been lovers then, we'd have bathed together like this."

He closed his eyes at the thought. "God, how I wish we had. How different our lives would have been. When I think that you might be ill now," he added, then instantly regretted that he had.

His words upset her. "Please don't say that. Please don't remind me."

Andrew climbed out of the tub first and after draping a towel around his waist, he immediately attended to her; she had begun to shiver to such an extent that her teeth chattered. He rubbed her arms and back to warm her, but he soon recognized that her chills were not brought on by the cold. She couldn't go on like this, he knew. "When we get dressed, will you do something for me?"

She knew what was coming and went into her bedroom to escape.

He didn't want to put undo pressure on her, but he also realized that if her former lover was well, it would put an end to her torment. "I want you to call this man you were seeing," he said as he followed her. "I want you to ask him about his test results."

She closed her eyes tightly. "Please Andrew, not now."

"Look at me, Annie."

Reluctantly, slowly, she opened her eyes again.

He grasped her upper arms. "Whatever happens, I'm not going to walk out on you. If it is bad news, it's going to come sooner or later, and won't it be better that I'm here with you?"

The tears were looming. "But I'm so scared."

"I know you are, and I'd be lying if I said I weren't, too," he admitted. "But it's time to know."

She looked at the clock on her dresser, then protested, "I can't call him now. It's too early there."

"All right, later then, but today," he insisted, "and I want your word on that."

She grimaced. "All right, goddamnit."

When he began to dress, Andrew expressed some consternation. "I have no fresh clothes to put on. I should have brought the things from the hotel."

"I've got a shirt that should fit you," she offered. "It's one of Mike's if you don't mind wearing it."

"Why should I mind?" he asked.

"I thought it might make you feel funny."

He considered that, then asked, "Funnier than I feel about sleeping with his wife, about being in love with his wife? What's funny is that I don't feel the least bit odd about any of this. What I feel is the absolute rightness of being with you."

She walked to the closet and removed a freshly ironed, blue Oxford cloth shirt, then helped him into it. It fit him well enough, although Mike's chest was broader from his days of playing football for Princeton. She thought of that strong chest now and reflected a moment on a beautiful fall day many years ago when they played touch-football with friends. She had the ball and was sprinting toward the goal when she felt his arms wrap around her and pull her to the ground. He pinned her with his powerful body, and despite the playful nature of the illegal tackle, he held her there a moment looking deep into her eyes. When they were on their way home that evening, he impulsively pulled the car into a secluded spot, then made love to her in the back seat with the energy and impatience of a teenager.

As she buttoned the shirt for him, she told Andrew, "I've always liked wearing my husband's things," and in this moment she realized why. "It was a way of feeling close to him when he wasn't around, which was a lot of the time."

"How do you feel about me wearing it?" he wondered.

She found herself staring at him, at the oddity of seeing him in something of Mike's. "Fine," she answered, though she wasn't quite sure.

"Would you tell me about him, Annie, tell me what went wrong?"

She shrugged before answering. "I don't know. He just sort of drifted away from me." She was still chilled from the bath and said abruptly, "I'm going to make some tea."

As they walked into the kitchen together, he asked, "Did things go bad early on?"

"No," she responded, as she filled the kettle. "In the beginning it was good, but there was always a tendency on his part to keep some distance between us. And it seemed the harder I tried to bridge that distance, the further away he pulled."

"Was this his first marriage?"

She shook her head and leaned against the sink. "That was part of the problem. His first wife was murdered."

He was sincerely shocked. "Dear God—how?"

"In a robbery," she told him, "and she was five months pregnant. The man shot her in the abdomen." If she was unemotional in the telling of this story, it was only because she'd lived with it for so long.

He lowered his head and closed his eyes as he conjured up the horrible image, saying only, "The poor man." He thought of his own wife in her pregnancies and how protective he'd been of her. The idea of someone assaulting a woman in that condition was inconceivable, and the reaction it would elicit in the husband and father was unfathomable in its fury.

The kettle whistled. As she poured the boiling water into the pot, the unmistakable fragrance of Earl Grey filled the tiny room. "They were young and in love, and it was their first child," she went on. "He was in court that morning, and he didn't even know until hours later. When he got to the hospital, she was already brain-dead, and he had to make the decision to stop life support."

"Dear God," he said again, nausea welling up in him. "Can it be any worse?"

Her eyes were focused on something in the nonexistent distance, and as she continued, she folded her arms. It was something of a defensive posture, one she unconsciously assumed when talking about this. "He wouldn't do it right away. He sat at her bedside for days, holding her hand, talking to her, trying to bring her back. And when it was finally over, Mike insisted they bury her with the little fetus they'd already taken."

The pain of that was incomprehensible. "How ever did he go on?" Andrew asked.

"Work was his salvation," she informed him, then added, "and now it's his hiding place."

As he contemplated the tragedy, Andrew began to understand something about Mike. How could anyone who'd been through what he had ever open himself up again? "Did he love you when you married?"

"In all honesty, I'm not sure," she answered, "but I think he started to. I think there was a point when he was beginning to forget, and he was letting himself love me and my son, then he just stopped." When she realized that she'd left out an important detail, she hesitated briefly. "Did I tell you that Marc is the just about the same age his child would have been?"

He shook his head as his understanding deepened. "Is that why you never had children together?"

Sighing, she answered simply, "Mike couldn't handle it." She poured the tea now, their mugs already prepared with one raw sugar cube and the cream that she preferred. "It did occur to me that he was afraid of losing us, too, so I tried to help him with that, but the more I tried . . ." She halted in mid-sentence.

"Ta," he said, as she handed a mug to him. "How about professional help? Did you try that?"

She wrapped her icy hands around the warmth of her mug and held it close to her face. "I suggested it, but he turned it down point blank. He'd been in therapy after Michele's death and thought it a waste of time."

"Did you love him, Annie?" he asked timidly.

She responded without hesitation, "Very much, and I still do. He's a good man, Andrew, certainly one of the best I've ever known. That's why it hurt so. That's why I've suffered for the loss of him." She swallowed some tea before adding, "It was another painful loss—like you, like my little brother. I do reckless things when I hurt like that, I do desperate things."

"Like having an affair," he finished for her.

Her brow lifted slightly. "It wasn't what I set out to do. He was one of my closest friends, someone I could talk to, and I was so lonely. I felt abandoned."

He reached for her hand just as the phone began to ring.

She let it ring several times before she picked up. "Yes, this is Annie d'Inard."

"Maxwell Brown, solicitor for the estate of Thomas Keegan, Ms. d'Inard. I wonder if we might have a word?"

"Yes, of course."

"There's a bequest, a personal request really, that Mr. Keegan made just ten days prior to his death. It asks if you might be willing to scatter his ashes. He was cremated yesterday, you see."

Annie swallowed hard. "Sure," she answered, in a near whisper. "I'll do that. Is there anything else?"

"No, that's the extent of it."

"What about his son, Mr. Brown? Are you trying to locate his son?"

"It was not requested."

She shook her head and dropped her gaze to the floor. "How do I, I mean, where do I go to get the remains?"

"I'll have them brought to you. Would tomorrow afternoon be convenient? Say, two-ish?"

"Tomorrow at two is fine."

"And there's a letter for you. My courier will bring that, also."

"Was that about your friend?" Andrew asked as she sat next to him on the couch.

"It was his lawyer, asking if I'd mind scattering his ashes. Tom requested it."

He enfolded her in his arms, and she rested her head on his shoulder.

"Will you go with me?" she asked.

He took one of her hands and kissed it, then held it against his lips as he answered, "Of course."

They sat in silence for a while before Andrew spoke again. It was almost too much for today, but he felt very strongly that it needed to be done. "What time does Glenn get to his office?"

Her eyes misted over instantly. "Oh, Andrew! Please don't make me do this now! It's not a good time."

"There's never going to be a good time," he said. He reached for the phone and brought it to her lap.

Trembling, she dialed the number, then anchored herself in his eyes.

Glenn was holding his morning meeting, but he abruptly ended it when his secretary told him who was on the phone. He quickly ushered the half dozen people out of the office. Feeling somewhat paranoid, he then locked the door.

"Annie!" he exclaimed. "I was beginning to think I'd never hear from you again. Where are you? Are you home?"

"No, I'm still in Scotland." Her heart was beating so fast and strong that it pulsated in her ears.

He continued in a quieter voice. "After my meeting with your husband, I thought for sure I'd hear from you."

His casual tone had reassured her heart and it had slowed a bit, but now it was her mind that raced as she attempted to make sense of what he'd just said. "You had a meeting with Mike?"

"I had to tell someone," he explained. "You said you were going to let me know how to reach you but you didn't, and I wanted you to get the news as soon as possible."

Oxygen seemed suddenly scarce in the room. "What news?"

Andrew watched her chest begin to heave. As he had on the beach, he took her hand and held it against his heart, exaggerating his own breathing with deliberate slowness.

Glenn's voice dropped to a whisper. "Just a second." After walking to the door and putting his ear to it, he came back to the phone. "I thought someone was outside, but it's OK. I was thoroughly tested, Annie, and I'm completely negative."

"Negative," she blurted out. "Did you say negative?"

"Yes, completely. You had me in a panic, so I went to Hopkins to see my cousin. He's an internist there. He did the tests twice, and there wasn't even a single antibody."

The return of breathable air made the room spin. "I don't understand."

"Mike didn't tell you?"

"No." To steady herself, she turned back to Andrew's eyes.

"I don't know why he didn't," Glenn told her. "I specifically asked him to. I wanted you to be reassured, about me anyway. There's nothing for you to worry about with me, and I wanted you to know that."

She stammered, "He never said—he never said he spoke with you." That part didn't seem real, and it lent a feeling of unreality to everything else she was hearing. "I don't understand that."

"Maybe talking to you about me is just too hard for him," he offered.

"But we've talked about you," she protested. She was trying to remember what Mike had said yesterday. Didn't he tell her to call Glenn? Why hadn't he told her then that he'd spoken with him? "When was this? When did you see him?" Maybe she could find an answer there.

"About a month ago. We met at Harry's for a drink."

She knew Harry's well, and she readily pictured Mike and Glenn sitting at a table discussing her and her faithlessness. That encounter had to have been perfectly horrible for Mike. But a month ago? Mike had known for an entire month?

Andrew didn't want to lose her eyes. They were his focus, so he lifted her chin to see them again. Tears were visible on her cheeks.

"Annie? You still there?"

"Yeah."

"Are you all right? Have you been tested again?"

"No, I haven't."

"Why on earth not?" he asked.

"I haven't wanted to know," she explained.

"That seems silly."

"I guess it does," she admitted.

"Are you going to come home now?" he wondered.

"No."

"Why not? What about your son?"

It was an effort to pull her thoughts together, but she managed. "He's coming here next week, and then he'll be in Spain the rest of the summer."

"Oh, I see," he responded. "I guess you've given up on your marriage."

Had she? His comment made her question that herself. "I'm working here. I've got a job here," she told him.

"I didn't know. What are you doing?"

"Consulting."

"Are they paying you well?" It was a typical question for him.

She answered bluntly. "Very. Look, I'm sorry, but I've got to go." She needed to relay this information to Andrew. Maybe he could make some sense of it.

"Me, too. I've got a meeting."

"Thanks for letting me know," she managed to add.

"I'm sorry you didn't get the news sooner, but it's not like I didn't try. Will you give me your number so I can call you sometime? Who knows but I might even get over there soon. We might think about getting together."

That suggestion was repulsive in so many ways, it was impossible to pick one. "It's better if we keep our distance," she told him in no uncertain terms.

"Right," he responded, then misinterpreted, "until you get things sorted out with your husband. Well, it was nice to hear from you. Really, it was."

"Yeah," she said curtly, "you take care." She hung up the receiver and stared at the wall.

"Tell me," Andrew demanded.

Still not quite grasping it, she said, "He's not ill. He's completely negative."

"My God," he exclaimed, "that's wonderful. That's perfectly, bloody wonderful!" Joy filled his face and voice, but it quickly faded when he realized that she was not smiling. In fact, she looked quite troubled. "What's wrong? Something's wrong."

"Mike," she answered, "he spoke with Mike a month ago. They met and Glenn told him he wasn't infected, and Mike never said a thing. He never said a word to me about it."

"What? Why, in God's name not?"

"I guess," she stopped herself.

He thought he understood. "God! It was his way of punishing you, wasn't it?"

"No," she protested, "he'd never do anything like that! He's incapable of anything as mean as that!"

"Then why, Annie? Why wouldn't he tell you? He's had to know the kind of anguish you've suffered. It was impossibly cruel of him to keep that information from you!"

"There had to have been a reason," she insisted. "You don't know Mike. He wouldn't have kept that from me without good reason."

"I can't imagine a reason good enough." He could see in her face that the doubts were creeping in, the same questions he was now asking himself, the most important one being, was it Mike who'd put her at risk?

Her mind was a battleground. No, she told herself, absolutely not. Mike said that he'd been faithful; there was no reason to question that. Still, I did catch him in a hotel room with another woman this morning, and it couldn't have been the first time, or was it? I trust him, she reminded herself, and I've no cause to do otherwise. This mess is my responsibility, but is it possible that he's guilty, too? No, stop doing this to yourself. It'll drive you crazy. There's only one way to settle this, one way to be sure. I have to see that doctor Andrew wants me to see, and I have to do my damnedest to keep this from my mind until then.

As her thoughts raced, she scanned the room, looking to see if she might find an answer buried among the ashes from yesterday's fire, or, perhaps, lying on the table, scattered among the remnants of breakfast. Her bewildered eyes finally settled on the window that looked upon the farm road where Andrew's Aston Martin was parked.

"Let's not talk about this now," she said in an unsteady voice. "I can't even think of it. Let's get out of here and go have our picnic. Please, Andrew, take me out of here."

He swallowed his upset so as not to distress her further. "Let me make a couple of quick calls first to see if there are any messages. I need to stay in touch with Janet and the children."

"Of course you do," she said. As he began to dial, she pulled on a sweater and walked into the yard, then stood near the collapsed cliff edge gazing into the sea.

Chapter 42

It was after two o'clock when they left the cottage. The day had grown warm and blue-white, and the gorse and fields of blooming rape seed were brilliant in the full light. They traversed the gravel farm road and turned south toward their destination; the top was down, and she tilted her head to let the sun touch her face.

"I think I know where we're going," she called to him when they were underway.

"Do you?" he called back.

As he downshifted to turn onto the narrow road, lined on either side with fieldstone walls, she ran her fingers through her hair to return it to order. When he brought the car to a stop, they sat in silence for a moment looking at the little church.

When they were standing inside, he asked her softly, "Have you been here—this time, I mean?"

"No, because I couldn't find it. I'm amazed that you remembered exactly how to get here."

He wondered if he should admit this. "Over the years, I've come here now and again."

"That surprises me," she said.

He might as well say the rest. "Everyplace else, all the places in town that reminded me of you, they're all too public. This was a place where I could be alone with my memories of you," he explained, then decided he'd said enough. "Come on, let's walk to the burn."

They followed the path along the cemetery wall that led downward through wooded darkness to the stream.

They stopped at the rock outcropping that had once sheltered the practice of Druidism.

"Does it upset you to be here?" he asked. "It frightened you before."

She scanned the area warily. "This is where we brought ourselves to their attention. This is where it all began."

He laughed at her, then squatted and sat cross-legged in front of the ritual basin. It had been used to catch the running blood of the sacrificed, but it now held only algae-ridden rainwater.

"What are you doing?" she asked.

"Defying your gods," he answered. "Come, sit beside me."

Her anxiety was growing. "It's not wise to get too uppity with them, Andrew. They don't like that."

He laughed at her again. "We've given your gods what they wanted. We sacrificed our youth to them. We gave each other up and lived in misery because of it. What the bloody hell more could the buggers want?"

It amazed her that he could even ask such a question. "Everything, they want everything!"

"To hell with that," he laughed, but it was less than genuine; it was angry. "They're not getting another thing from us, not one bloody thing more."

"Don't say that, Andrew, don't tempt them. There's still so much more we can lose. Please, don't say any more."

His teasing had been meant to allay her fears, but he could see now that it hadn't. "You really believe in the buggers, don't you? You really, truly do!"

"Please, don't tempt them to do us more harm," she pleaded. The air was dank and stale, and Annie was finding it increasingly difficult to move it in and out of her lungs.

He recognized the beginnings of another panic attack, so he said, "All right, I'll stop, but I do mean to defy them. Whether I believe in them or not, I intend to proceed with defiance. I refuse to let them take any more from me."

"Shhh," she whispered. "We should never have come back to this place. Can we leave? I'm afraid we've made an awful mistake coming here."

He took her hand and began leading her up the path. "Do you want to leave altogether, or can we go have our picnic?"

"Let's go to the open field. Let's go out into the sunlight again."

Her mood brightened considerably once they were out of the woods. They gathered the basket and two blankets from the car, and then walked hand in hand toward the field where so many years ago they'd brought another picnic. It was now planted with a crop of thick, green rye, so they chose a bare spot on a slope that the plow had been unable to reach.

"Feeling better?" he asked her once they were settled.

In the open air and light now, she was experiencing some embarrassment. "Sorry for getting so upset back there. I know I'm being silly."

He wanted to console her. "You're not alone in your beliefs. Crinan Castle is surrounded by places like that, you know, all sorts of cairns and henges that were sites for mysterious rituals. And plenty of people in and around Kilmartin regularly visit them to make their own offerings to the gods."

"Really?" she asked.

They lay on their backs and watched clouds glide over them, like a parade of silent passersby. The green blades of rye surrounded them and hid them from view.

"This is cozy. It makes me feel like a child in my secret place," Annie said.

"Did you have a secret place?"

"Of course! It was in the alley where my grandmother kept her garden. Timmy and I would hide behind the jasmine trellis and make plans for our futures." She turned her face away. "We were always going to be together, even when we grew up and married. We promised we'd never live far from each other."

He drew her back to him. "You needn't hide your grief from me," he said softly. "Tell me, what were you like as a child?"

"A stubborn little thing, always insisting upon having my own way—nothing like I am now," she teased. "And you?"

"Dutiful, dependable, boring. In fact, I never did anything wrong, at least not until the incident at school."

"Were you ever able to talk to your father about that later on? To sort things out, I mean."

"Once." As the memory surfaced, he sighed. "I was angry with him over some business decision he'd made and with which I was not in accord, and it just came out, as a 'you've never listened to me about anything that's important' sort of thing. He sat behind his desk and said, 'all right, let's have this thing out once and for all.' And we did." His face darkened. "I told him he was a horrible father, that instead of being understanding and forgiving as a father should be in a situation like that, he made me feel like the lowest form of life on Earth, and he took away all my self-esteem and joy. I said that because of him, I went about much of my youth hating myself." His expression turned quite sad. "I think what I said actually hurt him."

"I hated your father," she declared rancorously.

He turned his head to look at her. "That's odd to hear you say."

"Well, I did. I hated what he did to you. Every time you talked about him, even thought about him," she remembered, "this look would come over you, this forlorn, resigned expression—very much like the one you just had—and I'd feel you pulling away from me. You'd go right away from me and it would be hell to get you back."

A tractor started up in a nearby field. They couldn't see it, but they listened to its deep, grumbling voice, and soon they heard gulls gathering overhead, eager to partake of whatever it churned up and left in its wake. The pungent scent of freshly tilled earth grew heavy in the air.

Andrew didn't want to talk about this anymore, so he sat up and opened the basket. "Let's see what they've given us."

There was a risotto with white truffles, cold lobster and grilled vegetables, several kinds of cheeses and breads, and some delicate little cakes. He spread a linen cloth over the second blanket and began setting up their feast. He was dismayed to find a warm 1985 Taittinger, and an equally warm white Bordeaux.

"Blast! I forgot to chill the wines."

"Never mind," she told him, "we'll save the champagne for later."

"I'll have to do better by you next time," he said as they clinked their wine glasses.

"To many such next times," she responded.

He leaned forward and kissed her lips. "For one precious second this morning, I stopped worrying about you when you told me that Glenn was negative."

"Me, too," she frowned. "I had about two seconds of relief, and then there were so many questions. I need to see that doctor. I wish we were going today."

He was thinking the same thing. "What day is your son arriving?"

"Saturday."

He searched his mind, trying to determine how he could fit it in. "I could try to organize something. It would be tough, but I could try."

"No, let's not," she decided. "It'd be too crazy and I'm so enjoying this time together, this little bit of peace we have now." She looked down at the blanket and then back up at him. She dreaded the answer to this, but she had to know. "When will you leave?"

He touched her hand. "I thought Thursday. I need at least one day to catch up with business, then I should spend the weekend at home. The children . . ."

"Please don't feel that you have to clear things with me," she said with an awkward smile. "Your family has to come first, and I don't want to feel that I'm keeping you from them." She made every effort to cover the sick feeling that the thought of his leaving had brought on.

"It's not that they're first," he wanted her to understand, "it's that they're equally important." He watched her drink some wine, then offered her a plate.

"Tell me about your children," Annie said.

He swallowed his mouthful of food before answering. "You first. I want to know about your son."

"Marc's a great kid," she said proudly, "very intelligent and motivated and caring. It amazes me how independent and strong he is. We went through some rough times when he was little but I think it not only made him stronger, it also made him more sensitive and compassionate."

"You've never mentioned his father," he observed, just before taking a bite of lobster.

She grimaced. "Are you trying to spoil my appetite?"

"I won't press you," he said. There'd be plenty of time to fill in the gaps of their years apart.

"Your children," she reminded him, "you were going to tell me about your children, remember?"

"My children," his face softened and his eyes filled with warmth. "They're wonderful and very different from each other. Donald, the oldest, he was named for my father and is remarkably like him in that he possesses my father's better qualities. He's starting at university here in October, you know."

"Yes, you said that at John and Lena's party."

As he recalled his rudeness that evening, he cringed. "Now there's something I'd rather forget. Anyway, back to Donald. Unlike me when I was his age, he takes readily to his role. His brother Duncan, however, is a different sort. He's very creative and wants to go his own way in life."

"Is he more like you, do you think?"

He nodded. "He's less interested in following the traditions and more interested in finding things out for himself."

"I wish I could meet your sons," she sighed. "I wish I could know them."

"I wish you could know all of my children," he said with detectable regret. "Now the girls, Margaret and Catherine, they're very different, too. They adore horses and dressing up and being little social butterflies, but Maggie is quite outspoken and won't let anyone tell her what to do, and Cat is far more sensible and easygoing."

"Are they pretty?"

"They're lovely. They both have very sweet faces. Maggie is a redhead like her mother, and Cat's hair is the color of mine. They're both going to be tall, it seems, like their brothers."

"And Malcolm?" She sliced a bit of cheese and offered it to him.

"Ah, Malcolm," he grinned. "He's a different bird altogether. He's gentle and quiet, and you can see that there's a lot going on in his head. It's odd, but I feel more protective of him than I do the others, and I don't believe it's because he's the youngest."

"He sounds a little introverted," she observed.

"I didn't mean to give that impression; he isn't. He has a mischievous streak, too, and can be a right rascal when he's a mind to. No, it's just that his heart seems very soft and in need of protection."

His son's soft heart made her recall that she'd always felt that way about him, about the young Andrew she'd fallen in love with. She pushed her plate aside and wrapped her arms around his waist, then leaned into his shoulder.

He rubbed the arms that held him. "I try to be a good father to all of them. I make every effort not to be like my own."

"I doubt you ever have to worry about that," she told him.

"Sometimes I lose my temper and shout at them," he admitted. "But I never say the derisive, demeaning things my father used to say, no matter what they've done. I want them to feel good about themselves and learn from their inevitable mistakes, so they won't be undone by them."

She moved her head closer to his heart as she nestled into him.

"Janet's very good with them. She's been a wonderful mother."

"And wife," Annie added for him.

"Yes, and that. I can't deny that."

For a few painful moments, she was overcome with agonizing jealously. *It should have been me she bemoaned. I should have been his wife and the mother of his precious children.*

The tractor continued to drone on in the nearby field. It seemed for a few minutes as though it might be stuck, but then with a great straining lurch of the engine, it moved on and regained its steady, grumbling hum.

After a time, she said to him, "What we want, I think it's impossible."

He tightened his hold on her. "It can't be," he answered, then gazed off into the distance. "Being with you again, something's changed. Something feels very different in me. I don't want to lose that. I know I should be racked with guilt over this whole thing, but being with you feels so right to me."

"What are we going to do, Andrew?" Annie asked plaintively.

He couldn't think how to respond, so he stroked her head, then embraced her more tightly.

They dozed off for a time, lulled into sleep by the wine and warm sunlight. When they awakened, they packed up their picnic. Instead of returning to Annie's cottage, they drove farther southward, for there was plenty of daylight left in the spring evening. They didn't say much as they drove, holding hands whenever they could, turning toward one another and smiling when they did. They meandered through Stravithie and Dunino, then west to Lathones and Peat Inn. They headed toward the south again before making the turn back to the northeast at Earlsferry, then followed the coastal highway through Pittenweem to Crail. At one point, Andrew pulled off the road before a lovely old country house, set high atop a hill and surrounded by grazing sheep.

"That place resembles Crofthill," he informed her. "But Crofthill is somewhat larger."

She dropped her lower jaw. "That place is enormous! Crofthill is bigger?"

"And Crinan Castle is about four times the size of Crofthill."

"My God!"

"I want to take you there," he said now. "I want you to see it."

She looked toward the manor house again. "It would be nice, but I just don't see how."

"I'm going to do it," he said with an angry determination, as he started the car off again.

Crail was alive with activity on this night, and Annie and Andrew found themselves driving into the thick of a local festival. They were headed for a pub Annie knew kept a fire, though not the one they'd been to twenty-two years ago after their first picnic in the meadow. They found themselves unable to get near it for the traffic, so they parked at some distance and walked, going past the little church that was reputed to have been the target of Satan's wrath.

"Do you recall the legend regarding that rock?" he asked her, pointing to the dark boulder in the church yard.

"Let me see," she said, frowning slightly. "It's supposed to have been hurled at the church by the devil himself from the Isle of May, in a fit of rage at the inhabitants of Crail. Is that right?"

He laughed and said, "Well done."

As they walked, they became aware of music, the sound of a ceilidh band and the accompanying noises of a dance hall gathering. Soon they came upon the old town hall, its doors flung wide to welcome the breeze. They stopped a moment and peered in.

"God, but that brings back memories," he sighed.

She sighed, too, as she slipped her hand in his and led him away.

The pub was full and noisy, and they were grateful for that. A corner seat became available moments after they arrived, and they squeezed into it.

"This isn't the place we came to before," he commented.

"No, I haven't been back there. I don't want to go there," she answered him.

"Why not?" he questioned.

She answered readily, "Because it was one of the most perfect moments of my life, and I don't want to do anything that might disturb the memory."

Andrew said nothing in response. He stood and went to the bar, returning with two large glasses of Scotch. He put one in front of her, then stared into his for what seemed a long time. "Annie," he finally asked, "will you do something for me?"

She responded by touching his hand.

"Just for tonight," he said, "I want to forget everything that's happened since we parted. I'd like to walk these streets with you, go into that dance with you, whirl you around the floor and kiss you when I feel like it, in front of everyone. I want to feel that glorious freedom, that precious freedom." His voice faltered, and he took several sips of his drink before continuing. "That blessed freedom I felt when I was with you. The only time in my life I've ever felt that was then, with you, for a few fleeting weeks."

She slid her fingers between his and grasped his hand. The pub grew noisier as a newly arrived group pushed its way toward the bar, shouting for the attention of the bartender. Laughter burst from the corner near the dartboard, while a rough-looking boy carried in an armload of wood and added some to the fire.

"I've always been free," she told him, "too free. What I felt with you wasn't so much freedom as it was belonging. And it was one of the most wonderful experiences of my life, belonging with someone so fine, who made me feel my worth."

Her words heartened him, and he smiled slightly. "I believe those feelings, differently though we describe them, are one and the same, Annie."

Andrew recognized the strains of the Gay Gordons as they walked through the door, and he wasted no time in pulling her onto the dance floor.

"Wait!" she protested. "I don't remember how to do this! I'm going to embarrass you!"

He pulled her into himself and gave her a tight squeeze, then released her to join the line of dancers. An older gentleman heard what she had said and offered his assistance.

"Here ya are, lassie, follow me!" he told her, and whisked her away from Andrew.

Andrew laughed happily and partnered himself with someone else, all the while watching Annie out of the corner of his eye. They went through the first dance like that, Annie's eyes trained on the feet of her coach, and when it concluded she searched the room for Andrew. She found him standing aside, smiling contentedly at her.

"May I have this next one, lassie?" he asked, affecting the Scots accent he used to tease her with as a young man.

"I thought you'd never ask," she giggled.

The little band started into a droning sort of waltz, meant to please the ears and feet of the elderly, but Annie and Andrew danced as though Strauss himself conducted it. They moved with lighter feet than they had known in many years, and they listened to its strains with ears that were neither hampered by time nor experience. A few people near them chuckled when they were dancing still, despite the band having stopped.

"Must be newlyweds," they heard someone say.

"Let's not disappoint them," Andrew whispered, just before he kissed her.

The band struck up again, this time with a reel, and to this couple—dancing a reel together after so very long—it made the place they were in seem even more dreamlike. They wove in and out of the circle, whirling away from each other, linking arms with strangers, returning and finally bowing at the end to the one with whom the dance began. No partners in the room bowed more sincerely or reverently toward the other than Annie and Andrew.

Andrew's heart pounded, not from the dancing but from wanting to be closer to her, wanting to caress her. "Shall we go for a bit of air?" he asked.

Breathlessly, she answered, "Let's!" Her heart pounded, too, as she linked her arm in his.

The sweets table was near the exit and being tended to by three older ladies. As the couple passed it, they heard one say, "It is him! I tell you it's the earl!"

Both their galloping hearts seemed to stumble and fall when they heard those words, when they realized that they must keep walking and not return to the dance.

A tentative, trickling rain played itself out through the night, an annoying tat tat tat on the roof and glup glup glup down the chimney. Neither Annie nor Andrew slept well. They both turned and tossed and kicked their way through dreams unsettled by the rain's intrusion. Throughout the night, they reached for one another, holding on as long as they could before their night minds took them away, carrying them to other realities.

Andrew walked along the corridors of Crinan Castle looking for something. He opened doors upon bed chambers but found no one, only evidence—cast-off clothing, scattered toys, half-eaten plates of food. He walked on through the long galleries, past the frozen busts, the portraits of his ancestors—his footfalls echoing against the silence—still searching.

Annie returned to the ritual site and stood in the middle of the sacrificial bowl, naked, transfixed. She heard a rustle in the brush and meant to run but could not. She watched with horror as it came closer, ever closer, revealing bits of deep, dark red for her to see through the shadowy woods.

Chapter 43

The dawn brought an end to the rain and some sleep to Annie, but not to Andrew. Instead of finding her lover when she awakened, Annie found a note on his pillow.

Forgive me darling, but I awakened early, so I've gone to the hotel for a shower and change of clothes. I've also quite a few calls to make—business to tend to—but I should be back no later than ten. I'll bring breakfast!

He scrawled an elegant "A" across the bottom.

She looked at the clock and sighed when she saw that it was only just past eight. She made herself some coffee and then ran a bath, puttering around with things, adding water to the roses, tidying the bed, trying hard to keep her eyes from the clocks.

The phone rang at half past nine as Annie sat on the couch and stared out the window, watching for his car on the farm road.

"Sorry, darling," he said straight off, "but things are taking more time than I expected. Why don't you get in your car and come here? I'll order breakfast for us, and we can be together while I'm attending to things."

"You want me to come there," she questioned, "to the hotel? I don't think so."

He understood her concern. "I've had a discrete discussion with the manager, this chap Howard. He'll wait for you in the lobby and bring you up. So you needn't worry about being seen with me unless you feel it compromises you too much."

"No, it's not that," she responded. "I'm used to sneaking around with Glenn."

"I don't mean to insult you," he apologized.

"And I wasn't. I'm just being silly," she answered, "but I can't be skittish about things like this, can I? This is how we're going to have to do things if we want to be together."

"Look, never mind," he told her. "I'll finish up as quickly as I can. You wait for me there at your place."

She realized that she had upset him. Don't make things harder for him, she chastised herself. After all, he's a very busy and important man. "No, Andrew, it's all right," she said. "I'll come to you."

Andrew had described her to Howard as a tall, elegant brunette with green and amber eyes. He'd been watching the entrance for her, and when she came through the doors, he smiled to himself, instantly understanding why the Earl of Kilmartin had come to St. Andrews in such haste. He approached her when she was but a few feet inside the entrance and addressed her respectfully.

"Good morning, madam. Howard Connell, at your service," he said, then escorted her directly to the private elevator. A few people in the lobby turned their heads to look and wonder who she was.

Andrew was on the telephone, and he waved them in. Howard bowed slightly and backed out the door, closing it quietly behind him. Room service had already arrived and laid out a sumptuous breakfast in the dining room of the suite. Annie didn't go to Andrew, who was engrossed in a conference call and dressed in all new clothing. She went instead to the window that afforded a view of the West Sands.

It took several minutes for him to conclude his conversation. When he did, he came up behind her and wrapped his arms around her waist. "An ironic view, isn't it?"

She nodded as he brushed the hair from her neck, then kissed it repeatedly, breathing in the scent of her skin. His kisses raised goose pimples all over her body.

"I've stayed in these rooms before," he said softly, "twice actually. And both times, I did a lot of staring out the window."

"What would you think while you stared?" she wondered.

"What if," he answered, "what if I'd turned around to you and begged you not to go? What if we'd been lovers that night? What if I'd asked you to marry me?"

Hearing that, her heart felt suddenly heavy and she needed to sit down. When she did and Andrew saw her face, he expressed concern.

"You're very pale," he told her. "Come on, let's get some food in you."

"OK," she answered meekly.

She ate breakfast in silence, because Andrew was continually on the telephone. Among other things, he was making arrangements to be in New York the following Wednesday and arguing with his secretary about the necessity of the trip. Andrew felt it was important, but his secretary seemed to think that other things needed his personal attention more. He was stern and authoritative with his employee, and as Annie listened, she realized how much there was about him that she didn't know.

She'd been hungry when she arrived, but her appetite was fading fast. Something like fear was welling up in her stomach, some kind of worry. It nagged at her; it asked her what she thought was she doing, what was she letting herself in for, loving this man again.

"Make certain my wife knows that I'm due in tomorrow."

She heard him say that, loudly and clearly.

"Anything else, your lordship?" Nigel questioned.

"You and I need a one on one," he told him. "I don't like having to argue with you about things that concern my personal life."

"Yes, sir. I didn't mean . . ."

"I'll see you tomorrow, then."

"Have a pleasant flight home, sir."

"Right, thanks." When he'd replaced the receiver, he lifted the pile of papers in front of him. "Do you see all this crap? This was all faxed here because it was so damned important it couldn't wait another day." He slapped the desk with them, then walked to where Annie sat. His face had worn a distinct frown, but everything, including his tone, changed dramatically now, as he turned his attention to her. "I apologize for the telephone. How was your breakfast?"

"Fine," she answered, "and don't give it a second thought. I'm used to it. I've been married to one of the busiest corporate lawyers in America for the past ten years, you know."

"So you have," he said, pouring himself some hot coffee and taking a seat. "I did a little checking up on him, you know, to satisfy my curiosity. He has some impressive credentials."

"Princeton undergrad, magna cum laude, then Yale law," she casually acknowledged. "He was a few years behind them, but he's friendly with Bill and Hillary."

He raised a single brow. "The tobacco companies love him, don't they?"

"They do," she answered. "Mike's saved them billions. But between us, I think there've been many times when he's wished he was on the other side."

"Quite a lucrative profession, though," he observed.

She responded thoughtfully. "There's only so much money you can spend, especially when you don't have the time to spend it, and I don't know what good it does, putting it away and worrying over it. I think it becomes an addiction after a while."

"Has he ever talked about making a change?" he asked.

"Once," she recalled. "We have a beach house, near Cape Hatteras, North Carolina—a beautiful place right on the dunes. We don't get down there much, but once, about seven years ago, when he was particularly worn out after a big trial, I insisted we go down for a week so he could rest up. Marc was with his father, so it was just the two of us. We took long walks and talked about making some changes, about resetting our priorities. We thought we might move down there, be beach bums for a while. But when we got home, we fell right back into everything without missing a beat." She turned her head and looked out the window again.

"What are you thinking?"

"What if," she answered sadly.

He let that settle out of the air. "Would you have been happy doing that, do you think?"

"Who knows?"

"People like your husband," he told her, "like me—we thrive on our work. It feels a lot of the time like it's killing us, but we actually thrive on it."

"I believe that's a testosterone thing," she said with an ironic grin.

Andrew smiled at her. "You're probably right about that."

"Then again," she mused, "maybe it's a substitute."

Andrew rose from his seat and reached his arms out for her. "Come here. It's already been too long since I've held you."

They remained locked in that embrace until he asked her, "What would you like to do today?"

"We've got to be back at my cottage at two, remember?"

"Ah, yes, your friend's request. We've some time before then," he realized. "Is there anything you need to do in preparation for your son's arrival?"

"I need to shop, but I can't very well do that with you," she answered. "Your face is on the tabloid covers from the other day, you know, dancing with the Princess of Wales. I can see it now," she teased, "the twenty-fourth Earl of Kilmartin standing in the checkout line at the supermarket, while the other customers whip their heads back and forth, comparing you to your photo. Is it? No, it can't be! Wait, it is!"

Andrew laughed. "I could wear a disguise."

"And what would you disguise yourself as?"

He smiled mischievously. "As a young student in love with a wildly beautiful American girl, who drives a motorbike named Percy B. Think I could get away with it?"

"You're crazy," she giggled. "Not a chance. No one in his right mind would ever believe that."

The phone rang again, but before Andrew became too involved, Annie interrupted him. "How much longer do you think you'll be?" she whispered.

"An hour at most."

"I'm going, then," she decided. "You come to my place when you're finished, OK?"

He kissed her hand and went back to his call, watching with sad eyes as she crept out of the suite.

The courier was polite and somewhat embarrassed; delivering human remains was not something he was accustomed to doing. Annie offered him tea, but he clearly wanted to be on his way. She and Andrew watched him speed up the drive, his tires firing bits of gravel against the cottage as he pulled out.

She placed the urn on a windowsill and sat on the couch next to Andrew, pulling her legs up and tucking them beneath her. As she opened the letter and read the greeting, she wiped away tears.

Dear Friend Annie,

If you're reading this, you've been kind enough to take care of my last request, and I thank you with all my heart for that. Spending the rest of time closed off in a jar was not something I could bear the thought of, and though I would rather not have troubled you, asking my solicitor or some unknown person from the funeral parlor was just too depressing to contemplate.

It's been wonderful having you around these past weeks. Our chats over dinner have made my last days infinitely more pleasant than they would otherwise have been. Again, I thank you.

There's not much to be said for me, for my life. I leave behind no great accomplishments, no loving family, no deep abiding friendships. I sinned against life in the worst way. I was arrogant and unforgiving and locked myself away from love with my infernal pride. I now pay for these sins by dying alone and uncomforted. But I pray that I may be able, in this time that is left, to achieve a small amount of redemption if I open my heart at long last and share it with you.

I know that there are issues with you, I think having to do with your own sins, that have brought you to this place. I see you alone, going over and over the past, trying to find some clue, some answer in those things that are already fixed in stone. Annie, it's not there. The answer is not in the past—it is inside of you. Look there, look inside, to that part of you that is infinite, to your very fine soul, and let it lead you. Trust it. It will take care of your heart. It will bring peace to your mind, and it will nourish your whole existence. You talked about your forsaken spirit— that's the soulful you. Let it out, let it live.

I never trusted mine. I feared the hurt it could bring me, the vulnerability it generated, the needs it gave birth to. I shut it off and went about my life mechanically, logically, coldly. My miserable, regret-filled death is logic's harvest. Without my soul, I was forced to drag myself through the muck of mortal life; with it, I might have had wings.

My last request is that you take my ashes out to the pier, the one below the cathedral and say, if you can, a prayer for my soul—for my pathetic, smothered spirit, that it may somehow find peace now that it is released from the prison of my body. Give what is left of me to the North Sea and the wind, so that I might become a part of something wonderful, something spiritual, something so very much greater than myself. From my heart, I thank you.

Ever your grateful friend, Tom Keegan

She handed the letter to Andrew, then rested her head in his lap. As he read, she closed her eyes and let the tears flow.

Andrew held the letter in his hand long after he had finished reading it, clearly moved by its contents. "What a pity I'm not able to know him. He seems to have been extraordinary."

She wiped her eyes and blew her nose. "He was a widower, and he had a falling out with his only child years ago. His son didn't even know he was ill."

"God, that's pitiful!"

She looked to the sill where the small urn sat, then rested her head on his shoulder.

"When would you like to do this?" he asked her.

"When the sun is low on the water," she answered, "because that was his favorite time of day."

They left her cottage and went down to the beach for a walk, stopping first at the mound of dirt Andrew and Mr. McBain had covered with a plastic tarp.

"If you want me to dig that up, I'd better get on it now," he told her.

An enormous sigh escaped as she remembered Tom's words: The answer is not in the past—it is inside of you. "It's the past," she said to Andrew.

"Yes, it is that," he agreed.

"I need to let it go."

He reached an arm around her. "Can you?"

Before she could answer, there was something she needed to know. "Tell me first, what you said in the hotel. Did you really think of asking me to marry you?"

He sat on the sand and gently tugged at her to join him. He looked far into her eyes, as he confessed, "There was nothing I wanted more."

It made her gasp to think of it, and she put her hand to her heart. "I used to imagine it, you know. I'd daydream about it while I waited for you at the Whaum. Then I'd hear you come in. I'd hear the sound of the door, your voice as you sang sometimes. Remember that ballad you used to sing? The one about the tragic lovers?"

He nodded. He had often thought of that and how prophetic it had been.

"I'd listen while you put your books away," she continued. "I'd hear you coming to greet me. Then I'd see those eyes and I'd melt inside. I'd have given anything, Andrew—everything—for you to take me to your bed. I wanted with all my heart for you to love me."

They were sitting face to face, and their eyes were fixed in each others.

Powerful emotions had been churning in him since he'd seen her again—feelings that he was still afraid to give voice to—but with her admission just now, that fear vanished. He gripped her upper arms. "God forgive me, but I knew that, and I committed the sin your Tom spoke of, the unforgivable sin of turning my soul away from you, of not allowing it to guide me. And when it couldn't be suppressed any longer, it was too late. Every day since there's been a pain, an ache that comes from then, from the loss of you. It never goes away. Even when my children were born, even then I thought of you; I needed you." He let go of her arms and put his hands on her abdomen, caressing it as though she carried a child. "My children should have come from here. This is where they should have been given life, from you and me, loving each other beyond hope, beyond reason."

The magnitude of what they'd lost was difficult for her to fathom, and it was through her grief and bewilderment that she asked, "Why'd we let it get away from us? How could we have been so stupid?"

"We trusted in time," he answered. "We were young; we didn't know better."

"It kills me now to think of it," she nearly sobbed, "to know that you wanted to marry me."

It was pure torture for both of them to go where they were going, but neither of them could help it, because having so long suffered apart, they needed to feel the pain together.

"I imagined we'd do it in France," he recalled, "in a little village somewhere. I fancied you in your blue gown, the one you wore to the ball, carrying a bouquet of roses. I saw us spending the rest of the summer like gypsies, going wherever we wanted. And then, if my father disowned me, I thought we'd go back to St. Andrews. Robin would let us live at the Whaum, I was sure of that, and I'd get a job. I didn't worry about how we'd manage. I knew as long as we were together, everything would work out."

Her eyes filled and overflowed. "Oh God, oh God, I never knew. I never knew you felt that way!" she cried out.

He'd never told anyone this, but it came from him free of restraint. "Those were my thoughts, Annie, in the moments before the crash. That's where my mind was as I killed that man. It was in France with you, making love to you."

The anguish she felt over that imparted a wildness to her eyes. The next instant, she felt as though a giant vacuum was sucking the air from the beach. Mournfully, she cried, "We can't get it back—it's lost forever—when I think of that—it hurts so badly—it feels like I'm going to die—" She gasped and choked on her tears.

He saw her struggle for breath and pulled her head and upper body to him. "Shh, hush—I know," he said, while stroking her.

Molten emotion was liquefying all her defenses, claiming the excuses, all the explanations she'd placated herself with throughout the years. It left nothing in its wake but raw, excruciating pain—pain that made it impossible to breathe. Words became ludicrous, impossible, but between the gasps she released a cry so wrought with suffering that it startled the seabirds that had come to listen.

In his efforts to calm her, he pulled her even closer. "Let it go, Annie, let it go. It's time to let it go."

She was hyperventilating and rapidly reaching a dangerous point. Her lips were turning purple, and her skin was going pale blue. "No, I can't."

Recognizing that she was growing worse, he held her at arm's length to see her face. When he saw her color, it terrified him. "Look at you! Look what this is doing to you!"

The realization of what they had lost was too much, far too much for her to bear. "I don't want—to forget—" she struggled to say. "I don't care—if it hurts—worse than—anything—I don't want—to—forget!"

"We won't forget, but we have to stop reliving it," he understood. "We have to stop feeling that tearing apart; over and over again we feel that tearing apart!"

It was a futile effort now to get even the smallest amounts of oxygen into her lungs. "It's—all—I have—left—of—you—"

"Not anymore, Annie, not anymore," he said. "We have each other again."

Emotion was feeding on her, draining her life energy. Her limbs were going weak, her vision turning gray and spotty. She began to sense that there would be peace in dying—in sliding quietly into the grayness, her hearing shutting off, her muscles melting down. Andrew felt it as she slipped away from him, as her body became sponge-like and cool and her eyes lost their focus.

"No! I won't let you do that," he insisted, as he shook her.

Something pushed inside of her and forced itself through the collapsing spaces in her chest: a rush of warm life. The warmth escaped and it happened again; it pushed inside and got through to where it was needed. It felt good, so she relaxed into it, letting it happen again and again. As her mind became clearer, she realized that Andrew's mouth was on hers and that he was breathing for her, calling her cells back to life. Her limbs tingled as her circulation improved and her muscles regained some tone. She reclaimed her breathing for herself now, but he held onto her and stroked her forehead.

"There, there, that's my lass. That's my good lassie. Come back to me now, stay with me now."

She responded to him by breathing more slowly, more deeply, albeit still slightly gasping.

Color was returning to her skin. She turned in Andrew's arms to look to the pile of rubble that lay hidden under plastic, staring at it while her breathing settled to a more normal pace.

He saw where her eyes had gone and understood that she was thinking again of his letters. "We need to leave it in the past where it belongs," he tenderly told her. "It's crippled you. It's almost destroyed you. It's time for both of us to put it away."

The sea was closing in on them. The tide was rising and coming to the very edge of the heap that contained the broken flowers, the remnants of her garden bench, the letters from Andrew filled with his love and pain. The sea smelled strongly of itself, of iodine and seaweed and all the things it laid claim to. It filled Annie's nostrils and startled her like a whiff of smelling salts.

"I need to stand. I need to move my legs," she said to him. They felt heavy, pricked all over with thousands of pins.

"Of course." With difficulty he helped her to her feet. Though she looked and sounded considerably better, he was still deeply concerned. "Shall I go for your medication?"

"No, it's over. The worst is over."

"Are you certain? You looked positively dreadful, like you were—like you were dying." He had, in reality, been terrified that she would.

Her knees were weak, but he supported her and stood by as she carefully moved one leg and then another, testing them to make sure they would hold her up.

"All right?" he questioned.

She nodded and nudged him away so that she might stand on her own.

"No need to do that alone," he said. "I'll help you."

She held him off and staggered a little as she turned and walked toward the plastic tarp, lifting it up and pulling it away from the rocks that secured it to expose the pile of debris. Looking to Andrew for his reassurance, she beseeched, "We'll never forget."

He understood the gesture and was deeply moved by it. "No, we won't. We'll remember enough to remind us every day of how precious we are to one another."

"Yes, we'll do that," she agreed. She sat down again, this time where she stood, on the damp sand.

He sat next to her and enfolded her body with his arms. "Let me take you to the cottage and call a doctor. I'd feel much better if someone checked you out."

After the monumental effort she had just exerted, she didn't have the energy to answer, so she merely shook her head. They sat in silence for the next ten minutes or more, looking out over the water. Without trying to make it so, they breathed in perfect unison, in and out together like one person, as the tide crept toward them.

Bits of sea foam were blowing across their feet, when Andrew told her, "We're going to have to move. Let me take you in now."

"All right," she answered.

In this moment, she felt as she had the day her brother was buried. She'd refused to leave the grave site and had remained there alone until it was nearly dark, until her grandfather came back for her and convinced her to leave. And when she did, it was as another person, someone who'd been reduced to rubble by grief, then tenuously reconstructed by the stubborn persistence of her own life.

As he had that first day, Andrew took her hand and led her slowly up the path. Behind them, the sea covered the beach where they had sat with small but relentless waves, breaking over the mound of debris and then retreating, claiming memories that had already been laid to waste by yesterday's tide.

Chapter 44

It was chilly and damp in the cottage. Andrew wrapped a quilt around Annie and laid out a fire as quickly as he could.

"You've got to find a better place to live," he told her. "You can't go on staying here. Why don't you let me move you into the hotel?"

"I don't want to live there. There are too many Americans in that place," she said without hesitation.

Amused by that, he grinned. "Well, how about Rufflet's, then? That's a lovely spot and far more traditional."

She responded simply, "My son arrives on Saturday."

"That's even more reason to move."

"We'll be all right here, Andrew. Thank you, but we'll be fine."

Shaking his head, he frowned. "You can be very stubborn, Annie d'Inard. There's not even a proper kitchen to cook the child a meal in."

"We won't be here that much," she defended, "and we'll eat out."

He thought of something else now. "That reminds me. Will you keep my car for me? I know you're renting that thing you have, and there's no sense in it. Keep the Aston Martin for me, and let them come get that other thing."

She realized what he was doing, what he wanted to do. "You don't have to take care of me. I don't need you to keep me like a mistress."

"And why can't I take care of you?" he retorted. "Why can't I spoil you a bit? What on earth is wrong with that? Christ, I consign a third of my income to charities, and I've still got more bloody money than I know what to do with."

She cocked her head to one side and viewed him skeptically.

He understood the meaning behind the look. "How can that compromise you? Come on, we're so far beyond silly posturings like that it's ridiculous. Take the bloody car and don't say another word about it."

She wasn't thinking of herself. "It could compromise your wife."

"She can't be compromised if she knows the truth," he responded, "and I mean to see that she does."

Annie shook her head.

"What's the matter now?"

"Janet's never done me any harm," Annie persisted. "She's taken very good care of you and your children and yet here I come, insinuating myself into her nice life, messing everything up. I'm sure she's suffering because of it, and that's very hard for me to deal with."

"First off, you're not insinuating yourself," he argued. "I'm inviting you in. And secondly, it's not as though I've made the choice to hurt her. I'm doing the best I can with the circumstances, because our coming together couldn't have been prevented any more than an earthquake might have been." He reflected for a moment on the metaphorical truth in that, realizing that her return to his life had generated an upheaval that he'd been powerless to control. "Please, Annie," he implored her now, "I need you to be with me on this. You can't balk at every fence."

"I'm sorry," she said, from a confused and frustrated place. "I don't mean to make it more difficult for you."

His own sense of frustration turned his face slightly pink, and he rather impatiently demanded, "Then for Christ's sake, don't! Now I'm going into that pathetic excuse you have for a kitchen and make us something to eat. No, to hell with that," he decided. "I'm taking us to the hotel for dinner, and I don't want to hear another bloody word from you about it. Do you understand?"

She raised her voice. "Jesus, you're such a tyrant! Working with you on that commercial shoot should be a fucking laugh a minute!"

They stared each other down for a few seconds, then burst into laughter.

His voice turned soft and apologetic. "Pack an overnight bag, all right? We're staying at the hotel."

She curtsied as she answered, "Yes, your lordship. Whatever you say, your lordship." A silly thought occurred to her. "Why don't they call you your earlship?" she teased.

He scowled and playfully slapped her bottom, then scooted her toward the bedroom to pack.

Annie carried Tom's remains in her lap as they drove to St. Andrews. She and Andrew said nothing to each other during the ten-minute drive, nothing as they parked at the foot of the old stone pier, and nothing as they walked out onto it. It was a strikingly beautiful evening, and they stood admiring the softening evening colors for a minute before Annie removed the lid from the urn.

"Look at that," she exclaimed. "There's so little!"

Andrew peered inside. "Bloody humbling, isn't it?"

"I hate that about life."

He put an arm around her. "What do you hate?"

"That everything we think so damned important during our lives ends up being so insignificant. I really hate that."

"Is that your eulogy?"

"Of course not." She bowed her head and spoke into the ashes. "You were much more soulful than you knew, Tom. It was your soul that brought us together and made us friends. And your life was not a waste. You hung in there and you did the best you could with yourself. It wasn't your fault that you were afraid of your spirit; a lot of us are. But it came through in the end. It led you to reach out to help someone you barely knew. Thank you for sharing yourself

with me, Tom. I'll always cherish my memories of you. I
wish you well with whatever's ahead, and I hope it's a
peaceful place you go to."

"Peace," Andrew added.

Annie walked to the end of the pier and turned the urn
upside down, saying to the North Sea, "Take good care of
him." Some of the ashes blew off to the water and some
blew back in her face, causing her to breathe them in.

Andrew witnessed this. "You all right there?" he asked.

She blinked her eyes several times as they teared from
the ash. "Yeah, fine," she answered, then chuckled slightly.
"I guess Tom meant to stay with me."

"I guess he did," he smiled.

He took the urn from her and they clasped hands for
their walk back to the harbor.

They ordered dinner in the suite, and while they were
waiting, Annie decided to take a shower. Andrew used the
opportunity to ring up Janet.

"Yes, Andrew," she answered flatly, "I got your message."

"You were riding when I rang this morning. I hope I'm
not disturbing you now."

"I've just been nursing my bruises in a hot bath," she
informed him.

He was instantly concerned. "Did you take a tumble
today? You weren't riding that beast again, were you?"

"I was," she answered defiantly.

"Blast it, Janet. I don't want you on that stallion! He's
a mean streak a mile wide. He should be put down."

The seventeen-hand thoroughbred he was referring to
was named "Outrageous Fortune," but everyone called
him Rage, a most suitable nickname considering he had
the temperament of a cornered snake.

She was very calm in her response to her husband.
"Don't go on about this. He's my mount. It's not for you to
decide." Janet had purchased Rage at auction a year earlier. He'd been a winning steeplechaser with an impeccable
bloodline when he sustained a career-ending injury in a

spill. Although he was no longer race worthy, she had intended him for stud, but since his recuperation, she also fancied that she could make an excellent hunter out of him.

"I despise that animal," he told her, "and I don't want the children around him. Have you forgotten he tried to kill a groom?"

Maintaining her composure, she responded, "I haven't, and it wasn't entirely Rage's fault."

"Janet, be reasonable about this," he implored. "The girls are in and out of that stable every day. It's only a matter of time before there's another incident, and God help me, if he hurts the children."

"Steady on, Andrew, what's got you so overwrought?" she wondered. "Trouble with your mistress already?"

"No, there's no trouble," he sighed, "just a mountain of complications."

Realizing what he meant, she responded more soberly. "I see. I'd be one of those, I suppose."

"I'd like for us to have some time alone after dinner tomorrow, if you're up to it."

"Of course, I'm up to it," she answered. "It's not as though I've been busy. I've done nothing with myself this week but take care of his children and household while my husband cavorts with his mistress."

Andrew winced at that remark, then said rather timidly, "There's something I need to ask of you."

Her heart took one of those little galloping runs hearts tend to take when they anticipate a blow.

He filled his lungs with air. "I'd like to have Annie and her son for the Laird's Day celebration."

"What?" she asked in the midst of a swallow. "Have you taken leave of your senses? Bring her here, to my home, with my children about? You must be mad!"

"Hear me out, please," he beseeched.

She exhaled loudly, then railed, "How can you ask such a thing? I can't understand why you'd want to do that to me!"

His argument was untenable, he knew that, but he was going to try anyway. "Please listen to me for a moment. There'll be hundreds of people about, hundreds. It's the perfect opportunity for you two to meet and I think, no," he corrected himself, "I feel that it'll be a good thing somehow, to satisfy the curiosity you have about her and she about you. You needn't spend time with her. Just greet her like you will all your other guests and be your usual gracious self. That's all I ask of you."

"How can bringing her here be a good thing? I don't see that at all. And why do you presume I have curiosity about her? I don't give her a thought," she lied, "not one bloody thought!"

It wasn't an easy thing to say, but he knew he had to. "I can't separate her from the rest of my life, Janet. She's a part of it now, and I won't live my life in fragments."

It was hard to know if it were anger or shock she was experiencing, but it was likely a combination of both. "How is she to be a part of your life?"

"I don't know yet," he responded honestly.

Fear drove her to ask, "Do you have it in your mind to divorce me and make her your wife? Is that what you're after?" Her heart was pounding so wildly it was making her feel faint.

He could feel the agonizing pain that accompanied his wife's words. To ease it, he responded quickly, "I've no plans of the sort, and even if I wanted that, I don't think she'd have it. That's why I want you to meet. I think meeting each other will take away those sorts of fears."

Her heart settled down and she sighed exasperation. "Lord, this is just what I need!"

"I won't do it if you're dead set against it. It's your decision, your call. I just wanted you to hear me out and then give it some thought."

"And the children?" she wondered. "Just how would you introduce her to our children?"

"As my old and dear friend, nothing more than that," he assured her.

As she mulled over his insane idea, as the prospect of it seeped into her consciousness, she began to see some merit in it, some possibility of satisfaction in meeting this ghost woman who had always seemed to darken a corner of their bedroom. She would, after all, have the upper hand in this circumstance: in their magnificent house, her beautiful children in tow, in full command as the Countess of Kilmartin. She could see the strategic benefit in that. Better here in this situation, she told herself, than in some other where she had no such control.

Janet sighed again. "I'll probably regret it."

Her husband's relief was audible. "Thank you, Janet. I know how difficult this is, and I can't thank you enough."

"Lord," she said heavily. "I expect you'll want her to stay here, too."

"Have we the room?" he wondered. "I know we've usually a packed house."

She couldn't shift her thoughts there, because her mind was overloaded by everything else. "I'll have to see and let you know tomorrow," she said, exhaustion creeping into her voice.

"And if you can manage," he added, "there are two others I'd like to invite."

She rallied her strength to scoff, "Oh, do! Let's invite the whole ruddy world to come and meet your mistress! It should be great fun for all!"

Andrew closed his eyes and reminded himself that she had every right to react that way and that she deserved his forbearance. "It's John and Lena Millar-Graham," he explained. "I'm only asking because it'll lessen the burden on you if there is someone she knows besides me."

"Fine," she spat, recognizing the wisdom in that. "You'll invite them then, or shall I?"

"Whatever you prefer," he responded.

"Right, what I prefer. I'll remember that," she remarked caustically.

He understood that his request had put his wife in an impossible position, and it was somewhat apologetically that he asked, "Is there anything else you'd like to discuss, or shall we just close this until tomorrow?"

"There's nothing else," she answered, feeling utterly depleted.

"Then good night, Janet," he said, rather formally. "I'll see you tomorrow, and again, I thank you. You've been exceedingly generous, and I know that this is far from easy for you."

"Andrew?"

"Yes?"

She hesitated now. She could picture his face, sad and sweet, smiling slightly, still boyish despite the scars. It was the face that she had grown to love so very much, the one that had allowed him to get away with things he might otherwise not have. She wanted to tell him that he sounded different, very different from when they last spoke. She wanted to go on with the conversation, to find out more of what had happened these past three days, to tell him something about what she was feeling. But, "Never mind, see you tomorrow," was all that came out.

When Annie emerged from the bath, Andrew handed her a glass of neat Scotch. She had already dried her hair, but she was dressed only in the hotel bathrobe.

After watching her sip at it, he asked, "What do you think?"

She let the taste of it linger on her tongue before answering, "Not bad."

He'd taken a drink from his glass and he almost spat it out as he exclaimed, "Not bad? Well, thank you very much! That's our private reserve you're drinking, our very best. People downstairs are paying forty quid a glass for that! Not bloody bad, she says!" He slammed his glass to the table, all the while trying to keep from laughing.

"Jesus! Give me a minute, will you. I just brushed my damned teeth," she said, then decided to torment him all the more. "Maybe it'd be better with some ginger ale or a twist of lemon or something."

"Ginger ale! Lemon! Bloody, tasteless American!" he railed, then lunged at her, pulling her robe open and throwing her backward upon the bed. Her glass slipped and hit the floor, but neither one cared as they kissed, very deeply and passionately, forgetting for a moment her edict against it. He pushed himself against her naked flesh with a compellingly deep thrust that was at once a proposal, a plea, and an invocation from the past.

"Andrew," she whispered, as they ended the kiss, his penis throbbing against her. "I can't. You've got to help me with that."

His voice confident and strong, he told her, "I used to be terrified of my feelings for you. I'm no longer afraid of anything with you."

"It's not love I'm afraid of," she responded.

He reached his hand down and grasped her pubic bone, taking a forceful hold of the hairs. "I'm not afraid of you," he said into her eyes. "I don't believe you're sick, and I belong there, inside of you."

Her mind was chasing after her heart, trying to put it back in a safe place, reminding her that above all she needed to protect him. "Can we at least wait until I see that doctor? I promise you, whatever he says, whether he gives me good news or bad—"

"It won't be bad," he insisted.

"But if it is," she found it inordinately difficult to say, "we'll talk with him about protecting you. We'll find out if we can be reasonably assured of your safety. Please, help me with this," she implored. "I need to do it this way."

"All right, my love," he told her, moving his hand to rub her abdomen, then her breasts, his eyes still focused on hers. "And for the record, I'm not going to let you be sick, even if that doctor says you are. I'll never allow it."

She cupped his face in her hands. In this moment, her heart ready to burst with love for him, she thanked the fates for bringing them together again, and she prayed to know—how will I ever find the courage to do the right thing tomorrow, to say good-bye and send him home to his wife?

They dined in the suite on delicate lamb and fresh local vegetables, washing it all down with a divine Chateau Margaux. Knowing how resistant she was likely to be and not wanting to spoil her appetite, Andrew waited until they'd finished dessert to approach her with his idea.

He began somewhat awkwardly. "I rang up my wife while you were showering, because there was something I wanted to ask her." He lifted his snifter of Cognac and twirled it. "We celebrate Laird's Day at Crinan Castle next weekend, and I asked Janet if I might invite you and your son."

It was with wide, incredulous eyes that she responded. "I wish you'd asked me first. It would have saved Janet the embarrassment because I would've told you not to."

He responded calmly, "I asked her to at least hear me out, and now I'm asking you the same."

She hadn't really wanted more to drink, but she found herself in need of it just then. She held out her glass to ask for a refill. "Go ahead," she said after swallowing nearly half the glass.

"Laird's Day has been a tradition for more than 400 years," he explained. "We've hundreds of guests, many of whom stay with us, and the entire village is invited on Sunday. The point is to honor all the past earls, and for the present earl to pay tribute to all over whom he is laird. It's a tradition unique to my family and something I'm very proud of. I want you there. I want you to see who I am and where I come from. I want you to meet my children, my mother and sisters—and perhaps most of all, my wife. Janet's agreed to it, and I believe your son will enjoy it tremendously. So now that you've heard me out, what do you say?"

She was so astounded by this that she could barely respond. "Janet agreed, you said?"

"Yes," he answered, then added, "though reluctantly. For her part, I convinced her it would be better to meet you and have this out in the open. As I told her, I think meeting each other will take away a lot of your fears."

She finished her drink. "What do you mean, out in the open?"

"Not publicly open," he qualified, "open among the three of us." He softened his tone. "And there's something else. I'd like your permission to tell her about the situation with your health."

She lifted her eyes and let them find his. "I suppose she should know," she realized. "Anyone you sleep with has the right to know that you've been in contact with me."

He was instantly upset. "You speak of yourself as though you're carrying some dreadful plague!"

"Well, the fact is, I could be."

"Dammit, you're not!" he insisted. "And for the record, I'm not going to sleep with Janet. I've not been able to sleep with her since the day I saw you on that plane."

His admission shocked her. "Oh Andrew, that's no good! No good at all!"

He hadn't meant to reveal this, but sometimes there was just no stopping the truth. "How would you expect me to be with her, with any other woman, when my heart and mind have been completely occupied by you?"

"Oh, no," she murmured, "you can't do that. You can't let me mess everything up. It's not fair to Janet, or your children."

"You haven't messed anything up," he told her with a soft, affectionate smile. "But because of you, things have changed. I'm glad for that, because I think it's a change for the better."

She didn't see it. "How can any good possibly come of this?"

"Because it has to," he answered her, "because I intend to see to it that everything works out in the end for everyone, and that all wrongs are put to right." He almost left it at that, but seeing that she remained skeptical, he added, "I make you that promise, Annie, on my honor as Earl of Kilmartin."

As he spoke those words, Annie saw something in Andrew that distracted her. She'd seen it before, recently and many years ago, but tonight was the first time she understood what it was: It was his nobility, the cherished honor that made him who he was and directed him in all his actions. As she looked into his eyes, she recognized it, and it filled her with an electric sensation, that same surging warm current that she'd felt as a young woman whenever he was near.

It affected her now just as strongly as it used to then. "I'll come to Crinan Castle," she whispered, because she was powerless to say otherwise.

After dinner they went for a walk. Annie left the hotel first, and Andrew met up with her as she stood outside the Royal and Ancient.

"Remember Lord Cowan," he asked her, "remember meeting him here?"

"Very well," she answered. "I should have gotten some clue about who you were then, shouldn't I?"

"Cowan was quite taken with you," he informed her, "and the scoundrel reported to my father on how attractive you were. I'm sure that solidified Donald's resolve to keep us apart," he realized now. "He had no faith whatsoever in my judgment, and he believed you'd cast some sort of spell over me."

"Didn't I?" she teased.

"That's it, you're a witch!" he declared. "Well, you sly thing. I should have known, coming from New Orleans and all. It was voodoo, wasn't it?"

"Exactly. And watch out," she added with a lift of her brow, "because I'm not through with you yet."

"I sincerely hope not," he answered, only half teasingly. "By the way, when you come to the Laird's Day thing, there'll be one or two people there who know you."

"Oh?"

Grinning now, he asked her, "Remember Robin Keay from the Whaum?"

"Of course! You're still friends?"

"More than that. He runs the textile division for me."

"That's cool, and he'll be there?"

"He certainly will, and I've also invited John and Lena."

That surprised but pleased her. "I'm glad. I've grown very fond of Lena, you know. She reminds me of Susannah." Then, without thinking, she blurted out, "But that bugger John—can you believe he tried to kiss me the other day?"

They had been walking, but Andrew halted dead in his tracks. "Did he now?" He was clearly not amused.

She instantly and mightily regretted saying that. "Don't get the wrong idea," she told him, then nervously rambled, "because it wasn't a real kiss. It was just an impulsive, 'wanting to see if there was anything there' sort of thing, and when he realized there wasn't, well, that was the end of it." The pissed-off look on his face made her mouth grow dry. "Really, Andrew, that's all it was."

"I believe you," he said, then began walking again.

But she could see the wheels of his thought spinning, and she began to be worried for poor John.

They walked along The Scores as far as the castle, then stood outside its walls remembering that May morning when the world was fresh and time lay before them, like an abundant crop that could be endlessly harvested. When they headed back toward the hotel, the Whaum was tucked away for the night, its windows dark and reflective, and they both heaved heavy sighs as they walked past it for the last time.

* * *

His absence from the bed roused her from her sleep. She saw him standing at the window, searching the darkness that blanketed the West Sands.

"Andrew," she called softly, "what's wrong?"

He wiped his eyes before he turned around, then untied and removed his robe as he walked back to the bed. As he lifted the bedclothes, the scent of her reassured him, welcomed him. His naked body was cool, and he pulled her warmth in as closely as he could.

In a melancholy whisper, he told her, "The night is passing too quickly. It'll be dawn soon."

She nestled her head against his heart.

He remained deeply pensive. "Come October, I won't be able to visit you here."

She responded tenderly, "I realize it'll be too risky with your son in town."

"It's such a small place. It could be anyone who says to him 'I saw your father.' It could be just anyone."

"Then I'll move," she offered. "I don't have to live here."

He sighed before adding, "Anywhere we go in Scotland, or in Britain for that matter, we run that risk." He'd been giving this a lot of thought. "After the commercial's done, will you go away with me? Will you spend some time with me in France?"

She planted kisses all over his chest, as she answered, "Nothing could keep me from you."

Earlier that evening, they had gone over the plans for the upcoming days. A car was to come next Friday to take Annie and her son to Edinburgh and Andrew's waiting jet. They'd stay at Crinan Castle until Monday morning and then leave for Barcelona on his jet again. Andrew had arranged for her to see Dr. Coupau on Tuesday. By Wednesday, she was to be on location in the Pyrénées with John and company.

"Bring all your important things with you when you come to Kilmartin," he advised her, "because you may be in France for quite some time."

"That sounds mysterious," she said, "what are you up to?"

He smiled slightly. "Will you let me surprise you?"

"Yes," she answered, then kissed him again. As they lay in an embrace afterward, a thought occurred to her. "What are you going to do with the clothes you were wearing, the old ones?"

"Leave them, I suppose. I've no case to put them in."

"May I have them?"

His chuckling laugh was infectious. "Do you know what I have in my safe at home?"

"No, what?"

"An old pair of gardening gloves and a barrette."

"Really?" In this moment, she looked like a very young Annie who'd been surprised with something wonderful.

"Really." He reached and touched her lips, pursuing her smile, trying to capture it with a fingertip.

She closed her eyes and shut out the world so that she might be aware of his touch and only that, but as she did, an inevitable memory surfaced—inevitable because of the mention of the barrette. It overcame her with its ugliness.

He watched as her smile was chased away. "What is it?"

"I lost the Swiss Army knife you gave me." Her face was pinched with anxiety as she explained, "I left it in Amsterdam because I was in such a hurry to get out of there. It devastated me when I realized it, and I wanted to go back, but the circumstances were such that I was afraid to go back."

He stroked her hair. "Why were you afraid?"

She didn't want to spoil this last night together, so she answered, "I'll tell you some other time. I'll tell you all about it if you want. I'll go deep into all my hiding places with you, if you want that."

"I do want that, Annie, and you need that. You need someone to know it all and love you still, love you more because of it, and I want to be that someone."

They embraced again, arms and legs wrapped around each other, like seaweed clinging to a rock when the tide departs.

The first light of day was illuminating the misty beach and chasing shadows from the room. Through the heavy, insulated hotel windows, they could barely hear the birdsong.

"Will you be all right after I've gone?" he asked her, wondering the same thing about himself.

"It won't be easy," she said, "but I'll have my son with me, and I know I'll see you next Friday."

"I'll ring every morning, first thing," he told her. "And you've got the numbers where you can reach me. Nigel will be directed to get you through to me right away, no matter what I'm doing." He didn't at all like saying this, but he felt he had to. "When we meet again, I'll be different. I have to be careful how I behave with you in public, especially at Kilmartin."

In a quiet voice, she said, "I understand."

"It's the children I want to protect," he explained, "and Janet's dignity."

She tightened her embrace of him, as she responded, "We both want that."

He breathed in and out very slowly, as though he were preparing himself to lift something heavy. "Why has time been so cruel to us?" he wondered aloud.

She sounded almost angry. "They were jealous of us, Andrew. The powers-that-be were so envious of what we had, they wanted to destroy it."

Gently, he contradicted her. "They stole it from us, Annie, but they didn't destroy it."

"No, you're right, they didn't destroy it," she sighed. "But now they've made thieves of us for trying to get it back."

They were both impacted by the awful truth in that.

* * *

The helicopter shattered the peace of St. Andrews as it raced in over the bay and deposited itself on the dead-end road that separated the West Sands from the Old Course. Annie and Andrew sat in the Aston Martin watching it come for him; she clutched his hand as it touched down and whirled its arms impatiently. One uniformed man got out and took up a position outside the blades' radius.

They emerged from the car, and Andrew looked to the helicopter, then to Annie again. "It seems we've come full circle," he told her.

He heard the panic in her voice when she asked, "Is that thing safe?"

His amused smile reassured her somewhat as he recalled how worried he'd been about her, leaving for parts unknown on a motorcycle. "These gentlemen were trained in the R.A.F., darling. I've flown with them many times before. They've even brought the queen up to Balmoral. Would the British entrust the safety of their queen to anyone but the best?"

"No, I guess not," she responded, though still deeply anxious. "But I don't like those things."

Looking into her eyes, he told her, "It saves time, my love. Time is very important, especially now."

Everything in her wanted to reach out and embrace him once more, but she would not compromise him, so she balled her fists at her side.

He turned his back so the pilots could not see his face and found her eyes again. "The last time we parted in this place, I didn't tell you what I was feeling, and I've regretted it every day since." He had to swallow before he could continue. "But I want to tell you now. I love you Annie, with all my heart and soul, I love you."

She had no voice. She tried to speak, but only garbled, gurgling little sounds came from her throat—the precursors of sobs. He told her with his tender smile that he understood, then he turned and walked to the helicopter.

The storm the great machine generated blew her skirt and hair frantically as it lifted off. He could make her out for a little while, a fragile figure on the West Sands, her arm extended, her hand reaching as though it meant to pull him back. As she faded from view, he felt that familiar tearing sensation he had so often experienced as a young man, the one that always came upon him when they parted. He blinked away the tears and tried to hold her in his sight for as long as he could, while the ache settled into his bones.

The story continues in: *The Rape of Europa*